Lucy in the Sky

Lucy in the Sky

Anonymous

Simon Pulse

New York   London   Toronto   Sydney   New Delhi

SIMON PULSE

An imprint of Simon & Schuster Children's Publishing Division

1230 Avenue of the Americas, New York, NY 10020

First Simon Pulse edition May 2012

Copyright © 2012 by Simon & Schuster, Inc.

All rights reserved, including the right of reproduction in whole or in part in any form.

SIMON PULSE and colophon are registered trademarks of Simon & Schuster, Inc.

For information about special discounts for bulk purchases, please contact Simon & Schuster Special Sales at 1-866-506-1949 or business@simonandschuster.com.

The Simon & Schuster Speakers Bureau can bring authors to your live event. For more information or to book an event contact the Simon & Schuster Speakers Bureau at 1-866-248-3049 or visit our website at www.simonspeakers.com.

The text of this book was set in Adobe Caslon Pro.

Manufactured in the United States of America

20 19 18 17 16 15 14 13 12 11

Library of Congress Control Number 2012930474

ISBN 978-1-4424-5187-2 (hc)

ISBN 978-1-4424-5185-8 (pbk)

ISBN 978-1-4424-5188-9 (eBook)

Lucy in the Sky

July 4

~~Dear Diary,~~

That's ridiculous. Who writes "Dear Diary" in a diary? I mean, who writes in a diary at all? Shouldn't I be blogging?

This is lame.

July 5

Okay, so this isn't going to be a diary. It's a journal. I guess that's the same thing, but "journal" sounds less like I'm riding a tricycle or something.

Yesterday was my birthday. I turned 16.

It's so weird sharing a birthday with your country. Always fireworks: never for you. Mom always plans an actual birthday dinner—usually the Saturday night after July 4th so that I can have a day where we celebrate just for me. It's fun, kinda like having two birthdays in the same week.

We're not big July 4th celebrators . . . celebrators? Celebrants? People. Whatever—we're not big on July 4th. Usually in the afternoon we have friends from school over and walk down to the beach to play volleyball. There are lots of nets at the beach just down the hill, then we haul ourselves back up the canyon to our house for a cookout in the evening. My brother, Cam, invites his friends from the varsity soccer team. Mom gets my favorite cake (the one with the berries in it).

1

After we gorge on grilled meat and birthday cake, we all crowd onto the balcony outside my parents' bedroom and watch the fireworks down the coast. You can see the display at the pier really well, and the ones in the cities just up the coast shoot off too. Last year Cam (nobody calls him Cameron except Mom) climbed onto the roof from the front porch so he could get a better view, but Mom freaked and said, CAMERON! Get. Down. This. Instant. Mom's big on safety.

I got a lot of cool presents yesterday. Mom got me the swimsuit I tried on at the mall last week. It's a really cute two-piece with boy shorts, and this fun, twisty top. Dad's present to me was that he's taking me to get my license this week. I've been practicing with him in the parking lot near his office at the college. He gave me a coupon for one "Full Day with Dad." On the back it says, "Good for one driving test at the DMV, followed by a celebratory meal at the restaurant of holder's choosing, and a $100 shopping spree/gift card to store of choice."

He made it himself out of red construction paper and drew this funny little stick figure on the front. It's supposed to be him. He draws curly hair on the sides of the round head so the little man is bald on top like he is. The coupon is sort of cheesy, but so is my dad. I think it's funny. And cute.

Cam got me this journal. We've been going to this yoga

class together, and the teacher is this woman named Marty with bright eyes who talks about her birds a lot. She told us to get a journal and spend a few minutes each day writing down our thoughts and feelings.

I just looked back at everything I've written, and it's mainly thoughts. Not very many feelings. I'm not sure how I feel right now. I mean, I guess I feel fine? Happy?

No, just fine. I feel fine.

I also feel like people who have birds are sort of weird.

July 6

It's funny that Cam bought me this journal. It's one of those things I would never have bought for myself but secretly wanted. I don't know how he knows that stuff. I guess that's what older brothers are supposed to do: read your mind. I mean, who actually goes out and tries the stuff that their yoga teacher says to do outside of class?

Cam got way into yoga last summer when he had a crush on this exchange student from England named Briony—like Brian with a y. (Really? Who names their kid that?) Anyway, she wouldn't give Cam the time of day, so when he found out that she went to this yoga class, he started going to the same one. He bought a mat and this little bag to carry it in and just happened to show up in her class like, Oh my God! Wow!

What a coincidence. Briony never went out with him. I didn't even know she'd gone back to London until I was teasing him about how he should be glad Briony didn't do something like synchronized swimming. He was like, Briony moved back to London right after school got out.

I asked him why he was still going to yoga, and he said he really liked it. And he said I should come.

I'm not sure why I did, really. I guess I was just bored last summer. But now we go to yoga together. It's this really great studio a block off the Promenade, and they run it on donations. You just pay what you can or what you think the class is worth. I didn't think I'd like it at first. It was hard, and I got sweaty and slipped on my mat and couldn't do any of the poses. But I sorta like spending time with Cam.

Who am I writing that to? It's not like anyone is reading this but me. This is exactly how it feels when Grams asks me to pray over dinner. I feel like I'm saying all this stuff that is bouncing back at me off the ceiling and landing in the spinach salad.

Cam probably didn't have to read my mind about wanting a journal at all. He's really smart. His early acceptance letter to this great college up north came last week. He's going to be a biochem major, which just makes me want to lie down on the floor and curl up in a ball. He's a brainiac. And on top of it he's

nice and enthusiastic—which has a tendency to be dangerous.

Last semester Mom was always telling me to ask Cam for help with my geometry homework. I did, but instead of telling me what to do, Cam always talks and talks and talks. It's like he knows so much about stuff and likes math so much that he has to say it all instead of just the answer.

I stopped asking questions. It sort of annoyed me. Just did it myself, and didn't really understand it. I got a C in geometry. You'd have thought I'd flown a plane into a building. (That's bad to say, I guess. I mean, I know people died and everything, but it was a really long time ago.)

Dad came unglued. He's the chairman of the music department at the college where he works. He made me sign up for tutoring this summer with a student that his friend in the math department recommended. Our session starts in a few minutes. I was relieved when Nathan showed up the first time. I was afraid I'd get stuck with some weird math girl.

Nathan is a freshman. He's from Nebraska and has brown hair that's cut short. He works out a lot, and he wears these polo shirts with sleeves that are tight right around his biceps. I just stare at his arms a lot instead of listening when he's trying to help me find the answer.

I wish somebody would just tell me the answer.

Nathan's here. Gotta go.

Later . . .

OMG.

I TOTALLY JUST INVITED NATHAN TO MY
BIRTHDAY DINNER.

OMG OMG OMG OMG

And

He

Said

YES!

This is totally crazy. I can't believe I actually said the words
out loud. I didn't mean to. We were just sitting at the dining room
table and he was talking about the hypotenuse of a right angle,
and while he was looking at the protractor he was using to draw
lines, I was staring at the lines of his jaw and noticed that they
were almost a right angle, and the hypotenuse of the right angle
of his jaw was this line in his cheek with a dimple in the middle
that he gets when he smiles, and then I heard myself saying,
You should come to my birthday dinner on Saturday, and then
I realized that Mom was looking RIGHT AT ME like my hair
was on fire, and I realized that I'd just invited an 18-year-old over
for dinner in FRONT OF MY MOTHER. OMG. I just wanted
to CRAWL UNDER THE TABLE.

But he stopped with his pencil stuck into the protractor and looked up, and then glanced over at Mom like he was looking to see if she'd heard, and she smiled at him, sort of weakly. I guess he took that to mean that it was okay with her 'cause he looked me right in the eye and said, Sure. That'd be fun. Now look at this triangle.

I tried to look at the triangle for the rest of the half hour, but I have no idea what he was saying. When he left, I walked him to the door, and Mom said, Nathan, come by around 7:30. He said, Sure thing, and you can call me Nate. He waved at me before he got in his pickup truck and said, See you this weekend. Then, he drove away. Just like that.

I went running back up to my bedroom and buried my head in my pillow and did one of those silent screams where you just breathe out really hard, but with no sound; it's sort of a soft roar, but the excitement on the inside of me made it feel like my head would explode.

I could hear my heart pounding in my ears, and I took a couple of deep breaths and then I remembered what Marty said in yoga this morning about trying to meditate and how to focus on the breath, so I sat down on the floor and crossed my legs like Marty does in front of class, and I closed my eyes and took really deep breaths and tried not to think about Nate. I could do it for about 5 breaths at a time, but then I'd see that

line with the dimple in it behind my eyelids, and then the rest of his right-angle jaw would appear and I'd see a triangle fill in the space on his face.

I mean, it's really no big deal. My dad is two years older than my mom. Nate's only 18, and I'm 16, and it's not like he would be robbing the cradle or anything.

I think I really like him.

OMG I CAN'T BELIEVE THAT NATE IS COMING TO DINNER ON SATURDAY.

July 8

I was just standing in my mirror trying on a couple of different options for tonight. I passed my driver's test and got my license yesterday (YAY! OMG. Finally!), then Dad and I went shopping on the Promenade. I'm a really good bargain shopper. Cam worked at the Gap last summer and taught me to never EVER pay full-price for anything 'cause they just mark it down every two weeks. Primary, secondary, clearance. Primary, secondary, clearance. Every week on Tuesday night the markdowns would come through from the home office, and we'd all run around with those price-tag guns the next morning, marking down tops that some poor dope had paid $20 more for 12 hours ago. So, anyway, I got a lot of great stuff. Even Dad was surprised with how many items I got for $100. Well, then I splurged a little and added $40 from my savings to get these supercute sandals that I'd been wanting.

Anyway, I have all this stuff to try on, and I felt myself doing that thing I do where I put on, like, 12 different outfits and stand there and pick every single one of them apart, and I end up standing in front of the mirror in my underwear with this pile of really cute clothes with the tags still on them lying on the floor. I had just put on the second skirt I bought and could tell I was about to find something wrong with it, and then I just stopped, looked at myself, and thought: Don't be that girl.

I just don't want to be that chick who is always staring at herself in the mirror whining about how she looks and having a meltdown in the fitting room. I mean, I'm not a model or anything, but I think I look okay. I have already showered and straightened my hair. It's not frizzy or even curly really—just has some waves, and when you live this close to the waves it can get wavy. (God. Stupid joke.) Whatever, I stepped away from the mirror and saw my journal sitting on my desk, and I thought I'd write about it. I mean, this is a feeling. I'm not sure what kinds of feelings I'm supposed to be writing about in here, but maybe this is what crazy Marty the bird lady was talking about.

I'm SO EXCITED about Nate coming over and I want to look really hot, but the excitement also feels like nervousness, like I'm going to barf or something. Mom is downstairs putting a marinade on some shrimp that she's going to have Dad grill, and the smell when I walked through the kitchen made me feel like I was going to hurl up my toenails—and I LOVE shrimp.

I know I look good in this skirt. Dad told me it looked "far out" when I came out of the dressing room to check it out in the mirror. He said this in his I'm-being-a-little-too-loud-so-the-other-people-present-will-hear-me-and-think-I'm-hilarious-when-really-I'm-just-torturing-my-daughter voice. I told him to please be quiet and offer his opinions only regarding possible escape routes in the case of a fire, or a random stampede of wild bison. In all other matters, I respectfully asked him to please refrain from speaking to me until we had reached the cash wrap.

I looked in the mirror again just now. This skirt totally works.

Weird how excited and scared feel like the same thing.

July 8—11:30 p.m.

I shoulda known.

I shoulda known when he walked up the front steps with flowers and handed them to Mom.

But he brought me a card with a joke about having pi on my birthday instead of cake (guh-rooooan) and it had a $25 gift card for iTunes in it. Which was cool and so sweet of him, but he just signed his name. Shoulda known when he didn't write anything personal. Just "Happy B-Day! Nate."

But he was really funny and sweet at dinner. He sat across from me and told us all this hilarious story about when he was growing up in Nebraska and he and his brother raised sheep for the county fair. (Yes. Apparently people still raise animals and take them to fairs where they win ribbons and titles and scholarships. Thank you, CHARLOTTE'S WEB.)

One morning he and his brother went out to scoop food out of these big 25-pound sacks of feed for the sheep, and there was a mouse in one of the bags that ran up his little brother's jacket sleeve. He was telling us about how he thought his brother had been possessed by a demon because he kept screaming and shaking his arms and beating at his chest and running around in a circle while the mouse wriggled around inside his shirt. We were all crying, we were laughing so hard, and Cam almost inhaled a bite of shrimp, which sent him on a coughing fit that made the rest of us laugh even harder.

He jumped up and helped me clear the table when Mom asked who wanted dessert. When Mom told him he didn't need to do that, he smiled at me and said, Oh yes, ma'am, I do. My mama'd fly in from Grand Island and smack me if I didn't.

When we were in the kitchen, I started rinsing plates and he loaded them into the dishwasher like he lived here. We were laughing and joking around and no one mentioned geometry.

He was so easy to talk to, easy to be near. I didn't feel nervous even once. I couldn't help but wonder what it would feel like if we were married and this was our house and we were loading the dishwasher together. That's probably stupid, but it made me feel hopeful inside, like maybe something like that was possible.

When Nate bent over to put the final plate in the dishwasher, a necklace fell out of his shirt. It had a tiny key on it, and I was about to ask him where he got it, but Mom came into the kitchen to get some coffee mugs and the French press. Nate tucked the necklace back into his polo before I could ask him about it, but I shoulda known.

There's a long porch on the back of our house that looks over the bottom of the canyon out to the water. We ate dessert out there. Dad lit the candles in the big lanterns on the table outside. Cam sat next to Nate and they talked soccer. The flicker made their skin glow like they were on the beach at sunset. Nate looked all sun-kissed and happy. I felt a foot nudge mine just for a second under the table and my heart started racing. I was glad that it was just the candles outside in the dark 'cause I started to blush like crazy. I thought maybe Nate had touched my foot, and I kept sliding mine a little bit closer toward him under the table, but his foot never touched mine again.

It was almost 10 when he pulled out his phone and checked it, then said, Whoa. I gotta go.

I felt really bummed all of a sudden, and then silly. What was I hoping? That he'd stay and walk me down to the beach? He stood up and shook my dad's hand, then gave Cam one of those weird hugs that guys give each other where they grab hands like they're gonna shake and then lean in and hug with their arms caught in between them. He kissed my mom on the cheek and told her what a good cook she was.

Then he looked right at me and said, Will you walk me to my truck?

I got so many butterflies in my stomach, I thought they might start flying out of my ears. I said SURE, and realized that nobody had really heard him ask that because Mom was pouring more wine and Dad was pouring more coffee and Cam was texting somebody. So I slipped into the house and out the front door.

He'd parked on the street, and when he got to the door of his pickup, he leaned against it and looked up at the sky and said, Huh.

I said, What?

He told me that in Nebraska at this time of night you could see lots of stars. I followed his gaze up to the sky, but I knew there wouldn't be any stars. Out here, the sky just glows this weird purply color even on the darkest night here. It's the light pollution bouncing off of the marine layer, I said. It's what

13

happens at night when 8 million people get jammed up against the ocean. I turned around and stood next to him with my back up against the truck.

He said it was funny how you always hear about all the stars in Los Angeles, but at night in Nebraska, it's like the sky is covered with diamonds. Then he looked over at me, and I don't know what happened, but I just knew that I had to feel his lips on mine. So I leaned in and kissed him.

Nate jumped like I'd shot him with a taser. He said, WHOA, what are you doing? OMG! I was SO EMBARRASSED I couldn't even LOOK at him. It was like we were having this PERFECT night, and then BLAM-O: I broke the spell. I was blushing and stammering and then I felt the tears come to my eyes, and I didn't wait. I just sprinted back across the street toward the house. I was not going to let him see me cry.

As my foot hit the curb on the other side of the street, he said WAIT!

There was something in the way he said it that made me turn around. And then he shook his head and smacked his forehead, and he walked over to me, and just looked at me. He pushed my hair over my shoulder and said, No. I'm sorry.

He told me that I had come along two years too late. And that I was beautiful. And that he has a girlfriend.

I shoulda thought about that. I shoulda never invited him to dinner tonight.

I shoulda known.

July 10

Thank GOD I don't have a session with Nate this week 'cause of the midterm. I would never date a guy who drives a stupid pickup truck.

ALSO? He's a total liar. I am plenty of things, but I am not beautiful.

July 13

Took the geometry midterm in summer school today. I think I did okay. We don't have class again until Monday. Only 4 more weeks to go, then I finally get a stupid month off.

[Sad trombone . . .]

July 14

Cam and I got to go to the 1 p.m. yoga class today because I didn't have geometry. Usually I am in class until noon, and it's too rushed to go to Marty's 1 p.m. class, so we go to the 3 p.m. class. Of course, Cam always gets up early to run so that he stays in shape for soccer. Practices start way before school does and he always says that the only thing that sucks worse than two-a-days in July is two-a-days in July when you didn't run in June.

There's a whole different crowd at Marty's 1 p.m. class. I was not expecting that. It totally changes the feeling in the room. This class had more guys in it and a crazy lady who musta been like 45 years old who was wearing only her bra and some bicycle shorts—and not like a sports bra. She was wearing just a regular old ivory-colored bra. Lace on the cups. Underwire. In yoga. Like it was no big deal. I wanted to pull her aside and be like, um, okay. I know you probably don't understand that there's a difference between a regular bra and a sports bra because they cover about the same amount of skin and all that BUT. THERE. IS.

Siiiiiiiiiiiiiiiiiiiiiiiiiiiiiiiiiiiiiiiiiiiiiiiiigh.

July 15

I almost didn't go back to the 1 p.m. class with Cam today.

I'm really glad I did, though. And I know how this is going to sound before I even write it down, but fine: YES. It's because of a boy. There. I said it. I'm becoming one of those starry-eyed, dewey-cheeked bimbos. I can't help it.

I was staring at Crazy Bra Lady (today's bra was black) while we were doing side planks and I noticed this guy watching me watch her in the mirror. He was about my age and had longish brown hair that was kinda shaggy, but cool shaggy not

16

gross shaggy, and he was really tan. When I saw him looking at me, he got this little smile, like he knew a secret about me.

After class, Cam went into the bathroom to change shorts and I was waiting outside on the sidewalk, watching Crazy Bra Lady unlock her bike. She'd put on a big T-shirt that had the neck cut out of it so it hung off one shoulder. As I watched her pedal away, I heard this voice behind me say, She is totally wackadoodle.

When I turned around, it was shaggy brown hair guy who flipped his bangs out of his eyes and said, Hey, I'm Ross.

I told him my name, and he got that little smile again. I said, What? Do you know something I don't know? And he was like, Maybe.

I said, You gonna keep it a secret?

He grinned at me and said he was just hoping I'd be back. He said, I saw you yesterday but you and your boyfriend left before I could say hi.

I frowned at him and said, My boyfriend? right as Cam walked out the front door with his yoga mat slung over his shoulder and said, You have a boyfriend?

Ross frowned and said, Oh. Then . . . who are you?

Cam frowned and said, Who are YOU?

Finally I pointed at Cam and said BROTHER, then pointed at Ross and said ROSS.

Boys are so weird.

Cam and Ross shook hands and then we went to get smoothies and Cam gave Ross the third degree during which we learned:

1. Cam should play a detective on CSI.

2. Ross is 16 years old like me.

3. Ross just moved here from Florida.

4. Ross's mom got a job as an associate events manager at this big resort hotel on the beach.

5. Ross can go hang out at the pool at the hotel when his mom is working.

6. Ross has A-MA-ZING blue eyes.

Cam probably learned more, but when I noticed the eyes, I sorta stopped listening. As we walked back to our cars, Ross invited us to come to the hotel for a swim later, but Cam was headed to the beach, and I promised Mom that I'd vacuum and dust today 'cause I didn't do it on Saturday because it was my birthday (observed), and then I was sorta glum on Sunday. I think she knew it was something about Nate even though I didn't tell her about it.

Ross stopped in front of a pickup truck and I thought Holy. Hell. What is it with guys and pickup trucks??? But I just said, You drive a pickup? And he said, How else am I gonna haul my surfboard around? and all of a sudden, Ross was 27-times cuter than I already thought he was.

Then he said, I'm gonna paddle out tomorrow morning sorta early. Wanna come? We can hang out on the beach after I catch a couple waves.

I glanced at Cam, who punched Ross in the shoulder and said, Dude. You can't ask my sister out with me standing right here.

And I was like OMG CAM! SHUT UP.

And Ross got his little secret smile again, and Cam cracked up while Ross tapped my number into his phone.

He's coming by to pick me up at 7 a.m. tomorrow.

I have to go dust and vacuum now.

I AM SO EXCITED. HE'S SO CUTE.

Later . . .

I told Mom and Dad about Ross over dinner. They were all, We've never met this young man. We don't want you running around with kids we haven't met.

ARRRRRRRGH. They're sooooooooooooo uptight sometimes.

But Cam came to the rescue and vouched for Ross, and they finally agreed to let me go on the condition that they get to meet him first.

I texted Ross after dinner: My parents want to meet you in the AM b4 we go.

He wrote back right away: KEWL. C U AT 7 =)

Now if I can just keep the chitchat to a minimum tomorrow morning we'll be set.

Later . . .

Maybe I was wrong about guys with pickup trucks. Guess it depends on the guy.

July 16

I am writing this on the beach. I packed my journal and a pen in the bag with my towel and a couple of magazines, a bottle of water, and some sunscreen. I set my alarm for 6 a.m. so that I would be up early enough to take a shower and put on some waterproof mascara. I didn't want to look like I'd just crawled out from under a rock when Ross got here.

He rolled up right at 7 a.m. on the dot, amazingly punctual for a surfer. He was wearing a hoodie and a cap, and I could see the surfboard sticking out of his pickup truck in the driveway. I don't know if it was the fact that it was so early in the morning or what, but Mom and Dad were both really well-behaved. Mom smiled and was friendly; Dad didn't make any jokes that only he thinks are funny.

As we climbed into the truck, I was nervous that my brain wouldn't really work right as far as coming up with things to say. Ross was sort of quiet at first, and I felt that nervous feeling in my stomach like somebody was tap dancing in my rib cage. As we drove up the highway along the coast, Ross kept eyeing the water, like he had forgotten I was there. I felt my face get flushed, and I felt out of place, and then I felt embarrassed, and then I felt ... ANGRY.

I did NOT shave my legs and put on waterproof mascara before dawn to be IGNORED.

Almost, as if he could read my thoughts, Ross flipped his bangs out of his eyes and said, This part always makes me nervous.

I laughed, and said, ME TOO! I said it a little too loudly and with a little too much enthusiasm, but he smiled over at me and said, Yeah! I know, right? It's always like will there be good waves or not??? And I realized that we were talking about two completely different things. He wasn't talking about being alone in the truck with me for the first time and figuring out what to say. He was checking the coastline for waves.

I thought briefly about just opening the door and throwing myself out of the truck, but just as I was trying to gauge how soft the tall grass along the shoulder might be and whether I would clear the concrete and gravel part, Ross must've found what he was looking for and pulled off the road. I recognized this part of the coast. It's the place where the beach line dips in toward the highway and creates a little bay with a natural surf break. Ross eased his truck off the road and parallel parked between two other cars on the side of the highway.

He was all business, and I could tell he wanted to be in the water ASAP. He jumped out of the truck, pointed at the water, and whooped something that sounded like "hella goody nugs." Then he raced around to the back of his truck and pulled off his cap and hoodie and T-shirt all in one swift movement.

And I forgot that I was mad.

And I forgot that he hadn't looked at me twice.

And I forgot that he hadn't probably given a second thought to how smooth my legs were.

All I could see were his p-e-r-f-e-c-t chest and his ABS. OMG.

Ross.

Has.

Some.

ABS.

He wrapped a towel around his waist and traded his board shorts for a wet suit that was in the bed of his truck under his board. I'd always seen surfers with their wet suits peeled down on the one hundred zillion other times I've driven by this surf break. (Hey! Look! I sound like I know what I'm talking about!) I always just thought that they unzipped the back and pulled down the top part because they were hot. I didn't know that they were in the process of GETTING NAKED IN BROAD DAYLIGHT under a TOWEL!

I'm not even sure how he did it so fast, but about 30 seconds after we parked, we were picking our way down the path toward the beach. Well, Ross was like scampering down, balancing a board and pulling up his wet suit and using words I didn't really completely understand to describe the waves.

He's surfing right now. I can sometimes make out which one is him. There are about 10 people out there trying to catch a wave. One of them is a girl with blond braids. Sometimes I think it would be fun to surf, but the water is so cold that it makes me shiver just to think about it. The sun is already trying to break through the marine layer, and I hope that it will so I can take off my hoodie and T-shirt and get some sun. I have a really cute swimsuit on underneath my shorts.

I wonder if Ross will think I look sexy?

I've never really done anything with a boy except kiss.

OMG! Ross just caught a huge wave and rode it all the way in!

July 16, 2 p.m.

I just got back from the beach with Ross, and I can't believe what happened. He offered me drugs. I'm not even sure I should write those words down. I mean, what if my MOM FINDS THIS??? It's so weird. I had such a good time sitting on the beach watching Ross surf, and after a couple of hours he came and sat with me. He unzipped his wet suit and pulled it down halfway. He has those little V lines that plunged into his wet suit from his abs, and I had to concentrate so that I didn't just stare at them the whole time.

We talked for a while. Or, well, I talked. A lot. More than I usually do. Ross just kept asking me about my family, and growing up here and what it was like. He kept telling me that I have a really pretty smile. Like a movie star, he said. He laughed and called me Hollywood. It's funny. Now that I think about it, I didn't really ask him any questions at all. I felt so excited the whole time that he seemed to want to know all about me, and he just kept asking me questions.

THEN!

We headed back up to his truck, and after he slid his surfboard into the back, he shimmied out of his wetsuit using that little towel trick again. Some girls drove by in a silver BMW while he was pulling his suit out from under the towel and honked and screamed out the window. At first it made me blush, but then I thought how cool it was that I was the girl with the guy that other girls were honking at.

When we got into his truck, Ross popped open the console on the armrest between us and pulled out a little glass pipe and a lighter. He brought the pipe to his lips, sparked the lighter over the bowl, then sucked air in, causing the flame to dip into the bowl. A little cloud of white smoke floated up from the glowing embers in the pipe, and Ross held the smoke in his lungs for a second before rolling down his window a couple inches and exhaling out the crack at the top.

This weird, sweet, stinky smell filled the cab of the truck, and I knew that it was weed, but I have never smelled it that strong before. I was afraid my hair would smell like it.

I've seen people smoke pot in movies and on TV, but I've NEVER seen anybody do it in real life. I mean, I think Cam smokes pot. I've heard him and his friends joke around about it, but he's not like a stoner or anything. I felt my heart sort of speed up while I watched Ross smoke, then he turned to me and held the pipe toward me.

He asked me if I wanted a hit.

NO!

I said it fast like I was scared someone might be listening. I was just A. MAZED. that he even thought I looked like a girl who smoked pot. Then I was really worried that he would be mad at me that I didn't want any. I felt like I had answered too fast. I didn't want him to think that I didn't like him just because he smoked pot. What if he didn't like me now?

I shouldn't have worried. He just laughed and said he figured I was a straight edge but that you couldn't blame a boy for trying.

My cheeks are red again now just writing this down. I have to make sure Mom doesn't find this journal and think it's my schoolwork. Not that she'd actually read my journal on purpose; at least I don't think she would. Anyway, I'm going to hide it under some other stuff on my desk, just in case.

I like Ross. I don't want Mom not to let me hang out with him just 'cause he smokes pot.

Ross invited me to come over to the hotel where his mom works tomorrow after yoga and lie out at the pool with him.

Oh yeah, and when we were lying on the beach talking, he told me my suit was "cute." I think he really likes me.

July 17

CAM IS TAKING ME TO MY FIRST BIG PARTY!!!!!!!!!!
IT'S ON SATURDAAAAAAAAAAAAAY!!!!!!!!!!!!!!!!!
THAT'S TOMORROOOOOOOOOOOOOW!!!!!!!!!!!

I CAN'T WAAAAAAAAAAAAAAAAAAIT!!!!!!!!!!!!!!!!

I can't believe he said yes. I heard him talking to his friend Jason about it, and he was like, If Elizabeth Archer's sister is going to be there, I'm THERE.

Elizabeth Archer is this blond cheerleader in my class at school, and she's really pretty, and really nice, but is dumb as a stump. Her older sister is a freshman in college this year, and is just as pretty, only she has red hair and was valedictorian last year. She speaks French and Spanish fluently and is on track to finish her undergrad degree in 3 years. Cam has followed her around like a drooling puppy since he was in 9th grade and she was a sophomore.

I heard him hang up with Jason and go YES! really loudly, and that's when I wandered into his room and said, If Elizabeth Archer is going, can I go?

He opened his mouth to say NO like he always does, but then he looked up at me and really saw me. He sat and sort of looked at me for a minute, like he was taking me in, and then he smiled, and said, Why not?

I jumped up and down and screamed like a moron on a game show, and he laughed and said, But only if you stop screaming right now and promise never to do that again.

I immediately shut up and said, I promise I won't get in your way.

And then Cam said the nicest thing to me. He said, You're not in the way, sis. I like hanging with you.

Which is weird 'cause usually brothers and sisters our age don't always get along, but I realized that Cam is maybe the best brother in the whole galaxy.

July 19

Last night was the party and it was really awful and really great all at the same time. God, sometimes I write stuff down in this journal that just doesn't make any sense at all. If anyone ever finds this, they'll have me committed for being a crazy person.

I'm not sure how I feel about last night. I still can't believe how it all went down. The only two things I know for sure are:

1. Pot is GREAT.
2. Ross is AMAZING.

Cam drove us to Jason's place with strict instructions from Mom and Dad to keep an eye on me. Jason's house was already pretty crowded when we got there and Cam steered us through the living room to the kitchen where he gave Jason a high five and I saw Elizabeth Archer talking to this guy with shaggy brown hair who looked a lot like . . . ROSS!

It was totally him, and I felt my stomach drop like I was on a roller coaster. I couldn't believe he was here too. Elizabeth saw me and waved, and Ross turned around and got this big goofy smile on his face like he was really happy to see me. He came over to say hi to me and Cam and grabbed a couple of beers out of a cooler on his way around the island in Jason's giant kitchen. He handed one to Cam and then held one out to me.

I felt my cheeks go hot, and I glanced up at Cam like, Should I do this? Is this okay?

He laughed and said, You won't like it, sis.

Well, I wasn't about to let Cam tell me what to do for the whole night, so I grabbed the beer and took a big swig. It was cold and bubbly like soda, but as I swallowed it, the taste turned sour and sweet in a really weird way that made me start to gag a little, and I made a face that must've been really funny and a noise that felt like I was trying not to throw up, sort of an URGGGH sound, and Cam and Jason laughed as I handed the beer back to Ross.

Cam was right again. He's right about everything. Beer tastes pretty gross.

Ross got a phone call and held up a finger as he answered and disappeared around a corner toward the front door. Cam saw Megan Archer out by the pool and grabbed Jason and pushed him toward the glass doors that led out back. My face was still pretty red from the beer and the embarrassment. I was really worried that Ross thought I was a moron now. Elizabeth patted my back and smiled her big loopy smile. She said, I hate beer too. Let's get some wine coolers.

I told her I was okay and just wanted to go get some fresh air. She thought this was a good idea and grabbed a bright red bottle of something out of one of the coolers, then took my hand and dragged me out toward the pool and over to the fire pit.

Jason and Cam were over at the hot tub talking to Megan, and Elizabeth and I sat down by this girl I'd never seen before. She was sipping a wine cooler too, and she smiled at us as we sat down.

Elizabeth introduced herself, and the girl told us her name was Astrid. Elizabeth asked her what school she went to, and she told us she was transferring to our school for her senior year. Apparently, she was sick of the Catholic school she'd been attending and convinced her dad to let her go to public school for her last year. She'd come to the party with her boyfriend, who knew Megan and was getting a drink.

I sat there feeling sort of invisible. I wasn't nearly as pretty as Elizabeth or Astrid or Megan, and I couldn't shake the feeling that everybody at this party was older and cooler than I was. I mean, I know that Elizabeth is my age and not very smart where school is concerned, but she's so pretty, I sort of felt like I could have disappeared and no one would have noticed. I felt like a dweeb who couldn't even keep down a swallow of beer.

I wanted to go find Ross and hang out with him, but I was still feeling like I'd disappointed him somehow by not liking the beer he brought me. Maybe he was hanging out with other girls. Girls who drink beer. I was thinking about all of the ways that Ross probably thought I was lame when Astrid noticed I wasn't drinking anything and offered me her wine cooler.

She smiled and asked if I wanted to try some. She said, You look like you're not having a very good time. This will help.

And right at that moment, I DID want to try some. I DID want to have a good time. I just didn't want to be that quiet girl in the corner not talking to anybody at the party.

So I said YES.

The wine cooler was cold and not as bubbly as the beer. It was really really really SWEET. Like, too sweet. It felt like I was drinking snow-cone syrup straight from the bottle. But it was better than beer. At least this was fruity. I couldn't tell if it was strawberry or watermelon or cherry. It just tasted . . . red.

I smiled at Astrid and said thanks. She laughed and said no problem. Elizabeth jumped up and went into the kitchen to get more wine coolers and brought them back. I couldn't really tell any difference in how I felt. I've never been drunk, but I sort of felt . . . lighter somehow. I think it was probably because I didn't feel so lame. These girls were cool and pretty and they were sitting here talking to me like I was one of them, like I belonged there.

I took a drink of the new wine cooler that Elizabeth handed me, and then we were talking about the boys we thought were cute. Elizabeth asked me how I knew Ross, and I told her and Astrid all about meeting Ross at yoga and how we'd gone to the beach together. All of a sudden, as I was talking, I let out a little burp from the wine cooler and my eyes got wide and I slapped a hand over my mouth and started giggling.

Astrid and Elizabeth laughed really hard too, and it felt so good to share a funny moment with these girls who I barely knew. I felt my stomach turn a little bit, and I realized I hadn't eaten much dinner because I was nervous about going to the party. These wine coolers had a lot of sugar in them and maybe it was that or the alcohol that was making my stomach hurt. I told Astrid my stomach felt kind of weird, and she smiled and rubbed her hand on my back. She told me not to worry. You'll get the hang of it, she said, and nodded at the wine cooler. Maybe have a glass of water after that one before you have more. You know, pace yourself.

Then Astrid looked up as she saw a guy walk through the glass doors and come out onto the pool deck. She jumped up and said, Oh, there's my boyfriend. I'm gonna go say hi. See you two later. I watched as she picked her way through the crowd around the pool toward the stairs at the door. She walked up behind this muscular guy on the stairs and put her arms around his waist.

When he turned around, I gasped really loudly and Elizabeth looked at me and said, What?

It was Nathan.

Astrid was Nathan's girlfriend.

Now I really felt sick to my stomach and a little dizzy. I stood up quickly, and all of a sudden I felt the wine cooler hit me, and I sat back down really fast 'cause I thought I might fall down. I closed my eyes and turned away from Nate and Astrid. I didn't want him to see me. I didn't want him to know I was here. I leaned back into the shadows from the hedge at the back of the concrete bench that was carved around the fire pit.

Elizabeth was like, Do you know him?

I nodded. I told her he was my geometry tutor, but even as I said it, I wished I'd kept that to myself.

Elizabeth turned back to watch as Nate and Astrid walked over to join Megan, Cam, and Jason in the hot tub. I put down my wine cooler and stepped over Elizabeth Archer and all of her questions and ran into the house.

I had to find Ross.

When I didn't see him in the kitchen, I headed into the

living room and almost ran into him head-on. He started to say that he'd been looking for me, but I guess the look on my face made him stop short. He asked me if I was okay, and suddenly my eyes filled up with tears and I felt even more like a COMPLETE IDIOT. Oh. My. GOD. I was about to start crying in the middle of my first party, and Ross was completely cool. He looked over both shoulders, then grabbed my elbow and steered me across the living room and up the stairs in the entryway so fast it made me a little dizzy.

I followed Ross into the master bedroom, and he pushed out two French doors onto a balcony that overlooked the backyard. I could see the hot tub and fire pit on opposite sides of the pool. I stood at the rail and looked out at the shadows silhouetted by the flames of the fire pit and the lights under the water in the hot tub. I couldn't make out his face, but I knew Nate was out there. With Astrid.

Ross joined me at the rail and said, So. How's my straight edge?

I felt his arm against mine. It was warm, and he followed my gaze down toward the hot tub. I told him I wasn't such a straight edge tonight.

He laughed and said, Nah, you're just ON edge.

He nodded toward the hot tub and asked who I was looking at. It came pouring out. We plopped down on the patio furniture and I told him all about Nate and the night I tried to kiss him, and about Astrid and the wine coolers. As he listened, Ross pulled a joint out of his pocket and lit it. He took several drags and then held it out to me. I couldn't believe it, but I just took it from him. I told myself it was because I'd already drunk a wine cooler, but really it was because I just didn't want to feel like a loser. Ross is so cool and handsome. I want to feel like a really hot girl. I want Ross to want me the way Cam wants Megan Archer.

I put the joint to my lips, and Ross told me to suck slowly on the end and take a deep breath. I could taste the smoke as it rolled into my mouth over my tongue, then I sort of squinted and inhaled it in a quick deep breath. It tickled the back of my throat so bad that I started coughing really hard. I must've dragged in more smoke than I thought because I could see it puff out around me, even in the dark.

Ross tossed his bangs out of his eyes while he took another long, deep drag off of the joint. I watched the way he held the smoke in for a long time before he blew it out. He cut his eyes my direction with a little smirk and asked, Wanna try again?

I smiled back at him and took the joint. This time I was more prepared. I sucked in very slowly, and the tickle at the back of my throat wasn't quite as bad. Then I held the smoke in my lungs for as long as I could, and when I blew it out, I only coughed once.

Ross whistled and laughed. Dang, girl, he said. That's a big hit. You're gonna feel fine in about 5 minutes.

We settled back on the little patio love seat and kicked our feet up on the bench in front of us. He laid his head on my shoulder, and we looked up at the moon over the palm trees. For a second we were real quiet, and then he put his hand on my leg and said, Sorry about the thing with Nate. I shrugged, and my heart was beating really fast, and after a couple more minutes I started singing along with this song that was blasting out of the speakers by the pool. Then I started laughing, and Ross started laughing too. Uh-oh, he said. And I was like What? And he said, Somebody is stoned!

And then I realized that I felt good! Really good! Deep down to my feet good! I didn't even care about stupid Nate and Astrid anymore. I could sort of feel a weird floating feeling in my brain, like it was all calm and cool in there, and my toes were a little buzzy somehow, and all of a sudden I wanted a drink, something cool and bubbly and NOT a wine cooler.

Ross musta had the same thought 'cause right at that second he said, Let's get outta here, and I said, I want french fries, and he laughed like that was the funniest thing he'd ever heard.

He grabbed me and said, Of course you do. Damn. You're hilarious.

I followed Ross downstairs and waited in the kitchen while

he ran out to the hot tub to tell Cam he was going to take me to get some food and then home. Then we jumped into his truck and headed over to Swingers, where I had the biggest plate of french fries I've ever seen and I didn't give a crap about the calories because they tasted so good. We went through three sides of ranch and half a bottle of ketchup and we sat on the same side of the booth with our feet up on the other side.

The thing that makes Ross so different from other boys is that he listens. He just listened to me talk blah blah blah blah blah for like hours about Nate. And he just kept eating french fries. And ordering chocolate malts. And dipping french fries into the chocolate malts.

And then I felt all weird and spacey in my head, like maybe I'd been talking for at least 23 years without shutting up, and I was really thirsty, and I got worried. I was worried that Ross was bored and that he wasn't having a good time and that I was being one of those whiny girls who complains about everything all the time to everyone and turns everyone off. So I took a really long drink of my Diet Coke through a straw, and just as I was about to turn to Ross and ask if he was totally bored, I felt him lean over and kiss me on the cheek.

Then he laid his head on my shoulder and said, I get it.

We just sat there in the booth for a long time, and I felt his head on my shoulder and I stopped being worried. I got this really happy feeling, like this floaty place in my chest because I knew that Ross did get it. He didn't have to say another word.

We're going to the beach tomorrow.

I can't wait.

July 20

I just got back from the beach with Ross. We smoked another joint before we got out of his truck. It was so much fun! I feel like smoking pot used to be this thing that I was like TOTALLY AGAINST because of all the stuff that everybody tells you and because of the people who you see at school who do it. They're all like fuzz heads who need to clean their fingernails. But Ross is different. And now I'm different. Probably because I'm making the decision to do what I want. I never realized how much I let everyone else decide what I'm going to do. I mean, we started having policemen come to school in what—like 3rd grade?—to tell us that pot is so eeeeeeeeeeevil and WRONG. But, actually, I've smoked two joints now and I'm still going to my geometry class in summer school. No big deal.

Anyway, the beach was good. It was nice to lie in the sun while Ross surfed, and then he sat on the beach with me and we talked. Or, actually, I talked. I'm always the one talking. It was weird at the end. I asked him some questions about Florida and the move out here and the school he went to and his friends there. He didn't really talk about it. Just said that his dad was an asshole and that he was glad his mom got this job. And then he checked his phone and was like, We have to go, and he seemed to be in a really big hurry.

It kind of pissed me off. Totally ruined that floaty feeling I was having from the joint. I feel like he wanted to go hang out with someone else and he didn't want me there. I wish I had my own joint right this very second.

July 22

Tried texting Ross after summer school today, but I never heard back. It's weird. When we're together, he feels like my best friend, and then he just disappears. I wonder what it'd be like to hold his hand? I want to try to when we go to the beach the next time. Maybe when we're walking up to his truck. But he's always holding that damn surfboard. I really want him to text me back. Dad and Mom were all over me tonight about how geometry is going and I know they really care, it's just that I don't know how it's going. I mean, I guess fine. I passed the midterm. Got a B. No big whoop.

ROSS, TEXT ME BACK.

July 25

Oh. My. Gosh.

Just got back from hanging out with Ross and Cam at

the hotel where Ross's mom works. This morning Ross F-I-N-A-L-L-Y texted me back. He told me that Cam and I should bring our swimsuits and meet him at this new yoga class this afternoon. It's at the place where we usually go, but earlier. Luckily Cam had the day off from cleaning pools, so he came and got me at school and we went to meet Ross.

When I asked him if he got my texts yesterday, all he said was, Yeah. Sorry. I was busy.

I was like WHAT. EVER. But it was still really good to see him. Ugh! Sometimes I'm so like one of those dippy girls I just HATE who are like all gross over some guy who treats them like crap. I mean, not that Ross is treating me like crap. Maybe he WAS busy. Maybe it's something weird with his dad or something. I don't know. ARGH. SEE? THIS is why I need to smoke a joint sometime! My head just goes on this giant Tilt-A-Whirl and I can't make it stop.

ANY

WAY

We got to this new class and there was this teacher named Ian who Ross knows. Ian is a sophomore at the college where my Dad works, and he apparently teaches yoga on the side. Ross met him at a party at the beach on Saturday. He's got blond spiky hair and a friendly smile. He's a little too tan if you ask me, but I guess he and Ross are surfing buddies or something.

There was a lot of "whassup" and "dude" and "bro," only it sounds like they're saying "bra" and general weird boy talk. Cam even got into it.

I wish I had a friend who is a girl to talk to like that. I mean, not LIKE that, but someone who I felt like I was close to. It was sort of instant with these guys.

Anyway, after class we were all talking while we headed over to the hotel, and Ross told us that Ian has a friend named Blake who has a beach house up the coast. Then he said that Blake was having a party this weekend, and almost before he finished the sentence, I was like YES I WANT TO GO TO THE PARTY! That made Ross and Cam crack up, and I thought about how perfect this summer was turning out to be because I had met Ross and Cam was treating me like an adult.

When we got to the hotel Ross's mom was in meetings or something, but the concierge told us "hi" and joked around with Ross and then let us go lie out by the pool. We went and changed clothes in the locker rooms by the pool where they had towels and everything. It was SO NICE.

But then Ross and Cam went into the bathroom together and I think they totally smoked pot because when they came out, they were sort of giggling. Ross started talking on and on about how cool Ian was and how much fun they had the other night at the party, and I realized THAT was the night I was texting him, so he wasn't busy with anything like his dad, just at a big party.

I got really quiet because I was feeling left out. I mean, it wasn't fair that Cam and Ross got to get stoned and I didn't, and it REALLY wasn't cool of Ross to not return my text messages when he was just at a party. I mean HOW HARD IS IT TO TEXT AT A PARTY??? GRRRR.

Then the boys got hungry and Ross ordered food that they brought out for us right there at the pool, and we didn't even have to pay for it. He said his mom got an expense account at the hotel every month for clients and it was okay with her if he got lunch for himself and friends as long as he didn't spend too much.

The food helped, because I realized I was really hungry from yoga, but then Ross noticed I was being superquiet and asked what was up.

I just said, Nothing, but he wouldn't let it go, so I told him. Well, I whispered it. I said:

I want a hit.

And Cam heard me and said, You won't really like it.

And I shot him a look and said, I already really like it. You don't know everything about me.

Cam frowned for a second, and then Ross busted out laughing like it was the funniest thing ever. When Cam heard that, he started laughing too. I said, See? You're both high as kites so everything is funny. NOT. FAIR.

Ross promised me that he would smoke me out at the party on Saturday.

Cam was laughing too, but he kept looking over at me and then looking away on the drive home. I hope he isn't getting all Big Brotherly on me.

July 26

I just got back from Cam's bedroom and I'm SHAKING. I can barely hold the pen to write this in the journal. Oh my God. My handwriting looks like crap.

I can't BELIEVE what just happened.

Cam has to work really early on Saturday morning cleaning a pool for these people who have this big party planned for their kids. He told me that he couldn't go to the party because he has to get in bed really early.

I told him that Ross could take me to the party, and he said, I don't feel comfortable with that.

I told him that I didn't care what he felt comfortable with, I was going to this party with Ross and Ian no matter what.

He just stared at me. I was standing in the doorway of his room, and he got up and pulled me in and closed the door. He was like, Do you want me to tell Mom and Dad that you've been running around smoking weed with Ross?

I just stared at him. I said, Are you serious? Because I'll march right in there this second and tell them that you've been smoking pot with Ross in PUBLIC. At the HOTEL. And who knows where else? And I'll also tell them that you were standing right there when I had my first beer.

I sort of wished I hadn't said that because he looked hurt, but I mean, come on! You're going to THREATEN me? He rolled his eyes and said, I can't believe you've been smoking pot.

I said, Look. I've had two puffs off of two different joints. It's not like I'm some crazy stoner chick. I just liked it. It's no big deal.

Finally I got him to agree that I could go and he wouldn't tell Mom and Dad anything.

I just got a text back from Ross. He and Ian are going to swing by and pick me up in 2 hours.

OMG.

WHAT AM I GOING TO WEAR???

Later . . .

Cam came into the bathroom while I was putting on my makeup and just leaned against the door. He was watching me in the mirror while I put on mascara, and he asked how I could do that without poking my eye out. I told him I am talented. He cracked a smile for the first time all day. Finally.

Then he came over and hugged me and told me that I was pretty.

I laughed and told him to stop being a weirdo.

But really, it made me feel so good on the inside, like he finally accepts that I can make my own decisions, like he doesn't just see me as his stupid kid sister anymore.

Oh! He just called for me. Ian and Ross must be here. He's insisting on walking me out so that he can be all big brother and tell them to take good care of me.

July 27

Holy crap. HOLY CRAP!

I don't even know where to begin. My head is in 100 thousand different places. AND POUNDING LIKE A JACKHAMMER. This is the first time I've been able to sit up all morning, but I had to write all of this down so I don't forget!

First things first: So, Ross and Ian came in to meet Mom and Dad, because of course when they found out that Cam wasn't going to the party, Mom almost had a heart attack and wasn't going to let me go. Luckily Dad was cleaning up the flower bed out front when Ross and Ian pulled up, and he recognized Ian. Apparently Ian was in a section of music theory last fall that Dad teaches. He and Dad were laughing and talking when Mom stormed out to say that I couldn't go to the party, and Dad introduced her to Ian, and Ian was really charming and promised that they'd have me back home by midnight and that nothing bad would happen.

I HATE hearing people say that they'll "keep an eye on me." As if I'm some crazy person who might just EXPLODE at any moment. Whatever. Ian told Mom that he really loved her impatiens in the flower bed that Dad was weeding and how he used to work in a nursery. Then they talked for like 29 years about soil types, and Ross and Cam and I were almost comatose from boredom by the time Mom finally glanced over at me and said that it was okay if I went to the party.

So FINALLY we got in the car, and I was so happy to finally get out of there that I didn't even mind that Ross sat up front with Ian. I mean, I guess it would have been weird for him to sit in the back with me, but I thought that maybe he'd at least offer me the front seat. Whatever.

So we drive up the coast and get to this amazing house that's all glass and chrome and is perched on a cliff overlooking the ocean and there's this pool that looks like it flows off of the cliff—an infinity pool. It looks like it just goes on and on forever.

Ian's friend Blake answered the door barefoot in designer jeans and a bright green Lacoste polo that was tight around his biceps. He was handsome and had brown hair that was short on the sides and messy on top. Ian introduced him to Ross and then me.

When I walked in, Blake smiled at me almost like he was shy. Then he took my hand and said that Ian was the best friend in the world for bringing the prettiest girl to his party.

I was like WHAT? I looked over at Ross, who winked at me and laughed. Blake slid my hand around his arm like he was walking me down the aisle at a wedding and gave us the full tour. It was really crowded already. People were everywhere, and it seemed as if Blake knew every single one of them.

Upstairs in the master suite, Blake slid open the big glass wall and led me out onto the balcony, and Ian and Ross followed us. The view was so amazing that it took my breath away. I asked Blake what it was like to wake up in that bed and see this view every morning, and he turned and looked right at me and said, Why don't you stay tonight and find out?

I blushed really hard. I jerked my arm away from him and put my hands up to my cheeks. I didn't want to, but I couldn't help it! I felt so strange inside. Ian laughed and Ross whistled, and I just didn't understand what was happening. I mean, Blake is very, very handsome, and he's not that much older than I am. He just turned 20, so he's like 3½ years older than me, but I

47

really like Ross, and I couldn't understand why he was whistling and hooting, and it sort of made me mad at him because I realized that he wasn't acting like he liked me back very much.

When we got back downstairs, new people had arrived with bottles of white wine and vodka. Blake led the way into the kitchen, which was as nice as the master bedroom. It was like something out of a magazine. I looked around at all of the people who were there, and I pulled Ross aside while Ian was making us drinks and whispered, WOW we're like the youngest people here.

He smiled at me and said, I know! Isn't it better than those dumb high school parties?

I stepped out the big glass doors off the kitchen toward the pool to get a closer look. There were already a lot of people outside, and I walked down to the end where the pool seemed to flow over the edge of the cliff and looked past the clear glass partition at the edge of the pool area. The water flowed over a false edge into a trough below where it was sucked back into the pool filtration system. It created a pretty little waterfall.

When I turned around, there were two girls standing behind me, admiring the view. I say girls, but one was older than the other. She must've been in her 30s but she was dressed much younger. Her hair was red, but I don't think it was her natural color. She was standing next to a tall blond girl who looked like she was about my age, only she had really long legs and wore a

48

short black dress. She was holding a beer, and she looked like a high schooler on a TV show—you know, one of those shows where high school girls are really pretty and have million-dollar wardrobes and no zits, and they're constantly getting their moms out of trouble instead of getting into trouble themselves? Anyway, she looked like that, and when I turned around, I realized that she was closer to my age than anyone else at the party besides Ross.

Both girls smiled and said hi. The blond girl told me her name was Lauren. I introduced myself and then turned back to follow her gaze back out across the water. We both stared for a minute in silence, and then she said how amazing this place was. I smiled and agreed. The redhead said her name was Diane and asked who I was there with. I told her I was there with Ross. She asked if that was the guy who came with Ian, and I said yes. Lauren asked me how long I'd known Ross, and I told her we'd been going out for a couple of weeks. This made Diane start laughing really hard, and Lauren sort of looked at me like she felt sorry for me and elbowed Diane in the ribs.

I asked what was so funny. Lauren looked at me and said: Ross is gay.

I stood there at the end of the pool, and the first thought I had when she said it was that I was glad there was a glass partition behind me to keep me from falling over the edge of the cliff. I. COULDN'T. BELIEVE IT.

Diane was still laughing and told Lauren to come inside with her because there were a bunch of people Diane needed to introduce her to. She tried to grab Lauren's arm, but Lauren didn't even look at her. Just rolled her eyes and shook Diane off her arm. She told Diane to go ahead, that she'd come in a minute. Diane told her to hurry and then walked back toward the house.

I turned back around toward the ocean and closed my eyes really tight. I thought maybe Lauren would just take the hint and follow Diane back into the house. I didn't want her to see me cry. I didn't want to cry, but I couldn't help it. I knew that my mascara was going to run and I'd look like a raccoon.

I felt Lauren walk up next to me, so I opened my eyes. She was staring out at the ocean and the lights on the coastline in the distance. She was quiet for a minute, then I felt her pat me on the back and say, All the cute ones are gay. I tried to smile, but I was so embarrassed.

When I was quiet, she just kept talking—like it was easy. I could tell she was one of those girls who could talk to anybody. I usually hate them because sometimes it's really hard for me to speak up, but I was glad that she was there. Otherwise it would have just been me crying over the edge of the cliff at a party where I should have been having fun. I HATE that about myself. Most of the time I feel like everyone else is cooler and smarter and prettier than I am. It was nice that she was talking to me because it gave me a second to chill out and just listen.

Lauren told me that when she'd first met Ross at that party on the beach with Ian, she thought he was really cute too. And she told me not to feel bad because she'd thought he was straight 'cause of the truck and the surfboards and everything. She told me that she was new to town, too. She'd just moved here from New York to live with her dad. His name is Gerald (with a hard G, not a J sound) and he's a music producer. Blake's dad is a movie producer, so basically he is a rich kid who grew up in the Palisades. He dropped out of NYU and started a band. Lauren used to sneak out of the house in New York to go to Blake's shows, and she told her dad about his band. Her dad came with her to a show one night and signed the band, so Blake moved back out to Los Angeles.

I asked Lauren why she moved to Los Angeles. She was quiet for a minute, then looked at me and told me that she came to live with her dad because her mom's boyfriend in New York was a total creep who kept hitting on her. She took a sip of her beer, then offered it to me. I smiled at her and told her that I don't like beer.

She laughed really loudly and said, ME NEITHER, then reached over and poured the rest of her beer into the pool. I started laughing too, and it felt good to laugh with somebody. Lauren said C'mon and grabbed my hand and pulled me back toward the house. I asked her where we were going, and she said to find some good stuff.

I couldn't believe how cool Lauren was and that she was being so nice to me.

Lauren gave Diane the slip again, weaving past her near the door to the house. She said Diane worked at the label for her dad. Diane was trying to introduce Lauren to people, supposedly because Lauren was new in town, but really so that Diane could pretend to be important and cool by running around with her boss's daughter.

Lauren led us to the bar in the kitchen where Blake was mixing drinks. Ian and Ross were there, passing a joint back and forth. Ross came over and gave me a hug and kiss on the cheek. He said he was so glad Lauren and I had met each other. Lauren rolled her eyes and jabbed him in the ribs.

What was that for? Ross wanted to know.

Lauren said it was for being a heartbreaker and that we weren't here for hot gay guys, we were here for cosmos.

Blake laughed hard when she said that, shouted COMIN' RIGHT UP, then started pouring vodka and cranberry and some other stuff into a martini shaker. I had never had a cosmo, just seen them on TV. The women drinking them were always wearing high heels like Lauren's, and they didn't ever seem to feel ugly or at a loss for words, like me. I looked around at Ian and Blake and Ross and Lauren, and all of a sudden I didn't feel like a loser anymore.

Blake passed me a martini glass with cold pink liquid about to slosh over the rim. I took a small sip off the top as he held it. It was SO GOOD! It was sweet, but not syrupy like wine coolers. It was so cold and a little tart, but then as I swallowed it, I felt the warmth of the vodka all the way down. Blake grinned at me over the rim of the glass, like we were sharing a secret. He told me I had perfect lips, and when he said it, I blushed. AGAIN. He was so cute and had this little dimple when he smiled halfway. He actually reminded me a little bit of stupid Nathan—only Blake is MUCH COOLER.

By the time I finished that drink in the kitchen with Lauren, I was feeling SO BUZZED. It was so much fun, and Blake had cranked up the music in the living room. Ross grabbed Lauren's hand and reached for mine, and I pulled my hand back like Ross was a hot stove. I felt this weird stab in my chest and just looked at him. No matter how much I didn't want to feel it, I was hurt; hurt that he hadn't mentioned he was gay; embarrassed that I hadn't figured it out; afraid that he thought I was stupid for having a crush on him.

He must've seen it in my eyes, 'cause he tossed his bangs in that little way he always does, and said, I have to dance with you right now.

I crossed my arms, and said, Why?

He said because it's a rule that the gay dude has to dance with the two hottest girls at the party, and Lauren's already coming, so that just leaves you.

I peered up at him through my lashes and said, I flat-ironed my hair at 6 a.m. for you that first day we went to the beach.

Lauren threw her head back and laughed so hard she snorted. That made me start giggling, and suddenly I was leaning against Ross to keep from falling down. We all laughed so hard we almost cried, and just like that, with a group hug and a good laugh, all of the embarrassment melted away, and I realized that there was something better than making out with Ross would ever be: dancing with him at this party.

Blake followed us into the living room that ran the length of the house. It had gotten dark outside finally, and the pool was lit up, flowing over the edge of the cliff. The moon was high in the sky, and I felt so good! The cosmo made my head feel all warm and I was laughing with Lauren as we sandwiched Ross between us and danced with our hands up in the air.

Blake danced up behind me and I felt his hands on my waist. My heart started beating really fast, and at first I pulled away a little, but then he gently pulled me back into him and whispered in my ear. He said, I don't bite, and I laughed, and then he said, At least not hard anyway, and that made me smile.

I leaned my head back against his chest and he wrapped his arms around my waist and I felt him pressed up against me. I could barely breathe!

The doorbell rang, and someone answered, and a another big group of Blake's friends found us in the living room. As Blake kissed and fist-bumped and high-fived his way around the room, Lauren came dancing over and whisper-yelled over the music, OMG! BLAKE LIKES YOU SO MUCH. Then she said, C'mon let's go get more cosmos.

So we did.

Lauren's cosmos tasted as good as Blake's did! I asked her how she learned, and she just flipped a long strand of blond hair over her shoulder and raised her eyebrow. She said that some girls are scouts and learn how to sew buttons and tie knots. She'd been mixing drinks for her mom since she was 12.

We danced our way back to the living room with our glasses and danced with these two really tall guys who were twins, for what seemed like hours. As we danced, I kept looking over at Lauren and thinking how comfortable she was with all of this, and then I realized: SURPRISE! YOU'RE comfortable with all of this, and it felt so AMAZING. I knew that this wasn't just me being there with Lauren. It was the cosmos. They totally helped! I'd always heard all of this stuff about how dangerous it was to drink and how many teenagers get killed in drunk driving accidents, but no one ever told me how it actually FEELS to be buzzed on cosmos and dancing with two hot guys and your new friend at a party overlooking the ocean!

Somehow my glass kept getting refilled and it felt like we were dancing for hours. I was feeling really buzzed when one of the twins asked Lauren if we wanted to come outside with them for a cigarette. Lauren just laughed and said that tobacco was totally gross. Then she blew the twins a kiss and dragged me upstairs, giggling.

When we got to the master bedroom, Blake was leaning over a mirror on the bedside table. I didn't really see what he was doing, but when he saw us, he popped up and rubbed his nose, sniffing, and said LADIES! really loud, like us coming in was the best thing that had ever happened. Lauren sort of froze and was looking down at the bedside table. I followed her gaze and there was a mirror sitting there with a little pile of white powder on it. I was FREAKING OUT! I didn't even know anybody who KNEW anybody who did cocaine, and now there was a pile of it sitting right in front of us.

I felt an arm come around my waist and somebody kissed my neck, and I turned around to see Ross. When I saw him, he pinched my stomach, and it tickled, so I giggled and twisted around. Right then Blake pointed at the mirror and asked Lauren if she wanted to do a line. I guess he meant sniff a line of cocaine because I'd never actually heard anyone offer someone cocaine, much less SEEN IT RIGHT THERE IN FRONT OF ME!!!

I sort of held my breath. Ross was watching Lauren too. She flipped her hair over her shoulder and said, WE aren't doing any REAL drugs. But I might show a little leg for a joint! Ross whooped and shouted TAKE IT OFF, BABY! and pulled a little tinfoil pouch out of his pocket, waving it around. Blake cracked up, and before I knew it, he had set up this really big glass tube with about 3 inches of water in the bottom. Ross called it a bong and gave me a step-by-step on what he was doing as he loaded some brown powdery stuff into the tiny bowl on the side.

I was feeling all spinny from the cosmos, and when I saw the brown powder in the tinfoil I said, Oh no! Ross, your weed went bad. It's all brown! and everybody cracked up. Blake came over and told me I was his new favorite girl and that this was called hash—which Ross said is like just the part of marijuana that makes you get high, or something like that. I can't really remember. All I knew was that Lauren said if I liked pot, I'd REEEEEEEALLY like hash.

SHE.

WAS.

RIGHT!

OMG.

I took one hit off of the bong, and the smoke didn't even make me cough. When I smoked joints with Ross, it took a couple minutes to feel anything. Maybe it was 'cause I'd already drank three cosmos, or maybe it was just 'cause this was hash, but it hit me—WHAM! The minute I blew the smoke out I felt SO HIGH.

Only, this high was DIFFERENT. I didn't feel paranoid, like I sometimes do when I smoke pot. I just felt floaty, and good. I'm not really sure how we got downstairs, because the next thing I remember is Lauren kicking off her high heels and standing up on the diving board with me. Blake had turned the music on the outside speakers up really loud, and Blake and Lauren and I started dancing on the diving board.

Lauren saw the twins and jumped down to run over and say hi, and then it was just me and Blake dancing on the diving board over the pool. I could see Ian and Ross were down by the edge where the pool seemed to drop over the cliff. Ross had his arms around Ian's neck, and there was this smile on his face that made me feel so good inside.

I spun around a little too fast, though, and I guess I was drunker than I thought, or maybe it was the hash, but the next thing I knew I had fallen in the water. And the most AMAZING thing happened: I started laughing. I mean, usually I'd have just fallen apart from embarrassment and wanted to just drown. CAN YOU BELIEVE IT? Falling off the diving board right in front of a WHOLE PARTY full of people staring at me like that?

The water felt cool against my skin, not too cold, and I saw all of these bubbles burst up in front of my face and realized that I was laughing. I was laughing at myself, and how silly it was that I was dancing on a diving board with a 20-year-old boy anyway, and then OF COURSE that I was the klutz who would fall into the water, and it felt AMAZING!

Of course, it only took me about 10 seconds to think all of this, but the hash was still playing with my sense of time, I think, because it felt like quite a while. Only, I wasn't panicked from being in the water, just laughing at myself, and then through the bubbles from my laughter, I saw another body splash into the pool and then swim toward me. It was BLAKE! He had jumped in with all of his clothes on too, and I felt his arms around me as we swam up to the surface.

When our heads popped out of the water, I heard the music again and I heard Blake laughing. I turned toward him as Blake found his footing near the shallower end of the middle of the pool. He pulled me closer and said, Gotta be careful dancing on the diving board. He said it with a big sweet smile. Then he leaned in and kissed me. I closed my eyes and just felt weightless in the water, with Blake's arms wrapped around my waist and my legs tangled up in his.

Ross and Lauren were suddenly at the edge of the pool, and Ross shouted, OH JEEZ! Come up for air you two! And then I heard Lauren giggle, and I looked up just as she pushed Ross into the pool, then jumped in herself. All of a sudden the whole place turned into a POOL PARTY and about 20 people were in the pool with their clothes on, laughing and shrieking, and in the middle of it all Blake and I were floating around kissing. I can't remember when I've EVER had more fun in my entire LIFE.

After a while Blake helped me out of the pool and we went upstairs to get towels. When we were in his bathroom, he took off his shirt and jeans right there in front of me, like it was no big deal. He draped a white robe over my shoulders. Then we kissed for a long time. OMG! I HAD NEVER KISSED A GUY IN JUST HIS UNDERWEAR. He was just wearing a pair of black briefs, which I thought was sort of sexy because most high school guys wear boxers. Not that I've seen a lot of them except when their jeans are riding low. But Blake's underwear looked sort of expensive and made him seem like a grown-up. I was leaning up against the sink, and Blake was breathing really heavily. I could feel that he was hard through his underwear and it was pressed right up against me. I made out with Sean last year when we went to homecoming, and it was the same thing, but Sean was wearing jeans at the time, and he was kissing me like he was going to swallow half of my face. Blake is a MUCH better kisser, and he was kissing my neck and giving me goose bumps all up and down my arms (even WITH the robe on) when I heard Ian calling my name and coming up the stairs.

That's when I remembered I had a curfew.

Blake wasn't too happy that I had to be home so early. He kept pulling me closer to him and whispering "don't go" into my ear, but I finally giggled and pushed him away. Back downstairs, Ross, Lauren, and Blake traded cell numbers for everybody. Lauren kept laughing and hugging me and saying OMG! I'm so happy we met! We're going to have so much fun!

As I headed downstairs in my soggy clothes, my head was starting to feel a little heavy, like I couldn't hold it up by myself. Blake leaned in for one last kiss and whispered, When will I see you again? in my ear. I tried to say "soon," but the room was kind of spinning and it was like my tongue was made of a big cotton ball, only it was heavy and I couldn't make it move the way I wanted it to. Ross was laughing and said, C'mon, princess, let's get you to the car.

Somehow I got to the backseat of Ian's SUV, because the next thing I remember is Ross yelling, WHOA WHOA

WHOA, and Ian must've pulled over, because I felt the car swerve and then stop really fast. Ross opened the door, and I leaned over and barfed really hard onto the curb. My head was pounding, and Ross was there, helping me sit back up in the car.

I remember pulling up to our house, and I tried to get out, but Ross wouldn't let me. He was texting someone on his phone, and the last thing I really remember is Cam coming to the door of the SUV and telling me that I had to be quiet. I don't know what I was saying, really.

When I woke up this morning, I was in bed, and my head hurt so bad, I thought I might throw up again. I went into the bathroom and took some Advil and lay back down again. I must've drifted off, because I just woke up again to my phone buzzing. I have 3 text messages: Ross, Lauren, and Blake. THAT put a big smile on my face just now. I'm SO EXCITED to hang out with all of them again. I want Cam to meet them too. He'd love Blake, I think.

Only next time, no hash when I've had 3 cosmos. UGH. I don't EVER want my head to hurt like this again.

Later . . .

ARGH. Sometimes I just hate Cam so much.

He is sooooooooo pissed about last night. He said that he was almost asleep when he got a text from Ross that I was wasted and that he had to come get me out. He asked me if I even remembered walking into the house. I said yes, but I don't, and he knew it. He asked me if I remembered talking to Mom and Dad and I said of course I did, and he just shook his head and glared at me and said Mom and Dad were in BED. Then he called me an idiot under his breath.

I don't see what the big deal is. I mean, they don't know I came home drunk, and they're not going to find out. I told Cam he should just calm down. He said, CALM DOWN? You came home last night in a BLACKOUT.

I don't really think it was a blackout. I mean, I still remember most everything. I think a blackout is like when you wake up somewhere and you don't know how you got there, right? Either way, I got sort of scared when I saw how upset Cam was, plus my head still hurt and my stomach felt really gross. I started to cry a little bit, and Cam chilled out. He brought me some orange juice and told me that I had to be smarter about partying, but he was still really serious about everything.

I just don't understand why he has to be like that. I mean, nothing happened. Next time I'll just drink more slowly, and I won't smoke hash on top of it. It's really no big deal.

Lauren just texted me. She said she had fun last night and I should call her when I'm up.

She didn't seem too drunk at all last night. I wonder if she has some tips for not getting quite so wasted? OMG. LOL. Maybe I just won't drink ever again. Jeez. I'm gonna call Lauren. That'll make me feel better.

OH! AND! I'm going to pack for VACATION next week! That'll make me feel better for SURE!

July 28

Blake keeps texting me!

Okay, he's not really texting, he's sexting—all about how he wants to kiss me again. He said he wants to be in the pool with me again, only this time just us, and we'll take our clothes off first.

I sorta blushed when I read that one.

Lauren says he's a horn-dog and Ross says that he's a cokehead.

But I kinda can't stop thinking about him. I keep replaying that scene in his bathroom in my mind, and I get that same feeling, like I can't quite catch my breath, and my pulse races. Then he'll send me a text about wanting to feel my body against his or something, and I get all embarrassed by it, and nervous—like I'm ashamed of it. Yesterday the text he sent me just grossed me out, and I didn't even text him back.

It's confusing. I want him to like me and I want him to be

turned on by me, but I feel like the cosmos and the pot got me to jump way past this place where it was flirty and fun, and we wound up almost naked in his bathroom. Now it all seems to mean more somehow, or maybe I just want it to mean more?

Maybe it only means more to me, and I feel like every text he sends me is all about my body. That's why I feel weird about it. I'm not sure if likes anything besides my body.

Does that make me one of those crazy girls who is always asking for MORE? I mean, I only hung out with him ONE TIME, and now I am a complete LUNATIC thinking about him ALL THE TIME—his body in those little black briefs, the way he felt pressed up against me.

Maybe I just need to hang out with him again and see what happens. I want to, but he hasn't really texted me to ask me out on a date or anything. Maybe I can see if Lauren can set something up so we can all go hang out together.

July 29

Today was my last day of geometry summer school!

Cam dropped me off this morning, and Lauren and Ross were waiting for me when I got done taking the test. I'm pretty sure I aced it. And if I didn't, WHO CARES??? At least the tutoring with stupid Nathan paid off. Glad I got something out of that guy. HA HA HA!

Ross and Lauren and I drove down the beach and passed a pipe around. I asked Ross where he gets his weed because I feel like I smoke a lot of it lately. (Am I a total stoner now?) He said he gets it from Ian. Lauren said she's going to try to get a medical marijuana card so that we can go get it legally. I'd never thought about that before.

After we were good and stoned, we decided to drive up the highway along the water. Ross rolled down the windows and Lauren turned up the music, and I let my arm drift out the window. For a second I wondered if it was a good idea for Ross to be driving around stoned, but I couldn't worry about it for even 5 seconds. It was one of those beautiful days when the sky is so blue that you can't believe it's real, like you're watching a movie of the sky. The long grass on the hills along the road was yellowed from being baked in the sun all summer. I just decided it was too beautiful out to worry about Ross, or anything else, for that matter. I told myself that driving stoned is different from driving drunk. I've heard about drunk driving accidents, but I've never heard of a stoned driving accident. Besides, the breeze off the ocean was cool and everything smelled fresh. The salt air whipping through the truck, through my hair, through my fingers seemed to carry every worry away.

Ross pulled the truck off the road into a little parking lot by one of the state beaches and led the way down a flight of railroad tie stairs onto a stretch of sandy beach at the base of a steep cliff. At one end of the beach were huge rocks and boulders that led to a small cave where we could walk through to a secluded stretch of private beach (if we ducked). When the tide was out, you could make it through. Ross said we could hang for an hour before the water got too high to walk through.

We were the only ones on the beach. Lauren pulled off her top. Ross stripped down to his boxers and they both teased me until I took off my shirt too. At first I was like HELL NO, but then Lauren rolled her eyes, and said, Oh, c'mon, it's not like he's checking you out or anything. She had a point, I decided.

Lauren and I sat there next to each other in our bras, staring out at the water while Ross jumped into the waves and body surfed for a little while. (OMG. Lauren's body is CRAZY. She's so skinny!) After a while Ross came out of the water, all dripping, and golden brown, and gorgeous. He sat down, and the three of us started talking about school. Turns out Ross and Lauren are BOTH coming to my high school! I HADN'T EVEN THOUGHT ABOUT THAT! This school year is going to be SO GREAT!

They both had lots of questions about teachers and what the kids were like and who my friends were. I was sorta embarrassed because I told them that I didn't have many close friends and that I was really glad they were both going to be there. Lauren asked why I didn't have a lot of friends. She seems like one of those people who makes friends really easily without even trying that hard.

I told them I didn't know why I had a harder time making friends. I'm quieter than Cam is, I guess. I said that people seem so unpredictable to me, and that scares me. Ross laughed and said that he finds people TOTALLY predictable. I smiled and said that it really helped to smoke some pot. And also that Lauren's cosmos helped me be less quiet.

This made Lauren giggle until there were tears running down her face, and Ross laughed too. He said the funniest thing he'd seen all summer was the moment I fell off the diving board at Blake's house, and I started laughing too. We all lay there laughing for a long time. We'd finally get quiet, and then one of us would think about it again and start giggling all over, until finally my stomach hurt.

On the way home, Lauren and Ross took turns quizzing me about Blake, and Lauren almost made Ross run off the road while she tickled me until I gave her my phone so she could read all of the texts that Blake had sent me. Ross wanted to know if I was going to see Blake again, and I said I didn't know how to work that out. My parents would NEVER go for me dating a 20-year-old. I think that's part of the reason that it feels so EXCITING when he texts me: It feels dangerous. Lauren is going to see if she can set up another party with Blake when I get back from vacation.

When Ross dropped me off, Lauren said she was really going to miss me while I was away. Ross said he would too. I made them promise not to have too much fun without me.

July 31

It's so early in the morning I can barely keep my eyes open. Somehow I made it to the gate at LAX with Mom and Dad and Cam. Cam just asked me if I wanted to come with him to get coffee. I don't like coffee that much, but maybe I can get a vanilla latte. Ugh. How come vacation feels like a chore right now?

Later . . .

I never realized how much people drink on airplanes. The people sitting across the aisle from me and Cam are having Bloody Marys. They've both had 2, and the guy just ordered another one. It's, like, midmorning and this flight isn't that long. They're going to be wasted by the time we land.

I wonder what it would be like to drink on a plane?

I've really only drank once. I don't count that wine cooler at the party, but now I notice it more when other people are doing it. Last night at dinner Mom and Dad each had a glass of wine.

I sat there the whole time wondering what wine tastes like. I thought about sneaking a sip after dinner, but then Lauren called, and I forgot about it.

Later . . .

We just had lunch at a restaurant in the airport because our rental car was delayed.

EVERYONE was drinking. Except me and Cam.

Dad had a beer. Mom had a glass of chardonnay. Well, Dad convinced her to. He laughed and said, C'MON! We're on vacation, Margaret! She acted all giggly like she was going to get caught by the wine police or something.

Cam said that it was cocktail hour SOMEWHERE in the world. Mom shot him a look and said, Well, it's not cocktail hour for EITHER of you for at least another few years.

She. Would. Have. A. FIT. If. She. Found. Out.

Maybe I should start hiding this journal. I don't think Mom would ever go snooping. Still . . . Oh! Our flight's boarding.

Blake just texted me AGAIN:

THINK OF ME WHEN U RUB IN UR SUNSCREEN.

God. He's such a dirty boy!!!

(I kinda LIKE IT!!!)

August 2

Mexico is AMAZING.

We drove for about 30 minutes up the coast to this little beach town. Dad rented a house on the water here. The house isn't as nice as ours at home, but it's RIGHT on the beach! When we got here, there were two women in the kitchen who work at the house and make food and clean everything. It's like a hotel only the food is included and it's a lot cheaper to just rent the house for a week.

I am sitting writing this in a little hut that is right on the beach in front of the house. It's nicer than a hut, really. It's just a thatched roof over beautiful tile—sort of like a gazebo, only no walls or lattice. There's a little bar with a sink and some stools next to a grill, and big cushions on built-in benches all around the perimeter that face the water. I watched Cam head down the beach with a surfboard a few minutes ago.

It's so strange being in a place where my phone doesn't work at all. I didn't realize how much I'd been texting Ross and Lauren in the past few days. Or Blake. It's funny; when I think of him my heart races, but I'm not sure I even like him. I feel like he's the ocean and I've fallen in and the waves are too big; like I'm in over my head. I'm not even sure which way is up anymore.

All I can see in front of me is water. The beach seems to go on for miles, and miles. The sound of the waves hitting the shore is loud and the rhythm makes me take deep breaths. Everything just feels slower here—more relaxed.

Except for the waves, it's so quiet.

August 3

Today was so FUN! Dad booked this thing called a canopy tour for us and we went zip-lining through the trees. It was scary at first, but it made my heart race in a really fun way. That feeling of free falling really fast for just a few seconds always takes my breath away. It's SO SCARY, but SO FUN. When I was on, I looked down like 5 stories and thought, AM I REALLY ABOUT TO DO THIS??? I couldn't believe it, but I just jumped!

WWWWHHHHHHHHEEEEEEEEEEEEEEEE!

It was SO. MUCH. FUN!!! As soon as I did it, I couldn't wait to do it again.

Can't wait for dinner! I'm STARVING. The food here is SO GOOD. Tonight the cooks said they were making something called ceviche that is fish and lemon juice and other stuff. I can't wait to try it!

August 4

I fell asleep on the beach this afternoon, and I would've gotten SO sunburned except Mom came down to join me and woke me up just as I was starting to get a little pink. She rubbed some sunscreen into my shoulders, and then I did her back. It was actually fun to lie on the beach with her. She told me she thought Ross was really sweet. I told her about meeting Lauren at the party. At first I was worried that she was going to start grilling me, but she didn't! She said she was really glad that I'd made a friend, and she was excited to meet her.

I also told her that Ross was gay. She just smiled and asked me how I felt about that. All of a sudden I felt really close to her, like my opinion really mattered to her. I told her that I was confused at first because he hadn't told me right away and he was such a guy's guy. He liked surfing and sports and drove a truck and everything. Anyway, we talked for a long time. She told me about this guy she'd dated in high school who wound up coming out when he went to college, and the story was so funny. Maybe not the story, but the way she told it. It was like we were girlfriends sharing secrets.

Dad was reading up in the little hut-gazebo thing and came down after a while of hearing us laughing. He brought Mom a margarita and me a Diet Coke. We all sat there on the beach and watched Cam riding waves. It felt so good to be there with them, to feel like I was part of something special.

We had dinner outside tonight. Dad grilled burgers in the little outdoor kitchen. We all lounged around and ate until we were stuffed as the sun set over the ocean. Mom and Dad just went for a walk down the beach together after it got dark, and Cam is up at the house watching a movie.

I'm just sitting here listening to the ocean, thinking about how lucky I am that my mom and dad are still together, and how fun this trip is. And look! No drinking or drugs required. Mom left almost a full margarita after dinner, and I thought about trying a sip of it when she and Dad left on their walk, but you know what?

I'm good.

Just like this.

Just where I am.

August 6

Back on a plane.

Back to cell phone signals!

Next stop: home.

Later . . .

OMG.

Like a MILLION texts popped up on my phone the minute we landed.

Okay, not a million, but a lot.

A lot were from Ross and Lauren. Most of them were from

Blake. Blake sent me texts every single day. Lots of them. And every single night, he sent even more. Blake sent me a lot of texts in the middle of the night. The later the texts, the sexier they were. I was sitting next to my mom as the plane taxied to the gate, and I had to put my phone away because I didn't want her to see any of the really sexy ones. He texted me pictures of himself. Shirtless. And more. It's weird. I'm not really sure why guys think girls want to see that. I mean, I guess it's one thing to feel it pressed up against me in his bathroom, but . . .

I dunno.

Leave something to my imagination, will you?

August 8

Mom met Lauren yesterday, and she really liked her, which is very good news for me. That means I don't have to worry about Mom hassling me about hanging out with her. Lauren lives with her dad in this gorgeous condo near the water. I didn't mention to Mom that Lauren's dad is out of town a lot. He's constantly flying back to New York. I've just sort of let that go because I know Mom's rule that if I'm spending the night at a friend's house a parent needs to be there. It's such a lame, old-fashioned rule.

After we hung out at our house for a while, Lauren asked if I wanted to spend the night. Mom said as long as it was okay with Lauren's dad, it was fine with her. Lauren assured her that it was fine with her dad. Lauren's dad is in New York this weekend, so he won't even know, but obviously we didn't tell Mom that. The best part is that Lauren's dad has plenty of Absolut and Lauren made us cosmos. Ross came over and we all had a couple of drinks and smoked pot out of Ross's pipe. Ian came over too, and brought more weed because Ross was low.

It was SO FUN to be back with the gang! I couldn't stop thinking about Blake and texted him to tell him that we were all hanging out. He texted me back FAST and said he wanted to come but he was in San Francisco playing a show with his band. Lauren smirked and asked me who I was texting, really loudly in front of everyone because she already knew, and my face got totally red and they all whistled and teased me about dating an older man.

I said, We are NOT dating.

Lauren laughed, and said, Not YET anyway. Just wait until NEXT SATURDAY!

Ian smiled, and I could tell he knew what Lauren was talking about. I asked what next Saturday was, and Lauren said, We're going HIKING with your BOYFRIEND . . .

I was like, Hiking? Why are we going hiking? We'll be all sweaty and gross! I want him to think I'm pretty, not a big sweat ball.

Lauren poured more cosmo into my glass and said that we

weren't just hiking, that there would be a special surprise. Blake's uncle has a ranch up the coast and there are all of these trails through the foothills and even some horses that run free on the back acres. We are going to drive up and spend the day. I am excited but a little worried about spending a whole day with Blake. At least it won't be a hard sell for my mom. What could be more wholesome than a daytime hiking trip?

August 9

Cam can't go hiking with us because he has to clean pools all day. He's bummed. And I am too, a little. Blake keeps texting me about how much fun this hike is going to be. It's weird, but I never thought of Blake as much of an outdoors guy. Maybe this has to do with the big SURPRISE that Lauren keeps talking about. It's making me nervous. I wish she'd just tell me already, but she says that it would no longer then (by definition) be a surprise.

August 12

Lauren is spending the night so that we can get up first thing in the morning and get on the road to Blake's place up the coast, then get on the road to his uncle's ranch. It's about an hour's drive past his place, according to Lauren. I told her that we were NOT going to talk about Blake to my Mom and she gets it.

Mom is THRILLED that we are going hiking with Ian and Ross. Lauren told her that the ranch we're going to is owned by a friend of her dad's, which is sort of half true. I mean, technically, her dad DOES know who Blake's dad is, and knows that the ranch is in Blake's family. Anyway, Mom has packed us a cooler of sandwiches and cans of Diet Coke, and bottles of water, and made us promise to take lots of pictures, and call when we're headed back.

Cam is all mopey that he can't come. I told him he should just call in sick tomorrow, but Cam is very conscientious and says he needs the money.

August 13

Wow.

W-O-W.

I'm not even sure where to start.

When Lauren and I got to Blake's house, Ian and Ross were already there. I guess they'd spent the night there. I'd been chattering nonstop to Lauren all the way there about how crazy nervous I was about seeing Blake again, and what if this was all in my head, and Blake didn't really like me at all. She just rolled her eyes and said that I was very good at inventing reasons to be worried.

The minute he opened the door, Blake wrapped both arms

78

around me and kissed me on the lips really gently. He smiled and said, Finally. Then he sort of danced me into the kitchen so he could grab some water bottles. Lauren giggled and yelled TOLD YOU as she ran upstairs to get Ross and Ian. In the kitchen, Blake leaned me up against the island and kissed me so firmly that my knees went a little bit weak, and I was glad that I was leaning against something solid. He pressed his whole body into mine, and I could smell his skin, and the body wash he must've used, and the product in his hair that smelled like eucalyptus.

All of the worries I'd had about him melted inside of me. It raced out of me from every direction, through a buzz under my skin that came shooting out of my fingers and toes and the hair at the top of my head. What was left after all of the doubts were gone was the sound of my heart pounding in my ears and the heat of Blake's breath on my skin.

In that moment I just didn't care whether he wanted to date me or not; I knew that he liked me totally and completely, and I wanted to just stay right there with him all day long, kissing in the kitchen.

When we heard Lauren and the boys coming down the stairs, he grabbed my hand and dragged me out to the driveway with him. We all piled into Ian's SUV, then headed north up the coast to the ranch. When I took the cooler out of Lauren's car,

Ian asked me what it was, and I told him it was food and drinks for the trip. Ian laughed, and Blake said, We probably won't need any food today, but the drinks will come in handy.

I didn't understand what they meant right away, but once we got to the ranch and Blake jumped out to open the gate at the end of the gravel road we'd taken off of the highway, Ian turned around and said, Okay everybody! Time for the hiking surprise!

He pulled a Ziploc bag out of his pocket and handed it to Ross. We parked the SUV under a tree at the edge of a giant meadow that had a little gravelly stream running through it. The stream looked like it wound up into the hills, which were covered in tall, sun-bleached grass, yellow and waving in the breeze. The sky was bright blue and the clouds were big white billows, wafting slowly behind the mountains in the distance.

Lauren was passing around sunscreen for our faces and ears, and she helped me spread it onto the part in my hair so that I wouldn't get burned there, either. I started wondering how long we were going to be out in the sun, and when I asked Blake, he took my hand and said, Well, it all depends on how long the surprise lasts.

Ross and Ian had everybody huddle up and hold out our hands. Ross dropped one tiny square of white paper into each of our palms, and Ian told us not to drop it because this is all that there was, and he'd been through HELL trying to get it.

I asked what it was, and Blake said, It's LSD.

My eyes went wide as I saw Ross hand the plastic bag back to Ian, and then gently place the little square of paper on his tongue. I almost shouted, This is ACID? We're going to take ACID?

Ross giggled and said, We're taking a little trip today.

Blake rubbed his hand on my back and said, It's okay. I'll be right here.

Lauren laughed and said, C'mon! You're going to LOVE it.

I wasn't sure what to expect, but when I put the little square on my tongue, it tasted like . . . nothing. I looked at Ross for a minute, and then at Blake. I asked if something was supposed to happen.

Ian laughed, and said, Not yet. It'll kick in after about 15 or 20 minutes. Let's go hike!

Blake led the way down the trail along the little stream, which looked like it must have more water in it during the spring. Right now it was just a little trickle that ran over a few of the rocks at the center. We hiked along the stream for a while. Ross was running and jumping onto Ian's back and making him give him a piggyback ride for a few feet every so often. Lauren and Blake and I were walking together, and Blake had his arm draped over my neck.

After a little while the stream dipped in between two hills

and the trail led up the side of one of them. As we climbed up, I was telling Blake and Lauren all about our vacation to Mexico, and it must've taken a little while because I was just talking and talking, then we reached the top of the hill and I realized that I was breathing sort of fast, and when I lifted my eyes up from the path, I stopped midsentence and sucked in a huge deep breath of air. We were standing at the top of the hill and I could see the blue sky and the rolling hills of the valley below. The place where the blue sky met the yellow grass seemed miles away in the distance, dotted with bright, brilliant green trees, and when I stared out at the white clouds, they seemed to breathe in and then collapse a little, then breathe in again.

Then the green trees at the horizon begin to wriggle in this strange way, almost like they were dancing with one another. They would swirl together and reach up toward the white clouds, and then the clouds would answer back, swirling down toward the green trees, and all at once I was LAUGHING. I gasped and gulped in the air and I said, You guys, LOOK! The trees and the clouds are DANCING!

Lauren and Blake walked up on either side of me and I grabbed both of their hands and said, SEE?

We just stood there for what must've been an hour, or maybe it was 5 minutes? I don't know! That's the amazing thing about acid; you just can't tell how much time has passed. It's like someone has shuffled all the cards in your head, and you recognize people and places, but you can't quite fit together how you got here, or where you are, only that you feel AMAZING, and you're seeing these INCREDIBLE THINGS.

While we stood and watched the trees and the clouds, Ross and Ian suddenly let out a whoop and went racing down the hill through the yellow grass into the valley below, and as we followed them, I saw the yellow grass around me. I stuck out my hands as we ran and let my fingers brush through the tall thin stalks, only it felt like liquid running over my hands.

At the bottom of the hill we found Ian and Ross sitting next to each other on their knees in the middle of the tall grass. They had mashed down a little place in a circle, and they were sitting there, holding hands. Ian said, Look! We built a NEST.

Lauren and Blake and I saw this and laughed and laughed until the tears ran down our cheeks. I thought it was amazing and wonderful! I was going to build a nest too, but then Lauren saw a big boulder over by a tree near the stream and called us over to it. We all climbed up on top of the giant rock, and as we sat there, I saw a bee, lazy and slow, dance around, then land next to my hand. Any other time I would have yelped and tried to shoo it away, or run from it myself. But this bee seemed to be trying to tell me something. His hind end with the yellow and black stripes seemed to be wiggling in a strange rhythm, and I felt as though I was connected to this bee, that he had a message for me that only I could decipher because he spoke a language of bee dancing that only I could understand. I called Lauren over, and she watched the bee dance with me.

I just read what I wrote, and it sounds like a CRAZY person has hijacked this journal, but that's EXACTLY WHAT IT WAS LIKE! It was like the bee and I were TALKING to each other until eventually he flew straight up into the blue, and when he did, I followed him with my eyes, and WOW! The bright blue was dripping down out of the sky and landing with big silver splats onto the grass at the top of the next hill. I told Blake that I had to go see the sky waterfall, and he giggled like a little boy. Then I jumped down off of the Bee Boulder and led the charge up the hill in front of us, chasing the shadow of a cloud up the hill.

At the top of the hill I found myself back at the stream, and just as I turned around, 2 horses came walking up the hill, and I clapped my hand over my mouth and felt shivers of pure joy shooting up and down my spine. It gave me goose bumps all over. Suddenly Blake was at my elbow, and he whispered, C'mon. Then, very slowly, he walked up to one of the horses and held out his hand. The horse snorted and eyed us, then came closer and sniffed his hand, then licked it. Blake told me I had to feel that, and so I held out my hand too. The horse was so powerful, and muscular. It looked like it could just crush us both if it wanted to, but it was kind, and gentle, and when it licked my hand, its tongue felt like warm, wet sandpaper scraping over my palm. It felt AMAZING.

The whole day was like that. I wish I could do it justice as I'm writing about it. I feel like I could use all of the words that I have in my head 100 times each and never be able to tell exactly what it was like. There were so many amazing parts: sitting on the low branch of a big sycamore tree with Blake, and holding hands and talking about the way the sky looked. Then we were just quiet, and I saw sunbeams shimmering out from the edges of a giant cloud, and I felt for sure it was God sending me a signal—a signal that everything was going to be okay; that we were all connected: me, Blake, Lauren, Ian, Ross, the bee, the trees, the horses, the grass, the hills, the whole earth, and everyone on it.

Ross and Lauren and I lay on our backs in the grass and stared up through the leaves of a tree at the blue sky, and the leaves made a canopy that would snap into a grid, then swirl and snap into a grid again. Ross said it was like we were plugged into a big computer program, and Lauren said she thought maybe the acid allowed us to see the way the whole universe really worked. Then she said that she felt so peaceful and safe, and that she loved me and Ross so much, and we said we felt the same way.

Eventually the sun started to sink in the sky, and we started to come down. We walked back to the SUV parked under the tree and sat in it for a while, talking about everything we had seen and experienced, and eating the sandwiches my mom had packed for us.

I wonder how I could possibly explain it to my mom. I mean, I know I couldn't. But it was AMAZING! I wish that she could see it for herself, and Cam and Dad.

By the time we drove home, the sun had set, but it wasn't quite dark yet. I was leaning against Blake in the backseat, and he just held me close and kissed my ear from time to time. My head started to hurt a little, and he told all of us that we'd probably have a headache, so to be sure to drink plenty of water and take some Advil when we got home.

I'd promised Mom that I would be back for dinner at 8 p.m., and it was almost that time when we got back to Blake's, so I called her and told her I would be a few minutes late. She thanked me for letting her know and said she was glad I'd had a good time. Blake walked me over to Lauren's car. He told me he'd be out of town for 6 weeks because he was going to tour the East Coast with his band. UGH! 6 WEEKS???.

They have shows at small clubs in New York, and 2 weeks of rehearsal, then some shows in Boston, then they're going down to Florida and working their way back up to New York and

Toronto. They're playing little clubs, mainly, and opening for a couple of bigger bands. He told me that he'll be really busy, but that when he comes back, he wants to see me.

Then he kissed me again. Maybe it was the leftover acid in my system, or just him—I couldn't tell—but his lips on my mouth were almost electric, and I wrapped both of my arms around his neck and pulled his face into mine.

Lauren and I were quiet as we drove back toward my place, but it was a good, tired quiet. It was a comfortable quiet. The kind of quiet where neither one of you has to say anything because you can almost tell what the other one is thinking. When we pulled into my driveway, I smiled at her, and she reached over and hugged me.

I told her thank you for setting this all up.

She smiled back and said, It's a trip I'll always remember.

August 17

Blake leaves on tour tomorrow. I know he's busy, but he hasn't been texting as much. It makes me feel strange because I felt like we really had a connection last Saturday. Was it just the acid? Was it just because we were tripping? Does Blake text other girls the way he's texting me? I know he's always going to parties and stuff. I'd ask Lauren about it, but I sort of don't want to know for sure. It makes me feel so sad and upset when

I think about it too much. If I don't hear from him tomorrow, maybe I'll call him and see if he picks up.

August 18

BLAKE CALLED ME! I didn't even have to call him. He told me he was sorry that he hadn't texted as much 'cause he'd been rehearsing like 24/7. I told him "good luck" on the tour, and he said he didn't need luck because all he had to do was think about kissing me, and he kicked ass on stage.

Still, 6 weeks feels like an ETERNITY. It'll be OCTOBER when he's back in town. Ugh. Lauren says she's going to keep me distracted. It's going to have to be some pretty major distraction.

August 27

I was just reading over that last entry about Blake from last week, and I was right: Gradually, over the past week his text messages have gotten further and further apart. Although he still sends me a few from time to time. It's weird. Usually they come in the middle of the night.

ANYWAY!

Lauren has been very good about keeping me distracted! I've been having such a great time with her and Ross and Cam. We've been going to the beach a lot—trying to use up as much summer sun as we can before school starts again. Cam comes after he's done with soccer practice or cleaning pools.

Tonight is the last Sunday night before school starts, and Mom and Dad let me have Ross and Lauren over for dinner. Ian came by too. It was funny, because I don't think that Mom realized Ross was dating Ian for a little while. After dinner, Mom and Dad said they'd do the dishes, so Cam and I walked down to the beach with Ross, Ian, and Lauren to watch the sunset. Ross and Ian both had joints, and we passed them around and got a little stoned.

I just sat there thinking about how badly this summer started out and how AWESOME it has ended. I feel like I've got this great circle of friends, and for the first time in my whole life, I feel like I'm making my own decisions.

I watched the sun sink into the waves on the beach, and the colors were so bright and intense. I think pot actually makes sunsets more vibrant somehow. I mean, you're looking at the same colors, but the colors seem to MEAN more. Does that make sense? I mean, who am I asking? My journal? HA HA HA HA HA. I think I may be a little stoned still.

So we're sitting there and Ross put his arm around my shoulders, and I actually got a little teary-eyed. Lauren and Ian were laughing at this story Cam was telling about accidentally knocking one of his customer's cats into their pool with the end of the net and having to fish the cat out of the pool, so they didn't notice, but Ross did.

He asked if I was okay.

I smiled at him and nodded and said, Ross, I'm better than ever.

He smiled at me and kissed me on the cheek, and the two of us just sat there listening to our friends laugh and the waves on the beach, watching the colors in the sky as they became almost unbearably beautiful, and then, like someone had flipped a switch, the sun dropped under the horizon.

I feel like I'm not able to write it down in a way that describes it well enough. There's no way to explain what it feels like to be high, and happy, and held by your good friend as you watch the sun set.

August 28

School starts tomorrow.

Ugh.

I'm going to be a junior.

At least Lauren and Ross and Cam will be there. Mom took the day off work today, and she took Lauren and me school shopping. I've decided that all clothes should have to go through a rite of passage and be tried on by Lauren first.

It's just not FAIR. She's SO pretty. And she has such good

taste. She pulled out all of these really cute jeans that I wouldn't have looked at twice, and FORCED me to try them on. And you know what? She was right. I looked GREAT in them. Mom is always talking about how hard it is to buy me jeans because I'm so picky. She was so relieved that I liked them that she bought three pairs in three different washes. SCORE!

Lauren and Ross are going to meet me and Cam out front in the morning so that Cam can show Lauren around and I can show Ross around. I'm so nervous, I'm not sure how I'm going to fall asleep.

Well, here goes nothing.

August 30

Well, that was one for the BOOKS.

First of all, never underestimate walking into the first day of school with the hot new guy. (Even if he's gay.) It was like, all of a sudden people who had NEVER seen me before suddenly knew my name. Every single girl in every single one of my classes could not take her eyes off Ross. Elizabeth Archer made a beeline for us in her blue-and-gold cheerleader uniform as we walked into first period. Before Mr. Sanders had even finished taking role, she'd passed me a note that read: "Are you going out with Ross?" I almost started giggling. I mean, it's SO predictable. But Elizabeth is sweet. I leaned over and caught her eye and shook my head with a smile. Ross almost wet his pants, he was laughing so hard after class.

The next period Elizabeth made sure to sit down on the other side of Ross. Before the bell rang, she asked him if he had a girlfriend. He whispered, I play for the other team. Elizabeth nodded with that sweet blank look that just showed she had no idea what that meant, then frowned as she looked down at her books, like she was trying to figure out which sport Ross was talking about.

We all got passes to be able to go off campus for lunch, so at 12:35, when the bell rang, Ross and I headed out front to regroup with Cam and Lauren. When we walked out the front door, they were already there, talking with a girl who had light reddish hair—sort of strawberry blond. Cam saw us and waved, and the girl turned around.

It was ASTRID.

You could've knocked me over with a text message. I couldn't BELIEVE it.

All of a sudden the butterflies in my stomach were back. I remembered that at the party, where she and Nathan had materialized out of thin air, she'd said she was transferring schools, but I'd never thought about her coming HERE.

I thought I might have to throw up, but right at that second Ross leaned into me and whispered, It'll be cool. Then he sort of propelled us over to where the three of them were standing.

I could hardly think as we all stood there deciding where to go eat. Finally, as we were walking around the corner to grab sandwiches, Lauren fell in next to me and said, Okay, what's going on? I felt my stomach drop even more, because she could tell just from my face that something was up. She knew about the thing with Nate, but when I told her that Astrid was his girlfriend, her eyes went wide, and she whispered, WOW!

It wound up being okay, though, because at lunch Astrid and Cam were talking and Astrid mentioned that she had just broken up with her boyfriend. Ross and Lauren both shot me a look. I said, You broke up with Nate? I must've sounded like I thought she was crazy, because Lauren and Ross both kicked me under the table, but I DID think she was crazy. I mean who breaks up with a guy like that?

Astrid just smiled at me and said that it was too hard with their different schedules and schools. She said they were still friends and that the good part was Nate would let us know about UCLA parties. Cam jumped in and said that speaking of parties, Jason was planning a big blowout at his house on Labor Day—the last pool party of the summer.

Astrid said thanks for the invite but her parents were having friends over and she was supposed to be there. Cam made his puppy-dog eyes at her, and begged, literally begged her to come to the party. Astrid just smiled and said she'd see what she could do.

Later, when we got back to school, Astrid came to the bathroom with Lauren and me. As we were leaning in to the mirrors surveying the damage of the morning and touching things up, Astrid smiled slyly and said, I can't wait for that Labor Day party. I asked her if she was really coming, and she said of course. Lauren just started giggling. Astrid said she couldn't make it seem like she was TOO eager to go to the party with Cam or else he wouldn't have to work for it. I said, So you like him? And she just put her finger to her lips and winked. When Lauren and I were walking to our lockers, she told me I couldn't say a word; she said it was called playing hard to get and that I should pay attention because it was a necessary skill.

I asked her who in the world was trying to get me.

She raised an eyebrow and said, I think there's a certain up-and-coming rock 'n' roller who has been trying to get in touch with you, isn't there?

I thought about the texts from Blake. They'd sort of petered out. I told her I hadn't heard from him in a while. Lauren laughed and said, See? You're playing so hard to get he's leaving you alone. You know more about this game than you think you do.

Sometimes I think Cam is right. Girls ARE weird.

September 1

AP classes are KILLING me.

ARGH.

Luckily, Lauren and Astrid have chemistry with me, so we get to study together. They were both over tonight so that we could study for our quiz tomorrow. (What kind of sadistic teacher gives a quiz on 40 pages of reading on the FIRST FRIDAY of the school year?)

Anyway, we studied the periodic chart until our brains started to melt, and then I went downstairs to grab us all Diet Cokes. When I got back up to my room, Lauren said she thought chemistry would probably be more enjoyable with a shaker of cosmos.

Astrid asked if there would be booze at Jason's party on Monday because she was pretty sure she was going to have to be a little buzzed to be in a swimsuit in front of Cam and Jason. Lauren laughed and said she would bring a bottle of her dad's vodka just to be sure we could have cosmos. That girl is convinced that it's not a party unless there are cosmos. I said I would make sure that Ross was there with enough pot to smoke us all out. Astrid smiled and said she just might be able to wear her bikini.

Lauren raised her Diet Coke can and said that she was calling for a pledge: a couple hits of weed and cosmos–only school year.

And only on weekends. We all clinked cans in solidarity. Lauren said she'd seen some of the girls at her old school in New York go crazy on REAL drugs like cocaine and stuff. Astrid said that the white drug groups really scared her. I said I'd never even SEEN cocaine before we were at Blake's that one night.

It felt good to have agreed between us that we weren't going to become total party-heads. The girls just left, and I wanted to write this down because I feel so good about having my own group to run with. I've never really been that friendly with other girls before, because I could never predict whether or not they'd be friendly back. The dumb thing is that all that did was ensure that I didn't have any friends at all.

I can't wait for this party on Monday—but I'm also a little nervous. I always get nervous when I'm supposed to be in a bathing suit, and this is definitely a pool party at Jason's. I wish I had Lauren's boobs. Or was as tall and thin as Astrid. SIGH. Oh well. I'll have to get Lauren to help me pick out what I should wear.

September 2

Thank God it's Friday. I survived the chemistry quiz today. BARELY. It's a good thing we all studied last night. The SUPER FUN part is that Lauren and I both decided to audition for the choir and we BOTH GOT IN! She's an alto and I'm a soprano.

The bad news: When I came home, Mom made me help her fold laundry and dust and vacuum my room. Ugh. I HATE not having a housekeeper. Mom and Dad decided that we should Tighten Our Collective Belt and just have Maria come in to clean on special occasions, not once a week like we used to. I know that sounds bratty. I'm lucky that we can afford to have a nice house near the ocean. I guess the least I can do is clean my own room.

The good news: Cam just got home from soccer practice, and we're going to meet Ross and Lauren for a movie up on the Promenade. He told me that he asked Astrid if she wanted to come earlier, but she hasn't called him back or texted him one way or the other. I texted Ross to make sure that he brought some of the GREEN drug group as Astrid would call it. It will be fun to see a movie stoned! I've never done that before!

September 3

Last night was a bummer. Ross couldn't get in touch with Ian until later, so he didn't have any pot. It was still fun to hang out with everyone, but it would've been SO COOL to get stoned and see a movie. Oh well. It's not like the end of my world. I got sort of upset in the moment when I found out that Ross didn't have any, but I kept it to myself. I didn't want to seem like THAT girl, like a big whiner who couldn't have fun unless she had pot.

After the movie Cam went over to Jason's because they've got soccer practice tomorrow morning. The big homecoming game is in a few weeks. I didn't have to be home until midnight, so Ross and I went to Lauren's place. Her dad was there, and I met him. He's a nice guy, but we couldn't have cosmos then either. BUMMER.

Ross went out on the balcony to smoke a cigarette and Lauren and I went with him. While we were out there, his phone rang and it was Ian. After they talked, Ross hung up and was sort of quiet. Lauren asked him what was up, and Ross said he didn't really want to talk about it. I asked him if everything was okay with him and Ian, and Ross just laughed and said that even if it weren't, there were plenty of other guys. Lauren grabbed my phone to take a picture of me and Ross on the balcony, and after she did, a text message popped up while she was holding it and Lauren saw that it was from BLAKE.

She and Ross were both ON IT. They made me show them all of the texts from Blake and they were hooting and laughing so loudly that Lauren's dad came out onto the balcony to ask if everything was okay. My face was BEET RED. I was SO embarrassed.

Ross said that he wished he had a guy as cute as Blake banging his door down. Lauren asked me why I was so embarrassed. She said that this was totally a good thing. I just told her that I didn't know, but I always got so nervous around guys. Especially guys like Blake. The only time I've ever been brave around a guy was the night of my birthday with Nate, and that was a craptastic failure.

Then Lauren reminded me of the night at Blake's on the diving board, and I remembered how uninhibited I'd felt dancing with her. She also said I looked pretty at ease that day we all went hiking. I said, Yeah, but I don't want to have to drink until I hurl, or drop acid every time I want to feel comfortable with a guy. Ross agreed that was a good idea. (The not drinking till I barf/dropping acid part.)

Lauren said it was no problem. She has a prescription for something called Xanax that she got from a psychiatrist in New York. (I had to google how to spell it. I thought it started with a Z, like it sounds. Who knew?) Ross and I were just blinking at her, and she rolled her eyes and explained that it was no big deal, that he'd prescribed it because she was really anxious about her mom's boyfriend being a jerk to her.

We went back inside and up to her bedroom. She dug a bottle out of her purse and took out a tiny white pill that was like a rectangular bar. She broke two little parts off of the bar and gave one to Ross and one to me. She said we should take them before the party on Monday and we'd feel as relaxed as ever. EVEN if there were cute boys around.

I put the little pill in the small pocket of my jeans. When I got home just now, I slipped it into the bottle with my allergy medicine that I take sometimes.

Now I'm not nervous about the party on Monday at ALL. Somehow just knowing I have a pill to try makes me feel really excited about the party—but not worried excited, just FUN excited!

September 5

I have to get in bed right now. But I just wanted to write and say that we had a BLAST at the Labor Day party today. Astrid showed up and Cam almost had a heart attack. Jason's parents were in Las Vegas for Labor Day, so there were about 50 kids there from school. Ian showed up for a bit to hang with Ross.

That Xanax Lauren gave me made me feel loopy, but calm. It wasn't like smoking pot. It was less in my head and more in my body somehow. It was different because I didn't feel like I was underwater, the way that pot sometimes makes me feel— like I'm moving through Jell-O. This was different. It was slight, but it just took the edge off. It was like falling backward onto a really puffy pile of pillows.

HA HA HA HA HA HA

I think that's enough. RIDICULOUS. I must still be feeling it. I just felt really happy. It didn't even bother me that Lauren couldn't find any vodka there. I didn't even feel like drinking at the party. Cam had a couple of beers with Jason, and there were a couple of girls from school who drank so much beer that they threw up in the azaleas in the corner of Jason's backyard.

Anyway, I was wearing a little red bikini Lauren loaned me, and I felt like I could talk to anybody I wanted to. This guy named Mark who is in my English class came up and started talking to me. He's tall, and really cute, and on the football team, but he's also really smart. He won some sort of academic award last year. I've always noticed him, but he's one of those guys I would never just walk up and talk to. And HE came up and talked to ME! He saw that Lauren and I were just drinking Diet Coke and said something about how he didn't drink, and it was nice to see that there were girls at the party who weren't on anything either.

I just looked at Lauren. I saw her raise her eyebrows behind her big black Chanel sunglasses. I decided not to say anything. He didn't need to know that we'd taken Xanax. He's got this really cute dimple when he smiles. He told me he'd see me in class tomorrow. I felt this really warm feeling in my stomach about this Mark guy. He's the kind of guy my mom would be THRILLED about me bringing home for dinner.

On the way home, Lauren told Ross that he wouldn't have believed how chatty I was with Mark. Ross gave me a high five. Of course then Blake texted me again. Lauren asked me how long I was gonna string that poor boy along.

I'd never admit it to anyone, but it's kind of fun knowing that there's this 20-year-old guy who can't stop thinking about me!

September 6

Not much went on today.

Had choir with Lauren.

Lunch with Lauren and Astrid in the CRAPateria. Ross was out sick. Cam went off campus with Jason and a bunch of the soccer players.

Mark is in choir. He's a baritone. How did I never notice him before? He smiled at me today. I thought about going up to talk to him, but then I saw a picture of me in that red bikini on Facebook. UNTAG. It was a nightmare. I look weird, like my proportions aren't right. Lauren has these perfect long limbs, and I just looked skinny fat. I only ate half of my dinner tonight. Mom asked if I was feeling well. I said I was fine.

I wish I could sing more. When I'm singing and we're all following Mr. Brown and I hear the harmony with all of the other voices, I forget everything else. Or, not forget, but I can't think about anything else—just listening and singing the right notes.

September 8

Things get so boring so fast. I've got all this reading to do for AP English. I'm like 20 pages into THE GRAPES OF WRATH and I can barely keep my eyes open.

I can't even hang out with Ross while I do it because he always has the bright idea to get stoned and then read. Of course, we read for like 27 seconds and then sit around giggling and talking instead of actually reading. Yesterday we tried it, and he wound up painting his toenails green with this old nail polish he found in my bathroom. He's hilarious.

I just remembered HOMECOMING is at the end of the month. I'M SAVED! It's so much more fun when there's something to look forward to. Maybe I'll see if we can all figure out a place to have a party after the dance!

September 10

Tomorrow is a Sunday, and in the afternoon our choir from school is singing at a concert the city is hosting to commemorate the 9/11 attacks. I was so little when 9/11 happened; I just remember that Mom didn't go to work, and she kept Cam and me home from school, but we weren't allowed to watch TV. She put on a couple of movies for us, and when Dad came home, I remember that he and Mom were so quiet.

Now that I'm older, I've looked up the footage online of the planes hitting the buildings, and I can sort of understand why Mom didn't want Cam and me to see that when we were so little. I don't really understand it. It's like watching a movie.

I asked Lauren what it was like, actually being there in New York. She said that they were running late that morning and her mom was just dropping her off at school when the first plane hit the towers. She said that they could see this giant black plume of smoke coming from downtown, and her mom told her they were going back home. Her dad had a group of 8 friends who played poker together. Three of them worked in the towers. Two of them were killed. The 3rd one had called in sick that day.

Lauren still thinks that her dad and mom got divorced because of September 11. I asked her if it was because her dad was sad about his friends. She shook her head. She said she thinks it's because they weren't happy and 9/11 made them realize how short life was. She said they were divorced a year later.

That makes me sad to think about. I mean, not just all the people who died but that Lauren had to be so sad because her dad left, and then going through all those years of having her mom's new boyfriend hit on her.

That makes me so damn mad.

September 12

Today at school Mark followed Lauren and me to our lockers after choir. Then he asked me if I wanted to go to the homecoming dance with him. Right there! In front of Lauren, and the whole wide world. I was like, um . . . and Lauren closed her locker and said, Mark, you seem like a good guy. If you don't mind can I offer you some advice?

Then without waiting for him to say anything, she smiled and told him that probably there was a smoother way to ask someone to homecoming than a hallway ambush and that maybe he'd like to regroup and see if he could come up with some other way to catch my attention than just a surprise attack after 6th period. The whole time she was saying this she was opening a little spiral notebook that she always carries in her purse and scribbling something on a page, then she tore it out and handed it to him. She told him this was my phone number and that if he wanted to ask me out, he might try just calling first and seeing if I was interested in talking.

Then she grabbed my hand, told me to close my mouth, (which was hanging open), and then dragged me down the hall and out to the parking lot.

I'm glad she told me to close my mouth so I didn't trip over my lips.

We got into her car, and I just started laughing. I couldn't believe she did that for me. Astrid and Ross got into the car with us, and Lauren filled them in on what had just happened. I wasn't sure if I wanted to go to homecoming with Mark or not, but I sure didn't want to have to answer him right that second.

Lauren drove us around the block while Ross packed a bowl and passed the pipe around, and we all weighed the pros and cons of Mark Wilson. Lauren said that he is very cute but we hardly know him, and I agreed. Ross told me he thought I was crazy for turning down a guy that hot, and if I didn't go with Mark, he might try to. We all laughed about that, and Astrid didn't see what the problem was with saying yes. I told her I wanted to have a little party after homecoming and didn't want him to freak out if we smoked or had a couple of drinks. He'd made such a big deal about how great it was that Lauren and I weren't drinking at the Labor Day party, so I had a sneaking suspicion that he'd have a problem with dating a girl who did.

The pot helped me calm down a little. My heart stopped racing, and when I got home I ate half a bag of carrot sticks. I swear, if I give in to the munchies every time I get high I'm going to weigh 400 pounds by the time I'm a senior. Now I'm tired. I'm going to take a nap so that I can stay awake to finish GRAPES OF WRATH.

Later . . .

Mark just called while I was sleeping and left a voice mail. I don't know what to do. I am not really sure I want to go to homecoming with him, but at the same time I'm not sure I'm in a position to be turning down dates offered by cute, nice guys.

Do I just want to go with someone else so that I can party a little? Could I have fun with Mark and just stay sober? When I think about that, I get all disappointed and sad thinking about Ross and Lauren and Astrid and Cam having fun and me not.

OMG. I just wrote that if I couldn't drink or smoke pot I wouldn't have any fun. Do I really think that?

Now Lauren's calling me. Stand by.

Later . . .

Lauren is SO FUNNY. She's already found us dates who don't mind if we drink. LOL. She said I can go out with Mark whenever I want, but to tell him that I already have a date for homecoming. Lauren said there are these two senior guys named Andrew and Ryan in her British literature class who keep trying to ask her out. She said they're best friends and have this competition going to see who she'll go out with first. She called Andrew and told him that we would go to homecoming with him and Ryan just as friends. She said it's better anyway because now I'm playing hard to get for Mark.

I asked her if I was Ryan's date or Andrew's date. She just laughed and said, Oh c'mon. Who cares? Take your pick.

Ross just texted me: IF YOU BREAK THAT BOY'S HEART I'LL BE HAPPY TO BE THE SHOULDER HE CAN CRY ON.

LOL. I love my friends.

September 13

Told Mark today that I already had a date for homecoming but that we could go see a movie or something if he wanted. He was a little disappointed, but he smiled and that dimple of his poked in. He said that would be great. We made a plan to go and see that new superhero movie when it opens this weekend.

September 14

Astrid and Lauren had to rescue me from Cam a second ago. JEEEZ. I'm so glad I have a free period now so I can write about it. I was just at lunch in the cafeteria with Astrid and Lauren and Ross when Cam came marching over and said that he'd been in the locker room for PE and heard Ryan and

Andrew talking about this hot junior chick they were taking to homecoming with the new girl, and about how they were going to get me drunk and see how far they could go with me.

Ross started laughing and Cam slammed his hand down on the table and was like IT'S NOT FUNNY.

Lauren told him that he needed to take a big deep breath. Cam told her that she needed to back off, that I was his little sister and he was taking care of me. I stood up and told him to shut up, that he was embarrassing me and I could take care of myself.

He looked around and saw that everybody was staring at us. Astrid grabbed his hand and pulled him down next to her. He got quiet, but his eyes were still bright and angry.

Lauren told him that we were all just going as friends. She said, Besides, your sis has a hot date with Mark Wilson this weekend. You certainly can't object to that, can you?

Cam asked me if that was true. I nodded, and he smiled really big and said, That's awesome sis!

I swear, Cam can go from hot to cold and back in 12 seconds flat.

All I can think about is that two senior guys called me THIS HOT JUNIOR CHICK.

OMG! SENIORS THINK I'M HOT!

I know. I know. I'm supposed to not be excited about that.

Sue me. I don't see my brains when I look in the mirror. It wasn't the A on my GRAPES OF WRATH report that made Mark Wilson want to ask me to homecoming.

September 15

Mark Wilson is following me and Lauren and Astrid around like a puppy dog. Who knew telling a boy to cool his jets could be so effective? Today Lauren invited Ryan and Andrew to come to lunch with us, only I didn't know it. So, when I walked out front, there they were with her and Astrid. Of course, Mark had followed me outside and had just started to ask me to lunch when Lauren saw me and waved me over.

I smiled at Mark and asked him what time he was picking me up tomorrow night for the movie. He stared at Ryan (who was smirking at me) and Andrew (who was trying to pinch Lauren's butt until she smacked him) and looked like he'd just swallowed a golf ball.

He said 7. I said, make it 6:45 so you have time to meet my parents.

Then I turned around and walked to lunch with Lauren and the boys without looking back.

But my heart was totally racing! I could feel Mark staring after me. I felt so powerful!

I think Lauren is right: This is making Mark crazy hot for me.

September 16

Mark will be here any minute. I borrowed this little black skirt from Lauren that makes my legs look 27 miles long. He's not going to know what hit him.

OMG! I've NEVER felt like this before a date. Last year when Sean took me to homecoming, I was so nervous I threw up while I was doing my makeup.

I'm not even worried about this now. I mean, I know I don't look as good as Lauren or anything, but this boy is whipped for me. I wonder if I'll kiss him tonight?

Hmmmmmm. Maybe I'll make him suffer. HA HA HA HA HA. I'm so bad.

Oooh! That's him. Here goes nothing!

(I'll report back as soon as I'm home.)

September 17

Okay, the movie was SO LAAAAAAAAAAME. Superheroes who just magically win everything in the end are SO BORING.

And that was the BEST part of the evening. I mean, Mark is so sweet, but he's so . . . SERIOUS. After the movie, we went to get ice cream on the Promenade, and while we were eating, he told me all about how worried he was about me going out with Ryan for homecoming. He said that Ryan only had one thing on the brain, and it wasn't honorable.

Honorable.

Who uses that word?

I totally played stupid, and was like, What does Ryan have on his brain that isn't honorable, Mark? (Wide eyes, blinking, blank look, the whole nine.) Then I crossed my incredibly bare legs and tugged at Lauren's little black skirt. (Also, I cannot BELIEVE my mother let me out of the house in it. I saw the look on her face when I walked down the stairs, but then she met Mark and probably knew she had nothing to worry about.)

ANYWAY, Mark then spent like 20 MINUTES showing me this necklace he wears with a little key on it, and how it's part of this pledge he made at his church. Apparently, the key is the key to his "heart" and he's not supposed to unlock it until his wedding night with the woman who is going to be his wife.

I mean, WHAT? I get it that I am young and shouldn't just throw myself at the first guy I see. I'm a virgin, and I do want my first time to be special with someone who I really care about. But I have this idea that I'm going to probably have a boyfriend at some point before I get married who I'll want to sleep with. I'll use condoms and all of that; I'm not stupid.

But Mark was SERIOUS. I was like, Hold up. A big handsome guy like you is a VIRGIN? And then I sort of smiled, and he saw it and said, Are you making fun of me? And I giggled, and said, No. No, I'm not. But I couldn't stop smiling.

And then he started smiling because I was smiling and then we were both laughing, and he said, What?

I didn't say anything, I just got up and grabbed his hand and led him out toward the parking deck and his car. I held his hand while he opened the car door for me, and when we got in, I leaned over to kiss him. He actually put his hand on my shoulder and held me back.

Then he asked me what I was doing!

I said, What does it look like I'm doing? Is this a trick question?

He told me that he didn't want us to go too fast on our first date.

I almost busted out laughing right in front of him, but I just smiled really big and nearly chewed a hole on the inside of my cheek to keep from giggling. When he saw my smile, he sat back in the driver's seat and let out a big, relieved sigh, then took my hand and told me that he was so happy that I was smiling because he could tell I understood and felt the same way.

I was almost crying from holding back the laughter. All I could think about was winding up practically naked in Blake's bathroom that first night I met him, and how poor Mark would have a meltdown if he knew about that. I'm afraid all the circuits in his brain might melt and then he'd never be able to unlock his heart with that little key around his neck.

113

The minute he dropped me off I called Lauren and was like, OMG! Come. Over. NOW.

Mom was very pleased that I was a.) home early from my date, b.) that Lauren came over and wanted to hang out at our place. (She worries that Lauren spends so much time alone because her mom is in New York.) Mom made us popcorn and then went to bed. Lauren and I went up to my room to watch movies and Lauren had a surprise. She'd brought a pill for us to split. She said it was a muscle relaxer and gave me half. I asked her what it did, and she said, Just mellows you out.

That little pill was AWESOME. In my body, it was like I'd smoked pot, only my head wasn't cloudy at ALL. It wasn't like being drunk. I just wanted to lie really still, and it felt like I was melting into the bed, but I wasn't tired.

When I told Lauren all about Mark, she laughed her ass off—especially the part about his necklace and saving it to open up his heart for his wife on his wedding night.

I feel sort of bad writing that. I mean, Mark is very sweet. I don't want to make fun of him, but it's just FUNNY.

Anyway, I slipped off to sleep at some point and slept like a rock. Usually it's hard to sleep in my bed if somebody spends the night, but not with that little yellow pill we took. It was like I was sleeping on a cloud in a deep dark cave.

This morning Lauren went home to write a paper she has due for her British literature class.

It's a good thing we're both very together. See, All Adults Everywhere? Not all teenagers who swallow pills and smoke pot die in car accidents. Some of us are very responsible!

September 18

Nothing much.

Ross was going to come over today and have dinner with us, but his grandma is in town from Boca Raton, so he's eating at the hotel with his mom.

I'm all done with my homework.

I was bored and messing around on my phone, and I read a bunch of the texts that Blake had sent me. I haven't heard from him much since he left on tour. I felt sort of nervous when I thought about texting him. He's probably got girls in every town swarming all over him. But I texted him anyway, just to say hi. He texted me back like IMMEDIATELY. And it wasn't a sex text either. He just said: HOW ARE YOU BEAUTIFUL?

OH! THE BIG NEWS: Cam asked Astrid to homecoming. It's so weird that my friend thinks my brother is cute. EW. I mean, he's a nice guy, and I guess Cam is cute and everything, but I just keep thinking about what a pain in the neck he is sometimes and how he picks his nose in the car when he thinks no one is looking.

EW.

September 20

Ross told us today that Ian invited us all up to his parents' house in the Hollywood Hills after homecoming to hang and use the hot tub and stuff. Ian's dad is some big movie producer and he's scouting locations in Italy until Christmas. Anyway, Ian's got their big place to himself, and we're all invited. Astrid and Lauren and I are going shopping for outfits tonight. Homecoming is a pretty casual thing, so Mom put me on a strict budget: $50 toward an outfit. I told her that $50 MIGHT buy me one sleeve of a top. She said that maybe I'd remember this when I got Christmas money from Gramps this year. I told her maybe I'd just have to go topless.

She said that she'd be happy to give me just $25 if that would make me stop whining.

GOD!

I guess I should be glad that I'm getting anything at all. Dad just looked at me and said that I should be grateful. It's not that I'm not grateful; I just know that Lauren and Astrid will have all-new outfits that will make them look like a kabillion dollars.

Anyway, Astrid said she'd help me pick out stuff that would work, and Lauren said I could raid her closet for stuff. That'll be good because she has SO. MANY. SHOES!

September 22

Tomorrow is homecoming. It's going to be so much fun!

Ryan and Andrew actually took Lauren and me to lunch today. It was sorta sweet. Although, Ryan talks about himself a LOT. It's not so bad, but it just gets kind of boring. I saw Mark watching me as I walked down the hall with Ryan and Andrew. I smiled and raised my hand in a little wave, and he just shook his head and turned around. I wonder who he's going to go to homecoming with? He hadn't asked anybody last week when we went on our date.

Anyway, at lunch Ryan would NOT shut up about this point he scored in their beach volleyball game last week and how TOTALLY RADICAL the spike had been, and how Andrew had given him the assist. Apparently, they play every weekend down at the beach and won a 2-on-2 tournament.

Lauren rolled her eyes and interrupted him at one point and said, So, Andy, do you often assist Ryan with his balls?

They both acted all hurt and were like NO WAY, that's cold. Lauren said that it wasn't as cold as she would be if she had to fight to get a word in edgewise all night tomorrow night.

117

I just started laughing and told Ryan that I live right up the street from the beach. He smiled at me all bashful, like he was secretly pleased, and said that I should come check out a match sometime. I said that maybe I'd bring Cam down with me next weekend if things went well at homecoming. It effectively reminded them that Cam is indeed my brother, and that sort of shut both of them up for a second. Cam is probably a head taller than both of them and has bigger muscles, too.

While we were shopping on Wednesday night, Astrid told me and Lauren that Cam and Jason had tossed both of them up against the lockers and threatened to brain them if either one of them caused us any trouble at lunch or at homecoming. I actually don't mind that Cam is being so protective. Ryan seems nice enough. He actually held the door for me today, but I don't really know him.

Mom says that's what a date is all about: getting to know someone. Of course, she wants to get to know them first, so she made me introduce them to her last weekend after Cam's game.

I dunno. Maybe I'm just a dumb girl, but there is something about boys after a soccer game when they're all sweaty and gross that makes me think they're really hot. Mark walked up to say hi to my parents while we were all talking to Ryan and Andrew, and he looked really good, even though he smelled pretty bad. Of course, Mom and Dad were all smiley and like HI MARK!

as if he was their long-lost son or something. Ryan just looked at me like What. Is. Up?

AWK-WARD.

Anyway, Elizabeth Archer is our junior class princess on the homecoming court, naturally, although Ross said it shoulda been this kid in our chemistry class named Raymond. Raymond is SO QUEENY. All the girls think it's kinda funny in a cute way, but the older guys pick on him a lot, Andrew especially. Cam has told him to lay off several times, but when you come to school wearing eyeliner, there's only so much Cam can do for you.

Ross is out, at school, but he doesn't act any differently than Cam or Mark, or any of the straight guys. He just looks like a cute surfer. Guys like Raymond have it worse, 'cause they just come across as really different from everyone else. Ross will tell you he's gay if you ask, but he just kind of blends in. Raymond really stands out.

The worst part is that Raymond has this CRAZY CRUSH on Ross. He asked Ross if he wanted to go the homecoming dance, and Ross was kind, but firm. I can tell it bothers Ross that the guys will start picking on him the way they pick on Raymond. Every time Andrew is picking on Raymond, Ross clears out of there as fast as he can.

Anyway, Ian is actually going to come to the homecoming game with Ross, and then we're all going to go to the dance together. I already told Ross that I want to sneak back to the car with him before we go into the dance and smoke a bowl.

OH! And I have to remind Lauren about another little chunk of Xanax.

September 23

Holy. Moses.

Why do they even HAVE school the day of homecoming. It's taking FOR. EV. ER.

And we still have to get through the damn pep rally. Elizabeth Archer is so excited about it, she's about to explode. I am sitting behind her, and she keeps turning around to wink and smile at me and Ross. Elizabeth is wearing the new cheerleading uniforms she and the squad earned washing cars in their bikinis over the summer. The skirts are so short they're almost nonexistent.

Ross asked me if I wanted to get stoned at lunch, but I told him NO. Under no circumstances do we smoke during school. THAT would make us total STONERS.

And we're not stoners.

We smoke in the parking lot AFTER school.

He rolled his eyes, and shook his head.

Then Lauren walked up and said she had a quarter of a Xanax bar for each of us that she'd be handing out right after last period. Ross called her the Fairy Godmother of Pharmaceuticals, and Astrid laughed really hard.

Oh, crap!

Mrs. Winslow just called on me because she saw me writing and thought I was taking notes. I had NO IDEA what she was talking about. I haven't really had to pay attention in a history class in years. Newsflash: American history doesn't change much after 5th grade. Pretty much, you've hit the high points by then.

I better put this away. The last thing I need is for it to get confiscated. Jeez.

I CAN'T WAIT FOR TONIIIIIIIIIGHT!

September 24

I don't even know where to start. I'm in real trouble. Serious. Trouble. Last night was a complete nightmare. I am so scared. I don't even know who to talk to. I want to go tell my mom all about it right this second, but I can't. I'm so afraid that she'll never let me leave the house again. I can't even write about this. I'm crying so hard, I can't see what I'm writing.

Later . . .

Lauren just left. She came over to make me feel better. I love her so much. I know I've only known her for a couple of months, but I don't really remember my life without her. I don't know how I would've made it through the day without her. She gave me another little chunk of Xanax, and I'm finally feeling relaxed for the first time all day.

Mom must think I've lost my mind. She thinks I just had a bad date.

Jeez. That's the understatement of the year.

I'm too tired to even think about writing all of this down now, but I will first thing when I get up tomorrow. I need to write it down. I want to. Something about writing it down will make some sense of what happened last night.

I hope.

September 25

It's Sunday morning. I'm feeling better today. I was just lying here in my bed, and I felt the fear flood into my stomach again, like the fog that hides the sun on June mornings. I know I just have to keep moving this pen across the page, but everything in me says that if I tell the truth about what happened Friday night, that'll make it real somehow, and I don't know if I can even face the memory in my head, much less watch the words come out of the pen and onto the paper in this journal.

It started out easy, and bright. The pep rally was crazy, and then Lauren passed out the Xanax, and Ross, Lauren, Astrid, and I all headed over to Lauren's place to order food and get ready for the dance. Lauren's dad is out of town this weekend, so she mixed us up some cosmos as soon as we got to her place, and by the time we'd had one, the food had arrived and the Xanax had kicked in. We ate and then started getting ready.

We laughed until our mascara ran and we all had to do it again. That's what I mainly remember about getting ready: laughing.

Ross was SO FUNNY. He'd only had one cosmo 'cause they're too girly, but he'd smoked a whole bowl of pot himself, then finished all of our leftovers while we all got ready. He was ready to go in like two minutes. He had a new polo and a pair of skinny jeans that looked like he was melted and poured into them. He lay down in the Jacuzzi tub in Lauren's HUGE bathroom and cracked jokes while he smoked pot and we straightened our hair. Well, Lauren and I straightened; Astrid curled. There were lots of hair ironing devices.

Then finally we were ready and Ross let out a low whistle, and then we spent like 20 minutes taking pictures of each other in various configurations. Of course, then Andrew and Ryan showed up, and they'd brought beer that Andrew had nabbed out of his dad's beer fridge in the garage. Ross smoked them out and had a beer, and the three of them seemed to bond or something. At one point Andrew told Ross he was okay for a homo, and Ross told Andrew that he was not bad for a breeder, and the two of them collapsed on the couch laughing and blowing pot smoke all over the place.

At that point Astrid looked at her watch and herded us all out the door.

For some reason, stepping outside made me realize how hard the Xanax had hit on top of the cosmos. All of a sudden I was floating, but it wasn't as clean as just Xanax or a muscle relaxer. I'd only smoked one hit of pot, but on top of two cosmos and the pill, I was a little foggy, and as we crowded into the elevators at Lauren's condo, I wobbled a little on my heels. I was glad that Ryan had big arms. He smiled at me when I was teetering toward the wall, offered me his arm, and asked if I was okay.

I smiled and said that I was fine. He raised an eyebrow and said, Oh, I can see you're fine. You're the finest girl I've ever taken to a dance; that's for damn sure.

I blushed HARD when he said that. Then Lauren said, God, Andy, your friend RyRy is a total cheese ball.

And then we were laughing again.

Ian joined us in the stands at the game. He looked great, and Ross got that big goofy grin on his face when they sat down together next to me. The crowd was WILD. We all were. The air was crisp and you could smell the ocean from the soccer field. Elizabeth Archer cheered right at Ross during the big halftime routine. Then as the junior class princess she was escorted across the field by Jason. Astrid snickered when she saw this and said that Megan Archer wouldn't give Jason the time of day, so he was escorting Elizabeth to homecoming in hopes of showing up on her radar.

We won the game, and Cam joined us after he had showered and changed. Astrid went walking up to him in her impossibly high heels that made her almost come to his chin. He bent down and kissed her softly on the lips. Ross punched him in the shoulder and said that he didn't care what the two of them did behind closed doors, but he didn't want them flaunting their lifestyle choice in his face, which made Cam laugh so hard he snorted.

We didn't want to be the very first ones at the dance, so we walked to the back of the parking lot and took turns sliding into Ian's gigantic Land Rover to smoke a bowl. Then Lauren dragged me and Astrid into her car so that we could touch up. LAST LOOKS EVERYONE! she yelled. She said that's what they say on movie and music-video sets before they shoot the scene so that the makeup people know to dab powder and fix hair.

When we were in her car, she passed around a silver flask she said her dad keeps in the kitchen and never uses. It was filled with cosmos. Naturally.

Then we headed into the dance.

And we DANCED.

It was hilarious. Ian is SUCH a good dancer, and he's 20, so he doesn't give a crap about what high school kids think of him. Every girl in the place wanted to dance with him, and every guy in the gym wanted to BE him because every girl wanted him, but when there was a slow dance, he pulled Ross in, and held him close, and flipped off anybody who gave him a dirty look.

That's what I want. I want somebody who has my back.

Ryan was an okay dancer, but he was REEEEEALLY stoned and had slammed a couple of beers in the parking lot, so he smelled sort of skunky. Still, it was fun. He kept telling me how sexy I was and how I was making him crazy. He tried to press his junk up against me every 30 seconds, and I just let him. It was fun watching him get all red in the face.

Then I'd drag him over and make him dance with Ross and Ian and me. Lauren did the same thing with Andrew, and by the time we'd been in the gym for an hour, we'd danced ourselves as sweaty as Cam was when he'd walked off the soccer field.

And then we were leaving. Cam and Astrid hadn't moved apart from each other in like an hour, and Ian was trying to take his shirt off, which is against dress code at the dance, and Ross had to drag him out into the parking lot, laughing, and I looked at Lauren, and she said, Let's blow this joint. And I said, A JOINT sounds GREAT!

Lauren went over and tapped on Cam's shoulder. He finally came up for air with Astrid, and he said they'd meet us at Ian's dad's place.

I shoulda gone home right that second.

Crap. Now I'm crying again. And Mom just called up the stairs. We're driving up to have lunch at my grandparents' house. I'll have to finish this in the car.

Later . . .

It's too hard to write while we're driving. I can't tell if it's the butterflies in my stomach or the motion of the car. Either way, it's making me a little sick.

Later . . .

I feel better now that I've eaten. I think I was just hungry. Grams made a big pot roast with all the trimmings. She had this giant yellow cake with fudge frosting, like the ones you see on the commercials for Betty Crocker, only this one didn't come from a mix: She made it from scratch. It's Cam's favorite dessert. I had a very small slice. It was good to see Cam smile again, even if it was about cake. Sometimes he seems so easy. All it took to put him in a good mood again was food.

Cam dragged me into the kitchen with him to do the dishes so that Grams and Gramps could hang out with Mom and Dad for a while. Actually, it was so he could talk to me about what happened at homecoming. At least he's not yelling at me like he did on Friday.

It all happened so fast after we got to Ian's parents' place, which is this HUGE house in the hills. The whole place looks like it might teeter off the side of the hill with one stiff wind and we'd wind up crashing down the hill into the big strip of trendy nightclubs below.

The view took my breath away. You could see downtown to the left and all the way to the edge of city and the beach on the right.

Ian and Ross beat us there because Lauren wanted to stop and get cranberry juice so that we could make cosmos just in case they didn't have the right mixers. Ryan was driving because Andrew was totally tanked. He'd slammed like 3 of the beers he and Ryan brought during the dance. He kept whinnying like a horse and trying to slap Lauren's butt. Lauren was not amused.

When we got to Ian's, she made a beeline for the kitchen to whip up some drinks. Ryan and Andrew followed her inside, and I stopped by the pool to take in the view. There's something about being up in the air like this and seeing the whole city laid out below me that never gets old. It looks beautiful from so far away, like somebody lined up perfect strands of red-and-white holiday lights in a grid and then plugged in the whole city.

When you're driving around down in it, there's so much light, and noise and honking and screaming and laughter and music, but up in the hills, it looks so peaceful and everything is so quiet.

I was thinking about all that when I heard a voice behind me say, Beautiful, isn't it?

I knew it was Blake before I turned around, and before I could, I felt his arms slide around my waist. He pulled me in toward his chest from behind and whispered in my ear:

It's beautiful, like you.

Maybe it was the pot, or the Xanax, or maybe it was just how I felt in the moment, but before I knew what was happening, he had pulled me in and we were kissing! Right in front of everyone.

And I didn't care.

At that same moment Lauren came walking in the door with my drink.

What the hell are you doing?? She said it in a loud whisper that sounded angry, but when I saw her face, she was about to laugh. I stepped away from Blake, blushing.

I couldn't believe Blake had shown up! He said he'd just gotten back last night and Lauren had told him about homecoming tonight and invited him up.

Lauren handed me a cosmo and told me I better watch it because Tweedle Dumb and Tweedle Dumber are in there getting wasted right now and I didn't want to start a brawl by kissing Blake in front of my date.

Blake laughed and said he could handle a coupla high school guys.

That's when we went inside and I saw Ross bending over the mirror on the coffee table in the living room. Then I heard him take a huge sniff and throw his head back and shout, WHOO!

Ian was sitting next to him and kissed him and laughed. Only, it wasn't a normal laugh. It was sort of wild and loud. When he turned around, his eyes were wide and darted back and forth between us. When he saw me and Lauren, he yelled, LADIES!

Blake laughed and led us down two short steps into the living room. He asked us if we wanted any party favors. I looked at Ross and said, WHAT are you DOING? I couldn't believe he was doing coke. I could see that Ryan and Andrew were out on the balcony off of the living room smoking cigarettes.

Ian just laughed and told me to relax, that Ross just did a little bump.

Then, before I knew what had happened, Lauren was bending over the mirror. She came up, sniffed, and tossed her long blond hair over her shoulder. She turned to me and said a single word:

C'mon.

I looked down at the little straight line of powder next to the larger pile. There was a little straw in her hand. My heart started racing faster than the beat of the music.

I glanced over at Blake, who grinned at me and said, You're gonna like it!

I looked around at everyone else. Ian was tickling Ross on the couch. Ryan and Andrew were staring through the window with their cigarettes. I could smell the fingers of smoke tickling my nose through the partially opened door. When they saw me contemplating the mirror, they started chanting, DO IT DO IT DO IT . . .

Something in me knew that this was the only chance. If Cam were here, I'd never do this. But it was so . . . COOL. There was this big house in the hills and a pile of cocaine, and I wouldn't do a lot, just a little bump. Besides, it was an event! Blake was back, and we were all together, and it would just be this one special time.

I took the straw from Lauren.

I smiled up at her as she set the mirror down on the table. I slid in next to Ian and said, Okay! Okay! How do I DO this?

She giggled and said, Just put the straw down and sniff the line up into your nose.

I laughed and started to lean forward, but Blake yelled, WAIT!

I froze and looked up at him like I'd been caught or something.

He looked at me and said, Before you bend over the mirror, make sure you've exhaled so you can inhale through your nose. Otherwise you'll end up exhaling and blowing coke all over the room.

I breathed out.

I touched the edge of the straw to the little line and then put the straw in my nose and sniffed. I saw the white powder disappear up the straw, then felt a little sting in my nose. I dropped the straw and sat back on the couch and sniffed again.

I felt the little clump of powder in my nose hit the back of my throat and make my mouth water with a strange, bitter flavor that made the back of my throat numb.

Ryan and Andrew came into the living room, hooting. Lauren giggled. Ross jumped up, grabbed my hand, and yelled TO THE HOT TUB!

That's when things sped up. I remember the rest in snapshots.

I felt a WHOOSH of something that made me smile and laugh. It was like the first drop on a roller coaster; the excitement flooded my whole body, and I know this sounds completely made up, but I felt TALLER somehow, and prettier.

I remember saying things that made everyone laugh, but I don't remember what they were.

Suddenly we were all in the kitchen making more drinks.

Ryan and Blake went back to the living room and brought the coke into the kitchen. I remember doing another line with them while Lauren and Andrew made out in the corner of the kitchen.

FLASH—Running out to the hot tub with Ross. Laughing so hard I cried as he pulled off all of his clothes and jumped into the water naked with Ian.

FLASH—Another line with Lauren in the kitchen.

FLASH—Dancing with Blake on one side and Ryan on the other.

FLASH—Running into the kitchen for another line with Ross and Ian.

FLASH—Sliding down into the hot tub and realizing we're all in the hot tub. In our underwear. Nothing else.

I wasn't sure whose legs and hands were whose, but the buzz of the coke made me not really care. I felt like my face was lit up from a hum on the inside that made every word I said sound smart, and important.

Ian brought towels out and I caught myself staring at him. I'd never realized how muscular he was before. I nudged Ross and said, Your boyfriend is a hottie. He laughed and said, Let's go smoke out.

FLASH—Back in the living room, smoking a bowl. Ian sprinkling a little cocaine onto the weed in the bowl and saying, You're gonna love this. Smoking deeply, but not feeling that heavy feeling that pot always gives me.

FLASH—Making more drinks with Lauren back in the kitchen. I told her I felt like I could drink a lot more without getting really wasted. She laughed and said that was why cocaine was so awesome, but she said I should pace myself. I told her my stomach was feeling weird. She said that's because they cut the cocaine with stuff like baby laxatives so it's not 100 percent pure. She grabbed her purse and gave me another little chunk of a Xanax tablet.

FLASH—The Xanax and the pot took the edge off of the upset feeling in my stomach. I am laughing with Lauren about how drunk Andrew is, and I hug her and say, THIS IS PERFECT! She hugs me back and says, I know!

FLASH—Blake is sitting in the hot tub with me while everyone else is in the kitchen. We are staring at the lights of the city. I feel his hands on my foot under the water. He starts massaging my foot and it feels AMAZING. I lay my head back and close my eyes.

FLASH—Another bump of cocaine, this time with Ross and Blake. We're all wearing towels, and after I snort the line, I see Blake wipe the end of the straw with his finger and rub it across his top gum. He tells me to try it. The taste is metallic, like the drip in the back of my throat, but it makes my teeth numb, and suddenly I feel so clear and alive!

FLASH—Blake leaves with Lauren to go get more vodka. Ross and Ian have disappeared into the master bedroom. I'm in the hot tub with Ryan and Andrew. At first we were just laughing about the dance and Andrew is talking about school, and this house, and where he's going to college, and how he can't wait for their next volleyball tournament, and all of a sudden I feel lips on my ear and realize that Ryan has pulled me over to him, is nibbling on my ear, and it feels really good, so I lean into him and suddenly our lips have found each other and I feel his tongue on mine, and I put my arms around his neck.

As I'm kissing Ryan, I feel arms around my waist and realize that Andrew is kissing my shoulder! I try to pull away from Ryan, but he just holds me tighter, and I relax a little as I kiss him. We stay like that for a minute, and I feel the heat around my legs in the bubbling water spread up into my stomach and my chest. My breath gets shallow, and I press my mouth even harder into Ryan's. I feel Andrew moving his hands up and down on my stomach and then up to my breasts, and I pull away from Ryan and laugh. Andrew! What are you doing?

He just leans in behind me and whispers, Shhhhhhh, then smiles and says, You know you've wanted both of us since you laid eyes on us. All of a sudden my heart is pounding in my chest. I am NOT okay with this. I turn back to Ryan. I hope he will help me. I hope he will tell his friend to back the hell off. But he just winks at me and leans in to kiss me again.

I try to pull back, but Ryan tightens his grip around my waist while Andrew slides his hands down between my legs. I'm only wearing my underwear and bra, and I hear Andrew saying Sssshh as he slides his fingers under the fabric, pulling them to the side, exploring, exposing. I arch my back and try to throw him off with my hips as I push against Ryan. I yell: STOP. DON'T, ANDREW! But Ryan is pulling me down onto the seat in the hot tub. He pushes me down, hard, and I hit my back against the concrete edge of the tub.

The pain makes me go limp for a second, and Andrew takes this moment to pull my legs farther apart. Ryan is trying to kiss me again.

FLASH—Ryan's hands on my breast, kneading, pawing, squeezing.

FLASH—Andrew's breath on my neck, his fingers pushing further and further inside of me.

FLASH—Their arms holding me down. Their mouths clamped over mine, stifling my shouts. Andrew laughing as Ryan steps in between my legs, forcing them open with his. Screaming. My heart racing, where is everyone? Is Blake coming back?

FLASH—Ryan flies sideways, splashing across the hot tub. Andrew wheels around. I yell out for help. I see a fist connect with Andrew's nose. Blood spurts into the water. Cam is standing in the hot tub, fully clothed. Astrid is pulling me up onto the side of the tub, covering me with a towel.

Andrew is scrambling backward out of the tub toward his clothes. Cam has Ryan by the throat, one fist has already landed, and his arm is drawn back again. Every muscle in his body is strained. Ross and Ian are there, too, and Blake and Lauren are running toward us. Everyone arrived at once.

I've never heard Cam curse like this before: If you ever fucking look at her again . . . If you fucking look at her sideways . . . If you fucking bump into her in the hallway, your ass is MINE.

Ryan and Andrew run out. The party's over.

Cam dragged me into the kitchen. Astrid and Lauren followed us in with my clothes. I saw Cam spot the mirror covered in cocaine that was sitting on the bar in the kitchen. Everything stopped. It was like somebody threw the brakes on a semitruck going 65 miles per hour down the highway. The whole evening jackknifed across Ian's dad's kitchen, then skidded to a halt.

Cam got quiet. Really quiet. He turned to Astrid and said, I have to take my sister home right now. I'm sorry. She just looked at him and nodded. Lauren had helped me back into my clothes by this point. Cam looked at Ian and Blake and said, Who. Brought. The. Coke? One word at a time, like he might explode at any moment.

Everyone just stood there, silent. Cam grabbed my arm and said, We're out.

All the way home, he let me have it. What were you thinking? Do you know how dangerous coke is? He kept saying how he'd warned me about Ryan and Andrew, and that Lauren was a bad influence on me.

Then he said he was telling Mom and Dad.

I started sobbing, and begging. I told him that I'd do anything. He pulled the car into the driveway and turned it off, and we sat there for a minute. He told me to pull it together before we walked in just in case Mom was awake. I asked him how he was going to explain to Mom and Dad that he was wet from the waist down. He said he was going to tell them exactly what happened unless . . .

I said unless what?

He told me I had to stop. Everything. No more pot, or drinking, or pills, or anything. He said no more sneaking to Lauren's for cosmos with Astrid and Ross. They could come to our house for the next month, but that was it. If he saw anything going on, he'd tell Mom and Dad everything.

I felt desperate. I would've promised Cam ANYTHING to stay quiet. I felt my heart racing. I was so panicked that he'd tell Mom and Dad I'd done cocaine. I knew they wouldn't yell or scream. I knew they'd just look at me and tell me how disappointed they were with me. I couldn't face that. I couldn't stand to see the hurt in their eyes.

So I promised. I promised Cam that I would be done with it all.

That was late Friday night. Well, I guess it was early Saturday morning. Today is Sunday and I can't believe it's only been a day since all of this happened. From the back deck at Grams and Gramps's I can see a sailboat in the distance, a white blur against the bright blue sky. The boat seems so far away, sort of like Andrew and Ryan and what happened on Friday night.

Yesterday I just lay around with Lauren, feeling sick and sad. Somehow, today I feel numb.

Grams came out with a glass of iced tea for me. She's sitting next to me in the sun. Told me to keep writing, that it does her heart good to see how much I like it. Jeez. She'd fall over and die if she knew I was recording my first time doing cocaine and almost getting raped in a hot tub.

God. My life has become like a terrible Lifetime movie of the week.

Later . . .

We just got back from Grams and Gramps's. Lauren has been texting me all day. Ross is really worried about me. He's been hanging out with her today. Lauren wants me to come over and join them, but Cam is watching me like a hawk.

And you know something? I'm glad.

I'm glad I have a brother who was there for me on Friday night. I start crying every time I think of what would have happened if he hadn't shown up when he did.

I texted her back on the way home from Grams and Gramps's and told her that we'd regroup at lunch tomorrow with Cam. I leaned over and showed the phone to Cam before I pressed send. He read the text, then looked across the backseat and smiled at me for the first time since Friday.

Then I lay my head down on his lap and closed my eyes. I felt him put his hand on my arm and give me a little squeeze. We stayed like that for a long time, and when I opened my eyes again, we were pulling into our driveway back home.

September 26

We all made a pact today at lunch—Me, Lauren, Astrid, Ross: no more drugs. It was a fun experiment, but I'm done. It's just not worth it. Everybody agreed. Astrid said she was so glad that

Cam had shown up when he had. Lauren had tears in her eyes and said she was so sorry for even introducing me to Ryan and Andrew. Ross said that Ian and Blake felt really terrible and they are laying off the partying too.

Cam seemed satisfied, and it felt good. A clean start. It felt good to have everybody there at the table, and bonded together. I don't know what I was thinking. I guess I wanted them all to like me so much that I never considered that they'd be okay with not drinking; that they'd want to hang out with me just for the friendship part.

I have to admit it'll be strange. Most times, we've all gotten stoned together. Ross had a great idea, though—this weekend we're all going to go do yoga together on Saturday. Ian is teaching a class on Saturday morning, and Cam is jazzed about getting back into it now that soccer is winding down.

I feel happy in that satisfied, contented way that makes it seem like everything is going to be all right.

October 1

We all went to Ian's yoga class this morning. It was hard after not having been there in a while. Ian says yoga is surgery without knives, and he's right! That's what it feels like.

Afterward Cam and I went shopping for Dad's birthday

(which is today!) We got him some running shorts and a running shirt, the kind that wicks the moisture off of your skin while you sweat. Dad likes to run on the path along the beach in the mornings before he goes to teach. I'm really glad that my dad is such a health nut. It makes me feel like maybe he'll be around for a long time. I never really think about how much I like my mom and dad until I think about them not being around, and that idea is so weird that it's hard to wrap my head around it. Dad is turning 47 today. He was 30 when I was born. That seems so crazy to me.

What will I be doing when I'm 30?

I can't really imagine past being in college. I mean, I can sort of imagine myself graduating from college, but then I'm not sure what it looks like after that. I like to think about having a boyfriend.

For some reason, when I wrote that last sentence, Mark flashed into my head. Yesterday in the hall he asked me how homecoming was. I said it was fine. I asked him how it was for him. He said he went home after the soccer game.

Maybe I'll see if he wants to come to lunch with us on Monday.

Dad has invited his friend from college, Dale, and his wife, Karen, over for dinner tonight. They have a little boy named Nelson who is 9 years old. Mom is making Dad's favorite meal: lasagna, with German chocolate cake for dessert. Cam and I were allowed to invite one friend each as well. I like that about Dad. He always wants to make sure that our friends are included.

Cam invited Astrid, of course. I invited Lauren this morning after yoga class, but she said she is having dinner with her dad at some fancy place tonight, so Ross is coming instead. Mom said Lauren could come over for dessert if she gets done with her dad in time.

I texted her, but I haven't heard back. I hope she's okay. I know that the thing with Andrew and Ryan really upset her.

Later . . .

Dinner was delicious. Ross wore a bow tie, which was funny because he's got that shaggy surfer hair. He looked so cute! Mom really likes Astrid. I can tell. Astrid looked beautiful, and she always seems to know the right thing to say. She was able to talk to Karen and Dale like she had known them for years and years.

After dinner Cam and Ross took Nelson outside and kicked the soccer ball around for a while. I texted Lauren twice, but I didn't hear back from her. Weird. I'm sure she's just at dinner with her dad and some big-time rock star. Sometimes he invites her to dinner and she ends up sitting across the table from some world-famous singer.

October 3

Lauren isn't at school today. Ross and Astrid haven't heard from her either. Now I'm getting worried. I am going to walk down to her place with Ross at lunch. Mark will just have to wait.

Later . . .

The good news: Lauren is alive.

The bad news: She is not well.

When Ross and I got to her place, we signed in with the security guard at the front desk, then took the elevator up to the penthouse level. Ross banged on the door while I texted her that we were in her hallway.

Finally she came to the door. It looked like she'd been crying. Her eyes were really puffy and she was all sniffly. She said that she had gone to dinner with her dad on Saturday night and then had an allergy attack when she got home and couldn't sleep for two nights. I hugged her and told her that she should at least text me back so I don't send the Coast Guard out looking for her body.

When we were walking back to school, Ross was really quiet. I asked him if he was okay. He nodded and said he was fine, but he thought that Lauren wasn't.

I asked him what he meant, and he said it didn't look like an allergy attack to him. He said he thought it looked like Lauren had been partying. And by partying he meant cocaine.

I told him that was ridiculous. We'd all just made that pact last week.

Ross just shook his head and smiled at me, this weird smile like he thought what I said was sweet but that I just didn't get it. I told him he was crazy. He told me I hadn't been around cocaine very much. I asked him when he'd become such an expert, but right at that moment Mark walked up with Cam and Astrid. I told them that Lauren was fine; she'd just had an allergy attack. Ross snorted and rolled his eyes. Cam saw him and frowned, then asked what was up. Ross just shook his head and said, Nothing. A little Benadryl will fix her right up. Then he walked off to class.

GOD. Ross can be such a DICK sometimes.

October 7

School SUCKED this week. God. I am so happy I don't have to go back tomorrow, but I have so much homework, I won't be able to leave the house this weekend.

Lauren was back in class on Tuesday looking stunning as usual. Ross was sorta standoffish and quiet all week. He kept watching Lauren when she talked, like he was looking for clues. Astrid and Cam are spending a lot of time together, which is nice. I really like her. She's coming over later to watch

145

a movie with Cam, which is code for lie on the couch under a blanket and do God knows what. I have to write two papers this weekend—one for history and one for English. I don't have any idea how I'm going to get them done.

When I told Mom about it, she was very sweet and said she'd take me out to sushi on Sunday night to celebrate finishing.

I told her the thing that might be finished by then is ME.

I always feel so good when I make my mom laugh.

October 9

It's 4 p.m. and I feel like my fingers are going to fall off from typing school papers. And that my brain is going to leak out of my ears. It actually feels good to hold this pen and write on paper that isn't virtual. I have to finish the bibliography for the English paper and then I am DONE.

Later . . .

Just got back from sushi with Mom. In the middle of dinner she started asking more questions about homecoming. She said I had seemed sort of quiet after that night and wanted to know how my date with Ryan went. When she said his name, my heart started racing like I had been running a marathon and I felt all sick to my stomach. She asked me if I was feeling okay, and I said I was fine, but I wasn't. Just the thought of him pushing me down in that hot tub gives me a panic attack.

I told her that Ryan just wasn't my type. We're not a match.

Now I'm freaking out. I'm not sure how I'm going to get to sleep thinking about that all night. Jesus. I'd just started to forget it. I wish my parents didn't want to do such a Good Job parenting sometimes. I mean, I know you're supposed to ask your kids questions and stay engaged in their lives, but some things I just don't want to talk about.

I wish Ross were here right now with his pipe so we could smoke a bowl. I know I promised Cam that I wouldn't smoke out anymore, but UGH. This SUCKS.

Later . . .
It's 1 a.m. and I'm still not asleep. I'm going to be a zombie at school tomorrow.

Later . . .
1:30 a.m.

I just texted Lauren to see if she's still awake. No response.

Then I texted Blake 'cause he used to send me texts in the middle of the night all the time. I guess he's always up late playing music with his band and stuff?

He texted right back. I haven't really heard from him since

the Homecoming Hot Tub Fiasco. He asked what I was doing up. I said I couldn't sleep. He wrote back:

SLEEPING IS OVERRATED . . . ;)

October 10

Elizabeth Archer just poked me in the back with her finger because I was asleep in class. Ross is sitting in front of me and I had laid my head down on my desk. How do teachers expect you to stay awake when they turn off the lights and close the blinds so that they can use a projector? Thank God I have this journal to write in so I can stay awake.

Mark walked me to class this morning. He was hanging out by our lockers when Lauren and I walked in today. Lauren saw him standing there and elbowed me. She said, Don't look now, but All-American Mark is lying in wait. Then she giggled. She's taken to calling him All-American Mark, and he does look like something out of an Abercrombie ad. At least he doesn't use their cologne. I can always smell that crap a mile down the hallway. The boys in my school are obsessed with it—that and Axe body spray. Ross has a theory that they wear it because they think it will make them look like the guys in the commercials for it. The guys in the ads all have chiseled muscles and look like they haven't ever eaten a french fry in their lives. Cam looks like that, mainly because he runs nonstop and plays soccer. Thankfully he doesn't wear too much of anything that smells too strong.

Anyway, when Lauren and I walked up, I invited Mark to come to lunch. He frowned and said, Isn't the guy supposed to ask the girl out?

Lauren snort-laughed when he said this. I just looked at him until he said, What?

Lauren said, Oh nothing. Maybe after lunch you can slay a dragon for us and kill the evil witch. What century are you living in?

Which was funny, but it made Mark blush, and for some reason I feel badly about that. I'm not sure why. I mean, he's SOOOO old-fashioned in some ways, but there's something about it that seems . . . I dunno. Sweet? Yeah, it seems sweet, like he wants to be Proper with a capital P.

I'm just not sure what he sees in a girl like me. It makes me wonder why he's so interested.

October 16

I can't believe I haven't written in almost a week.

Actually, yes I can. Midterms start tomorrow.

I'm doomed.

October 19

YAAAAAAAAAY!

MIDTERMS ARE OVER!

Ross and Lauren and I are going to the movies tonight. Astrid and Cam might join us. I am SO RELIEVED. I don't think I did very well on chemistry. We had a marathon study session at our place last night. Astrid, Lauren, and I all sat at the dining room table until Lauren actually fell asleep with her head on a book and I couldn't see the flash cards Astrid was holding to drill us. (Astrid is crazy when it comes to studying. Who makes flash cards?)

We blew up the air mattress in my room for Astrid, and Lauren slept in my bed with me. I got up to go to the bathroom in the middle of the night, and no one was on the air mattress. This morning in the kitchen, Mom was making us a big "Last Day of Midterms" breakfast (BEST. MOM. EVER.) and I pulled Cam aside and said, So . . . funny thing. Astrid wasn't on the air mattress when I got up to go to the bathroom last night. He didn't even LOOK at me, just poured some coffee and said, I have no idea what you're talking about, little sister.

But his ears were bright red.

LOL. Gotcha.

Later . . .

Ian showed up at the movie last night. Ross doesn't talk a lot about what's going on with the two of them, and he hadn't really mentioned Ian since homecoming. It was a little tense because Cam showed up too, and he's still a little touchy about Ian and the whole cocaine thing. But we went to the movie, and then out to get milk shakes and french fries at Swingers. Mom let us stay out until midnight, even though it was a school night. By the time we were all piled into the booth at the restaurant, Cam and Ian were joking around again and things seemed back to normal.

Then Ian dropped the bomb: Blake is throwing a giant Halloween party.

Lauren threw both hands up in the air and squealed like an 8-year-old.

Cam got really quiet. Lauren saw this and said, Oh, don't worry, Cam. We all took the pact, remember? No scary party drugs. Besides! You and Astrid will be there.

Cam shook his head and looked uneasy.

Astrid put her arm around him and buried her nose in his neck.

Whatever she whispered to him were the magic words, 'cause his ears went red again and he got this sort of wicked-looking smirk on his face.

I smiled at him across the table and said, I promise we'll be good, Cam. I PROMISE.

He grinned at me, but there was caution in his eyes. He said he wasn't worried about me being good. It was the rest of these yahoos he had to keep an eye on.

OMG! I'M SO EXCITED. This Halloween party is going to ROCK.

Let the costume planning commence!

October 22

I think my feet might fall off. We walked up and down to every costume store on Hollywood Blvd. today to get the stuff for our costumes, but it was SO WORTH IT.

We're going to Halloween as a HAUNTED CIRCUS.

Lauren: Ring Mistress Dominatrix

Ross: Lion

Me: Sexy Clown

Astrid and Cam are going as Antony and Cleopatra. Jason and Elizabeth Archer are coming too, but I'm not sure what their costumes are going to be yet.

Cam is really excited about the party now. I think he just needed some reassurance from me that we're all staying on the straight edge. Well . . . mainly.

I wasn't even sure if I should write this down, but after we got our costumes, Lauren and Ross and I were in his truck on the way back. (Cam and Astrid went in Cam's car.) Anyway, Ross had his pipe and smoked us out.

I don't think Cam would really care, but I'd rather not give him any reason to be upset, so that'll just be our little secret.

God! I forgot how great it is to get stoned and laugh my ass off with Lauren and Ross.

Cannot. Wait. For. Next. Weekend!

November 1

I feel so fucked up right now, like I don't know what's right and what's wrong anymore. Thank God Cam left early last night. I'm still in deep shit with him as it is, but at least he doesn't know about the Ecstasy yet, and if I can help it he WON'T.

Lauren did a really good job talking Cam down over the last week. He was still a little leery of going to Blake's for the Halloween party because of the whole homecoming thing, but most every day at lunch last week Lauren and Astrid talked about their costumes, and how great the music was going to be, and blah blah blah. Cam was finally getting really excited.

Everybody came over here to get ready last night before we went to Blake's. Mom and Dad could not take enough pictures. Lauren looked AMAZING in her black shiny vinyl high-heeled boots that went up to her thighs, and her fishnets. She wore a black leotard with a bow tie and a tuxedo jacket that had long tails. Her top hat was bright red, and she had this long gold whip that was wound up and hung from her belt. She piled her long blond hair up on top of her head in a tight French twist with little ringlets down the side of her face and crazy dramatic eye makeup. She was a KNOCKOUT.

I could tell Mom thought Lauren's costume was a little trampy because when we were planning what I would wear, she made sure that mine covered a little bit more skin, which was fine with me. My body's nowhere near as amazing as Lauren's is, but my costume was so FUN! I had a tiny purple skirt that poofed out with crinolines underneath. I wore bright red fishnets and heels that Lauren loaned me. The shoes were this vintage pair of old-fashioned character heels that made my legs look great! I had a silver corset and loooooooong fake eyelashes. Astrid and Lauren spent like an hour curling my hair into these tiny ringlets that they pinned up in the back so they could perch a tiny clown hat with a GIANT plume sticking out of the top. I had white face paint and tiny red heart lips, sort of like a clown from Paris. At least that was the idea according to Ross who found this picture online. I also had a tiny parasol. When we were all done, I looked in the mirror and hardly recognized myself. I looked amazing.

I realized while I was getting ready that my tummy was all

jumpy, and every time I looked in the mirror, I realized I was thinking about what Blake would think when he looked at me. I kept remembering our kiss by the hot tub on homecoming night. He had pulled me in so tight, and kissed me so hard, like he was drowning and I was the only way he could get oxygen. He texted me yesterday and said, CAN'T WAIT 2 C U.

I was texting him back when Ross came out of the bathroom where Astrid and Lauren were doing his makeup. Ross had a fake fur mane and was covered in gold glittery powder dusted on his face and bare chest. He had skin-tight black jeans that had a tail sewn onto the back that Lauren linked to his wrist with a little bit of clear fishing line that Astrid got out of her dad's tackle box. (Astrid and Lauren are like crafting GENIUSES.)

Astrid had this AWESOME black Cleopatra wig that had straight bangs. Her long linen robe had a jeweled collar. She looked like some sort of Egyptian goddess. Lauren had found these gold snakes with wires in them that we wrapped around her arms and wrists.

When Cam came out in his Mark Antony Roman war-hero getup, Lauren and Astrid and Mom and I hooted and whistled. He was wearing sandals that had long leather straps that wrapped all the way up to his knees and a short tunic with armor that covered his chest. The breastplate was shiny plastic, but it looked like metal and he had a shield and a helmet with red plumage at the top.

Mom and Dad took pictures like somebody was getting married; then they made everyone promise to drive the speed limit.

Cam and Astrid drove to Blake's together, and Lauren drove me and Ross. When we got to Blake's and parked, I still couldn't believe the view. My stomach was all jumpy because I hadn't seen Blake in a long time, but BOOM: There he was. He was dressed as a mummy . . . or I guess I should say UNdressed as a mummy because very little of him was actually covered. He had these strategically placed strips of cloth wrapped around his head, arms, and legs, but his chest was mainly bare. I just stared. I guess I had been pretty drunk and high the last time I was here and we were in his bathroom together. I hadn't really noticed what an AMAZING body he has.

Then, my stomach REALLY got jumpy because Cam walked right up to him and I realized I was holding my breath until they smiled at each other and shook hands. Then Blake winked at me and threw his arm around Cam's shoulders and showed him around. The tour was equally impressive the second time around, only this time there were WILD Halloween decorations everywhere. There were black lights making stuff glow purple and the pool lights had red gels in them so the water looked like blood as it flowed off the false edge of the concrete deck. But even cooler than the pool was something that Blake had kept a surprise:

There was a giant bouncy castle inflated next to the pool. There were already 3 or 4 people in it jumping up and down and screaming like maniacs. Lauren and Astrid and I were like NO WAY. Cam just shook his head and gave Blake a high five. Ross didn't even wait. He'd seen that Ian was one of the guys in the castle and took off running in a cloud of gold body glitter.

Astrid and Cam were talking to Blake, and Lauren and I wandered down to the clear glass wall at the end of the pool. The moon was a tiny waning crescent (SEE? I DID learn something last year in physical science), and there was an eerie blanket of fog rolling in off the ocean. It was PERFECT for a Halloween party.

I leaned close to her, and our arms touched. I said, Remember? This is where we met. She threw her head back and laughed, and hugged me. She said, I can't even remember not knowing you. What did I do for fun before you?

Couldn't focus on the fog for very long because right about that moment, the DJ started spinning. YES. There was a DJ. One of Blake's friends (who also has a deal with Lauren's dad's record label) was spinning. Lauren and I stood there looking around as people in the CRAZIEST costumes poured out onto the dance floor that was set up near the house. Lauren grabbed my hand and yelled cosmos!, then we took off running for the kitchen.

Cam and Astrid were already there with Blake. The guys had beers and looked like best friends. Astrid was drinking sparkling water, and when Lauren offered her a cosmo, she just shook her head and winked, then whispered, I'm going to try to get Mark Antony out of here a little early to have some ALONE time. Lauren said that she'd drink to that, and we clinked glasses, then pushed everybody out onto the dance floor and danced our asses off.

Ross and Ian joined us and Ian had gold body glitter all over his costume because he'd been jumping around in the bouncy castle with Ross. Ross pulled Cam aside and the two of them disappeared for a little while, and I KNEW that they were smoking out.

I got SO JEALOUS at that second. I mean, how can CAM be telling ME not to do drugs and smoke out and hang with these guys if he's going to do it? I tapped Lauren on the shoulder and said, Did you see Cam and Ross just leave to go smoke out? She smiled a wicked Ring Mistress smile, then adjusted her top hat with one hand as she pressed a little chunk of Xanax into my palm with the other hand and said, One step ahead of you, sister.

I looked down at the tiny pill in my hand. I said, What about our PACT? She said, We've been really good! We've proven that we can handle it. Besides, it's not like we're doing coke or something.

I felt weird about it, like I wasn't sure what would happen if I took this little pill, but the music was so loud, and we looked so good, and Lauren was laughing and dancing and telling me to C'MON!

I grinned at her and we danced over to Astrid who was refilling her sparkling water in the kitchen. Lauren scooted around a man dressed as a rapping rhinoceros and grabbed the martini shaker. She mixed us an extra-strong round of cosmos and we washed down our Xanax. Ross came around the corner with Cam. I raised an eyebrow and asked, How is the smoke this evening?

Cam was totally caught and he knew it. He looked at Ross, then back at me and said, Okay, but just a couple tokes. I don't want you throwing up again.

I raised my cosmo glass and said, No, no. It's fine. I don't need to smoke pot to be cool.

Lauren and Astrid cracked up. Cam just rolled his eyes and shook his head, then Astrid led him back out to the dance floor.

Ross asked if I wanted to get stoned, but I didn't. I realized that I was just jealous that Ross had asked Cam first, and I was pissed that Cam was trying to act like my dad or something by telling me that I should stay totally clean while he went and had fun. I told Ross that maybe I'd want to later. I remembered how NOT fun it was to throw up on the way home. My clown outfit was way too cute for that. Ross pulled me into the living room where we started dancing with two girls who were dressed as sexy cats.

Blake, Ian, and Lauren came over, then Cam and Astrid joined us. We all danced our way out by the pool, and slowly everyone in our party became covered in Ross the Lion's gold body glitter. At some point I had put down my parasol in the kitchen, and Lauren's top hat wound up on Blake's head. Blake kept dancing back and forth to the kitchen with a shaker of cosmos, and Lauren kept making sure our glasses were full. Cam must've been on his 4th beer when Astrid checked her phone and whispered in Cam's ear.

I don't know what she said, but it worked. He came dancing over to talk to me. Actually, he walked like an Egyptian over to me, following Astrid, who held his hand over her shoulder. His breath was hot on my cheek and smelled like beer, but his smile was so wide, I couldn't resist smiling back. Astrid was going to drive him back to Egypt, he said, giggling. Then he tried to get as stern as he could after 4 beers and made sure that Ian knew how important it was that I got home by 1 a.m. because that was curfew and he'd promised Mom and Dad that he'd look out for me. He turned to leave with Astrid and then pulled Ian in close and yelled over the music: Don't make me regret this.

Lauren ran up and hugged Astrid, then kissed Cam on the nose and said she'd take good care of me. Cam rolled his eyes and said that's what he was afraid of. Then Lauren dragged me down to the bouncy castle, and before I knew it, we'd kicked off our high heels and we were jumping around, shrieking and laughing like idiots. It made me think of when I was a little girl at the carnival down by the pier at the beach. Cam had eaten too many hot dogs and got a stomachache from jumping around too fast, but Dad had to come in and drag me out when it was time to go home. I never wanted to leave.

Lauren double-bounced me at one point, and I crashed into her, then we both collapsed and lay on our backs laughing and listening to the music. She propped up on her elbow and asked me if I thought Astrid and Cam were going to go all the way tonight. I was like, AAAUGH. He's my BROTHER! And she giggled and tickled me between my corset and my skirt until I yelled that I was going to wet my pants if she didn't stop. She grabbed my hand and said, Why didn't you TELL me you had to go to the bathroom. C'MON!

We went running into the house. Blake called to us, but Lauren was on a mission. We ran up the stairs to Blake's bedroom and closed the door. I was peeing while Lauren reapplied her lipstick, and when I stepped over to the sink, she opened the cabinet under the vanity and pulled out a mirror that had a giant pile of white powder on it. She shot me a mischievous smile and asked if I wanted a bump.

I stopped short and asked, Where'd that come from? She said Blake told her he always has a stash under the sink at parties.

I could hear the music down by the pool, but it sounded so far away, like the DJ was on the moon. I watched as Lauren used the razor blade Blake had left behind to cut lines, bigger than the ones we had done the night of homecoming. Then she picked up a little glass tube that was lying on the mirror and snorted one of the lines—half of it up each nostril. She did a little head shake that made her ringlets bounce, then turned and motioned me over.

I felt my throat get tight. It was CRAZY. I wanted to snort that line SO BADLY, but I stood there frozen. I told her I couldn't. She laughed, and said, Of COURSE you can. Cam's gone. Nobody will know. And it'll make you feel DELICIOUS.

The thing was that I knew she was right. I remembered after homecoming how I'd felt like a rock star when I had my first line. I felt like I was a giant magnet and I could pull anybody to me that I wanted. Every word I said sounded hilarious, and smart, and made people love me.

And then I remembered the hot tub: Andrew's hands on my butt, the hard edge of the hot tub digging into my back as Ryan tried to force my legs apart, and I felt like I was going to throw up. Lauren saw the look on my face and put the coke back under the sink, then ran over and hugged me. She whispered into my ear, said that it was okay. That she was so sorry that happened. That I didn't have to do anything I didn't want to.

As we stood there, I felt her arms around me and I felt better. I started to breathe a little slower, and the memory of the terrible drip from the coke in my throat on homecoming night finally subsided.

There was a knock on the bathroom door, and we heard Blake's voice asking if everybody was okay. Lauren pulled back and asked if I was okay. I nodded and smiled. She opened the door, and Ross and Ian and Blake pushed into the bathroom and closed the door again. Ross had his pipe and a Baggie of weed out before I could say hello, and I realized that was exactly what I wanted. Ross packed a bowl, and I took a long deep hit, and then another. Instantly I felt more calm.

Blake had brought up the martini shaker and a couple of glasses. The vodka was so cold against my lips after the smoke, and it tasted like SweeTarts. I had a big gulp, and felt the icy splash on my tongue. Lauren's eyes were wide, and darting around. I knew she was feeling the buzz from the coke. My eyes felt a little droopy, but I wasn't sleepy, I was relaxed. I sat down on the edge of the bathtub as Ian and Ross repacked the bowl of weed, and I felt warm strong hands on my bare shoulders. It was Blake.

His hands felt so good massaging my neck and shoulders. I closed my eyes and leaned back against him. He was standing in the tub and I felt his lips on my neck, then his breath against my ear: You look so beautiful.

When I opened my eyes, Ross was smoking the pipe, and Ian was offering Lauren a mint from a little red tin he'd opened up. She popped one in her mouth and sucked on it, then her eyes got wide and she swigged the last of her cosmo. One gulp and the mint was gone.

Ian was laughing, and Lauren playfully smacked his arm. I asked what was wrong with the mint. She said, Nothing, it just wasn't a mint. Genius here just gave me a tab of E.

Maybe it was the pot, or Blake's hands working the tension out of my neck, but I guess I didn't understand right away what she meant. Then it hit me: Ecstasy.

I sat up on the edge of the tub and looked around. Ian was still laughing, and Ross was sitting down with his back against the cabinets in the bathroom, holding the pot pipe in one hand and watching his other hand as it ran back and forth across Blake's plush silver bath mat.

I looked at Lauren and said, They're all on Ecstasy, aren't they?

Lauren followed my gaze to Ross, then Ian, and then she looked at Blake and sighed, nodding. She said that it looked like everybody was rolling but me.

I knew right away that I was not going to just sit there while everybody else did Ecstasy—no matter what I had promised Cam. I stood up from the side of the tub and held out my hand to Ian, who looked at me, then down at my hand, and then smiled when he understood.

Without a word, he pulled the red tin out of his pocket and opened it.

The pills really did look a lot like mints. It was a smart way to carry them around. He plucked one out of the pile. It had a little heart stamped into it. He smiled as he dropped it into my hand and said, Enjoy the ride.

Lauren grabbed my arm as I lifted the pill toward my lips. She asked if I was sure. In response, I put the tablet on my tongue and took a long drink of my cosmo. She jumped up and squealed, THIS is why I LOVE you.

We all went back downstairs to dance, and after about 20 or 30 minutes, I was feeling hot, and a little drunk, but nothing else. I went to the kitchen and grabbed a bottle of water out of Blake's fridge. The clock on the microwave was glowing a bright blue 11:47, and I realized at that there was no way that I was going to get home at the right time tonight.

The party had thinned out a little, and I found Lauren by the pool and pulled her into the kitchen. I told her I needed a favor. She just smiled and shook her head and said not to worry. The minute I'd swallowed that tab of E she knew we weren't going home before 4 a.m., and she'd called Cam to tell him that I was spending the night at her place.

YES! I threw my arms over my head and spun around in a circle, and it felt like a big wave of pure happy crashed down on top of me. I almost felt like I was going to cry because I was so happy. When I looked up, Ross, Ian, and Blake were standing behind Lauren in the kitchen watching me spin around. I caught myself, and said, WHAT?

Ross handed me a grape-flavored candy lollipop and said, Feeling anything yet?

I took the sucker and unwrapped it and put it in my mouth as I thought about it and said, I don't know. But Ross! This sucker tastes AMAZING!

They all burst out laughing, and Blake said, You're rolling!

And it was like the minute he said that I felt another big wave of pure happiness crash over me, stronger this time. It made my knees feel weak and my jaw a little clenched—almost like I was going over the first drop on a roller coaster, and I was glad that I had the sucker in my mouth. This wave made me take a great big deep breath, and suddenly I felt a wave of heat that made my forehead a little sweaty and I took another big deep breath. The waves were coming with my breath and Lauren took my hand and said, C'mon! Let's go outside.

As I stepped out onto the back stairs that went down to the pool, a crisp breeze came blowing off of the water and the red lights of the pool seemed to glow brighter in a flash. The grape sucker in my mouth tasted like the best thing I'd ever put on my tongue, and Lauren's hand felt so soft in my mine. Suddenly I stopped and closed my eyes and took another deep breath as a big wave of intense feeling rolled through my body.

I felt Blake's hands on my shoulder, and my eyes flew open. The lights in the pool flashed 100 times brighter than they had been, and as I looked up at the sliver of moon reflecting off of the ocean, my eyes wiggled back and forth really quickly for just a second, and I saw these AMAZING streamers of light flying off the moon and the lights in the pool. I felt Blake's lips at my ear, and my whole body shivered like I was cold, but I wasn't.

Blake whispered, This is why they call it Ecstasy.

And as he said it, I felt another wave of pure happiness wash over me, and I realized THIS is why they say you're ROLLING. I pulled Lauren's hand closer to me and said, It's coming in WAVES!

I've always had fun dancing, but after a couple of songs, I get bored, or sweaty, or tired, and usually take a break. Dancing on E was like NOTHING I'd ever experienced. I couldn't get my body close enough to Blake's or to Lauren's. Every touch felt like an electric wave of tiny tingles that spread slowly up my fingers and arms down my whole body into my legs and feet. The music sounded like something coming from inside of me. I wasn't HEARING the music, I was FEELING the music, and we danced, and danced, and danced, until all our makeup had sweated off, and we'd kicked off our shoes, and Blake had wrapped his arms around me. I felt like I could dance all night long.

The funny thing is that writing this now, there are so many problems that I can think of. There are so many things that I feel aren't right about me, about my life, about how I look, about how I feel, about my friends, about my family. I have so many fears, and worries, and I think too much about all of those things.

But dancing by the pool with Blake and Lauren, and Ross and Ian, I didn't worry. At all. I wasn't afraid. Of anything. It wasn't that I had all the answers to all of my questions, it was that I didn't have any questions. Everything felt like it made sense, and not just in my head, it made sense in my heart, in a way that I can't explain. My stomach was calm and I felt a beautiful, glorious, peaceful excitement. Peaceful excitement? I sound like a CRAZY person. But that's what it was like—that there was nothing wrong. It felt like "wrong" wasn't even an option, as if nothing had ever been wrong, or ever COULD be wrong.

At some point, we all ended up in the jumping castle. If bouncing around had been fun BEFORE, it was AMAZING on Ecstasy. As I jumped up and down, the lights at the pool squiggled in bright plumes around me. My eyes would wiggle back and forth really fast a couple times a minute, and great big waves of happiness swept over me until I was breathless.

Finally we all collapsed in a heap in the castle and lay there talking, talking, talking. Ross talked about how glad he was that he'd met Ian, and Ian talked about how he couldn't believe that Ross was into him, and when I looked up, he had the most beautiful smile and there were tears sliding down his cheeks. His whole face looked lit up from the inside, and his eyes almost seemed to be glowing.

I felt so happy in that moment that Ross and Ian had found each other. Lauren took my hand, and Blake pressed his body against mine on the other side and ran a hand through my hair. I said how great it was that I'd met Lauren and Ross this summer, and suddenly my eyes were filled with the happiest, warmest tears I'd ever felt. I had to take several deep breaths as I talked. Lauren had tears in her eyes too. As the drops brimmed over my eyelids and slid down my cheeks, they felt thick and warm, like syrup or glycerin, and another wave of pure joy washed over me. We all lay there for a few minutes listening to the music, and then Blake said:

Let's go put our feet in the hot tub.

So we did.

The DJ was playing slower songs now, and people were leaving.

Somebody gave me a water bottle, and the warmth of the hot tub on my feet and legs felt like a delicious caress. Lauren and I talked and talked about how wonderful it felt, and how amazing this night was, and how we wished that Astrid and Cam were here with us. Slowly, somehow, it got quiet. The music finally faded away, and everyone left, and Lauren looked at me and smiled. She didn't even have to say any words. It was just the two of us sitting here under the moon. And I felt so connected to her, like we'd be best friends forever.

Blake must've seen everyone out and paid the DJ, because he came to the back door and said, Hey you guys! C'mere.

Lauren and I got up and walked into the house, and there in the living room, Ross and Ian were lying on the shiny silver shag rug in the living room. The fibers were thin and stringy, soft and smooth. I don't really remember how it happened, but soon we were all lying on the rug. It felt SO GOOD running our hands and feet through it.

We stayed there for a long time on the rug. Blake disappeared into the kitchen and brought back ice cold cosmos for me and Lauren. I remember drinking it and thinking that my eyes hadn't gone wiggly in a little while. And then Blake was back on the rug with me, running his hands over the long silky silver fibers, and over my skin. Then we were kissing, and I closed my eyes and felt his body pressed against mine, and it was like we were moving together and breathing together and thinking together. His tongue felt so amazing against my own, and his hands were electric on my body.

I felt his fingers unlacing the corset of my costume, and I looked around and realized that everyone else was out back in the hot tub, and it was just us. Then we're upstairs somehow in Blake's bedroom, and sinking, sinking, sinking down into the soft mattress. I'm naked, and Blake is naked, and he's pressed against me so tight that it makes me gasp. His breath is on my ear and neck, and his hands are on my breasts. My arms are wrapped around him, my fingers sliding down his back and across his thighs, pulling him into me closer and closer until I feel like we have somehow merged into one another. I can't feel where I start and he stops, and the waves of warmth and feeling roll through me and I have never felt like this before, but I never want it to stop, and then . . .

I wake up.

When I opened my eyes, the light was bright outside the window. I lay there for a minute before I remembered where I was. I had a terrible headache and my jaw felt sore, like I had been gritting my teeth all night. I felt so achy and I stretched my legs slowly under the covers. I felt an arm around my waist and suddenly I realized that I was in Blake's bed. With Blake.

He ran his hand up and down my back, and whispered how beautiful my body is, and how amazing I felt last night, and in a flash I remembered:

We had sex.

I froze, and my stomach dropped, but not in a happy way. My head hurt so badly that I closed my eyes for a minute. Blake gave me a soft kiss on the forehead and slipped out of bed into the bathroom. I heard the shower turn on, and I grabbed my underwear off of the floor. It was the only thing I saw of mine in the room. Then I remembered the rug.

I pulled a blanket off of the bed and wrapped it around my shoulders and headed downstairs. My phone and purse were on the counter in the kitchen. I walked into the living room and felt a flood of relief when I saw Lauren curled up on the couch under a blanket.

Then I was shaking her awake, and we both checked our phones and it was after noon. The only thing that went running through my head was that I needed to find my skirt and shoes.

I collected the pieces of my costume, pulled the skirt on, and carried the corset back upstairs.

Blake came out of the bathroom in a towel as I sat down on the edge of the bed to buckle my shoes. He asked why I was leaving so soon. I asked if he had a T-shirt I could borrow so I didn't have to lace myself back into the corset, and as he fished through a dresser drawer, I realized there was something else in my head besides the pounding:

A nagging question.

As it formed in my brain, it sank down into my stomach, and I felt another wave wash over me. This one was a wave of pure undiluted terror that forced the words from my stomach up into my mouth and flying out of my lips:

Blake? Did we use a condom?

The way he smiled at me was different from the smiles I'd seen from him before. He handed me the T-shirt, and he tried to lean in and kiss my neck. I pushed away from him and looked into his eyes.

He said, What? You're on the pill, right?

The room started to spin a little bit when he said it, and I took a step backward. My cheeks were hot and I gulped a deep breath. Blake saw the answer before I even said the word no.

He shook his head and snorted a short laugh through his nose. He looked at me like I was the silliest, stupidest girl he'd ever met.

As Lauren drove us down the highway along the coast, I couldn't help but think that he was right. Lauren grabbed my hand and held it as I told her everything. She told me that I didn't need to worry: She had morning-after pills at home. She got them from her doctor in New York.

I leaned my head against the window and just stared at the gray clouds and the angry waves that pummeled the rocks along the beach where I first went to watch Ross surf. I thought about that girl who'd sat on the sand and watched Ross ride that day. She was so different from this girl: the one who had done Ecstasy last night, and had sex with a 20-year-old with no condom. This girl who was going to her best friend's house to take a morning-after pill.

Who am I now?

How did this happen?

That's when Cam texted me: WHERE ARE YOU?

I texted back: AT LAUREN'S.

He called me, and when I answered, he yelled into the phone: NO YOU'RE NOT!

When I didn't answer his texts this morning, he'd driven over to Lauren's and knocked on the door. Her dad told him that Lauren had spent the night at a friend's last night and that I wasn't there.

I hung up on him. We raced back to Lauren's, I gulped

down the morning-after pill, then she dropped me off at home.

Mom and Dad met me at the door, and I was terrified that Cam had already told them I hadn't actually spent the night at Lauren's, but he hadn't. They wanted to hear all about the party. The very last thing on the entire earth that I wanted to do was sit down to brunch with Mom and Dad and tell them about the party, but as I did, I realized they didn't know that Cam had left early with Astrid.

By the time we were done eating, I felt terrible. My headache had gotten steadily worse after I took the pill, and now I felt sick to my stomach. I was dizzy as I left the table, but Cam followed me to my room and hissed: What the HELL are you thinking? Did you spend the night at Blake's?

I just stared at him and then said, Why do you care?

His face got bright red and he said, I swear to God, if I find out that asshole laid one finger on you, I'll kill him.

I told him to calm down. That I could take care of myself.

He left in a huff, and I've been lying here, thinking about last night, and trying not to throw up.

Blake just texted me. He says he wants to see me again soon. Tonight. I texted him back and told him I have homework to do. We have essays due in American government tomorrow. It's the last thing I want to do.

All I want right now is to feel Blake's arms around me

175

again. I want to hear him tell me I'm beautiful. I want to feel those amazing waves of pure happiness crash over me again and again.

I don't care what Cam says.

I don't care what anybody says.

November 2

Didn't finish my American government essay. I've never not turned in an essay before. Lauren didn't have hers either. Mr. Daniels made us stay after class so he could talk to us. He told us we could hand it in during class on Thursday or he'd drop our scores one letter grade.

I don't care about Abraham Lincoln and the treaty that ended the Civil War. Writing this essay is going to be like pulling teeth.

Blake keeps texting me.

I haven't texted him back. Lauren says I should play it cool. I really want to see him again, but I am still pissed at him for not using a condom.

November 3

I handed in my freaking essay this morning.

While I was proofreading it last night after dinner, Blake

texted me. He was driving through our neighborhood. I decided that I deserved a little reward for finishing my essay, so I met him down at the end of the block, got in his car, and made out with him for a minute. He had a one-hitter with him, a little metal tube that was painted to look like a cigarette. He loaded it a few times, and we smoked out and talked and kissed for a while. I was maybe gone for like fifteen minutes. No big whoop. If Mom saw me come back inside, I was gonna tell her I was looking for my gym bag in her car.

When I walked through the door, Cam was standing in the entryway with his arms crossed. He came to my bedroom and gave me the 3rd degree. Said he followed me out and saw me get in Blake's car. Asked what was going on with me. Threatened to tell Mom and Dad that I was going out with a 20-year-old.

I told him he was being a moron and that if he said a single word to Mom and Dad I would make sure that they knew he and Astrid had left the Halloween party without me and that he was wasted so Astrid had to drive.

Thank God Cam's got his big invitational soccer tournament out of town this weekend. That means he'll leave tomorrow with the team after school and be gone until late on Sunday night. I need a break from him.

November 4

This.

Day.

Will.

Never.

END.

Lauren and I have one more class after this one: choir. Then we're going to her place with Ross, and Blake and Ian are going to meet us there. Lauren's dad is in New York for the weekend, and Astrid is going to watch Cam play soccer, so it's going to just be us.

This week I have felt like I'm walking around under Jell-O. I just want to feel good again. At lunch I asked Ross if he had pot to bring to Lauren's tonight. He smirked and said, But what about the pact?

Lauren rolled her eyes and laughed, but something about his question stuck in my stomach. I realized I wanted to feel good, and it didn't matter how much I promised myself I didn't want to do drugs anymore. What did it matter? What was the point of being so good? Wasn't it so I wouldn't do stupid things like sleep with boys with no condom? And I'd taken care of that. I can handle this. I can make my own decisions. I don't need Cam or anybody else telling me what to do. If I want to have a drink or do a line, or smoke a joint, it's nobody else's business but mine.

I must've made a funny face because Ross asked me if I was okay, said he was just teasing. I said the pact was pretty much broken last weekend.

I cannot wait for this class to be over. All I have left today is choir with Lauren, then we're headed to her place. First stop: cosmos. And some weed. Then I'm gonna drag Blake into the master bedroom and make out with him. Maybe more.

Lauren asked me how the sex was the other day. I told her that I thought it was incredible, but of course I don't have anything to compare it to. She said that if it was good, it was good, and that I shouldn't question it. She said you don't have to have lots of experience to know when something feels right.

I always feel like she has way more experience than I do. She's like this grown-up version of a teenager. She never makes me feel like a moron, though. She's always really kind to me. In all of this craziness, she's been the one person I can count on.

Lauren's friendship makes me feel really special, like I'm worth it.

November 5

~~I am so upset I don't even know how to put it into writing. I can't even sit up and hold my pen. I can't stop cry.~~

LAUREN IS A FUCKING BITCH.

179

November 6

I am never speaking to Lauren again.

I am never speaking to Blake again.

I am never doing drugs again.

Cam had a gut feeling about Lauren and Blake and Ian, and he was RIGHT about ALL of them. I feel so shitty for not believing him. I should have listened. I should have trusted him. Instead, I trusted these so-called FRIENDS.

I'm not even making any sense. If anyone ever read this (which would be like my WORST NIGHTMARE) they would think I am a lunatic. Maybe I am a lunatic. Maybe I'm the stupidest woman to have ever drawn a breath on the planet.

I don't even want to write about it.

I don't want to think about it.

I don't want to feel this feeling in my stomach. I can't eat. I can't sleep. I can't think.

Mom thinks I have the flu. She keeps coming to my room with saltines and 7Up and asking if I want any soup. She's being SO SWEET to me, and it just makes me feel EVEN WORSE for doing all of these things that she would be so upset about.

I can't stop crying.

I HATE THIS FEELING.

Later . . .

I know if I don't write this down, I'll never get it out of me. So, I'm just going to write it as fast as I can. Just the facts. Just what happened.

On Friday I left school and walked down to Lauren's place with her and Ross. We went inside and Ross packed a bowl, and we all smoked out. Lauren made cosmos and we raided the fridge while we watched TV. Blake and Ian showed up and we all headed down to the Promenade for Mexican food. Ian has a fake ID and ordered a pitcher of margaritas. Lauren and I finished our water and Blake poured margaritas into our glasses.

I was feeling really buzzed when we got back to Lauren's and Ross was smoking more weed. I said I was getting too tired from the weed and the drinks and the food. Blake looked over at Ian and said, Well, I've got a solution to that.

Then he pulled a big bag of cocaine out of his pocket and Lauren clapped her hands. Ross and Ian said that they were staying away from the blow as much as they could, but after Blake and Lauren both did lines, we all decided that we'd just do a little bit and then go get in the hot tub on Lauren's roof.

The coke instantly perked me up and I felt so much more awake. Lauren dragged me back to her room to put on swimsuits. We must've taken a long time because Blake poked his head into her bedroom, and was like, Ross and Ian are doing another line. You girls want more?

That's the bad thing about cocaine: Even when you say you're only going to do one line, you end up doing more because it makes you feel so on point. I had been making Lauren laugh, and I felt beautiful in the little white bikini she gave me. I waltzed out into the living room in nothing but her swimsuit and Blake convinced me to let him do a line off of my stomach. I lay down on the couch, and he poured a little line of coke out right under my belly button. I was laughing so hard when he snorted it because it tickled, and then he licked the place where the cocaine had been, and ran his tongue all the way up to my breasts, then between them up to my neck, and kissed me in front of Ian and Ross.

Lauren walked in and saw us kissing, and was like, You two get a ROOM! Blake said he was fine with that idea and picked me up and threw me over his shoulder like a sack of potatoes and headed down the hall over my giggling. I tickled him until he dropped me and then we all went upstairs to the hot tub.

Lauren and Blake brought up two shakers of cosmos and plastic glasses for everybody. Lauren's hot tub on the roof is AMAZING. You can see the pier with the big Ferris wheel and roller coaster all lit up, and it was a clear night at the beach. We laughed and talked about God knows what, and Ian smoked some cigarettes because he does that when he does cocaine.

I kept sniffing and feeling the cocaine drip down the back of my throat and I realized that I kind of liked that feeling now. I remembered how weird it had felt at first, but now I could feel the buzz of the coke—making me want to talk and laugh. Coke makes everything interesting, and alive feeling, for about 20 minutes or so, and then I always want more.

Lauren went back downstairs to fill up the martini shakers again, and Blake followed her down to help out. I was trying to take deep breaths in the hot tub and just relax, which is hard to do on coke. Ross was talking about how his mom was going to have to work on Thanksgiving, but that was okay because the hotel had an amazing 5-star restaurant and he was going to get to hang out there with Ian, whose mom and dad were still in Italy.

I started feeling this weird anxious feeling in my stomach and asked Ross if he was feeling it too. He said he was, and Ian said it was because they must've cut the cocaine with something speedy. He said that some Xanax would help level out that feeling, and I remembered that the last time I'd done coke Lauren had given us Xanax.

I told the boys I'd go get us some, and I grabbed a towel. Ross whistled at me as I got into the elevator, and I blew him a kiss. When I walked into Lauren's place, I heard music coming from the speakers hidden in the ceiling and walls of the condo. Lauren and Blake weren't in the kitchen, so I walked back toward Lauren's bedroom. I saw her door was open about a foot, and I opened my mouth to call her name, but that's when I heard it: a gasp.

I've been thinking about that gasp for two days now. Wishing I would have just turned around right then, and gone back into the kitchen, and mixed another drink, and gone back up to the hot tub.

But I didn't.

I couldn't.

Maybe it was the coke, or the vodka, or both. I felt my heart start to race like a locomotive about to pound through my chest. I smelled the coke in the back of my throat, sort of greasy like gasoline, and I felt the bottom drop out of my stomach. It was fear and rage all rolled into one. My hand was shaking as I touched the doorframe, and I held my breath as I peered into the room.

I saw Blake's naked body on top of Lauren on the bed, her legs wrapped around him, her fingers running down his back, and that's when I heard the second gasp. I saw the mirror of cocaine on the bedside table, and something in me snapped. I kicked the door so hard that it slammed open and hit the wall.

And as I kicked the door, I screamed.

I cried and screamed the words that echoed in my head as Blake scrambled for his jeans, and Lauren pulled the comforter over herself, the words I repeated over and over as she cried and begged me not to be upset, the words that Ian and Ross heard me sob as they drove me home:

HOW COULD YOU?

Later . . .

Blake and Lauren have both texted me a gazillion times. Finally I turned off my phone.

Cam came home a little bit ago and poked his head in my room. He closed the door behind him, and walked over to the bed, and sat down really gently, like I was a glass of wine balanced on the pillow and might spill all over the place.

He looked at me, and then down at the striped rug that pokes out from under my bed. He told me that Lauren had texted Astrid while we were driving back.

I was silent for a second. We just sat there looking at each other. Cam could have said anything at that moment:

*I told you so.

*You're so dumb.

*What did you think was going to happen?

*Did you think he actually liked you?

But that's the thing about Cam: He doesn't care about being right. He cares about me. He reached over and took my hand, and instead of saying any of those things, he said:

I'm sorry.

Something about those words knocked me over, and I spilled out all over him. I cried, and he leaned over and hugged me and I pressed my face into his shoulder and that's how Mom found us when she came in. She wanted to know what happened, and once more I held my breath and waited for Cam to spill the beans.

But he didn't.

He just said that Lauren had been unkind to me.

Unkind.

Who talks like that? But you know what? He was right. It wasn't that I cared so much about Blake. It was that what Lauren did . . . well, it's not what friends do to each other.

Blake didn't break my heart.

Lauren did.

November 7

I am leaving for school in 2 minutes. I don't know how I'm going to make it through this day. I don't even want to SEE

Lauren, let alone TALK to her. We've eaten lunch together almost every day this school year.

How is this going to work?

Later . . .

Turns out it's not so hard not to speak to Lauren today. She walked up to me at our lockers and said, I'm sorry. I didn't look at her. I didn't answer her. I just closed my locker and walked away. She didn't even try to meet us for lunch. I walked down to the cafeteria with Ross and Cam and Astrid. Astrid gave me a hug and asked me if I was okay. I smiled and told her I would be.

But I don't think I will.

Not because of Blake, or Lauren, or what happened last Friday. It's because I feel this sense of dread in my stomach since I've sworn off drugs and drinking again. And something in my head feels like I'm going to miss out on all of the fun. Isn't that CRAZY? After everything I've gone through? After all of the bad stuff, and tears, and feeling terrible?

But it's true. I feel like I won't have anything to look forward to. The excitement about drinking cosmos with Lauren, or smoking out with Ross, or doing lines with Blake is over now. What am I supposed to do for fun? Go to movies with Mark?

I'm afraid.

Afraid this can't last.

November 11

Ross and Lauren didn't show up today. I texted Ross, but I didn't hear back from him. Of course, he's not really tied to his phone so I guess I shouldn't be surprised. Still, I can't shake the feeling that it's weird. I feel like I'm being petty and stupid, but I have this feeling in my gut that they were hanging out together all day.

ARGH. I feel like a psycho.

Ross can hang out with whoever he wants. It's not my business. I just don't want to be around Lauren anymore.

Tonight I'm helping make the shopping list for Thanksgiving. It's less than 2 weeks away. I can't wait. I love the holidays. We have my dad's whole family over for Thanksgiving, and then a bunch of Dad's college students who don't go home because the break is so short. It always feels so great to have a full house and lots of food and a big fire in the fireplace. Dad always borrows folding tables from the college and we set them up in the living room.

I'm kind of relieved that I don't have to go out with everybody tonight. I just want to go home and put on my sweats and watch TV. Maybe Mom will order pizza.

Later . . .

When I was on my way home from school with Cam, Mark texted me.

Cam asked who it was, and when I told him it was Mark, he didn't say anything for a minute. As we pulled into the driveway, he said he knew that I thought Mark was a dork, but that he was actually a really nice guy.

I just can't. I don't have the energy. I don't need a date.

I need a nap.

November 15

I was singing in choir today, and I heard Lauren's voice over the melody, and I got SO ANGRY that I wanted to march up the stairs in the choir room and SMACK HER.

After school yesterday we were both at our lockers at the same time. I've been waiting at the end of the hall until she finishes getting her books, then going to my locker so we don't have to stand there in silence while she fidgets and keeps looking at me to see if I'm still upset with her.

Like I'm ever NOT going to be upset with her.

Hello??? What planet is she on? I'm just going to MAGICALLY be okay with all of this one day?

Anyway, yesterday I just didn't give a crap and she was taking forever, texting somebody in front of her open locker instead of getting her shit and getting out of there. So, I just walked up and opened my locker and got my stuff, and closed it, and as I was walking away, I heard her say my name, and then she yelled my name, and it was like this bizarre moment where everybody sort of froze, and our little section of the hall got momentarily quiet.

I turned around and looked at her, and I could tell. I just knew: She was doing coke. Her eyes had that wide, wild stare in them, and her nose was a little red. And right as I turned around, she made a quick little sniff.

The screwed up thing is that this look passed between us where she saw that I knew.

And she gritted her teeth and blinked hard and then said, Are you just never going to look at me again?

I stood there, then I shook my head slowly, then turned and walked around the corner.

The worst thing about this is that I'd never really had a BEST friend before. Lauren was the first person I'd ever been close to like that, and as much as I know that I can't be friends with her anymore, I also MISS having a friend that close. I miss being able to laugh with her about stuff. I miss that excited feeling I got when we were mixing cosmos and how "bad" it felt and how we were partners in crime. I was also WORRIED about her. I couldn't believe that she had done a line at SCHOOL.

I mean, that's INSANE. If she gets caught, she'd be expelled and be in HUGE trouble.

I miss Lauren. But not this Lauren. I miss the Lauren I met that first night at Blake's.

I wonder if she exists anymore?

November 17

It's so weird how things change so fast. Those first couple months of school, I just assumed that we'd be one big gang the whole year. We were all together all the time. I let myself imagine how we'd all give each other Christmas presents and go to parties together, and winter formal. Hell, I let myself imagine going to prom with all of them.

Ross still sits by me in our classes, but I feel like there's this thing between us that's holding us back from being the way we used to be. It makes me SO UPSET because he was MY friend first, and now I feel like Lauren is coming between us. I mean, he doesn't really hang out with her at school or at lunch either, but he's not totally present with us on the days he joins us for lunch.

I talked to Astrid about it. She isn't really hanging out with Ross or Lauren anymore either. She and Cam go out every Saturday night, like clockwork. This week Cam wants me to come and bring Mark.

He's been following me around again.

November 20

So, Mark came with us to the movies last night. It was me and Cam and Astrid and Mark.

AND IT WAS SO BORING.

Ugh.

Cam kept smiling at me like SEE? ISN'T THIS FUN? And I tried. I reeeeeally did try. But I just can't. Mark was sweet and he even held my hand during the movie. He smells good, and he has really big arms. They stretch out the band on the sleeve of his T-shirt. He's cute.

There's nothing wrong with him.

There's something wrong with me.

I just kept thinking how much more fun the whole thing would've been if I was stoned. Or had a drink.

Now I wish I'd never EVER even taken a tiny toke off of the pipe Ross handed me. I wish I'd never laid eyes on Lauren or taken a martini glass full of ice-cold cosmos from her. I wish I'd never swallowed that hit of E or snorted that first line of cocaine.

I wish I'd never done ANY of it.

And it's not because it made me feel so bad.

It's because it made me feel SO GOOD.

And now . . .

I can NEVER not KNOW how good it feels. Now I'm trapped knowing how great it is, and not being able to do any of it.

Later . . .

Cam just came in and saw that I was writing. He thought I was doing homework. Lately I usually am because there's nothing else to do. It's not like I'm going to go hang out with Ross and get high, or go party with Lauren. My grades have been WAY better on quizzes and stuff, which is good. Cam wants to go to yoga. There's a class at 4 p.m. on Sundays that Marty teaches.

I think I'll go.

It's not a party, but something inside me feels like it's a good idea. I can't shake the feeling that maybe if I'd kept going to yoga, I wouldn't have started drinking and doing drugs. Or maybe that's crazy. Whatever.

At least it'll be something to do that isn't homework.

Later . . .

Yoga was good.

I feel more peaceful on the inside, more content, maybe. Mom and Dad wanted to know if Cam and I wanted to join them for a game of Scrabble.

SCRABBLE. Like a board game. Yes, an actual BOARD is involved. Not on an iPad, not on a laptop, like little pieces of wood, on little pieces of cardboard.

I said yes.

And usually I HATE playing word games with my dad

because he's like super-duper reader guy and knows all the vocab stuff that I have to study my ass off for.

But I think I said yes because I'd been to yoga. I felt calm. And I dunno. It seemed like a nice idea to hang out with our family.

Just us.

OH! And at yoga, I was looking at the schedule and I noticed that Ian's name isn't on the schedule for the next month ANYWHERE.

I asked Marty if Ian was taking a break, and she said that nobody had heard from him. He'd stopped coming to class, and when they called him, he said he wasn't going to teach anymore.

I started to text Ross to see what was going on, but Ross hasn't really been returning my texts. Or hanging out with us at school that much. I have this nagging suspicion that he's hanging out with Ian and probably Lauren. If that's the case, I know what they're doing. I don't have to ask.

As much as I don't want to admit it, I feel completely left out.

November 21

I just finished my last chemistry quiz before THANKSGIVING! I'm SO GLAD it's a short week this week. Lauren is in New York with her mom for the holiday. She texted me before she flew out early this morning to say that she hoped I'd have a good holiday and that she was "thankful" for me.

Whatever.

Ross asked me if we could go to lunch today. I said yes. He seemed like he wanted to talk about something. I almost asked him about Ian, but I decided not to. He can tell me if he wants.

Later . . .

Cam saw me leaving for lunch with Ross and gave me the eagle eye from down the hall. GOD. I HATE THAT. I've been the perfect student for the past couple of weeks, and he acts like I'm about to run around the corner and snort a line every time he looks the other way.

Ross and I had fun at lunch. He didn't mention Lauren. We talked about Thanksgiving, and what he usually does. This year he can't be at his grandma's in Florida with all of his cousins, so he's just going to the hotel where his mom works. I told him he'd said that he was going to do that with Ian.

He got really quiet when I mentioned Ian's name. This faraway look came into his eyes.

I hope he's okay.

(Ross. Not Ian. I mean, I hope Ian's okay too, but I care less about Ian than I care about Ross.)

November 24

THANKSGIVING!

Today was so great. Mom made us banana bread and pumpkin bread to eat while we watched the parades. Then we helped Dad move all the furniture and set up the tables in the living room. I couldn't believe that we fit everyone in there! We had 35 people eating at tables in the living room. Dad was up at 5 a.m. smoking a turkey on the grill, and Mom had one going in the oven. They had a contest to see whose would turn out the prettiest. Dad's won. Mom's tasted really great, but something about smoking it on the grill made the skin on Dad's all crispy and bronze colored, and it tasted DELICIOUS.

We all sat down to eat around 3 p.m., and I can't believe the amount of food I was able to fit inside my body. I ate like I'm going to be shot the next morning.

Okay. I have to make a confession: I DID have a drink of wine. But not a lot! Just a glass! It was a mug, actually, so Mom and Dad couldn't see. I saw Cam had swigged a little bit out of Mom's glass when he went to refill it this afternoon, and so when everybody was having coffee with their pumpkin pie, I just poured some of the leftover wine out of one of the bottles into a mug, and everyone thought I was drinking coffee.

It was so fun! I got a little warm buzz, and I felt all cozy and perfect. I mean, all of the grown-ups were drinking wine, and I'm 16. It's not like I'm a kid anymore.

Anyway. We just got back from a movie, and Dad pulled out all of the leftovers, and Mom started talking about putting up the Christmas decorations next weekend and pulled out a tin of fudge she made last night. Mom's homemade fudge is always the symbolic kickoff of Christmas. She never puts it out for dessert on Thanksgiving. She always waits until everyone leaves and it's just our family.

Cam and I are watching TV. He's texting Astrid like every 37 seconds. She's in Phoenix with her family visiting her mom's family. We are also GORGING ourselves on Mom's fudge. I think I may slip into a diabetic coma.

I AM SO HAPPY. These are the moments when I think that WOW: Maybe I do have the BEST family EVER.

It's true: I really do have a lot to be thankful for.

December 3

I had a HUGE FIGHT with Mom today. She wanted me to come with them to pick out the Christmas tree. I told her I didn't want to go, and she made it like this federal case. It was like I'd told her that I'd decided to become a stripper.

ARGH.

Then Cam came to my room and tried to talk me into it, all puppy dog eyes. I was like, LOOK! I have cramps. I just spent ALL DAY on a SATURDAY writing a paper for English. I want to have a Diet Coke and a painkiller and sit and watch TV on the couch. I don't wanna go stand in the cold while Mom makes us look at every single damn tree on the lot and then ends up buying the display tree anyway. Which TAKES LONGER because they have to retie the whole thing up.

It's not personal. I just don't want to go.

And then Cam started acting all high and mighty and talking about how I had been doing so much better, but he wonders sometimes if I've really changed, or if I'm just acting like it so that he'll get off my back.

I HATE IT when he acts like that—I mean, HE'S the one who gave me my first beer, and I've smoked pot with him like a billion times now. I couldn't hold my tongue and told him that the quickest way to make me want to take a big bong rip was to stay on my case like this.

Now he's mad at me too.

CRAP.

I guess I should just go and get it over with.

WHY IS THIS STUFF SUCH A BIG DEAL???

Later . . .

That was the most monumental waste of time ever.

One and a half HOURS.

Bought the display.

But it smells nice. And I dunno . . . there's something about Christmas that just makes you happy no matter what's going on inside of you. Like cocaine. Only it lasts for like a month instead of 12 minutes.

HA HA HA HA HA HA HA HA HA.

Omg. Lauren would think that was so funny.

ughughughguhguhgugh UGH

THESE are the moments when I really MISS her.

December 7

They should just CANCEL school between Thanksgiving and Christmas. The teachers are either COMPLETELY stressed out because they've got to do all of this stuff besides teach, or they're like CRAZY Christmas spirit FREAKS in sweaters with sparkles and jingle bells on their shoes. Our U.S. history teacher has worn a Santa Hat EVERY. FREAKING. DAY. since we got back from Thanksgiving.

I love Christmas as much as the next person, but really?

Lauren has missed two days of class every week since

Thanksgiving. Astrid said she hasn't heard from her at all. I think the only one she's talking to anymore is Ross, but Ross isn't saying anything to me about it.

Today at lunch he asked me if I was ever going to forgive Lauren.

I asked him if Lauren wanted to be forgiven.

He just shrugged and looked off like he always does.

Mom told me to invite him over for dinner next week. Cam got his boxers in a bunch about that. I told him to chill out.

December 16

I got an A on my English paper!!!

Maybe it was the good grade, or maybe it's the fact that Mom has the house DONE to DEATH, or maybe it's the lights outlining the roof of the house that Dad risked his life to hang. Whatever it is, I'm officially in the Christmas spirit. I've been CHRISTMAS SHOPPING!

EEEEEEK!

I LOVE GIVING PRESENTS!

I had exactly $147 dollars that I could spend. I got Cam a new yoga mat because his is totally gross from being sweat on all the time. I also got him one of these little terry-cloth towels cut the same size as a yoga mat to CATCH the sweat so that he doesn't have to keep rearranging his towel on the mat when we're in class.

Mom is always the hardest person to buy for because I'm never sure what she really wants, but we were shopping the other day at the new mall at the end of the Promenade, and she tried on this really cute pair of shoes that were marked down like a bazillion times to $49. They were orange satin heels with a little open toe and they looked SO CUTE on her foot—like something out of a '50s TV show. She kept looking at her feet in the mirror and talking about how fun they were. But THEN she put them BACK and went on and on about how they weren't practical and she would rather spend the money on Christmas presents blah blah blah.

SO I WENT BACK AND GOT THEM!

I was really worried that they wouldn't be there, but they were. SCORE.

Dad is easy. I think Cam and I are going to go in on a couple of records that he really wants. (Yes. Vinyl records. The kind you play on a rotating disc with a needle. Sigh.) We're also going to get him a new warm-up suit because his is looking a little worse for wear.

Ross is on his way over for dinner, and Astrid will be here too. I'm really glad that they're coming.

Later . . .

Tonight was really great. Well, not at the beginning. It started out weird because Ross made some reference to Lauren and homecoming and Cam got all bristled up and didn't talk a lot. But then Ross was telling us about Thanksgiving at the hotel where his mom works, and how the chef had come out to their table to say hello and wish them a happy holiday, and this old lady at the next table pushed her chair out into a waiter who had a bottle of wine, and the bottle hit the floor right at the chef's feet and exploded, drenching the chef in pinot noir.

Ross is hilarious when he tells stories, and by the time he was done, Cam was gasping for breath and my dad was laughing so hard he was crying.

It felt just like old times.

Well, I guess, it felt like this summer.

Funny how "old times" is only about 4 months ago.

It seems like it was a lot longer ago than that.

December 24

I love Christmas Eve.

I am sitting in the living room staring at the lights on the 9-foot Douglas fir. Dad just walked into the living room and gave me a kiss on the cheek. He turned up the lamp and said I'd go blind if I kept writing in the dark.

I remember when I was a little girl, Dad would always help Cam and me leave a plate of cookies and a glass of milk for Santa before we went to bed on Christmas Eve. I guess I was about 6 years old the year that Cam got out of bed to check and see if the cookies and milk were gone and discovered Dad eating them. He cried and cried—not because there wasn't a Santa Claus, but because there weren't any more cookies left and now Santa wouldn't come.

I didn't cry, and Cam got upset with me for not caring. Dad just winked at me and smiled as he rocked Cam back and forth. Dad knew I knew about Santa being make-believe.

I don't know how I knew.

I just always did, I guess.

I've always thought that the invisible and the imaginary are the same thing.

I guess that's why I like Christmas Eve so much. It's the one night where I feel like things that aren't seen have a possibility of existing: angels, elves, flying reindeer. It all seems possible somehow.

I've been thinking about Lauren a lot lately. She still texts me every once in a while. I mean, it's not like I don't see her. Ross calls me the Ice Queen because I haven't actually acknowledged her since that night last month.

But tonight, staring at the lights and the star at the top of the tree, I realize that I've been thinking more and more about the good parts of Lauren and the weird space that's been left in my life for the past 7 weeks without having her in it.

Who knows? Maybe the ice will melt one day. It hasn't yet, but tonight is a night about magic that makes everything feel . . .

Possible.

December 25

OH MY GOD!

MY PARENTS GOT ME A CAR!

YAAAAAAAAAAAAAAAAAAAAAAAAAAAAAAAAAAAAAAAAAAAAAAAAY!

I can't even BELIEVE IT!

It's not a new car or anything. It's a Certified Pre-Owned Jetta. It's two years old, but it was at a used car dealership and it still has that NEW CAR SMELL. Dad said I'd done such a good job this fall in school and had been so responsible lately that he and Mom felt like I was ready.

THIS IS SO AMAZING!

I'm going to pick up Ross and then we're going to go get hot chocolate and see a movie.

Later . . .

I was just sitting in my car in the driveway listening to music after I dropped Ross off. I still can't believe it. I just want to be in that car ALL THE TIME!

Mom just walked through the living room in the shoes I bought her and her bathrobe. She stuck out her foot like a movie star and laughed and smiled at me.

I think she was really surprised that I was paying attention to what she wanted.

Cam and I are going to go to yoga every day this week since we're off from school. He loved his yoga mat.

January 1

I can't believe it's a new year already. Tomorrow we go back to school, and for the first time EVER I'll get to drive my NEW CAR into the parking lot.

Dad surprised Mom with a night of dinner and dancing in a supper club at the top of a skyscraper downtown. Cam got permission to go to Astrid's and Ross invited me over to dinner because his mom was having a New Year's Eve party.

When I got there, the place was already packed and Ross dragged me upstairs to his room away from all of the adults. He was totally annoyed because he wanted Ian to come over but his mom wouldn't allow it. She said that Ian is a bad influence on Ross. He said he yelled at her and said that Ian wasn't an influence, that he was a BOYFRIEND. His mom thinks that Ross is just going through a phase, apparently. Ross thinks his mom is under the impression that I want to date him, so she's always saying that he should invite me over.

I was giggling SO HARD when he told me that, partly because early on that was true, and partly because it's SO RIDICULOUS. I guess after being around Ross so much, I wouldn't want to imagine him any other way.

I asked Ross where Ian had been, and a stormcloud passed across his face. He went completely silent, and finally I just tossed myself back onto his bed and yelled REALLY? You're just not going to TELL ME?

He looked at me long and hard, then said to wait a second, he needed "supplies." Then he ran out of the room. In a minute he came back, only he was wearing a snowboarding jacket. He unzipped the coat and pulled a bottle of champagne out of the sleeve. He popped the cork and said, Happy Frickin' New Year, then took a big gulp that made the bottle foam up and spill all over him. We laughed and he grabbed a towel out of his bathroom and mopped it up.

When he handed the bottle to me, I took it, but I immediately heard an alarm go off in my brain: YOU'RE DRIVING YOU'RE DRIVING YOU'RE DRIVING.

I shook my head and reminded him that I had a car now. When I handed the bottle back to Ross, he rolled his eyes and handed it back. He said, Gimme a break. You're not going to get tanked, you're just going to have a couple sips and then I'm going to tell you about Ian.

I decided he was right.

I took the bottle.

I took a drink.

The alarm stopped.

And then Ross told me about Ian. Apparently they broke up about the same time I found out that Ian wasn't teaching anymore. Ross said that Ian had dropped out of school and stopped teaching yoga.

Then Ross got really quiet, only I could tell that he had more to say. He went over to his dresser and opened the top drawer, pulling out a little brown box. He slid off the top that was fitted so tightly it looked like a solid piece. He pulled out his pipe, packed a bowl, took a deep toke, then handed the pipe to me and waited until I put my lips to it. He sparked the lighter and I pulled the smoke through the purple glass into my mouth, then breathed it deeply into my lungs.

It didn't take very long for me to feel the floating sensation in my head, and when I opened my eyes, Ross was staring at me, smiling so sweetly. He said, You missed it, didn't you. I giggled and nodded. I said, Don't think this is going to become a habit or anything.

Ross took another couple of hits until the bowl was cashed and then he tapped out the ashes in the trash can and put the pipe back in its secret box in the dresser. Then he turned around and told me that the day he and Lauren missed school together was the last time he'd seen Ian. They'd been up all night long the night before doing blow at Blake's house. Ross said Ian had been sort of a jerk lately, making comments about how Ross owed him for all of the free drugs he was getting.

Ross said, I looked around and realized that I had school in the morning and that I wasn't going to make it. And then I realized I wasn't having fun.

He told Ian that he didn't want to do any more coke that night, that he needed to get home. Ian laughed at him and said that was fine, he could just leave.

Ross was quiet for a minute after he told me all this. Then he looked at me and asked me a question:

How could a drug be more important to him than I am?

The hurt in Ross's eyes made me catch my breath and I felt myself tear up. I gave him a long, tight hug. He buried his face in my shoulder and cried. We sat like that for a long time.

He said that Ian had texted him a few times, but Ross had

told Ian that if he was doing cocaine, Ross didn't want to be around him.

I told Ross he was smart. I told him how strong he was, and what a good friend he was being to Ian to stand up to him like that. That he'd done the right thing.

Then he looked at me and tears ran down his face, and he said, Then why does it feel so wrong?

I didn't have an answer.

January 2

I just passed Lauren in the hallway on my way to first period. I couldn't believe it. I haven't seen her in a few weeks, but that's not really that long. I don't know what happened, but she looks TERRIBLE. Her skin is almost gray, and her hair is a mess, but the most shocking thing is that she looks like she lost 10 pounds over the holidays, and BELIEVE ME when I say that Lauren did NOT have 10 pounds to lose. She looks like a skeleton.

Later . . .

I didn't mean to talk to her.

I was standing at my locker and I felt her come up next to me, in a hurry. She was in a hurry because Cassie and Bethany were following her, laughing. They've been after Cam since they were in 7th grade and he's never given them the time of day.

When Lauren showed up this year and fell in with our group, they were silently pissed. Today they broke their silence.

I heard Cassie cough the words COKE WHORE as she passed, and I felt Lauren whirl around. She told them to fuck off and Bethany stopped and said, OR WHAT? I was trapped in the middle of this, trying to look busy with my gym bag. Bethany was in full-on bitch mode. She called Lauren a druggie and when Lauren said it wasn't true, Bethany just laughed. Cassie said really loudly, We all KNOW it's true. I mean, your own best friend won't even LOOK at you anymore.

I don't know what it was, but something about that comment made me SO PISSED OFF. In a split second I realized that I was WAY more angry at Cassie Wasserman than I could ever be at Lauren. I slammed my locker so hard that I felt Lauren jump beside me. I turned around very slowly and looked at Cassie like I might decide to take a bite out of her head. Very softly and slowly I said, While we'd love to stay for more of your enlightening banter on the nature of our friendship, Lauren and I are headed to lunch. I looked at Lauren. Her eyes darted to mine as if she were afraid to look at me, like she was staring up at the sun after being locked in a dark closet for a week.

I smiled at her and jangled the keys to my car: I'm driving.

I saw tears fill her eyes, but before they could fall, I grabbed her arm and sped her outside to my car in the parking lot.

We hit the McDonald's drive-thru for fries and Diet Cokes. Then I opened the sunroof because it was a beautiful day, turned the heater on full blast because it was a little crisp, and drove toward the highway along the beach. I pulled off onto the side of the road where Ross had parked the first time that he took me surfing, and put the car in park.

Then we talked.

She told me how sorry she was about the thing with Blake. She told me he'd tried to pressure her and Ross into selling drugs for him. He'd offered them free coke, but they'd refused. Ian took Blake up on the offer, and the two of them had been selling drugs to Ian's college friends like crazy.

I asked her why she looked so awful.

She said she'd gone to New York to get away from Blake and Ian over Christmas break but that a guy she'd been dating off and on before she came out here invited her to a party on Christmas night, and he'd had an 8 ball of cocaine. She said they were awake for 2 days, and then he just kept getting more.

We sat there in silence for a while, staring at the waves. Then I reached over and took her hand. She started crying. After she stopped, she wiped her face with her free hand and squeezed my fingers tight. She thanked me for standing up for her today, that she almost didn't come back to school because she couldn't take it anymore. She said she'd thought about just getting her GED and going back to New York to start college.

I smiled at her and said, You CAN'T go to college yet. We haven't gone to winter formal and PROM!

She smiled at me cautiously. I said, But first things first: You look like SHIT.

Her eyes went wide, then we both busted out laughing. We laughed until the tears ran down our cheeks and we couldn't breathe and we were late getting to school from lunch, but I don't care.

I have my best friend back.

January 3

Astrid and Cam almost fell down when they saw Lauren and me walking toward them for lunch today. Ross broke into a big smile and said, The band's getting back together, dude. Cam was really quiet during lunch, and tonight after dinner he came to my room and said he was worried about me. He said he was afraid I would start. I threw a pillow at him.

He was all, WHAT? I'm just concerned.

I told him he had nothing to be concerned about. I mean I have MORE than proven that I can stay off drugs. I'd only had that tiny hit of pot with Ross on New Year's Eve. That's IT. Well, and a couple sips of champagne that night.

Cam reminded me about the mug of wine at Thanksgiving, and I told him that he needed to back off because I saw him swigging out of Mom's glass that day in the kitchen before he refilled it.

GOD. He can be SUCH a hypocrite.

I told him I could take care of myself.

He got this snotty tone and said he hoped so because he wasn't going to ever cover for me with Mom and Dad again. I told him he wouldn't have to. He said, I better not, then he stalked out.

GAAAAAWD! Why does he ALWAYS have to have the last word?

January 6

Lauren asked if she could come spend the night tonight. I texted Mom and she said it was fine. It's only Friday, but Lauren is already looking more normal. For one thing, I've been making her EAT! I told Ross he should come over too, and we'll order pizza and watch movies.

January 8

This weekend was just like old times, only better! I forgot how much Lauren made me laugh. We had such a good time on Friday night with Ross. We were all up until like 3 a.m. watching TV and eating leftover Christmas fudge and cookies and stuff. Cam even warmed up and hung out with us. He and Astrid had gone out for dinner, and when they came back, we were all having so much fun that Astrid called her mom and got permission to stay over with me and Lauren.

Ross got a call from Ian. We told him to ignore it, but I could tell that it bothered him. He said he wouldn't call back, but he left a little bit after that, and I'm sure he called him.

ANYWAY: We all made plans to go to the big winter formal which is the last Saturday in January.

January 13

Friday the 13th. The scariest thing about the month of January is that sometimes I feel like it will

NEVER END.

GOD. It's INTERMINABLE.

(That's the word I got WRONG on the vocab quiz today in English. SHEESH.)

January 18

Lauren and I are going to look for outfits for winter formal after our choir sings at the chamber of commerce luncheon on Saturday at City Hall. I can't wait. Ross said he's going to come hear us sing. Who knows? Maybe we'll drag him along with us to shop. He's been no help at all when we've taken him before. He's not one of those PROJECT RUNWAY gays. He always wants us to just buy whatever is the lowest cut, and the shortest.

He's such a perv.

January 21

Okay okay okay okay. I KNOW I said I was DONE with drugs, but Ross had his pipe with him today, and we smoked a little. Just a COUPLE HITS EACH.

Lauren and I found the CUTEST outfits for winter formal today. There were racks and racks and racks of stuff at Nordstrom marked down like 70 percent off. I guess stuff doesn't sell very well after Christmas. Ross met us afterward at Lauren's place. Her dad was watching a basketball game on TV, so we all went back to Lauren's room and we tried on our stuff for Ross. I got the cutest little black dress with sequins at the neck, and Lauren got this silver dress that I LOVE.

After we tried on our dresses, Lauren said she wished her

dad wasn't home so she could make us cosmos to celebrate our good bargains, and Ross pulled out his pipe and wiggled his eyebrows up and down.

Both he and Lauren just turned to look at me like I was the one who had to give the okay.

I just looked at them both and said, LOOK, you losers. We can smoke pot, but we are NOT doing coke again. EVER. Or Ecstasy or anything else. And on the night of the actual dance we ARE NOT DRINKING. Because I have to drive, and if I can't drink, you two aren't drinking either. Got it?

They both nodded and then I said, JEEZ. When did I become JIMINY CRICKET?

When I said that, Lauren busted out laughing, and pretty soon we were all giggling like lunatics. Lauren put on some music and we just hung out in her room for a couple hours, smoking pot, and talking and laughing. I forgot how much fun we have when we're stoned.

Next week is going to be SO MUCH FUN.

I'm so glad we're not taking dates and stuff. Mark keeps asking me but yesterday I told him that I think we're just better as friends.

God, I hope he GETS THAT this time. I mean . . . even if we dated, would he KISS me? NO. Would he want to make out? NO. So . . . we'd be friends anyway, right? Because what fun is it to go out with a guy who won't kiss you??

January 26

I tried on my new dress for winter formal today and went to show Mom, and DAD walked into the living room and had a minor meltdown. He went OFF on how it was too short, and it looked like I was cheap and all of this complete CRAP.

Mom was trying to stick up for me and saying that she thought I looked really mature and the dress fit really well. She said that I wasn't a little girl anymore, and I was going with a group of friends, and Cam would be there, and Dad just got all red in the face and was like MARGARET, WHY ARE YOU TRYING TO TAKE HER SIDE?? And then he stomped into his study and told me that I would wear that dress to winter formal over "his dead body."

WHO SAYS THAT?

Is this like a MOVIE FROM THE '80S???

I just started BAWLING and ran into my room.

He came in later, all hanging his head and telling me that he was sorry. He said sometimes he forgets that I'm not a little kid anymore, because when he looks at me he still sees that little girl. I was really quiet as I listened, and then I told him that he really hurt my feelings because I wasn't trying to be CHEAP. I was trying to look pretty.

He just looked at me and said, To who?

January 27

Today is Friday and the dance is tomorrow, but I can't get that question my dad asked me out of my head: To who?

Who do I want to look desirable to? I mean, it would be one thing if I had a date, or even a crush on somebody. The thing that I keep thinking about over and over again is that I just want to look like Lauren. I mean, I never will because her legs go all the way up to her chin and she's like a head taller than me and has beautiful (NATURALLY) blond hair. But I want to feel like I'm as stylish as she is.

I'm wearing the dress.

January 28

Cam is picking Astrid up at her place, so Ross is coming here, and then we're going to go over to Lauren's to get ready. Mom wanted us to all come here so she could take pictures, but I was like NO. I am NOT going to have Dad FREAK OUT again because of my dress, or my makeup. Besides, the shoes I'm wearing are at Lauren's. Her dad got her these AMAZING Jimmy Choos for Christmas. Well, he gave her his Amex and SHE got these AMAZING shoes for Christmas. Like, 10 pairs. She's actually going to let me wear this pair that she hasn't even WORN YET!!!

How amazing is THAT?

Our friendship is even stronger, I think, because of what happened.

Cam texted me and was like, I want to see you at the dance as soon as you get there. I know he's afraid I'm going to drink and drive. ARGH.

I wish he'd lay off of the LAW & ORDER routine. GAWD.

Oooh! I think I just heard Ross pull up. YAY.

January 30

My whole life is a FUCKING NIGHTMARE.

I keep thinking that at any moment, I'll just wake up. Poof. Like that. It'll be easy, and all better, and none of this will have happened.

But I'm awake. I'm sitting here in my bedroom actually about to write these words in my journal:

I got a D.U.I.

Yep. I was Driving Under the Influence.

We got high at Lauren's. Ross had plenty of the "cronkest cush" as he likes to call it. We smoked until I could barely stand up on my Jimmy Choos, but we had NO cosmos. As I drove us to the school, I got a little paranoid. I'd never driven stoned before, and it was sort of stressful. I kept checking my speed, and all of the mirrors, and this guy honked at me when I was turning right. I guess he thought I was going too slowly, but I didn't care. I wanted to make sure that I didn't have a wreck or something. I was relieved when we finally got to the school and parked.

The formal was lame. Astrid and Cam were there, and they were dancing with Jason and Elizabeth, and they all went out to the bleachers on the football field to make out. Of course, at that precise instant, Mark spotted me and started walking toward us with a girl from his church who goes to this private Christian school. The girl Mark was with was pretty, but as he approached us, Mark couldn't stop staring at my legs. Ross whispered to Lauren that Mark was getting as much as he'd ever get before his wedding night right this second while he stared at me. That made me laugh right as they reached us and I think the girl from the Christian school thought I was laughing at her, which was TOTALLY AWKWARD.

When they finally walked away, I turned around to glare at Ross, who was sending a text message. Lauren looked at me and then she looked at Ross. Then she said, OMG. LET'S GET OUT OF HERE. Ross grinned up from his phone and said that he had an idea. I said I was too stoned to drive and handed my keys to Ross, who jumped behind the wheel.

Ross took side streets and drove through a beach neighborhood south of ours, then parked on the curb at the edge of a little neighborhood that has houses built along some canals. Lauren and I teetered across a little wooden bridge at the end of the sidewalk, and Ross led us through a low wooden gate and to the front door of one of the houses.

The first person I saw when we walked through the door was Blake, and I caught my breath. I hadn't seen him since that night at Lauren's, scrambling for his clothes, and I felt this stab in my chest that took my breath away for a second.

He was in the kitchen with Ian, leaning over a clear glass pie plate filled with cocaine. He was skinnier than I remembered, but he looked up at me and smiled.

Right at that moment, I knew.

I knew I'd be doing some coke that night. It's so weird, but it wasn't even a question. It was like a door clicking shut behind me. As I saw Ian bending toward the mound of white powder, every ounce of willpower I'd had in the last few months, every conversation I'd had with Cam and Ross and Lauren about not partying, just floated away.

In that moment I realized something: What I wanted, and what Cam wanted in this moment, were two different things. I WANTED to do a line. I WANTED to feel that rush. I WANTED to laugh like crazy and do another line and maybe steal one of Ian's cigarettes and have a big gulp of an icy cosmo and hear Blake tell me I looked like a billion dollars.

And you know what?

That's exactly what I did.

I marched into the kitchen where Lauren and Ross were standing looking sheepish, and Ian stood up in a flash, looking panicked like he'd been caught, and I took the straw out of his hand, and I snorted a GIANT rail as Lauren gasped, and Blake laughed, and I tossed my head back and felt the quick burn in the back of my nose, and I felt the delicious bitter taste in my mouth, and I closed my eyes and said, AAAAAAAAAAHHHH.

And then it was ON.

Lauren was making cosmos, and Blake was making passes, and Ian and Ross were making out, and BLAM: my phone exploded with text messages from Cam.

WHERE ARE YOU?

DID YOU LEAVE THE DANCE?

IF YOU'RE NOT HOME ON TIME I'M TELLING MOM AND DAD EVERYTHING.

I realized we'd been there for 2 hours, and it was almost curfew time for me: 1 a.m.

I downed my cosmo and did one more line, then I grabbed the keys from Ross and headed toward the front door and yelled, CAM PATROL! I'm heading out! Blake asked if I was okay to drive. I assured him I was. Nothing makes you more alert than coke, no matter how much you've had to drink.

Lauren came running after me, laughing, and Ross followed. I turned the key in the ignition. Ross turned up the music. I turned onto Pacific.

I felt my phone buzz in my lap. I knew it was another text from Cam. I glanced down at the screen.

Lauren screamed. Ross yelled, LOOK OUT!

BLAM!

The light had changed, and the car in front of me stopped short. We weren't going that fast, but there was a police car at the opposite corner. Suddenly there were lights and sirens, bright lights, and loud questions. The cops had flashlights, and they asked us to step out of the car.

They called a backup squad car. They put Lauren and me in one and Ross in the other. I have never felt so scared in my entire life as I did when I was sitting in the back of that car. The cuffs cut into my wrists and all I could think about was how my mom and dad were going to kill me. We all got taken to the police station and booked: Ross for marijuana possession, Lauren for underage drinking, and me for driving under the influence.

I felt like crying, but I couldn't. We were taken into the juvenile detention center, and I didn't see Ross and Lauren again until they had taken our fingerprints and our mug shots. Lauren's dad was actually the first to arrive. Ross said his mom was working at the hotel, but she showed up before my parents did because they'd been out to dinner and a play with friends.

When they showed up, it wasn't pretty. Dad was stonily silent. Mom had been weeping all the way home from the theater. Cam was waiting when we got home, and the minute we walked in the door, it started. He spilled everything:

Every drink.

Every joint.

Every snort.

Every party.

Everything.

When Mom stopped crying, she got very quiet. Dad got loud. Then he started crying, which was the WORST THING IN THE WORLD. Then Cam got an earful from both of them for not telling them what was going on sooner.

Cam turned to me and cried and said that all he wanted was for me to be happy.

Dad talked about how lucky I was that no one was hurt.

Mom talked about how lucky I was that no one had died.

Everybody kept saying that this could have ruined my life. I knew they were right. Suddenly everything that had happened, and sitting in a cell and being handcuffed, washed over me and I couldn't stop crying. I told them how sorry I was for not being the girl they thought I was, for not being the person they wanted me to be. Worse than that, I realized I wasn't the person I wanted to be. I was a criminal now. I had a police record.

Worse than that, I could've died. I could've killed someone.

I have to change.

January 31

Lauren's dad got a lawyer friend to argue her case. He's offered to have him argue for me and Ross as well. When Lauren's dad called my parents with his lawyer friend, he explained to them that since I failed the Breathalyzer test, my license would be suspended until I was 18 years old.

I'm totally screwed.

February 8

It's all over school. Cassie and Bethany have been total BITCHES to me and Lauren. Lauren keeps telling me that we'll get through it, but she's not the one whose license is suspended. She's not the one who will have to endure another YEAR of high school without a car.

Cam is really quiet around me now. He can barely look at Ross and Lauren. Mom has been checking my phone for texts or calls from Blake and Ian. I can barely text Ross and Lauren.

THIS IS A FUCKING NIGHTMARE.

I've been trapped in the house every night and the weekend

and don't get to hang out with Lauren or Ross by myself. Mom and Dad walk around like somebody has died. I just want to SCREAM and shake them and say SNAP OUT OF IT!

I can't wait to get to school tomorrow.

I can't believe I just wrote that sentence.

February 14

When I pictured the way my Valentine's Day would go this year, it never involved going to court for a DUI. I knew my license would be suspended (it was), but nobody had told me about the REST of the punishment. Ross, Lauren, and I have to do 50 hours of community service AND we have to go to two AA meetings every week for the next two months.

AA stands for "Alcoholics Anonymous," and I am mortified about having to go. I was serious about making a change and really becoming the person that I want to be, but I'm not a DRUNK. Yes, I like to have a cosmo with Lauren and Ross, and smoke a joint, or do a line every once in a while, but an ALCOHOLIC? I wanted to go back into the courtroom when I found out what that was and ask the judge, Do you REALLY think I'm a drunk? I mean, LOOK at me. My hair is FLAT-IRONED, for the love of God.

Anyway. We start AA and community service this weekend.

Later . . .

Oh, yeah.

Mark slid a valentine into my locker. It had Daffy Duck on it and reads, "I'm all QUACKED UP over U!"

Stellar.

[Rolling my eyes on paper.]

February 17

AA is so weird.

Ross and Lauren and I just sat there, staring. It's in the basement of this Catholic church around the corner from where Ross lives. Cam dropped me off and sat in the car with me until Lauren and Ross walked up. He said it was because he wanted to be supportive, but really I think it was because he was afraid I'd ditch, or get high with Ross and Lauren before we went.

Anyway, we have these little attendance sheets from the court that we have to get signed. Lauren wore tight jeans and a low-cut cashmere sweater and looked like something out of a magazine. She sidled up to this older guy who was telling people where to put the chairs when we got there and asked if he was the one in charge. He introduced himself and said that he was the secretary of the meeting. His name was Al. Lauren handed him our forms and asked Al if he would sign them. He said that was the job of the person in charge of "court cards" and that we should drop them in the basket when it was passed during the meeting.

We did.

But man, oh man, did we have to sit through a lot of talking first.

They read all this stuff out of a notebook, and by they I mean all the people at this meeting who were my mom and dad's age. It was so weird. They'd see us and smile really big like it was SO GREAT that we were there and then come running up and introduce themselves and shake our hands. Then they'd say WELCOME! KEEP COMING BACK.

Ross told one of them, Oh, I will be so I can get this court card all filled up.

Anyway, the stuff they read out of the notebook was all this stuff about AA not being a religion, but then they all said a prayer together about having the strength to accept things and the courage to change things. Then this woman who must've been my grandma's age got up and talked about her life for 20 minutes. This woman used to keep a bottle of scotch in her GLOVE COMPARTMENT. She said she was late for her own wedding because she was drunk. By the end, her husband left her and her kids still don't talk to her.

But then the weirdest thing happened: She started crying

with this big smile on her face and she talked about how AA had saved her life. She said she'd met some woman who helped her work the steps (whatever that is) and that she had found a higher power that helped her stay sober because she couldn't do it on her own.

Then, after she was done speaking, they passed a basket around. They said there are no dues or fees for attending AA, but if you feel like it, you can give a couple bucks, and they use it to pay the church rent for letting them meet there. Most people put a dollar or two in the basket, and we all put in our court cards. Turns out they don't hand them back to you until AFTER the meeting. (TRICKY! That way you have to STAY for the whole thing.)

After the basket was passed all these people shared all sorts of things, mainly about how they either wanted to drink and didn't that week because they called somebody at the meeting, or because they prayed and the urge went away, or they read something in this blue book that everybody had called The Big Book, and it spoke to their heart and gave them the strength not to pick up a drink.

Afterward we finally got our cards and walked outside. Mom was supposed to come pick me up, but she'd texted me during the meeting that she was running 15 minutes late. I called Mom and told her we were done and that I was walking over to Ross's apartment. She said she was on her way and would pick me up there.

We went up to Ross's room, and Lauren said that she didn't know if she could take another 15 AA meetings. I said it was the most religious nonreligious meeting I'd ever been to. Ross lit a bowl and passed it around to us.

And there was this weird thing that happened. As I reached for the pipe, I realized that I had this URGE to smoke weed. (And probably do whatever else I could.) I thought about what that lady said, about the urge being removed. I wondered if this was the urge she was talking about.

But it couldn't be, right? I mean, I'm not drunk every day. I'm not a mess. I haven't lost a husband, or been late to my own wedding. I mean, I'm not even 17 yet. This isn't even alcohol. How could I be an alcoholic?

I took a long, slow hit on the pipe and passed it to Lauren. She smiled and laughed and said that THIS was her idea of serenity.

God. What a way to spend a Friday night.

February 19

Lauren and Ross and I had to pick up trash on the side of the highway for 8 hours yesterday. It was my entire Saturday. I have to do homework all day today.

It. SUCKED. By the end of the day we were so bored and so tired that we all got kind of grouchy and stopped talking to one another.

I can't believe we have to do that for the next four weeks.

I'm so jealous that Ross got to go home and smoke pot.

February 24

I can't take it anymore. I just can't. Mom and Dad are treating me like a PRISONER. Cam is trying to "help" by taking me places with him and Astrid, as if I need a babysitter. I have to go to another AA meeting, and Mom is taking me this time. She said she wants to sit in on the meeting and see what's going on. So, of course, we won't get to go to Ross's tonight to smoke pot afterward. Or at least I won't. Lauren and Ross will, I'm sure.

February 25

Community service SUCKS. Today we picked up trash on the beach. It was FREEZING. We have to wear these little orange vests and we have these sticks to stab the trash and put it into bags. After lunch they moved us down onto one of the pedestrian bridges that takes you over the highway along the coast down to the beach. We had to scrub and paint over graffiti.

We were almost done when I saw a car pull up, and Ross said, Hey. That's Ian.

Lauren sauntered over to the window as Ian rolled it down and grinned out at us. Lauren talked to him for a second before our supervisor yelled at her to get back to work.

When she came back over, Ross asked her if she knew Ian was coming. She smiled and said that she'd texted him and that she had a surprise for us as soon as we were done. When we finished painting the wall, they took us back to the check-in office where my dad was going to pick me up. Lauren grabbed my hand and said, You better go to the restroom before you go home. She pressed a little plastic square into my hand and closed my fingers around it.

I knew what it was before I even looked. I was standing there holding a tiny bag of cocaine. Everything in my head screamed DON'T DO IT. But it was like my body couldn't resist. My heart was racing and I could hear the blood pounding in my ears. The excitement was delicious. Ross whispered that I should hurry, and I did.

I went to the bathroom and locked the stall door behind me. I poured a tiny pile of the white powder out of the Baggie onto the top of the toilet paper dispenser. Then I reached into my pocket and rolled up the receipt from the salad I'd bought at lunch. I stuck one end of the roll into my nose, held the other over the little pile of powder, and sniffed. The sniff echoed in the bathroom, and I flushed the toilet before I sniffed again, just in case anyone was listening.

When I came back to where Ross and Lauren were standing, I saw my mom had pulled up. I hugged Lauren and slipped the Baggie back into her pocket. Mom got out of the car and asked Lauren and Ross what they were doing for dinner. They both shrugged. Mom told them to come over to our place at 7.

As we drove home, Mom looked at me and said that she thought I'd been doing really well with all of this, and that she was fine with Lauren and Ross being my friends as long as we hung out at our place.

I feel SO GUILTY now that Mom is trying to be so nice to me, and I was sitting there, high on cocaine! She was telling me what a good job I've been doing, and I'm just a total fraud! I have to tell Lauren and Ross that I'm not doing it anymore, but every time they have it around me, it's the ONLY THING I can think about.

March 1

I think I'm afraid of being bored. Actually, it's not so much boredom I'm afraid of. It's that I'm afraid of not having anything to look forward to. Getting to hang out with friends used to be enough. Then I met Lauren and Ross and it was hanging out with COOL friends who I could party with. It's the excitement I miss. I miss knowing that Friday night we'd have cosmos. This guy in AA the other day said he'd been a periodic binge drinker. He used to go weeks and weeks without drinking and then he'd just get HAMMERED. I mean, that's what I did, I guess. I just don't know what's so wrong with it.

Besides the obvious, I guess? I mean, I did get a DUI. AAARGH.

I just want to get drunk and smoke pot and do some blow with my friends and have it not be like this HUGE deal. My life wasn't RUINED. If I hadn't checked that text from Cam, no one would have even KNOWN about all of this.

I mean, I really DO want to have a good life. I want to be able to go to college, and maybe even grad school. (Dad's always going on and on about grad school.) But I'm not ready to NEVER DRINK AGAIN. I mean, my God, I'm not even in college yet, and what fun will college be if I can't drink and smoke pot?

THAT'S WHAT COLLEGE IS FOR! You work hard, you study hard, and you get to go to lots of parties and have a lot of fun. Every movie ever made about college is all about that.

I just feel so torn on the inside. I know that this hurt my family. I'm just not sure why. I mean, what does it matter to them if I decide to drink and snort some cocaine?

Speaking of colleges, we're going to look at Cam's college

next week over spring break. Lauren is going to New York for the week.

She's so lucky. I bet she's going to have a WILD time.

March 10

Dad is making this trip to Cam's college like a mini vacation. After we spend the weekend at the college, we're going to a really nice hotel. Cam likes the college. Yay.

UGH! Why can't I get excited about anything?

March 12

Cam got to sit in on some classes today and go to a soccer practice. He's all jazzed, and I can totally see how he's going to LOVE it here. I haven't seen him smile this much in a long time.

Astrid is with us, and she's thinking about coming to school here too. Although, I don't think her parents are wild about her moving. They want her to stay close and go to a college nearby. Cam says her mom thinks she is "following a boy."

SEE? That's what I'm talking about.

Why do moms and dads always get so worked up about stuff like that? SO WHAT if Astrid wants to "follow a boy" to college. WHO CARES? I mean, she's going to college, right? So what does it matter? I'm going to go to college too. It's not going to hurt if I smoke a little weed, right?

Speaking of, there are TONS of weed shops up here. They are called "medical marijuana dispensaries" and the state has made it legal to get a PRESCRIPTION for marijuana. I knew that because I heard Ross talking about it with Ian and Blake one time, but I've only seen an actual store once.

While Cam was at soccer practice, Astrid and Mom and I went shopping at some of these cute little places in Berkeley, and we must have walked by 5 places where you could buy either pot, or pipes and bongs, and other stuff.

It made me miss Ross. He'd LOVE it up here.

I texted him a couple of pictures from my phone, but I haven't heard back yet. He said he was going to spend his spring break sitting in the hot tub at the hotel where his mom works. I'll bet he's getting BAKED in his truck before he does . . .

Lucky.

March 17

This has been a really exciting week.

I know.

It's not what I expected to write, either. I just realized that I've been having a lot of fun with Cam and Astrid, and even Mom and Dad. And I didn't have any drugs to look forward to, or drinking. In fact, I barely thought about that at all after we left the college.

Excitement without drugs. Who knew? I've looked forward to stuff every day!

We went to these AMAZING museums this week. There was an exhibit at one about the history of fashion and I couldn't stop looking at it. The museum was in this beautiful park, and I wandered around looking at the plants and trees. Then we drove over the bay on a bridge that was so beautiful it gave me goose bumps.

As I stood there, staring out at the water, the sun broke through the clouds and glinted into my eyes. I squinted at the fire-colored arches of the bridge as an idea tried to take shape in my head: college, fashion, the museum. Something about this place feels right. I don't know what it is. I could imagine going to work at that museum. Do they have a graduate degree for that? I should ask my dad.

I texted Ross and Lauren a picture of me with the bridge in the background. Lauren texted me right back: SOOOOOOOOOOOO GR8!!!!!

I am still laughing about that. Usually she's the one who takes forever to respond. It's weird that I haven't heard back from Ross at all.

Tomorrow we drive back home. I guess I'll call Lauren when I get there. Usually I don't look forward to a car ride that long because reading or writing, or even playing around on my phone, makes me a little carsick. I wish I had some of Lauren's Xanax.

Oh well.

At least Astrid is here. She's been really fun to talk to. Cam has been less crazy, too, probably because I'm not hanging out with Lauren and Ross. This has been a fun time. I keep thinking about college and the museum. I'm not sure what it is, but something about that place made me feel so good, so peaceful on the inside. I kind of wish I could go there every day.

March 18

Lauren just finally went to sleep.

Oh. My. GOD.

This is fucking crazy.

We got back home, and Lauren was at my place hanging out on the front porch, which is fine, I suppose, except she's never done that before. She gave my mom this big hug, and then me and Astrid. Mom was all happy because she worries about Lauren sort of being by herself all the time, so she was happy that Lauren was there, and even though she was tired from the trip, she insisted that Lauren stay and have dinner and even invited her to sleep over and go to school with me tomorrow.

The minute we were all inside, I grabbed Lauren by the

elbow and pushed her up the stairs to my bedroom. I could tell she was H-I-G-H.

But it was weird. It didn't seem like it was a coke high.

Because it wasn't.

She was on METH. Fucking CRYSTAL METH. Her eyes were all darting around and she wasn't making a lot of sense. I got Mom to let us order pizza. Told her we had to study for a big chemistry test. Luckily Astrid had already headed home so she wasn't around to verify.

I got back to my room after I ordered the pizza and closed the door behind me. Lauren had one of my dresser drawers open and was organizing and refolding all of my T-shirts. While we were waiting for the pizza to come, Lauren told me all about it. Her ex-whatever in New York had started dealing meth. Lauren had always been really snobby about it. She said she'd always laughed at people who did meth because they were poor and meth was cheap and dirty and cooked up in a trailer.

But they were out of coke one night in New York, and so she tried it. She told me she tried to snort it, but it burnt like hell, so she smoked it out of a pipe, and she said it was amazing. She got so high on just a little bit of smoke, and it lasted for a LONG TIME. Hours instead of minutes. She said it made you feel like you were alert and awake like coke, only less happy, more warm and safe and secure. And like cleaning.

Luckily she'd taken some Xanax. I texted Ross and told him to get over here QUICK with some weed because Lauren needed some help coming down. NOTHING. I was starting to get worried, so I texted Ian and asked if he'd heard from Ross because I hadn't. I found some Tylenol PM in the medicine cabinet in Mom and Dad's bedroom and forced Lauren to take two with a slice of pizza that I had to almost shove into her mouth so she would eat it. She kept laughing and saying she wasn't hungry.

Then we watched two movies, and she finally started to doze off.

March 19

Lauren is still zonked out. I have to wake her up soon so that we can take showers and get to school on time. I'm sort of exhausted. I didn't sleep very well last night thinking about Lauren doing meth. Part of me wants to try it, but I know that it's one of the most addictive drugs that there is. I mean, I've seen all of the videos in health and read all of the pamphlets and the warnings. The police come and talk to us about it every year. They show us picture of people with TERRIBLE acne and abscesses who are delusional. None of them look like Lauren, that's for sure.

But I wonder how long it will take for Lauren to start to look like them?

And if Lauren does it, I don't know if I can say no.

Sometimes I think I'm just not a very strong person when it comes to drugs and drinking. Fuck. That's a really scary thought, and now I'm crying.

I'm going to talk to Lauren about it. I'm going to tell her that if she doesn't stay off crystal, we can't be friends.

Later . . .

I'm sitting in U.S. history. I had The Talk with Lauren. She started crying immediately and saying, I know, I know, and promising that she would never do it again. She hugged me so tight that it almost hurt, and she begged me to help her. She said she needed my help.

I told her I would help her; that we'd go to AA and actually talk to some of the people there about it. I was scared enough to actually get one of those blue books and read it. She nodded and said that was a good idea. She was crying and said that she knew this was her last chance, that none of the other girls at school would even look at her and that if she lost me as a friend again, she couldn't handle it.

I hugged her and said: Then stay off of crystal.

I haven't seen Ross this morning, which isn't that big a surprise. He's been late a lot this semester. But it's totally weird that he hasn't texted me or anything. I have this sick feeling in the pit of my stomach that he and Ian got back together.

March 20

It is 4 a.m. on a Tuesday, and I am high on meth.

I didn't meant to be.

But I am.

I'm not tired at all. I feel like I could go to school and take a test right this second. I feel good, and in control, and really . . . peaceful, somehow. I feel like everything is going to be just fine.

Ross finally called me back after school yesterday. He asked if he could come over. I said yes, mainly because I wanted to talk to him about Lauren, but also because I was hoping he'd have some weed on him, which he did.

When he came in, we said hi to my parents who were headed out to dinner with friends, then a concert series at Dad's college. Thank God they were. And thank God Cam was over at Jason's. He's spending the night over there, working on some project they have due next week.

We went to my room, and I was talking to Ross about Lauren and how she'd been doing crystal, and he asked if I wanted to smoke some weed. I didn't think it would be that big a deal.

But it was. Once we were really stoned, Ross looked at me and said, I need to tell you something.

He said that he was bored during spring break. When Lauren

got back, she called him and said she was over at Ian's place. She and Ian kept texting him to come over, so he finally did. He said that when he got there, Blake was there too, and all of them were smoking meth. Ross said he almost turned back around and walked out the door but that something in him wanted to try it. Ian told him meth would make him feel like a god.

Ross said, I just needed to try it. Just once.

It was so great that he smoked it for 4 days. He said that the sex was incredible—the best he'd ever had.

My heart was racing as he told this story. I felt the tremble in my knees and the sweatiness in my palms return. The old excitement was back, and even before he finished talking, I knew I had to try it too.

When I told him, he smiled and pulled out a clear glass pipe about the size of a pencil, but a little wider. Carefully, he took three tiny pebbles from a little plastic Ziploc bag and placed them in the end of the pipe. Then he took out a special silver lighter and flipped open the top. A blue flame sparked to life, but this was not the flame from a regular lighter. It was a steady burning flame that was hotter. He held the flame under the pipe until the rocks at the end melted into liquid, then bubbled slightly and boiled into a white vapor. Ross carefully sucked the white vapor out of the glass tube, then held it and exhaled.

The smell was acrid and chemical. Not skunky like pot, but sharp and toxic.

He held the pipe out to me, and I carefully placed the end in my mouth while he held the lighter. As the smoke filled the tube, I inhaled.

The taste was bitter and metallic. My mouth and eyes watered as I held the smoke in my lungs. Then I exhaled.

We both did this again.

And by the time I took the second hit . . .

I understood.

Ross texted Lauren after I smoked, and she was there within minutes, it seemed. I can't really be sure. She came armed with painkillers and muscle relaxers, which she said would help us go to sleep when the time came. Eventually they both went back home, but the time to sleep never came.

I've never felt so sure of myself as I do right now on this drug. I feel this level of certainty and safety that I've never possessed before. I feel like I could easily explain why this was the best choice I could've made to anyone who asked: Cam, Mom, Dad. I feel like even questioning my judgment would be foolish.

I feel like THIS was how I was MEANT to feel: confident, perfect, beautiful, sexy, in control, smart, and more certain of myself than ever.

I was grinding my teeth a little, and Lauren told me that's just an effect of the speediness of the drug. She told me to take half of a muscle relaxer or a little bit of Xanax.

I heard Mom and Dad come home several hours ago, around 11:30 p.m. I turned off my lights and crawled under the covers in my bed. Dad peeked his head in my door, and I pretended to be asleep.

But I don't need to sleep tonight.

I don't want to miss a single moment of how I feel.

Later . . .

Ross and Lauren and I left campus for lunch before Astrid and Cam could find us. We piled into Ross's pickup truck, and he drove toward Venice. I didn't even have to ask why. Ian was happy to see us. He said Blake had just been by. We hung out for about a half hour, and he gave us each a small hit of meth, just so we could get through the day at school in case we started to feel tired.

It's so funny, sitting here in class, high as a kite, but hearing everything and watching everyone around me. No one knows that I'm high. No one even suspects it.

I'm just following Ian's instructions: Talk as little as possible. It's when you start talking that people might be able to tell.

Later . . .

It's almost midnight, and I finally feel just a little bit tired. Not really sleepy, but I can tell my body needs to rest. I took a muscle relaxer that Lauren gave me. It seems to be helping a little bit.

I'm only sad that this feeling has to end.

I'm going to lie down and close my eyes to see if I can sleep.

March 21

Today sucks.

I slept for about 5 hours, and when I woke up, I felt like the underside of my shoe. My head hurts and I was so groggy I could barely talk. Mom said I looked pale and put a hand on my forehead to see if I had a fever.

Something about the way she did that just made my skin crawl. I told her I was FINE. I could tell I hurt her feelings when I snapped at her, but Cam was sitting across the table giving me the damn stink-eye. I can tell he thinks something is up.

Oh. My. GOD. This day cannot end soon enough.

Lauren isn't here, and Ross was about 10 minutes late. He said he wouldn't have come except his mom is off today and the only thing worse than being at school is being at home with her. We're walking over to Lauren's at lunch.

Later . . .

Ross smoked us out at lunch, so I feel softer around the edges somehow, a little less like I've been hit by a dump truck. I still don't know how I'm going to make it through the rest of the day. Ugh. Now I'm in this weed haze and I feel miserable. I'm not sure what I liked about pot before. It seems like such a lame high next to Tina.

LOL. That's what Ian calls crystal: Tina.

He texted Ross and told him that he should have the girls over this weekend because his friend Tina was coming.

March 22

School has been a complete fog for the past few days. I barely passed our chemistry test on Tuesday. I was stoned, and sore, and hadn't even studied. I've never made a D on a test before. Something in me doesn't care. I hear this voice in my head say that I should care, but I just don't.

I went home yesterday after class and crawled into bed and went to sleep. I slept until about 10 p.m. and wandered into the living room while Dad and Mom were watching TV. Mom jumped up and reheated some chicken soup she'd made me earlier. She asked if I was okay and said she'd thought about waking me up for dinner but wanted to let me sleep because she knew I was fighting something off.

Can you imagine if I told her I was fighting off meth?

The soup was delicious, but I still felt like I was moving under Jell-O. After I ate, I curled up on the couch with her and Dad. Mom put her arm around me, and I closed my eyes on her lap. There was something so peaceful about it. I felt like a little girl again, like I didn't need to worry about anything. It made me miss being little. It made me wonder who I was growing up to be. My eyes were closed, but they filled up with tears, and I got a big lump in my throat. When I got up to go back to bed, there was a wet spot on the throw Mom had spread across her lap.

She looked up at me and asked if I was sure I was okay. I wanted to shake my head and let it all out. I wanted to tell her everything, and crawl back onto the couch and bury my face in her lap again and let her keep me safe.

But I'm not a little girl anymore.

So I nodded and kissed her good night.

Now I'm sitting in American government, and I can't pay attention. We just took a quiz that I knew about 4 answers on. I'm pretty good at guessing, but I don't think Ross did as well.

Later . . .

Cam and Astrid came to lunch with us. They brought Mark with them.

A-W-K-W-A-R-D.

248

Lauren and Ross and I had to keep kicking each other under the table to keep from laughing. Every time Mark opens his mouth, he just sounds ridiculous.

It's weird having had the experiences I've had now and hearing people talk who haven't. It's like they wouldn't be able to even FATHOM some of the shit I've done.

When I was in the bathroom after lunch with Lauren, Cassie and Bethany came in to reapply their eyeliner as is their custom every other class period. When they walked by us on the way to the sink, Bethany groaned and said, Burnouts, under her breath.

Before I knew what I was doing, my hand jetted out and grabbed her blond ponytail and pulled her backward. She shrieked like she was being boiled in oil. I pulled her head back toward my mouth, and very quietly I said, Shut up, Bethany.

Lauren snorted with laughter, and Cassie got all sputtering and flummoxed, and said, Well, SCREW YOU! Really loudly. I said, You'd probably like that because nobody else has, that's for sure. Then Lauren and I walked out.

God, I hate most girls my age.

Later . . .
Ross just texted me and Lauren that he's skipping school tomorrow to go hang at Ian's. Lauren said I should go to school with Cam and then come to her place instead of going to class.

I can't take another day like today. I need to feel good again.

Screw AA. Screw community service.

I'm going.

April 1

I'm writing this in a new notebook.

I'm writing this in a new city.

It's Sunday now. I'm a couple of hours away from home, a little town out in the desert.

When I woke up on Thursday, I wasn't sure where I was. Turns out I was on the psych floor at the hospital. They wouldn't give me anything to write with. They were afraid I was going to stab a pen into my throat or something. Or probably stab it into somebody else's throat. Apparently I had been unconscious for a day and a half. When they finally let my parents come in to see me, my hands were still in restraints. I'd been scratching off my skin, and fighting the nurses and orderlies.

I finally started to piece it together. A week ago last Friday, I remember walking to Lauren's. She had mimosas ready when I arrived. They were delicious—orange juice with champagne. We finished the bottle, then she drove us over to Ian's. Blake and Ross were there already, and when we walked in, Blake said he had a surprise for us.

Blake took us up to Ian's bedroom. It had a pretty view of

the canals out the window, and Ross was already standing on the balcony outside in the spring sun smoking a cigarette. There was a tray lying on the bed with a pipe, a big Baggie of meth, a lighter, and a pile of syringes with orange plastic caps.

When Lauren saw the syringes, her eyes got big and she got quiet. She looked at Blake and said, For fuck's sake. Are you kidding me?

But I saw them, and I knew. I felt the queasy feeling leap into my stomach. My mouth flooded with the metallic taste of meth. I wanted it again. That feeling. I didn't cut school for the same old feeling. I wanted it different.

I wanted MORE.

Are those for shooting up Tina?

When I said the words, everybody's head turned at once, and Blake smiled at me.

Why, yes, they are, he said.

Before anybody could move, Ross stretched out on the bed next to Blake and pulled up his sleeve. Lauren rolled her eyes and said, Oh my GOD. I HATE needles.

Ross just said, Whatever. You've done it before.

Lauren froze. I just looked at them both. Ross was staring out the balcony door. He had made a fist and shook his outstretched arm. C'MON DUDE. LET'S DO THIS.

Blake smiled. Ian held a spoon with its handle bent and

filled it with crystal meth, then held a lighter beneath it until it was liquid. Blake pulled the orange cap off of a syringe, sucked the meth up into it, then he held it in his teeth while he swabbed Ross's arm with an alcohol pad. Carefully he eased the needle into a vein. Ross flinched and then closed his eyes as Blake pushed the plunger on the syringe, then pulled it out, recapped the needle, slid it into a small coffee can on the bedside table, and said, Who's next?

I turned to Lauren and asked, You've done this before?

Ian just laughed. I realized he'd already shot up. He said of course they had. Where did I think they'd been when they missed school those days since I'd walked in on Lauren and Blake?

I knew one thing for sure in that moment: I would not be left out again.

Ross opened his eyes with a loopy smile and quietly said, Hell, yeaaaaah.

Ian walked over and squeezed in behind him at the headboard of the king-size bed. He bent over and kissed him long and hard on the lips. He smiled and said, Feel good, mister?

Ross focused his eyes back on me and said, Better than good. I'm freaking Superman.

I rolled up my sleeve. Lauren just looked at me, then shook her head.

I said, Lauren. I want this. I'm not getting left out again.

Blake got everything ready and told me to make a fist. I did, and he tapped around on my arm, then took an elastic strap and tied it around my arm near my shoulder and told me to squeeze my fist harder. I looked down and saw a light-blue spiderweb of veins start to pop up from the bend at my elbow.

The alcohol swab was cold.

The prick was fast.

As Blake pushed down the plunger, I heard bells. I kid you not. BELLS. INSTANTLY. Some people will tell you that it takes a while, but not for me. At that moment I was the sexiest, smartest, funniest, most powerful, amazing person in a perfect universe that I created. I felt the tension drop out of my shoulders, and I lay back on the bed, laughing. The sensation was instant, and delicious, and I knew right then and there that everything was warm and perfect, that everything had always been perfect, that everything would always be perfect.

Everything else comes in snapshots.

Lauren finally agreeing, and Blake shooting her up.

Running along the canals with Ross.

Taking my shoes off at the beach with Ian.

Finding Blake and Lauren naked in Ian's bed. Laughing and joining them.

Feeling Blake's body and Lauren's body and my body warm and naked and perfect.

Seeing my phone across the room, ringing and ringing. The text messages flashing across the screen: CAM CAM CAM CAM MOM MOM CAM DAD DAD DAD CAM MOM MOM MOM CAM HOME HOME HOME DAD CAM MOM . . .

I guess we were there at Ian's for a long time. Days. The nurses in the psych ward really wouldn't tell me much, just that I was checked in on Sunday, one week ago today. I finally came to around Wednesday. I was released from the hospital early this morning, and Mom and Dad walked me to the car in the hospital parking deck. We stopped at home so that I could pack a bag. Mom told me I'd be leaving town for a month. Dad told me he had my cell phone for now, and that I couldn't call, text, e-mail, or even leave a note for Lauren or Ross.

Cam came into my room as I zipped my suitcase and sat down on the bed next to me. I asked him what happened.

He said that Mom and Dad called the police when he got home from school on Friday night and no one had seen me. He said that the police told Mom and Dad they had to wait 24 hours. Cam was sure we were at Blake's and had driven up to Malibu with Astrid to check. He'd also gone to see Ross's mom

254

at the hotel. She didn't think it was any big deal, as Ross was usually pretty much on his own.

By Sunday morning Cam was sure I was with Ian somewhere, but he'd never been to Ian's place, so he didn't know where he lived. That's when he went to the yoga studio and explained the situation to Marty. She looked up Ian's address in the computer at the studio and gave it to Cam.

Cam raced back home to tell Mom and Dad he'd gotten Ian's address and we needed to go over there, when his phone rang and it was Ross calling him. He said that when he picked up, Ross was hysterical. Crying and shouting. He kept yelling SHE'S DYING. SHE'S DYING.

Cam started crying while he was talking, slow tears flowing out the corners of his eyes as he soldiered through the story. Calling an ambulance, giving them the address, certain I'd be dead before they arrived. He said, I really thought I'd never see my little sister again.

I asked him why Ross thought I was dying.

He looked at me and said, You don't remember, do you?

I shook my head.

April 2

I'm at a rehab in Palm Springs. It used to be a motel that was built back in the '60s. The rooms are all centered around a swimming pool. Sounds nice, I guess. I wish it felt nice. I went to my first meeting today. The rules are strict. Up at 7 a.m. I have to make my bed, then report to the kitchen for breakfast. Afterward we all have chores, then group therapy starts at 10 a.m. and goes until 11:30.

It's part 12-step meeting, part counseling. I'm the youngest person here. There are mainly gay guys, one grandma who got busted cooking meth in her mobile home, and two girls who used to be strippers.

We have lunch next, then more chores, an hour of free time, then another group session. After dinner, we all load up in a big gray van and go to an AA meeting someplace in the city.

April 3

I had an individual session with the therapist at the rehab this morning. He had a mirror that he handed me and asked if I knew how I got the scratches on my face.

I've been putting some ointment on them that Mom gave me when they dropped me off. The scratches on the right side are deep, and hurt when I roll over in the night accidentally. I'm really worried they're going to scar.

I told him that I don't remember.

He said it was from the heroin.

I told him that I didn't do any heroin.

The he handed me a photocopy from a file folder he had in his hand. He said it was the toxicology report of what was in my system at the hospital. He said that the paramedics had wheeled me in dead, pumping air through my lungs with one of those squeeze thingies like you see on the emergency room shows. They gave me the highest amount of epinephrine you could give someone, and then shocked me twice before my heart started again.

The word "heroin" was circled on the report.

Later . . .

I was cleaning the toilet in my bathroom for inspection and I had a sudden flash. I don't know when it was, but I saw Blake grinning at me and saying, This is even BETTER than Tina. Don't worry. You'll love it.

I don't remember anything else.

April 5

I didn't have time to write yesterday because I had to go to the doctor for a checkup during free time. I am so pissed that they make you keep your lights off at night. I can't really sleep and I wish I could write in my journal.

I don't really know how I feel about being here. I said that in group this morning.

Randy, the counselor who runs group, said that was okay. That the reason we're here is to start feeling better.

I told him I didn't know if I felt bad.

He said, No, no. I mean we're here so that we start FEELING better; feeling EVERYTHING better. Right now, you don't know what you feel. We're here to get you in touch with what you're feeling.

April 6

I don't know if I can take it here anymore. I still feel like a zombie. Last night I woke up having bad dreams and cold sweats. I dreamed that Lauren and Ross were out by the pool. They were trying to get me to sneak out with them, and when I finally did go out by the pool, Blake was there, holding a scalpel. He had a big grin on his face and he kept saying, IT WON'T HURT! IT WON'T HURT.

I sat up in bed, panicked and sweating. I went into my bathroom and turned the water on in the shower as hot as it would go, then I sat down in the tub and cried for a really long time.

This all feels so hopeless.

What am I doing here?

Later . . .

I told the group about my dream today. Randy said that it
sounded like I was feeling BETTER. I got SO MAD when he
said that. I started crying, and I yelled I FEEL LIKE SHIT!

He just said, But you can feel that. Your feelings are starting
to work again.

I told him I didn't want to feel the bad stuff better. That I
just wanted to feel GOOD.

He said that's the tricky part about feeling better. You
don't get to pick what you feel, you only get to start feeling it.
All of it.

Later . . .

The weirdest thing happened tonight at the AA meeting we
go to in town. This girl who was maybe only a year or two
older than me spoke. She talked about all of this stuff that I
TOTALLY related to. Her name was Amy, and she was the first
person I ever heard speak at an AA meeting who said anything
that remotely sounded like me.

This girl TOLD MY STORY!

She was 14 years old and a freshman in high school when
she and her friend started drinking. Then smoking pot. Then
doing Ecstasy. Then doing coke. Then doing meth.

She talked about how all of these things made her feel in

control, and pretty, and confident, and happy, and like she had something to look forward to.

Eventually she said she was shooting meth and then shooting heroin.

She ended up going to juvenile hall and being locked up there for 6 months. While she was there, she started going to an AA meeting they held, and she got a sponsor who walked her through the 12 steps. She said that she didn't really believe in a "capital G" God, but that her "higher power" was the accountability that she'd found in the rooms of AA. She said that even if you didn't believe in a god or a higher power, you could still come to AA and you didn't have to drink or use just for today, no matter what.

I think my mouth must have been hanging open, because she came up and talked to me afterward. She gave me her phone number and her e-mail address. I told her that I didn't have a phone right now because I was at the rehab.

She smiled and said that she went to that rehab too. She said she'd see if Randy would let her come visit me.

For some reason when she said that, I started crying.

Then this girl named Amy who I don't even know hugged me. She whispered into my ear, Let us love you until you learn to love yourself.

I hope she comes to visit.

April 10

I'm so excited! Amy actually came to visit me today. She said that Randy was glad she wanted to come and talk with me. During our free period, we lay out by the pool. She's one year older than me and is graduating from high school next month. Then she told me that she was going to the college where my dad works this fall to study to be a music teacher. When I told her my dad runs the music department at that college, she was like NO WAY. She'll have my dad for a class next fall!

Amy said I should watch out for little coincidences like this. She said some people in AA call them "God shots." When I laughed, she said, Yeah. That's kind of silly. I just like to think of it as all things working together for good.

Before she left, I asked Amy to be my sponsor in AA. I don't really know what all that means, but I know that you're supposed to have somebody to show you how to work the steps and to check in with if you feel like drinking or doing drugs. I'm not even really sure that I'm an addict yet, but I feel like most teenage girls probably don't get DUIs and then overdose on heroin and end up in rehab.

I know that in a couple of weeks we have "Family Day" coming up, where Cam and Mom and Dad will come down and I'll have to talk to them about all of this. I'm not sure what I'm supposed to say. When I think about it, I get that nervous feeling in my stomach. I feel so guilty and so ashamed that I've put everyone through this.

The first step in AA says, "We admitted we were powerless over alcohol—that our lives had become unmanageable." Amy said that I could substitute any drug I wanted for the word alcohol if that made it easier to understand. She also said that overdosing and getting a DUI and being high on crystal at school sounded pretty unmanageable to her.

And you know what we did when she said that?

We laughed! 'Cause it was like the UNDERSTATEMENT OF THE YEAR!

It felt really good to laugh with Amy, especially about something that has been so bad. Maybe all of this will work itself out after all.

April 18

I have been working on my AA steps so much that I haven't had much chance to journal! Doing the steps involves a lot of writing about a lot of different stuff, mainly about the people you resent, and what your part is in those resentments. Eventually I'll have to make a list of people I've hurt by drinking and using drugs so that I can make amends to them, but that's later, and Amy says not to worry about that yet.

Anyway, here's what's been going on:

1. I've been talking to my parents and to Amy on the phone every day.

2. Things are rocky with Mom and Dad. Mom still cries every time she talks to me. Dad is really quiet, like he doesn't know if he can still trust me. They're getting ready for Cam's big graduation party, even though it isn't until next month.

3. I've been allowed to check my e-mail a couple of times. Ross sent one e-mail that said he was sorry about everything that happened. Lauren sent an e-mail saying she was sorry that my parents shipped me to Palm Springs. She said that school is lame without me. I wrote both of them back and told them all about my rehab and Amy and how I felt really good about the changes I was making. I told them that I hope they check out some other AA meetings back in LA. I said that it made a big difference when I heard someone who was our age talk about addiction.

4. I'm working on Step 2 right now with Amy: "Came to believe that a Power greater than ourselves could restore us to sanity." Amy told me that Albert Einstein once said that "insanity" is "doing the same thing over and over again and expecting different results." I realized that's exactly what I'd done: continued to drink and do drugs and hang out with the people who did those things with me, even after I started getting into trouble.

I want to do things DIFFERENTLY now.

I finally feel like I have so much to look forward to. One of the guys in our group therapy told me that now I'm on a "pink cloud." It's this term in recovery that means I'm really happy and I think everything is going to be just perfect now.

I don't think everything is going to be perfect now.

But I sure do feel better.

April 27

Mom and Dad and Cam were here for family night tonight. It was hard to face them, but the looks on their faces when I asked their forgiveness for the way I treated them for the past year—for the lies, and the craziness—well, that made everything worth it.

Tomorrow I get to go home with them. I'll have been here for 28 days. It will be sad not seeing Amy as often, but she'll be moving to college this fall, and she's promised that we'll talk every day on the phone as long as I check in with her the way you're supposed to when you have a sponsor. We're getting ready to start on Step 4, which is a big list of all the people and places and ideas that I've ever resented in my life. The step says to make "a fearless moral inventory." It's actually really scary, but Amy said not to be scared of it, just to do it. There are really specific instructions about how to write it out in the Alcoholics Anonymous Big Book. She sat down with me by the pool the other day and made a little chart in my notebook with 4 columns so that I have a guide of how to do it.

I can't wait to get back home and share what I've learned with Lauren and Ross. I e-mailed both of them this week about going to meetings together when I get back home. I haven't had a chance to check my e-mails yet, but I'm excited that I can share what I've learned in my time here with them.

When I got here, I wasn't sure that I'd ever feel hopeful again. I felt like all of the good times of my life were over—behind me. I didn't want to even think about the idea of NEVER being able to party again.

Now I feel like I have everything to look forward to if I just don't drink or use a drug TODAY. If I can just remember that I only have to worry about TODAY, nothing seems so terrible or overwhelming.

April 28

I'M BACK HOOOOOOOOOOOOOOOOOME!

You know, I never realized how BEAUTIFUL our house is, or how BIG my bedroom is. After living in an old motel in the desert for a month, I walked in and our place looks like a PALACE. I stood on the back balcony for a while and stared out at the ocean. Mom came up and stood behind me and wrapped her arms around me. Then she whispered into my ear how proud of me she was.

She said, You're a different girl now. I can see it in your eyes.

I got goose bumps when she said it. I felt tears come into my eyes, and I squeezed her fingers in mine, and I said, Yes, Mom. I AM different.

Later . . .

Dad just gave me back my cell phone! He said he and Mom discussed it and they can't believe the difference in me. I gave him a big hug and kissed him on the cheek.

I am going to yoga with Cam tonight for the first time in over a MONTH! I am so excited. I have to go grab my mat and get changed. Cam hates to be late.

Later . . .

Ross was at yoga! It was so good to see him!

When I walked into the room, he came running over and gave me a hug. We talked about what rehab was like for a little bit after class. I asked him how Lauren was, and he said she was okay, that they really missed me at school.

I told him Mom had sent my books to me and I had been doing as much schoolwork as I could at rehab but that I was still way behind, and I'd need his help to get caught up. He smiled his crooked little smile and said, I'm glad you're okay.

I hugged him tight and said, I'm more than okay. I'm better than ever. See you Monday.

Teen Found Dead of Accidental
Overdose, Coroner Rules

May 5th, _____—The 16-year-old girl whose body was recovered from a _____ beach house by police late Friday evening died of an accidental overdose the _____ County sheriff-coroner has declared.

The man whose father owned the house, Blake _____, 20, and his friend Ian _____, 21, were both retained for questioning in the matter. Two teenage friends of the victim, a boy and girl who were present at the scene but whose names have not been released, were also taken into juvenile custody.

Toxicology reports indicate that the young woman, the daughter of a local college professor and his wife, had taken lethal intravenous doses of crystal methamphetamine and heroin. Two journals found in the young woman's bedroom have been turned over to detectives by her parents.

A spokesman for the district attorney's office would not speculate on whether or not criminal charges would be filed in the case, but a full investigation is under way.

TURN THE PAGE FOR
A GLIMPSE AT TWO NOVELS
BY AMY REED

CLEAN

KELLY

My skin looks disgusting. Seriously, it's practically green. I have big gray bags under my eyes, my hair is all thin and frizzy, and I'm erupting all over the place with giant greasy zits. I look like a cross between a zombie, a hair ball, and a pepperoni pizza. Have I always looked like this? Was I just too high to notice?

OLIVIA

Did I pack my AP Chemistry book? I can't remember if I packed it. I am not ready for this. I am so not ready.

EVA

This place is a body. The walls are its bones or its skin, or both—an exoskeleton, like a crab has. A crab's shell is meant to keep it safe, to protect it from the world; it is made to keep things out. But this shell is meant to keep us in, to protect the world from us. We are cancerous cells. Quarantined. An epidemic. We are rogue mutations that cannot make contact with the outside world. We're left in here to bump around like science experiments. They watch us pee into cups. They study our movements. One doctor says, "Look, that one's slowing down. There may be hope." Another says, "No. They're all doomed. Let's just watch them burn themselves out."

CHRISTOPHER

Everyone's looking at me weird. They probably just had a secret meeting where they voted on how lame they think I am, and the verdict was "very lame." Add that to the fact that they can all most likely read my mind, and basically I'm doomed.

JASON

Fuck you fuck you fuck you FUCK YOU.

EVA

And the halls are like tongues, fingers, toes, like so many appendages. Dislocated. And these rooms are the lungs—identical, swollen, polluted. This one is the stomach, churning its contents into something unrecognizable.

CHRISTOPHER

That's it. They all got together and compared notes and have unanimously decided to look at me weird.

JASON

If I don't get a cigarette soon, I'm going to fucking kill somebody. We can smoke in here, right? They said we could smoke in here.

KELLY

They took everything, including my astringent. Now how the hell am I supposed to clean my face? Do they really think I'm going to *drink* astringent?

EVA

All these rooms—body parts with mysterious names and functions.

OLIVIA

When was the last time they cleaned this place?

JASON

Fuck this place.

BEAUTIFUL

I don't see her coming.

I am looking at my piece of pizza. I am watching pepperoni glisten. It is my third day at the new school and I am sitting at a table next to the bathrooms. I am eating lunch with the blond girls with the pink sweaters, the girls who talk incessantly about Harvard even though we're only in seventh grade. They are the kind of girls who have always ignored me. But these girls are different than the ones on the island. They think I am one of them.

She grabs my shoulder from behind and I jump. I turn around. She says, "What's your name?"

I tell her, "Cassie."

She says, "Alex."

She is wearing an army jacket, a short jean skirt, fishnet stockings, and combat boots. Her hair is shoulder length, frizzy and green. She's tall and skinny, not skinny like a model but skinny like a boy. Her blue eyes are so pale they don't look human and her eyelashes and eyebrows are so blond they're almost white. She is not pretty, not even close to pretty. But there's something about her that's bigger than pretty, something bigger than smart girls going to Harvard.

It's only my third day, but I knew the second I got here that this place was different. It is not like the island, not a place ruled by good girls. I saw Alex. I saw the ninth grade boys she hangs out with, their multicolored hair, their postures of indifference, their clothes that tell everybody they're too cool to care. I heard her loud voice drowning everything out. I saw how other girls let her cut in front of them in line. I saw everyone else looking at her, looking at the boys with their lazy confidence, everyone looking and trying not to be seen.

I saw them at the best table in the cafeteria and I decided to change. It is not hard to change when you were never anything in the first place. It is not hard to put on a T-shirt of a band you overheard the cool kids talking about, to wear tight jeans with holes, to walk by their table and make sure they see you. All it takes is moving off an island to a suburb of Seattle where no one knows who you were before.

"You're in seventh grade." She says this as a statement.

"Yes," I answer.

The pink-sweater girls are looking at me like they made a big mistake.

"Where are you from?" she says.

"Bainbridge Island."

"I can tell," she says. "Come with me." She grabs my wrist and my plastic fork drops. "I have some people who want to meet you."

I'm supposed to stand up now. I'm supposed to leave the pizza and the smart girls and go with the girl named Alex to the people who want to meet me. I cannot look back, not at the plate of greasy pizza and the girls who were almost my friends. Just follow Alex. Keep walking. One step. Two steps. I must focus on my face not turning red. Focus on breathing. Stand up straight. Remember, this is what you want.

The boys are getting bigger. I must pretend I don't notice their stares. I cannot turn red. I cannot smile the way I do when I'm nervous, with my cheeks twitching, my lips curled all awkward and lopsided. I must ignore the burn where Alex holds my wrist too tight. I cannot wonder why she's holding my wrist the way she does, why she doesn't trust me to walk on my own, why she keeps looking back at me, why she won't let me out of her sight. I cannot think of maybes. I cannot think of "What if I turned around right now? What if I went the other way?" There is no other way. There is only forward, with Alex, to the boys who want to meet me.

I am slowing down. I have stopped. I am looking at big sneakers on ninth grade boys. Legs attached. Other things. Chests, arms, faces. Eyes looking. Droopy, red, big-boy eyes. Smiles. Hands on my shoulders. Pushing, guiding, driving me.

"James, this is Cassie, the beautiful seventh grader," Alex says. Hair shaved on the side, mohawk in the middle, face pretty and flawless. This one's the cutest. This one's the leader.

"Wes, this is Cassie, the beautiful seventh grader." Pants baggy, legs spread, lounging with arms open, baby-fat face. Not a baby, dangerous. He smiles. They all smile.

Jackson, Anthony. I remember their names. They say, "Sit down." I do what they say. Alex nods her approval.

I must not look up from my shoes. I must pretend I don't feel James's leg touching mine, his mouth so close to my ear. Don't see Alex whispering to him. Don't feel the stares. Don't hear the laughing. Just remember what Mom says about my "almond eyes," my "dancer's body," my "high cheekbones," my "long neck," my hair, my lips, my breasts, all of the things I have now that I didn't have before.

"Cassie," James says, and my name sounds like flowers in his mouth.

"Yes." I look at his chiseled chin. I look at his teeth, perfect and white. I do not look at his eyes.

"Are you straight?" he says, and I compute in my head what this question might mean, and I say, "Yes, well, I think so," because I think he wants to know if I like boys. I look at his eyes and know I have made a mistake. They are green and smiling and curious, wanting me to answer correctly. He says, "I mean, are you a good girl? Or do you do bad things?"

"What do you mean by bad things?" is what I want to say, but I don't say anything. I just look at him, hoping he cannot read my mind, cannot smell my terror, will not now realize that I do not deserve this attention, that he's made a mistake by looking at me in this not-cruel way.

"I mean, I noticed you the last couple of days. You seemed like a good girl. But today you look different."

It is true. I am different from what I was yesterday and all the days before that.

"So, are you straight?" he says. "I mean, do you do drugs and stuff?"

"Yeah, um, I guess so." I haven't. I will. Yes. I will do anything he wants. I will sit here while everyone stares at me. I will sit here until the bell rings and it is time to go back to class and the girl named Alex says, "Give me your number," and I do.

• • •

Even though no one else talks to me for the rest of the day, I hold on to "beautiful." I hold on to lunch tomorrow at the best table in the cafeteria. Even though I ride the bus home alone and watch the marina and big houses go by, there are ninth grade boys somewhere who may be thinking about me.

Even though Mom's asleep and Dad's at work, even though there are still boxes piled everywhere from the move, even though Mom's too sad to cook and I eat peanut butter for dinner, and Dad doesn't come home until the house is dark, and the walls are too thin to keep out the yelling, even though I can hear my mom crying, there is a girl somewhere who has my number. There are ninth grade boys who will want it. There are ninth grade boys who may be thinking about me, making me exist somewhere other than here, making me something bigger than the flesh in the corner of this room. There is a picture of me in their heads, a picture of someone I don't know yet. She is not the chubby girl with the braces and bad perm. She is not the girl hiding in the bathroom at recess. She is someone new, a blank slate they have named beautiful. That is what I am now: beautiful, with this new body and face and hair and clothes. Beautiful, with this erasing of history.

She was an athlete

with a bright future. She only wanted
to lose a few pounds.

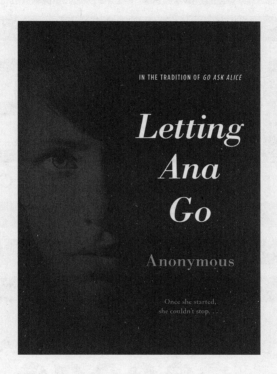

*Read her devastating journey in her own words,
in the diary she left behind.*

Breaking Bailey

Breaking Bailey

Anonymous

Simon Pulse

New York   London   Toronto   Sydney   New Delhi

SIMON PULSE

An imprint of Simon & Schuster Children's Publishing Division

1230 Avenue of the Americas, New York, New York 10020

First Simon Pulse paperback edition June 2019

Text copyright © 2019 by Simon & Schuster, Inc.

Cover photographs copyright © 2019 by Thinkstock/Yasinemir

Also available in a Simon Pulse hardcover edition

All rights reserved, including the right of reproduction in whole or in part in any form.

SIMON PULSE and colophon are registered trademarks of Simon & Schuster, Inc.

For information about special discounts for bulk purchases, please contact Simon & Schuster Special Sales at 1-866-506-1949 or business@simonandschuster.com.

The Simon & Schuster Speakers Bureau can bring authors to your live event.

For more information or to book an event contact the Simon & Schuster Speakers Bureau at 1-866-248-3049 or visit our website at www.simonspeakers.com.

Cover designed by Tiara Iandiorio

The text of this book was set in Adobe Caslon Pro.

Manufactured in the United States of America

10 9 8 7 6 5 4 3 2

Library of Congress Cataloging-in-Publication Data

Title: Breaking Bailey / by Anonymous.

Description: First Simon Pulse paperback edition. | New York : Simon Pulse, 2019. | Summary: Sent to a fancy boarding school by her stepmother, a prominent attorney, Bailey keeps a journal chronicling her involvement in a "Science Club" that makes and sells crystal meth.

Identifiers: LCCN 2018039720 (print) | LCCN 2018046846 (eBook) | ISBN 9781534433083 (hardcover) | ISBN 9781534433090 (pbk) | ISBN 9781534433106 (eBook)

Subjects: | CYAC: Drug traffic—Fiction. | Substance abuse—Fiction. | Boarding schools—Fiction. | Schools—Fiction. | Diaries—Fiction.

Classification: LCC PZ7.1 (eBook) | LCC PZ7.1 .B751547 2019 (print) | DDC [Fic]—dc23

LC record available at https://lccn.loc.gov/2018039720

September 3

Dear Diary,

Does anyone actually say that anymore? Maybe some fifth-grade girls. The type who have unicorn-and-rainbow diaries with easily picked locks and "I heart Billy" drawn on every page. This one doesn't have unicorns, which is surprising since it's from Dad. He probably thinks I still play with Barbies. It's not that he doesn't care about me. Just more like he doesn't notice me anymore. He hasn't since he started dating Isa. Truthfully, he hasn't really noticed me since Mom died, but I can't blame him for that. The past couple of years have been a giant blob of suck. At least Dad has Isa, though. I guess one of us should have someone.

Isa. That stupid name makes me want to scream. I almost poked through the page with my pen writing it. Any normal person would shorten Isabelle to Belle, or even Isy, if they wanted to be cute. But Isa? EEEESUHHHH. God. Most Pretentious Nicknames for a thousand, Alex.

But she's the reason I'm here, at Prescott Academy, where graduation nearly guarantees you a spot in an Ivy League. And she's the reason Bex gets to go to the Campbell School, which means she'll get into Prescott, too, when she's old enough. Dad can't afford fancy private schools, but Isa the Bulldog Lawyer can. So I guess I can put up with a stepmother when I'm required to come home. Holidays already suck without Mom, and the same fake smile hides both grief and irritation.

Bex hugged me so tight before they left. She's scared to go to a new school, and she's never been away from home before. She's never been away from *me*. That's going to be hard. As cool as it's going to be on my own here, what am I gonna do without Bex's hugs? Her nonstop chatter? Her—

Sorry. My roommate showed up. Her name is Emily. She seems cool, and she didn't bring anything annoying like wind chimes or beaded curtains, but she did bring chocolate. :) Off to the dining hall for dinner.

September 4

Okay, so I think I'll try to write in this thing every night before I go to sleep. I don't know why. I've never really kept a diary before, but . . . I don't know. I guess it's nice that Dad got something for me. And it will be fun to document what it's like to go to Prescott Academy. Maybe years from now, when I'm a famous chemist, I'll use it for reference when I write my memoirs. But anyway . . . about that documentation. Here I go. . . .

Today was just so weird. Prescott isn't just a different school, it's a different planet. I got to my first class, English, and sat at an empty desk. Everyone around me was talking because they all know one another, but it wasn't like home. At home, if someone asked how your summer was, you'd say it was lame or talk about a summer job or something. These Prescott kids . . . It was all "Oh, Paris is just so lovely in the summertime!" and "Daddy's new yacht couldn't even fit at the dock in the Hamptons" and "I tried amazing caviar on solid gold plates!"

Okay, it wasn't that bad, but it wasn't much better. These are the kinds of kids who clearly never had to wonder IF they'd ever get a car, just when. Oh, and also, since we all have to wear the same uniform, apparently the trend is to show off the only things that we can individualize: makeup, jewelry, and what brand of flats you wear. Seriously. I'm guessing my Payless fake leather won't get me into the upper echelon at Prescott. I suppose I could ask Isa for better flats, but . . . honestly, I'd rather die than feel like I owe Isa anything.

Thank God Emily and I had calculus and civics together, and we found each other at lunch so I didn't have to eat by myself. She told me last night that she's a scholarship student. That's the only way her parents can afford this place. She begged me not to tell anyone, but she didn't have to. I get it. I told her about my dad and Isa. I didn't mention Mom.

Emily wants to be a writer. Like movie scripts and stuff. She's pretty quiet, but if you get her talking about movies, she could go for days.

That's another thing that's different about the kids here.

They're really focused on the future. Everyone seems super smart and ambitious, and they take classes seriously. Back home, classes were just sort of a necessary evil until summer. And they certainly weren't supposed to be interesting. Here, even my least favorite classes are going to be interesting and challenging.

Speaking of favorite classes . . . There's a guy in my chemistry class. His name is Drew. Definitely not a scholarship student. His dad owns a restaurant chain or something—at least that's what Emily said. Anyway, he's kind of cute. Preppy, but his hair does this floppy thing that's truly adorable. I saw him later at lunch, too, sitting with a very serious-looking bunch of people. Serious but glamorous. They were just sitting at a dining hall table together, but they might as well have been posing for a *Vanity Fair* cover. The girl had the prettiest, thickest black hair and dark red lipstick. She had large black rhinestones on her flats. At least I think they were rhinestones. For all I know they could have been real gems from Tiffany. It wouldn't surprise me in this place.

I'm going to have to buy some better shoes.

September 5

Day two at Prescott was just as weird as the first, made even weirder when Drew actually spoke to me about halfway through chemistry.

4

Drew: Bailey, right?

(I nodded dumbly, like I'd forgotten the
English language.)

Drew: You seem like you really know this stuff.

Me: Um. Yeah. There was a really good
chemistry teacher at my old school. I used to
do extra assignments for her. For fun.

Drew, looking amused: For fun?

Me: Well, um, yeah. I was kind of good at it,
so she let me work ahead of the class.

Then he just nodded, sat back in his desk, and locked eyes
with Dark Lipstick Girl. They looked away from each other
at the same time. He said nothing else to me, after class and
all day. But when I walked by his table of glamorous people at
lunch, he and Dark Lipstick Girl stared at me in this sort of
predatory way.

What is this? Am I the girl who accidentally stumbles upon
a group of vampires and werewolves at her school?

I asked Emily about Drew. She warned me to stay away from him while also drooling over the way his Prescott uniform sweater tightens over his chest, so . . .

September 7

Tomorrow is the first Friday here at Prescott. In other words, it's the first Friday night I've ever had without parents around. Prescott has a curfew. We have to be back in our dorms by eleven, but that doesn't mean we have to sleep. I've heard a few people talking about parties in the dorms, but no one's invited me. It's okay. Emily and I have decided we're going to stay up all night and watch movies and pig out on chocolate. I guess she wasn't invited to any parties either.

September 8

The plot thickens.

Mr. Callahan asked me to stay after chemistry class today, so the whole class I was sick to my stomach with nerves. Turns out he wanted to know about my old school back home. He said he noticed I seem to be ahead of what he's teaching at Prescott.

Ahead of a class at Prescott!

So I told him about Miss Beverly at my old school and how I'd spend a lot of days after school in the lab, doing special stuff that no one else got to do. I also told him that I want to be a chemical engineer. He laughed when I told him I hadn't even known that was a thing until Miss Beverly told me about all the jobs that use chemistry, but now it's the only thing I can see myself doing. He asked if I'd thought about college, like I haven't been dreaming about Harvard since I was three. He said he'd help all he could.

I thanked him and walked out the door, and that's when Dark Lipstick Girl grabbed my arm and dragged me into the ladies' restroom.

> DLG: Bailey, right?

Huh. The same way Drew greeted me the first time. Weird. Definitely vampires.

> Me: Yeah. Were you listening to me talk to Mr. Callahan?

> DLG, shrugging: Not on purpose. You're pretty good at chemistry, then?

> Me: I guess. I'm sorry. I didn't catch your name.

> DLG: Katy. Katy Ashton. Your last name is Wells, isn't it? Are you on scholarship?

I got super uncomfortable with our conversation at that point. The assumption felt awful. Maybe it was my cheap flats? Or maybe it's just that my family doesn't summer at the same vacation spot as everyone else? Whatever. She sort of backtracked after that. She put her arm around my shoulders and started walking with me toward my next class.

Then she invited me to Science Club. Seriously? This gorgeous girl is part of something like the Science Club? Prescott isn't like my old school AT ALL.

> Katy, formerly known as DLG: It's
> Saturday night. Herschell Hall. That's the
> upperclassmen boys' dorm. Seven o'clock.

> Me: The Science Club meets in a dorm on
> Saturday nights?

Katy just smiled at me, all secretive and glamorous, and told me she'd see me there. Seriously. If Science Club is code for Vampire Club, I will be not be surprised. Pissed at how clichéd it would be, but not surprised.

~~September 8~~ Sorry! It's actually September 9 now!

Emily is fast asleep. I'm about to pass out too. I know it's probably lame that we stayed in and watched movies, but I had

8

a lot of fun. She's really down-to-earth. Honestly, she seems like she could be from back home. We watched *Notting Hill*. Emily had never seen it before and seemed to love it, so maybe she won't mind watching it again sometime. It was Mom's favorite. We used to pop popcorn and put on fleece pajamas and watch romantic comedies all the time. We'd both cry at all the sad parts and some of the happy parts and tease each other about being saps. When Bex got a little older, she'd stay up late with us too. She'd always have a box of tissues ready for when Mom and I would start sobbing.

I wonder how Bex is doing. I miss her.

I really miss Mom.

September 9, later

Walking over to Herschell Hall was the most I'd really seen campus since orientation day over the summer. So far I've kept to the class buildings and Baker Hall, my own dorm. Herschell, though, is on the other side of campus, and there's a pretty pond and park in between. The leaves are starting to turn and I can tell it's going to be gorgeous here in the fall. Maybe I should start studying outside.

Katy met me at the entrance, holding the door open for me so it wouldn't lock us both out. When she told me we were going to meet in Drew's room, my stomach did a massive somersault. How is he in Science Club? I've never heard him answer a single question in chemistry. Of course, everyone here at Prescott is a genius, or at least that's what their glossy brochures try to tell you.

We walked up three flights of stairs and into a dorm room that looked a bit like mine, only it had window seats and a slanted ceiling on account of the room being on the top floor. I guess I expected the room to be gross and smelly, like frat houses in movies or something, but Drew's room was tidy and, maybe I'm mistaken, but I think it had been professionally decorated. It kind of looked like the reading room at the New York Public Library. Soft lighting, dark wood furniture, everything just a little gilded.

Drew was smoking a cigarette on one of the window seats, the window wide open, no screen. He took a big puff and then handed what was left of it to a boy who sat on the floor by his feet. And while Drew looked like he'd stepped out of a Burberry ad, the other boy was every bit the geeky kind of person I'd been hoping to meet since I got here. Like a lankier but more rugged Harry Potter, the boy took the cigarette, braced it between his lips, and stood, extending his hand to me.

He introduced himself like James Bond. "Clark, Warren Clark," he said. Crystal blue eyes locked onto mine and didn't look away, even when I did. Drew started talking about me,

10

about how I really knew my stuff in chemistry class. He said Warren was just like me that way. That, and Warren is a scholarship student too. I told them I'm not on scholarship and they acted totally surprised until I told them that my stepmother is Isabelle Marlowe, which made Drew chuckle, and Katy said her own father had been up against Isa and lost on more than one occasion. Then Drew started talking about how Katy's father had represented his in some sort of embezzlement charge and got him out of it with just community service, and then everyone was talking about people I didn't know, places I'd never been to, and stories I wasn't a part of. Weekend trips to sunny beaches, cabins in the Berkshires, wrecking a Porsche and getting a replacement the next day. And they were funny but I felt even more out of place than ever. Even Warren has history at Prescott. It sounds like he spends a lot of time with Drew, and spends just as much money. He didn't mention having a job, but maybe he does. How else does he have that kind of money?

But at some point I noticed he was looking at me again, his blue eyes kind but intense. I met his gaze and did my best to smile back.

At no point did we talk about chemistry, or even science.

When Katy walked me back to my dorm, she hooked her arm through mine and tossed her gorgeous hair over her shoulder and told me I was welcome at the next meeting. I feel like I passed some sort of test I didn't even know I was taking. Of course I told her I'd go.

September 11

I guess I thought Katy would invite me to sit with them at lunch, but she didn't. They only nodded slightly as I passed by their table on the way to sit with Emily. Warren was wearing a beanie, which is against the uniform code, but I get the feeling that the so-called Science Club can get away with anything. I've asked a few other people about Drew. Turns out his family owns most of the neighboring town of Wiltshire, so I bet the headmaster is afraid to touch him. He flat-out put his head down and slept during chemistry today, and Mr. Callahan didn't do anything about it. And I looked out the window during civics this morning and Warren was sitting in a tree, feet and overcoat dangling, smoking a cigarette. Smoking on campus, sleeping during class, skipping classes . . . All of those things are against the rules at Prescott, but I haven't seen Drew or his friends face any consequences.

Oh, and Warren is in English with me. Or he's supposed to be, when he bothers to come. I didn't realize that because I guess he always sits in the back, and I always sit in the front and don't turn around much because I'm trying so hard to focus on the merits of Shakespeare. (Okay, I actually hate Shakespeare. I know it's a necessary evil in school, like eating four servings of vegetables every day, but really. So stuffy. No wonder I have to focus so hard. Everything else I can ace in my sleep, but not Shakespeare. Oh no. He demands undivided attention.)

I asked Emily about Warren. She told me he was a scholarship student, which I already knew, and that he's from her hometown. She said nothing about his personality, and I could be wrong, but I think maybe she doesn't like him. There was something kind of cold in her eyes when she talked about him. When I pressed her further, all she said was that he spent last summer at Princeton in some sort of science program, so he'll probably go there when he graduates.

Well, at least one person in the Science Club seems to like science.

September 13

I feel like maybe I'm getting the hang of Prescott. I mean, I still wear my Payless shoes, but I'm getting used to everyone being so rich. And I feel like I can kind of fake it, or at least play along when I have to.

The classes aren't as hard as I expected, either. It's a lot more work than my old school, and I feel like all I do at night is homework, but it's not harder, really. It's just like they expect more. It's kind of weird not having parents around. You'd think everyone would slack off with no one telling them what to do. But everyone seems to try harder because of it. I even keep my side of the room clean. Well, sometimes.

Mr. Callahan had me stay after school and balance some really challenging chemical equations today. He didn't tell me I did well—I think compliments are going to be hard to come by with him—but he was smiling ear to ear when he checked my work. I asked him about the Science Club. He just chuckled like I'd said something funny and told me I didn't need a club. Then he told me I didn't have to do the chemistry homework tonight. I might have some free time!

September 14

I don't even know where to start today.

Emily and I were about to go to dinner when Katy showed up and told me it was time for the meeting. I felt really bad leaving Emily to eat alone, but I had a feeling that if I turned Katy down, I'd never get a chance to hang out with her again. I'd be out of the club, so to speak, and I just can't give up this chance. It will be so nice to have a group again. Somewhere I belong. I hope Emily isn't too mad.

So we get outside and I start walking in the direction of

Herschell Hall, and Katy grabs my arm and turns me in the opposite direction, almost off campus, to a building that looks like it hasn't been used in years. It's creepy as hell. The old walls kind of sag in places, several of the windows are busted out, and there are no streetlights in sight. It looks sort of like a big, yawning stone monster.

Me: Here? Is this even Prescott's building?

Katy: Of course. We use the old science building for our meetings. Come on. I promise there are no ghosts.

Me: Not my main concern. More scared of rats, live wires, dead bodies . . .

Katy just laughed and pulled me through the doors. We went down some stairs and a beautiful smell hit me. Chemicals! It was GORGEOUS down there. There's a fully equipped lab. Something simmered and steamed and hissed pleasantly on a burner. Tubes and beakers and vials and jars and all kinds of equipment lined the shelves and was scattered on old lab tables.

Okay, and I admit it. An even prettier sight was Drew and Warren, both of them in lab coats, hair pulled back by the goggles they'd pushed above their foreheads. They were leaning over the simmering brew, looking like they knew exactly what the hell they were doing. To a girl who loves chemistry, there's nothing hotter.

Drew smiled at me, but it was Warren who met my gaze and, with a slight jerk of his head, beckoned me over. I don't know why, maybe it was because I finally felt like I wasn't so out of my element, but I walked right up to him and asked him what he was working on.

When he answered, the room spun. I can't believe I'm going to write this. I should definitely get a lock for this thing.

Drugs. Warren was working on making crystal meth. That's what he said.

And I laughed because I was sure he was joking, but he wasn't. Katy started explaining what they do, how they sell to local dealers, and how the area around Prescott is kind of depressed and has a lot of addicts, so it's easy money. Warren said he needed the cash to get by, and it sounds like he's the real talent. Katy and Drew make the sales and manage distribution. They explained it to me like it was no big deal. Like it's completely normal to do something so illegal. Like it's just a little side business like making decorative wreaths for Etsy.

It was so surreal. The more they talked, the more I felt like I was dreaming or I was the butt of a terrible joke. As they explained, my ears started ringing and I couldn't breathe. And I didn't say good-bye or anything. I just ran out of the building and all the way back to my dorm.

Diary, I need to hide you now.

September 14 again, later

I could be imagining it, but I swear Emily knows. I keep catching her looking at me like she's suspicious or something. And again she warned me to stay away from Drew. This time she threw Katy's name in there too. Do you think she knows what the Science Club is up to? I wonder if I should tell her? I mean, of course I shouldn't. I don't want to get Warren or any of the Science Club in trouble, but this is just . . . too much. Telling her would be a relief. Someone to share the load, so to speak.

I guess I'm telling this diary, though. It can be the secret keeper for me, since obviously telling someone is out of the question. And I'll definitely have a lot to tell if these first few weeks here are any indication. Sheesh. What a strange place Prescott is.

September 15

I tried to avoid Warren when I saw him in the hallway but he wouldn't let me. He asked if we could talk and then pulled me into an empty classroom.

Warren: Are you okay?

Me: How could I be?

Warren: Look, I know it's a lot to handle, but it's not what you're thinking. It's really not that bad at all.

Me: Oh really? What's not bad about making drugs to sell to the poor addicts in town?

Warren, looking at me like I'm adorable for having a conscience: They'd do it anyway, Bailey. At least if they get it from us, it's safe. We're not like those guys that throw poisonous fillers in to make more money and end up getting their clients killed.

Me: Clients? Is that what you call them?

Warren: It's business, so yes. But not like you see on TV, okay? No cartels, no one who's going to shoot your kneecaps or something

18

for breaking a deal. No one is dissolving dead
bodies in bathtubs. We just provide a product
and make a sale.

Me: With people buying who are slowly
killing themselves.

Warren, with a huge, impatient sigh: If
someone wants to eat burgers and fries for
every meal and they die of a heart attack, it's
not the manager at McDonald's who is to
blame, is it?

I still felt uneasy, but I had to concede that point. Then
Warren started talking about how much he can use the
money. I get the impression his parents aren't in the picture
anymore, but he didn't seem to want to explain why, just that
they don't help him financially. And Princeton is going to be
incredibly expensive. But he hopes he can eventually become
a scientist who could find a cure for addiction. I'm not sure
if it's hypocritical or just poetic that that's what he wants
to work for, but I assured him I won't tell anyone about the
Club.

He asked me if I'd come by the lab again. Apparently they're short one chemist after a Science Club member graduated last year, and Warren can't do it all.

I told him I'd think about it, but how can I even consider this?

September 16

I got to talk to Bex! Turns out Isa got her a phone so that she can call home, and she called me, too! She sounds super happy at Campbell. It also sounds like she's popular. She rambled on about all the kids she's friends with. Doesn't surprise me. Bex is the opposite of me in a lot of ways. She's really extroverted, athletic (she's going to be playing soccer for Campbell's junior girls team), and even though she's ten and should be kind of awkward, she's not at all. I got all the awkwardness, I guess. But Bex never makes straight As like me, so I'm fine with the way the current flowed in the gene pool.

She asked how I'm doing, and I told her about Emily, and I told her there are some cute boys in my class. Of course I didn't mention the Science Club. There are some things that even Bex can't know about me, and I wouldn't want her to know this. She'd be disappointed. Or worried. Or both. That's the last thing either of us needs.

Before we hung up, Bex told me she wishes she could tell Mom about Campbell. I told her to tell Mom anyway. Is it silly to think she listens? Probably. Probably clichéd, too. I don't think there's anything about Prescott I want to tell Mom yet, but I did put her picture in this journal. There's a little pocket in the inside of the back cover where I can keep it safe and sound.

Maybe, in a way, I'm *am* telling her things.

September 17

Warren came to my room. I opened the door and he was smiling in that reserved way of his, and he asked if he could show me something. Super weird—Emily, who was doing homework, barely even looked at Warren. He didn't say anything to her, either. It was like they were trying really hard not to notice the other. What is up with that?

I went with him, even though I still had homework to do. The members of the Science Club have been a little cold to me since I ran out of their lab the other night, and I wanted to at least prove to them that I'm not going to rat them out, even if I didn't join them.

Neither of us was in uniform, since classes were over. I was in jeans and a comfy tee. Warren was wearing his long overcoat, even though it wasn't that chilly out. I asked him why he always wears it. He said it belonged to his brother but didn't say any more. I didn't press. I barely know him but I can tell talking about his family is off-limits.

It didn't take me long to figure out that Warren was leading me to the lab. When I hesitated, it was as if he read my mind. Not breaking eye contact once, he told me there was nothing to be afraid of. The rest of the Science Club wouldn't even know I was there. That the decision was completely up to me and there was no harm in just coming in and learning.

Going with him wasn't a commitment. It was just . . . learning. And I thought that maybe it could help me decide.

In the lab there's a station for every step of the process, so that they can have multiple batches cooking at once. He said he makes it a point to stop by every few hours during the day, and that for the most part, nothing is running at night. Apparently the old building has most of the equipment they needed. It's the ingredients they get elsewhere. Whatever money is left after reinvesting in ingredients, that's what the Science Club gets to keep, and apparently there's generally a lot left over. He explained a bit about the group dynamics, how they absolutely trust each other, always, 100 percent, and are completely loyal and dedicated to each other. Warren gets the biggest cut, since he's the brains of the operation and has the biggest job. Drew and Katy make the deals, handle the logistics, things like that. That Warren makes a lot of money became evident the more he talked. Underneath that dingy overcoat, everything he wears is designer. He doesn't seem like the type of person who actually cares about brand names, but then, if he's making as much as he intimated, I can't blame him for buying the best. Goodness knows my first purchase would be better clothes.

As Warren explained the chemicals, the reactions, and the methods to what he was doing at each station, I realized something: This is just chemistry. All of it. I could almost forget what we were making, and what it was meant to do, when we were talking about formulas and ratios. It's actually fascinating. The things I'd done for Miss Beverly were like this, but making meth is even more involved. More nuanced, even. Warren talked about how he's constantly coming up with new ways to produce it more efficiently or more cleanly, and I could feel myself getting excited too. His passion was contagious, and it was the same passion as mine. This is what I like to do. It's what I want to do with my life, really. I want to make the world a better place, one ion at a time.

I started asking questions, and Warren was really eager to talk about everything. And he actually wanted my opinions. We started bouncing ideas off each other. Warren almost became a different person. Instead of reserved and stoic, he became animated and witty. We joked, and laughed, and it felt so good to have someone who had the same type of brain that I do. I honestly forgot about the final product until I was back here, in my room.

As I'm writing I'm realizing something, though . . . Warren never pressured me to join the Science Club. Not once the whole night. In fact, he didn't even bring up me joining. I have to admit, the money would be nice, but more importantly, the group itself would welcome me in. It's not just that the Science Club is so mysterious and glamourous, it's that they clearly look out for one another. Their loyalty is fierce.

Loyalty is something I need, I think. After Mom's death, some friends fled from my grief, some stuck around for a while but ultimately couldn't handle it; even my own father abandoned me. Knowing that this group wouldn't do that, even if the reason has to be kept a secret, is so tempting.

Maybe it wouldn't have to be permanent, either. Maybe I can do this, just for a while, just until they find someone else. Long enough to get to know Warren some more, and maybe earn a spot in their tight-knit circle. Maybe I can even give Warren some advice on how to perfect the product, without actually doing it myself. Maybe this might work.

September 20

At breakfast, I asked Emily about Warren. Why she doesn't seem to like him. She shrugged and said he was just kind of a jerk. I don't know what's up with this school and everyone acting like everything's a big secret.

I had lunch with Emily, but Katy brought over a wrapped brownie for me. It had a note attached:

(Katy's note, taped to the diary page, in Katy's girly handwriting):

> *Drew's driving into Wiltshire tonight. Want to go*
> *with and shop? I need new shoes. Herschell Hall, 6 p.m.*
> *Shh, don't tell.*

I doubt Katy needs new shoes. Not in the same way I need new shoes. And I have no money to spend, but this isn't about shopping. And it's a secret.

Looks like I've got secrets too.

September 20, again.

I'm back from shopping with Katy and Drew, and oh my God, you should see the shopping bags sitting here. I can't even believe how many there are and what stores they're from. I feel like I'm a movie star or something.

At Prescott there are specific rules to going off campus. Only upperclassmen are allowed to, and you have to be back before curfew. You can't spend the night elsewhere, and you cannot go to what our rule book calls "unsavory establishments." I'm assuming that means bars. It could mean brothels and strip clubs too. Ha. I guess it's kind of a catch-all rule for that purpose. Very clever.

So Drew's car. I mean, I have to say something about it. I don't like to think of myself as a shallow, materialistic person, but maybe that's just because I've never had a car like this. It's nicer than Isa's, even. Drew said his dad bought it for him for his birthday last year. That's just amazing. I think I got a gift card to Bath & Body Works. Anyway, it's this dark silver sporty thing. Hardly a backseat, but I didn't mind. It seriously sounded like a race car as we roared down the country roads we had to take to get into town.

Drew dropped us off at the mall. When I asked Katy if he didn't want to shop with us girls, she said that he had business to take care of. I know, of course, what that meant. Drew was going to check in with the dealers, maybe even drop off the, um, product. I hadn't thought of that. If he'd been pulled over for speeding and the car had been searched . . . I got kind of sick thinking about it, but . . . I felt a bit thrilled at the idea. Like we'd gotten away with something. I asked Katy if they are afraid of getting into trouble. She obviously didn't want to talk about it in public. She whispered and looked around nervously as she answered, but she said they aren't. That between her father being a lawyer and Drew's dad owning a good chunk of the town, they figure they'd get a slap on the wrist at most.

Then she bought me a pair of flats like hers. When I protested, she held up her hand and said she likes to buy her friends things. She also noted, somehow not unkindly, that I could use a better pair. And she wouldn't hear of me trying to pay her back. She repeated that at four different stores, big department stores that I usually don't even go into. I have a new wool coat, a makeup palette specifically matched to me from a glitzy-looking makeup counter, some hair products that Katy promised would make my frizzy hair smooth, and some new sweaters for our days out of uniform. Every time, Katy took out a credit card that had her name on it. She never minds paying for quality, she said. But I'm not sure if she really meant herself or her father. Who pays the credit card bill?

We met Drew outside one of the department stores. Katy asked if he'd been successful, which he answered by showing her a huge wad of cash. He said we should go eat somewhere fancy, so we did.

He chose a place with a French name, which turns out is owned by his family. The staff called him "Mr. Richmond" the whole time and kept bringing us complimentary appetizers and glasses of wine. *Real* wine, not like the sugary cheap stuff my friends from home would get if their older siblings were in a good enough mood to buy for us. I find it kind of hilarious that they were complimentary, since the whole meal was on the house, or on Drew's house, I guess. I had thought his father owned only a few fast-food chains, but Drew explained that they'd bought some nice restaurants all around the state as well.

They did ask me to join the Science Club again. In a way. Katy and Drew talked about the advantages to having disposable income and not ever having to ask their parents for money. And of course it's good to have nice things: brand names, high-end makeup, trendy clothes. I had to agree. If I do this with them, I'd never have to ask Dad (or worse, Isa) for anything. I might even be able to buy stuff for Bex. And if what Katy said is true, I won't have to worry about getting into trouble. I can't afford to have a record if I want into Harvard.

It's no problem, Drew said when I asked about getting into trouble again. There's no way their families would ever let them get a record. Drew and Katy both have their eyes on Yale. They can't afford trouble either, and with Warren wanting to get into Princeton, it has to be the same with him.

By the time we got back to Prescott, I was feeling much better about the Science Club. I asked them when the next meeting is. Katy and Drew seemed incredibly happy that I was interested.

Emily looked at my (Katy's) purchases and seemed curious. I told her I'd gone shopping with Katy Ashton and her eyes almost bugged out of her head. She told me to be careful around Katy. She said Katy only *seems* nice. I think Emily's just jealous, honestly. The more I hang out with Katy, the more I like her. But I have to admit, I'm afraid she won't like me back. I know she bought me all this stuff, but I feel like I have to impress her somehow, if that makes sense. Drew, too, although now that I've talked to Warren more, I think Warren is definitely the cuter one. Maybe not as classically handsome, but definitely smarter and more intriguing. There seem to be a lot of Drews around here, but there's clearly only one Warren.

September 22

Another Friday night with no invite to a party, but that's okay. I know it's just because there aren't any parties, at least any I'd want to go to. I heard Drew tell Katy in chemistry that they need to do a lot of work this weekend, so I know they're at the lab. I could probably join them, but I'm still not sure I want to. Plus I kind of feel like I haven't fully been accepted yet. I don't know how or when I will be, but I'm almost 100 percent sure I'll have to prove myself. Like an initiation or blood oath or something. Or maybe I've seen one too many mob films. Still, I have no doubt that they are serious about secrecy and loyalty, so with all I know, they have to make sure I'm not going to rat.

Emily and I skipped the dining hall and ordered a pizza and did our movie thing again. She has a whole collection of DVDs. She keeps them in one of those old-school flip albums like my dad has to store his CDs. She organizes them by director, not alphabetically or even by genre. I let her choose tonight. She decided on a movie called *High Fidelity*, which I'd never seen before, but I can see why she likes it. The main character reminded me of her a little because he was so into music, but in this cool way, like he could recall the history of the songs he liked and random trivia about musicians. Emily is like that with movies.

After the movie we sat around talking. She asked me about my mom and I told her a few things. Then she asked me what happened to her. And it's okay. I mean, I'm used to getting asked, I guess, and it's nice that she cares. I told her about how Mom was driving me to get some school supplies. Luckily, Bex was home with Dad. We had a green light. Mom even looked both ways before she started to go through the intersection. She was always cautious like that. It was just that this other car was so fast. And the driver was texting, not paying any attention. She hit Mom's side of the car and we spun so hard that I hit my head on my window. I passed out. At the hospital I was told I had a concussion. I was also told Mom didn't make it, but they didn't have to tell me. I remembered—still remember—every detail of the last time I saw her alive. The side of the car was folded in over her. She was covered in sticky red. It smelled like metal and burning. Her mouth was open, frozen in a scream. She didn't answer me when I called out to her, before I lost consciousness.

I didn't actually tell Emily the gruesome parts and I don't know why I wrote it down just now. I guess it feels good to write it, like something I needed to get off my chest. The girl who was texting walked away with hardly more than a scratch, like she hadn't irrevocably changed anyone's life. That girl is still alive. I am too. At least, mostly alive. I've heard people say that a part of themselves died when they lost someone they loved. I'm not sure any of me died with her. But I am sure that I'll never be the same. It's been two years now and I still don't really feel like myself. I managed to keep my grades up, and I went through the motions at school, but I didn't make any friends. The ones I had got tired of me being not much more than a zombie who did homework. I never went out with them anymore. Pretty soon I just wasn't invited. I'd like to say it hurt, but it didn't. Not really. I was kind of relieved that I didn't have to act normal around anyone.

Dad was kind of like me, too. He'd be better around Bex, because Bex needed both of us to show her that we were okay, that we were all okay, or we were going to be. But when it was just us, Dad and I were the same. Until Isa came around. Then Dad wasn't just pretending that things were fine, he actually was fine. He pulled himself out of the hole we'd made for ourselves and cleaned up the house, bought new furniture, got rid of Mom's clothes, and, I noticed, he took down the pictures of Mom in his room. Meanwhile, I kept her picture by my bed and slept with her pillowcase on my pillow, still deep in the grieving hole. And I guess that's what I'm mad about most. Not that Dad found someone new or even that he's over Mom. Just that he left me behind, and now it feels like I'm the only one still grieving.

I didn't tell Emily any of that, either. She started talking about movies where moms die, like they could be some kind of therapy for me. It's sweet of her, in her own nerdy film-buff way, but I don't need therapy. I don't need movies. I just need Mom back. Failing that, because of course I can't have her back, not being alone would be nice. And now that I think about it, having new friends who know nothing about my mom . . . Honestly, it would be kind of a relief. A fresh start. I could eliminate the sad elephant in the room and just try to be Bailey again.

I think maybe I should just flat-out ask Katy what I need to do to become an official member of the Science Club. It would be amazing to be part of a group again. I had a decent-sized group of friends back home. Two of them, Jess and Anna, had been my friends since first grade. Evan, Cat, P.J., and Chelsea were added in middle school, and we oddly stuck together through high school. I thought they were going to be there through thick and thin, but I realized that wasn't going to happen after Mom died.

I can't really blame them for not understanding, and they were just amazing before then. Very accepting of my know-it-all-ness and Ivy League ambitions, even if they would have rather spent their nights driving around aimlessly in the country and hardly ever read books unless they were for school. As fun as they were, though, it would be great to have a group of friends with ambition like mine, and of course the chemistry part of it would be fun. Plus, well, Warren. Maybe it's too soon to say this, but I think there's a connection there. I can already see how great it would be to have a boyfriend who wants to go to Princeton and loves learning and chemistry. Back home, I think it intimidated most of the guys I knew, how focused I was on college. And let's face it, if I join, I'd certainly never have to be lonely, because it's clear the Science Club takes care of their own. And if my mom's death taught me anything, it's that being lonely and not understood is the worst thing in the world.

I guess I've made up my mind.

September 24

I found out what the Science Club initiation is.

I went to the lab again. It was Sunday afternoon and I was bored. Emily was elsewhere—she didn't tell me where she was going. I assume the library, or Prescott's AV room. I'd finished all my homework, even the extra set of formulas Mr. Callahan had me work through. There was nothing to do except watch sitcom reruns or read, and the rest of the dorm was too quiet. I threw on one of my new sweaters and went to the old science building.

The doors outside were locked, but I could see lights on through the frosted glass of the basement windows. I knocked as loud as I could. Katy laughed when she opened the door and saw me there.

Katy: Password?

Me: Um, *labor omnia improba vincit*?

Katy: You honestly think Prescott's motto is going to be our password?

Me, stuttering: Um, okay. Etlay emay inyay, easeplay.

Katy, smiling: Glad to see you here, Bailey. We were hoping you'd join us. You do want to join us, right? (I nodded.) There's something we need from you before you do, though.

Me: Is this the initiation?

Katy laughed, like I was such a kidder, but she got serious really quickly. Then she explained what they needed from me.

Collateral. They need something to make sure that I won't rat them out. Something to make the consequences horrific for me if I did.

And as Katy explained exactly what I needed to do, I started to realize exactly how horrific.

She must have been able to see my thoughts on my face because she told me to think it over and to come back when I was sure.

I don't know how I could ever be sure of this.

September 25

Something truly weird just happened. Emily and I were doing homework after dinner when there was a knock at the door. She went to open it, and there was a package sitting in the hallway. No one was there. Pretty handwriting on the top announced that the package was for me.

It was wrapped in simple brown paper and tied with twine, like an old-fashioned Christmas present. I opened it immediately. Inside there were two chemistry textbooks. Textbooks I know plain well are used at Harvard. Both are written by professors there.

Emily asked me if they were from Mr. Callahan, but they're not. I know exactly who they're from.

September 27

This has been, by far, my best day at Prescott, and I owe it to the Science Club. It was like they planned a wooing coup (God, that sounds ridiculous, but I don't know what else to call it). I don't have much time because Katy's going to be here in about twenty minutes to go get coffee and study for our civics quiz, but here are the highlights:

Warren showed up after my first class with a cup of coffee for me. He walked me to my next class, looked me straight in the eye and told me it was great to see me again, then walked away. Swoon. For such a chemistry geek, he has swagger for DAYS.

At lunch I walked by the Glamorous Table like usual, but this time they waved me over to them. And then they slid over and made room. Just like that. It was SO COOL.

Katy taught me how to use lip liner between third and fourth period. Then she gave me one of her dark lipsticks. It was Chanel. I told her I couldn't possibly accept it, since they're so expensive, and she just shrugged and said, "Please. That's pocket change compared to what we make in a week in the Club." And then she asked me to get coffee with her tonight.

Drew announced to the whole class that I am brilliant with chemistry. He actually called me the Chemistry Queen. It was embarrassing and also amazing and I think some of the girls wanted to kill me.

Emily is gone again. No idea where she goes, but I'm okay with that for now. She isn't happy that I ditched her at lunch, I don't think. But I did ask everyone if she could join us. Warren said no, absolutely not. I feel really terrible about that. Emily doesn't seem to have many friends here at Prescott. She's not exactly a pariah, but I don't think she MEANS to be a loner either. Maybe something happened with her before . . . like maybe she used to have a lot of friends but they don't talk to her anymore for some reason. Which leads me to the next point:

I'm beginning to feel like maybe Emily and Warren used to date or something? I can't help but wonder . . . Why does Warren seem to dislike her so much, and vice versa? Must ask Katy later.

I promise I'll write more tomorrow, but for now, all I can say is I feel like I'm "in." And it's wonderful. The best I've felt in ages. And I can't be out again. I just can't.

I know what I have to do.

September 30

This time when I showed up at the old science building, it felt like everything had changed. Everyone was a lot more serious, but I also felt a lot more welcome. Like I belonged.

Drew helped me give them what they needed for collateral. I feel this weird sense of trust with him now. And I know he will use it only if absolutely necessary. But I also feel like he was completely understanding about how hard it was and how scary. I feel like he truly cares.

Katy and Warren hugged me, and we all promised to protect one another. Then they gave me a new lab coat and a pair of goggles. Warren took my hand (!!!!) and led me over to the first station, and my first official lesson in making meth began.

Over the next three hours, I was on a different planet. It was just us and the reactions of chemicals, the only real magic there is. But to be honest, it wasn't even about the chemistry. Or that what we were doing was going to make us rich. It was that I felt like a part of something, and not just any part, but a truly integral part. I felt needed and wanted.

And when we were done, Warren walked me back to my dorm. :)

October 3

I managed to do two steps of the process completely by myself tonight. Warren stood there watching me, like a proud parent or something. And I was proud of myself too. In a way this is some of the hardest chemistry I've ever done. It's not that I can't understand it. No, it makes perfect sense the way the chemicals mix and break down and react. It's just that everything has to be perfect and precise; otherwise it won't be Science Club–worthy. Apparently there's some competition that isn't so careful and doesn't produce excellent results every time, but the Science Club prides itself on being consistently superior. That's our gimmick, if it can be called that and if our specific type of product can have gimmicks.

Warren handled the rest himself, but I could tell he was happy and maybe a little bit surprised at how well I did. He said he'd be back tomorrow, same time, and would love it if I could help. Of course I agreed. He walked me home again.

Emily asked me if I'd been with Warren and I told her yes. She didn't say anything else, but she seemed so judgmental about it. Maybe even angry. She told me she had to run to the AV building and left, but I think she was just trying to get away from me for a while.

I'm going to have to talk to her about it. I like Emily and I want to get along, especially since she seems so lonely, but Warren is a part of my life now. Hopefully he will be an even bigger part. I need to figure out why she dislikes him so much. I hope it's not something that will be a Big Deal or anything. I'd like to be her friend, but I can't be as isolated as she is. I can't go back to that, and I can't let whatever happened to her dictate my friends here at Prescott. I need people.

Oh, also, Drew told me tonight how much of a cut I'm getting.

Yeah. I'm going to be able to buy all the flats I want.

October 5

Mr. Callahan had me stay after class again today. He wants me to apply for a chemistry program for high school students that would mean spending most of my summer at Princeton. Of course I was flattered and I said yes, but I have to admit, part of me is super excited about possibly spending the summer with Warren. Or near him, if he's still doing the science program there. Perhaps it's even the same program?

Mr. Callahan said I'd have to keep my grades up in all subjects because entry is determined by GPA and a few other things, like an essay about your career goals and recommendations from teachers. I'll be fine in everything but English, so I'm going to have to work extra hard in that. I know, I know. I write all the time in this thing, but give me a literary metaphor to explain or a story's theme to dissect and I cannot put a proper sentence together to save my life. I'd much rather deal with numbers and formulas. Even the guesswork with those is logical. English makes no sense!

I've been in the Science Club lab almost every night this week. It's mostly just me and Warren who cook, but Drew sometimes pulls out some rubber gloves and helps. Katy, for the most part, is just there to keep us company and to talk to our customers. Last night she quizzed me on *Macbeth* while I worked. When I got the answer wrong, Drew would make this annoying buzzer sound and shout out the right one. Apparently his talents lie in the written word. It was funny and made studying tolerable, but I got too many wrong. I'm going to have to study hard for the midterm.

When Drew and Katy left, I asked Warren if they were together. They seem to be a little . . . overfamiliar sometimes. Warren laughed and rolled his eyes and said that they weren't together, in spite of themselves. I told him I was sure most of the girls at Prescott would be relieved to hear that.

> Warren, quietly: Yeah. Drew never lacks attention from the girls. Hell, some of the boys.

> Me: Well, he's cute and smart and charismatic. That's everyone's type, right?

> Warren, even more quietly: And is it your type?

> Me, with a shy but hopefully suggestive glance in his direction: No. I prefer stoic over charismatic, actually.

> Warren, smiling and looking down at his hands: Noted.

We were quiet and kind of awkward after that, but when he walked me back to my dorm, he put his arm around me. He was warm, and I fit so well, and he smelled great, like subtle spices and ocean waves. Probably a very expensive cologne. I have to admit, I've never had a boyfriend before, just a few flirtations that amounted to nothing in the end, so I didn't know what to expect. Would he try to kiss me? Would he go for the mouth or just the cheek? Or should I kiss him? I was super nervous and even more nervous since I didn't know what to do. In the end, he didn't try to kiss me, he didn't even hug me, but it's okay. Honestly, just his arm around me was the sexiest thing I've ever experienced in my life.

October 6

Well, I officially feel terrible. I think Emily assumed we'd be spending another Friday night watching movies and eating popcorn. She started talking to me this morning at breakfast about possible themes for tonight and I had to break it to her that I actually have plans with Katy. I mean, she took it okay, but I could see she was disappointed. She just kind of sat there drinking her orange juice quietly.

Then she said: So are you part of their group now?

Me, trying to keep my face neutral: What
group?

Emily: You know. Katy and those guys. Drew
and Warren.

I noticed she didn't call them the Science Club, but she
could have just been keeping that a secret, like I'm supposed to.
I told her that yeah, I guess I'm part of their group now, and she
asked me why I'd want to be.

Me: Why not? They're fun. And smart.

Emily: And snobby. They're only friends with
themselves. They don't hang out with anyone
else. I'm really surprised they let you in, no
offense.

I defended them, of course, which only made Emily double
down. Again, I had to wonder if Emily had been cast out of a
social group, maybe even the Science Club itself, by the way
she was acting. The weird thing was, I realized she's right:
I'd never seen any of them associate with anyone outside the
Science Club. They talk to other people here at Prescott, but

it's not like they'd ever invite them anywhere with us. Half the time we're in the lab.

I wonder how much of it is really snobbery and how much is just secret keeping?

I do feel bad, though. Emily reminds me a lot of me at my old school, without any real friends. What I could STILL be if I hadn't decided to join the Science Club, I guess. At least I have them now, and thank goodness for that, but Emily doesn't seem to have anyone.

I think I smoothed things over by offering to spend most of Sunday watching movies with her, but I'm not sure. I didn't sit with her at lunch. I didn't see her at lunchtime at all, actually, and I probably wouldn't have sat with her anyway. Warren patted the seat next to him when he saw me walking through with my tray, and draped his arm over the back of my chair. Katy raised a brow and gave me a look, so I guess we'll be talking about *that* tonight.

October 7

I feel awful, but I think last night was so worth it. We met at the lab, me and Katy. Drew and Warren were already there. Warren looked AH-mazing. He was wearing this dusty-blue turtleneck sweater, all studious and preppy and sexy. How does anyone manage to make a turtleneck look hot? And it was super soft.

Cashmere, he said. Some brand name he told me that I don't remember. All I know is that when I leaned against him, it felt so wonderful on my cheek.

Drew passed out our shares. My first "paycheck." I can't even believe how much money I have right now. New shoes are definitely a must, and maybe something for Bex. Maybe I can even get Drew to drive me over to Campbell and give it to her in person.

Then Drew brought out a bottle of champagne and we toasted the "new" Science Club and our first payday together. Warren and I checked on the progress of our latest batch and it was good to go, so we went to Drew's room and he had even more champagne there waiting for us. It was so classy. Honestly, just being around them makes me feel cool by proxy. And considering what Emily said yesterday, I kind of feel lucky to call them friends. They don't let just anybody in, after all, and they chose *me* for some reason. And I don't think it's just for my chemistry skills because Katy asks me to hang out, no chemistry involved, and Warren . . .

I don't know. Sometimes he looks at me in this way that makes me tingle all over. I'm rolling my eyes at writing this because I can't stand puns, but really, with him it's all a different kind of chemistry.

I had a lot of champagne. I swear, the bottles just kept

appearing, and I clearly don't have the experience with alcohol that they do. They acted like it was nothing, like they do this every day, so I kept the slight scandalized feeling I had to myself. I felt light-headed after my second, and we were all laughing like idiots. I don't even remember most of what we talked about. Okay, I do remember doing a pretty nasty impression of Isa once, and they gave me a standing ovation for it. And I *definitely* remember sort of settling against Warren at some point, his arm around me again, his soft sweater and his warmth. The next thing I knew, he was gently waking me up, telling me I should probably get back to my dorm before we all got caught. He was smiling so sweetly at me as I struggled to keep my eyes open, and I was so grateful that he was looking out for me.

I didn't really want to leave Warren there all snuggly and warm, but getting caught would be ugly. So Katy and I left. I somehow managed to get in without waking Emily and fell asleep. Now my head is pounding and the thought of eating breakfast is horrifying. But . . . I have money, I have friends, I have (maybe only kinda sorta) Warren. I have found my place, and it's probably the coolest place at Prescott. I will deal with a hangover every day if I get to have nights like that.

And now back to bed I go.

October 7, later

Drew picked up pizza tonight, so we took a break from chemicals and chowed down. A batch was nearly done, so he'd been out taking orders, so to speak, and it looked like our next paycheck was going to be pretty great as well.

We were sitting there, no sounds but chewing and bubbling chemicals, when a thought occurred to me.

> Me: So, how do we *know* this is quality? I mean, Warren and I have been making some subtle changes, but how do we know it's working? That it's making our, um, recipe better?

> Drew, around a mouthful of pizza: A couple of the sellers are also users. Not badly enough that we should be worried about them holding up their end of the bargain, but enough to dip in every now and then. They give us feedback.

Seemed like a decent system, with no danger of any of us getting hooked or anything, but I was curious about what we'd been busy making. What was it like? What did it make you feel? What did it DO?

Me, looking at all of them: But have any of you ever tried it?

Katy, laughing: Not me, but these two idiots have.

Warren, with a shrug: We thought we'd better know, is all.

Me: And . . . ? What's it like?

Drew and Warren exchange a glance. Then, Warren: I felt like it gave me superpowers. I felt smarter and faster and stronger.

Drew, nodding: Totally like superpowers. The comedown sucked, though. You instantly miss feeling powerful. Did you want to try it, Bailey?

Of course I said no. I know I'm the world's biggest hypocrite here, but anything that could make you addicted terrifies me. I don't even understand how someone could inhale something or stick a needle in their arm knowing they might not ever want to stop. It scares me a little that the boys have tried it, that they've risked addiction or even flirted with the idea of it. They seem so rational and in control, and they certainly don't seem like the type to do drugs. Just make them.

How does that even make sense in my head? But it does. Drew and Warren are too smart to be addicts, I'm sure of it, and maybe that's why they felt like they could try it. I wanted to ask them more, but I also . . . didn't want to know more. I don't like thinking of either of them like that.

We worked until about one in the morning and crept home. I promised Emily the movie day tomorrow, and I'm glad I did. I could use a day to just relax.

October 8

Emily and I had a really good time watching movies, and we went to dinner together. She talked to me about her parents (both are teachers, both pretty strict, but both encourage her to write). She's an only child, so her parents are her entire family. I can't imagine that. I love Bex so much, it almost makes me feel sorry for Emily even more, that she doesn't have a little sister to share with. Maybe I'm just lucky that Bex is so awesome and we're far enough apart that we hardly ever fight.

Afterward, we helped each other with homework. There was a chemistry question I got stuck on and nearly texted Warren for help, but thought better of it. He hasn't texted or even mentioned how I fell asleep on him the other night, but maybe he's trying not to embarrass me. Maybe he's trying to gently show me he's not interested? I don't know. It's just that I thought for sure he was thinking what I was thinking, but he hasn't really made a move, other than putting his arm around me. Maybe he moves slowly? Maybe since I have no idea how this works, I'm expecting too much?

Or maybe . . . and I hate to even list this as a possibility, but . . . maybe he's just not that into me.

I didn't ask Emily about him again. I think, whatever it is that makes them uncomfortable around each other, I'd rather hear it from him. She seems angry or at least cold whenever we talk about him, but Warren just seems . . . I don't know. Indifferent? I think his perspective might be better. At least I think I'd rather deal with indifference than anger when asking about a possible past relationship with a guy I would like to have a possible relationship with in the future. Ugh.

October 11

I had a ton of homework tonight, so even though I was "helping" at the lab, Warren did most of the work and I sat there studying and writing civics notes. I swear, I could feel every time he looked at me like it was a physical thing. And he seemed to look at me a lot. Maybe he's trying to figure out if he likes me? I don't know. But I could actually hear my heartbeat in my ears at one point, it was so nerve-racking to be so close to him and not know what he was thinking. I kept my eyes on my homework, mostly, and didn't talk much. I was too afraid I'd say something stupid. Warren, on the other hand, seemed to want to fill every silence. He talked about all of his classes.

Me: How do you keep up? You're always here, and I hardly ever see you in class.

Warren, smiling slowly: I go to class.

Me: Not . . . enough. How do you do it?

Warren, still smiling, though it's cockier now: I don't sleep much and I have a really high IQ.

Me: Must be nice. Jerk.

He laughed and had me come over to help him transfer a particularly heavy container of chemicals into the first station tub. Then he let me run the first part of the process, which I'm getting super good at, while he quizzed me about civics and wrote my answers down for me.

Me: I think Mrs. Goodman might be a bit suspicious about the change in handwriting.

Warren: Then tell her you were dictating to your personal secretary, Warren Clark.

Me: Secretary? That sounds so . . . mid-century. How about "assistant"?

Warren: Personal slave?

Me, giggling: Deal. (Pause in which I work up the courage to ask him the hard questions.) So . . . why do you hate my roommate?

Warren, looking up from my notebook with surprise: Emily? I don't hate Emily.

Me: You wouldn't let her sit with us.

Warren: We don't let anyone sit with us. We might need to discuss business.

At least that explains the elitism.

Me: Well, when I asked her about you she got pissy. So I guess I thought . . . I don't know. Maybe you two had something going on, and now you don't? Bad breakup?

Warren takes a long moment, seeming to collect himself, then: You're not wrong, exactly. Emily and I had a thing last year, I guess you could say. It wasn't long, but it was really intense. Not healthy. I had to end it.

Healthy or not, I am not sure I love the idea of Warren having any sort of intensity for anything outside of me and Science Club, but I put my jealousy in check. He hasn't even wanted to hold my hand yet, after all.

Me: I guess some people just don't click, huh?

Warren, looking at me, intense but sweet: Right. But some people click. They really, really click. Perhaps right from the start.

Me, blushing as I picked up on his meaning: Really? I thought maybe I'd misread you. I mean, you haven't been very . . .

Warren: Forward? Pushy? Those kind of guys
are the worst, Bailey. I'm not one of them. Not
my style. There's an art to waiting for the right
moment. Don't want to mess anything up.
Don't you agree?

I very much agree.

And I don't think I'm going to be able to handle it if he ever
feels it's the "right moment."

October 12

I didn't do as well on the civics test as I'd hoped. It isn't a
terrible grade, but it isn't Princeton Summer Program/Getting
Into Harvard good. I'm going to have to study harder. Prescott
is more challenging than I thought it would be. At my old
school I would hardly study and still get As. Trying to slide
by like that at Prescott means my grades will slide too. I'm
just going to have to spend more time with the books. Warren
seems open to me studying in the lab while we work, so that
will help.

Dad called. I realized it was the first time he'd called me
since I got here. I've called a few times, but this was his first.
He wanted to talk about holiday plans. Prescott has two
weeks off at the end of the year and most of the students go
home or travel somewhere fun with their families. But Dad

told me Bex wanted to go to New York with a new friend for skiing and shopping, so she wouldn't be home much, if at all.

I'm not 100 percent sure, but I kind of got the impression he was hoping I'm not coming home, either. He and Isa probably want to go somewhere by themselves and not have a teenaged third wheel tagging along. Especially one who is still in the grieving hole, missing her mother and being a total downer and all.

That hurt, but it also made me angry. So I sucked up my pride and made up a lie about possibly going with Katy instead of coming home, and I definitely heard relief in my dad's voice then. I know I talk about Mom all the time, mostly just because I want to remember her and know that someone else misses her too. But it's got to make Dad feel super awkward and probably irritates the hell out of Isa (which I count as a bonus).

I might actually check with Katy to see if I can tag along, wherever she's going. Even if Dad was happy about me coming home, I'm not sure I'd want to go. It hasn't been the same without Mom. She'd always insist on letting us open one present on Christmas Eve, usually something she'd picked out herself, especially for us. The year before she died, she got us matching pajamas. The year before that, glass ornaments we could paint. But of course it was never about the gift. It was just that we did something together, just us girls.

I'm a little sad that Bex wants to be anywhere else for Christmas. I really wanted to see her. Maybe she doesn't want to be home without Mom, either.

Does it make me a horrible person to hope that's the reason why?

October 13

Turns out I didn't even have to ask. An opportunity presented itself in an awesome way. At lunch today, Drew announced that his family would be spending Christmas in Vermont at a resort. He said his mother has some sort of fantasy-land hope that it will be just like *White Christmas*, and somehow they'll all miraculously get along and sing carols and sip hot chocolate and stuff like that.

That's exactly the kind of Christmas I'd like, but I kept my mouth shut, since everyone else thought it was ridiculous.

Katy said she's going to St. Lucia with her family, which sounded fun and warm but not like anything I'd probably get invited to. I turned to Warren, who had his arm around me again, and asked him where he was going.

The whole group got quiet, so I knew I'd stepped in something. It was Drew who answered for him.

Drew: Warren stays at Prescott.

Warren: Someone has to be here, making the product. Supply doesn't go down because of the holidays.

Drew, smiling: Nope, it goes way up. The holiday season makes everyone tense. Our clients especially.

Drew was basically saying that we needed to sell more of our product because addicts might be especially upset or depressed or lonely this time of year. And for the first time in weeks, I remembered that there is someone on the other end of all this work. There is someone on the other end of the money I'm handed once a week. I lost my appetite.

Katy must have noticed, because she smiled really big and reassuringly at me.

Katy: Are you going home, Bailey? What does your family do for Christmas?

Me, shrugging: I don't know. I think my dad and Isa really want to be alone. My sister is going skiing with a friend, so if I didn't come home, he and Isa could have a few weeks to do whatever they want.

Warren: Then stay here. With me. I certainly wouldn't mind the help. Or the company.

Me, my heart thundering in my ears: Really? The school doesn't mind?

Warren: There's hardly anyone here. It's nice, actually.

Me: It's not . . . lonely and sad?

Warren, his blue eyes staring straight into my soul: It wouldn't be if you stayed with me.

It was so intense I could have sworn the rest of the dining hall disappeared and it was just me and Warren and him basically asking me to stay with him, alone, for two weeks.

But then Katy let out the type of squeal I was kind of mentally doing inside and told us we were beyond cute. Which made me blush and Warren laughed. Then it was time for class and Warren walked me there, apologizing for Katy being so Katy about it. I told him I was happy that perhaps someone else thought we had potential. His blue eyes danced with laughter at that, and I spent all afternoon thinking about holiday break and being alone with Warren instead of listening to my teachers.

October 13, later

I called Dad and told him I also had holiday plans and not to expect me home.

I'm not sure what I hate more: the relief in his voice or that he didn't even ask what I was doing.

October 16

Mr. Callahan gave me the application for the Princeton chemistry program. It doesn't look too bad, just a bit longer than I expected. They want two teacher recommendations. I think I'll steer clear of my English teacher. Ha! The second page asks for transcripts of science-related courses. I'll have to go to the guidance office (always a bit awkward and scary) to get that, I guess, and maybe call my old school. Twice as awkward.

Midterms are coming up, so I'm really going to have to buckle down. I have a routine, at least. After classes, I catch dinner with Emily or sometimes the Science Club, depending. Emily seems to shut herself in the AV room quite a bit, so a lot of the time she's not around. Sometimes Katy and I go for coffee and study together (i.e., gossip), or I just go straight to the lab. Depending on where Warren and I are in the process and how many batches we have going, sometimes it takes only an hour. Sometimes, though, we're in there until midnight or one a.m. After the long days, I feel like I could sleep for a week. I wish I could be like Warren and get by doing the bare minimum in class, but it just doesn't come that naturally to me. I hate admitting that, but there it is. He's got to be amazingly smart. I mean, I don't think I'm dumb or anything, but I'm nowhere near his level. It's incredible the way his brain works. Just as sexy as his blue eyes or his slow smile.

Sexy, sexy, sexy.

ANYWAY.

As hard as the long nights are (and the mornings after), at least I'm spending time with Warren, getting to know him more, and he's helping me study. For the most part. Also, Drew dispensed cash again. Katy's promised me she'll shop with me this weekend.

I'm thinking new ski boots for Bex.

October 21

Drew didn't have any business in town on this fine Saturday afternoon, so he let Katy borrow the car. I couldn't believe it. And I couldn't believe it even more when we got in and Katy revealed she was actually terrible at driving a stick. It was hilarious. She accidentally killed it about four times before we even got off campus. I'm pretty good at it (Dad insisted on teaching me how to drive a stick when I had my permit because he's one of those Boy Scout types and didn't want me to ever be stranded somewhere with only a manual transmission and not be able to drive). So . . . Katy let me drive! With the caveats that we did not tell Drew, that I did not wreck, and that we switched back once we were on campus again.

I got us safely to the mall, where there was a sporting goods store that would have everything Bex needed.

We lingered by the cute workout clothes before we made it to the ski section, naturally.

Katy: Sooooo Warren . . .

Me, grinning like an idiot: Yes?

Katy, taking pointed interest in yoga pants: Is it, like, official yet?

Me: I don't know? He hasn't kissed me or anything. We just . . . hang out. Talk a lot. He makes me laugh. But he's not in a hurry. At all. Like, frustratingly.

Katy: No, that's not Warren's way. But he's
soooo into you.

Me: How can you tell?

Katy: The way he looks at you! Oh my God.
It's like . . . so intense, you know? Like he's
seeing your soul or something.

Me: . . . So did he look at Emily like that?

Okay, so at that point, Katy got really quiet and wasn't
laughing anymore. She told me Emily was selfish and kind of
weird and blamed Warren for a lot of things that weren't his
fault. Serious issues. That's what she said Emily had. Serious
issues. Then she said after it ended between them, the Science
Club decided without really talking about it that they were
pretty much going to pretend she didn't exist. Loyalty, and all
that.

I suppose Emily could be seen as weird, since she doesn't
really have friends. But didn't the Science Club basically create
that situation? Seems kind of harsh to punish someone for
being an outcast when you're the one who did the casting out.
But I didn't say that to Katy. I don't want to seem disloyal either.

Me: She is kind of weird, I guess. And she's not around much. It's like I can't find her some days, and sometimes she's even later than me getting home. She's super into her films and stuff.

Katy: Yeah. She gets kind of obsessive about things. Anyway, now you're with Warren, or you will be, and none of that matters anymore. Trust me, he may take his time, but that's only because he wants it to be *perfect*.

That made me grin from ear to ear, then we went and picked out new ski boots and a matching coat for Bex. She'll be the best-dressed girl on the slopes, even among the other Campbell students. And all thanks to Big Sis's new "job."

October 22
I was beginning to wonder exactly what criteria Warren was using to measure the perfect moment. I guess I know now: anticipation, a beautiful fall night, and fire extinguishers.

We were in the lab, just me and Warren. Katy and Drew had been there but had already left, claiming studying and homework. I'm not even sure how it happened, really. I mean, chemically, I know. Ammonia and heat don't mix well. But I'm not sure how either of us was so distracted that we didn't catch our mistake.

Okay, well, I guess I know the answer to that, too.

It really was a beautiful night. The air was cool with a crisp promise that winter was on its way. All of the trees seemed to change color at the same time here on campus, and they're all bold oranges and bright yellows and deep reds. The breeze picked up just enough that while I was walking to the lab, I had a magical moment where the leaves were swirling around me. I felt like I was in a movie, and I was smiling and practically giddy by the time I got to the lab.

Drew and Katy were soon off, and Warren and I were deep into a groove with the process.

I've done a little research online about making meth, just to learn, and only when I was certain I could erase the browser history. Most makers have a two-day process. Warren likes to spread it out over four days, just to guarantee perfection and quality. He likes to examine it between each step and let the finished product breathe a little before handing it over to our sellers.

My research let me learn not only how to make it but how to do it well. Each step is nicely drawn out and meticulous, and now that I have some experience under my belt, Warren and I circle around each other to different stations like a well-choreographed musical scene.

And I guess that's why it was probably easy for him to predict where I was going to move next and . . . suddenly I was in his arms.

I laughed and blushed and immediately felt like it was all a little too much. I had the basic shape of him mapped out in my head, thanks to his well-fitting clothes and the occasional falling asleep on his shoulder. But when he pulled me close I started to understand how swooning was a thing.

He's lanky, sure, but he's *fit*. Maybe it's all that time he spends climbing trees around campus. I didn't expect his strength, and I really didn't expect how assured he was. He turned me, leading me into an ungraceful spin, and then pulled me back to him again. And he leaned close like he was going to kiss me, and there was fire.

A literal one, unfortunately.

I'd set down a beaker of ammonia too close to the burner and it went up in flames.

I panicked, but a different kind of self-assurance kicked in with Warren, and he spun for the nearest fire extinguisher. It wasn't a big blaze, luckily. It didn't even set off any alarms (although I'm not honestly sure the old building has any working ones). Basically once the liquid dispersed onto the floor and everywhere else, the fire didn't have much life in it, and what it did have, Warren easily put out.

> Me, hands over my mouth: Oh shit, I am so sorry.

> Warren: Okay, new rule—no dancing while we work?

Then we both broke out into hysterical laughter, fueled by adrenaline and relief.

Then Warren set the fire extinguisher aside, took a moment to make sure we were safe, and pulled me into his arms again. He kissed me then, and it was like another fire started, this one much more welcome but just as sudden and hot. And he is just as much an expert at kissing as he is at everything else. His arms encircled me, lifting me up slightly, and his lips were soft and tempting and gave and took. When he pulled away, those dazzling eyes stared straight into mine.

> Me: You're right. Timing is everything.

> Warren, laughing: Worth the wait, I hope?

Me: Yes, but I'm not going to let you make me
wait that long again. In fact . . .

This time I was the one to kiss him. And we kissed and
kissed, so much that I was light-headed by the time we were
done, and I don't think it had anything to do with the lab's toxic
fumes.

October 24

Another perfect day at Prescott. Warren walked with me to all of
my classes (holding my hand or with his arm around me always,
like he can't resist me or something). Mr. Callahan was super
impressed with the extra assignment I'd turned in for fun. Neither
me nor Katy had a lot of homework, so we got to spend extra
time obsessing over the kissing with Warren. Then Warren and
I had the lab to ourselves, so there was chemistry and *chemistry*
happening (last time I'll let myself make that joke, I promise). He
asked if he could call me his girlfriend, and of course I said yes!!!!

And . . . I got to talk to Bex!

She is SO excited about her ski trip, and she's going to go
wild when she sees what I got her. We made plans to see each
other Saturday, contingent on Drew letting me (or Katy) borrow
his car, of course. Campbell isn't that far away, really, so I'm
banking on him saying yes.

I asked if she was at all sad that she wasn't going to get to see Dad, and she said she was but that she was more afraid of going home and missing Mom the whole time. That made me think, and I've come to the conclusion that I'm the same way. I might miss Dad this Christmas, but the void Mom left is so much bigger. Plus it would have been so weird to sit there with Dad and Isa and pretend I was happy, or even comfortable with this new arrangement. All in all, I think I made the right decision not to go home.

I told Bex a little about Warren. Not that we are official or anything. I'll save that news for in person. But just about him and what he's like. She's starting to pay attention to boys now, so she was pretty curious, and I loved being able to share some girl stuff with her.

I'm headed to bed relatively early and all my homework is done. Feels like it's been weeks since both of those things happened at one time.

Like I said: perfect day at Prescott.

October 25

Okay, so a really weird thing happened just now. Warren walked me home tonight after we finished up at the lab, and we were at the gate to my dorm and Emily was returning from wherever she goes. If she didn't already know Warren and I are a thing, she does now. No way she could have missed him kissing me.

But it was like she didn't even see me standing there with him. She got super close to him, almost pushing me away in the process, and told him they needed to talk.

Emily seemed so different from when we were just sitting around watching movies. It was like total tunnel vision, and Warren was at the end of that tunnel and nothing else existed. I can see what Katy meant by "intense." It almost seemed stalkerish.

Warren was cool as could be and smiled at her. Sweetly, even. Then he said he'd talk to her and looked at me with an expression that was apologetic and also calm, like he was trying to tell me it was okay and he would be okay. He told me he'd see me tomorrow and to sleep well, and they walked off.

I don't even know how to feel about this. It's been two hours and Emily still isn't home. I could text Warren or something but I don't want to seem just as intense and possessive as Emily, so I'm not going to. Where could they be? What on earth did she want to talk about? And Warren didn't seem surprised or even nervous that she asked, or that she was in his personal space bubble. It was almost like he was . . . used to it or something.

I won't text Katy, either. I'm just going to try to go to sleep. Failing that, I'll pretend I am, so Emily won't think I've been freaking out all night long.

October 26

Okay, I guess my freak-out last night was over nothing, at least as far as Warren is concerned. He was waiting for me outside of English, cup of coffee in hand. He smiled and handed me the coffee and told me it was very cool of me to be okay with him talking to Emily last night. He thanked me for being supportive and understanding. I asked if they got everything sorted out, and he shrugged.

> Warren: I'm not sure. She will have to sort out a lot on her own, you know? She's got some issues that go far beyond me and our whole thing, and she's got to learn how to get those under control. I can't hold her hand through that. That's not my job. It wasn't really even my job when we were together.

I nodded like I totally understood what he was saying, but I didn't get it at all. I wanted to ask about a billion more questions, but after he'd thanked me for being so chill about it, I didn't feel like I could.

> Warren: Did she come home last night? After we talked?

Me: I don't know. When did you finish talking?

Warren: We only talked for about an hour.

Me: She must have gone somewhere else, then.
She wasn't there when I woke up this morning,
either. Maybe she went to a friend's? Or to the
AV room? I guess I can understand if she didn't
want to be around me. If I'd known . . .

I stopped there, shook my head, and smiled at Warren.

Me: Okay, if I'd known, I probably wouldn't
have done anything differently. Am I a
horrible person?

Warren, laughing: No! I liked you from the
moment I first saw you. I probably would
have been relentless if you'd turned me down,
especially if it was because of something silly
like your roommate.

Me: Well, hopefully she'll get over it. I have to
live with her until summer.

Warren: She'll have to. You didn't do anything
wrong. Our breakup was mutual, really. Just
do me a favor?

Me: Sure. Anything.

Warren: She'll probably try to convince you
that *I'm* a horrible person. Don't believe her.

Me, leaning up to kiss him in spite of the
harsh penalties at Prescott for PDA: I could
never believe that about you.

The rest of the day was fine. I sat with the Science Club at
lunch, I went to the lab after classes, and Warren and I quizzed
each other about chemistry as we worked, because we have a test
coming up.

I stayed pretty late at the lab. We didn't even have that much
work to do, but I really didn't feel like dealing with Emily yet.
I'm not afraid she'll be angry, more like I'm afraid of that weird
kind of intensity that she had with Warren last night. I don't
think I could handle that if it was focused on me. Also, I'm
really curious about her and Warren. Oddly obsessed. I don't
really want to know, but I also *really* want to know. And I guess

I'm kind of scared too that maybe he'll make me as nuts as Emily. I'm already scared of losing him, and I think about him nonstop. I mean, it's not out of the realm of possibility that I'd take it pretty badly if he broke up with me. Maybe not stalkerish and trying to talk to him in the middle of the night months later, but . . . it would really hurt.

But I didn't have anything to worry about. Even though it's really late, Emily still isn't back in the room.

October 30

Not much to report today. I thought Halloween would be interesting here at Prescott, but it turns out they have strict rules against dressing up and celebrations because of a couple of pranks that went south a few years ago. So lame. I feel like these rich kids could really do Halloween right, but I guess it's not worth the risk of punishment. The teachers, to their credit, have largely ignored that and passed out candy in every class I've been in. I thought about asking Emily if she'd want to watch a scary movie or something, kind of an olive branch, but I haven't seen her at all since the whole thing with Warren, mostly because she's been elsewhere. I feel like I should be there for her. She's obviously not dealing well with everything, and I think I might be her only friend, but I have no idea how to navigate this now that I know about her and Warren. Added to that, school is getting increasingly difficult. Maybe the teachers are just piling on the work because it will be winter break soon, and then we'll only have a few weeks before midterms. I don't know, but between homework, Emily, the Club, and break, I have a lot to juggle.

And UGH. I have to write an essay about *Macbeth*. I really do not want to write an essay about *Macbeth*. Please, God, anything but *Macbeth*. Katy said she'd help me, which might be the only reason I'll get a good grade. I've decided to write about the prophecy and how it influenced Macbeth's actions. I personally don't think he and Lady Macbeth would have acted the way they did if they hadn't been convinced that the witches had predicted their future. But then, maybe the witches knew that telling him would lead to that, so they were right anyway? Either way, I think they felt justified and maybe even absolved sometimes because they believed so strongly that ruling was their destiny. I don't know. It's all so confusing. Maybe I'll just do what everyone else is doing and write about how Lady Macbeth manipulated her husband into doing awful things. I only have a little over two weeks to get it done.

Drew actually wants to come to Campbell with me, so he's going to drive. I guess he has a little brother there. Katy is going too, so naturally Warren is coming along. I can't wait to see Bex. I wonder what she'll think of Warren???

I wonder what Mom would think of Warren too. And would she be happy for me that I finally have a boyfriend? And about how happy I am?

And is it . . . is it okay to be this happy? I mean, this is what I've often wondered about Dad and Isa. I know Mom would be happy that I'm happy, but I don't know. It feels somehow disloyal to Mom to be smiling when she's gone.

November 1

I finally talked to Emily. It was sort of hard to read her, really, because I got the feeling she was being overly . . . well, overly enthusiastic about me and Warren, actually.

I basically told her I hoped it wouldn't be a problem that I was seeing Warren now, and she assured me it was fine. She said the other night was just about some stuff she had to get off her chest but that she is completely, 100 percent over him. Then she rambled for a while about how she realizes now how unsupportive he was and how he never really understood her. She also said it was pretty much all lust between them, which made me a little angry and jealous if I'm being honest. It was like she wanted to remind me that she'd also kissed him and she was there first. But really, she's over him and I shouldn't be worried about anything.

Oh, and she threw in this comment about how she hopes I

won't believe everything he says about her, which is exactly what he said about her.

I told her that if it made her uncomfortable, I'd never bring him around her, and she snapped at me and said it was all fine and she didn't care at all. I left it alone after that and we both did our homework in silence. Then about twenty minutes later, unprompted:

> Emily: Warren can't just ignore me all the time, you know.

> Me: I don't think he would do that. Maybe he's just nervous that you're still upset with him.

> Emily: That's totally something he would do, Bailey. But you don't know him that well, do you? Not like I do.

At that point I put my headphones in and listened to music until I was done with homework. I'd have given anything to go to the lab and stay there instead or something, but it was late and I would have been busted for curfew. Luckily, Emily turned off her light and went to sleep and I didn't have to deal with her anymore.

I think she's just trying to get in my head, but she's definitely managed it. I wish I'd seen Warren tonight, even just a little, but with all the studying and homework I had to do, I'd told him earlier there was no chance of helping him tonight. It will be all right, I know it will. I just haven't had a relationship before, especially not with someone as amazing as Warren. So I'm paranoid that he's not as into me as I am him, and I think that's only natural, right?

And of course I realized as I was writing this that I didn't work on my *Macbeth* paper. I'm in no frame of mind for that tonight. I'll have to start tomorrow. I can't stop thinking about what Emily said.

Like, I am trying SO HARD to be there for Emily and to make her feel like she's got someone to talk to. So why would she pick at me like this? I hate to say it, but maybe the Science Club has the right idea about her. Who would blame me for ditching her with her acting like this?

November 4

Bex! Oh my God. When I saw her, we hugged and hugged and laughed and then hugged some more. I've been so busy and distracted (a good thing, I guess), I hadn't realized how much I've been missing her until I saw her. I feel like this is something only an old person would say, but she looked like she'd grown about five inches. And she's learned how to fix her hair, a necessity at boarding school. She's clearly rocking a straightener.

And everyone at Campbell loves her. That's clear. I swear everyone we walked by said hello to her by name, even some of the older kids. Of course. Who wouldn't love Bex? She's funny and caring and pretty and tough.

The drive didn't take too long, and Warren and I snuggled in the backseat the whole way there. We split up when we pulled into Campbell's visitor parking lot. Drew and Katy went to go find Drew's little brother, and Warren and I headed to Bex's dorm. Her face when she saw Warren was with me and I introduced him as my boyfriend! Priceless. I thought she was going to fall over dead of shock. We took her to lunch. She requested a restaurant off campus, naturally, and a kind of funky one that wasn't a chain. A gastropub, she said, like she knows all about gastropubs or something. So sophisticated now. Ha. Warren, sweetly, picked up the check. And when Warren went to the bathroom and we had a moment alone, she told me she liked him. She said he was funny, and cute in a geeky way, which is Bex speak for "not my style but I can see why you like him."

We met up with Drew and Katy and Drew's little brother Matt. Matt and Bex know each other, even though Matt is a year older. Bex got a little quiet around him, and I will definitely be teasing her later about that. How funny would it be if Bex's first crush was Drew's little brother? He's like a miniature version of Drew, but maybe a little sweeter, so why not?

Bex loved her boots and coat! She couldn't believe I got them for her, and she was super impressed that I'd picked that particular brand. She asked how in the world I could afford it, and Warren answered her by saying that since I'm not going home for the holidays I could give her Christmas now. Bex accepted that pretty easily, and I was grateful to Warren for covering for me. I feel stupid for not thinking about how to answer that question before.

It was kind of weird (and awesome, really) to see how much Bex looks up to me. She clearly had heard my friends' names before, so now I'm the coolest ever in her eyes. But I could see it even more when I told her I was thinking of doing a summer program at Princeton. I always think of her as naturally so much cooler and social than me, so it never occurred to me that she would admire me for anything other than just being older.

Now I'm sitting here wondering what Bex would do if she found out about Science Club. She's too young to understand, really. She would just see it in black and white; one mention of drugs and she'd be mad, disappointed, and probably scared for me. How could I possibly make her understand how I see it? Would she get how much I need loyal friends? Or that I've been so lonely? Or that it's helping me get out of the grieving hole?

November 6

The high of a carefree day with Bex wore off, and I was slammed back into the reality of unrelenting work at Prescott.

At least, thank goodness, Emily seems to be back to her old self. No more mention of Warren. No more snarly, jealous comments. She actually suggested we go to dinner together, and we did, but I had to bail on watching movies tonight. I'm just too panicked about all the classwork piling up.

That *Macbeth* paper is like a rain cloud looming over me constantly. Mr. Callahan continues to give me extra work on the side in chemistry, and it's challenging but also fun, so I never dread it and do it first. Calculus is the same way. Civics is tougher. With everything going on, I feel like it's hard to keep all the civics stuff straight, and since I certainly have no aspirations to be a politician or lawyer, there's no reason TO keep it all straight.

I did my calculus and started on my *Macbeth* paper, even though everything I wrote sounds stupid and I'll probably have to redo it. I finished most of calculus and then packed up and headed to the lab.

I actually beat Warren there, and he was startled when he walked in. He seemed a little frazzled, but then he just seemed grateful to see me. He kissed me so hard we almost tumbled into some chemical bottles.

Me: Rough day?

Warren: Much better now. What is with everyone demanding everything all at once?

Me: I think our teachers are all freaking out that they still have so much to cover before the end of the semester and are taking it out on us. Did you get all your work done?

Warren: Yeah. You?

Me, pushing my chemistry book toward him: Go over these with me? I just want to make sure I'm right.

Warren, taking the book and a kiss as well: You usually are. You're the most gifted chemist I've met. At Prescott, anyway. Genius.

Me: Ha! I'm not the one who manages to
gets straight As while also running a full-time
business. How do you do it?

Warren: I've made a clone of myself so I can
be in two places at once. Which Warren is the
real Warren? Maybe I'm the clone. What if
I'm the clone, Bailey?

Me, swatting at him playfully: Seriously!
How?

Warren, suddenly sobering: Magic, I guess.
And luck. And I never get much sleep.

I laughed, but . . . I don't know. It was like I suddenly
NOTICED. I looked at him and didn't just see my adorable
boyfriend; I saw the dark circles under his eyes, the slight droop
of his shoulders, and how thin he really is.

I'm going to help more. I told him I could be at the lab
more to check in on our work and do more of the process than
I usually do. He told me not to worry about it, but I saw relief
flash in his eyes, so I insisted.

I don't know how exactly I'll put in more time at the lab, but

I have to. I'll just work on homework here more often or get less sleep myself. But I do know I can't let Warren take on all of this by himself.

It will be fine. That's what I keep telling myself, anyway.

November 8

Had the scare of my life tonight. I legitimately believe it took a few years off my life.

I was in the lab alone, just me and my civics book and the quiet bubbling of all the tubes and pots around me, when I heard the doors open and shut above me. I called out, thinking I'd hear Katy or Drew answer back, or even Warren if he decided to come in after all. But instead a superdeep male voice answered, and an imposing shadow appeared in the doorway.

My heart nearly stopped.

Not only was I alone, I was also surrounded by evidence of a highly illegal business.

The figure stepped down into the basement's fluorescent lights and it was a police officer. Campus security, I guessed. He had a badge but also a hat that had Prescott's crest on it. In the light, I could see that he was just as surprised to see me as I was to see him. I stepped in front of the largest vat of chemicals, futilely.

Officer: You're not Katy.

Me: No, sir. I can, um, call her if you need her.

Officer: No, it's okay. Are you the newest
member?

Me: Oh. Um . . . I . . .

Officer, smiling: I'll take that as a yes. I'm
Mark. Campus security.

Me: I gathered. Um, what can I help you with,
Mark? I'm just here doing homework.

Officer: You can drop the pretense.
Apparently they haven't explained how things
work.

He walked toward me, hand extended to shake. I shook it,
in shock.

Me: Hi . . . Mark. I'm Bailey. I'm sorry, but
what exactly have they not explained to me?

84

Mark: Oh! Right. It would be better if they explained. Plausible deniability and all that. But Drew or Katy was supposed to meet me here tonight.

Speak of the devil, Drew appeared, thundering down the stairs in a rush. He and Mark greeted each other, smiling, with a macho hug like guys are prone to doing, while I'm standing in the background with all my blood in my feet and not breathing well. They chatted like old friends for a few minutes, catching up on each other's lives. Apparently Mark's wife is expecting another child in May. Then Drew took out a thick envelope from his back pocket and slipped it into Mark's breast pocket. Mark thanked him, said he'd keep in touch, and was on his way.

I sat down on a metal stool and tried to breathe.

Me: What the hell was that?

Drew, sheepish: I'm sorry, Bailey. I should have told you this before. Mark is a security guard.

Me: I can at least follow that, thank you. Why the hell didn't he arrest me? Or you? And obviously he knows about what we do?

So Drew told me. For as long as they've had Science Club, which has been three years now, they've had Mark. Drew discovered he was easily swayed by money, and so they made an arrangement: Mark gets paid a tidy sum monthly in exchange for his silence to Prescott and the police about us, he makes sure his reports about this building always say it's secure and untouched, and he gives us any info that may be valuable, like if the janitors decide to come in and clean or if the admin gets suspicious.

It all makes total sense, of course, but I feel like I'm in a movie or something. A mob movie. This can't possibly be my life, that I'm doing something a crooked cop covers up for a price, right? But I am. This is reality. I am making drugs that are sold. And if Mark cracks or something goes wrong, I could go to prison.

> Drew, his hand on mine comfortingly: We
> have to involve others. It's just the nature
> of the game. But I make sure we can trust
> them. Don't worry, okay? I have this covered.
> Trust ME.

And the strange thing is, I do. I trust him, and Katy, and Warren. They really know what they're doing.

I guess you could say I trust them with my life.

November 13

Another night that I just cannot concentrate enough to work on that damned *Macbeth* paper. I got everything else done, though, and I still have a few days for the paper, so it will be okay. I worked at the lab with Warren (and okay, there was some pretty heavy making out in addition to work, but nothing blew up this time) for a few hours and came back to the dorm. Emily was here working, and she asked me if I'm ready for the civics test, and I think I am. Then . . .

Emily: Did he ask you to stay with him over holiday break?

Me, awkwardly: Warren? Um, not like WITH him. Just that we will both be here. Are you going home?

Emily, totally ignoring my question: I thought he'd come home.

Me: Right. You're from the same town. I kind of forgot that. It's right outside of Wiltshire, right?

Emily: Kingsley. It's not far from here. I can come back if I need to.

Me: Um, sure. I'm sure I'll be fine, though.
I mean, it will be nice to have free rein of
campus with almost everyone gone.

Emily: Yeah. Have fun.

She threw her headphones in and started watching a movie
on her laptop, jotting notes in a little notepad she always carries
around with her. It shook me a bit, that she just basically wanted
to know about Warren. A little of that weird tunnel vision. I don't
feel like she's abnormal in any way except for that, this obsession
with him, and when she slips into it it's really uncomfortable. He
told me she has a lot to sort out, and I can be patient while she
does, but this part of it, with Warren, is going to get old soon.
I may have to confront her about that, and that's really the last
thing I want to do. She needs to understand that it's over between
them, and he's with me now. Undoubtedly with me.

What could Warren have seen in her? I don't consider
myself pretty, really. I'm certainly no Katy Ashton, but I'm not
plain. Emily . . . is. She's got kind of rounded, soft features and
big eyes, but her hair is medium length and stuck in a weird
in-between shade of brown and blond, she's not too tall and not
too short, and she's not thin but she's not curvy, either. There's
just nothing that really stands out.

I shouldn't say that. She's super smart. Probably smarter than me in a lot of ways. And goodness knows Warren isn't in it for looks with me. I guess I'm just curious and a little . . . Wait. Am I jealous? Is this what jealousy feels like? Ugh. I suppose I could talk to Katy about it, maybe get her advice about how to talk to Emily, but I have a feeling Katy would tell me to go full nuclear on her, and I don't want to do that. It wouldn't go over well with us being roommates, not to mention her issues, but I also just don't want to do that to Emily. Everyone else has deserted her, and I know all too well how that feels.

Mom would know how to handle this. She was always so patient with everyone, always gave people the benefit of the doubt, and always looked for the best in people. She'd help me with Emily. But I guess I'll never know what advice she would have given me.

November 15

Yeah. You know how I've had some really good days at Prescott and it's been amazing?

This was the worst day I've had at Prescott.

I stayed up all night to do that stupid *Macbeth* paper, and it still turned out like actual crap. And I should have spent more time studying for civics, or at least getting some sleep last night. The teacher handed the graded tests back and I got a B-. I've never gotten a B- on anything in all my life. That's only a small step up from a C! And a C is as good as failing.

The Club tried to comfort me by taking me for a burger and fries at a little diner not far off campus, but I felt guilty spending that time away from my books. Warren asked me if I wanted to stay the night with him. Just sleeping, he clarified, and I'm glad because I'm not quite sure I'm ready for anything else yet. He's amazing but . . . I never have, so . . . yeah, nervous and I feel sort of embarrassed, I guess, that I'm so inexperienced. BUT ANYWAY. That said, I'm not sure "just sleeping" would be a thing that could happen if I was allowed to be next to him all night. But God, his arms around me all night after the day I've had? Hard to turn down.

We said good-bye to Katy and Drew and he walked me home. He kissed me really sweetly and hugged me close and told me all we had to do was make it until the holiday break. Then we could be alone and not have to worry about classes or homework or anyone else but the two of us. And sure, all that time alone with Warren is a little scary, too, but in a good way. A really good way.

He's right. One step at a time. And there's so much to look forward to.

November 20

C.

That's what I got on the *Macbeth* paper.

90

I don't know what I'm going to do. I have a few more small assignments and the exam, but basically, this paper is such a huge part of my grade that I'd need to be perfect on all of those things to average a B.

I didn't tell Warren or Katy or Drew. As a matter of fact, I didn't even go to the lab tonight. I asked Warren if he could handle doing it all on his own and he said of course. He looked concerned and I could tell he wanted to ask, but I quickly made an excuse and came back to my room as fast as I could. I suppose if he texts tonight I'll tell him, but I'm so embarrassed. Especially since he has it together so well.

Emily, however, was amazing tonight. She was here when I got home from classes and immediately knew something was wrong and I . . . I just broke down. I told her I was afraid that I couldn't keep up with Prescott's classes and that with everything else going on (I did not say what, but I'm sure she thought I meant Warren and nothing else), I was falling behind.

She handed me a box of tissues and talked me through it, but first she picked up her laptop and ordered pizza for us.

By the time the pizza arrived, she'd talked me safely out of the panic attack zone. She also admitted to me that she has a hard time keeping up too. I should have realized that. Of course that's why she's always gone. She's working on her writing or her films in addition to all the classes we're taking. She puts in as many hours as I do. Probably more. She never seems to sleep.

Then she told me she'd help me with English if I wanted, and suggested asking the teacher for some extra credit. Apparently this teacher gives it out like candy if you ask.

I thanked her, and confessed that I kind of thought maybe she hated me. Just a little.

> Emily: I don't hate you. I mean, I kind of
> think we're friends? At least I'd like to be.

I didn't realize what a relief it would be to hear that. Because that meant maybe living with her while dating Warren wouldn't have to be so hard. But also because . . . well, if I'm honest, if Emily can still want to be friends with me even if she's still not over my boyfriend, she's going to be there through thick and thin, right? And I could use a friend like that.

> Me: We're friends. I just thought that maybe
> things had changed. Because of Warren.

> Emily: I was upset, I guess. Kind of mad,
> actually. I was just so into him. He's so
> confident and smart and . . . all of those good
> things, you know? He's perfect. Or at least I

thought he was. But he's soooo not. And I can see that now. You know what I mean. I'm sure you've seen it by now too.

Me, not at all sure I "know" what she's talking about in the slightest: Sure.

Emily: Thought so. Just be careful. He'll get you hooked.

Me: I'll be careful.

When I was stuffed with pizza and feeling much better about things, Emily said she was going to go to the AV room for a while, and I was truthfully a little happy to have some time to myself. I took a long shower and sulked and I'm going to take advantage of Warren working for me tonight and get to bed early.

November 22

So tonight, Warren and I were alone in the lab, which isn't unusual. Katy and Drew stop in a lot but are rarely part of the process. Things are going so well with the product. He and I have found such a great rhythm together that we practically communicate with our own language. With a glance or hum or slight shake of our heads, we tell each other everything we need to know.

And, uh, there are times when those things communicate another type of message entirely, and we tug off our gloves and goggles and his mouth meets mine without a single word ever having been exchanged.

Tonight we were probably fifteen minutes into a heavy make-out session when Warren pulled back and looked at me with those gorgeous eyes of his.

> Warren: So, holiday break . . . Drew is going home.

> Me: So is Emily.

> Warren: So, we'll both be alone. In our dorms. With no one there to interfere.

> Me: Or miss us if we're gone. But what about the dorm advisers? Won't they be patrolling?

> Warren, shaking his head: Not as often, and they really don't care.

> Me, cocking my head at him: Have you paid them off too?

Warren, laughing: No, although I think they'd
be easy to bribe. So . . . does that mean you'd
want to stay with me?

I do, I really do. But I'm nervous. I tried to explain my
nervousness to him, telling him how I have no experience
whatsoever (so embarrassing) and how I'm not sure if I'm
ready. But as usual, words and I do not mix, and it all sort
of tumbled out like incoherent nonsense. And I must have
went on and on because suddenly he stepped close to me,
took my hands in his, and silenced me with a short, sweet
kiss.

Warren: Bailey, we will take all the time you
need. You know how I am about finding the
perfect moment. And . . . (he ran his fingers
through my hair soothingly) don't worry
about any of that. I mean, everything we've
done together so far has turned out pretty
great, hasn't it?

He was right, of course. And this is Warren, after all. He'll
make everything perfect. So it's settled. I'll stay with Warren
overnight when I'm ready.

I'm already so nervous I could puke.

December 7

Last night a snowstorm passed through and the entire campus was covered in a foot of snow. It was gorgeous, but of course, the drawback to being at a boarding school is that no one has any excuse to miss class. Even in a foot of snow, classes are happening, and you're walking. But they do allow boots in the snow, so at least my feet weren't blocks of ice by the time I reached my first class.

This isn't the first time it's snowed on campus, but it's the first time it's snowed enough to do anything with it. Everyone was antsy to get classes over with and get outside, even the teachers. It was like, for the day, we were all little kids again.

Warren met me before first period with a coffee, and it felt so warm and cheery in my hands. He seemed to be in a really good mood, just like everyone else. I swear the whole campus got quieter. Even some of the teachers took a day off, so to speak. In English we were allowed to read all period. Mr. Callahan had us do our work individually and silently at our desks, and in civics the teacher showed us a video about John F. Kennedy instead of actually teaching anything.

Let's be honest, they were just as excited as us and wanted to get home and enjoy the snow or hibernate or whatever teachers do in this kind of weather.

The day seemed to fly by, and as soon as I got out of class,

I ran home to change into something warmer and snugglier. Emily was home, doing the exact same thing. She said she was going with some of the AV kids to sled behind the arts building. She said it was pretty much Prescott tradition. I told her I hoped I'd see her there, and I was going to check in with Katy and the gang first.

I didn't have to wait long. Katy, Drew, and Warren showed up at my door (literally, my door. The dorm mom let them up). Drew had a plastic sled.

Me: Behind the arts building?

Katy, winking: For a while, then we have even better plans.

Emily wasn't wrong. All of Prescott, freshmen to seniors, was behind the arts building, where the steepest and biggest hill on campus was. It was already getting a little dark, but there were some lights coming from the arts building and beside it from the parking lot.

Katy and I sledded down together the first time and came to a crashing halt at the bottom, flipping over a few times before landing hard in the snow. We both lay there giggling like idiots until Drew and Warren came over and practically

97

carried us back up the hill, we were laughing so hard. Everyone was going down so fast and it was so crowded, it was pretty dangerous.

Some of the kids even got creative and were using things like trash can lids and cafeteria trays as sleds. So hysterical. As Drew and Katy went down together, I looked around for Emily and saw her with a whole group of people I recognized but hadn't spoken to much. AV kids. She looked happy. They were laughing just as hard as me and Katy, and I don't know why, but it made me so happy to see her smiling. I don't see her with other people much. She disappears all the time, sure, but she never really talks about anyone else, so maybe she does have friends and it's just that they're all as busy as she is.

Then Drew and Katy were back, and it was me and Warren's turn. He sat behind me on the plastic sled and wrapped his arms around me as we coasted down. We glided easily all the way to the bottom until another sled rammed into us and we had to help each other up. We kept slipping and grabbing for each other all the way back up the hill, absolutely cracking up at how clumsy we were.

I'm not sure how long we stayed out, but it was cold enough that my toes and fingers were completely numb. And that's when Drew and Warren signaled to each other and grabbed me and Katy and pulled us off the hill.

We went down through the courtyard area and then back behind the freshman boys' dorm, which is famously the farthest dorm away from the school. Then, without a word, we slipped into the woods behind the dorm and walked until we could no longer see any of Prescott's lights.

To my surprise, we were not the only ones there. There was a fire pit in the center of a small clearing, and it was blazing brightly. (I later learned that a senior had stolen it from a local hardware place years ago, and the delinquents of Prescott have been using it ever since.) There were people everywhere, mostly upperclassmen from what I could tell. They were gathered around the fire, talking in small groups. Some stood a little farther away, talking in hushed tones, and then there were couples at the very fringes of the fire's light, taking advantage of some time away from the watchful eyes of teachers and dorm parents. First Snow Bonfire: the other Prescott tradition, my friends explained.

Warren and Drew had disappeared somewhere, and when they came back they had cups of hot chocolate for us. I sipped it, then turned with surprise to Warren, who winked. Someone had definitely spiked the hot chocolate. It was a little minty, and it was good. Katy and I settled onto a fallen tree branch and talked to some people around us, and with each other, as Drew and Warren worked the crowd. I noticed that Katy mostly watched Drew but thought better of pointing out that fact.

Katy introduced me to people I already knew from classes, it's just that I'd never seen them in this particular context, and if Katy was taking the time to introduce them, they were probably somebodies in the Prescott world. I nodded my head and drank as she did most of the talking.

I looked over at Warren at some point. He and Drew were with a group of boys I knew were sort of jocks. Prescott didn't have a football team or even a basketball team. We were too small for that. But we had lacrosse and crew. And those boys were athletes. Warren and Drew were doing their silent communication thing—I could tell even from the distance—and when one of the jock boys gestured in question, Warren and Drew nodded at each other before reaching out and shaking the jock's hand in turn. Then the whole group, Warren and Drew included, went off into the woods for a while.

The alcohol hit me all at once and I started giggling out of nervousness. Katy thought it was terribly amusing and went to get us refills. By the time Warren and Drew were back, I was sufficiently warm and tipsy.

The boys got us yet another refill and I sort of just slumped against Warren, letting him hold me and keep me warm, and I felt incredibly happy to be here, at Prescott, with Warren and my friends, who were obviously amazing, in the snow.

I heard Katy ask Drew about the boys, and their voices got quiet but I could tell from their tones they were excited about whatever they were discussing. I mumbled something to Warren about it and he chuckled, all low and sexy, and told me that yeah, things were good, and things were going to get better if we played our cards right.

I'm not sure what cards we are playing, and I'm not sure how anything could get any better, but I'm up for it, whatever it is.

December 8

Emily and I both slept until lunch today. Whoops.

Apparently, most of the school did, or at least the upperclassmen. Emily followed the proper Prescott procedure and called the school secretary for both of us, thank goodness, and the secretary sarcastically said something about a sudden illness raging on campus.

She and I went to lunch together and headed off to class. I do wonder why Emily slept in, though. I didn't see her at the bonfire at all, but I didn't ask. Maybe she did something with the AV kids, and that's a good thing, right? I'm certainly paying the price for all my fun. My head is STILL killing me.

Warren was just fine. As a matter of fact, he seemed to be in a great mood. Perhaps it was because things were going to get better, like he said last night. I didn't ask, honestly. I just tried to absorb some of his good mood. He was so calm and lovey tonight at the lab, exactly what I needed as I recovered. He even did most of the work tonight since I was still nauseated. I swear he's the perfect boyfriend.

The countdown until break is creeping by. I can't stand it! I'm soooo nervous, but also, the anticipation is KILLING me. I want everyone to go away so it's just me and Warren. I think I'll fill the time with more shopping with Katy and, of course, some extra time at the lab. ;)

December 19

Today is the last day before the holiday break, and even though the teachers assigned homework for the next two weeks, everyone seems to be in a great mood.

To my surprise, Emily gave me a present this morning, explaining she'd be leaving for home right after classes are over, so we probably won't see each other again. It was a copy of *Notting Hill*, the director's cut with all these extra features on it. It was amazing of her, really, to get me something that kind of bridged our worlds, with her love of films and . . . Mom. She knew it reminded me of Mom. I'd gotten her something too, though my gift was nowhere near as cool. Just passes to the movie theater in Wiltshire, which I knew were useful if not creative. She seemed really happy to get them. Maybe she and I can go together sometime, if things are still going okay between us.

I gave Katy a scarf-and-gloves set I'd seen her admiring on our last shopping trip. Katy got me an adorable travel bag for makeup and toiletries, perfect for spending the night in the boys' dorm, she added with a wink. She also gave me some, um, pointers for my first night with Warren, and it was honestly the sweetest thing anyone's done for me so far here at Prescott. It wasn't just stuff about how to make Warren feel good but a few tidbits for me, too, to make sure it wouldn't hurt much the first time. She told me about losing her virginity last year and it was sort of a cautionary tale, I suppose. Some older guy she wanted to impress who broke her heart after, so she told me to be absolutely sure I wanted to be with Warren. We kind of bonded over it all, and that was truly the best gift she gave me.

Drew and I exchanged nothing except an awkward hug and he gave me a very pointed and knowing "Have a great time here alone over break." I guess Warren told him, which is fine. I can't really expect Warren not to tell his best friend, and it's not like he told the whole world. It's just kind of embarrassing, and . . . I don't know. It's like it adds to some of the buildup or something.

Like the more we talk about it, the more I can't possibly compare to whatever people are thinking.

I didn't have any idea what to get Warren. Not one thing seemed good enough, so in the end I got him a few things to make up for it: a Princeton hoodie, a fur-lined hat that I thought would look Russian chic and perfect with his ever-present coat, and a metal paperweight for his dorm desk that was made to look like a molecule.

We aren't exchanging presents yet, though. We're going to wait until Christmas.

Drew isn't gone yet, but Emily and Katy are. I've got the room all to myself tonight, which I kind of feel like I need. Honestly, I had myself a good cry about Mom while no one was around to see. It's the second Christmas without her. Last year everyone was down and missing her so much. Now Dad has moved on. How is he okay with not decorating the tree with her or making her ooey-gooey fudge? I used to complain about having to stir that chocolate for so long on the stove; now I wish I could get every minute back.

December 21

It's day two of holiday break and everyone is gone except for me and Warren. There are probably some other people here, but honestly, it feels like he and I are the last two people on earth.

In a really, really good way. I'm not sure I'd even notice other people on campus anyway. It's just us and the lab and the work.

We pretty much spend most of our time in the lab. We go straight there after breakfast and work until lunch, then we walk to the coffee shop and grab a sandwich. Yesterday we had to go back to the lab right away because of where we were in the making process, but today we spent the afternoon watching movies curled up in his bed, dozing or kissing or both. We had to go back and work late afterward, but it was worth it. We are absolutely swamped right now with orders or whatever you want to call them. Drew was right about that: The holidays have driven demand right up. He'll be here tomorrow to get the product and make deliveries. Mark stopped by and I watched, kind of awestruck, as Warren handed him a thick stack of bills. I didn't ask how much it cost us. I don't want to know some things. Also, I'm more than satisfied with my own cut, so it really doesn't matter to me.

Speaking of my own cut, Warren and I have gone to a nice restaurant for dinner every night, once in Wiltshire, and we went to Kingsley tonight, and we're thinking of heading to Covington tomorrow for a seafood place, if there's time. For the first time ever, I don't even glance at prices. Warren drives. Warren bought the car by himself. I get the feeling his parents don't buy him much of anything. I haven't asked him outright, but he's said as much. Maybe I'll ask him tonight at dinner. I don't know much about his family, and that's part of being a girlfriend, right? I could bring up my family first. Even Mom.

It would be really nice to talk to someone about Mom. Especially Warren.

Okay, I need to get ready for that dinner. We'll probably have to go back to the lab when we get back, just to check on things. Then I'll go to his place.

So far I haven't been ready, exactly. But Warren is super sweet about everything and there's been no pressure. I don't know how I got so lucky, with him and Science Club in general. They may not be a secret coven of vampires, but it feels just as cool.

December 22

Wow. Just wow. I asked Warren about his family and I am still kind of reeling from everything he told me. We'd had some wine with dinner (it was one of Drew's family's restaurants, so they knew Warren and it was on the house, no questions asked), so I'm not really sure if he'd have been so honest without it, but I'd like to believe he just trusts me that much.

Really, I only asked because I told him about Mom tonight. He asked me about her, and I don't know, it was like a dam broke, and a rush of emotions spilled out. I told him how she died, how I tried to be so strong for Dad and Bex, how Dad found Isa, how sometimes Bex seems to not remember as much about Mom as I do, and how I feel like sometimes I'm the only one still grieving.

He reached across the table and took my hand, and he was a little teary as he listened. And that's when I worked up the courage to ask him about the family he never mentions.

He started telling me about his parents and what happened with them in a rush, just like I had, and I am certain he needed to tell someone. I think this might be eating him up inside, and he can't afford to keep it in anymore. I'm not sure he even talks to Drew about this, although I'm sure Drew knows. I don't know. I just feel very, very honored that he opened up to me about it. And knowing what I know now, it's no surprise he felt he could: We actually have a lot in common.

Warren had an older brother named Mitchell. Mitch was a lot older, meant to be an only child, but Warren was an "oops" for his parents eight years later (we both had a good laugh when he said that). When Warren was in middle school and his brother was in college, though, things went really sour. His parents kept it from him for a while but he figured it out soon enough: Mitch was an addict. What had started off as an addiction to pills—something to soothe the pain of a baseball injury from high school—had become more. Unable to get enough pills to satisfy him through a prescription, he'd turned to getting them on the street. When that became too hard and too expensive, he'd found something cheaper and easier to get: heroin.

Warren said all he really remembered about that year was his mother crying a lot, his dad constantly leaving, looking for Mitch, who had disappeared again. There was a stint in a good rehab, an even longer visit to a great rehab, and a period of sobriety. Then a setback, then again, days of not hearing from him, not knowing where he was. It was his father who discovered Mitch after a long disappearance, blue and swollen and alone, a needle still in his arm.

Though that hadn't been easy for him to tell me, the next part seemed even harder for Warren to speak out loud.

It was like a light went out in his mother. It wasn't just grief or even depression, it was . . . more. She lost her job, wouldn't leave the house; she barely responded when spoken to. Warren's father tried to help her. He had all sorts of therapists and doctors come to work with her, but nothing worked. He even sent her away for a while, to a facility in Florida, thinking some warmth and like-minded people would do her some good, but she came back virtually unchanged. After a while, Warren's father gave up, or at least he accepted that nothing was going to change. He started to stay late at work, went away for long business trips, anything he could do to avoid home. They never officially divorced; his father still takes care of his mother in most ways, but he no longer lives there.

And meanwhile, Warren was growing up, and they didn't notice. The only way they seemed to acknowledge his existence at all was when he would do something truly extraordinary, like getting into Prescott, being accepted into Princeton's summer program, getting the Headmaster's Award for chemistry. Sometimes they would be sad about it, saying it was something Mitchell should have done, but it was still attention. It was still some kind of recognition. So that's what he tried to do, all the time. Excel in everything. To make them see, to be seen. To make up for Mitchell's loss. To do the things Mitchell would never do.

So when I ask him how it's possible that he does all that he does, I guess I know how. He doesn't really see any other choice.

We were quiet for a while on the way home. I kept replaying the things he'd said over and over in my head, trying to grasp the scope of it all, how shaped Warren was by his brother's choices and by his family. But as I was sitting there, trying to comprehend everything Warren had to go through and everything he's still dealing with, Warren started asking me about Mom. Not asking me about her death or how much I missed her or anything, but just MOM in general. What she was like. What was my favorite thing about her. And I found myself smiling, remembering things I hadn't let myself think about in a while and telling Warren all about them. He was smiling too, laughing along with me at my stories, and I realized: I'd never felt so close to him. Our pasts tied us together somehow, two scarred people just trying to keep going. I admire him so much for that ability to go on, and my heart breaks for him, for how hard he works to be noticed. He's really amazing, and I think . . . I think I'm in love with him.

At that moment I decided I didn't want to wait any longer. I squeezed his hand and told him so.

Warren: You mean . . . ?

Me: Yes.

Warren: You're sure?

Me: I'm sure.

Warren: Because if you're not . . .

Me: Warren. I'm sure. I know you're all about
finding that perfect moment. I think this is it.

So we went back to his dorm.

That's all I can write right now. I'm finally back in my room,
and . . . well, I need to get some sleep. More to come . . .

December 23

Okay, back to it. I'm not supposed to meet Warren at the lab
for a half hour, so I have time to write. It's sort of embarrassing
to write all this down, but I want to remember, later. I want to
remember everything about last night. Honestly, I might veer
into a sappy romance-novel kind of thing, but that's what it felt
like, so it's just the truth. Last night could not have been any
more perfect. Warren was perfect.

After I told him I was ready, we both kind of sat there in
dumb silence for a moment and I almost started to panic, like
maybe he was going to change his mind, then I looked over at
him and he was grinning like an absolute idiot and I started to
giggle. Then he started to laugh and it was like we couldn't stop
laughing. I think it was just nerves or something but whatever it
was, it totally relaxed me.

We parked and checked for the dorm mom when we
sneaked in the front door. She was nowhere in sight, and it was

late enough that maybe she wouldn't do rounds again. When we got to Warren's room . . .

Okay, so I won't lie. At first it was like this totally intense making out. Greedy and needy and hot. The kind of thing you see on TV where it's out of control and clothes get torn. But it was like Warren came to his senses at some point, or at least had the decency to step back and, like he promised, be patient enough to make it right.

So he lit some candles and everything got a lot gentler and slower and he was so sweet. Intense, but focused on me totally, and it was amazing to feel like the center of his universe.

I can't even believe I'm going to write this down but here it is: It didn't hurt like I thought it would, just kind of foreign feeling and new. And . . . good. Very good. He looked in my eyes and kept mumbling my name in my ear and afterward he made sure I was okay and held me like I was something really precious to him. Then we talked all night, getting to know each other even more. Things we remembered from our childhoods, before things got hard, dreams for the future, the pressures we're facing now at Prescott. We just . . . we just click. He's wonderful in so many ways.

I am seriously the luckiest girl in the whole world that I got to lose my virginity to Warren Clark.

We have a full day ahead of us at the lab, and we're going to try to get homework done today.

You know, if we don't lose our focus. ;)

January 2

I feel bad that I haven't written in a while, but I'm not really sure why. I guess because Dad got this diary for me, so I feel like it's an obligation to him, even though he'll never read it. It's not like he feels any obligation to me.

I shouldn't have written that. It's just that I've barely heard from him at all. I spoke to him on Christmas, but I have to wonder if it's only because I called him. If I hadn't picked up the phone to call, would he have?

He said he and Isa had a wonderful Christmas. They visited her parents and spent a weekend at a cozy bed-and-breakfast. He inquired about my Christmas and I told him it had been great (it had, even if it was just me and Warren and Chinese takeout, which I did not mention), and he asked how school was. I kept that brief too. He asked if I'd received his presents and told me he enjoyed the ones I'd sent to him and Isa (gold cuff links for him, now that he has to attend fancy events with her all the time, and emerald earrings for her. No one seemed to notice that emerald was Mom's birthstone). He did not ask how I'd afforded them. I hung up the phone feeling like we hadn't really spoken at all.

I don't know what I'd expected or hoped for. Maybe an "I missed you so much, Bailey!" or an "I feel terrible that we didn't get to spend Christmas together." And of course he made no mention of Mom.

And I don't really know why I'm complaining. I did talk to Bex on Christmas and she has decided she was basically meant to ski. She said she was a natural on the slopes, which I don't doubt. And it *was* a great Christmas. Warren loved his presents. He got me a cashmere sweater in forest green (to match my eyes, he said), a sapphire necklace (his birthstone), and a pair of really good safety goggles, which we both had a good laugh over. He told me they were for Princeton, not our "work," and I was touched.

He got a little fake tree with lights on it and we sat in the glow of the lights and ate the takeout and laughed and he held me all night again.

I don't know what I'm going to do when everyone else gets back tomorrow, and the dorm mothers are going to be patrolling regularly again. For a while it was just me and Warren, and no stress or worries other than making sure the process was still going smoothly. I wish we could go on forever like this.

January 3

Well, I think Emily is back to hating me, or whatever it is she called it. She came in and dumped her suitcase on her bed and asked how break was. I told her it was fine. Quiet. Hardly anyone around. I guess from there she must have deduced that I spent most of the time with Warren and went silent. When I asked about her break she was completely bitchy. Like me talking to her was irritating. Thank God I got a text from Katy that she was back and so I ran out the door to meet her.

Katy got her hair cut! I can't believe it. There's no way, if I had her hair, I'd have chopped it off, but of course, this haircut just makes her look more sophisticated and fashionable. It's a shoulder-length bob now. I swear she needs a beret or a cigarette holder or something and the look would be complete. Très chic.

Drew and Warren met us for dinner but afterward we sneaked off again for girl time. Warren promised he'd handle the lab, so Katy and I got ice cream and I dished about my break with Warren. She faked tears and put her hand over her heart and said she was a proud mama. I swear, we went over every detail, and she properly reacted to it all, giving me more advice when necessary and beaming proudly at other times. I also told her about Emily being kind of awful.

> Katy: Yeah, well, that's Emily. I'm surprised
> she hasn't made a voodoo doll of you or drawn
> some kind of curse symbol under your bed.
> Even now she still follows Warren around.

Me: Wait, what? She follows him around?

Katy, licking her spoon: Yeah. Sometimes she
talks to him. Sometimes she just trails him.
It's creepy.

Me: So Warren knows?

Katy: Yeah, of course, but Warren's too nice of
a person to do anything about it. Every time he
talks to her I can tell he just feels sorry for her.

Like, I don't know why it bothers me that Warren hasn't
told me about Emily, but it does. It's not like I suspect there's
anything going on between them, but that seems like something
I should know. What if she's watching us? Following us around?
It's creepy. I feel like I should start carrying Mace but . . . I live
with her. It's not like I can protect myself too much. Thank
goodness she's not there most of the time.

Katy had continued talking but I only noticed when I heard
her say:

Katy: . . . but Warren's a fantastic kisser, so I'm
sure he's good at everything else, too, right?

Me: How do you know he's a fantastic kisser???

Katy, laughing: Don't worry! It was a long time ago. Eighth grade. We made out at a party at Campbell. I think we were dared to, actually. But I had braces so he probably thought I sucked. I don't know. I've never had the courage to ask him.

I laughed, amazed and surprised that Katy Ashton, of all people, didn't have the courage to ask Warren about a kiss three years ago. And that she'd had braces! I assumed her straight teeth were a result of great genes, just like her hair and high cheekbones and body, magically toned even though I know she never sets foot in the gym.

There is a weird part of me that is super glad Katy Ashton had flaws at some point. It makes me feel way more hopeful about the future.

January 8

Ugh. I don't know what's gotten into me, but I totally forgot that I should have been working on the Princeton science program application over break too, because it's due next week.

Luckily, Mr. Callahan already had a letter of recommendation drafted for me, so all I have to do is find another teacher to have my two. But there's an essay due as well, plus my transcripts. So now I'm going to have to get those expedited to Prescott in some way. Maybe my old school can fax them? Are faxes still a thing?

And don't even get me started on the essay. Macbeth was bad enough. I should have been working on this for weeks. At least it's only five pages, but I'm supposed to talk about how I want to use chemistry to achieve my goals. It SHOULD be easy but it's not because, honestly, I don't really know what my goals are. I just know I'm good at this, so I want to keep being good at this and get into a great school for it, but it's not like Warren. He wants to find a way to cure addiction. Of course he does, after what he's gone through with his brother. What can I say? I want to cure cancer? Embrace a cliché? Maybe I can say, "Hey, Princeton. I don't really have any original goals on my own so I'm just going to say I want to help my boyfriend do all these amazing things," because really, what else have I got?

Ugh. I've got to get my shit together.

January 9

So, after thinking about it all through classes today, I think I'm going to write my essay about making drugs that will help people who are in pain but aren't addictive. So it's LIKE Warren's idea, kind of piggybacking on it, but a different way to think about it. I'm happy with that, and it's a good goal. Maybe I'll actually adopt that as a goal.

I was writing the essay tonight at the lab, thinking about Warren and his brother, and for some reason, I just couldn't keep my mouth shut.

Me: Warren? Can I ask you something?

Warren, looking up from mixing a compound in a beaker, his goggles making him look like an owl: Anything, Bailey.

Me: Does it ever bother you that you're doing this? Making meth and selling it?

Warren, pushing his goggles up on his head: Haven't we talked about this before? I thought you were okay with this?

Me: I am. I think. I was mainly trying to ask about you. Since . . . since your brother and everything.

119

Warren set aside the chemicals and leaned on a stool, looking at me all seriously. Then he started talking, and although he seemed just as sincere as he had the other night when he told me about Mitchell dying, there was something almost robotic about it. Like he'd given this speech a hundred times before. So much that it was memorized.

I had to wonder if it's because it's something he has to constantly tell himself.

He said his brother is the whole reason why he does it. He went into more detail about Mitchell's death, saying that the heroin he'd used the night he died was laced with fentanyl, which is a thousand times stronger than heroin. And that even though his brother was an addict, he'd still be here if he hadn't gotten a product that was bad. If the product had been reliable and safe. So he wants to make sure that what's available is good and pure.

But he also told me that meth is different. He said a meth overdose is really rare and that usually, if it happens, it's because the person was sick in some other way, in addition to being an addict. Not that I'd imagined people dying because of what we were doing (don't get me wrong, I knew it was a possibility, but I keep that far from my mind because I know we make something safe), but I do feel better knowing it's rare. Like Warren said, people are going to do drugs. We just need to make it safer for them.

Maybe I can put something like that in my essay.

January 15

Okay, is it just me, or did the teachers literally double up the amount of homework now that everyone's back from break? I have to read two chapters of *Canterbury Tales* tonight, solve about a bajillion calculus problems, and answer all the chapter review questions for three chapters in civics. Just tonight! Even Mr. Callahan assigned twice the equations to balance that he usually does. I don't even know why I'm bothering to write in this diary right now. I have too much other stuff to do. I'm beginning to think maybe it's my way of telling Dad what's going on with me, even if he could just ask.

Or maybe it's my way of telling Mom. . . . I don't know. I don't have time to psychoanalyze myself tonight.

I talked to Mr. Callahan a little after class about maybe backing off on the extra work for a little while. He said that adjusting to Prescott's expectations can be difficult for a first-time student because the work definitely gets harder as you go, and there's more of it. He said in a few weeks I'll get the hang of it and know how to balance my time, and we could resume then. He didn't seem angry or even disappointed, so I was relieved. He asked about the essay for the Princeton application and I told him it was done.

It's not. It's not anywhere close. I have two more days. But I DID call my old school and they said they could scan and e-mail my transcripts to my adviser here. Thank goodness. I feel so behind and so unorganized, which is totally UN-Bailey, really, but . . . let's be honest. A lot about this year has been pretty un-Bailey. I'm part of a pretty elite group, I have extra money to spend, I have a sexy boyfriend, not to mention my "side job." It's no wonder I'm a little behind, but who could blame me? And honestly, it's worth it. I DO need to get more organized, though. I can do everything if I just focus and schedule myself better.

I didn't feel like I could skip out on Warren at the lab tonight, even though he said he'd be fine without my help. We're still trying to meet a high demand. Almost everyone who, um, distributes for Drew is out of product, so we're trying to build up a supply again.

Warren was super sweet, though, and mostly handled everything while I did my civics and calculus. He looked over my calculus homework and I only missed one. He takes that class as well, just a different period than I do, so I told him just to copy my work and get a different question wrong. Hey, at least one of us won't have to do it all tonight, and it was the least I could do since he handled the lab work. He said he'd do the work tomorrow, and that sounds like a good deal to me.

By the time I got back, Emily was asleep, which is just fine because I'm in no mood to deal with another human being, even if she decided to be Nice Emily. Ha. Maybe that's how

I should refer to her from now on. She's either Nice Emily or Scary Emily.

Just a few more chemistry formulas to balance and I can go to bed. I swear I could sleep for days, that's how tired I am. But there's no way I can slack off now. In fact, I need to do more than usual to keep on top of things. If I don't, I swear all this work is just going to pile up and suffocate me, like a big giant stress monster swallowing me whole. Okay, that's the weirdest sentence I've ever written, but also so true. I feel like I'm barely ahead of all of this, and if I don't keep up or I falter in any way, it's going to get me.

January 16

I wrote part of my essay in chemistry today. If there is any class I can afford to not pay attention in, it's chemistry. Plus, it's chemistry related, so I think it counts. It's too bad Mr. Callahan can't give me extra credit for all I do with Science Club. Ha! He didn't notice that I wasn't working on his stuff, I don't think. We weren't doing a lab today at all. He was lecturing about acids, stuff I know pretty well from my old school. I got the notes from Katy later anyway.

Everyone was at the lab tonight, and it was funny because I guess Warren and I are kind of used to having it alone now. We were doing our dance, mind-meld thing as we worked and Katy

123

and Drew thought it was sickeningly cute. And once, after we finished an incredible-looking batch, Warren picked me up and spun me and kissed me like no one was around. Drew started whistling and clapping. Honestly, it's really cool that they're so happy that we're happy. And I really miss alone time with Warren. . . . I wonder when Drew will go home next. Ha.

The only downside to having everyone there was that I didn't get nearly as much homework done, so I had a lot to do when I got back to my room. Emily was still up, doing her own homework, and she smiled at me and we commiserated about how much we had to do before settling back into it. She finished before I did and crawled into bed. I should have worked on my essay more before writing in here, but I'm just too tired. Katy's notes were good. Maybe I can write more in chemistry again tomorrow. I have another day. All I really have to do is type it up. The rest of the application is done.

January 17

Okay, well, I have GOT to get ahold of myself.

I overslept this morning. I hit snooze, only it wasn't snooze; I turned my alarm off. Luckily, Emily shook me awake and asked me if I was sick. While she was trying to inform me about sick day procedures at Prescott, I jumped up in a panic and pulled on my uniform. I barely had time to comb my hair.

I went to class without makeup and without a shower. I wanted to disappear all day long and just go home. I even thought about skipping lunch but I was starving since I didn't have any time to grab a bagel before classes started. Warren, bless him, didn't say a word about how awful I must have looked but hugged me hard after lunch, like he was concerned for me. Katy pulled me into the girls' room and let me use her concealer. Thank goodness for good friends.

I tried to work on my essay during chemistry but my brain felt like it had been fried. I barely got more than two paragraphs done, which left me tonight to finish it and type it up on top of all the other homework I had.

When I got to the lab tonight, I started to tell Warren about the essay and how it still wasn't done (I hadn't wanted to admit that to him. He's always so on top of things. I feel so stupid around him sometimes, I swear). Then I don't know what happened. Something in me snapped. One minute I was explaining about the essay and how I needed time to work on it tonight, the next I was apologizing for being such a screwup and sobbing into his chest while telling him about how hard Prescott was for me. Well, and not just Prescott. But my father being distant, missing Bex, missing my mom. . . . It was so bad I soaked his uniform sweater. I think . . . I think maybe I didn't realize how stressed I've been until I started talking about it. I don't think I knew how much I was missing my family, either. And how tired I really am. Even on good nights I'm hardly in bed by midnight, and classes start by seven thirty. At most I get six hours' sleep, if I can sleep well at all.

He held me, stroking my hair and telling me to tell him everything. Then he lifted me on top of the counter, kissed me, and started working through the problems with me in this amazing, confident, calm way. Exactly the opposite of me.

> Warren: Everything is okay here, Bailey.
> Don't worry about the product. I can
> handle it.

> Me: But . . . but you have a lot of work too.

> Warren: Yes, but you have the essay to do.
> That's an extra thing I don't have, since I've
> been admitted to that program before. So go
> ahead and work on it. Use my laptop to type
> up what you have, and write the rest when
> you're done. That way you're not writing
> it twice. You can e-mail it to yourself and
> print it in the lab in the morning. I'll give
> you my calculus homework to copy, and

chemistry, too, if you haven't done it. I can't do your reading for you in English, though. If you can do it after your essay, great. If not, read it this weekend and catch up. If you're called on in class, tell her you think the stories are metaphors for sex or politics or something. That will make you sound like you know what you're doing. Works like a charm, trust me.

Me, grabbing his face and kissing him: You're wonderful, you know that? I'm a mess, but you're wonderful. Thank you.

Warren, smiling, intense gaze on me: You're not a mess, Bailey Wells. You can do this. And I'll help you.

And that's just what he did. I somehow managed to get everything done, and for the first time since break, I feel relaxed. It's late now, and I'm setting two alarms for tomorrow, just in case. And even though it was late when I went to bed and I set two alarms for myself just in case, for the first time since break, I felt relaxed.

January 19

I got my application in on time. I'm not sure the essay was the best it could be, but at least I got it done. I did decide to write about making drugs that are non-addictive in the future, and I managed to work in some info about the drug problem in the local area as well. No outside sources needed.

Warren insisted we go into Wiltshire to celebrate, and since Drew needed to make a few drops, he and Katy went with us. It turned into an excellent evening. Drew suggested we catch a movie while he was out taking care of business, so Katy and I overruled Warren to see a romantic comedy. We kept joking around that Warren had a harem, since it was like he was taking us both on a date. It totally embarrassed him, I think, but it was so fun to watch him blush and seem awkward for once. We were the only people in the theater, and so we got a little rowdy and had a popcorn fight and kept a running commentary of the movie as it played.

When we came out, Drew was waiting by his car for us, mission completed. He gestured to Warren, and Warren nodded, then the two boys went off a little ways to talk alone. Katy and I crawled into the warm car to wait, me in the back and her in shotgun.

Me: What's that about?

Katy: Probably just business. Who knows?
They do this all the time.

Me: And it doesn't bother you that you're not
included?

Katy, shrugging, focusing on her phone: Nah.
The less I know, the better, really.

Me: But won't we all get in trouble anyway? If
one of us is caught? Don't we all . . . you know,
go down with the ship?

Katy, finally looking at me: Oh, you sweet,
innocent child. Of course not. If Drew gets
caught making drops, it's all on him. Or if you
and Warren get busted in the lab one night,
Drew and I don't know you. No, if you get
caught, you take one for the team. Why do you
think I always let Drew do the drops alone?

Me: So . . . cut and run?

Katy: Cut and run. As much as we can.

Me, squinting at her: Save yourself instead
of all of us in it together? That doesn't seem
very loyal.

Katy, snapping: Loyal? You don't think that's
loyal, Bailey? If I got caught, I'd do everything
I could to keep the rest of you from getting
caught too. I'd take all the blame. You guys
could go on with your lives while I rot in
prison. I'd do it for all three of you, and I
know Drew and Warren would do the same
for me.

Me: Okay, okay. Sorry. I didn't understand. I
get it now. I'd do it too. I just . . . didn't see it
like that before.

Katy, softening: In this business, it's about
doing the least amount of damage to ourselves
that we can. You got me?

I think I got her. There is honor among thieves, so to speak.
The most honorable thing you could do if you were caught
would be to keep your mouth shut about everyone else and

their involvement. And for some reason, it makes me feel safer. I mean, of course it's nice knowing that if one of us got caught, we wouldn't all go down. But it is also good to know that we'd all go to such lengths for each other. Again, I feel that weird sense of trust in this little group.

Of course there's the collateral to consider. Which would be used if we ever betrayed one another. But we would never do that.

Warren and Drew got back in the car, none the wiser to the conversation Katy and I had just had. Warren took my hand.

Katy: Everything okay?

Drew, smiling: More than okay. You know that thing we talked about? How we could expand? It's gonna start next week. One of our dealers has made a few connections, so there will be about five degrees separating it from us.

Katy: Excellent.

Drew: But that means Bailey and Warren will have to cook even more. Can you handle it?

Warren, squeezing my hand: We can handle it.

But . . . I'm not sure I can. I'm barely making it as it is. And I want to know more about this so-called expansion. Where are we expanding *to*? But then again, the less I know, the better (Katy's words). I think I should probably heed them. The less I know, the fewer lies I'd have to tell, and the more I can keep the distribution part of this process far, far away from me.

January 21

I have literally all my books piled up with me on the bed right now. Emily wanted to know if we could go see a movie with those passes I gave her and there's just no possible way I can. It's Sunday night, and it's my own fault because I left all of this to do until now. After the news Friday that we'd be expanding, Warren and I kicked up our production majorly yesterday, and we were there until late (luckily, no one else was, so we got in some great making out while things cooked around us), and we were at the lab most of today, too.

I apologized to Emily, saying it was bad planning/ procrastination and totally my fault, and she nodded understandingly. She said the workload this semester was overwhelming, even for Prescott. We joked that the teachers are all involved in a conspiracy to drive us insane. Then she asked if Warren and I are pretty serious.

Emily: You're just spending a ton of time with him is all.

Me: You really want to know?

Emily, rolling her eyes: It's fine. I'm fine.

Me: Then yes, I think we're pretty serious.

Emily: But you're not hanging out with him tonight? He could probably help you with homework. He's smarter than anyone else here.

Me: I'm aware. But he's got his own work to do.

Emily: I'm sure he does.

I didn't really appreciate her talking to me like I don't know Warren or something. I'M his girlfriend, after all, and pretty soon he and I will have been together longer than he and Emily were. She was barely a blip on his radar. And I didn't like the knowing way she said, "I'm sure he does." She doesn't know the half of it. If she knew how he keeps up with his classes while also basically running a whole business . . .

Deep breaths, Bailey. Emily is no longer your competition. He broke up with her. And he's with you now. Relax. Okay, self. Good talk.

I just don't know why Warren seems to bring all the jealousy out of me. And really, thinking about our conversation, she could have meant everything she said innocently. It's just that I already have my hackles up with the stress and . . . yep. The jealousy. I vowed to give her the benefit of the doubt. Maybe this is more MY issue than hers.

Anyway, as we were working, Emily got a text. She glanced at it and got up, throwing her coat and boots on. She looked at me and shrugged, saying she'd be back later.

I was trying to seem calm and casual (I hope she couldn't tell that she'd gotten a rise out of me), so I didn't ask her where she was going. She can do whatever the hell she wants, as long as it's not with Warren.

January 27

I haven't written in a few days again. It's not just that I'm busy. It's that my hand actually hurts from writing as much as I have been. Warren and I are basically working from the minute classes end for the day until ten or eleven at night, then I come home and do

134

any work I still have left, and fall asleep, usually on a book.

At least I'm not the only one. Emily's obviously been just as stressed-out. If she's here at all, she's sometimes passed out in her bed, snoring slightly. I can totally understand where she's coming from, so I just throw a blanket on her and let her sleep. We've both had to wake each other up for classes in the morning a few times now. Emily's incredibly hard to stir, so I sort of hate it. She acts like she doesn't know where she is for a while, and she always wants food first thing. Sometimes we're both so late there's no time to get breakfast, so she gets into our stash of granola bars and takes five or six for herself. I don't mind it, really. But I feel like if she's going to take a whole box of granola bars, basically, in one day, she should probably pay for the bulk of them. Whatever.

Mr. Callahan said I'd hear from Princeton in about a month, so nothing to report there yet.

In other news, I got a B on another English paper. This time about Chaucer. She said it was a good premise but not enough support with the text, and it lost its focus. I'm upset, but only at myself because she's right. The paper is a mess. I'm lucky she gave me a B, honestly.

But between that and the bad civics test, I've got to double my efforts in those two classes. I still have a chance to pull all As, if I can do phenomenally well in the next few assignments.

I'll start tomorrow. I'm just too tired tonight. I can't wait to get in bed and sleep. I feel like I could sleep for days.

January 28

Nothing really to report except to say I'm super pissed at myself. First day of trying to double my efforts in civics and English and I got home later than usual from the lab and fell asleep with my English book on my stomach.

I just can't stay awake, but if I can't stay awake longer, how can I get everything done???

January 29

Tonight I actually fell asleep in the lab. I woke up hunched over a lab table to Warren rubbing my shoulders. When I asked what time it was, Warren told me it was just after ten and that I'd been out for almost a half hour. A HALF HOUR.

Then he told me to go home and rest, that he could handle all the product tonight. And I looked at him and his bright blue eyes and sweet smile and I looked at all the books spread around me on the table and all the things we had simmering and smoking and cooking and . . . it just hit me that I'm failing everything. I'm failing school, I'm failing my friends, I'm failing Warren. I'm even failing Bex. I haven't called her for ages. I can't keep up with it all, can't hold up my end of the bargain.

All I do is disappoint, let people down, and break promises. Everything feels so out of reach and I can't remember the last time I had a break to rest. No break in sight, and only constantly disappointing everyone I care about and I . . .

I just lost it. Completely lost it. And it wasn't like I let out this big scream or sob or anything. I just sat there numb and tired and silently crying. That was the worst of it, I think. That there was no warning. The nervous breakdown sneaked up on me, and I was completely unprepared.

So was Warren. His eyes got as big as I'd ever seen them and he hugged me hard. Then he knelt in front of me, holding my hands while I cried and cried and cried.

> Me: I can't leave you to do all this alone anymore. I'm not being a good partner. Or girlfriend. Or sister or student or roommate or friend or . . . or anything right now. I just can't get it all done. All the homework and the Science Club. I thought it would get better, or I would, and it just hasn't.

> Warren, squeezing my hands: Bailey, it's okay. Everyone is struggling right now. Drew and Katy, even.

Me: What? They are? See? I don't even know that. I hardly see Katy. I haven't really seen her since before break. Just that dinner we had.

Warren: And I'm sure she misses you. But we're all really busy right now. Katy and Drew have a lot of responsibilities too, even though they don't have to work here as much. It's just hard right now. We'll get through it.

Me: What about you, Warren? I mean, you don't seem like you're tired like me. I know you're supposed to be a genius and all, but it can't be that easy for you, right? Please tell me it can't. Lie. Just for my sanity.

Warren, laughing: It's not that easy, Bailey. I promise. It's hard for me, too.

Me: But why aren't you tired?

Warren looked at me for a long moment, like he was considering his answer very carefully. Then he stood and took something out of his back pocket. He handed it to me. It was a plastic bag with small orange pills inside. They looked like candy. I stared at it. Oddly, I wasn't shocked or surprised, but I WAS curious. Scarily curious.

> Warren: I AM tired all the time, Bailey. But I have a little extra help. From these.

> Me: But . . . what are they? A prescription?

> Warren: A mixture of amphetamines and dextroamphetamines. And yes, a prescription.

> Me, knowing enough of those chemical names to understand now: Stimulants.

> Warren: Adderall. I was prescribed it after Mitch died. Couldn't concentrate.

> Me: And it helps keep you from falling asleep on your books at night?

> Warren, nodding: And it makes me super focused and confident. Like I can do it all. And with the energy it gives me, I can.

Me, shaking my head: Why didn't you tell me before? I mean, don't you trust me?

Warren: No. Nothing like that. I guess I just hate admitting that maybe I can't do it all on my own, you know?

Me, nodding: How much do you take?

Warren: Whatever I want, really. Depends on the day and what I'm doing. I don't remember what the prescription was for. Two a day, maybe? Doesn't matter. I can always get more. It's an easy trade for what we make, and so many people around here take them.

Me: And it really helps you?

In answer Warren took my hand and folded it into his, around the bag of pills. He said they were mine, and I could try it and see if it helped. He said it was absolutely up to me and also that I could trust him.

They're sitting here next to me as I write, and I feel like I'm in a cartoon with a devil on one shoulder and an angel

140

on the other, thinking about what I should do. Emily is fast asleep, so there's no worry about being found out. Warren told me if I want to take one, wait until tomorrow so I won't be up all night.

On one hand, it's a pill. On the other, they could obviously help me right now. I could be like Warren and actually get through the day and do the things I need to do. I could stay on top of my work and have energy. I mean, look at him. He takes them, sometimes more than he was prescribed, and he's doing so well. He's practically a model student.

Is he right? Can I trust him? Of course I can. I know that. Not only that, but he knows chemistry inside and out. If there was a real danger to these, he would have said so. Besides, he was prescribed this as medication. It's meant to be used for focus.

I tucked them under my pillow. I think I've decided. I'll see how tomorrow goes.

February 1

By third period today, I felt like I was dragging. I could feel the pills in my jumper skirt pocket. They felt heavy as lead but so did my eyelids. I kept thinking about how easy it seemed for Warren to do everything, and I raised my hand and got permission to go to the bathroom.

Inside the bathroom I slipped one pill out of the bag and into my hand. I looked at myself in the mirror, like I was asking permission of myself or something. Or maybe advice. My reflection offered neither; the Bailey who stared back at me looked exhausted and scared, terrified of failing, and barely hanging on. I wanted to help her. I turned on the water and cupped my hand, ready to toss the pill back, and the door swung open. Luckily it was Katy.

Katy: Hey. You all right? Saw you leave calc.

Me, nodding and balling up my fist around the pill: Yeah. Fine. Thanks. You okay?

Katy: What's that?

And because it's Katy, and because I feel like I need some advice from someone who isn't just a reflection, I opened my hand. Katy snatched the pill from my palm and a huge grin spread over her face.

Katy: An Addy? Bailey! Did Warren give this to you?

Me, apprehensive: Yeah. Is that a problem?

Katy, snorting: Yes it's a problem! He's been
holding out on me. Said he couldn't get me
any until next week.

Me: You take these?

Katy: Yeah. Who doesn't? Wait. Don't tell me
this is your first time. . . .

I stared at Katy dumbly. All of a sudden it was like a door
had opened into a world I hadn't been able to see before. Or
maybe it was just that *Wizard of Oz* kind of thing. . . . Suddenly
I was seeing things in color.

Katy's world, apparently, was already in Technicolor. She
was laughing, calling Warren stingy, then she asked me if I had
any extra.

In answer I pulled out the bag.

Katy, laughing harder: Mind if I join you,
then? I don't think I'm going to get through
this day without something.

Me: Sure. But . . . why does Warren get them
for you? Aren't you the contact?

Katy: I make the contacts. I don't necessarily keep them. Sometimes they like to deal with Warren directly.

Me, not sure what to make of that, so switching the subject: Are you serious, though? Everyone here does this? It's no big deal? I mean, it's not dangerous?

Katy: Hell no. I think it's how most of us survive Prescott.

So Katy took one of my (Warren's) pills out of the bag and handed it back to me. We both swallowed them at the same time and headed back to class, giggling like idiots. I felt good. A little nervous about how it might make me feel, but good.

When fourth period came around, something changed. I just felt more ALIVE. Like everything was super interesting. Even Shakespeare. I didn't feel high or anything, just energetic. Almost hyper. And very, very capable.

I'm noticing as I'm writing that it has worn off a little, but I still feel better than I have in weeks. Honestly, Warren was right. This was exactly what I needed.

February 2

Yesterday was amazing. I did well in all my classes, did my homework, and helped Warren at the lab until it was time to go home for the night. (And since we were alone in the lab, we took advantage. At least we pretty much always know ahead of time when Katy and Drew are going to stop by, so we didn't worry about getting caught.) He walked me home, and as we were walking he smiled at me and said I seemed to be having a pretty good day. I got his hint and played along. I told him I was and asked if I could take more than one. He laughed like that question was adorable or something. Then he told me not to take both at once but to spread them out. He said I'd be able to tell when it was leaving my system, and I could take another then. We talked for a long time about what it felt like, and he was so amused by how excited I was. He said he could tell it was really working for me.

I don't know why I doubted him there for a little bit. Warren really cares about me. He's not going to do anything that would hurt me.

He did tell me it would make me feel like crashing later. He said I'd feel really aware and kind of hyper still, but also tired at the same time. He told me to drink lots of water and eat something, even if I didn't feel hungry yet. He also gave me a bottle of melatonin, which he said would make me sleep even if my brain felt really active still.

He was right about all of it. As soon as my energy waned, I felt thirsty and hungry and a little grumpy. I took one of the melatonin and lay down. Emily wasn't home, thank goodness, so she wouldn't know something strange was going on. Luckily, I didn't have long to think about any of it. The melatonin kicked in, chasing out the energy left over from the Adderall, and I went to sleep. I think I slept like a baby. I woke up early and ready to do it all over again. I felt like I could take on the whole world.

February 9

So, when Drew said we were expanding, I guess it didn't really compute with everything else going on that we would also be making more money. A LOT more money. Warren and I have nearly doubled our output and . . . the money appears to have doubled as well.

I've been keeping money in an extra makeup bag I had, but now it's almost too small for that. So, naturally, the only solution is to go buy something else to put it in.

When Friday night rolled around and Drew had to make his deliveries, Katy and I caught a ride into Wiltshire with him, and of course Warren came too. We didn't have to cook tonight. We'd decided we'd take most of tomorrow to do that. Sunday, Emily and I are going to the movies, so it makes sense to get the bulk of the supply started Saturday.

Warren didn't come with me and Katy to the mall, though. He said he was going to help Drew. That worried me a little. I like thinking Warren's not directly involved like Drew, but I guess Drew needs extra help now, so this is going to be a regular thing. He told me not to worry about it. He said Drew's good at what he does and they always deliver on their promises. Essentially, they're too valuable to be hurt or ratted out. When I pressed him a little further, he told me Drew had protection taken care of.

I'm not sure what that means. Do they pay someone to be their muscle? Does Drew pack a weapon? Have I watched far too many gangster movies?

So I tried not to worry while the boys were doing business. Neither of them seemed like they'd be useful at all in a street fight (I can only write that here. They'd probably be so mad at me for thinking it, but come on, they're brainy boys who don't even play sports).

To keep myself from worrying, and also because I had more money than I knew what to do with, Katy and I went into Sephora and had them do our makeup. I ended up buying every single thing they put on my face, as well as a few other things they recommended, and something they promised would keep my hair super soft, which was more for Warren than me. Katy bought some Dior lipstick and

a French perfume I've seen Isa ogle before. Then we left
in search of purses. I picked out a really cute brown-and-
turquoise purse and matching wallet—for all my extra money.
Katy assured me the designer was worth the price, even if it
was half a week's "paycheck."

We tried on dresses for fun. I guess Prescott has a formal
(they don't dare call it prom—proms are for peasants) in the
spring, so it's months away still. Only juniors and seniors can
go. I assume Warren will ask me, if that's his type of thing. Katy
said he'd take me even if it wasn't. I asked her if she'd go with
Drew.

> Katy: Why would you think that?

> Me: You guys do everything else together, I
> guess, so why not formal? And you flirt all the
> time.

> Katy: We do not.

> Me: Liar. Come on. What is up with you two?

> Katy, pretending to be interested in a black
> sequined dress: Okay, don't tell anyone I told you

this. Even Warren, though I'm sure he knows. What's up with me and Drew? I really don't know. Sometimes he acts like he wants to be together, then he doesn't. So, it's confusing, and I feel like we're always kind of together but not, but I'd feel weird about being with anyone else. I don't know. I guess it's friends with benefits, but a little more sometimes and a little less other times.

Me, shocked: So . . . you fool around with him and stuff but you're not really together?

Katy: Oh, come on, Bailey. Don't be a prude.

Me: I'm not! I'm just surprised that it's not official. I never see him with anyone else. So what's his deal?

Katy: He's so busy, I guess. The business is his first love, you know?

Me: Yeah, but . . . Warren's busy too. He still finds time for me.

Katy: Yeah, because you're both in
the lab all the time. Drew and I are
constantly out making connections in
different places.

Me: Yeah, okay. And you two must have done
a hell of a job with this latest expansion.
Warren and I can barely keep up.

Katy, grinning like the cat who caught the
canary: Yep. And it's not going to slow down.
The market's getting huge. And you know
what? It was all my idea.

I didn't ask what market or what, exactly, her idea was.
Again, there are some things I don't want to know. And also,
it doesn't really matter. We're doing this safely, for people
who are already addicted. It's not like Drew is pushing meth
on anyone who hasn't been using already. He's not even a
dealer himself, just a supplier. It is as innocent as we can
possibly make it.

When I got home I put my money in my new wallet, in my
new handbag, and slid it under my bed. Innocent or not, Emily
doesn't need to see it and get nosy.

February 12

Yesterday was fine. Emily and I went to see a rather serious film about World War II and went to dinner afterward, and she didn't mention Warren once. But she did seem particularly restless. During the movie she kept squirming, and she rushed off after dinner. Maybe she had a lot to do as well. I ran to the lab when we were done and helped Warren all I could before I had to finish up what was left of my homework. I got it all done before midnight and actually got about six hours of sleep.

But still . . . classes were the last thing I wanted to do today. What I really wanted to do was spend all day with Warren. Preferably alone. In his bed.

It feels like break was forever ago, okay? And it's hard that we don't have that much time alone anymore.

I ended up taking another one of the Adderalls that Warren had given me. I hadn't all weekend, but I felt like maybe it was the only way to face this stupid day. It kicked in after breakfast and I felt good to go. I swear it gives me more brainpower or something. It's like it unclutters my mind and lets me focus on the important things. I don't find myself zoning out, even when Mr. Callahan is working over the sixth equation in a row, and they've all been things I could solve in my sleep.

Then in the afternoon, after classes ended, I took another

one. I was starting to feel that downward slide Warren warned me about, and I still had most of my day to go. I'm so glad I did. I had the energy to do all my homework and still stay in the lab until late. Warren was so entertained by how talkative I was, and I could tell he was also super impressed with how much I did tonight in the lab. I usually let him handle the bulk of the work so I can get my homework done, but tonight it was completely equal.

I thanked him for the pills and told him they were helping. He said they've been helping him for years. If he's been on these since middle school and he's so completely together and brilliant, it clearly doesn't have any bad side effects. I've heard pot can make you lose brain cells and be lazy, and people do that stuff all the time. Of course, Adderall is a prescription, so it must be safer anyway.

Going to turn in. Another long day ahead of me tomorrow.

February 19

It's been a while since I've written. Again. I probably should get better about this, but honestly, with everything going on, the diary my father gave me is just not a priority. Besides, Isa was probably the one who picked it out or told him to get it for me. It wouldn't surprise me if Isa still keeps a diary *insert massive eye roll here*. It's probably filled with things like "Got Greg to spend Christmas with me instead of his horrible brats!" or "Convinced Greg to send the ugly stepchildren to boarding school. It means one fewer trip to Paris this year, but c'est la vie!" But it's weird. I feel bad when I don't write. Guilty. Like I'm not holding up my end of the bargain, even though I never really made one with Dad. I guess maybe I'm hoping that one day he'll want to know what's been going on with me.

Also, I have to admit, there's something about writing down what's going on with my life that feels a bit like therapy. It kind of helps me sort out my thoughts, which seem to be scattered at best. I'm just SO busy, so tired, and I feel like I will never catch up.

Not that there's much to report at the moment. Every day is just like the last. Too much homework, not enough time with Warren, Emily is sometimes restless or complains about Warren but is mostly okay and usually absent from our room anyway, and Katy and I have been meeting in the bathroom every morning to throw back an Addy before classes. We've been out for coffee only once this week, but she's so busy too, all we can do is check in. She and Drew stop by the lab a lot, though.

And Warren. I swear, he's gotten even better over the last few days. I don't know how. Maybe it's just that I haven't had a freak-out for a while, so he feels like he can relax around me again. It's some kind of record for me or something. Whatever it is, I swear he's more awesome than ever before. I've never seen him smile so much. And he's just as anxious as I am to find some time alone together, but he's never pushy about it. I really could not have asked for a better first boyfriend.

Oh, and did I mention how beautiful his eyes are? Not lately? Ha. Okay.

Anyway, off to bed. It's 12:30 a.m. Tomorrow morning is going to be a bitch.

February 21

You know how the last time I wrote I was praising Warren for being so awesome?

Well, we had our first fight tonight. It's okay. He's still awesome and all. It's ME who's not awesome. I'm just so afraid I've let him down somehow. He seemed disappointed. It was almost like what I felt like when I'd get in trouble with Mom: not scared about the consequences so much, just afraid that she thought less of me.

It started at the lab. It was all fine. We were joking around and having a great time. We were even going over some ways we could maybe tweak our process to make it more streamlined, or at least a lot less messy. I'm not even sure how we even got on the subject from there. . . . I think I may have asked him what meth was really like. If it was like Adderall but stronger. And he asked me how much of the Adderall I'd been taking.

> Me: A couple a day. I'm about out, actually. I was going to ask for more. If that's okay.

> Warren: How are you out? I gave you a couple dozen pills. It's not even been a week. Are you lying?

> Me, horrified: No! I'm not lying. I've just been giving some to Katy. I didn't realize she took them sometimes. So she and I have been taking a few together every day.

> Warren: (cursing like I've never heard him curse before)

> Me: I'm sorry. Was I not supposed to give any to her?

> Warren: No, Bailey. You weren't.

Me: Okay, well, I'm sorry. I won't give her
any more. I didn't realize it was a problem.
She kind of implied that you knew, that
everyone did it, so I didn't think it was a big
deal.

Warren, snapping: Of course not. She's
getting all the pills she wants. You don't have
any left?

Me: No. Did you . . . did you need some? Did
you give me all of yours?

Warren, sighing: No, I . . . I shouldn't
have used so many. I just figured you'd still
have some. And I can't get you more until
next week. I can't get US more until next
week.

Me: Okay. I'm really sorry. And I was going
to ask how I could pay you for them, I guess?
They probably cost a lot, right?

Warren: Yeah, Bailey. They cost a fucking lot.

At that point I made myself really busy with chemicals and started crying because I'd screwed up . . . just one more thing I was screwing up in a long list. And honestly, because I'd never seen Warren this angry. I'd never seen him angry, period. He's always been so patient and understanding. Now he was beyond irritable.

I wiped at my eyes and that's when he must have noticed I was crying. He immediately pulled me into his arms and kept saying, "Shhh," over and over, even though I wasn't talking. I buried my head in his chest and he stroked my hair.

> Warren: I'm sorry. I shouldn't have snapped at you. I shouldn't have expected you to know. It's just that they're not easy to get. Not in that kind of quantity. And I'm . . . I'm a little over my head right now in what I owe people.

> Me: Can we make more product? Exchange it or sell it to make up for it?

> Warren: No. I don't owe anyone money for drugs. That's not what I meant. I owe for my car. For Princeton's program. And I owe

it to my parents. They pay for everything;
I just pay them back. So finding some
extra for pills is hard, even with all we're
raking in.

Me, understanding now why everything was
so serious and important: Then take some of
what I'm making.

Warren: I couldn't . . .

Me: Come on. This is for me, too, right?
And honestly, Warren, this week . . .
having that extra energy? I finally feel like
I can handle everything. And I won't share
with Katy again. Unless she gives me a
cut too.

Warren, kissing me hard on the lips: I really
am sorry.

Me, kissing him back, but sweet and long: I
know. Me too. Everything's going to be all
right.

We ignored the chemicals simmering around us for a while and got quite lost in, um, apologizing to each other after that. As much as I don't like fighting with him, I certainly LOVE making up with him.

February 26

I was a little off today. Just . . . sluggish. Kind of short-tempered. I was even a little rude to Mr. Callahan after class when he asked me if I'd heard from Princeton yet. I don't know why. I just have this sinking feeling that it will be bad news and I don't know why he has to bug me about it. So I said something snarky like, "I'll let you know when I get my rejection letter," or something and pretty much fled the classroom before he could say anything back. The last thing I needed today was him trying to convince me that I'm good enough to get in. I don't need that kind of pity.

At least I got all my homework done, but it was at the expense of spending time in the lab, and I really could have used some more time with Warren tonight. Like, a lot more time. After the little fight we had the other night, I've wanted nothing more than to be with him and let him convince me that everything is okay. But I had to leave the lab early to do my reading in civics and English.

Emily was in a foul mood tonight too. I don't know what's going on with her and I probably should have asked, but quite frankly, I don't have the energy to invest in her right now. I'm just scraping by as it is. And if it's about Warren, I don't want to hear it anyway. So when I got in and she snarled something about "trouble in paradise" with me and Warren, I pretty much threw in my earbuds and buried myself in my civics textbook. She stayed up even later than me and I nearly screamed at her for drumming her fingers on her desk and keeping me up with her impromptu percussion solo.

Thank God I'm about to fall asleep from pure exhaustion, or it might have come to blows.

February 27

Everything seems to be fine with Warren, and he's getting more pills tonight, but something about that fight has been bugging me since it happened. And it took me until tonight to figure it out:

If he thought I'd taken all those pills, shouldn't he have been concerned about me? Not the pills?

But that's silly. I told him I'd been sharing with Katy right after that. He probably didn't even have time to worry about me. And wasn't him thinking I was lying concern for me anyway? I mean, if I'd taken those all myself and lied to him about it, of course he'd be concerned. Obviously he was just trying to make sure I was taking them properly.

. . . Right?

March 3

I went with Warren and Drew to make deliveries tonight.

Katy thought I was nuts and asked to be dropped off at a frozen yogurt place. She said she makes enough connections, she doesn't want to be seen with them too. But Warren and Drew said it would be okay, as long as I waited in the car.

I don't really know why I wanted to go. For one, Katy has been a little cold to me since I told her I was out of Adderall and that Warren didn't want me to share anymore. She said Warren was always selfish like that, which I thought was uncalled-for and completely untrue, so we haven't been talking as much as usual. I mean, really, how dare she? He's trying to help me, and she's only focused on the pills. She hasn't asked me how I'm doing at all.

But other than that, there was no good reason for my sudden desire to stick with the guys. I've been pretty happy with keeping my distance from this part. Blind eye and all that. But now that Warren is involved . . . now that I know why he did this and why he works so hard . . . and also, now that we are making more than we've ever made before, I want to know how it works. I want to at least understand every cog in the machine, even if it doesn't really touch mine.

We dropped Katy off (after she asked me again to be sane and come with her instead) and headed to the east end of Wiltshire.

As we drove, we literally went across some train tracks like some horrible cliché to a part of town I was completely unfamiliar with. As soon as we were on the other side, everything changed. The houses were more run-down. There were bars on the storefront windows. There were people out walking, and none of them were dressed well, like the people we saw in the mall in Wiltshire. We passed under a bridge and there were tents there.

Me: So, when you said we were expanding . . .

Drew, shaking his head: This is our territory, Bailey. All of it. Has been for a few years. The expansion was less about an area, more about attracting a new type of clientele.

I wanted to ask, but I didn't. I was beginning to think this was a mistake. I didn't know any of the people we were passing by, but I saw their faces now. Their eyes. Their hopelessness.

Warren, disgusted, turning away from the window: There's lots of heroin down here too. But, as you know, we wouldn't ever get into that scene.

Drew: No. The guys that deal it too . . .
straight-up frauds. They put all sorts of shit in
their product. Or they don't even know where
it's coming from.

Me: Fentanyl?

Warren, visibly agitated: Yeah. Fentanyl.
Whatever they can get their hands on.
(Cursing under his breath that I couldn't quite
make out.)

Drew slowed to a stop. I couldn't help but think his fancy
car stood out in this area like a sore thumb. The dome light
came on as Drew pushed open his door. I felt like it was the
only light around for blocks.

Drew: Lock the doors. Don't you dare leave.
And on the off chance that something bad
goes down, do not under any circumstances
call the cops. Drive away. Park a mile or
two from campus, leave the keys inside, and
walk back.

Warren, handing me the keys to his car: And
come back to pick up Katy with mine.

Me, staring dumbly at the keys: There's a
possibility that something bad will happen?

Drew, smiling warmly: Usually not. But
sometimes people we don't know show up.

I noticed that nowhere in this plan did they want me to
come back for them. Meaning they would either be in jail or
dead. Panic seized me, and I must have been showing it on my
face because Warren reached out for my hand and gave it a
squeeze, promising everything would be fine. Then he pecked
me on the cheek and they both climbed out of the car, taking
several duffel bags with them. I saw them disappear into a
house that was mostly dark. A light flipped on inside, but only
one. I locked the doors and waited, watching and listening.
Anxious. Time moved so slowly I thought I was going to grow
old and die in that car. But then I heard voices. Drew and
Warren were back.

Me, more relieved than I'd ever been in my
life: Everything went okay?

Drew, smiling: Yep.

Warren: I think perhaps we should up our prices.

Drew: Maybe. In a week or two. Materials are getting expensive. (He turned back to me.) Okay if we make one more stop?

I said sure, because I'd survived one, so I could surely survive another. Unlike the last place, though, we didn't stop at a house. We were outside of what looked to be an abandoned gas station. The boys told me it was the same deal as before, and left me. This time, by way of the streetlights, I got to see what went down.

I felt like I was watching a movie. Like this couldn't possibly be part of my life.

As Warren and Drew headed toward the station, a solitary man came from the other direction, shaking their hands like they were old friends. There was some talking, some laughing, then Drew pulled out what was obviously a wad of cash. I started to worry, because this seemed so public. So VISIBLE. But the man didn't hold on to the cash for long. I don't even think he counted it, just pocketed it and withdrew a couple of small bags from the inside of his coat. Drew took one, and

Warren took two. Even from this distance I could see the pale orange color inside one of them. The guys all shook hands again and then it was over and they were back in the car.

Warren slid in next to me, letting Drew play chauffeur. I looked at him questioningly, and he pulled out the bag of orange pills. We smiled. So that was it. Not that hard. And the guy had just wanted money in return, not our product.

When we crossed back over the train tracks, Drew pulled something out of his coat pocket and tossed it unceremoniously into the glove compartment. As he shut the door I caught a glimpse of a dark metal barrel and a leather grip. It was a small gun, but I had no doubt it would do the job and that Drew knew how to use it. The protection they'd mentioned before. But somehow, it didn't make me feel safer.

I curled into Warren and he wrapped himself around me. When Katy got in, she leaned over and whispered something into Drew's ear that made Drew turn back to us and ask if it was okay if we split up for the night. It meant that Katy wanted Drew to come back with her for a while. It also meant Drew and Warren's room would be unoccupied.

I put the worry out of my mind so that I could enjoy having some time alone with Warren, but now that I'm writing, I have to wonder . . . if you have to bring a gun to feel safe, do you really feel safe?

March 7

Today I saw for myself what Katy was talking about with
Warren and Emily. I'd gone into the dining hall between first
and second periods to grab some coffee (the dining hall coffee
is rather horrible and weak, but I don't have time to get to
the coffee shop until after school) and as I was walking out, I
spotted them. They were deep in conversation by the English
building, exactly where I needed to go. I could tell by both their
expressions that the conversation wasn't pleasant.

I felt absolutely ridiculous and kind of paranoid, but I totally
hid behind a tree and watched.

We have fifteen minutes between periods so we can all get
to the other buildings on campus, and getting the coffee couldn't
have taken me more than five, if that. Which left nearly ten
whole minutes of them talking to each other. Emily's brows
were furrowed and she spoke through a clenched jaw. Warren
seemed impatient, shrugging and shaking his head. I think I
even saw him roll his eyes once.

Then, to my horror, she stepped closer to him and took his
hand. He let her take it for a moment, then dropped it, and his
lips formed a forceful "No."

I was so relieved. It was like seeing that everything he and
Katy had ever told me about Emily, and how Warren felt about
her now, was completely true. I mean, I knew deep down he

wasn't lying to me, but I guess there was a part of me . . . that scared and paranoid part, probably . . . that still thought maybe he had some feelings for her. Or, if I'm really honest with myself, he didn't feel that strongly about ME.

I figured it was time to mark my territory, so to speak, so I wandered over to them, gave Emily the brightest smile I could muster, and kissed Warren on the cheek. He shot me a grateful look and reached down for my hand. The warning bell rang, so Emily excused herself, and Warren gave me another kiss before we went into the English building.

Me: Everything okay?

Warren: Great now that you're here. Sorry about that. She seems to find the worst times to corner me.

Me: What did she want?

Warren, with a sad smile: She just wanted to remind me, again, that I'm a horrible person and everything is my fault. Don't worry about it. Coming to the lab tonight?

Me: Wouldn't miss it.

Warren, wrinkling his nose: Unfortunately
we won't be alone tonight. I think Drew and
Katy want to have a little meeting. I swear,
every time Katy has a whim to hook up with
Drew, we have to rehash everyone's roles
again. It's like they forget how to be normal
around each other.

Me: She obviously wants more and he won't
give it to her. It's sad, really.

Warren stopped walking, right in front of our classroom,
and looked at me strangely.

Warren: Is that what she told you?

Me: Yeah. Why? That's not what it's like?

Warren, laughing: Not at all. Drew's been
crazy about her for years but Katy only wants
him when it's convenient.

Me: So Katy's lying?

Warren: Katy's a master manipulator, Bailey. I
know she's your friend, but she only looks out
for herself. She's incredibly selfish.

It was weird that he called her that, when she'd used the
same word about him last week. But I had to admit, in Katy's
word against Drew's, I'd believe Drew first. Maybe I'll try
talking to Katy again, though. Selfish or not, she's super fun, and
I miss having her to gossip with. And we haven't even discussed
the other night yet. Plus, with my only other female friend
actively trying to hold my boyfriend's hand, I think I'll take the
lesser of two evils, thanks.

I'm so mad at Emily I could scream. Honestly, there's no
way to deal with her and maintain peace in our room. I guess
I should just accept that and tell her to back the hell off my
boyfriend. Or maybe I should take a kinder approach.

Ugh, Mom. I'd give anything to talk this over with you. . . .

March 8

To say that Emily and I had it out tonight would be the
understatement of the year. Maybe even the century.

I got back from the lab and she was sitting at her desk,

doing her homework and tapping her fingers like she does in that way that grates on my nerves, and I don't know what it was, but I snapped. There was no way I was going to take the "kinder" approach when I'd seen her try to hold hands with my boyfriend earlier. I just couldn't take it.

I threw my bag down and just kind of unleashed. Then she accused me of spying on them and being paranoid. I told her I wasn't paranoid when I'm clearly seeing things with my own eyes. Then she fed me some bullshit about how she wasn't trying to hold hands with him, just trying to make him listen. She kept saying he was cutting her off, and I screamed that of course he was, they were no longer dating and she needed to leave him the hell alone. She yelled back that she'd leave him alone if he would leave her alone, whatever that means. Probably just trying to make me doubt Warren.

It was so bad the dorm mom came up to investigate, but luckily, Emily had already stormed off. After I apologized and the dorm mom left, I called Warren and told him what happened and warned him that Emily might come looking for him and that she seemed especially bad at the moment. He promised he knew how to handle her and told me not to worry. He thought maybe I was mad at him, but I assured him I wasn't. None of this is his fault; it's hers. She can't let him go and I think she's delusional. He told me he'd call if

Emily shows up or something, but if I don't hear from him, everything is good.

I can't do the homework that I still have to do. My nerves are completely frayed. So I took a long, hot shower, checked my phone to make sure I hadn't missed a call from Warren, then settled into bed with this diary. I am so done with today.

And just WHAT did Emily mean about Warren not leaving her alone??? I mean, she's the one who follows him around. Katy says that. Warren has implied as much. But . . .

I don't know. It totally could be my mind playing tricks on me, but sometimes I swear he ENJOYS the attention. From her, but then from me, when I get upset about it. And I don't know. I know everyone close to me says Emily's a bit on the unstable side but . . . she's never struck me as mean or vindictive. Or even a liar.

I don't know. Maybe I fought so hard with her because I'm confused and I don't know who to believe. But they both can't be right.

March 9

So Katy wasn't exactly the nicest last night in the lab. She wasn't mean; she was just kind of cold. She pretty much just reminded all of us that she and Drew take care of the selling, while Warren and I are to stick with making the product. I felt like the whole thing was meant to put us back in our place, like me going with the boys the other night was crossing some kind of line. And it was definitely a reminder to Warren that he's just helping, that he's not as important as Drew.

Such a laughable thought. If they didn't have me and Warren, they'd have nothing. And Warren is the whole reason our product is the best around.

But when Katy showed up in the girls' restroom when I was about to take my first Adderall of the day, I couldn't be mad at her. Katy is who she is, and I kind of admire how strong and honest she is.

So I pulled out a pill for her and gave it to her. She looked at it, confused, and asked if my "master" was allowing me to share again.

The "master" barb stung. I mean, I was sort of following his orders, but this was a totally abnormal situation. I shrugged her off and told her I'd cover if he asked, and claim to have taken the extra one myself. Still, even for Katy, the remark was a little below the belt.

> Me: Why are you so pissed at me, anyway? Because of Warren and not sharing?

> Katy: No. Not really. I don't know. It's a bunch of stuff. And only some of it even involves you.

Me: Well, I'm listening.

We took our pills and I swear I started to instantly feel better. Perhaps it was just a placebo effect, but just knowing the pill was in my system now made me feel more ready for whatever Prescott or Katy threw at me. I honestly don't know what I'd do without them at this point, which is a little scary but . . . it's okay. It won't be for much longer. After that, Katy suggested we blow off class and go elsewhere. I shouldn't have missed English, but I hated thinking I was somehow not in Katy's good graces, especially with things as bad with Emily as they are. So I said yes. Moments later we were walking away from the English building and wandering in the direction of the coffee shop.

Katy: So part of it is that you and Warren are so intense. I'm jealous, I guess. Drew would never act like that with me. But also, I swear he's all you think about. It's like we haven't had girl time since break.

Me: Well . . . he kinda is all I think about. I'm sorry. I'm just so into him. I can see why Emily's so . . . irrational.

Katy, rolling her eyes: He is hot, in a sort
of subtle, nerdy way. And I get it. You're in
love with him. But between you and Drew
not paying attention to me, then Warren
apparently not even liking me enough to
share Addys with me, I just feel sort of . . . I
don't know. Left out. When you went with
them the other night . . . I was worried for
you. And worried I'd be on the outside even
more after that.

I think I stared at her for a full minute, mouth hanging
open, because I couldn't wrap my head around the impossibly
cool, glamorous Katy Ashton feeling left out or caring about
what anyone else thinks, period. But I thought about it, and, as
loyal as the SC is to each other, we're also super isolated. If Katy
or any of us feels left out, we don't have anyone else to turn to. I
suppose it's for good reason, but it means I've got to keep myself
in. I regained myself and tried to say something useful.

Me: First of all, I just wanted to see what went
down. I won't go again. And I do think Drew
would pay attention to you any time you
wanted him to. Clearly. I mean, he dropped

everything for you the other night. Lastly, I don't think Warren's not sharing because he doesn't like you. They're just expensive and hard to get.

Katy, snorting: No they're not. Warren gets whatever pills he wants, any time he wants them. Everyone wants to keep him happy because his product is so good. Your product too, I guess. But he won't even share his sources.

Me: Wait, pills? Like plural?

Katy: Of course. You know Warren by now. He wouldn't touch heroin or, you know, ACTUAL drugs. But Oxys, Percs, whatever you want, he can get them.

I thought about the other night, how I'd seen Warren pocket the Adderall but something else as well. Inwardly I started to panic, thinking about what else Warren could be taking, but I tried to be as casual as possible.

Me: Right. The other pills. Sure.

Katy: What I don't get is that he knows I
need them. And I hate begging. But I made
our contacts, damn it. I don't see why he gets
to use them but I don't. He says it muddies
the waters, whatever that means.

The Addy had taken full effect by the time we made it to
the coffee shop, and it was like Katy's voice was a buzzing bee
in my ear. I let her drone on until she seemed satisfied but I was
no longer listening. I was thinking about Warren and that other
bag of pills.

What else is he keeping from me?

March 13

I'm so upset but I don't know who to be more mad at: me, Mr.
Callahan, or Princeton.

Mr. Callahan told me after chemistry that he heard from
his friends at Princeton that I didn't get into the summer
program. Not officially. I got wait-listed. I guess that's still
good. Out of all the people that apply they take only twenty,
and twenty more go on the wait list. But that means there
were twenty people who were better than me. More, maybe.
And it means that unless someone drops out, I won't be
spending the summer with Warren.

It was the essay. I know it was. Sure, my grades slipped some for a while there, but not that much. Thanks to the Adderall, I've been keeping up okay again. But my grades from my last school and first quarter here were amazing, and Mr. Callahan would have given me a great recommendation, so the only thing it could be is the essay.

I know I didn't do that great with it. I kind of left it to the last minute. But Mr. Callahan said it was fine. Shouldn't he have known if it wasn't? And if it wasn't, shouldn't he have helped me make it better? He just nodded his head and sent it in.

I'm so mad I could scream.

I'm home now. It's lunchtime. I couldn't face anyone in Science Club yet. Especially Warren. But I'll have to tell them soon. Will they even still want me making product for them? Me, the girl who got wait-listed at Princeton?

The room is a freaking wreck. I didn't see Emily at all last night. She must have sneaked in while I was sleeping and slept late. It looks like she couldn't find something to wear, even though we have uniforms. Her clothes are everywhere. If I hadn't seen this from her a few times before I would think we were robbed.

Whatever. If I'm going to deal with another afternoon of stupid Prescott and having to tell my boyfriend I'm not as smart as he is, basically, I'm going to need another Adderall. Warren said I could take more as long as I space them out. I usually wait until after school, but I'll take another one now, and another later. I just can't deal with this on my own.

March 14

Warren can be the sweetest sometimes.

When I got to the lab last night, he took one look at my face (yeah, I'd been crying. It started after dinner while I had a moment alone in my room and I couldn't stop it) and asked Katy and Drew if they'd excuse themselves so we could talk. I told him between hiccups that I didn't get in, all panicky and hyper because of all the Adderall in my system.

He told me that he was wait-listed his first year, which made me feel infinitely better even though that was three years ago, and that I'll probably still get in anyway. He said a lot of people apply then realize they can't give up their whole summer or can't spend that much money.

I told him I feel stupid and not good enough and it makes me doubt I can even get into Harvard. Or anywhere, for that matter.

Then he did the most amazing thing. He scooped me up in his arms and set me on the counter and told me every single thing he likes about me. He told me I'm brilliant and beautiful and sexy and funny and sweet, and kissed me SO passionately in between every word he said. He made me feel like I'm all those things, if only to him, and that's really all I need. He truly does believe those things about me. The best part was that he acted like he couldn't get enough of me tonight, like he was drunk on me, like he'd do anything as long as I kept kissing him. And we totally took advantage of being alone in the lab. But I have to admit, even though I feel special every time with him, tonight was so different. I wondered briefly if that's what it felt like to be a drug, and craved and needed all the time. I found myself wanting to be HIS drug.

His only drug.

Regardless, he definitely made me feel better about myself. If Warren loves me, that's all that matters. Screw Princeton.

March 15

After the high of Warren wore off, I woke up this morning accepting Princeton's decision but faced with the cold reality of it: I won't be seeing Warren at all this summer, I'll be spending it in misery with Dad and Isa instead, and I have no one to blame but myself.

Warren was extra wonderful today. He brought me coffee and walked me to all of my classes and told me I don't have to tell Katy and Drew if I don't want to. I took three Adderall again today, because it was really hard to focus on anything while I was so depressed about not getting into the program.

By the time I got to the lab tonight, I was a mess again. Probably shouldn't have taken that extra Adderall because it seems to make me more anxious somehow when I'm upset, but at least I could get all my homework done.

Drew and Katy were just leaving, and judging by the looks on their faces and the speed with which they excused themselves, they had plans. Warren looked up from the chemicals he was stirring and shrugged, a cute smile on his lips.

Me: Well, maybe it will be more official after all?

Warren, not-so-subtly flirting: Or maybe there's just something in the air in this lab.

Me: Yeah, noxious fumes.

Warren, laughing: Are you feeling okay?

Me: Not really. I'm so sad I won't be with you over the summer. I can probably get over not getting into the program if I never get off the wait list. But I'll miss you. And I do feel stupid. And I've felt anxious all day.

181

Warren hugged me and I felt better, but I was also wondering about what Katy had told me the other day, about how Warren could get anything I wanted, and if he was taking more than Adderall. I was scared to just straight-up ask him; sometimes direct isn't always the best approach with him, but I thought maybe there was a chance I could lead him to telling me on his own.

Me: Does the Adderall make you feel sort of . . . jittery? Like you could have a panic attack but you never quite reach that level?

Warren: It never makes me feel anxious, but if you were already anxious . . . maybe it could do that.

Me: Huh. Well, I love being focused and having energy, but now I feel like I need something to calm me down, too. Kind of ironic, isn't it?

Warren, studying me intensely: Well . . . maybe you do need something else. Okay. Promise me you won't freak out?

Me: Uh, sure, I guess.

Warren looked at me for a long moment and then went to his overcoat, which was hanging on an old coatrack in the corner. When he came back to me, he had a bag of pills in his hand. I took them from him. At first glance I thought they were white, but they were actually just this side of yellow. One side said "10/325" on it, the other spelled out the answer to my question: PERCOCET.

> Warren: Maybe these would help you more. Just to relax. Probably not when you're in class. They sometimes make me drowsier if I'm already tired. But these would probably help you calm down when you're upset.

> Me: These are what you bought the other night? I saw you slip more than the Adderall into your pockets. (Warren nodded.) So . . . you take these too?

> Warren: Sometimes, yeah. When I don't want things to bother me. When I'm stressed or angry or . . . whatever. Like, if my parents

183

call, I'll definitely have one. It's just peaceful,
you know? Like how Addys make you feel
like you can do anything? Percs make you
feel like nothing can upset you. Takes the
sting out.

I eyed the bag of pills for what seemed like an eternity.
What he was saying they could do for me . . . that sounded
exactly like what I needed. What I wanted. And he was
TELLING me. He was being honest. He'd told me he used
them completely on his own. He folded his hands around mine.

Warren: Take them, Bailey.

Me: Okay. Do you . . . do you want money
for them?

Warren, with a soft laugh: No. No, not from
you, baby.

I thanked him and pocketed the bag. When I got home,
Emily was asleep. I turned her desk lamp off and slipped the bag
of pills into my purse, with all of my money.
Warren was sweet to offer them to me. It was a sweet

gesture, wasn't it? He knows I need to feel calm right now. He knows how anxious I've been.

He also knows how much I need them. How tempted I'd be with them.

In most cases, giving someone something they need is a good thing. But . . . but maybe in this case, it's the worst thing you could do for someone, and Warren had just done it to me. And what about his own habit? If he's doing these, what else is he doing? Could it be that there's more he's not telling me?

I took the pills out again and memorized them, planning to do some research on them later. I held them in my hands for what felt like an hour, thinking about them, about Warren, about what they meant, about how I wanted to be calm for once.

I didn't take one.

March 16

I tried not to take any Addys today because I didn't want to feel so on edge. I thought maybe that would help me feel calmer, or at least more normal.

But by the time I got to third period I realized it actually had the opposite effect. I was way more jittery than normal, and I felt like my eyes were crossing or something. I couldn't focus at all on the reading in English. Not like I just couldn't concentrate, but like my eyes wouldn't work correctly.

I felt right as rain, though, after I took one between classes and went to chemistry.

Mr. Callahan is disappointed that I didn't get selected for the Princeton program, but he said he'd talk to someone at the school and see if he could pull some strings. I asked him why I wasn't accepted, if maybe it was my essay. He said it might have been, but not for the reasons I thought. Turns out the selection committee probably gets tons of essays every year about wanting to make drugs that aren't addictive. He said the opioid epidemic is so bad around here, it's a common theme for hopeful young chemists.

> Me: I've heard this area is seeing a lot of heroin addiction.

> Mr. Callahan: Heroin, but prescription drugs too. The kind usually prescribed for pain treatment. Things like OxyContin and Percocet or Vicodin. Oxycodone, hydrocodone, morphine. You know. But then people get addicted and can't stop.

> Me, alarmed: So Percocets ARE really addictive?

Mr. Callahan: Oh, I know they are. All opioids are. Studies show it affects the body in more permanent ways than other drugs, so the body ends up craving more, and addiction happens faster.

Me: So . . . it's more addictive than something like, say, meth?

Mr. Callahan: Well, everything like that is addictive, Bailey. One isn't better than the other. Meth, for example . . . the users sometimes go through withdrawal or comedown for days. Users can hallucinate or get very depressed when they don't have a supply, which makes them need more to get rid of the feeling. So, like I said. Neither is particularly better than the other. Are you worried about someone?

I looked at him, confused as to why he would assume that. I shook my head and, luckily, was quick enough to cover.

Me: I just feel silly for thinking I had an original idea, I guess, and I realized I don't

really know much about drug addiction.
Thanks for talking to me about it.

Mr. Callahan: Of course. I'll call my friend at
Princeton tomorrow. See what he says.

I thanked him and got out of there, but honestly, I couldn't
stop replaying what he said over and over inside my head. Meth
causes depression? Hallucinations?

And perhaps more important, considering what my
boyfriend gave me last night, Percocet is highly addictive?

March 19

Well, the second fight with Warren is down in the books.

I don't quite know what happened. What I do know is that
when I went to the lab tonight, it was just us, and everything
was going fine. Then I guess since he told me he takes
Percocet, he's super comfortable with taking them in front of
me. Warren joked that he really needed to relax because the
day had been such a pain in the ass, and he took a Perc out of
his pocket and threw it back and panic sort of seized me. I was
scared for him.

Me: You know those are really addictive.

Warren, actually rolling his eyes at me, which pissed me off to no end: They're just Percocets, Bailey. It's fine.

Me: Just like the Adderall?

Warren: I thought the Adderall was helping you.

Me: It is. But I tried not taking it, and I was a nervous wreck. Seriously. I felt weird.

Warren: Well, yeah. You have to go off slowly. It's medication. Come on. Plus, you've been sort of a mess for a while now.

Me, stunned and feeling betrayed: *I've* been a mess?

Warren: Since Christmas. At least.

Me: Well, I'm sorry I can't do all of this effortlessly like you. I'm sorry I have to study and sleep and go to classes.

Warren: Hey, this isn't my fault. I'm trying to help you. I help you study, I do most of the work in this lab, I gave you the Addys to help you focus. What else do you want from me?

Me: How many of the Percocet do you take a day, anyway?

Warren: Don't try to turn this around now. You're angry at me because this is easier for me than it is you.

Me, ignoring him: Those are opioids, you know. Addiction to those leads to heroin.

Warren, with a shocked laugh: Been on the Wikipedia page, Bailey? Suddenly you think you know everything? And do you actually think I'll get addicted to heroin after what happened to my brother? You think I'm that stupid?

Me: Well, how much do you use? I bet your brother didn't think he'd get addicted either.

That was it. I'd crossed a line. If there's one thing I've learned about Warren, it's that you can't talk about his brother that way, even if what you're saying is true. Warren's pretty blue eyes turned to ice.

> Warren: Not that it's any of your goddamn business, but I'm fine, Bailey. I don't take that many. I'm not addicted. It just helps me relax sometimes.

> Me: I don't see how it's not my business, since I love you and you love me. Isn't that what relationships are about? (He didn't say anything to that, so I went on.) So you think you could stop taking them and it would be fine?

> Warren: I know I could. Here. Take them. Take the whole damn bag.

He put on his coat and reached into the pocket, removing a bag full of yellow pills. He threw the bag at me and I barely caught them before they hit me in the chest.

> Me: You don't have to. . . . I'm sorry.

Warren: No, let me prove it to you, since you obviously don't trust me.

Me: That's not how I meant it.

Warren: Whatever, Bailey. Do me a favor and finish up here tonight. I'm done.

Me: No. Warren, don't go. I'm sorry. Please.

Warren: I'm just going home. To be sober. But if you don't trust me, ask your roommate for stalking tips. She always seems to know where to find me.

Because I was all alone, I didn't finish up work at the lab until one in the morning. When I got home, Emily was still up, and I must have looked like hell because she immediately asked if I'd fought with Warren. I couldn't help but wonder if she already knew that we had. She told me she was sorry, but she was also glad I was finally seeing this side of him.

And the thing is, she sounded genuinely worried for me, and . . . kind. I mean, if you can possibly believe that someone would want you to think of your boyfriend as a bad person and that would be kind, but it threw me for a loop. Especially since the last time we really talked was a fight.

I thanked her for her concern but swore to her that Warren treats me well, although I have to admit it was more trying to convince myself than her. I think Warren has good intentions. I think he truly wants to help me. But I can't help wondering if he's really helping me at all.

I fell asleep with my uniform still on, most of my homework undone.

March 20

Warren wasn't waiting for me before class today, although that could have been because I was so late I didn't even have time for breakfast. And honestly, I didn't have time to shower, either. Emily was just as late. She stayed up even later than I did last night. It's gross, but I was kind of lucky I was still in my uniform. I sprayed on extra perfume so I wouldn't smell like BO (or chemicals) and that was all there was time for.

But during first period, a page showed up at the door with a note asking me to come to the principal's office.

I immediately panicked, thinking perhaps someone had found out about Science Club or the Addys or even me staying the night with Warren. Then I thought maybe Mr. Callahan's call to Princeton actually did some good, and got excited.

It wasn't anything related to school, though. Good or bad. It was a giant vase of purple hyacinth. There was a card, and I opened it and read it to myself several times.

Bailey:

I was a giant asshole last night. A giant STUPID asshole. Please forgive me?

Love, Warren

I tucked the card back into its holder, smiling. I asked the school secretary what I should do with the flowers and she told me to take them back to my dorm and then come back to class. So I took them to my room and I'm here now, enjoying a moment with them. They're gorgeous, and they smell so wonderful, plus I got out of most of first period. The fight was terrible but . . . maybe this is a sign that he's trying, and he does love me. At the very least, he understands how terrible it was.

March 20, later
Well, I think Warren and I are okay. He told me that his brother is just a touchy subject and he tends to get overly emotional

194

when he's brought up. I told him I was just worried about him and that I still am, and that I sometimes feel like I don't know what's going on with him, and he promised me he would talk to me more about everything. We held each other for a long time at the lab tonight. Not really talking, which was probably the safest thing we could have done, but just leaning on each other. He asked if I liked the flowers, and I really do. They're sitting here at my desk, all cheery and bright and perfect. Mom would have loved them, I think. She liked girly things, so the purplish pink would have suited her.

I wonder if Mom would have had that superpower that some moms seem to have, that they can tell if a guy is right for their daughter or not.

The thing is, I really love Warren and I know he's got a good heart, and I think he wants the best for me. But there's something about the way we fight . . . I feel like the fight always turns on me. And I just never feel like I get the whole truth from him. Just bits and pieces of it. That's how I feel about Emily sometimes, and really the Science Club too. It makes me feel a little like I'm still on the outside of everything, which was what I wanted to avoid with joining the Science Club in the first place.

I'm probably just overthinking as usual and making myself depressed, so I'm going to go to bed and try to rest.

March 23

It turns out I'm not that far down on the waiting list for the Princeton summer program, and Mr. Callahan was able to get me bumped to the top spot, so as long as I can keep my grades up, I'm in if anyone drops out or can't go.

I feel so much better about everything right now because of that. For some reason, my whole perspective is more positive. I feel like I'm actually doing okay with all the work, school and otherwise. It's like the perfect reward for how hard I'm working, and all the hours I'm putting into everything, school and otherwise.

Well, that and the money. It keeps rolling in like it's the tide or something. I'm literally to the point where I don't know what else I really could buy. I'm not out of uniform enough to justify a huge wardrobe (plus the closet space in the Prescott dorms seriously sucks), and I can wear only so many pairs of flats. I bought a few new coats for myself and sent one to Bex as well. I wish I could have made the time to go visit and deliver it in person, but I'm way too behind with schoolwork and the lab to give up a weekend day.

Maybe it's time to start thinking of a little trip. Spring break is perfectly nestled between third and fourth quarters this year. Most likely, Dad won't want me home so he and Isa can be gross and happy together, and Bex will probably have made plans with all her new friends. But should it be only me and Warren? Or should we include Katy and Drew?

Hey, maybe a little trip together, all four of us, would push Katy and Drew together. For real.

Okay, I'll bring it up at the lab later, assuming everyone will be at the meeting tonight.

March 23, later

Tonight it was just me and Drew for a few minutes. Katy was late, as usual, and unusually, so was Warren.

It's silly, but it's hard to remember that I actually thought Drew was cuter than Warren at first. I guess I'm so into Warren, all I see when I look at Drew now is a friend. Or Katy's potential boyfriend, which is considerably more important.

> Me: How long have you and Warren been friends?

> Drew: Since Campbell, really.

> Me: So you knew him before his brother died?

> Drew, shrugging: Yeah. I only met Mitch once. I went home with Warren one weekend

197

because Mitch was home from college. But he was pretty messed up already. And I mean, Warren totally didn't exist.

Me: What do you mean?

Drew: His parents acted like they only had one son. It's no wonder Warren's so screwed up.

Me: You think Warren's screwed up?

Drew: Yeah, don't you? I mean, I love the guy, but he's got serious issues. I'm surprised he even told you about Mitch. Usually that's verboten. Especially with girlfriends.

Me, suddenly curious: You make it sound like he's had a lot of girlfriends. Has he? I mean, how many are we talking?

Drew, shaking his head and laughing: Nope. Huh-uh. Against the bro code. You'll have to ask him yourself. But why? Obviously it's

different with you if he trusts you enough to
tell you about Mitch. My advice? Don't worry
about it. Digging around like that is asking for
a ride on the pain train. Let it go.

Me, deciding to let it go (for now anyway):
So . . . are you worried about him? I mean, do
you think he's okay?

Drew: Warren's okay, Bailey. He deals with
shit his own way. Seems to work for him.
That's what we're all doing, right? Just trying
to deal with shit in our own way.

Drew was right, I suppose. I know I'm certainly trying
to deal with things in my own way, and I can hardly blame
Warren or anyone else for trying to deal with them in his.
I thanked Drew for the chat, and we spent a few minutes
joking about teachers or a few of the ridiculous rumors around
school. When Warren and Katy showed up, the lighthearted
atmosphere in the room changed. Warren and Katy had
obviously been fighting. But Katy, in typical Katy fashion,
pulled out her lipstick and applied a fresh coat, and plastered a
smile on her dark lips.

Katy: So what are we talking about?

Me: Drew was going to update us on numbers and probably insist that Warren and I increase production again. (Everyone chuckled, and the tension dissipated somewhat.) But more importantly, I wanted to ask about spring break.

Katy: Ooooh, I like this subject much better.

Me: Do we have to keep the lab open? In other words, any chance of us all getting away for the week?

Warren: I love the way my girlfriend thinks.

Me: I was thinking of somewhere secluded and warm.

Warren, pulling me to him and stealing a kiss: I REALLY like the way my girlfriend thinks.

Katy, shooting Drew a rather seductive look: I like the way she thinks too.

Drew started talking seriously about production then and what we'd have to do to be able to take time off but also keep our buyers happy. What it amounted to, realistically, was that Warren and I would have to work our asses off in the weeks leading up to it so that we could have enough of a supply to take time off. Drew and Katy said they'd pitch in, if we thought they could measure up to our standards. Warren and I exchanged a look, silently communicating that we doubted they could, but we agreed to keep an open mind. It would be worth it if we all got to go somewhere together.

Then the conversation turned to plans. Wouldn't you know, Drew's family has a time-share in the Cayman Islands?

I am just full of excellent ideas.

March 25

I just keep screwing up with Warren. It's like I can't help myself. I must be incredibly bad at being in a relationship. I mean, what's wrong with me???

First, I asked him what he and Katy were fighting about, and he kind of shrugged it off like it wasn't a big deal. Asking isn't a crime, right? Seems pretty normal in a relationship. But when he wouldn't say, I kept pressing him about it. He finally admitted that it was about two things. One, they'd fought about Adderall. Katy wanted him to get her some, and he wasn't comfortable with the idea so he told her no and she went off on him. The second was the expansion of our sales. Warren isn't very happy about having to do so much of the actual delivery and thought Katy should take over, but she refused, and they said some pretty nasty things to each other. He reiterated how selfish Katy is, saying that she's willing for everyone else to take a risk but won't take any herself.

I trusted my gut and didn't ask about the expansion, again. But for some reason, my stupid gut asked Warren if he'd been the one to give Adderall to Katy for the first time. Honestly, it's been bothering me that he's given me something that is so addictive, and so easily. And he's done it twice. It made sense in my head that maybe he'd given it to Katy, too. But when I asked, everything changed.

The look in his eyes was clearly a warning, but he did answer me. He said that it was actually Drew who'd brought out Adderall the first time. So I guess maybe it really is as common as Katy said, if even Drew does it? Everything seems so easy for him, even easier than Warren, so it makes a lot of sense.

But something was nagging at me. It was the way Warren and Katy were late, and how they seemed to truly despise each other on occasion. It reminded me too much of . . . well, of Emily and Warren.

So I asked Warren, flat out, if he and Katy had ever been a thing. And if maybe leftover feelings were why they fought.

It was just as bad as the other night, if not worse. He accused me of not trusting him. I tried to defend myself, saying I'd heard that he'd had a lot of girlfriends, and then of course it became about how I must be gathering information on him, like a spy or something. At that point I'd lost any control of the conversation and it was in a spiral. I kept trying to defend myself or tell him it wasn't that I didn't trust him, that I just wanted to understand, but it seemed like everything I said just dug me deeper into the hole I'd made for myself, so I gave up and started crying.

That's when Warren apologized and pulled me into his arms. He told me over and over that there was nothing with him and Katy and that anyone who came before me didn't matter. He said I was the only thing that mattered now. He said he just wanted me to be happy. Then he asked me if it was all right if he took a Percocet to calm himself down.

Yes. He had more of them. I don't know when he got them or if maybe he didn't give me all of them in the first place, but when I told him it was okay, he pulled one out of his pocket. His hand was shaking a little as he put it in his mouth, and I felt terrible then for even bringing any of this up. He's working just as hard as me, harder, really, and then I go and put him on edge with all of my insecurity and immaturity. I apologized to him over and over and he held me for a long time as I cried more.

He finally got me to smile by talking about spring break, and I felt like things were going to be okay.

I think the stress of everything is getting to me. And I'm just so afraid I'll lose Warren. Like, any minute some cuter/richer/smarter girl is going to take him away. He'll wake up and realize he's wasting himself on me or something. Me, the girl who can't handle Prescott academics and can't even get into Princeton's summer science program. And obviously, every girl around me could be the one who does it. Katy's so gorgeous and sophisticated, and even though she seems to be really into Drew, she'd be the obvious choice. I'd like to think I'm cuter than Emily, but that doesn't stop me from wondering where Emily goes all the time, especially when it's while I'm not with Warren.

I'm such a mess. God, it's like I cannot keep it together at all. The Adderall helps me with energy and focus, but how do I get rid of paranoia and jealousy? Do they make a drug for that?

Sadly, I'm not even sure I'm kidding about that question. If something like that was available, I'd take it in a heartbeat. I just so want things to be easier than they are. I'm so tired of things being so hard. . . .

March 26

Got the BEST compliment from Katy today. Drew and Warren had to run into town (I know, not even on a Friday, but business is booming) and so we tagged along and went shopping. Naturally, because all we can think of is being on the beach with our boyfriends (okay, whatever Drew is to her), we tried on bikinis.

Katy looked amazing in everything she tried on, because of course she did. And I tried not to think about how that meant Warren would be seeing her in a bikini but whatever. She finally chose a retro-looking suit that was like something a pinup would wear in the forties. Kind of sailory, with a bow at the chest and little sailor stripes in blue and red.

I tried on a few that were a little flattering and some that were terrible. But when I walked out of the dressing room with a gold string bikini on, Katy shrieked and said it was the one.

She walked around me like she was inspecting a racehorse to purchase or something, and proclaimed: "You lost weight!"

And I have to admit, I've never been one of those girls to obsess about the number on the scale or even the number inside of a dress, but I looked at myself tonight in the mirror and I could see hip bones, and my stomach was super flat, and I looked pretty good (for me) in the bikini.

> Me: Maybe skipping a few meals in the
> cafeteria is paying off.

Katy, winking: Maybe it's all the extra cardio you're getting with Warren.

Me: Ha! I wish. We never have enough time alone.

Katy: The beach will fix that. So will this bikini. He won't be able to think of anything else.

Me: You're sure this is the one? I mean, it's not like I can't afford it, but it's pretty steep for a swimsuit.

Katy: Oh, it's definitely the one. You look SO sexy in it. Plus, Warren's such a geek, he's going to think about *Star Wars* and Princess Leia, and trust me, that's a fantasy every geek boy has.

Me: You've sold me. As long as I don't have to put my hair in buns.

Katy, laughing: Nope. Not a good look. Okay, well, as long as we're shopping for vacation, I think we both need to hit up the lingerie, yes?

So Katy dragged me off to buy more things to tempt Warren with, and I admit it, it was fun and kind of hot to think about him seeing me in a pretty bra-and-panty set. I have a few cute things to wear, but nothing like what Katy talked me into buying for the trip. Warren is going to LOVE IT. I'm not sure I'd have bought it normally, but the comment about losing weight? I mean, it was a straight-up shot of self-esteem for me. Katy's not fat or anything, far from it, but she also has some curves that I don't. I have practically nothing up top, and I've always been self-conscious about that, but if I've lost weight, what I've got going for me is a flat stomach, right?

I don't have a scale in my dorm room, so I have no idea how much weight I've lost, but I did try on a pair of shorts that I wore last summer for a comparison, and I could pull a few inches of material from around my waist.

I wonder if Warren's noticed?

March 29

I called Bex today. It's been too long, and I just needed to hear her voice. I almost called Dad, too. Almost. But I wasn't ready to talk to him about spring break yet, and I figured it would come up because he's probably anxious to know what my plans are so he can make plans of his own. To be honest, I just didn't want to hear the hopefulness in his voice when he asked if I'd already made plans.

So it was just Bex I talked to. She sounds SO happy. I've always been a little jealous of her because everything comes so naturally to her. She got all the cool factor our family had to give, I think. But tonight especially, I was super jealous of her life. She's so happy. So stress free. So INNOCENT. She doesn't have to worry about all the stuff I have to worry about, like her boyfriend dumping her for someone else. Or making enough product to keep a business going and keep everyone's pockets flush. She's not worried about keeping on top of classes and getting into Ivy League schools or summer programs. And I know for sure she's not worried that all of it is going to explode one day because someone finds out something they shouldn't have.

She thanked me for all the gifts I've been sending. She said she's pretty much the most stylish girl at school when they can be out of uniform. (I'm not sure she really is. She prefers wearing sporty clothes, things I'd work out in. That's her regular style.) So I've sent her all the best brands for workout clothes, and maybe it's a trend at Campbell. I know here Katy wouldn't be caught dead in yoga pants unless she was actually doing yoga.

Bex asked me tonight where I'm getting the money. Somehow (maybe the Adderall?) I was sharp enough to come up with a fake job: I told her I'm tutoring underclassmen on the side for some extra cash, and the students here pay top dollar.

She thought it was so cool that I'm doing that and didn't ask any more questions. So, phew. I felt bad about it later, but it's so much better than telling Bex the truth. Not only do I not want her to know, she CAN'T know. Not only because I have to protect her from it but because . . . what would she think of me? What would she say? She'd be so let down, and I can't face that.

She did say she's thinking about traveling with friends for spring break, and so I told her I'm going somewhere with mine, too, and my boyfriend, and she's under strict instructions not to mention the boyfriend part to Dad.

She's actually thinking of New York, which would be amazing for her. But she said she's totally jealous of me going to the Caymans. So . . . I guess we're even. Ha.

March 30

Today was both great and terrible.

The terrible part was English class. My teacher asked me to stay after class. Warren skipped out, luckily, so he didn't see her ask and doesn't know. And I don't think I'll tell him anything. After all we've been through (really, what we've put each other through) the last few weeks, I don't want him thinking there's another thing I can't handle. Or that he's going to have to do even more to pick up my slack. So I'm just going to have to work harder.

I have a C in English. I honestly don't know how it happened.

I've done all my work, on time, and I've made sure to meet all the requirements for each assignment. But my teacher says that my essays are meandering at best and nonsensical at worst. (Whatever that means. Honestly, I thought the last two flowed pretty well. I was typing like a madwoman.) I explained that for some reason, English and I don't get along, and her reply was basically that I need to figure out how to get along with English because no school is going to take someone who can't write an entrance essay. And she wasn't even talking just Ivy Leagues.

Plus, a C at Prescott is failing. Literally. In any other school, a C would be average, right? Passable at least. Not at Prescott. You have to repeat the class if you get a C. I'm not sure if Dad and Isa know about that policy or not, but can you imagine if I had to repeat a class? All that money down the drain. My teacher says I can bring it up if I do stellar work the rest of the quarter, and I suppose I can.

The thing is, I can probably sacrifice some time on chemistry assignments and even calculus. Maybe even not do some of the work in those classes, period, because I can ace the tests no problem. So I can devote that time to English instead and . . . I'll have to ask for Katy's help. Maybe even Emily's.

When I got to the lab tonight, I smiled and laughed and pretended like everything was fine. I think it worked. Warren seemed happy too and kept his arm around me pretty much the whole time. While he and I worked, Katy booked our flights and transportation. So it's official! I'll be spending spring break with the coolest people I know, including my boyfriend, who will see me looking hot in a gold bikini. That was the single good thing about today.

I just have to survive this quarter, I just have to survive this quarter, I just have to survive this quarter ...

March 31

So here's a small bit of good news: Prescott grades don't get sent home in the mail. They're all available online, through the student or parent portal. I assumed Dad and Isa were getting my grades at home but they're not. And they're not even logging in to see my grades or Dad would have called, angry. I can't believe I didn't realize this until now.

So they don't know I'm not doing great.

But they also haven't even been checking?

Okay, but let's look at the silver lining here and just be happy for now. Maybe by the time they think to check, my grades will be back up.

April 1

I walked into the lab tonight. I must have been pretty quiet because Warren didn't hear me. When I came in he was bent over one of our tables, and I saw him snort up white powder.

I absolutely freaked. The only time I've EVER seen anyone snort something is in movies where they're all using cocaine, using rolled-up money on a mirror. So I naturally flipped out on him. Not only for doing cocaine, but for lying to me. Keeping it from me.

And as I was freaking out, demanding to know what the hell he was doing and how long he'd been doing it and why he was keeping it from me, he grabbed my wrists hard enough to bruise.

> Warren: Bailey. Bailey! Listen to me. It's not coke. Calm down. It's not coke.

> Me: Then what the hell?

> Warren, pulling me to him: Just the Percocets, baby. Just Percocets. It's okay. I wouldn't do coke. Okay? And I wouldn't keep it from you if I was.

> Me: Wait, so if it's Percocet . . .

> Warren: I crushed it up. I just . . . needed one. Faster. It takes effect faster this way.

> Me: But isn't it more dangerous?

Warren: No, it's not going to hurt me any
more than . . .

Me: Than taking it as a pill?

Warren: Right. I'm sorry. I really am. That had
to have spooked you.

Me: I mean, I guess I thought when you told
me the other day that you could stop, and
gave me what you had . . . I thought you'd
actually stop.

Warren pulled back a little and wiped at his nose. His hand,
I noticed, was shaking again, and something about seeing him
shake like that made me realize how on edge he was. How
possibly out of control. And it broke my heart and made me all
the more worried for him. I decided not to badger him about
it, and tucked the worry down deep inside. I didn't want to be
another source of stress for him.

Warren: I can. Of course I can. I just thought
it was okay, after you told me the other night
that I could take one.

Me: Of course it's okay. I didn't mean to imply that you have to have my permission or something. I'm not Emily, right?

Warren, smiling: Right. Thanks, baby. I love you, you know that?

Me: I love you too.

We got to work after a few minutes of kissing. I could literally feel Warren relaxing into my arms, the Percocet taking effect. After that his smiles came easier. There was a little dullness in his eyes, but the sharp, panicked look was gone, so that was good. At least I think it's good. Is it really Warren, though, if the smiles come so easily?

We worked almost completely in silence for a while; the only sounds around us were those of the process, and sometimes some sweet humming coming from Warren's direction. Then he got really still, and I looked at him, thinking he needed an extra hand with what he was doing. But no, he was staring at me, smiling bigger than I'd ever seen him smile.

Warren: You are gorgeous, you know that?

Me: Stop it, you big liar.

Warren: You are!

Me: I'm nothing compared to Katy Ashford or most of the girls at this school.

Warren: You're the liar now. Katy has nothing on you. And you look especially beautiful tonight.

Me: I think that's the Percocet talking.

Warren: Nope. Just a guy in love.

Me: Well, I have lost a little weight.

Warren, sliding his arms around me: Yeah, I can feel that. But that's not it, although you look great. I really think it's because I know you have my back. You worry about me. And I know I get upset sometimes about that, but . . . I don't think I've ever had anyone worry about me like that before.

Me: I'm sure your mom—

Warren: No. Not my mom. Trust me. And definitely not my dad.

He put his head on my shoulder, and I don't think he was crying, but I think he was definitely trying not to. I held him really close, just like I had the night he told me about Mitchell dying and losing his parents, in a way.

Me: I do care about you. And I'm sorry I sometimes let that make me into a jealous idiot. But, Warren, are you really okay? You are sorta worrying me tonight. Is something wrong?

Warren, letting me hold him: Honestly, yeah. I, um . . . well, two things. My dad actually called. He said Mom is going to go to a different facility and wanted to let me know. And he wanted to make sure I wasn't coming home for spring break. You know, the usual "Please don't come home, we'd rather not see you" crap.

Me, with a bitter snort: I know exactly how
that feels. What was the second thing?

Warren: Well, I have a C in English. Probably
because I don't go most of the time.

I busted out laughing, half crying with relief that someone
else (and Warren of all people!) was in the same boat as me, and
also with relief that neither thing was very serious. With what
Warren's into, with what we're ALL into, it could have been
really bad.

Confused, Warren looked at me as I laughed until I was
full-out sobbing.

Warren: Okay, now I'M worried.

Me: No. Don't be. I have a C in English too.

We both burst out laughing then, and we held each other
some more and talked about ways to pull our grades up, and
we ended up actually scheduling out time for ourselves to do
English homework together (at the expense of some making
out and possibly some time with Drew and Katy, but not at the
expense of the work in the lab).

So . . . in a weird way, this is good. I'm not alone in this. And he's going to be just as supportive to me as I'm trying to be with him. He loves me, I love him, and we will both work together to get our grades up. Everything is fine. I HAVE to believe that.

April 3

I can't believe it. It snowed again yesterday, a LOT. It's like we were all expecting spring, thinking warm thoughts (and beach vacation thoughts), and bam! Mother Nature threw us a curveball.

We went sledding again but we didn't stay long. We went pretty quickly over to the bonfire again; the boys seemed way more interested in that. Almost immediately, they went off to talk to a group of kids I only kind of know. I saw Warren hand one of the boys something, just as another boy handed Drew a wad of cash. The boys took off, going deeper into the woods, and Drew and Warren bent their heads together, talking.

I knew what it was, what had just happened. I wasn't stupid. I'd seen it go down just a few weeks ago in the Wiltshire slums, but I hadn't ever seen it at Prescott. That was new.

No one had spiked hot chocolate this time. I'm guessing no one was prepared for this snow. But Katy came prepared.

She drew a silver flask out of her coat pocket and we shared the strong-tasting stuff in it. I didn't ask how she'd acquired it. I'm getting really used to not asking questions.

Katy seemed pretty intent on asking me questions, anyway. She asked how much Adderall I'd taken that day. I honestly didn't remember. It was such a good day. I told her three, maybe. Three usually did it for me now. She told me to be careful drinking while I had Adderall in my system. She said sometimes it makes it harder to feel the alcohol so it's easy to have too much. I noted that but took her flask every time she offered it anyway. She perked up when Drew looked like he was coming in our direction, but he was only going to talk to someone close by us. Katy nearly deflated.

Me: You've got it bad.

Katy: Hello, Pot, I'm Kettle.

Me: Shuddup. So why don't you let it be more with him? I think he wants it. For sure.

Katy: No. I can't.

Me: Why? Is he not good enough for you?

219

Katy, snickering: No, darling. I'm not good enough for him. Just like Warren isn't good enough for you.

Me: Why would you say that? Warren's good enough for me. Why don't you like him? Honestly?

Katy: Oh, I adore Warren. When he's not being an asshole. But you're far sweeter than him. Nicer. Probably even smarter. But Warren has to have everything just so, doesn't he? His way. That way he can always be ahead of every situation. Always a step ahead. Always in control.

Me: I don't think he's controlling. Meticulous, maybe. Precise and methodical, more like.

Katy: Those things too. You know it was his idea to film collateral.

I didn't know that. I'd assumed it was Drew who thought to do that, and I honestly hadn't thought about the collateral since just about the day we filmed it. Most likely because it wasn't ever something I'd have to think about again. I trusted them. They trusted me. At least, that had been the premise.

I looked over at Warren. He was smiling, and I think he must have said something funny because the people around him laughed. He seemed calm, happy, even animated, and I had to wonder sardonically what chemical I had to thank for that.

I don't remember how I got home, but apparently I set my alarm. I got up when it went off, called myself in sick for the day, and went back to sleep. I mean, at this point, what does it matter?

April 5

The shine has definitely worn off the winter, literally and figuratively. Any snow we have left has turned into gray slush all around campus, and I'm now tired of wearing my boots instead of my cute flats. Now it seems like we're all sick of winter and ready for spring. Or moreover, spring break.

I've refused to ask Warren to do more in the lab or to ask for time away so that I can study more. Now that I know he's failing too, it doesn't seem right to ask. We have been working on English together a bit, not as much as I'd really like. He's almost exactly like I am, with having a better head for numbers than words, but it still comes relatively easy for him, and he's incredibly good at bullshitting his way through essays. I'm not, so I feel like I need more practice.

So what I've been doing is staying up later these past few days. Sometimes it's one or two in the morning by the time I finally fall into bed. But I think I'm doing all the assignments a lot better than I was.

Truth be told, it's hard for me to fall asleep anyway. I feel so amped up at night, and thirsty like Warren warned I'd be. I know it's the effects of the Adderall, but if I don't take it, I'm super unfocused and I just CAN'T be unfocused right now. Besides, when I don't take it I turn into the Incredible Hulk or something. Just super irritable and completely restless. Either that or all I want to do is sleep.

I guess I should be honest in my diary, because where else can I be really honest, right? Most nights when I can't sleep, I swear those Percocets are calling to me from inside my purse, under my bed, like something trapped inside of Russian nesting dolls. I haven't taken one, but I want to. I want to know if I could sleep better or fall asleep faster. Hell, even if it just made me calmer and more chill like Warren seems to be about everything, I'd take that too. There is nothing worse than being completely on edge at two in the morning, not being able to sleep, teeth chattering, and tossing and turning.

Emily hasn't noticed, that I can tell. She's either not here or she's fast asleep when I get home. She's never awake when I come in late from the lab. And the lab . . . we're keeping up with production, but we're tragically behind right now on making any extra for spring break. But we HAVE to. We just do. We have to go to the beach and relax and not worry about anything for a week. I swear, if we don't go, the stress is literally going to kill me.

Mr. Callahan was not impressed that I missed chemistry yesterday. He says he wants to be able to say, with absolute certainty, that I'm a good candidate for the science program if his friends at Princeton call with an opening. All I could do was apologize and tell him it won't happen again, but let's be honest here: I'd do that whole night over again every night if I could. It was absolutely amazing to hang with everyone in the woods, and I have to say, everyone at Prescott treats Katy and Drew like the king and queen, and me and Warren since we're with them. I think Warren would be really popular if he wasn't so aloof. It's almost like he chooses to be a mystery to the rest of the school. I will say this: People seem to trust him. The jocks weren't the only ones who approached Warren the other night. I remember that, even if the rest of the evening got a little hazy after the tenth time I swigged from Katy's flask.

Katy said she was the one who put me to bed and told me to drink some water and to take ibuprofen, NOT aspirin or Tylenol. Thank goodness I have friends who know what they're doing.

Anyway, nothing interesting to report, I guess. Still struggling, still tired, still extremely happy that we're going to the beach, still extremely in love with Warren. And the beat goes on . . .

April 6

I feel incredibly bad for even writing this, but it wasn't until I got to civics and put today's date at the top of my quiz that I realized: Today's the anniversary of my mom's death. It was this day, two years ago, that Mom and I went out to shop and she never came home.

I took the quiz but I couldn't tell you a thing that was on it. I'm not even sure I could tell you if it was multiple choice or fill in the blank. Then when I turned it in, I asked if I could go to the restroom. I sat in the girls' room for the next two periods, perched on a toilet, crying as quietly as I could. I was already so on edge that I didn't want to take an Adderall, but I also knew it was the only prayer I had of getting through a whole day of classes. So I took two. Some days I'm so thankful that Warren gives me these pills. I'm a complete mess without them anymore, and there's no way I'd be doing even half as good in my classes if I didn't have them. Maybe when I'm home over the summer, if my dad is willing to listen, I can tell him how unfocused I am at school, and he'd take me to the doctor and they'd prescribe them for me and then it would be legit, and I wouldn't even have to get them from Warren anymore.

Anyway, I got through the day but it was all a blur. I seriously felt like Mom was there today for some reason, just this presence next to me as I went through the motions. Or maybe it wasn't her presence I noticed so much today but the lack of it.

God, what would she think of me? Of what I'm doing? Of any of it?

Would I have been able to tell her how I'm struggling and stressed? Would I be able to tell her how in love with Warren I am? Or that he was my first? Could we have had that conversation? The truth is, I miss it even if we couldn't have. If I'd been afraid to approach her about sex and birth control and my first time, that would have been okay, because she would still BE HERE.

I went home after classes and instead of lying on my bed, jittery and nervous, I went to sleep. I think all the crying exhausted me. . . . At the very least I was exhausted by trying to keep myself together all day.

I slept until eight, way past time when I'm usually at the lab. When I woke up, there were texts from Warren asking where I was and if I was okay, and one from Katy, too, asking me what was up. I threw on my coat and went to the lab, still in my uniform.

Warren stopped everything he was doing when he saw me and pulled me into his arms.

Warren: You've been crying. What happened?

Me: Oh. I'd meant to fix my makeup. It's nothing. It's . . . Today's the day Mom died. The anniversary of it. And I couldn't keep my shit together. And I went home after school and slept until . . . well, until ten minutes ago.

Warren, looking alarmed: That's nearly five hours, Bailey.

Me: I know. And I'm so sorry. I should have been here. I was just so tired.

Warren, pulling me to him again: No, don't apologize. I'm sure today has been really hard for you. I'm sorry. Why didn't you tell me? I could have helped. You could have stayed in bed.

Me: You're already doing too much. And
I don't know why I didn't tell you. I mean,
honestly, I didn't even realize myself until it
was practically lunchtime. What's wrong with
me that I didn't realize?

Warren: Nothing, baby. Nothing is wrong
with you. You've got a lot on your plate is all.
And maybe . . . maybe it's kind of a good sign?
I've done it, with Mitch, I mean. I remember
halfway through the day. Maybe it means
you're healing.

Me: Maybe. I don't know. It doesn't feel like I
am. Not today, anyway.

Warren: Go on home, Bailey. You need to
rest.

Me: But . . .

Warren, cutting me off with a kiss: Go home.
Sleep. Cry. Do whatever you need to do. I'll
stay here and get this done.

I looked at him, realizing I'd wanted him to tell me he was going with me, so that he could hold me and let me fall apart. But of course work needed to be done at the lab. We couldn't both have the night off. Of course he couldn't come.

But couldn't he? Just for a while? Wasn't I more important than making this batch perfect or being on schedule or the money we'd get from it? So I decided to suggest it.

Me: You could come with me.

Warren, smiling gently: I think you need your rest, Bailey. That would be better for you than anything else right now. Take a Percocet. It will help.

The suggestion, from him, made me mad. He wants to fix me with pills, like I need fixing instead of support. I'd be easier to deal with to him on a drug.

Me, shaking my head: No. I know you can take them without getting addicted, I'm just not going to take that risk.

Warren: Okay, I understand. They just always help me.

Back in my room, Emily isn't here, so it's just me alone. All I can do is think. About Mom. How much I miss her, how much I want her to be here and see how I'm growing up, how much I need her love and support and her smile. And I can't stop hearing the sound of metal hitting metal. I feel so lonely. I'm trying to convince myself that Warren is right. I need rest and it was smart of him to stay at the lab. But it wasn't what I'd wanted from him. I'd wanted him to comfort me. I'd wanted him to come back with me and listen to me talk about Mom or just hold me or sit in silence even. And if I'm honest, I wanted him to show me that I'm more important than our next batch of product.

Now all I want is to fall asleep, get some rest, and stop thinking.

So I'm going to take a Percocet. Just one. Just one can't hurt me, right? And it might help, just tonight. Maybe it will do all that Warren promised it could.

April 7

I woke up this morning feeling rested. I slept, without waking up, for a solid seven hours. I didn't think about Mom. I didn't think about Warren. I didn't dream once. Instead, I woke up this morning and felt peaceful and ready for the day. It felt amazing.

Too amazing. Which is why I reached under the bed, pulled out the rest of the pills, and went into the restroom with the intent of flushing them all. But when I held them over the water . . . I just couldn't. I kept thinking about how good it had felt to sleep and not feel stressed. So I put them back in their hiding spot. I won't take them unless I really need them, but I think I should keep them around . . . just in case.

April 8

Shit. I am the worst sister in the world. Add that to the ever-growing list of my failures.

Not only did I forget the anniversary of Mom's death, I didn't call Bex.

When I did remember, and called two days late tonight, Bex was crying when I picked up the phone. I told her how sorry I was. I even explained that I'd been so exhausted with crying myself that I had fallen asleep for most of the day, and Bex swore it was all right but I could tell how hurt she was that I hadn't called.

We had a long talk after that. She told me how wonderful everything is at Campbell, but that she sometimes feels guilty for thinking everything is wonderful without Mom. I lied and told her I feel the same way about how happy I am at Prescott. I think it made her feel better, even if it kind of threw my unhappiness into stark relief. Then we spent the next hour or so sharing memories of Mom. I was super late to the lab, and didn't get most of my homework done, but it was worth it. I got to be there for Bex, better late than never, and I got to talk about Mom for a while.

But this does go on the list. I have to be better about checking in with Bex. Apparently that's another thing Dad dropped the ball on. I have to do everything now, I guess.

April 10

Mr. Callahan asked me to stay after class today, and I thought for sure he was going to "have a chat" with me about skipping class the other day again, but it wasn't that at all. It wasn't Princeton, either, though. It was bad news.

He asked me if I remembered our conversation the other day, about my essay, and of course I did. Then he set a newspaper in front of me before he went on talking. I glanced at the headline, which read, "Meth Addiction on the Rise in Highland County." I don't think I caught much of what he was saying, because I was thinking about just that headline and what it meant.

> Mr. Callahan: So not to make you feel bad or anything, but this is why your essay probably didn't seem groundbreaking to the admissions committee at Princeton. Addiction is bad

everywhere, even Wiltshire. Wiltshire has been a small, safe town since it was founded, but now . . . now drugs are taking over. And not just heroin. I mean, we had some incidences of crack addiction and trafficking in the eighties, but nothing like this. People are ruining their lives. So, you see, everything is equally bad. And these meth addicts, some of them get so tweaked out when they go through withdrawal, crime rates are up because of it.

Me, scanning the article: It says meth use is up eighty percent. Eighty percent?

Mr. Callahan: I know. Again, I'm sorry, but this is probably why the admissions team wasn't as impressed as they could have been. I'm sure almost every kid applying has a similar desire. At this point, hardly anyone is untouched. Doesn't matter your background, your class, your school.

Me: School? You think it's happening at school?

Mr. Callahan: You would know better than I would, I suppose. It's not like the students here ever tell us teachers anything.

Me, nervous: You're not like the rest of the teachers, though. But . . . where do you think it's coming from?

Mr. Callahan: The meth? Could be anywhere, Bailey. That's the thing about that drug. It's not like heroin, which isn't produced here, so you can trace a route. Meth can be made in basements, garages, trailers. . . . And there's not much stopping anyone from producing it, and it's relatively easy to make, as long as you can get your hands on the ingredients. But I'm sure the police are working on tracing it.

Me: How do you know so much about it? I'm sorry, that was personal. And I didn't mean to imply anything.

Mr. Callahan, smiling gently: It's okay, Bailey. I know so much because my brother was an addict.

Me: Was?

Mr. Callahan: Was. He's okay now. Sober for five years. He actually goes around to schools and helps with drug resistance programs in the area.

Me, not knowing why I'm telling him, but telling him anyway: You know Warren Clark's brother was an addict.

Mr. Callahan: I'd heard that. I'm glad you two seem to be getting along well. You could be good influences on each other.

I blushed at that, and Mr. Callahan sent me to my next class with an excuse for being late. He also let me keep the paper, which I read during downtime in English. The rise in meth addiction is concentrated in Wiltshire proper, in the east end. Police reports of dealers and drug use, statistics on the rise of crime, everything was included in the article. One of the addresses listed was for a street name I recognized as the street where our first drop had been, the night I'd gone with Drew and Warren.

But it isn't because of us. It couldn't be. I know how much of the stuff we make every week, how much goes out into the town, and how much we added on in recent weeks. It was a lot, but there is no way it could account for all this. There are other people out there making this stuff, and like Warren said, there is no way their product is as high quality and safe as ours. So our customers are probably not the people committing crimes. And we didn't create the problem. Obviously the market is there, or the Science Club wouldn't have gotten involved at all. Again, these people are going to do it; we're just trying to make it safer. That's all.

Only that doesn't quite add up, and I can't quite convince myself of it.

After English, I threw the newspaper away. I tore it into pieces first.

April 11

I seem to be doing all right in my classes, for now. Even English, although I'm not sure at all that I'll be able to get my grade up before the quarter ends.

Emily and I had been getting along well too, or at least better. We seemed to have reached an understanding about Warren, or perhaps the understanding was just that we wouldn't talk about him much. But yesterday she saw me looking up information about the Cayman Islands on my laptop and asked what that was about. I told her I'm going with Warren over break. I may have purposely left out that Katy and Drew are going too, but quite frankly, I don't care. It's like the second she notices something about Warren, she has to mark her territory or something. Yes, I know, Emily. You were his before. I just want to scream at her sometimes, "He doesn't want you anymore! He dumped you! HE GOT RID OF YOU!" But I can't bring myself to do it, no matter how good it would feel. Mostly because she acts like such a sad puppy most of the time about him and I can certainly understand how losing Warren would hurt so much. But I swear, Emily gets me so close to that edge sometimes. And it probably didn't help that she brought this up when I had layered two Adderall so that I could be sure to stay up late and work on English after I got done at the lab.

So I told her we're going, and that creepy switch flipped, and it was Obsessed Emily again.

Emily: For the whole week?

Me: Yes. The whole week.

Emily: Sounds boring.

Me: Trust me, we will not be bored.

Emily, snorting: I guess not. But I'm surprised
he wants to go anywhere.

Me: What do you mean?

Emily: Just that he doesn't seem to like
leaving Prescott much if he can help it.
Obviously. He stayed over Christmas break,
didn't he? He can't be away for long.

I understood immediately what she was implying and . . . I
felt stupid. Stupid for not realizing that Emily would possibly
know about Warren's extracurricular activities or his drug use
or anything else for that matter. That she perhaps knows, that
perhaps Warren had told her, made my temper (and jealousy)
flare and I lost the cool I always tried to maintain around her.

Me, snapping: Perhaps he just never wanted
to go anywhere with YOU.

At that Emily blanched, but after the initial shock of what
I said to her wore off, she nodded and looked like she totally
accepted my words.

Emily: You're probably right. Maybe it was just me. Maybe he would have taken one of the other girls always sniffing around him. I mean, he's taking you.

Me, ignoring her jibe momentarily: What other girls?

Emily, sincerely: Come on, Bailey. Think he's the type of guy to be faithful? Even if he's not cheating, he's all too happy to let you think he could, right? He plants all these little seeds of doubt on purpose.

Me: No. You're wrong.

Emily: He pushes you away or gets incredibly angry at you for questioning anything he does, right? So it makes you feel like he could easily drop you. And you don't want to even bring up anything anymore, so it's like he trains you to keep your mouth shut. So when you suspect he wants someone else, like Katy—

Me: Katy? You've got to be kidding me.

Emily, rolling her eyes: Come on. Do you
think all that fighting and stuff is actually
because they hate each other? They need to
get a room more than any people I know.

Me: But Katy's into Drew.

Emily: Uh-huh. And I bet she's hoping that
will just tear Warren up inside.

I don't think she's right about that. She may even be trying to
make me paranoid. Warren loves ME, I know he does. He tells
me so and he cares about me. He comforts me and listens to me.
Okay, maybe he didn't on the anniversary of Mom's death, but
he was doing what he thought was right. And maybe he doesn't
listen to my concerns about him and the pills but . . . Warren has
some issues. He's just working through them the only way he can.

Me, trying to feel confident: Warren loves me.

Emily, rather gently: I'm sure he says he
does. Mostly after a fight, right? Or when he

239

needs something from you? Or he's trying to
get out of being blamed for something?

We got quiet for a while, and in the silence my head
was spinning with what she was saying, trying to find
arguments against it, and even for it. But nothing was clear
to me. I believed him when he said he loved me. I still do.
At least I think I do. I decided to try to shift the focus of the
conversation.

Me: I think maybe he just doesn't know how
to really be with someone. He was so hurt by
his parents and his brother and everything.

Emily: What are you talking about?

Me: Oh, he didn't tell you? Never mind, then.

It felt spiteful to say that to her, but it got the job done.
Now she knows Warren shared something with me that he
hadn't with her. At least I had the upper hand back in our
conversation.

Emily: No, what did he tell you?

Me: It's not my story to tell. Forget I said
anything.

We went back to doing our homework, and I felt vindicated.
I was the only one Warren had told about his brother. The other
girls didn't really matter, then, did they? He felt more for me, he
knew he could share more with me. I win, I win, I win.

And maybe . . . maybe if she doesn't know about that, she
doesn't know about anything else, either. Maybe I mistook what
her words meant.

Me: You do know where Warren gets all his
money, right?

Emily hesitated, or maybe she'd gotten back into her
homework enough that it took her a while to answer.

Emily: Of course. I know he's on
scholarship and everything like me, but his
grandparents are loaded, so it's kind of an
illusion that he's poor. He likes to play up
the "woe is me" scholarship student thing.
He probably thinks it adds to the intrigue
or something.

I didn't know what to make of her answer or the hesitation. But something tells me Emily knows more than she let on.

And this isn't the first time someone has said something to me about Warren having a lot of girls around. I mean, Drew's said as much. Now Emily. They can't possibly both be lying, right? And why would Drew have any reason to make me feel like I can't trust Warren? Emily, sure, but not Drew.

I don't know how to ask Warren about it and not sound like I'm accusing him. And if I'm being honest, even asking him as gently as possible will make him angry. I guess it's in the past, right? And I shouldn't worry about the past. Unless it's a pattern for him . . .

God, I have no idea who to trust. I'd give anything to talk this through with Mom.

April 12

Warren found me before lunch yesterday and pulled me into an empty classroom. It was thrilling, not going to lie. But he wasn't there to steal a kiss. He asked me if I could make sure that Katy wouldn't go to the lab that night.

I jokingly asked if it was because he was desperate for some time alone with me, but my laughter sounded so fake and tinny. At the mention of Katy's name, all I could think about was what Emily had said about her and Warren.

Warren didn't notice my thoughts were elsewhere and told me he had ideas about the product that he wanted to try. I promised I'd do my best to keep her away, even though I was nervous about what he was up to. I haven't mentioned the news article to anyone in the Club yet, and honestly, I was feeling guilty enough about what we're doing. If he wanted to make the product stronger or something, I don't know if I could handle it.

At lunch I brought up that I'd heard Drew talking about a movie Katy wanted to see, and the two of them made plans to go see it, leaving Warren and me tons of time in the lab alone.

When I got there, he was already inside, in his coat and goggles. Something was brewing, but the smell was a little . . . off. Not in a bad way. Just different from what I'm used to. Sharper, somehow.

Me: So what's going on?

Warren, turning to me with a huge grin:
I think I've figured out how we can make something better.

Me: Better? Like better meth or something different?

Warren: Better meth. Essentially. Purer. Stronger.

Warren pulled out a notebook, an old spiral-bound thing that had seen better days. He flipped it open to where his scratchy handwriting revealed some touch-ups to the formulas we always use.

I took the notebook and studied what he'd written, and although I understood the formulas, I paid more attention to how quickly he'd written it, considering how sloppy and pointed his letters and numbers were. He'd obviously been hit by a flash of inspiration.

Me: So . . . basically we'd use more of the catalytic ingredients?

Warren: I think so. I think we'll be able to make it faster, and I think it will leave more of the actual high-inducing ingredients more pure.

Me: So it will cause a stronger high?

Warren, shaking his head: No. I mean, yes. It would. But they wouldn't need to use as much of it either. What do you think?

Me: I think we should try it. But how will we know if it works?

Warren, with a shrug: I'll be guinea pig. Or Drew. We've done it before. We can handle it.

Me: Okay. I trust you. I didn't know you wanted to change anything. I mean, I'm all about it, I just thought we were doing fine.

Warren: We are. But . . . there's always a better way, Bailey. And I'm always looking for it.

I had a feeling it wasn't just making the product that he was talking about. Was he always looking for better in everything? Like, a girlfriend? Emily's and Drew's words creeped back into my head, and I knew I had to know. Perhaps if I wasn't direct about it . . .

Me: Can I ask you something? (His pretty eyes clouded over, but he nodded.) We're . . . we're safe, right? I mean, you and me. I shouldn't get tested or anything, right?

245

Warren, his eyes now dark: Are you asking me
if I have an STD?

Me: I realize it's a little late to be asking, and
I know we take precautions but . . . I mean, do
you know for sure you're clean?

Warren: Let me guess. Emily told you I
sleep around? Probably insinuated that I'm
cheating, too, didn't she?

Me: She didn't insinuate that, but yes, she did
say you had a past. And she hasn't been the
only one to say something like that.

Warren set his jaw, and for one frightening moment I
thought he was going to yell. What he actually did was far
worse. He cleared his throat and looked at me evenly, and his
voice was smooth and emotionless when he spoke.

Warren: And you believe I'd put you in
danger? You believe Emily?

Me: No . . . I . . . maybe. I mean, you've kept
things from me before.

Warren: When?

Me, scrambling to think of examples: You said you wouldn't take any more Percs, but you did.

Warren, raising his voice: You told me I could, Bailey!

Me: Okay, well, you didn't tell me about the Percocets when you bought them.

Warren: Come on. Surely you've learned by now that the less you know, the safer it is for you. I'm just trying to protect you. Everything I've done is to protect you.

Me: And the Adderall? Giving it to me?

Warren: Has it helped you or not?

It has. It has helped me. On the surface. But now I can't sleep. And now I'm not just thin, I can actually feel my hip bones against my clothing every time I move. And now I can't NOT take it.

Me: And you sell to people here? At Prescott?

Warren, with a frustrated groan: Fine. You
want to know it all? Here. Here's my phone.
Read my texts. Memorize my schedule.
Follow me around. Know everything.

He took his phone out of his back pocket and tossed it
toward me with a little more strength than one could say was
friendly. I held it in my hands. The screen was lit, waiting for a
passcode to be typed in. I stared at it for a moment, then flicked
it off and tossed it back (gently) to Warren.

Me: I don't want it. I'm sorry. Emily got into
my head. That's all. Warren, I'm sorry.

Warren: You don't trust me.

I wanted to ask how I'm supposed to trust him when it feels
like everything is a secret, but he would just argue with me again.
And . . . in truth, he's right. He has an answer for everything. The
less I know, the safer I am, and he understands that.

Me: I'm sorry. I didn't understand. I love you.

Warren: I'm sorry too.

I was stunned to hear him say it back, and the shock of it made me realize how often he doesn't say it at all. Then there was a moment when I thought maybe he would reach for me or at least seem open to me touching him. But neither of those things happened. And, I realized, he hadn't told me he loves me back. We just stared at each other, my blood cold, his eyes tired.

Warren: I'm, uh. I'm going to go, but I'll leave
that notebook here.

Me, nodding: I'll finish up a batch and then
see what I can do with the formula. Warren,
please don't be mad at me.

Warren: I'm not. I'm just . . . tired. I'll see you
tomorrow.

He left, and I stayed at the lab until 1 a.m., trying to follow Warren's new instructions perfectly, so that he'll be pleased. Even if I would dare try it myself, I wouldn't know anything about what I'm supposed to feel like, so I'll leave it up to the boys, but I hope it's good. That would make Warren right about his theory and prove that I know what I'm doing with this and can be trusted to do it alone.

Emily wasn't home when I got here, which was weird, but I'm grateful. I think I probably would have taken all of my emotions out on her. I didn't fall asleep until it was nearly morning, but I wouldn't let myself take a Percocet, either, so that's at least good. I can do something right.

April 12, later

I didn't see Warren this morning, which means he is definitely still angry, or at least that's how I have to take it. My stomach twisted into a knot that stayed all day. Between second and third, Katy and I met in the bathroom. I wanted so badly to ask about Warren, to either confirm or deny what Emily said, but I let it go. I can't keep doing this to myself and to Warren. I can't keep letting Emily inside my head; I can't keep getting inside my own head like this.

And besides, the thing is, even if Katy wants Warren, she also clearly wants Drew more. I just have to have a little faith that Warren and I are more solid than that and that he truly loves me enough to turn down someone like Katy Ashford.

I did tell Katy about the fight, though, and she hugged

me and touched up my makeup out of her bag. Then I shared some Adderall with her. That's about the only thing that got me through the day. Warren was in English but came in late, so I didn't get to talk to him. When the bell rang, he was already out the door.

I went to the lab tonight, fully expecting that Warren wouldn't even come there, and I was right. When I got into the basement, Drew was there, suited up in coat and goggles.

Me, sighing: He's really that mad?

Drew, with a shrug: He'll get over it.

Me: What do I do?

Drew: Help me with this batch. It's been a while since I've had to do this. And Warren ... Give him time. He gets in his little moods and there's no talking to him. But I've never seen him so affected by a girl, so you've got that going for you.

Although my heart leaped at that, I don't know if "affected" is necessarily a positive thing.

On the other hand, maybe I'm just reading into Drew's words too much, just like I'm probably reading into everything else too much.

Drew, gesturing toward Warren's notebook:
What is this?

Me: Warren adjusted the formula. He thinks we can make it purer and more potent.

Drew: That's good. That's really good. We could probably make less of it and sell it for more. Did he try it?

Me: No. I made it last night, according to his instructions. He said he'd test it.

Drew: I'll do it.

Me, concerned: Okay, well. You won't need much, if Warren's right. And . . . I mean, I made it by myself, so . . .

Drew: Bailey, for fuck's sake, do you doubt everything you do?

I drew in a breath sharply. It wasn't just that Drew had never spoken to me like that before, it was the question itself. And I knew the answer: Yes. Yes, I do doubt everything I do. It's not just Mom dying or Warren's games that have me so off, it's Prescott, not feeling like I'm on top of things for once in my life. And joining Science Club. I don't know who I am anymore. That is the reality of it. And if I don't know who I am, how can I trust myself?

I felt like a scolded child, so I merely nodded, then I opened one of our storage units and took out the batch I'd made. It was clearly marked so I would know, and so would Drew or Katy, that it was different. It looked different too. Slightly more cloudy than the other batches Warren and I had made. I wasn't sure if that was a good thing or not. Usually I thought our finished product looked almost pretty, like crystal or glass. This looked more like shards of table salt.

Drew studied it, then, without a word, went to his coat and withdrew a glass pipe with a bulb on the end.

It occurred to me that I'd never actually seen anyone use what I'd been making for months, and I was suddenly seized with the urge to run out of the lab. I couldn't explain it; I just knew that if I saw it, saw what it did to people, I could never go back from that. I could never NOT know again.

While I was freaking out, Drew was oblivious, doing the drug like it was second nature. I watched as he loaded the pipe (um, is "loaded" the right word? I don't even know) and flicked a lighter underneath the bulb. Pure white smoke drifted, tranquil, around the bulb, and after a passing moment Drew inhaled it.

When he breathed out, I stared at him, looking for some sign of being high on meth. Like maybe it would change everything about him.

A slow, languid smile spread across his mouth.

> Drew: Oh, Bailey. You . . . Warren . . .
> whoever . . . round of applause.
>
> Me, heart leaping: Really?
>
> Drew, taking another hit: Really. This is going
> to make us bank. Rich, Bailey.
>
> Me, smiling: I thought we were.
>
> Drew: No, this is next-level rich. I gotta call Katy.
>
> Me: Oh. Um, can I ask you something about
> Katy?

He nodded. There is something so casual and unassuming about Drew that I feel okay asking him anything. Even this.

Me: Have she and Warren ever . . . you know,
liked each other?

Drew let out a burst of laughter and smoke. The smell hit
me then. It was like what I was used to smelling while making
it, but burnt. God, people put this crap in their bodies?

Drew: Hell no. I know. It sometimes seems
like it's sexual tension, but believe me, no.
Never. Not even when we were kids.

Me: Thank you. I feel stupid for asking. Emily
said Katy was into him.

Drew: You've got to stop believing that girl.
She's a damn mess.

Me: Apparently. And I need to start believing
Warren more.

Drew, nodding, slightly nervous and with
quicker movements than usual: Warren is
the only person I'd take a bullet for, Bailey.
He'd do the same for me. And I know he'd

do the same for you. He's hard to put up with sometimes. He's kind of an asshole. But you have to trust him. He sees the long game like we can't, you know?

I'm not sure I do know, but his words made me feel better. Drew and I finished up a batch (he was surprisingly knowledgeable about the process, even if he was sometimes too hyper and scattered to really help), and I went home, finished my homework, and even had a nice conversation with Emily about normal things.

I think I need to apologize to Warren. I'll find him first thing in the morning and do just that.

Warren and I are going to be okay. And I actually feel sleepy at a normal time (for the first time in what feels like months!!!), so hopefully that means I can finally get some rest.

April 13

I didn't have to find Warren this morning. He found me. He was waiting for me with coffee in hand, and if he hadn't had a sad, droopy smile on his face, I would have thought it was the same as every other morning since we started dating. He handed me the coffee and asked if we could talk, and I was suddenly seized by panic that this was it: This was the day he was going to dump me.

I agreed, and he started heading toward the exit. I grabbed his hand and stopped him, and he didn't pull his hand away. So that was a good sign. I told him I couldn't miss English. He promised to get me back before then.

So we went out, he still held my hand, and we sipped our coffees in silence for a moment. I was the one to break the silence.

> Me: I'm sorry. I can't tell you how sorry I am, really. But I think I realize now how much everyone else is getting in my head, and I shouldn't let them. I need to listen to you and trust you.

> Warren: No, I'm not sure you should. And I should be the sorry one here, Bailey.

With those words, I got truly scared. He must have noticed, so he pulled me to a bench outside the math building, uncaring that the very teachers marking us absent would be able to see us from the window. He held me close to him. The air was chilly and slightly damp, like the fog from the morning hadn't quite cleared.

He started by thanking me for doing so much work in the lab to help him, even though I've been stressed out about school.

257

Then he confessed that he feels like his life is a mess right now. It broke my heart to hear him say it but . . . honestly, it was also such a relief. On so many levels. I wanted to know that he could see that he wasn't doing well, and I have to admit, a huge part of me wanted to feel a little less alone in my messy life.

> Warren: Things have been awful with my
> dad lately and . . . I should have told you that.
> You let me in about your mom, and for some
> reason I have a hard time letting anyone
> else in about my family's issues. I shouldn't.
> Especially with you.
>
> Me: How can I help?
>
> Warren: You can't. I mean, not with my family.
> It's all too messed up. There's nothing anyone can
> do about that. I try to . . . I try to ignore all the
> shit and bury myself in the work or the money
> or you, sometimes. (He squeezed my hand hard.)
> And I try to bury it with other things.
>
> Me: Percocets.

Warren: Sometimes. Sometimes other things.

Me, panicking: Not ... please don't tell me ...

Warren: No, not heroin. I wouldn't stomp on my brother's grave that way. But ...

Me: How much? How often? What else?

Warren, rubbing his forehead: I don't know. I honestly don't know. Anything I can get my hands on. Anytime.

My heart ached for him so much then. The desire to medicate himself is only a desire to heal, to fix, just the completely wrong way to go about it.

Me: What can we do? Can I ... take you somewhere? Rehab?

Warren: No. I can't. My family can't know. It would destroy them all over again. It's okay. I can deal with it.

Me: But ... but you're around it all the time, Warren. Because of what we do. (I was suddenly seized with an idea. A way to make everything better. Perhaps the ONLY way.) Can we ... can we stop? Just quit? Tell Drew and Katy to find other chemists?

Warren: I can't do that, either. I need the money. I need them.

I thought about what Drew had said about taking a bullet for Warren, and I realized the feeling is mutual. And whatever animosity he and Katy have for each other, we are still a team, a family, and he knows he can rely on her.

Me: Okay, then what can we do? What can I do?

Warren: I don't know. . . . Do you think you could just ... let me be?

Me: You're asking me to leave you alone? Do you ... do you want to break up with me?

Warren: Oh, no! No, baby. That's not what
I meant at all. I mean, can things just be
normal again? Back to being happy and not
questioning everything?

Me: You want me to pretend this isn't
happening? That you're not taking pills just to
get through the day?

Warren, with a slow nod: Yes. At least for a
while. Just . . . just let me get to the summer,
you know? Then I can figure it out. And I can
be away from here and at Princeton.

How on earth can I just pretend that everything is okay? I
can't help but think it's the last thing he needs, but I was scared
to push him. I'm afraid of losing him but, honestly, more afraid
of how he'd react. His anger is intense, plus it might trigger him
into using more pills. So I told him I could try. That was the best
I could do.

He walked me back in time for second period. I should have
felt good, but I didn't. Not at all. Then when Katy and I met up
in the bathroom and I swallowed down two Adderall, I told her
everything. She didn't act surprised about his apology or about

his admission that he's using pills regularly, more than Percocets. What she did act surprised about was that this was the first time he and I had talked about it.

Did everyone know? Everyone but me?

I asked Katy what to do. What WE could do, as his friends and partners. She shook her head and laughed, and maybe she didn't mean it to be cold but it felt so icy I nearly started crying.

She said he is the smartest person she knows, that he can play all of us like violins. I asked her to explain what that meant.

> Katy: He got you to apologize, didn't he? And he got some sympathy. And he got you to say that you'll leave him alone about it.

> Me: That's not what he was doing. He's hurting, Katy. And he just doesn't know how to stop hurting.

> Katy: I don't doubt he hurts, Bailey. The problem is he makes everyone around him hurt too. See you at the lab tonight.

It's one in the morning and I'm still not sure how to interpret her words or the whole conversation in general. And I still feel unsettled about the talk with Warren. Even more than I was before.

I just don't know what to do. All I know is I can't give up on him. What kind of person would I be if I did?

April 17

After school today I didn't go with Katy to get coffee, and I put off doing homework or going to the lab, and headed to Mr. Callahan's classroom. I'm not sure why I wanted to talk to him. Maybe it was just that he seems so . . . adult. Wise, even. Warm, at least, unlike how most of my friends are at the moment. He was still there, sitting at his desk grading what looked like freshmen-level homework. He was delighted to see me. He asked me how things are going, and I told him that things aren't that great, if I was being honest. He gestured to a seat in the first row, and I sat.

I chose my words carefully, and of course I didn't tell him anything that would get me into trouble. But I did tell him that my grades are abysmal, at least to my standards (and sometimes to Prescott's standards as well), and that I feel that my friends here are confusing. I told him about the problems I'd been having in my relationships with Emily and Katy, and I also told him about Warren. I said it feels like Warren is such a big part of my life, and it's affecting everything else.

I could tell he was glad I confided in him. He said he'd been worried since I stopped coming in after school to do extra chemistry but he knew how hard Prescott could be. He also, sort of awkwardly, told me that first love can be intense and often confusing. He said he imagined Warren could be extra intense. I asked if he knew anything about Warren's family, and to my surprise, he did.

> Mr. Callahan: We were told. The staff, I mean.
> There are certain things in a student's file
> that are essential to teaching them . . . things
> like learning disabilities or perhaps a mental
> disorder. But there are also cases like Warren's,
> when something in a student's personal
> history needs to be known, because the
> student . . . well, the student was changed so
> much by it. It helps us teach that student, to
> get through to them. It's not salacious gossip,
> I want you to understand that.
>
> Me: I didn't think so. When you say
> "changed" . . .

Mr. Callahan: Well, I didn't know Warren as a child, but I have good friends at Campbell. Warren's parents are not exactly warm people. But when his brother was found dead . . . it was in all the papers locally, and the family was really under the microscope, considering their standing in the community. And if his parents were distant before that, they were downright neglectful afterward. Warren's mother took precedence. I can imagine that a boy like that, who believes he's not good enough to get his parents' attention . . . well, I imagine that his brother's death and his parents disappearing almost completely just proved that to him.

Me: He always seems sure of himself, though.

Mr. Callahan, looking at me with a gentle but probing expression: Does he really?

Me: I don't know. And I don't know how to help him.

Mr. Callahan: I wish I had an answer for you. I have a feeling that your loyalty and empathy for him have done more for him than most people in his life have, but it's probably also hard to trust that or accept it. Maybe he even wants to refuse it sometimes, because he may not think himself deserving. But . . .

Me: But?

Mr. Callahan: I hope you're not giving so much of yourself that you're giving up who you are.

Me: I'm not sure I know what you mean.

Mr. Callahan: I mean, Prescott's coursework is substantial, but you're extremely intelligent, Bailey. You shouldn't be having this kind of trouble with it, if you don't mind me speaking frankly with you. There's quite a difference between not being able to handle the work and just not doing it. And I hope

you don't give up on Emily. It sounds like
she could really use a friend right now.

At that point I could only nod to him because I was unable
to speak in the face of the harsh truths he was telling me. I
looked down to hide the tears in my eyes and my gaze landed
on a newspaper on his desk. The headline read, "Toddler Found
in the Cold." There was a picture underneath the headline of a
small, run-down house.

Tears forgotten, I turned the paper so I could see it better.

Mr. Callahan: Yes, terrible thing. Luckily the
boy will be all right. He'll be in foster care,
maybe until he's of age, but he'll live.

Me, scanning the article: What happened?

Mr. Callahan: Neighbors saw a little boy, a
two-year-old, out in the cold and rain the
other night in Frenchtown. Know where that
is? (I shook my head.) It's a trailer park in
the east end of Wiltshire. He was wearing
only a diaper, no clothes, walking in the
road. A kind soul took him in and called the

267

police. Turns out his parents were so high on meth they didn't even realize he was missing.

Me, heart galloping a syncopated beat: So he got out in the street?

Mr. Callahan: Could have been seriously hurt. Or taken. Or could have frozen to death. The temperatures were in the freezing range that night.

Me: How could his parents not even realize?

Mr. Callahan: When you're that high, I don't think you even know where YOU are, let alone a small child. But thank God, he's been placed in a home where he'll be safe and cared for.

Me: I don't understand how . . . how someone could let themselves get that way. That they'd not notice their kid was gone. That they'd thinking getting high is more important than their kid.

Mr. Callahan: That's how addiction works,
unfortunately. Addicts often can't think about
anything but their next fix.

For a moment I thought about Warren and the pills he
takes. And I thought about myself and the Adderall.

But I could stop taking that, couldn't I? I don't NEED it.
But I'm craving it. I'll start to want it whenever I feel my energy
fading. Or when I feel like I can't focus. Or when I have a lot of
work to do. But wanting isn't the same thing as needing.

. . . Is it?

I asked Mr. Callahan if I could have the newspaper and
he let me take it. Then he told me I could always talk to him.
About anything. I thanked him and went home.

I have to head to the lab in a few minutes, but I'm nowhere
near done with homework. Every time I try, I look at the picture
of the little house where the toddler lived with his parents. Even
if I hadn't read it or Mr. Callahan hadn't told me, I would have
known it was east-side Wiltshire.

I tucked the paper inside my purse, with the Percocets.

April 18
Drew was at the lab last night, as was Katy, and when I got
there they had my particular batch of the product out and were

in deep conversation. Apparently, Drew had filled Katy in, because when she saw me, she threw her arms around me and squealed. That was when Warren walked in.

Drew then told Warren about how he'd tried some of the batch I'd made, how it made him feel, and that I'd followed his instructions perfectly. Warren smiled, gave me a proud nod, and took out some of the new product for himself.

Drew didn't even need to be asked. He just got out his pipe and handed it over to Warren. I did my best, I think, to not look completely panicked. After all, he'd basically admitted to me that he is an addict but also that he can handle himself. Still . . . he doesn't need THIS addiction. He doesn't need to become the type of person who would let a child wander out into the winter cold without clothes and not even realize it. Will he one day do that to me? Metaphorically? Will I become just another distraction from the next high, something he'd rather forget?

But at least if I looked anxious, maybe my friends thought it was because I was worried I hadn't done a good enough job. I watched Warren heat the pipe with a lighter, watched him draw the poisonous fumes into his lungs. I wish I could say he looked awkward doing it. Or maybe that he had no clue what he was doing, or that he coughed and sputtered and rejected the drug with his body and his voice. But of course, he looked used to this. He looked as practiced and sure as he could be.

After a minute or two, long enough for the high to set in completely, a smile spread Warren's mouth wide. He started describing what he was feeling, his voice a little tighter and rougher than I was used to. There was something different about his pretty eyes, too. Less warm, more sharp. He talked to Drew and Katy, mostly, and avoided looking at me much, and honestly, that was just fine with me. I wasn't sure what to make of this new Warren, like he was more a stranger now. It wasn't just the change in his demeanor that bothered me, the obvious shift in his motor skills or the intensity of him with the high, it was something else. I watched him talk to our friends, trying to figure out what it was, exactly, that bothered me so much, and it hit me like a freight train: This was the most satisfied I'd ever seen him. I can't put into words how much that hurt, how much it felt like a betrayal that he needed a high and craved a high more than he did me, but there was no denying that it seemed in that moment he finally had what he'd been longing for.

And it made me realize that maybe . . . maybe I'll never be that important to him. Maybe nothing can be as important as a high to him.

He told us the new version of the product is stronger. He already felt like he'd used a lot more than normal, even though

271

that was the amount he would usually use. He talked about a sort of euphoria, a powerful feeling, like he could do anything. It was like Adderall times ten, if what he was saying was correct. He felt like he could run for miles without stopping. He felt like he didn't need to eat ever again. He felt like he could ace tests, write books, recall every fact known to man. It was that kind of invincible. But of course he was talking about nothing, really. Rambling on too fast and gesturing more animatedly than I'd ever seen him. He was truly enjoying the high, and the sad part was, I wasn't surprised in the slightest.

Drew agreed with him, and then they got to work. All of them except me. Katy started talking about her contacts, how to basically pitch the new version to everyone. Drew started talking logistics with Warren: how much of what ingredient and where they could get it, how much it would take up front to manufacture this version on a larger scale, and also where we could cut back since we were using less of some of the ingredients. Then, of course, they all talked about how much to charge.

It was more than I'd ever heard them talk about prices. So far, I knew only what came to me each week. How much I could stick into my pocket when Drew distributed payment. I'd never known anything about what we were selling it for versus how much money it actually took to produce.

The markup for our labor, logistical planning, and artistry was around 400 percent.

I felt tears form in my eyes and closed them so that they wouldn't fall.

Not only were we giving addicts the means to forget about their children in the cold; we were charging them through the nose for it.

I listened to the group make plans and work out numbers. I nodded along at appropriate times. I answered questions or gave my thoughts when asked my opinion. I even laughed when they talked about how if they started selling this now, we'd have extra money to blow while we are at Drew's beach house, when I really felt like puking on their shoes I was so disgusted. But in truth, I wasn't really listening. I was obsessively going over things in my head, getting my mental files in order: how I'd joined, how the Club worked, the collateral, Warren's addiction, my own (I think I have to put that name on it now) addiction, the consequences of leaving the group, how alone I'd be, what trouble I might get in, what I might possibly lose, how I'd survive without Warren. And as I turned those things over and over in my head like some sort of nightmarish carousel, one thing became crystal clear—I had to get out of the Club. It was the only right thing to do. And I had to do it without ruining my life.

As I'm writing tonight, I'm still thinking it through. Every scenario I've come up with, from simply telling the group I'm leaving and promising to never say a word to anyone, to going full-out nuclear on them and turning myself and everyone else in, means that life will never be the same. I might be going to jail. Or they are. Or more people will end up addicted.

One thing is for damn sure: If I get out, I'll lose them. All of them. Even Warren.

Maybe especially Warren. He is the one who will feel most betrayed, because if anything gets out about the Club, his own drug use is going to come out, and the ripple effect will go through his family. And I know Warren. There won't be any understanding or forgiveness for this. I'll be dead to him.

Another thing is certain as well: If I CAN get out of this without much collateral damage, without ever telling another soul and the group letting me go without a fight, I will no longer be able to get Adderall. The thought alone makes me nauseated and shaky. If I'm going to do this, I'm going to have to stop taking it first.

I can do it, I think. I can stop. Maybe I can even get Katy and Warren to stop with me. Maybe I can convince them it's for the good of the Science Club.

Maybe there is no chance in hell.

April 19

Of all things, my father called today.

I was so startled to see his number pop up on my phone that I sounded weird when I said hello and he immediately asked if I was okay. I told him I was. What else am I going to say? "No, Dad. I'm not. I think I'm addicted to Adderall and my boyfriend is addicted to way more than that, and oh, by the way, I'm totally in the drug business now. Cool, huh?"

I shared more than I ever meant to with Mr. Callahan, so let's just leave it at that, okay?

I asked how he was, and he said he was doing really well. He said Isa's had a pretty lengthy and intense case, so he's been on his own in the evenings more than he'd like. I could hear the sadness in his voice. The loneliness. And I felt for him, as much as I don't love Isa. Loneliness for any reason sucks. I've felt incredibly lonely in a room full of people before. I felt lonely last night at the lab, being the only person who seemed to see a problem in what we are doing.

He asked if I'd be home for break, and there was some hopefulness in his voice. That was more shocking than him calling me. Then I immediately felt like crap for saying I'd be elsewhere. Dad had obviously talked to Bex. He knew of her plans to go to New York, and I wondered how often they talked. Then, as if I wasn't shocked enough, he apologized for not calling on the anniversary of Mom's death. He APOLOGIZED.

> Dad: I'm really sorry, Bail. I wish I had a
> better excuse. I just couldn't pull myself
> together that day.
>
> Me: You mean . . . you were upset?
>
> Dad: Yeah. I think things have happened so
> fast for me, with Isa, I mean . . . I'm not sure
> I really had time to properly grieve for your
> mother. Not the way I needed to.

I didn't know what to say to that. Part of me wanted to yell and say that of course he hadn't grieved properly; he'd barely grieved at all. I also wanted to say terrible things about Isa and how she just distracted him from pain or something, but none of that makes real sense when I think about it. Of course she distracted him, but he obviously cares about her too. Most of all, though, I wanted to tell him how he'd left me all alone and moved on from Mom when I needed him most.

But I didn't say anything like that.

Me: Well, I'm not sure I've been coping in the healthiest ways, either.

Dad: What do you mean? Are you okay?

Me: I'm fine, Dad. Just . . . angry.

Dad: At me?

Me, swallowing hard: At you, yeah. I guess I felt like it was too soon for Isa. It felt disrespectful to Mom. But I'm mad at everything, Dad. Mad that she's gone. Mad at all the good things I do because she can't see them. Mad at all the bad things I do because she's not here to help. I don't know.

I have no idea if it was simply because he asked, and asked so sincerely that I truly thought maybe he wanted to know, or if with everything going on it felt good to unload something on him, but for whatever reason, I was honest. And yeah, it DID feel good to finally say it. Maybe we can understand each other a little better now. At the very least, there's not such a wall between us.

Dad, after a moment of silence: I'm really sorry, Bailey. I should be doing more. And I hope you understand about Isa. . . . She's not a replacement.

Me: I know. I understand, Dad. It's just weird to see you happy, I guess? I feel like you should still be angry like me. And sad.

Dad: I'm both of those things, Bailey. Every day. Every day I miss your mother. Is school really going all right? Have you made friends?

Me, trying to sound happy: Yeah. Friends, and a boyfriend.

Dad: Bex may have mentioned that, but don't get angry at her; she only told me because I was worried about how you were adjusting.

Me: I can't ever be mad at Bex, Dad. You know that.

Dad: So who is he?

I told Dad a little about Warren and about my friends. All the good stuff, none of the bad. I also told him I'm not doing as well as I want in my classes, and he confessed to me that he'd never been good at schoolwork and was impressed and proud that I was even in Prescott considering my genes. The conversation sputtered out, and Dad excused himself, saying he needed to get dinner on the table by the time Isa was home. He told me he knew I could handle Prescott and knew I'd get into Harvard or wherever I wanted to go. I didn't tell him about the wait list for the Princeton program. No need to disappoint him with that. If I actually get in, then I can tell him I applied.

When I hung up the phone I felt both better and worse, and bereft of a friendly voice. I considered calling Bex to give her a gentle teasing about not being able to keep a secret, but decided to let it rest.

It's almost eight o'clock, and I have a few more things to do for tomorrow's classes, but I don't feel like being alone. I need Warren. I need to know that he cares too. So I'll head to the lab and keep him company while I finish my homework, and if he really needs a hand, I can help too. It's okay. I can keep doing this. I have to, I think, until I have a better plan.

April 20

Although last night went okay at the lab (Warren mostly kept us talking as I did my homework, and even when I had to jump in and help him a bit, he kept my mind off what we were actually doing enough that I didn't have to think about it much), I just couldn't face it tonight. I wanted to be around Warren, even though I . . . I think I'm sure we can't go on like this. But I wanted to be with him tonight and kiss him and feel some of that heat. Just to feel normal. Maybe to distract me. But in the end, the image of the cold, abandoned toddler won out. I just couldn't bring myself to go through another four or five hours of pretending I was just fine with destroying lives. But I did go to the lab. I had another idea.

Warren was there, looking gorgeous in his blue cashmere sweater, his hair slightly mussed. I could tell by his eyes, though, that he'd had a lot of Percocets. Weird how I couldn't see that before. Now it's so obvious.

I asked him for his car keys. He cocked his head at me in question. I somehow, miraculously, came up with an excuse that would mean he wouldn't want to come along.

> Me: It's Bex. She needs some, um, girl help.
> She's really upset that some of the girls in her

grade already have real bras, so I'm going to
take her to get something pretty. Shouldn't
take more than a few hours. Unless you need
me here?

Warren, pulling a face: No, by all means, help
Bex with girl problems. And I'd prefer to
never think of your little sister and bras in the
same context ever again. You know how to
drive it, right?

Me, laughing: Thanks. And yes. I promise I'll
drive as carefully as possible and I won't let
Bex eat anything inside it.

Warren handed me the keys and reminded me where it was
parked. Then he reached for my hand and I let him take it.

Warren: Are you really okay? You've been kind
of weird these last few days.

Me: Weird?

Warren: Distant.

Me: Oh. I'm worried about you and trying
to control my worry for you, I guess. Trying
to leave you alone. But it's not easy, Warren.
I really care about you, and seeing you high
or not completely in control of the situation
scares me. You're high now, right? What if you
blow yourself up?

Warren, eyes flashing with anger before they
softened: You're right. I am. But I'm used to
this, Bailey. I'm okay. Don't worry. We'll get
through this. You love me, right? That's really
all that matters.

He kissed me sweetly, and my heart ached. For him. For
US. The truth was that maybe loving each other isn't all that
matters. Not when we're hurting others. Not when he really
needs help, and I do too. Not when we're in so deep that we
might all end up in prison. Some things are bigger than even
love can handle.

I promised I'd be back soon and left.

His car was in a student parking lot next to the senior
boys' dorms. I'd never paid attention to the exact make and
model before, but tonight before I got in, I circled around it

once. It was a relatively new BMW. Not exactly inconspicuous for his favorite hobbies but something with a lot of speed. I felt the power in it as I hit the gas the first time and shifted it into gear.

At a stoplight close to the center of Wiltshire, I took the folded-up newspaper out of my purse. The article about the toddler didn't mention an actual address, but based on Mr. Callahan's words about it and the trail we took the night I was with Drew and Warren, I could figure out a general area. Frenchtown, they'd called it. A trailer park. I drove over the bridge and Wiltshire changed over instantly from affluent and clean to poor and dingy. Fires were lit in what looked like a homeless camp.

I slowed to a stop across the street from that first house where Drew and Warren had left me in the car to go inside and work their deals. There was a lot of activity. I could see several silhouettes in the weak window lights. But nobody came outside, and no one stopped and went in, either. I took the car out of park and turned on the street closest to the house, following its backside half a block. The house seemed to go on forever, like over the years, people had haphazardly thrown a new house together behind it, then another behind that one. It was clearly broken up into quite a few apartments, with several mailboxes at each oddly placed entrance. All the houses around it were the same, even if they weren't as big. These were all apartments, not well kept, and I had to wonder what these people paid to live there. Probably some slumlord fleecing them for every penny.

At the next stop sign, I took a minute to get my bearings and look around. I didn't have to look far. One more block and there was a crumbling brick wall with a sign on it that, in its heyday, would have looked nice. Now it was missing a few letters and slightly crooked. It read: FRENCHTOWN CIRCLE. The trailer park.

I drove forward slowly. It didn't take me long to find the house I wanted to see. A little white thing that looked barely big enough for one person, let alone a family. I glanced from my newspaper to it, then back again. It was a match. Like before, I pulled to a stop across the street from it and turned off my lights. There were people inside. I could see someone's head through the front window, the closely shaved head of a man. The TV was on. Some show about cops, of all things. A woman walked through the room and sat by the man, her head on his shoulder.

So these were the parents of the toddler, sitting there like their world wasn't over, like their child wasn't at someone else's house because they couldn't get it together to take care of him themselves. These were the people I was cooking drugs for. The people I was enabling. The people I was making sicker. The parents I'D distracted from their son.

I glanced down the street. It was a flat street, but it was dark and muddy. Farther down the road was a tree line and, beyond that, if I had the map right in my head, the river. If the child hadn't been carried off by some devious stranger or hit by a car before that tree line, he might have gone in there and not been found in time. He might have even made it to the river. He wouldn't have meant to fall in, or maybe he would have wanted to play in the water, not understanding the insidious current beneath the surface.

I looked away from the tree line and wiped tears from my eyes. Back inside the trailer, smoke was rising in small, opaque tufts. The man moved, and the reflection of the TV caught the glass bulb just right. I started shaking from pure rage. I wanted to burst into that house and scream at them. Instead, I put Warren's beautiful car in drive and pulled away, still shaking violently. I shook all the way home.

But it's two in the morning now. I think I'm going to take a Percocet to calm myself down and knock myself out. And I think I'm finally understanding that I'm not mad at the parents of the toddler.

I'm mad at myself.

April 21

I went into the lab last night with one mission only: to convince Warren to stop. Stop it all.

The whole walk there, I felt like I was going to throw up, I was so nervous. Conversations not even half as important as this had ended badly, with him lashing out in anger or shutting me out, and there were about a billion ways talking to him could go wrong. Not the least of which was him thinking I was being disloyal to the Club and what kind of consequences that could have. The collateral was majorly on my mind.

He greeted me with a passionate kiss and I could tell he was really excited about something, and that made my heart sink and my stomach twist into a knot. I could also tell it was Adderall in his system, not Percocet. He told me, proudly, that he'd gotten the new recipe down to an art. He promised it would change our workflow a lot, but for the better.

I let him show me every change he'd made in every step of the process, only vaguely noting how it would change the product and cut down on time and some of our more expensive ingredients. He was so proud. Even a week ago I would have been proud too. Now all I felt was sick. I asked him if we could talk for a minute and watched a parade of emotions cross his face (anger, suspicion, curiosity, resentment) before he said we could.

> Me: I read the other night about a mother
> and father who were so high they hadn't

noticed that their baby was wandering around in the freezing cold for almost an hour.

Warren: Heroin?

Me: Meth. And here, Warren. In Wiltshire.

Warren: Let me guess. East side? Perhaps even Hodgkins Park? Or Frenchtown?

Me: Frenchtown.

Warren, shaking his head: That's terrible. It probably happens more than we know.

Me: But doesn't it bother you?

Warren: Of course. It's sad.

Me: Warren, it's more than sad. And it's our fault.

Warren, with a slight laugh: No, Bailey. It's not our fault. These people . . . they'd sell their souls

for another hit. You know that. They practically
do. My brother would have sold my mother
into a trafficking ring to get more heroin. He
was out of his mind. Addicts are the most
selfish people on the planet, trust me.

Me, before I could stop myself: And what
does that make you?

The light in Warren's eyes went out, then his gaze became
a cold, black stare. Fear shot through me, but I shoved it aside,
more determined than scared. He HAD to see. He HAD to
understand.

Warren squeezed his eyes shut. I watched as he balled up his
fist, raised it, and sent it down with a crack on the lab table. A
glass beaker fell on its side.

Warren: What does it make YOU, Bailey?
We can't help anybody. All we can do is keep
them safe.

Me: You keep saying that, but that's not all we
can do, Warren. We can take ourselves out of
the equation.

Warren: You want to stop making.

Me: I want us to stop being responsible for
children being left out in the cold and people
being too addicted to care about their lives!
And I want you to stop taking pills. I want
ME to stop taking pills.

Warren: Have you tried? (I shook my head no.
I hadn't tried yet. It was part of my plan, but
I couldn't convince myself, every day between
second and third periods and every day after
school or whenever, that I didn't HAVE to
take them. That I didn't need them. Warren
snorted at me.) If you tried, you'd know.

Me: I can. I will.

Warren: And how many Percocets do you
have left?

Me: I've only taken a few. I'm fine.

Warren: But what did it feel like?

Me: Good. I mean, I got calm. Sleepy. I slept.

Warren: You need the sleep. It does feel good, doesn't it? But you know you can stop.

Me: Yes.

Warren: I know I can too. So what's the harm?

Me: It isn't right. None of this is right. You should feel worse about this. You lost a brother to this, Warren. How do you not feel anything?

Warren pulled me into his arms then, his body pressing heavily against mine. His weight and warmth felt so reassuring because he wanted me close, but also because it felt human. He was human, not like a soulless, unfeeling robot.

Warren: No, Bailey, the problem is I feel too much. Isn't it? I feel too much for my parents. For Mitch. For you. Even Drew

and Katy. I'm not abandoning them. Are
you? Are you going to? Are you going to
abandon me?

Me: No! No. I just want you to come with me.

Warren: No, just don't go. Don't go in the first
place. It will be fine. We'll get through this
year and we can stop everything. Okay? Just
like I promised.

He kissed me before I could give him an answer, and I
kissed him back, letting that be my answer because I couldn't
seem to find my voice. What I wanted to say and couldn't was
that I didn't think we'd get through the year, not this way. And I
didn't think it would all be fine. But I don't know how to stop or
stop him or get out. I don't know how to get off this ride I'm on,
but I certainly don't want to make anything worse. I'm trapped.
All I can do is walk a tightrope right now of getting by and
trying to do the least harm I can, to anyone.

So I let him kiss me until we were both so wrapped up in
each other that everything else faded away.

I have to admit I don't remember much else about last
night. When he took out some Percs to calm himself down, he

offered me some as well, and I took them. Every single one he offered. Not because I wanted it or even needed to, but because I needed to do something with him. To show him I was with him. To feel that connection. I do know that Warren and I held each other for a long time and that he did cry on my shoulder, shaking as he asked me over and over again not to leave him, and I promised I wouldn't. I remember him walking me home and stopping me outside my dorm's gate, where he held my wrists in his hands hard and told me he wouldn't speak a word to Drew or Katy about me wanting out, since I'd promised I'd stay in.

And I remember yanking my hands away and that his voice hadn't sounded reassuring. It sounded like a threat.

April 24

The last thing I needed today was Emily being Scary Emily.

I woke her up because she was clearly going to sleep through class, and she seriously growled at me like some kind of animal. She looked like hell, and honestly, it was the first time I'd really looked at her in a while. Her eyes seemed sunken in, rimmed in purple, almost like bruises, and her face looked gaunt. When she rolled out of bed, fumbling around for the pieces of her uniform, I could see that she'd lost a lot of weight too. Maybe Prescott was taking its toll on everyone this year.

Me: Wow, did the AV club have a party last
night or what?

Emily, with a sneer: Did your snobby friends
have one? You were home later than me.

Me: I had a lot of work to do. Are you okay?

Emily: I'm fine. God. What time is it?

Me: Ten till. We've got to get to class. And
you're welcome, for waking you up.

Emily: Just consider us even. Do we have any water?

I took a bottled water out of the package we kept under our
window and tossed it to her.

Emily: Thanks. How's the Prince of Darkness?

Me: He's fine.

I'd be damned if I would ever tell her he was anything but
fine. Or that we weren't doing well. Or anything else for that

293

matter. Though sometimes she acts like she's a friend, when it comes to Warren she is 100 percent enemy. Briefly, a flash of last night appeared behind my eyes . . . Warren offering me pills, telling me to stay, me being so out of it that I barely remembered a thing. I looked down at my wrists and noticed bruising, in almost a complete circle around each.

Enemies. Sometimes they're the last person you'd expect. Sometimes they're people you really care about but you find yourself on opposite sides.

> Emily: Glad to hear. I'm sure all his money makes it easy.

> Me: I'm not with him because of the money.

> Emily: Not you. I'm sure it makes it easy for HIM. He can buy himself another toy and not think about it anymore.

> Me: Go talk to him about it. I'm sure that's what you'll do anyway.

I felt no more obligation to her and left our room, headed toward my first class. Warren was outside the building, waiting with coffee, and I swear his whole body somehow softened when we made eye contact. I pulled down my sleeves, not wanting him to see the marks he'd left. He wrapped his arms around me and I felt relief. He thanked me for talking things through with him last night, as if I'd helped him make up his mind, which was almost laughable because it was clear it had already been made up. The addiction decided that for him, and I'm beginning to think it's going to decide everything for him. But not for me. I just need to figure it out.

I was so stressed thinking about it that I took my first Addy of the day before first period even started.

April 25

When Katy walked into the bathroom today and bummed an Addy, she grabbed my hand and spun me around. Even though she looked completely flawless and like she'd had a solid nine hours of sleep, she complimented ME. She told me it was totally showing how much weight I was losing (not that I was fat before, she clarified) and said I looked like a model now.

She went on, joking about how maybe it was me being in love with Warren that was making me glow from within, and I don't know, something about talking with her while she was all bright and happy made me think it would be a good time to bring up the Club.

Me: Hey, can we talk?

Katy, applying more lipstick: Isn't that what we're doing?

Me: I mean seriously, though. Something's really bothering me.

Katy: Of course, sweetie. That's why we're friends, isn't it?

I told Katy as gently but matter-of-factly as I could about the articles I had seen in the local paper, about how I was worried we'd be caught but even more worried that we were contributing to the skyrocketing addiction around Wiltshire.

Katy: Well, what did you expect?

Me: I don't know. I guess I didn't realize we'd be making so much. Or that we'd be impacting people like this.

Katy, rolling her eyes: I know Warren talked to you about this when you joined. Users are

going to use, Bailey. What sets us apart is that
we are safe about it. And smarter, really.

Me: Safe or not, we're still putting it out
there. We're the ones making it available and
turning a profit on it.

Katy: Better us than anyone else.

Me: So you don't care?

Katy: Of course I do.

She cares. At least she said so. And this is Katy, right?
Fabulous Katy, who has been there so much for me this year
and who is fierce and loyal and ambitious but also good. She
IS good. But she's also THE Katy Ashton, fierce and loyal
and ambitious, and perhaps all of those things to a fault,
who might see me as a complete traitor and has the power to
destroy me.

But still. It's Katy. I just can't believe she wouldn't listen to
reason. That she wouldn't see the truth.

Me, taking a shaking breath: Then we should stop.

Katy took a step backward from me, like I'd struck her. Some underclassman girl came in and used the bathroom. Katy and I stood there silently until the girl had finished and vacated the bathroom.

> Katy, whispering: You want out?

> Me: No. I promised Warren I'd stay in. But . . .
> I thought that maybe if you wanted to stop too,
> we could all agree to it, so Warren would as well.

> Katy, eyes steely: I don't want out. But if you
> do, if you want to leave us, and betray us to
> anyone, you know what happens.

The collateral. I promised Katy I wouldn't say a word.

> Me: I don't want out. Unless we all do. I'm
> just . . . worried. And I think we're probably
> going to get discovered.

> Katy: And you're bailing before that happens.

> Me: No. It's not like that.

Katy: Sure it's not. Are you going to rat? (I
didn't answer, and Katy grabbed my wrist,
right where the bruises were that Warren
had left. When I squeaked at the pain, a
flash of a smile perked up Katy's mouth,
then was gone. She squeezed my wrist
harder.) You can't tell a soul, Bailey. You
know that.

Me: I'm not. I promise. I don't want to leave.
I'm sorry, I'm just scared.

Katy, letting go of my wrist and patting it
softly, like an apology: We all get scared,
sweetie. It's okay. But sometimes a reminder
of the consequences can keep that fear in
check. Know what I mean?

I knew exactly what she meant: I needed to shut up, or
they were going to make me, and their way of making me
would destroy my life. I would go to jail, I would never get into
Harvard, I might not be able to even graduate from high school.
And the pain I'd put Dad and Bex through . . .
So Warren won't budge and Katy not only doesn't want out,

299

she's ready to let me take the fall. I don't know who else I can trust. I feel even more trapped than before.

I have a thought, though, and it's either the smartest or the dumbest idea that I've ever had in my life. I have this diary. Maybe it wouldn't count for much to the police, but if they WOULD use the collateral, at least I have my own record of events.

I can't believe I'm thinking like this. Just a few weeks ago I would have done anything for them. Now all I can think about is how to get away and possibly how to make sure they'll go down with me if they frame me.

April 26

I was catching up on homework when there was a knock at the door. Emily and I exchanged a look of confusion, then I got up to answer it. It was Katy. She said there was going to be an emergency meeting and I needed to come with her now. I shut my books and left with her, heart beating a frantic, uneven rhythm in my rib cage.

We walked across campus to the lab without speaking a word. When we got there, the boys were already there, sitting on stools. There were two empty ones in front of them. Katy and I sat on them.

Drew spoke first.

Drew: Bailey, Katy told me about the conversation you had with her recently. About wanting out. It's understandable. I think we've all had moments where we've been scared, and we've thought about leaving the group. But then I brought it up to Warren, and he admitted he'd had nearly the same conversation with you a few days ago.

Me: No. I don't want out. I told Warren that.

Drew: I don't think we need to waste time arguing about whether you do or not. We have two people here who can attest to you saying as much. So let's talk about what happens next.

Me: But there is a reason to argue. I told Warren and Katy that I'd stay until summer. That I'd keep working and I wouldn't tell a soul.

Drew, looking more like a parent running out of patience than a friend: Bailey. You've expressed interest in leaving to two people in this group, and you told them that individually, while also trying to persuade them to leave with you.

Me: Well, I mean, of course. Warren is my boyfriend. Katy's my best friend. I trust them. I wanted to talk about what I was worried about. And I'm worried about them, too. And you.

Katy: And what if I wasn't your best friend? Or Warren wasn't a boyfriend? Would you run to someone else, someone outside the club, to get advice?

Me: No. Of course not. I know the rules.

They continued grilling me for what felt like hours, asking me about Mr. Callahan, how close we are, and how much I'd told him about any of the Club, its actions, OR its members. I didn't fare well under the pressure, because some of what they were insinuating was partially true, at least without context. I WAS close to Mr. Callahan, we had discussed drugs (generically

speaking) and especially meth, and we'd even discussed Warren.
I'm sure the guilt was all over my face, even if I didn't feel what
I'd done was wrong.

I ended up reiterating my stance that police are really
cracking down and we need to lay low for a while, maybe
stop making until we are sure we won't be caught. Maybe
even until after summer. They stared at me, all of them with
expressions that oscillated between embarrassment and flat-
out anger.

Drew: You sound like a coward, Bailey.

Me: It's not cowardly to want to be sure that
we don't get into any trouble.

Warren: The only way we get into trouble is if
someone talks. Someone like you.

Me: No. I won't talk.

Katy: You say that now, but what happens
when there's some pressure on you?

Me: I'll be fine.

Warren: Bailey. You're not fine. You're about
ready to crack just because of Prescott's
classes. Your grades are bad, you've said so
yourself. You barely sleep. You have a hard
time keeping up with the lab work. I mean,
you're barely keeping it together.

He was being extremely unfair. He knew how hard I was
trying. He also knew that I knew he was struggling too. That he
was so stressed and his emotions so unmanageable that he was
self-medicating just to get by.

Me: What do I do? What do I do to prove to
you that I'm in, that you can trust me? I mean,
I gave you collateral. I've promised I won't talk
and I will keep doing this. What can I do to
convince you?

Again the three of them exchanged a look.

Drew, clearing his throat: I don't think that
we can be convinced, Bailey. You've already
betrayed us, really, by trying to break us apart.

Me: I swear that wasn't what I was doing. I just needed to talk things out. Please. What can I do?

Drew looked to Warren, then away, and I knew something bad was coming.

Warren: We think perhaps it's best if you take some time and think about this. Think about what you really want and what it means to be part of this group. Alone.

The boys again exchanged a look. Katy didn't even raise her eyes and kept them glued to her polished nails. And it was then that I understood.

Me: No. No. Please. We were all supposed to go together. It was supposed to be our trip, our reward for all the hard work we've done. And I was part of that hard work.

Katy: We're not sure we're comfortable with you being there at the moment.

Me: But . . .

Warren: Our buyers want the new version of
the product. In two weeks. Obviously I won't
be able to help get the batch ready. But if you
decide you really want to stay in, and that
you can handle it, you could prove it to us by
making this batch.

It was so unfair. So cold. I'd worked just as hard as them.
Harder, sometimes. And here I was, ultimately just trying to
protect them, even if they couldn't see it. It felt like a huge
betrayal. They are shutting me out and I know it's just because
they are in denial or in too deep to want to hear what I'm
saying. Now it's clear: I'm totally alone in this.

Me: I don't know why you're doing this.
I don't understand. I was just worried for
you. You're my friends. I didn't want any of
us to get in trouble. I haven't betrayed you
at all. In fact, it's the opposite. I'm trying
to help.

And then . . .

Drew: Your method of "helping" is going to
land us all in prison. If you can't shut up and
get it together, the collateral goes out.

Katy said nothing. Neither did Drew. No one could meet
my eyes, like they couldn't stand to look at me. Voice shaking, I
appealed to the one person in the room who might care enough
to be sympathetic.

Me: Warren? You know I can be trusted,
right?

Warren raised his gaze to mine. His pretty eyes were dull,
filled with disappointment and, I think, disgust. He gave a short
shake of his head.

Warren: I don't think so, Bailey.

They left me in the lab, crying and stunned, with no one to
turn to.

I took a Percocet to help me sleep, but I'm truthfully so
exhausted I probably didn't need it. I'm sitting here writing,
still in shock. If I don't keep my head down and do what they
say, my life will be ruined. I'm so angry and so . . . I don't know.

Is there a word that's worse than devastated? Even Warren wouldn't speak up for me. How could he? After all I've done for him, after all we've been through and the things he's said to me. How could he say he loves me and then just talk like that to them about me? And THEY'RE concerned about betrayal? What do they think this is?

I've got to get out. At this point, maybe all I can do is do the things that will cause the least amount of problems for me: stay here, make the next batch, keep my mouth shut, do as I'm told. Then once it's summer I can be home and beg Dad to let me go back to my old school. Maybe I can disappear and never see any of the Science Club again.

May 4

I've been aimless for days. And utterly alone. They left Sunday, but even before that . . . I just sort of wandered in and out of classes, went to the lab, did what was expected of me. I wish I could say I tried to talk to them, tried again to get them to understand or change their minds about the trip, but I didn't. I can't decide if I'm cowardly or just too tired. Maybe I'm just done caring.

Warren talked to me. He kissed me too but gave up when I was unresponsive. It's weird. It's like I'm not even really angry now. I just feel empty. He told me not to be upset, that when they got back and the new batch was done, everything would be okay again. He told me it was just business and not to take it personally. But how can I not? It WAS personal.

And I can't stop thinking about how Warren didn't defend me. He didn't tell them how hard I'd been working. And he had no defense for not defending me, other than telling me this was for the best. How could it be for the best to spend a week apart when we could have been on a warm beach together?

And ... HOW COULD HE DO THIS TO ME? To someone he loves? Or maybe ... maybe that's just it, isn't it? Or he does love me but not nearly as much as he loves himself or his money or pills.

And Katy. She didn't defend me either, and she knew the stress I'd been under. She'd been helping herself to my Addys for weeks, for Pete's sake. But apparently all that meant nothing.

I considered calling Dad and telling him I was going to come home for break, and maybe going home and staying home. That would show them. The more I thought about it, though, the more I realized that wouldn't fix anything. My grades would still be abysmal and I'd have no chance of pulling them up, not to mention I really wouldn't have any friends. I didn't keep in touch with my old friends at all, so I'd be alone there, too.

Added to that, I didn't want to have to tell my dad that I wasn't going on the trip. I have to hang on to what little pride I have left, and besides, he'd ask so many questions. Also, there's no way I want to go home and be a third wheel with him and Isa. That would make everything so, so much worse.

I thought about calling Bex, too. But I didn't want to worry her and I really didn't want her to invite me to New York with her friends out of pity or something. Talk about pathetic, having to hang out with your little sister's friends over break.

So I am alone.

Plus I have to make the batch of new product. And I knew I was going to and that I have to do a perfect job. I've already made it once before and I'm certain I can do it again. I need to show them I'm serious, I'm in this, and I'm not going to let them down, because I need to buy time. I need to figure out how to get out of this without landing myself in jail. And if I'm honest, I need time to wean myself off pills, too. Needing them means needing Warren, and I still need both.

Warren did come to say good-bye, so that's something. He pulled me into his arms and apologized over and over, and told me he hoped I would understand. If not today, then sometime in the future. How the hell will I ever understand what he's done to me? I loved him. I DO love him, even if I know I won't ever mean as much to him as money or a quick high. I've only ever wanted to help him, to make sure he was okay. In exchange he's given me what? Pills? Paranoia? He certainly hasn't given me any reason to believe he wouldn't let me take the fall for everything if he felt like he was in trouble.

And he can talk all he wants and try to make it sound like no big deal, that he's leaving without me, but it's a punishment, I know it is. It's like when my mom and dad used to make me sit in a corner and "think about what I've done." It's not even about the thinking. They want it to sink in just how miserable they could make me. And I know that somewhere on Drew's hard drive is the video he took, the collateral I gave them, and he's just itching to use it, should I step out of line and narc on them.

To top all of this off, report cards came out for third semester. As in chemistry and precalc, naturally. A B- in civics and Spanish. C- in English. C MINUS.

I'm failing English, officially. I have an appointment with my guidance counselor for tomorrow, and I expect that she will tell me I have to retake English over the summer. I mean, she scheduled me during a student break . . . the news can't be good.

English aside, Bs have never been a thing for me before. Never. I feel like I'm failing those, too. The teachers say my work is sloppy, careless, thoughtless. That I'm not thinking critically enough, writing well enough, whatever. I don't know how. I feel fine about my assignments and tests when I turn them in. I feel like I've focused so well during my classes, even when I'm tired or stressed or worried about Warren. The Adderall really helps with that. But maybe it's all an illusion. Maybe the Adderall only makes me feel that way, but that's not the reality. Obviously they don't think my work is up to par.

I'm scared. Harvard doesn't exactly take B-average students. They certainly don't take students who can't write a coherent essay. I don't know what I'm going to do. Prescott was supposed to improve my chances, but I think it's done the opposite. I can't keep up. Even when I try my hardest. And it's not just the schoolwork; I'm obviously failing at everything. I disappointed my friends; I let my business partners down. Even my own boyfriend would rather go on vacation without me.

And ugh, Emily is staying over break too, and she seemed too distracted to even notice that I'm not in the Cayman Islands. Honestly, she's been a wreck. I don't know. Maybe my nerves are so shot they're rubbing off on her. She seems jittery and stressed. She won't stop moving when she's in our room. She's either bouncing her leg while she's reading or tapping her pencil or her fingers on the desk. And even when she's asleep she's restless. I think she tosses and turns all night long, and it keeps me up too, even when I take a Percocet.

And I don't even want to admit how many of those I've taken this week. I know I shouldn't, but I can't convince myself to care when I'm finally, FINALLY falling asleep. Everything seems so peaceful, like none of this stuff matters.

The Science Club is probably on a beautiful white, sandy beach, staring at a gorgeous blue ocean. The kind where you can't even tell when it ends and the sky begins. Probably drinking piña coladas and laughing and not missing me at all. And Warren is probably massaging sunscreen on Katy's shoulders and back, seeing her curvy body in a revealing bikini. She's probably trailing a hand lightly down his chest and speaking in double entendres that make him blush and plant all sorts of ideas in his head.

I sort of hate them right now. I hate everyone. I hate me, too.

May 6

I was right. Kind of. I will have to retake English, maybe. IF I can't keep my grade above a C the last semester. And honestly, since I thought my work was okay and it obviously wasn't, I can't see how I'll keep my grade higher than a C next semester. I don't even understand what I'm doing so wrong. There's a snowball's chance in hell that I'll be able to pull it off, especially if I'm going to keep up the workload in the lab like I promised.

At least it will be summer class. Which is good. That way I'm not held back an entire year. But it also means there's no way I could go to Princeton's summer program, even if I get in.

So, you know, I HAVE to keep this grade up, but I probably can't, so I'm probably not going to Princeton.

My anxiety is out of control. I don't want to keep taking Percocets and end up like Warren, but the Adderall isn't cutting it anymore. I have much bigger problems now, but what can I do? Go to a therapist and tell her I'm stressed out because I'm afraid I'm going to get caught making highly illegal drugs?

I think I need to be honest here: I can't talk about this with anyone, so no one can help me.

I'm completely alone.

May 7

I've spent eight days in a row by myself, save only for Emily, who has tried to be kind, even, but I'm so irritable I can't even deal with her voice. Besides, she's so annoyingly restless I find myself staying in the lab even longer just so it doesn't rub off on me. I sometimes eat some cereal in the dining hall in the morning and maybe get a piece of pizza or some mac and cheese sometime in the afternoon. But other than that, I don't eat. I think I'm losing more weight, but that could just be my imagination.

I do some extra work for English in the hopes that I might be able to salvage my grades (and the entire course of my life, while I'm at it), then I go to the lab.

It's weird keeping it running all by myself while everyone is gone. It's lonely and it's very, very quiet. If the Club truly wanted me to think about what I've done and what it means to be part of their group, well, I've had nothing but time. Mark came by to grab his money, which Drew had left for him in a drawer, and I nearly begged him to stay and keep me company.

But the work isn't hard. The instructions are clear, and Warren is nothing if not precise, so it's no trouble. I've looked at his notes and worked the equations out myself just to see if I could. Everything is sound; Warren truly knows what he's doing. Maybe he can find the cure to help addicts, once he stops making drugs for them and all.

I stay until late, make sure everything is off that should be, and lock up. It's usually midnight or after before I'm back in my dorm room and back in bed. Emily's usually there sleeping restlessly, but once she wasn't, and I couldn't bring myself to care. I'm just grateful we're not fighting and she hasn't said anything about not going with Warren.

Warren and the rest will be back tomorrow. The batch is nearly done. If it passes muster, maybe I can regain the Club's trust so maybe they won't be watching me so closely. After all the thinking I've done this week, I know for sure: There's only one way to keep going. They're not going to just let me out of this. They're too afraid I'll narc. And what else or WHO else do I have at this point? I have nothing. So I'll do what it takes to stay in. It's the only way I can get through this year. Then . . . then I'll be able to get out somehow. I'll vanish. I just need to make it through for right now.

I will just have to keep my head down, keep those blinders on, and not think about what happens after our product leaves our little lab. Or who it affects.

It's better this way. For everyone.

May 8

Warren is back.

He came by, knocking on my bedroom door. When I opened it up, I didn't really know what to do. Part of me wanted to shut the door in his face and shut him out of my life forever. But there was another part of me that just wanted things to be okay. I wanted him to hug me like everything was going to be all right. And . . . I guess old habits die hard. I wanted his approval. I wanted him to let me back in and accept me. I've held him up on that pedestal for so long, and I've felt so low and beneath him . . . and I know he's part of the reason I've felt so low . . . but I was just so tired. So tired and so desperate to have SOMEONE. I'm so tired of not having someone. Mom, Dad, Bex . . . all my old friends and now my new. Something about seeing Warren made me cling to that last bit of hope I had that maybe things could change. That maybe I'm not alone.

In the end, Warren made the first move and pulled me into his arms.

> Warren: God, Bailey. I've missed you so much.
> It's so good to see you. I'm so, SO sorry.

It was probably a lie, but I let myself believe it. Maybe holding on to the fantasy of how things could be would get me through the end of the year. Emily was there and saw the whole exchange. She shot him a particularly grouchy look, which he shrugged off, then asked me if we could go to dinner.

> Me: Are you sure? I mean, are you allowed to?
> Is this okay?

> Warren: Of course! All of this . . . It's not
> about us. You understand that, right? This
> wasn't about you and me. This was about trust.

Trust. Yes. Trust is a funny thing. He thinks I can't be trusted because I talked about wanting to stop the Club. While he's the one who didn't defend me and didn't have my back. And now I need him and the rest of the Club to trust me again so I can get out.

I threw on a sweater and went with him. We got in his car and drove into Wiltshire, saying nothing to each other most of the way there. But he did put his hand on my knee when he wasn't shifting gears. His touch was somehow both reassuring and sad at the same time. He was wearing a short-sleeved shirt, and his skin was a deep golden tan. When he pulled to a stop in front of one of the best restaurants in town, he looked over at me, smiling. Neither of us was in any hurry to go in, though. I noticed Warren wasn't fidgety, nor were his movements sluggish. He was as sober as could be, and I silently thanked my luck that we could talk without any chemicals . . . assisting. Or getting in the way.

He confessed that he made a reservation at the restaurant, thinking I'd probably turn him down. I almost laughed. How could I turn him down? If I broke up with him right now, he and Drew and Katy would probably panic and threaten me with the collateral. Or worse, just hand it over to the police. It was easier to just smile and act like there wasn't any reason for him to think I wouldn't come with him.

I asked him about the beach, and he talked about how high and drunk he was the whole time. He said nothing about how pretty the water was, how the sun felt, or what it was like with the sand between his toes. Instead he told me he'd found a good combination of pills that let him sleep through Katy and Drew

318

fighting, which apparently they did the whole time, and bragged a little about not having any hangovers because of yet another concoction of pills.

Maybe I should have been concerned, but I certainly was not surprised. Besides, that kind of conversation always led to a fight, and I couldn't afford a fight with him now. Head down, blinders on.

We got really quiet, both of us, and I looked at Warren, but he wasn't looking at me. He was staring straight ahead. It was starting to rain a little, and the mournful patter of raindrops on the roof was the only sound for a moment or two. Then Warren spoke.

> Warren: Bailey, I can't tell you how sorry
> I am. I wanted so badly to just have a nice
> week with you, relaxing and fun and sexy.
> I've wanted so much more for us, and for
> you. I wish we were just normal, you know?
> Just normal kids. No Science Club. No
> demanding Prescott classes. No worrying
> about colleges or summer programs that are
> incredibly hard to get into. And no . . . no
> family problems or pills or . . . anything else.
> Just you and me.

He wasn't crying, exactly, but he had his eyes so tightly shut that no tears could have fallen, which might have been precisely his goal. It struck me again just how similar Warren and I are, how abandoned we both feel, and my heart broke for him all over again, but I couldn't let myself lean into him or even put a hand on his to comfort him. As bad as I felt for him, as much as I felt he was telling me the actual truth this time, I also couldn't let myself soften toward him when he'd so coldly and easily told the Club that I shouldn't be trusted. I leaned against the car door, away from him, instead, and did my best to tell him what he wanted to hear even if my body language was saying something else entirely.

> Me: We aren't normal, though. And we can't be.
> But we're not alone, are we? We have each other.

> Warren: We do? We do. I just . . . I wasn't
> sure. I thought when we left without you, that
> maybe that was it. You'd decide it wasn't worth
> it. That I wasn't worth it. And you wouldn't
> want anything to do with me when I got back.

> Me: I was really upset. Really angry. I won't
> lie to you about that. And I still think it was
> unfair.

Warren: It was. I've made mistakes too, but Drew and Katy were never that harsh on me. Hell, Drew and Katy have made mistakes themselves. I tried to tell them they were overreacting, but they wouldn't listen to me.

Me, heart skipping: So . . . it was them?

Warren: Oh, baby. Of course it was. I wanted to just forgive you and let it all go and let you come along with us. They wouldn't let up, though.

Me: But . . . but . . . you didn't defend me.

Warren, taking my hands in his: Baby, I defended you all I could. By the time we talked to you about it, though, I couldn't do anything. They'd already made up their minds. Arguing with them then would have probably just made it worse. But I tried, I really did. I hope you're not angry with me.

Me, honest: No. I'm not angry. I've had a lot of time to think, which is what Katy and

Drew wanted. And I understand why what
I did made everyone freak out. I won't do it
again. I want back in. I want everything to be
our normal again.

Warren: It will be, soon. And if you made this new batch
correctly, you'll prove it to them. So . . . we're good? We're okay?

Me, forcing words and a smile: Of course. I
love you.

Warren: I love you. And I'm so glad to be
back here with you. Honestly, I couldn't stop
thinking about you the whole time I was gone.
Everything would have been so much better
with you there.

Although that was nice to hear, I was thinking about his
explanations. Plausible or not, none of it meant he couldn't
have fought for me more. And he'd left me, thinking that might
possibly mean I'd break up with him. There were alternatives.
He could have stayed with me. But clearly, the Club was still
more important to him than I was.

We went into the restaurant then, and I let him treat me to

lobster. And since it was the last night of break and the dorm parents weren't too inspired to make the rounds religiously, I went back to his room with him since Drew was spending the night at his parents' house. I wish I could explain it. Maybe I should have just gone back to my room alone but . . . it felt good to be wanted. And maybe I just wanted to feel normal for a while.

Maybe I just wanted to feel anything at all.

May 11

It's Friday night and I'm not sure what we did tonight was the best idea.

The Science Club had to let our, um, investors try the new product because of course they were skeptical, and they weren't going to give us a penny without making sure it was good. Drew was going, naturally, with Warren as the extra male muscle, I guess. And Katy insisted on going too, because she's the contact maker and she wanted to make sure her people were satisfied. As for me, well, I couldn't NOT go. I didn't want to be left out of one more thing, to be honest. Plus, I was the one who actually made the new version of the product. I had to see for myself.

We loaded up Drew's car, and a few minutes later we were in Wiltshire's east side, in front of a house I recognized from that initial trip with the boys, and then seeing it when I went to find the trailer park. Drew turned to me and Katy in the back before we got out.

> Drew: Let me and Warren do the talking. I
> know they're yours, Katy, but they're used to
> us now. We deal with them every week. And
> let me do all the negotiating. The money is
> MY thing. If they have any questions about
> the product, though, Bailey and Warren
> should answer. And dumb it down, okay? They
> don't need to know our formula, just that it's
> safe. Capisce?

Warren laughed. He was especially mellow tonight, so if I had to guess, I'd say Percocets. Snorted. Or perhaps something even stronger. I didn't even acknowledge it. I think I'm slowly starting to realize that he'll never stop. It reminded me that I need to talk to him about something for my nerves. I want that kind of mellow, and at this point, it can't hurt. Just one more thing I have to stop.

> Me: Drew, what if they don't like it?

Drew, shrugging: Then we go back to the old formula and keep our rates the same for a while so they forget about it.

Me: Yeah, but . . . what about me?

Katy, glaring: You'd better hope to hell it's good.

Me: I followed Warren's instructions exactly! I'm sure it will be.

Katy: You follow a recipe okay. Instructions, like keeping your mouth shut, seem to be different.

Me: I haven't talked to anyone but you guys since. Well, Emily, because I had to. But I swear, not another word to anyone.

Drew: Yeah. We'll see. We do appreciate you making this batch, though. It was nice not to have to worry about anything for a few days.

Me: So . . . I'm in? We're good?

Warren, now serious: Yes. We're good. (Katy
and Drew looked at him. He looked at me.)
We ARE good. C'mon, guys. She's learned.
And it's my fault if they don't like this batch,
not hers. It was my idea.

Finally, FINALLY, he defended me. I should have been
happy about that, perhaps, but I was just tired. All I could do
was give him a weak smile.

So we went inside the house, Warren carrying a plastic bag
in the pocket of his overcoat. I'm not sure what I expected when
I got inside. Perhaps an old-fashioned mob movie scene . . . guys
polishing guns and cooking marinara while smoking cigars and
talking business. Or maybe something like out of a true crime
show, with high people and drug paraphernalia everywhere.
Neither of those things awaited us inside.

The house wasn't exactly clean; it looked really run-down,
with yellow walls and stained carpet and secondhand furniture,
but there were only three people inside the house that I could
see. All three of them seemed so young and all three of them
were sober from what I could tell. They were also surprisingly
clean-cut and wearing clothes that, though not up to Prescott

standards and trends, were clearly of a style and brand they loved. An expensive brand.

Katy and I hung back, letting the boys do the work. She and I didn't talk. We didn't look at each other. I hadn't seen Katy much this week, probably because she knew exactly how to avoid me, but something told me it wasn't all because she was angry with me, either. Even when I saw her and she didn't realize I was there, she was distracted, angry, and very irritable. I know Warren said she and Drew fought a lot, but I had to wonder if she'd fought with Warren, too. I knew he was her source, and if she'd gone without during their vacation, Warren would have been to blame. And honestly, it felt like something Warren would do . . . deny her, maybe for revenge for not letting me come. Maybe just because he wanted to remind her who was really in charge. But the way Katy was acting . . . so on edge . . . well, I know that feeling acutely now. I feel it every time I don't have an Addy in my system.

The three men didn't introduce themselves but they definitely wanted confirmation that I wasn't a snitch. Katy snorted, and Drew shot her a murderous glare before telling the men that I could absolutely be trusted and, as a matter of fact, I was the "head chef," so to speak, for this particular batch. Then the three guys really got down to business, taking the bag from Warren and proceeding to get high from the crystals I'd created.

It took a few minutes, and the three men exchanged looks between them before one of them said, "This is some really good shit," and the rest echoed that exact phrase.

I breathed out a breath I hadn't realized I'd been holding, and Katy grabbed my hand, anger forgotten, squealing with delight. Warren came over and kissed me and whispered how amazing I was and how we'd done it, we'd done THIS together, and we were perfect together, and he loved me, which made my stomach turn.

Of course. For this he loves me. What would he have done if the product hadn't been perfect? Would they all have turned their backs on me or sold me out?

While this was happening, Drew started negotiations for price on the new product. By the time we left, he'd secured significant raises for all of us, with the promise that our product was going to be even more famous now. On the way home, Katy proposed we celebrate in Drew and Warren's room, so that's where we went. We finished our planning with a bottle of champagne Drew had been "saving for a special occasion." Drew did some quick math and we realized exactly how much more we were going to be making per week, and we toasted. Then Katy brought up that we could also push this product to our newest expansion, and I agreed it was a good idea, even though I still wasn't clear where exactly we'd expanded to. Then Katy and I fell asleep in Drew and Warren's beds, respectively, and had to sneak out at dawn. Honestly, it was nice to feel like she liked me again. Being on Katy Ashton's bad side feels absolutely terrible.

I DO think I can keep doing this until the summer. I think this will work. Warren will be at Princeton, so we can't cook, and I won't be able to get my pills. I can stop taking them then, and then the plan is to fade away. Not come back after summer. They'd have to be okay with that, right? If I didn't come back? What could they do? At the very least, it might even be worth my while to keep working on the product. Maybe I can make it even safer and assuage some of my guilt. And hey, if I fail out of Prescott, at least I'll have a backup career waiting for me. Ha, I'm hilarious.

May 14

I haven't written for a few days. I've just been so busy and I've been trying so hard to get my life back on track, in every department.

First, I've been working a lot on English. I was allowed to work on some extra credit, so I did all of that and maybe I can pull up my grade some. Mr. Callahan has actually put me in touch with one of the professors from Princeton that's in charge of the summer program. He thinks that maybe if I can make a personal connection and show this prof how much I want in and what I'm capable of, he might bend some rules and get me into the program this summer anyway.

Second, Warren has been extra sweet this past week. We haven't fought at all. He's super proud of the way I've made the product lately, so maybe it's that, that the business is going well. I often wonder, though, if he's being so nice because he feels guilty. I even told him about my anxiety, and he promised he'd get me something to help. I don't think I'll take whatever he gets me, but I suppose it's just his way of trying to help. In the meantime, he got me more Percocets. He got me more Adderall, too, and even though I had decided to cut back, it seems to help me focus on schoolwork, which I really need right now. Like Warren, I can just keep on keeping on until summer. I think that once I push through that shaky, irritable feeling, I should be fine after a couple of days. I won't ever have to take it again. I didn't tell him about how many Percocets I took over break, or anytime, really. It's not like I'm lying. I just don't want him thinking I'm a hypocrite for asking him to stop.

Third, Katy has been incredible this week. She really has. She's been so happy about the new product and getting it out to everyone that she's been the same fun Katy she was when we first started hanging out. She even promised a shopping trip this weekend. After all, we'll be making a bit more money this week, if everything goes according to plan. We're thinking Saturday. Clearly, as long as I do what the Club wants and keep my mouth shut, they'll act like they like me.

Last, there haven't been any new developments in newspaper coverage of the drug problem in Wiltshire. I heard some of my classmates talking about it in passing, but they all agreed that heroin is a bigger problem. Around here, they said, it's almost easier to get heroin than meth, and it's not like people die from meth like Warren's brother did from heroin. You're not going to find a meth addict dead with a needle in his arm. So I've been able to let it go, keep my mouth shut, and do my work.

The only thing that hasn't gone well this week is Emily. I walked in the other day and she demanded to know where Warren was, and we got into a huge argument. She was super aggressive, almost hyper or panicked. She reminded me of a hummingbird or something, the way she was pacing the room, back and forth, quick and with sharp movements. It actually reminded me of the way Warren and Drew were when they tried our meth, but I realized there was no way she was on meth of all things. Ridiculous. Emily seems pretty straitlaced, really. Not exactly a Goody Two-shoes, but nowhere near the Science Club. It was probably my own paranoia that made me even think it.

She was driving me so nuts I finally told her Warren was with Drew in their dorm and she left. I think it would have bothered me more if she'd tried to hide that she was going to him, but I knew exactly where she was headed. I texted Warren to warn him, and he told me later that he cut her off right before she tried to get in the dorm and talked her down from this particular episode. I told him it wasn't his responsibility to do that for her, but he said he felt bad for her and felt obligated because before him, she wasn't so bad. He said he felt terrible for being the one to cause her to spiral.

I had to wonder about that, why he would have been the cause. It was one thing for Emily to imply it, and another for Warren himself to say something.

Things almost felt "normal" with the SC this week. I must be doing an okay job of seeming normal myself.

May 18

Oh my God. Just got back from the lab, where Drew handed out our "paychecks." I can't even believe it. Not only are we selling the product for more, while our ingredient costs are down, we are selling more product itself. Word definitely got out that we have something of better quality, which doesn't take as much for a high. It's worrisome; that's going to make it easier for the police to track us down, not to mention maybe even make more addicts. But like everything else right now, I'm shoving those feelings aside so I can finally get out of this.

Warren is going to be here in ten minutes to take me

to dinner at a swanky place in the country. . . . He said it's somewhere his dad used to take his mother for anniversaries. I hope he won't be uncomfortable there because of that family history. Anything that reminds him of his parents usually is upsetting to him. But this seems like a good memory, and I won't lie, I want to try this chocolate dessert he was raving about. I've gained some of my appetite back.

Speaking of, Katy and I are going to breakfast tomorrow morning. (She's thinking IHOP or even a Waffle House. "Slumming it," she says. I just shook my head. Those are normal breakfast places for me and my family. At least they were before Isa.) Then we're off to shop. She reminded me that I need a dress for the formal, not that Warren has asked or I've even thought about it.

If I'm being honest, getting dressed up to go out in public and act like everything is great with me and Warren, or just ME, is the last thing I want to do.

May 18, later!

Okay, just writing to say that Warren has now officially asked me to the formal. He did it tonight at the restaurant. It was like a marriage proposal. He literally got down on one knee and asked, and he had a bracelet for me in a pretty turquoise box. The bracelet was gorgeous. White gold, with his birthstone, a sapphire, in a very delicate filigree link. I put it on, since at that point everyone in the restaurant was watching, but I took it off immediately when I got home. It feels so . . . permanent. And public, maybe? Like this is a symbol to everyone that I'm Warren's. Really, the whole "proposal" felt like it was just for show. At least it was for me, and I have to wonder if it was for him, too. A way to show everyone what an upstanding guy he is.

Katy texted while we were at dinner. It seems the boys had planned it: Drew asked Katy as well.

So tomorrow we'll get our dresses, and I'll smile and laugh with her and act like I'm so, so happy that Warren Clark is taking me to formal, and I'm the luckiest girl alive to be in their group and have all this money.

May 19

Oh God. Oh God oh God oh God.

I don't know what to do. I can't . . . I can't even think. I'm trapped in a nightmare.

I came home from shopping with Katy, and Emily was in her bed, taking a nap. Or I thought she was. But then I realized that she was in a weird position. I turned her over and her lips were blue. HER LIPS WERE BLUE.

I screamed for help down the hallway. I screamed for the dorm mom. Then I called 911. I don't even remember what the person on the phone said to me. I think she got my address and asked if Emily had a pulse. I couldn't find one. Oh my God, I couldn't find a pulse. The woman on the phone made me keep talking to her until the paramedics arrived, and my dorm mom came in and was trying to do CPR for a while, but it wasn't working. Other girls were gathered in the hallway, whispering and scared. I just sat by Emily, my whole body shaking, hoping to feel a pulse.

The paramedics arrived and put her on a stretcher. I couldn't stand, I was shaking so badly. When they laid her down . . . it was like she didn't have any bones. Her arms hung down . . .

Lifeless. She was lifeless.

I think she's dead.

I wanted to go to the hospital with her but everyone told me to stay there. To go back in my room and wait. So that's where I am. I'm all alone, sitting on Emily's bed. I haven't heard from anyone yet. I don't know what caused this and I have no idea if she . . . if she made it or not.

I didn't tell Warren. I didn't want to hear him talk about Emily negatively, not now. And also . . . I can't explain it, but my gut was telling me to keep this from him for now.

I have buried myself in blankets and I'm going to stay here until I stop shaking or until I warm up or until someone comes to talk to me. I don't know what else to do. I'm just so, so cold. . . .

May 19, later

About two hours later someone knocked on my door. It was a woman and a man, both police officers in uniform. They flashed their badges to me and wanted to know if I could answer a few questions for them.

I told them yes, even though at that point I was close to throwing up or passing out from fear. What were POLICE here for? What was going on?

They came in, standing awkwardly in the neutral space between my and Emily's desks. It was the woman cop who talked to me most. They asked for my name and age, and I could barely remember. I asked them if Emily was okay.

> Cop: They're working on her at the hospital right now, but that's why we wanted to talk to you.

> Me: Okay. Sure.

> Cop: So can you tell us what happened?

I told them all I could remember, that I'd returned home from shopping with a friend and thought nothing of Emily sleeping until I realized she looked weird. Then I called 911.

Cop: Are you and your roommate close?

Me: Um, not really, I guess. We're only kind of friends. Sometimes we didn't get along too well. She had, um, dated my boyfriend last year so there was a bit of jealousy and tension sometimes.

Cop: Are you aware of any mental health issues such as depression? Anxiety?

Me: Emily is kind of off sometimes. I don't know how to describe it. Like sometimes she gets really angry and upset but other times she's completely happy and fun to be around.

Cop, scribbling on a pad of paper: And how would you describe her mood lately?

Me, shrugging: She seemed better than usual, I guess. I don't know. She's not home much.

Cop: Where is she when she's not here?

Me, feeling suddenly guilty: I'm not sure, honestly. I assumed she was with her friends or the AV club. She was really into movies. IS. Sorry. She IS really into movies.

Cop: How often would you say she's gone, and for how long?

Me, suddenly feeling chilly: I don't know. I'm sorry. I've been so busy myself that I haven't really kept up with her. She seems to be gone a lot in the evenings. She gets back later than me and sleeps later. I sometimes have to wake her up so she doesn't miss class.

Cop: And when you wake her up, how does she seem? Moody and confused? Or lucid and calm?

Me: Very moody. Sometimes like she doesn't know where she is. She's always pretty mean when I get her up. She's a heavy sleeper. She usually just barks at me to get her water and leave her alone.

Cop: How often do you have to wake her?

Me, shrugging: Once or twice a week.

Cop: Do you have any reason to believe that Emily may have been under the influence of illegal drugs?

Me, my heart dropping into my stomach: What? No. Emily was a good student. IS a good student. I don't think she ever missed school unless she was sick.

But as I was giving the cop my answer, things started locking together in my brain like pieces of a jigsaw puzzle. Her near-instant switch of moods, her restlessness, irritability, odd hours, lack of a social life here at Prescott . . .

Her always wanting to know where Warren is. How she seemed to find him out of the blue, usually where they could be alone. Her exaggerated need to see him. Her angry accusations that he's basically the devil incarnate.

Just be careful. He'll get you hooked, she'd said.

My whole world shrank down to the realization:

It was Warren. Warren gave her meth. Warren probably got

her started on drugs, just like he gave me the Adderall, then the
Percocets. He probably told her how much he cared about her,
swore that it was okay, she wouldn't get addicted . . . they would
help . . . and maybe, when he broke things off and no longer gave
her Adderall for free, maybe she started using meth. And where
else would she have gotten that? The ex-boyfriend that was still
playing her every emotion and vulnerability like a violin, naturally.

Panic seized me; bile rushed up my esophagus. I tried hard
to focus on the policewoman.

Me: You think Emily was on drugs?

Cop: We have reason to believe so, and that's
the reason for her medical condition.

Me, thinking of Warren's brother: Like an
overdose? Heroin?

The cops looked at each other, then back at me,
communicating something silently. The cop who wasn't talking
to me walked slowly around my dorm room.

Cop: No. Not heroin.

Quiet Cop: Hey, Gina. Look at this.

The cop named Gina nodded and walked over to where he was, and I could see they were holding a small plastic bag in their hands, which the male cop had pulled from behind Emily's desk. They shook out something from the bag and it landed in Gina's palm. I knew instantly what it was.

I knew instantly because I'd made it.

I flexed every muscle in my body to keep myself from vomiting, and tried to steady my breathing, hoping the cops wouldn't see how panicked I was. This couldn't be happening. Meth didn't hurt people like this. It made them hallucinate, maybe. Made them addicted and they committed crimes, but it didn't make people's lips turn blue.

Cop, to me: Is this yours?

Me: No.

Cop: Do you know what it is?

(I shook my head, afraid to speak in case they could tell I was lying.)

Cop to the other cop: Call the chief. We're definitely going to need some help from narcotics. (Turning back to me.) Ma'am, we need to hold this room for search. You can either consent to a search of the room or we'll need to obtain a search warrant. Either way you'll need to be removed and detained during its duration.

Me, thinking quickly: Oh, um, you can search. It's fine. Could I take some books and my purse? I need to do homework, and I'll probably get something to eat while I'm out.

The cops looked at each other, then the woman nodded.

Cop: Normally we wouldn't, but if you give us consent to search now, we can oblige, since you're cooperating so well. Give us about an hour? And here's my card. If you can think of anything that may help us, please call. Anytime.

Me: I will. Thanks. Is Emily okay? Is she going to make it?

Cop, patting me on the shoulder: She's in a
coma right now. And I don't know. I'm sorry.

I quickly grabbed my purse (with all my money and my pills
tucked safely inside) and a few books, including this diary, then left
as quickly as I could. Outside the building, I headed around the
corner, waiting only until I was out of sight to lean up against the
wall and let myself fall apart. I cried and cried, until the nausea hit,
then I vomited too. I don't know how long I stood there, hidden by
the sophomore girls dorm, crying and vomiting bile. Long enough
that I was truly dehydrated, but I was, remarkably, starting to think
more clearly. Then I headed to the coffee shop, forced myself to
drink some herbal tea, and sat down to write and think.

I don't know what to do, but I do know one thing: I have to
tell the club.

May 20

It's Sunday. Really early in the morning. I can't sleep. Not even
the Percocet helped. The headmaster called. He said there's been
no change in Emily's condition and her parents have arrived.
He told me to please come forward with any information I may
have about Emily. It felt . . . accusatory.

But I've had some time to pull myself together. To think.
And here's what I've decided:

343

I have to get out of the Science Club. Somehow. I can't wait until school is over anymore. I don't have that much time.

The Club may or may not be responsible for Emily. As the articles in the paper said, meth is really common around here. And I know we have competitors locally. There's a small chance that it wasn't us. Until I talk to Warren, there's no reason to believe definitively that Emily had the meth I'd made.

I won't tell anyone here about the Club, not even Mr. Callahan. I certainly will not tell the police. If I do, the Club will just give the police my collateral, which is a video in which I take the blame for everything and confess to blackmailing the rest of the Club into working for me. I'll go to prison; they'll get off scot-free. If we're going down, we're all going down together. That was our whole philosophy. That's what they tried to teach me.

But . . . I think I need to tell my dad. Or maybe just Isa? She could help me, legally, if it comes to that. And I've heard for a long time about how she's the best. She could help. It's a terrifying thought, but I don't know where else to turn.

I'm going to try to sleep some more. Then I'm going to call my dad. Warren's been texting, but I don't know what to say yet. I need a plan on my own before I can talk to him. I need . . . well, I need someone I can trust helping me right now and I'm afraid Warren would only look out for himself. Apparently the rumors haven't spread too far. Prescott staff must have threatened my dorm mates to remain silent.

I'll have to talk to Warren soon. Very soon. But first . . . I'm calling home.

May 22

I told my father about Emily, and then about Science Club. Everything. About how they approached me, how I was fascinated by them and felt so amazing being part of their group, how I'm in love with Warren, what I do know about the group and their business actions, and what I've purposely avoided knowing, even how much money I've been making. I told him about the collateral, too. At some point, probably when he realized just how deep in trouble I was, he put me on speaker, and I could hear Isa humming as she took in the facts.

I didn't tell them about the Adderall or Percocets. I didn't tell them about my abysmal grades.

I'm completely surprised that my father revealed only a small amount of disappointment and frustration with me, and instead jumped into action alongside Isa, who was in full-blown lawyer mode by the time I finished my story. It makes my heart kind of break all over again, for even doubting that Dad was on my side and for thinking such awful things about Isa.

       Isa: Do you think your group has been selling to students at Prescott?

       Me: I don't know. . . . We expanded recently, but I don't know where or to whom. I . . . I once saw Warren make a deal with some students, but I'm not sure it was for meth.

       Isa: Good. It really is best that you don't know much. Katy was right about that. But you need to distance yourself from them. All of them.

       Me, heart sinking: Even Warren?

       Isa, sighing loudly: I think maybe especially Warren. But if you care about them, you need to make sure they're not selling to anyone on campus, and you need to try to make them see reason. They've got to stop selling, period.

Me, near tears: I tried. No one wants to drop out. It's like they see it as betrayal.

Isa: You can only try, Bailey. But try, and then get away, you understand? This could really impact your future. And do what you can to remove any evidence that you were in that lab.

Me: So . . . lie? I mean, what about the collateral? Even if I don't tell the police about them, they could use that to frame me.

Isa: I could get around that in court. I think. It's coercion at the very least. But if you have any documentation that would prove otherwise . . . that would be extremely helpful.

Me, remembering my idea about this diary: What about my diary? I've written about everything. Real names. I know it was probably stupid because it implicates me, but . . .

Isa: No. If they do try to blame you for this, that would be a good tool to fight it. But . . .

we have to keep it out of the hands of the police. For right now, we wait and see. If it's meth that put Emily in a coma, they might try to trace it, but with the way things are in Wiltshire, it would be hard to trace back to one source. Emily could say who she got it from, though, and if it's anyone from your group, we'd better pray they take the fall, as they so HONORABLY swore they'd do. But let's not panic. Let's wait and see.

Me: Okay. Thank you, Isa. And Dad. I'm so . . . so sorry.

There's a pause, then only Isa answers.

Isa: I know. We are too, Bailey. I'll . . . I'll tell your father.

Me: Wait. Where is he? I thought he was listening.

Isa: He was. I think he went outside. You know how he gets when he needs to cry. He

can't stand anyone else to see it. We were
actually talking last night about how bad we
feel about not being there for you this year,
like we should have been.

Me, stunned: . . . What?

Isa: Your dad and I. We should have been
more supportive. We know you're still grieving
for your mother, and with switching to a new
school, a difficult school at that . . . we should
have called more. Visited. I'm really sorry,
Bailey. There's no excuse. Your father is sorry
too. More than I can tell you.

Me, trying to make my voice neutral: It's
okay. Really. You two are really happy
together, and I'm glad for that. I'm glad Dad
has you, and you need some newlywed time.
I understand.

I told her that, but the truth was I didn't really
understand at all. I HAD felt unsupported, unloved, even. I'd
wanted so badly for my father to call, to check in, just to talk.

I've been so lost without Mom, and all the changes recently left me even more unmoored, if possible. The Science Club and Warren especially had helped fill the void. Until they hadn't.

My dad got back on the phone and told me he loves me and thanked me for coming to him and Isa about it. They promised to do all they could to help. I was so overwhelmed with gratitude that I sobbed out my good-byes.

But as soon as I hung up the phone, the hope drained out of me. Isa had sounded so worried, like even she might have trouble in court with this. And Emily's bed is still empty and mussed, from how she left it. There is still no word on her. What if she never comes back?

What if what I made is the reason why? How am I ever going to forgive myself?

May 23

Emily is gone. She's . . . dead.

May 23, later

I am . . . I'm going to try to write this down but . . . I just don't know how. I don't know how to say any of this. It doesn't feel real. I keep thinking I'm going to wake up and it's all going to be some horrible dream from stress or the Adderall or . . .

something. I can't even feel the pen in my hands, but I've got to try.

During first period, our headmaster got on the intercom and informed us that Emily had passed away.

Metallic ringing filled my ears. I left class. I went to the restroom and vomited. I nearly went to sleep with my head propped up on the toilet seat, I don't know why. Exhaustion? Emotional overload? Maybe my body was just trying to shut itself down so I wouldn't feel anymore.

When I came out, the headmaster and the school counselor, the one who had informed me I was dangerously close to going to summer school, were waiting. They spoke to me like I was a fragile thing, telling me that they were very sorry and that I could talk to a professional counselor on staff. They told me her parents would come by to get her things. They told me the funeral would be in two days. I think they said other things, but I don't remember. I nearly collapsed. I realized I've barely eaten since brunch with Katy four days ago. They also told me that if I knew anything at all that could help Prescott or the police, to please say something. Then I asked. I asked what had killed her.

Drugs, my headmaster said. He said that, unfortunately, the doctors could tell Emily had been using for a while but that for some reason, the last dose she had was different, and it sent her into cardiac arrest. By the time she got to the hospital, her brain had been cut off from oxygen for too long.

For some reason, the last dose she had was different.

Different because Warren and I had changed the formula. We'd made it stronger. We'd made it, like he said, more effective.

We killed Emily.

May 23, even later

The headmaster and counselor offered to walk me home, but I promised them I would be all right and that I could use the time alone. But I didn't go home. Home was the last place I wanted to go, to see Emily's empty bed and know I was the reason it was empty. And what if her parents came to get her things while I was there? How could I face them? How could I even be in the same room with them? So I went to the lab like a coward. I sat on a stool and looked at Warren's formula and for the first time realized . . . we'd nearly doubled the toxicity of it. Sure, meth was all poison, but what we'd done . . . if Emily had built up a tolerance to our previous recipe, then tried the same amount with this . . .

As I was sitting there, horrified, the rest of the Science Club came in, tiptoeing, almost like they didn't want me to notice. I looked up and caught Katy's eye.

Katy: How are you doing, sweetie?

Me: How do you think?

Drew: We're really sorry for your loss, Bailey.

Me: MY loss? She was OUR loss. Ours. Her
friends'. Prescott's. God, her parents' loss.

Warren, almost angrily: Yes. It's sad, but this is
what happens when you let addiction get the
better of you. Just like my brother.

I noticed that he wasn't anywhere close to me. That he hadn't
hugged me or even taken my hand. He felt light-years away.

Me: But it wasn't like your brother, Warren. It
wasn't anything like that. Sure, she chose to do
drugs. Got addicted. But she had no way of
knowing that we'd made something far more
toxic than she was used to.

Drew: Wait. What?

353

Me: Yeah. Emily died because our new formula was too strong. She didn't know to use less.

Katy, shaking her head: No. They can't prove that. They couldn't possibly know that.

Me: I know that. Warren does too. (I threw the notebook with his formulas in it like a frisbee to him. He caught it but didn't look down at the pages.) We need to track down every bit of this that we sold so more people don't die.

Katy: No. No way. That's pretty much admitting that it's us. EXPOSING us.

Me: Maybe we need to be exposed!

Warren: God, Bailey. Don't be stupid. We'll lie low for a while, go back to making the old formula. Maybe stop selling around campus.

Me: That's another thing. No one told me we were selling to Prescott kids. Was that your expanded market?

Katy: You didn't want to know. You never asked. I'm just doing my job. My job is to get buyers.

Me: Something like that, you should have told me.

Katy: I didn't tell you so I could protect you!

Me: And how's that working out? My roommate is dead. They found our meth in my room. What do you think the next step is going to be? They'll trace it. It'll come back to us.

Warren: Oh, Bailey. Don't be stupid. It's not like our fingerprints are on it or something. No one's going to talk.

Me: Yeah? Want to bet your future on that? Have we given all the dealers enough money not to squeal? What about our friend Mark?

Warren, rolling his eyes: Don't be dramatic. It was one incident. Compared to what's going on, police will hardly be bothered.

Me: One incident? Is that how you think of Emily's death? An incident?

Warren, biting: Yes. An incident. An unfortunate accident because she made a stupid mistake. She always made stupid mistakes. Completely led by emotions.

Me: Yes, and you knew that about her, but you kept selling to her anyway, didn't you? Was it just the money or did you like having that power over her? Did you love how she'd come running to you, needing a hit, begging for one? You love to see people at their lowest, don't you? Makes you feel better about yourself.

Warren, emotionless: Going to blame me for your own stupid mistakes too, Bailey? You think I don't do the math? I know exactly how many Adderall you need to get through the day without the shakes.

For one terrible moment, I thought I was actually going to kill him. The urge to run at him and wrap my fingers

around his neck and squeeze . . . for what he'd done to me,
for what he'd done to Emily, and probably Katy and Drew
and who knows who else. . . . That urge was so strong I
actually pictured myself doing it like some sort of fever
dream. But I didn't. I had too much blood on my hands
already. I took a deep breath.

> Me: Our whole goal, in your words, was
> to make our product safe for addicts who
> were going to do this anyway. (I pointed to
> the notebook in his hands.) You made it
> lethal.

> Warren, unfazed: WE. WE made it lethal.
> You saw the formula and you said nothing.
> Either you understood and you didn't care,
> or you are terrible at chemistry. I've seen
> your work, Bailey. I know you're not. And
> now your roommate is dead. But it's no
> more my fault than it is yours. We didn't
> force her to use.

> Me: . . . But you did get her into it, didn't you?
> You gave her that first hit.

Warren's eyes widened, like he was stunned that I figured that out, but somehow I'd known it since I found Emily with her lips blue. I'd known Warren was involved.

> Me: You dated her. Don't you feel anything at all? Sadness? Guilt? Don't any of you?

Drew and Katy looked away from me, but Warren kept his eyes on mine. Steely.

> Me: And what about me? Did you ever actually love me? Or was I just another Emily to you? And we were just so easy to control, weren't we? Once you got us hooked on pills, we needed you. Desperately. We couldn't leave you. Couldn't give you up.

He didn't answer. Honestly, his silence was answer enough. I picked up a glass beaker off the nearest table and threw it on the floor. Everyone flinched as it shattered, and the sound pushed me onward, like it was the auditory equivalent of my own heartbreak. I reached for another beaker, and another. I don't know how many I smashed before Drew grabbed me from behind, holding me in a violent hug so I couldn't use my arms. I screamed in frustration and kicked until I landed one, my heel meeting his shin with a painful-sounding thump. He let me go and I turned around, facing all of them, tears blinding me to their horrifyingly blank faces.

> Me: This has to stop. We have to turn
> ourselves in. Emily's parents deserve to know
> why their daughter is dead.

> Katy: You know what happens if you talk,
> Bailey.

> Me: Maybe you should consider what
> happens if you don't.

I ran out of the lab. No one tried to follow me, either to try to convince me to stay in the group or to shut me up. If it was the first, they didn't want me; the latter, they think I'm too cowardly to actually turn myself in. Or maybe it's both.

But I'm not too cowardly. I'm done with them and their lying. I'm done with Warren, too. If it weren't for him I wouldn't have lost sight of the important things. I would have noticed Emily's decline. I would have noticed my own. But then he would just say it was my own choices that did this, wouldn't he? He had nothing to do with it. I was the one who took the Adderall when he offered, knowing I was too tired to get all my work done. I was the one who joined the Club, even though they all knew I had no other friends. I was the one who didn't know enough, even after they all swore it was best for me not to know. I was the one who took the Percocets when he offered, knowing that I was depressed about my mother.

Mom. God, I miss my mom. And I've missed my dad so much, and now I won't see him for a long time. I know what will happen now. I'll call up the cop, the nice lady one. I'll tell her everything. And if the Science Club tries to use that collateral against me, it's okay. Because I'm going to give that cop this.

My diary. Maybe it won't count for anything. Maybe I'll still take the fall. But if they corroborate the events in it, find some evidence that I haven't lied in these pages, maybe . . . just maybe, it will clear my name.

So that's what I'm going to do. I'm going to call that cop.

I'm in my room now. Emily's room. I wish I'd been a better friend to her. I wish I'd listened to her warnings. I wish I'd just listened to her. Maybe then I would have understood that the girl who seemed so bitter and jealous sometimes was a product of Warren Clark.

I am probably going to prison. I will never do the Princeton program, never go to Harvard. I may never graduate from high school.

I guess Warren is right, though, even if he is partly to blame as well. This is all because of what I did, choices I made. My heart hurts so bad, almost as bad as when Mom died. I've done so much the last couple of years, hoping to make her proud if she can see me from Heaven, if Heaven exists. Now I know that if she's looking down at me, she must be so disappointed.

I need to calm down. I can't think when I'm hurting this bad. I'll calm down, then I'll call the cop. Maybe a Percocet won't hurt. How could it hurt now? Soon enough I won't be able to take them anyway.

I took one. It looked so small in my hand. Such a tiny thing to help me face such a huge problem. Emily is gone. Forever. It's my fault. And these pills are so damned small. They can't change that. But another can't hurt. I know I've built up a tolerance. That's what addicts do, and I'm an addict, aren't I? That's why I get shaky without pills. That's why I've lost all this weight. Just a few more. Just to stop from feeling so much. Then I'll call the cop. She seemed so nice. Maybe it won't be so bad. Something about her smile kind of reminded me of Mom.

It's not that many. They're so small. I'll just finish the bottle and it will all be okay.

Just days after Prescott Academy was left reeling from the drug-related death of one of their students, the academy is again facing the loss of another promising young life.

A seventeen-year-old girl, a junior at the academy, was found dead in her dorm room yesterday after a brief search by campus security when the young woman failed to attend classes that day. She was the roommate of the other teen who died unexpectedly this week. Though the first death remains a mystery—crystal meth was found in her system but has yet to be directly tied to her heart failure, according to the county coroner—the newest death was likely caused by drugs. According to the police report, the seventeen-year-old girl was found holding a handful of Percocets that were not prescribed.

Headmaster William Stevens issued a formal statement calling on all students to come forward with information about drugs and drug use on campus and asking that space and privacy be granted to the grieving students at this time.

Headmaster Stevens also went on record earlier today to say that there has never been a drug problem at the prestigious boarding school before, but that this year, in particular, the community of Wiltshire and the surrounding areas have been hit hard. The headmaster stated that he expects the students of Prescott to rise above the temptations of peer pressure and believes that the school provides plenty of support and care for the student body. He added that counselors and therapists will be on hand for the next week so that students can work through their grief.

A Prescott student who wished to remain anonymous said that the headmaster's view of the drug use at Prescott is naive at best and willfully ignorant at worst. He said the pressure the school places on students to excel in every subject and task often leads the students there to turn to chemical stimulants keep their heads above water academically.

Though there are no leads as of yet as to how the drugs are finding their way onto school grounds, Detective Gina Eisley of the Wiltshire Police Department believes several pieces of evidence found at the scene could lead to answers the shaken school community so desperately needs. In a small press conference this morning on the stairs of city hall, Detective Eisley revealed that one item, a leather-bound book believed to be the journal of the most recently deceased junior girl, was being analyzed by the narcotics department for any information it could provide.

The Wiltshire Police Department urges anyone with information on the deaths of the two Prescott students to call their tip hotline at 555-6384.

READ ON FOR A GLIMPSE AT ANOTHER
RIVETING TALE OF ADDICTION....

July 4

~~Dear Diary,~~

That's ridiculous. Who writes "Dear Diary" in a diary? I mean, who writes in a diary at all? Shouldn't I be blogging?

This is lame.

July 5

Okay, so this isn't going to be a diary. It's a journal. I guess that's the same thing, but "journal" sounds less like I'm riding a tricycle or something.

Yesterday was my birthday. I turned 16.

It's so weird sharing a birthday with your country. Always fireworks: never for you. Mom always plans an actual birthday dinner—usually the Saturday night after July 4th so that I can have a day where we celebrate just for me. It's fun, kinda like having two birthdays in the same week.

We're not big July 4th celebrators . . . celebrators? Celebrants? People. Whatever—we're not big on July 4th. Usually in the afternoon we have friends from school over and walk down to the beach to play volleyball. There are lots of nets at the beach just down the hill, then we haul ourselves back up the canyon to our house for a cookout in the evening. My brother, Cam, invites his friends from the varsity soccer team. Mom gets my favorite cake (the one with the berries in it).

After we gorge on grilled meat and birthday cake, we all crowd onto the balcony outside my parents' bedroom and watch the fireworks down the coast. You can see the display at the pier really well, and the ones in the cities just up the coast shoot off too. Last year Cam (nobody calls him Cameron except Mom) climbed onto the roof from the front porch so he could get a better view, but Mom freaked and said, CAMERON! Get. Down. This. Instant. Mom's big on safety.

I got a lot of cool presents yesterday. Mom got me the swimsuit I tried on at the mall last week. It's a really cute two-piece with boy shorts, and this fun, twisty top. Dad's present to me was that he's taking me to get my license this week. I've been practicing with him in the parking lot near his office at the college. He gave me a coupon for one "Full Day with Dad." On the back it says, "Good for one driving test at the DMV, followed by a celebratory meal at the restaurant of holder's choosing, and a $100 shopping spree/gift card to store of choice."

He made it himself out of red construction paper and drew this funny little stick figure on the front. It's supposed to be him. He draws curly hair on the sides of the round head so the little man is bald on top like he is. The coupon is sort of cheesy, but so is my dad. I think it's funny. And cute.

Cam got me this journal. We've been going to this yoga

class together, and the teacher is this woman named Marty with bright eyes who talks about her birds a lot. She told us to get a journal and spend a few minutes each day writing down our thoughts and feelings.

I just looked back at everything I've written, and it's mainly thoughts. Not very many feelings. I'm not sure how I feel right now. I mean, I guess I feel fine? Happy?

No, just fine. I feel fine.

I also feel like people who have birds are sort of weird.

July 6

It's funny that Cam bought me this journal. It's one of those things I would never have bought for myself but secretly wanted. I don't know how he knows that stuff. I guess that's what older brothers are supposed to do: read your mind. I mean, who actually goes out and tries the stuff that their yoga teacher says to do outside of class?

Cam got way into yoga last summer when he had a crush on this exchange student from England named Briony—like Brian with a y. (Really? Who names their kid that?) Anyway, she wouldn't give Cam the time of day, so when he found out that she went to this yoga class, he started going to the same one. He bought a mat and this little bag to carry it in and just happened to show up in her class like, Oh my God! Wow!

What a coincidence. Briony never went out with him. I didn't even know she'd gone back to London until I was teasing him about how he should be glad Briony didn't do something like synchronized swimming. He was like, Briony moved back to London right after school got out.

I asked him why he was still going to yoga, and he said he really liked it. And he said I should come.

I'm not sure why I did, really. I guess I was just bored last summer. But now we go to yoga together. It's this really great studio a block off the Promenade, and they run it on donations. You just pay what you can or what you think the class is worth. I didn't think I'd like it at first. It was hard, and I got sweaty and slipped on my mat and couldn't do any of the poses. But I sorta like spending time with Cam.

Who am I writing that to? It's not like anyone is reading this but me. This is exactly how it feels when Grams asks me to pray over dinner. I feel like I'm saying all this stuff that is bouncing back at me off the ceiling and landing in the spinach salad.

Cam probably didn't have to read my mind about wanting a journal at all. He's really smart. His early acceptance letter to this great college up north came last week. He's going to be a biochem major, which just makes me want to lie down on the floor and curl up in a ball. He's a brainiac. And on top of it he's

nice and enthusiastic—which has a tendency to be dangerous.

Last semester Mom was always telling me to ask Cam for help with my geometry homework. I did, but instead of telling me what to do, Cam always talks and talks and talks. It's like he knows so much about stuff and likes math so much that he has to say it all instead of just the answer.

I stopped asking questions. It sort of annoyed me. Just did it myself, and didn't really understand it. I got a C in geometry. You'd have thought I'd flown a plane into a building. (That's bad to say, I guess. I mean, I know people died and everything, but it was a really long time ago.)

Dad came unglued. He's the chairman of the music department at the college where he works. He made me sign up for tutoring this summer with a student that his friend in the math department recommended. Our session starts in a few minutes. I was relieved when Nathan showed up the first time. I was afraid I'd get stuck with some weird math girl.

Nathan is a freshman. He's from Nebraska and has brown hair that's cut short. He works out a lot, and he wears these polo shirts with sleeves that are tight right around his biceps. I just stare at his arms a lot instead of listening when he's trying to help me find the answer.

I wish somebody would just tell me the answer.

Nathan's here. Gotta go.

Later . . .

OMG.

I TOTALLY JUST INVITED NATHAN TO MY
BIRTHDAY DINNER.

OMG OMG OMG OMG

And

He

Said

YES!

This is totally crazy. I can't believe I actually said the words
out loud. I didn't mean to. We were just sitting at the dining room
table and he was talking about the hypotenuse of a right angle,
and while he was looking at the protractor he was using to draw
lines, I was staring at the lines of his jaw and noticed that they
were almost a right angle, and the hypotenuse of the right angle
of his jaw was this line in his cheek with a dimple in the middle
that he gets when he smiles, and then I heard myself saying,
You should come to my birthday dinner on Saturday, and then
I realized that Mom was looking RIGHT AT ME like my hair
was on fire, and I realized that I'd just invited an 18-year-old over
for dinner in FRONT OF MY MOTHER. OMG. I just wanted
to CRAWL UNDER THE TABLE.

But he stopped with his pencil stuck into the protractor and looked up, and then glanced over at Mom like he was looking to see if she'd heard, and she smiled at him, sort of weakly. I guess he took that to mean that it was okay with her 'cause he looked me right in the eye and said, Sure. That'd be fun. Now look at this triangle.

I tried to look at the triangle for the rest of the half hour, but I have no idea what he was saying. When he left, I walked him to the door, and Mom said, Nathan, come by around 7:30. He said, Sure thing, and you can call me Nate. He waved at me before he got in his pickup truck and said, See you this weekend. Then, he drove away. Just like that.

I went running back up to my bedroom and buried my head in my pillow and did one of those silent screams where you just breathe out really hard, but with no sound; it's sort of a soft roar, but the excitement on the inside of me made it feel like my head would explode.

I could hear my heart pounding in my ears, and I took a couple of deep breaths and then I remembered what Marty said in yoga this morning about trying to meditate and how to focus on the breath, so I sat down on the floor and crossed my legs like Marty does in front of class, and I closed my eyes and took really deep breaths and tried not to think about Nate. I could do it for about 5 breaths at a time, but then I'd see that

line with the dimple in it behind my eyelids, and then the rest of his right-angle jaw would appear and I'd see a triangle fill in the space on his face.

I mean, it's really no big deal. My dad is two years older than my mom. Nate's only 18, and I'm 16, and it's not like he would be robbing the cradle or anything.

I think I really like him.

OMG I CAN'T BELIEVE THAT NATE IS COMING TO DINNER ON SATURDAY.

July 8

I was just standing in my mirror trying on a couple of different options for tonight. I passed my driver's test and got my license yesterday (YAY! OMG. Finally!), then Dad and I went shopping on the Promenade. I'm a really good bargain shopper. Cam worked at the Gap last summer and taught me to never EVER pay full-price for anything 'cause they just mark it down every two weeks. Primary, secondary, clearance. Primary, secondary, clearance. Every week on Tuesday night the markdowns would come through from the home office, and we'd all run around with those price-tag guns the next morning, marking down tops that some poor dope had paid $20 more for 12 hours ago. So, anyway, I got a lot of great stuff. Even Dad was surprised with how many items I got for $100. Well, then I splurged a little and added $40 from my savings to get these supercute sandals that I'd been wanting.

Anyway, I have all this stuff to try on, and I felt myself doing that thing I do where I put on, like, 12 different outfits and stand there and pick every single one of them apart, and I end up standing in front of the mirror in my underwear with this pile of really cute clothes with the tags still on them lying on the floor. I had just put on the second skirt I bought and could tell I was about to find something wrong with it, and then I just stopped, looked at myself, and thought: Don't be that girl.

I just don't want to be that chick who is always staring at herself in the mirror whining about how she looks and having a meltdown in the fitting room. I mean, I'm not a model or anything, but I think I look okay. I have already showered and straightened my hair. It's not frizzy or even curly really—just has some waves, and when you live this close to the waves it can get wavy. (God. Stupid joke.) Whatever, I stepped away from the mirror and saw my journal sitting on my desk, and I thought I'd write about it. I mean, this is a feeling. I'm not sure what kinds of feelings I'm supposed to be writing about in here, but maybe this is what crazy Marty the bird lady was talking about.

I'm SO EXCITED about Nate coming over and I want to look really hot, but the excitement also feels like nervousness, like I'm going to barf or something. Mom is downstairs putting a marinade on some shrimp that she's going to have Dad grill, and the smell when I walked through the kitchen made me feel like I was going to hurl up my toenails—and I LOVE shrimp.

I know I look good in this skirt. Dad told me it looked "far out" when I came out of the dressing room to check it out in the mirror. He said this in his I'm-being-a-little-too-loud-so-the-other-people-present-will-hear-me-and-think-I'm-hilarious-when-really-I'm-just-torturing-my-daughter voice. I told him to please be quiet and offer his opinions only regarding possible escape routes in the case of a fire, or a random stampede of wild bison. In all other matters, I respectfully asked him to please refrain from speaking to me until we had reached the cash wrap.

I looked in the mirror again just now. This skirt totally works.

Weird how excited and scared feel like the same thing.

July 8—11:30 p.m.

I shoulda known.

I shoulda known when he walked up the front steps with flowers and handed them to Mom.

But he brought me a card with a joke about having pi on my birthday instead of cake (guh-rooooan) and it had a $25 gift card for iTunes in it. Which was cool and so sweet of him, but he just signed his name. Shoulda known when he didn't write anything personal. Just "Happy B-Day! Nate."

But he was really funny and sweet at dinner. He sat across from me and told us all this hilarious story about when he was growing up in Nebraska and he and his brother raised sheep for the county fair. (Yes. Apparently people still raise animals and take them to fairs where they win ribbons and titles and scholarships. Thank you, CHARLOTTE'S WEB.)

One morning he and his brother went out to scoop food out of these big 25-pound sacks of feed for the sheep, and there was a mouse in one of the bags that ran up his little brother's jacket sleeve. He was telling us about how he thought his brother had been possessed by a demon because he kept screaming and shaking his arms and beating at his chest and running around in a circle while the mouse wriggled around inside his shirt. We were all crying, we were laughing so hard, and Cam almost inhaled a bite of shrimp, which sent him on a coughing fit that made the rest of us laugh even harder.

He jumped up and helped me clear the table when Mom asked who wanted dessert. When Mom told him he didn't need to do that, he smiled at me and said, Oh yes, ma'am, I do. My mama'd fly in from Grand Island and smack me if I didn't.

When we were in the kitchen, I started rinsing plates and he loaded them into the dishwasher like he lived here. We were laughing and joking around and no one mentioned geometry.

He was so easy to talk to, easy to be near. I didn't feel nervous even once. I couldn't help but wonder what it would feel like if we were married and this was our house and we were loading the dishwasher together. That's probably stupid, but it made me feel hopeful inside, like maybe something like that was possible.

When Nate bent over to put the final plate in the dishwasher, a necklace fell out of his shirt. It had a tiny key on it, and I was about to ask him where he got it, but Mom came into the kitchen to get some coffee mugs and the French press. Nate tucked the necklace back into his polo before I could ask him about it, but I shoulda known.

There's a long porch on the back of our house that looks over the bottom of the canyon out to the water. We ate dessert out there. Dad lit the candles in the big lanterns on the table outside. Cam sat next to Nate and they talked soccer. The flicker made their skin glow like they were on the beach at sunset. Nate looked all sun-kissed and happy. I felt a foot nudge mine just for a second under the table and my heart started racing. I was glad that it was just the candles outside in the dark 'cause I started to blush like crazy. I thought maybe Nate had touched my foot, and I kept sliding mine a little bit closer toward him under the table, but his foot never touched mine again.

It was almost 10 when he pulled out his phone and checked it, then said, Whoa. I gotta go.

I felt really bummed all of a sudden, and then silly. What was I hoping? That he'd stay and walk me down to the beach? He stood up and shook my dad's hand, then gave Cam one of those weird hugs that guys give each other where they grab hands like they're gonna shake and then lean in and hug with their arms caught in between them. He kissed my mom on the cheek and told her what a good cook she was.

Then he looked right at me and said, Will you walk me to my truck?

I got so many butterflies in my stomach, I thought they might start flying out of my ears. I said SURE, and realized that nobody had really heard him ask that because Mom was pouring more wine and Dad was pouring more coffee and Cam was texting somebody. So I slipped into the house and out the front door.

He'd parked on the street, and when he got to the door of his pickup, he leaned against it and looked up at the sky and said, Huh.

I said, What?

He told me that in Nebraska at this time of night you could see lots of stars. I followed his gaze up to the sky, but I knew there wouldn't be any stars. Out here, the sky just glows this weird purply color even on the darkest night here. It's the light pollution bouncing off of the marine layer, I said. It's what happens at night when 8 million people get jammed up against the ocean. I turned around and stood next to him with my back up against the truck.

He said it was funny how you always hear about all the stars in Los Angeles, but at night in Nebraska, it's like the sky is covered with diamonds. Then he looked over at me, and I don't know what happened, but I just knew that I had to feel his lips on mine. So I leaned in and kissed him.

Nate jumped like I'd shot him with a taser. He said, WHOA, what are you doing? OMG! I was SO EMBARRASSED I couldn't even LOOK at him. It was like we were having this PERFECT night, and then BLAM-O: I broke the spell. I was blushing and stammering and then I felt the tears come to my eyes, and I didn't wait. I just sprinted back across the street toward the house. I was not going to let him see me cry.

As my foot hit the curb on the other side of the street, he said WAIT!

There was something in the way he said it that made me turn around. And then he shook his head and smacked his forehead, and he walked over to me, and just looked at me. He pushed my hair over my shoulder and said, No. I'm sorry.

He told me that I had come along two years too late. And that I was beautiful. And that he has a girlfriend.

Letting Ana Go

Letting Ana Go

Anonymous

Simon Pulse
New York   London   Toronto   Sydney   New Delhi

SIMON PULSE

An imprint of Simon & Schuster Children's Publishing Division

1230 Avenue of the Americas, New York, NY 10020

First Simon Pulse paperback edition June 2013

Copyright © 2013 by Simon & Schuster, Inc.

All rights reserved, including the right of reproduction in whole or in part in any form.

SIMON PULSE and colophon are registered trademarks of Simon & Schuster, Inc.

Also available in a Simon Pulse hardcover edition.

For information about special discounts for bulk purchases,

please contact Simon & Schuster Special Sales at 1-866-506-1949 or business@simonandschuster.com.

The Simon & Schuster Speakers Bureau can bring authors to your live event. For more information or to book an event contact the Simon & Schuster Speakers Bureau at 1-866-248-3049 or visit our website at www.simonspeakers.com.

Designed by Lissi Erwin

The text of this book was set in Adobe Caslon Pro.

Manufactured in the United States of America

10 9 8 7 6 5 4 3 2 1

Library of Congress Control Number 2012956565

ISBN 978-1-4424-7213-6 (pbk)

ISBN 978-1-4424-7223-5 (hc)

ISBN 978-1-4424-7214-3 (eBook)

Letting Ana Go

Friday, May 18

Weight: 133

Breakfast: Bagel (toasted), light cream cheese, orange juice (fresh squeezed! Thanks, Mom!).

A.M. snack: (Who has time for this?) Jill gave me a Life Saver in English. (Does that even count?) It was green.

Lunch: Turkey wrap with Swiss cheese, SunChips, Fresca, ½ bag of gummy fruit snacks.

P.M. snack: Other ½ of the gummy fruit snacks.

Dinner: Lasagna (1 square), Caesar salad with croutons. Dad made brownies. Ate two.

Now I'm supposed to "write a few sentences about how I feel." I feel this food diary is strange, and sort of funny. When Coach Perkins handed them out brouhaha ensued. ("Brouhaha" was a word on my final vocab quiz of sophomore year today. As was the word "ensued.")

Coach Perkins passed out pamphlets at practice. Not really pamphlets but I like all those *p*'s. Journals, actually.

Coach: It's a "food diary."

Vanessa: What is this *for*?

Geoff: Why don't I get one?

Coach: Only the ladies.

Coach said girls on other cross-country teams have been

using our sport to hide their eating disorders. They run until they collapse from not eating enough, not drinking enough, not knowing enough. Hello? Dingbat? Running four to eight miles per day? You're going to need some calories. (At least two brownies after dinner.)

Naturally, the adults are only now catching on. They thought that's just what runners look like. Parents: sometimes clueless.

As a result of not eating, these girls get sick, and we girls get to write everything down.

Our food.

Our feelings.

I still feel it's funny, somehow . . . or maybe absurd. (Also on the vocab quiz.)

Not Vanessa: This is unfair! What about the guys?

Or Geoff: Yeah! This is cool! I wanna do it too!

Ugh. Lovebirds. Too cute = puke.

(COACH PERKINS: If you're actually reading this, that was a figurative "puke" not a *literal* "puke.")

Coach says she'll be checking the diary every practice, and then over the summer when we meet up to check in once a month before school starts. Coach Perkins is pretty.

Ponytail, push-up bra, probably pushing forty. Not one to be trifled with. Tough as nails.

Jill was painting her nails in my room after practice during our weekly Friday-night hang out. I told her about the food diary, and how I found it preposterous.

Jill: Please. I've been keeping one for six weeks.

Me (laughing): WHY?

Jill: So I can lose ten pounds.

Me: You'll disappear.

Jill: Shut up.

Me: Seriously. You already look like a Q-tip on toe shoes.

Jill: The Nutcracker Nemesis must be vanquished.

Me: You're losing ten pounds for *Misty Jenkins*?

Jill: I'm losing ten pounds for *me*. I will be Clara this Christmas or you have seen my last pirouette.

She blew on her nails and looked at me with the same wide-eyed stare she has presented each Friday night past when making pronouncements of epic proportions over popcorn. These are not to be pooh-poohed, and I made the mistake of laughing.

She pounced with a pillow.

A brouhaha ensued.

Saturday, May 19
Weight: 132
Breakfast: Dad's omelets—eggs, cheddar cheese, tomatoes, bacon.

3

Vanessa and Geoff came over this morning and we ran before breakfast. Dad cooked us all omelets afterward. Mom was still in bed because she gets off so late at the hospital. I don't know how she stays awake enough to give people medicine in the middle of the night, but she says you get used to it. I turn into a pumpkin at about 11 p.m. every night.

Dad was doing his cooking tricks because Geoff and Vanessa were watching. He can toss eggs over his shoulder and catch them and break them into the bowl with one hand. He was spinning the whisk around his fingers and juggling tomatoes. He was a short-order cook before he started selling cars and he loves an audience. I've seen all his moves before, but Geoff and Vanessa were cracking up. It made me feel good—proud of my dad. He never went to college or anything, but we have a really nice house and great cars and everything because he's so smart and worked his way up until he was able to buy his own dealership.

I texted Jill and she walked over while we were eating. Dad tried to get her to have an omelet but she would only eat a bite of mine, then immediately pulled out her phone. Vanessa and I had just been saying we didn't know how we were going to remember every single thing we ate every single day without carrying these food diaries around with us all the time, and Jill smiled and waved her phone at us.

She was using this app called CalorTrack, which helps you keep track of what you eat. Everyone who uses the app can go online and enter the nutritional information and serving size of the foods they are eating. In the app, you can search for the food you have just eaten or are about to eat and it records the calories. You can set goals to lose weight or gain weight, and it charts your progress online. You can even print out a report of what your calories are over a week, or a month. This was a revelation. Vanessa and I immediately downloaded this app. Naturally, Geoff did too. Dad watched us all being absorbed into our phones and started doing the funky chicken dance in the kitchen using oven mitts as wings to see if he could distract us. We all started laughing at how ridiculous he looked. Jill and I had tears running down our faces.

I like Dad so much when he's in a good mood. I can't even be mad at him for behaving in a way that is completely and utterly mortifying because he's so funny.

Mom wandered into the kitchen, bleary-eyed, in her sleep pants and T-shirt. She saw Dad and started laughing with us. She kissed my head, and Jill and Vanessa said good morning, but when Dad saw her it was like somebody threw ice water all over him. He stopped dancing and started doing dishes. I don't think anyone else noticed.

Except Mom.

I don't know why Dad won't let her be part of the fun. He handed her a plate with an omelet without smiling, and turned back to the sink. Mom sat and talked to us while she cleaned her plate, but I couldn't take another bite. I just wanted Dad to come sit down with us.

Mom: These are so good! Dale, come sit down and have one with us.

Dad: (grunt from sink)

Geoff: His cooking is almost as good as his dancing.

Vanessa: Do the funky chicken again.

Mom: I always miss the good stuff!

Dad (under his breath): Not much of it . . .

No one heard Dad but me because I was sitting closest to the sink, and because Geoff was trying to demonstrate the funky chicken dance. Mom laughed at Geoff's attempt, then asked me if I was going to finish my omelet. Dad turned around and shot daggers at her. He opened his mouth to say something, but then glanced at Geoff and Vanessa and Jill, and turned around again.

Me: It's all yours, Mom. I'm stuffed.

Dad didn't think I saw him roll his eyes, but I did. How can he go from somebody I love to somebody I hate in the span of four minutes?

A.M. snack: Nothing. (Still full from breakfast. Dad's omelets are huge.)

Lunch: Tuna fish sandwich with tomato, carrot sticks, BBQ potato chips.

P.M. snack: YouGoYum yogurt—chocolate swirl, small, with bananas, pecans, chocolate chips, and hot fudge.

After her rehearsal at City Youth Ballet, Jill texted me and asked me if I wanted to get yogurt. She drove by my place and picked me up, her hair in the signature bun of ballerinas everywhere. YouGoYum is one of those "pump it yourself" places that seems to be sweeping the nation. There's even one in my grandma's town, a wee town with a single stoplight where the Starbucks recently closed. I chose a small cup and took pride in my perfect loops of classic vanilla-and-chocolate swirl. Making a picture-perfect soft-serve cup topped by a tiny twist like the ones in TV commercials requires both patience and precision. When I'm successful it pleases me beyond words.

I placed my yogurt on the scale at the register and turned around to see what Jill was having. Her fingers held only her phone, upon which she was typing out a text message.

Me: Where's your yogurt?

Jill (pointing at mine): Right there.

Me: You aren't getting anything?

Jill: Just a bite of yours, thanks.

Me: But . . . you texted and asked if I wanted to come get yogurt with you.

Jill (wide-eyed pronouncement face): No, I asked if *you* wanted to get yogurt.

Me: That bun is restricting blood flow to your brain.

Dinner: Buster's Burgers—junior double cheeseburger with ketchup, tomato, lettuce, mayo, crinkle-cut french fries, Diet Coke, half a chocolate shake. (Split it with Dad.)

I get the family-tradition aspect, but I'm not sure why Dad still insists on Buster's Burgers every Saturday night. Lately, every time we go, he gets all hot and bothered if Mom orders a burger that isn't "protein-style" (no bun), or we'll be standing in line and he'll start saying things like, "Wow! That new Garden Chicken Salad looks great! You want to try that, Linda?" He says it in this voice like he's never *seen* a Garden Chicken Salad before, as if he can't *imagine* such a thing, full of wonder and awe and a tempered excitement as if at any moment, he may simply *explode* with the rapturous joy of grilled chicken and tomatoes on a bed of mixed greens. It's the voice I suspect scientists used when they first saw satellite photos of the rings around Saturn.

It is the most annoying thing in the world.

News flash: if you are so concerned that Mom eat a salad with lo-cal dressing on the side, maybe Buster's Burgers isn't the place to come for dinner every Saturday night. Just a thought. I'm almost sixteen years old. Our family unit will undoubtedly survive if we take a weekend off.

Mom sat there across the booth from me picking at her wilted greens, watching Dad munch his BBQ Bacon Double Trouble and drink his thick, dark beer while he plugged quarters into the tiny jukebox they have mounted on the wall over every table. When he got up to order another one at the counter, Mom snuck a couple of his fries and scrunched up her eyes at him like a little kid who was going to do something she shouldn't just for spite. That made me laugh, and I was still giggling when Dad walked back to the table and wanted to know what I thought was so funny.

Mom: I was just telling her about our first date here and how you wore those snakeskin boots and black jeans you thought were so rock 'n' roll.

Dad: They *were* rock 'n' roll back then.

Mom (to me): They were so tight he could've sat down on a penny and told you if it was heads or tails.

Dad: And I could still fit into those jeans.

What he meant was *you* couldn't fit into what you were wearing back then. Of course, he didn't actually have to say those words. He just looked at her the same way he did at breakfast this morning when she ate the rest of my omelet. Nobody talked on the car ride home, but I knew the silence was the calm before the storm. When we got home I kissed them both good night in the kitchen, and before I got to my room, the terse whispers had exploded into an all-out battle. Name-calling, dish clattering, counter banging, door slamming, the usual. Our usual. I caught words here and there:

Late shift
Hospital
Lard ass
Disaster
So mean
How could you
Not with a ten-foot pole
Cleaning lady
Pigsty
Secretary

Finally, I put on my headphones and pulled the covers over my head to drown out the rest. I've heard it all before.

Sunday, May 20
Weight: 133

Vanessa texted me and came over to run before Mom and Dad woke up. I snuck past Dad, who was sleeping on the couch, and met her in the driveway. We ran by Geoff's house and he joined us for a five-miler. When we got back to my place, Dad was headed out to the dealership. Sundays are big sales days. He grinned as he saw us coming up the drive, but I couldn't smile back. I hate it when he and Mom fight. I was sweaty and gross, but he insisted on a hug, and told me he'd left us a surprise on the counter for breakfast....

Breakfast: Two doughnuts: one round glazed, one chocolate long john.

Mom woke up while Geoff was polishing off the last of the doughnuts and Vanessa and I were stretching in the living room. We were watching an episode of this reality show we love where drag queens redesign each other's bedrooms. It always devolves into somebody throwing a wig at the camera. Mom paused and looked at the doughnuts but didn't have one. In fact, she didn't eat anything, just sat on the couch with us staring at the TV until the show ended and Geoff left to walk Vanessa home. I was starving again and made an . . .

A.M. snack: Protein smoothie with strawberries and bananas.

There was extra left in the blender, so I offered a glass to Mom. She shook her head. I asked her if she was going to eat anything and she just looked sad and told me she needed to save her calories for dinner. I asked her if she was writing down what she was eating. She sighed and didn't say anything. Mom has this big, epic, end-of-the-world sigh. It's almost as annoying as Dad being a jerk about what she eats. If you want to change something, change it. Don't just sit around sighing all day like a balloon losing air. I feel sorry for Mom, but not as sorry as she feels for herself.

Lunch: Deli turkey and cheese slices, rolled together like little burritos. Wheat crackers, baby carrots dipped in ranch dressing.

I was studying for our biology final tomorrow. Stopped to enter all the stuff I was eating into the app on my phone. When I punched in two tablespoons of ranch dressing I was astounded. The little dollop of dressing had more calories than all of the carrots and turkey I ate *combined*. How is that possible?

When I took my plate back down to the kitchen, Mom was standing in front of the refrigerator holding the package of cheese slices. I saw a bag of potato chips on the counter.

Me: Want me to make you some turkey roll-ups?

Mom: No! I told you I want to save my calories for dinner.

Me: Just because you don't put the food on a plate doesn't mean the calories don't count.

Mom: *SIGH.*

P.M. snack: None.

I got lost in a biology blackout. I didn't even think about eating until I heard the garage door opening. Dad was home and brought barbecue takeout with him. The smell made my mouth water and I ran downstairs. He was grinning ear to ear as he laid out ribs and pulled-pork sandwiches, coleslaw, and baked beans on the island in the kitchen.

Dad told us the new salesperson he lured away from another dealership was already the best producer this month. He said she's already sold more cars in two weeks than his top seller sold all of last month. Mom did a double take when he said the word "she."

Dad: What?

Mom: *SIGH*.

Dad: Are you going to eat with us?

Mom: Yes. I've been very good all day today.

Dad: I can make you a salad if you want to keep it up.

Me: *Dad.* Lay off. She hardly ate anything all day.

Dad: I'm just trying to *help*.

Mom: *SIGH*.

Dinner: Six baby-back ribs, baked beans, coleslaw, half pulled-pork sandwich.

We ate in the living room. Dad wanted to watch this zombie show on cable, which was fine until the last five minutes, when six of the undead jumped out of the woods and chased the hero's wife across a grassy country field. When she got hung up in a barbed-wire fence and ran out of ammo she had to kill the last one by jamming the gun in its skull. Thankfully, I was finished eating by then. Mom was still holding a baby-back rib, but she yelped, then put it down and pushed her plate away.

Zombie shows and barbecue: not a good recipe for dinner, though perhaps a good way to diet.

After dinner I went back up to my room and tried to study

for biology some more, but everything ran together in front of my eyes, then my phone buzzed with a text message:

Jill: Biology brain bleed. Help me.

Me: Ur text = last thing I saw. Blind. Pls send future texts in Braille.

She called me laughing and said her head was going to fall off. I told her I was officially a member of the phylum Exhaustica. There was a lot of noise in the background and she was shouting into the phone. I asked if there was a tornado at her house. She explained her brother, Jack (yes, her parents named their children Jack and Jill—as Mom would say: *SIGH*), and his friend Rob were studying vocabulary for their Spanish final. Jill thinks Rob is the hottest guy on the soccer team.

Me: Sounds like some pretty aerobic studying.

Jill (yelling): Rob read some article online about retaining things more quickly if you're doing something physical while you memorize information. They are kicking a Nerf soccer ball back and forth down the upstairs hallway.

Me: And you're watching Rob run past your door as a studying technique?

Jill: He's so cute.

Me: It sounds like a crop duster.

Jill: Rob's calves are so sexy.

Me: Fourscore and seven years ago, our fathers brought forth on this continent a new nation, conceived in liberty.

Jill: Totally. Have you noticed Rob has this little divot in his chin that—

Me: I'm hanging up now. Enjoy the view.

I'm pretty sure Jill talked to me for at least five minutes after I hung up before she realized I wasn't there anymore. I love her, but I'm no match for Rob's legs. Mom walked by on her way to her bedroom and told me there was clean laundry for me in the dryer. I went down to get it, and Dad grinned and waved me over to the couch. He was eating ...

Dessert: Five bites out of Dad's Ben & Jerry's pint.

Ironically, Dad's favorite flavor is Chubby Hubby. Of course, he's not chubby at all. He's in great shape. He goes to the gym three or four times per week and lifts weights and runs on the treadmill. He used to run half marathons, and still talks about training again. He was watching some talk show with a politician and some comedians on it. They were in front of a studio audience and kept zinging each other, then sipping something out of mugs with the show logo on it. Zing! (Sip.) Zing! (Sip.) Zing! (Sip.)

We watched the show and passed the pint back and forth.

After five bites I held up my hand. Dad took one more big bite with a smile, and then paused the DVR. He put the lid back on the ice cream, then got up and put the pint in the freezer. He asked if I was ready for finals. I pulled a throw pillow over my face and collapsed on the couch.

Dad: What?

Me (muffled by pillow): I hate that question.

Dad (laughing): Why?

Me (throwing pillow at him): Because how the heck would I know if I'm ready? You never know if you're ready for a test until you are actually *taking* the test in question.

Then we both cracked up and Dad said he was sorry, that he would never ask if I was ready for a test again. I like him so much sometimes. I wish he were as nice to Mom as he is to me.

Monday, May 21

Weight: 134

Breakfast: Raisin bran with soy milk, orange juice.

A.M. snack: Nothing.

Lunch: 2 tacos—ground beef, lettuce, tomatoes, cheese, Spanish rice. Fresca, split a Twix bar with Jill.

P.M. snack: Trail mix from the vending machine: almonds, dried cranberries, raisins, white chocolate chips.

Dinner: Leftover lasagna (one square), spinach salad with tomatoes, avocados, and balsamic vinaigrette.
Dessert: 100 Calorie Snack Pack of mini-Oreos.

The best parts of today ranked in order of excellence:

1. Biology. Is. Over. For. Ever. (And I think I did okay on the final.)
2. Taco bar for lunch.
3. At practice, Vanessa showed Coach Perkins the CalorTrack app and we gave her our printouts from the last few days. Coach said we could continue using the app, and could bring our printouts to her during our summer practices.

Jill came over to study for our English final tonight. Dad worked late at the dealership and Mom leaves for the hospital around 4 p.m. She usually works four twelve-hour shifts every week. I was making leftover lasagna and a salad when Jill arrived in her post-rehearsal warm-ups. I offered her lasagna but she'd only eat salad. And by salad, I mean the raw spinach leaves with tomatoes—no avocado or dressing. We reviewed the English study guide for a long time, then we reviewed how hot Rob's legs are for an even longer time. If there were a final on Rob, Jill would ace it.

Thursday, May 31
Weight: 132
Breakfast:
A.M. snack:
Lunch:
P.M. snack:
Dinner:
Dessert:

I've been keeping track of my calories on CalorTrack for the
past week since Coach gave us the go-ahead, but I just saw this
food diary while I was cleaning out my bag. I realized there's
no place in the app to write about our feelings. I guess Coach
Perkins forgot about that part of the assignment. Not that it
matters so much to her about how we feel, although that makes
her sound like a terrible person, and that's not what I'm saying.
I just meant the point of her having us keep track of our food
intake is so we stay at a healthy weight for running. I'm sure she
doesn't miss having to wade through all of this babbling.

I guess I sort of miss writing it all down.

There's something about seeing my words on these pages
from the past week that gives me a feeling inside I'm not sure
how to describe. It's like when Mom tells me I have to clean
out my dresser drawers because they are such a jumbled mess

she doesn't know which one is for socks and which one is for underwear or T-shirts. I hate the feeling of dread, which starts with me basically dragging myself into my room by force and dumping out the drawers on my bed. It feels like an impossible task—like I'll never get everything folded neatly and put back into the dresser.

But then, little by little, it just happens—one T-shirt at a time—until finally, I slide the last drawer into place, and then I feel a big wave of relief in my chest. For the next few days at least, I try to keep the drawers as neat as possible. I become extra-diligent at folding things up when I put them on and don't wear them, and I make sure to put everything back in the right drawer, tucked away just so. Having a clean dresser affects my whole room, too. It makes me not want to leave my clothes on the floor at night. I always try to put them in the hamper, or hang them back up. I guess it sounds ridiculous, but I love that feeling I get in the morning when I open my eyes and everything is put away.

Of course, eventually, I get in a hurry, or I'm running late, or I can't decide what to wear on the way out the door and change twelve times, and then I come home to an avalanche of stuff to deal with. If I don't do it right away, the dresser gets messy again in a hurry—I just start shoving things wherever they'll fit. But while it's clean it seems I have all this space and freedom in my room, like the bedroom itself is bigger and has more space and air.

It's the same way with this food diary. Today was the last day of school, and I dragged home all the crap from my locker. I was unpacking my book bag in my room, and when I saw this diary, the first feeling I had was how glad I was that I didn't have to write in it anymore. Still, I flipped it open and read over some of what I'd written, and all of a sudden, I felt this urge to write again—like somehow it would be sad if I just stopped. It's only been a little more than a week and I'd already forgotten about telling Jill that her bun was too tight when we went to get yogurt, and it made me smile to remember that. I wonder what else I've forgotten because I didn't write it down?

As I looked back on all the pages I'd written so far, it was like seeing clean dresser drawers in my brain, and my heart. It's like I've taken this tangled mess of thoughts and feelings and things that happened and stuff people said and folded each one carefully into a little entry about what happened that day.

So I dug out a pen. The minute I was holding the pen in my hand, it felt impossible to write anything down. Then I saw the first blank for my weight, so I weighed myself and wrote that down. I've already typed all of my food into the app so far today. I decided to skip all that and just write what is going on today.

Today, my sophomore year is officially over. Next year, I'll be a junior. Vanessa got all weepy when we were cleaning out our lockers because she and Geoff won't see each other every single second of every single day anymore, although that's not really the case. We'll be running together practically every day, and usually we hang out in the afternoons, too. Geoff will probably get a summer job working construction for his dad a few days a week. I promised Vanessa that we would go and take him lunch if she wanted to, which made her smile and wipe her eyes.

She said it wasn't just Geoff she'd miss, it was *this*, and then she waved her arm around the hallway.

I don't know how to explain it, but I knew what she meant. We'll be back in school in twelve weeks—same buildings, same hallways, same people—but we'll never be sophomores again, and we'll never take biology together again, and we'll never be exactly the same as we were right in that moment. This afternoon when she said it, I understood what Vanessa meant, but now that I'm thinking about it, folding it up in these sentences and sliding it into the drawer with all my other thoughts and memories, it makes a knot swell up in my throat and my eyes sting a little bit. Who knows how this summer will change us?

I guess this is one of the reasons I like Vanessa so much. She remembers how special these little moments are while we're still having them.

I'm glad that I decided to write this down. Now that I'm

finished, it feels like I have all of this brain space left over to use for thinking about other things. I don't have to worry about forgetting this either. It's all right here, tucked neatly away for the next time I need it.

Friday, June 1

It felt so nice to sleep in this morning and not have to go to school. Coach Perkins ran us hard yesterday because it was our last practice before summer, and I was sore when I walked downstairs. I poured myself a bowl of Lucky Charms and plopped down in the corner of the sectional and flipped on the TV. Last night was Mom's fourth shift, so she'll be off for the next three nights, but I tried to be superquiet because she's always exhausted from working four nights in a row.

I was catching up on this show Jill and I always watch where this comedian cracks jokes about videos from the Internet. He's really tall, and skinny, and he's not drop-dead gorgeous or anything, but he has this handsome smile and he's so funny that he's one of those guys who gets cuter and cuter the longer you look at him. Sometimes he shows videos where somebody breaks an arm, and I have to fast-forward through them. You can always tell it's coming, just from the setup. Usually it's somebody on a bike getting ready to ride down a set of stairs, or some idiot pulling a bozo in a shopping cart behind a pickup truck. The thing Jill and I are always amazed by is that most of the time, you can tell that the person who is in the video doing something completely deranged is also the *person who uploaded this video*. Which begs the question, why would you want the *entire world* to see you do something so stupid? Isn't it enough that you came two inches from death and wound up in the hospital with a cast on your leg? Must you advertise this fact? When I do something that's embarrassing, I just feel like dying. I want to curl into a tiny ball and crawl under my bed.

Anyway, Mom stumbled into the kitchen and said good morning. I smiled and she came over and kissed me on the top of the head, then walked back across the great room and stood in front of the open refrigerator for what seemed like forever. Then I heard her *SIGH*. After that, the pantry opened, then closed. Then the cabinets next to the refrigerator opened, then closed. Then the pantry again. Then another *SIGH*.

And finally, I couldn't stand it one moment longer. I turned off the TV and marched into the kitchen with my empty bowl, rinsed it out in the sink, dried my hands, turned to my mother (who was peering into the refrigerator again), and said:

Mom! This is ridiculous. Just eat something for breakfast.

Mom: But I'm so fat. I just need to save my calories for dinner tonight.

Me: Stop. Whining.

Mom (shocked): Wha—?

Me: You are not fat. You need to lose twenty pounds. You are a *nurse*. This is not rocket science.

Mom: But I've been trying to diet and . . .

Me: Mom, dieting doesn't work. You *know* this. This is about changing the way you eat. Calories in versus calories out.

Mom: But I don't eat that much!

Me: No, you do eat that much, you just don't know what you're eating because you don't sit down and make a meal. You graze all day long and pretend that you're saving your calories for dinner, but really, you're eating all these little bites of crap all day, and then eating way too much at night because you're hungry from not eating the right stuff during the day.

She started crying at this point, and I gave her a hug, but I am just tired of this. Dad's always giving her a hard time about it, true, but if you want to fix something, you just have to start somewhere.

Me: How much do you weigh?

Mom: I . . . I don't know. I'm afraid to look.

Me: Jeez!

I grabbed her hand and dragged her up the stairs to her bathroom. I pulled the scale out from under the sink and pointed to it. I told her I wasn't leaving until she weighed herself. I quoted Coach Perkins. She said, just like performance in a sport, weight is one of those things you have to measure. Coach Perkins always tells us if you don't know where you're starting from, you don't know where you're going, and only the things that get measured get changed.

So she stepped on the scale. Honestly, it wasn't as bad as I thought, but she needs to lose about twenty-five pounds. At that moment, Jill rang the doorbell, and we went back downstairs. She saw that Mom had been crying and asked if everything was all right. I told her it was, and then Vanessa and Geoff showed up. We are all going to the pool at the club Jill's parents belong to today to lay out and get our tans going for the first day of summer. Right there in the kitchen every single one of us whipped out our phones and showed Mom CalorTrack. I downloaded the app on Mom's phone while Jill set up her account on the laptop and Vanessa showed her how she could type in the first few letters of the things she ate every day and they'd pop up on the list. Before we left for the pool, we helped her set a goal, and Geoff confiscated most of Mom's stash of Snack Packs and lo-cal treats and low-fat everything as snacks for the pool.

Vanessa pulled some cottage cheese out of the fridge and measured a three-quarter-cup serving. Jill cut up a cantaloupe that was sitting on the counter. Geoff put water in the electric kettle and brewed some tea. Then I went and got my swim stuff while they kept her company and talked about what she could eat for a morning snack, and lunch, and an afternoon snack.

Finally, everybody piled into Geoff's car, only I ran back inside to get my sunglasses, but couldn't find them. As I was digging through the junk drawer under the key hooks at the kitchen island, Mom grabbed me around the waist and squeezed me extra tight. She whispered the words "thank you" into my ear really softly.

I kissed her cheek, told her to be sure to eat lunch and take a walk, then ran for the car. As Geoff pulled out of the driveway and Vanessa cranked up the music, Jill reached over and handed me my sunglasses. I put them on and she smiled and said, Welcome to Your Summer. We're So Pleased You Could Join Us.

Then Geoff let out a whoop and sped down the street.

Monday, June 4

As I picked up the pen to write this I realized my cheeks were aching because I've been smiling all day.

This morning I ran the mile and a half to Vanessa's place. Geoff was already there, stretching in the driveway, and we did a middle distance at a pretty fast pace. When we ran by my place I went in and showered, while they ran back to Vanessa's. Mom was sitting at her laptop entering her breakfast meal—half a grapefruit, egg whites, and one piece of whole-grain toast. She looked up and smiled at me, and for the first time in as long as I could remember, she seemed excited about something.

I kissed her on the cheek and she pointed at the screen to where she'd just entered her weight from that morning. She's already down one pound since she started keeping track last week! I gave her a high five, and she giggled.

After I got cleaned up, Geoff came by and we drove over to meet Jill at her parents' club again. They've got such an awesome pool with a couple of springboards, and the snack bar is to die for. Jill got all As last semester, so as long as she gets permission her parents let her sign for all of our food on their account. It's not that we eat a lot or anything, but it's a great deal. It's one of the reasons we studied so much last year. Jack and Rob were with her, and Geoff challenged them to a cannonball duel to see who could splash the most water out of the pool onto Jill, Vanessa, and me. Naturally, the results were hilarious and disastrous with Geoff, Jack, and Rob ultimately being called into the head lifeguard's office. I, personally, had been unaware of the lifeguard hierarchy at the Fielding Club Aquatics Center until today, but suffice it to say watching the Cannonball Splash-O-Rama (as Geoff called it) being referred up the chain of command in a series of stern warnings and whistle blowing over approximately two hours was among the funniest things

I have ever witnessed. While Jack was being threatened with a suspension of his membership privileges at the pool by a red-nosed sophomore from the local junior college named Rusty, Rob and Geoff were firmly tutored in the Guest Behavioral Guidelines by Becky, the "assistant head lifeguard." A curly-haired woman who coached the club's master swim team, she made it clear that if the guys continued to give "her staff" any more trouble, they would be put on the Fielding Club Aquatics Center watch list for the next month and not be allowed into the facility as a guest.

All of the cannonballing and lecturing had made the guys hungry, and after our run, I was starving myself, so we went to the snack bar. When we arrived, Rob gave an order to Jack that was roughly as long as the Bill of Rights, then he and Jill went to nab us a table on the sundeck that overlooks the lap pool. Jack called after her to see what she wanted to eat, but she just shook her head and waived her bottle of water at him.

Jack: She never eats at the pool, does she?

Me: Did you just meet her today?

Rob: I'll get her to eat a nacho if it kills me.

Jack: It may.

Rob: Dancers and runners, world's fittest women everywhere I turn.

Geoff: We are some lucky bastards, aren't we?

Me: Like the three of you can talk. Your abs belie your 8 percent body fat.

Rob laughed, and walked as quickly as he could without drawing a whistle from a lifeguard. He joined Jill, who was pulling up enough chairs for all of us around a single table in the corner.

As we stood in line under the snack bar awning, Geoff draped his arm around Vanessa's shoulders and she leaned into him. His chin sat perfectly on top of her dark, wet ringlets. They were doing that thing they do where they somehow tune out the entire world by touching each other, which left me standing there next to Jack, suddenly shivering in the shade. I crossed my arms over the top of my suit. I've had breasts for a couple years now, but I don't need to be shivering and flashing my high beams at my friend's older brother in front of God and the world.

Jack's hair was still wet, and he tossed his bangs out of his eyes with a little flip of his chin and smiled at me.

Jack: You cold?

Me: A little.

Jack: I'd put my arm around you like Geoff here is doing for Vanessa, but that might be weird.

Me (laughing): Yeah. Might be.

Jack: Although, I hate to see you shiver like that.

Me (taking two giant steps out from under snack bar awning): Maybe I'll just stand over here in the sun and wait for you to get the food.

Jack (loudly): Yeah, but now I feel lonely.

Me: We regret to inform you that your loneliness has been trumped by our lack of body heat. We sincerely apologize for any inconvenience and look forward to seeing you in the sunshine again very soon.

Jack's laugh was infectious and I couldn't resist joining him. It was strange. In all the years Jill and I have been best friends, I don't remember being around Jack without her being right there with us. Standing there laughing, six feet apart, him in the shade, me in the sun, it was like I was meeting somebody new. Right before he stepped to the counter to order enough nachos and Red Vines to sink a submarine, he flipped his wet bangs off his forehead again, and for the first time ever I noticed his eyes.

As blue as the bottom of the pool.

Wednesday, June 6

Dad took me to dinner tonight. Mom is working shift three of four.

When I was little he used to do this Dad and Daughter Date Night where we'd go eat pizza and see a movie. I can't remember when we stopped doing it. I think around the time I went to middle school. I started running track that year, and Dad got the opportunity to open the dealership. It's one of those things you never mean to stop, but you don't notice when it does. Then one day you look up and it's over almost before you realized it was happening.

We went to this Korean barbecue place downtown where you cook your own meat on the grill in the middle of your table. It was delicious and we ate until we were stuffed. I thought about how much Mom would have liked this place. I wondered why he never brought us here. He'd obviously been here before. He knew the hostess by name, the waitress asked how things were going at the dealership, and the chef came out to make sure everything was okay.

Dad read my mind: I come here for work lunches a lot.

Me: It's a long way from the dealership for lunch, isn't it?

Dad: Yeah, but it's such great food. Sometimes it's worth the trip.

I remember a lot of things about our Dad and Daughter Date Nights when I was little. I remember the place we used to go for pizza with the stage full of singing puppets at the end of the dining room. I remember putting a dollar bill in the machine and the *kerchink* of tokens tumbling into the silver tray. I remember the feeling of Dad's arms around me as he helped me toss the

Skee-Ball into the 100-point hole. I remember squealing with excitement as the endless tape of tickets came spouting out as the sirens rang and the lights flashed. I remember the candy and tiny monkey doll for which I exchanged the tickets. I remember the doll was fuzzy and brown. I remember how she sucked her hard plastic thumb in a perfectly round, hard plastic mouth.

I don't ever remember Dad lying to me on one of our Dad and Daughter Date Nights when I was little.

This was a first.

Dad scribbled a tip and a signature across the credit card slip, then pocketed his card and headed for the door as if he were being chased. Just like that I looked up and saw our dinner was over—almost before I realized what was happening.

Saturday, June 9

It began as a cookout.

It turned into a freak-out.

It ended in a walkout.

First there was Dad firing up the grill, and me turning up the music, and Mom whipping up the fixings. She was whistling as she seasoned that ground beef and smiling to herself as she rolled it into balls and smashed them into patties.

I knew she was feeling good about herself. I can't really tell the four pounds are gone, except when I look in her eyes. For the first time in a long time, she's got that twinkle back. She doesn't look tired. She looks as if she's remembered some sort of good news she'd almost forgotten about.

The smell of the burgers was making my stomach growl as I carried the place mats and utensils out back to the patio table by the grill. Vanessa and I ran this morning even though Geoff slept in. I knew I'd have to eat two burgers to hit my calorie goal for the day, and that was fine with me.

Mom raised her can of Fresca once we all sat down: To my beautiful daughter, whose beautiful friends helped me start to feel beautiful again.

I laughed: Oh, please, Mom. You're beautiful all the time.

Mom: I was telling your dad I've lost four pounds already by keeping track of everything in that app you showed me.

Me: I'm very proud of you, Mom.

I looked at Dad. I looked at Mom, who was looking at Dad. Dad was biting into his burger as if nothing was happening at the table, as if nothing important was being said, as if it didn't matter that Mom had lost four pounds.

As if he didn't care.

I saw the hurt in Mom's eyes as she reached for the tray of burgers and wrapped hers in lettuce instead of a bun. She gave a halfhearted laugh and told me this was "protein-style," without the carbs.

Dad asked me how far we ran this morning. He asked me what we'd been doing since school got out. He laughed when I told him about the Cannonball Splash-O-Rama and the "assistant head lifeguard."

I reached for a second burger and another slice of cheese: These are delicious, Mom.

Mom winked in Dad's direction: Well, your father sure can cook on a grill.

Me: You should have seen him at the Korean barbecue place. He's practically a pro.

The minute the words left my lips, Dad looked up and stared into my eyes. It was a hard stare, one that said he wished I hadn't said what I'd just said.

Mom and I both said, "What?" at the same time. Me to him. Her to me. She looked at Dad and said she'd always wanted to go there, but he'd always said he was afraid they served mystery meat. I turned to her and told her about our Dad and Daughter Date Night on Wednesday. How Dad is like a celebrity at this place downtown. Something in Dad's stare told me to shut up. Something in Mom's eyes told me to keep going.

I could hear the words coming out of my mouth, but it was like someone else was saying them—like I couldn't have stopped them if I wanted to:

He knew everybody's name.

The chef came to our table.

It was delicious.

The waitress asked about the dealership.

He goes there all the time for lunch with clients.

There was a strange silence when I finished. It lasted for what felt like forever. Mom reached for another burger. This time, she took two slices of cheese and a bun.

She gave me an awkward smile: I've been so good this week.

I felt Dad's long, cold stare leave my face as he shook his head: Not *that* good.

I'd never heard my mother curse before today. Never once. Nor had I ever seen her throw anything besides a towel, into the hamper. The burgers must've still been pretty hot because Dad yowled like an alley cat when they hit him in the face, and the ceramic platter bounced off his chest and broke across his knee. As the pieces clattered to the concrete patio and shattered into a thousand bits I had the sudden thought that we'd never be able to put this back together if we tried, and as Dad raced into the kitchen for a towel to stanch the blood pouring from his knee and Mom yelled words I'd never heard her say before in a voice I could not recognize, I slowly climbed the stairs to my room, closed the door, and put on my headphones.

I fell asleep listening to a singer I love who plays the piano in a minor key over wailing guitars. Her voice is full and lush and I dreamed of falling endlessly backward into a rich velvet darkness.

When I woke up Dad was gone.

Mom was sitting on the couch, staring at the television screen with the sound muted, eating a pint of Dad's Chubby Hubby. I sat down next to her, and she tried not to look at me, but I could see her eyes were almost swollen shut from crying.

I put my arm around her shoulders: Is it over?

She nodded: Yes.

I'd always wondered what it would feel like if my parents split up. Sitting there, holding my mother as she buried her face in my shoulder and cried until my T-shirt was soaked, I didn't feel anything at first. Somehow, it made a strange sort of sense. It seemed this wasn't about me. This was about them. So shouldn't they be the ones with the feelings? Wasn't it right for my mom to be the one crying?

Then I felt something wet and cold against the leg of my jeans. The ice cream Mom was holding had melted and was oozing out of the container, a thick, cold pool across my thigh. Something about it made me gag. We were a mess. This was a mess. I was covered in tears and mascara and stickiness. I pushed my mother away from me, grabbed the carton and the spoon from her hand. As I ran to the kitchen, a chill went up my spine as her tears trickled down my neck and over my clavicle. I looked back at her as I wiped the ice cream from my jeans and washed the stickiness from my fingers and arms. In a flash, I felt something:

Disgust.

And guilt for feeling disgusted.

And certainty that we'd never be able to put this back together—even if we tried.

Sunday, June 10

I can't stop crying. I can't eat anything. I don't know why. It's not like they were such a barrel of laughs when they were together. Jill showed up and rang the doorbell because I turned off my phone. She sat in my room on the bed and didn't say a word for three hours. Just handed me Kleenex while we watched reruns of that Internet video-clip show with the comedian. It's one of the reasons Jill is my best friend. She knows when to be quiet.

I even watched the broken bone videos. Didn't bother me at all.

Monday, June 11

Vanessa and Geoff came over to pick me up for our first summer cross-country practice. They barely noticed I wasn't really speaking until we got to the parking lot at school. Vanessa just kept talking about this movie they went to see last night and how awful it was. How the lead actress is supposed to be a teenager in love with a zombie slayer but couldn't even move her mouth. Geoff parked and turned around to do his impression of her happy face, her surprised face, and her sad face, which were all the same face. I started laughing, and then burst into tears like one of those girls I hate. I am not a public weeper. Vanessa is a public weeper.

I told them about my parents. Vanessa was shocked about what had happened, shocked that I hadn't called her, simply *shocked*. (She can really be a drama queen.) I assured her I was fine.

Vanessa: You don't look fine.

Me: You wouldn't have answered your phone anyway.

Vanessa: What's that supposed to mean?

Me: Nothing. You were in a movie. Can we please just drop it?

Vanessa: Um, your parents just split up. I don't think that's something we can drop.

I told her I was far more worried about these stupid printouts. I haven't been able to eat anything in two days. Vanessa and Geoff assured me Coach would understand, although I didn't see how. Either I had eaten enough or I hadn't. Why would my parents or my feelings have anything to do with it?

But they did.

Coach Perkins isn't exactly the touchy-feely type. She has a very finely tuned BS meter, and the second she saw me, she asked me what was wrong. Her exact words were: You look awful.

Something about the way she said it made me laugh. I *did* look awful. I thrust my CalorTrack printouts at her. I told her I hadn't been eating. She pulled me aside and asked me if I was upset over a boy.

Me: Kind of. My dad left.

Coach: I'm sorry.

Me (starting to cry): I'm not.

I've run cross-country for Coach Perkins since the summer before freshman year. For the first time in two seasons, she wrapped her arms around me and hugged me until I pulled it together.

She said: You don't have to run today.

I said: Yes, I do.

Tuesday, June 12

I told Geoff and Vanessa I needed a day off from running this morning, but really I needed a day off from them. I didn't sleep very well, and when I woke up in the gray light at six thirty this morning, I clamped my eyes closed again as if I could shut out the day, but it was too late. The feeling in my stomach, the one that won't let me eat much, seems to kick-start my brain into hyperdrive:

Who was Dad taking to that Korean barbecue place?

Why wouldn't he take Mom?

Why would he lie about it?

Why didn't Mom try harder to lose weight sooner?

Why didn't Dad try to be kinder and help her?

Why did he have to leave?

Does he still love me?

I can never let myself go like Mom did.

But she works so hard.

Still, that's no excuse.

My mind seemed to be on a runaway raft in the middle of a river, bouncing down level-five rapids, until eventually, it tossed me out of bed. I didn't know what else to do before 7 a.m., so I pulled on my running shoes and put in my earbuds.

I ran in the opposite direction of Vanessa's house just in case. I ran toward the mountain, staring up at the top of the peak, turning down my thoughts by turning up the music, and letting the cadence of my feet on the pavement focus my breath in a steady rhythm: in-two-three-four, out-two-three-four, in-two-three-four, out-two-three-four. Breathing in for four strides then out for four strides gave me something to focus on besides the thoughts crashing through my head, and then the sun must've broken over the horizon behind me, because it drenched the mountain with a splash of crimson across the top that bled into the indigo at its base. There was something so big about the mountain canvas, and so bold in the colors, that all I could do was drink them in with my eyes like a thirsty little girl with a cold glass of grape Kool-Aid.

My eyes began to water and tears mingled with the sweat running down my temples onto my cheeks. These tears were different from the others I'd cried since Sunday. They weren't directed at my dad or my mom. These tears were squeezed out of me by the colors of the sun's brush on the sky, and clouds, and rocky peaks. These tears streamed out of me in answer to the magnitude of what they saw. I ran for farther than I might have otherwise, if only to keep the mountain in my vision, and by the time I turned around to run back home, I felt very small against the massive summit. What a tiny speck of dust I am compared to the rest of this universe. I could no more control the colors of the sunrise than I could my mother's weight, or my father's roving eyes.

I realized the only person I can control is me, and as I turned the corner down my street and headed for my driveway I realized one more thing:

I was hungry.

Jill was waiting for me on the porch. It was almost 8 a.m.

and I couldn't believe she was even awake, much less dressed and waiting on the stairs.

She smiled and waved: There you are. I've been texting since dawn.

I opened the front door and she followed me to the kitchen, where I gulped down a glass of water, then rounded the island into the den to stretch on the carpet. I asked her if everything was okay.

Jill: Better than okay. Don't be alarmed.

Me: You understand my concern? It is a summer day before 10 a.m. and you seem to be showered, clothed, and in your right mind.

Jill: I bring important news.

Me: By all means, share.

Mom wandered into the kitchen right at that moment looking out of sorts. She was rumpled and dazed. Ever since I left her sitting on the couch Sunday, she jumps when she sees me as if she's startled, as if she's forgotten I'm here. She turned suddenly when she realized Jill was with me, then stopped and slowly turned back around, continuing into the kitchen to open the refrigerator door. She took out a carton of cottage cheese and bravely tried to smile at Jill. It was almost convincing.

Jill smiled and said good morning, and Mom asked what

the important news was. Jill told Mom it was a good thing she was here, because it concerned her, too.

Jill: Mom and Dad are letting Jack and me each bring a friend on our annual boat trip at Lake Powell this year.

I should note here that Jill squealed this information, which was startling. Jill is not particularly known for any sort of girlish excitement. She is typically droll and measured. Also, it was early for squealing.

I grimaced: So, who are you going to take?

Jill: *You!*

This was also a squeal, but Jill was bouncing up and down on her knees, which made me feel extremely fond of her, so I couldn't frown. In fact, as I pulled my left calf toward my chest in a stretch, I felt my mouth spread into a smile across my face, and turned my head to look at my mother.

Mom had opened the cottage cheese over the sink and appeared to be staring into it for the answer to an unasked question. So I asked it.

Me: Mom, can I go?

Mom: Huh—?

Me: Can I go with Jill to Lake Powell when they go on vacation next week?

Mom (blinking): Oh. Oh, sure. Yes.

Jill: (SQUEAL)

Me: Mom, are you sure you'll be okay?

Mom: Yes. Yes, of course. I'm fine. It'll do you good to get out of the house.

I smiled and stood up. Jill threw both arms around my neck and jumped up and down, causing me to move with her, and as she squealed I couldn't help it: I laughed, and for the first time since Saturday, I felt like maybe the world wasn't coming apart at the seams.

Mom smiled at us jumping up and down in the living room. This was the first true smile I'd seen from her in four days. She glanced back down at the cottage cheese, then said, screw it, and dumped the container into the sink.

Who wants breakfast? she asked.

Mom grabbed her keys and a baseball cap she sometimes wears when she plants impatiens in the flower bed by the pool, then she drove us to IHOP and ordered chocolate chip pancakes for each of us.

To my complete and utter amazement Jill cleaned her plate.

Friday, June 15
Weight: 128

We're leaving tomorrow. I'm excited, but nervous—about going, about staying, about Mom and Dad, about being basically naked for a week on a boat with Jack. Jill says she always wears a bikini with shorts on the boat, and just slips off her shorts when she gets in the water. I've seen pictures from this trip. Usually they go with her cousins from Arizona, but this year her cousins are going to Mexico or someplace. When I asked Mom if I could have some money to go shopping for a couple new pairs of shorts and a bathing suit, she handed me her debit card and told me the PIN without looking up from the papers she was sorting through from the lawyer. I asked her if there was some sort of ballpark figure she'd like me to stay within for budgeting purposes. She looked up at me and blinked, then back down at the papers and said something about how my dad could afford it.

I walked down the driveway to get into the car with Jill. Jill was far more pragmatic about the situation and wore her "buy them both" face a number of times at a number of different cash wraps two days in a row. In the end, I have three new pairs of shorts, a new one-piece, and three new bikinis, two with trunk shorts, one with little ties on the sides. Jill insisted I get it. She said I've never looked better than I do right now. I was in the bathroom trying everything on when I got home tonight and weighed myself. I've been forcing myself to drink protein smoothies for the past week because my stomach is still too upset to eat anything. When I handed Coach Perkins my printouts today she patted my shoulder and told me I was making a good effort, but I know I'm nowhere near close enough to the number of calories she wants us to be eating. I told her I'd be on the boat all this week and she said she thought that was a good idea.

Coach: Take a break from running.

Me: I'll sort of have to.

Coach: Didn't want you making laps around the lake or anything.

Me: I hadn't thought about that.

Coach: Don't. And eat lots of chips and pizza and laugh a lot.

Jill said she's paring down her calories starting tomorrow because she won't be rehearsing. She did say we could do her "aerobics routine" on the boat. Whatever that is. She said she'd show me, but the idea of dancing around in place drives me crazy. That's the thing about running I love: I get to *go somewhere*.

Maybe that's why I'm nervous. I'll be stuck on a boat in the middle of a lake. With Jill's mom, who is nice, but let's face it, maybe a little . . . ice queen? She's like one of those blond politician's wives: hair always up, makeup always perfect, nothing out of place, eagle eyes—doesn't miss a thing.

I feel sort of guilty for leaving Mom, but she hasn't been

able to complete many sentences since the lawyer dropped off the divorce papers on Tuesday. She's plowed through two different sets two different times, initialing, crossing out, underlining, writing notes in the margins. She told me we're keeping the house. At least Dad isn't going to make us move.

Thinking about that makes me want to leave right this second. I want to be out of here and away from all this. I have to go to sleep now. I'm not sure how I'll do that. Jill and her family will be here to pick me up at 6 a.m.

Saturday, June 16

It's a nine-hour drive to Lake Powell. Jill's dad rented an SUV so large I'm not sure how we're going to make it without stopping for gas every twenty-nine miles. Rob and Jack were firmly ensconced in the very back seat when they rolled into our driveway this morning at 5:55 a.m. They were both wearing noise-canceling headphones, and their faces were obscured by flat-billed baseball caps with NBA logos and gold stickers proclaiming the size still affixed to the bills. They looked like extras from a music video.

Jill was comatose in one of the captain's chairs. She gave a grunt and tried to smile when I opened the van door, but it was halfhearted at best. I'm pretty sure she was asleep again by the time her dad pulled out of the driveway.

Mom worked last night to get some overtime, so I tiptoed into her room and kissed her on the cheek at five forty-five. She stirred and muttered something about waiting twenty minutes after I ate to go in swimming. I giggled and whispered: I love you. I'll text you when I get there.

Susan and James, Jill's parents, are as awake as I am. Her dad smiled like a news anchor when he tossed my bag behind the seats where Rob and Jack are sleeping. He said Jill was really jazzed that I could come. Jazzed. I don't think Jill has ever been "jazzed" about anything, or if she had indeed felt "jazzed" she would most certainly never have used that word. Still, I couldn't help smiling when her dad said it. When we were all settled in, he leaned over and kissed Susan on the lips—maybe a little longer than was entirely necessary—then glanced into the rearview mirror and said, "Head 'em up, move 'em out," as if he were a cowboy.

Jill groaned and readjusted her angle in the seat. The boys behind us remained silent, slack-jawed, and completely indistinguishable. Susan rolled her eyes and smirked, then turned back to me and sighed: Can you believe this guy?

I thought about my own dad. I thought about how clever and funny and charming he could be, and how more often than not, he was none of those things—like he was purposefully keeping it from us when my mom was in the room. It made my

49

stomach turn with a familiar wincing pang of longing, a longing for something I'm not sure my parents ever had. Did my dad ever kiss my mom for a little too long? I tried to remember.

Of course, my mom never looked like Susan. She had perfect makeup at 6 a.m. Not too much makeup like a Real Housewife, just precision eyeliner and mascara, and possibly some powder? Her skin was luminescent in the glow of the dome and dashboard lights. Her platinum-blond hair had been flatironed and twisted up. She looked a lot like the wife of that old guy who ran for president a few years back—lean and pretty, but somehow pointy around the edges. My mom's edges are all soft and full, and usually straining at the fabric somehow. Susan's entire essence appeared tailored to fit even (somehow) in a predawn appearance. She offered me a bottled water and quietly chirped about how I had my own climate control for the vents above me in the armrest to my right, and how we'd stop for a bathroom break and coffee and snacks around ten; told me to just let her know if I needed anything, and in the meantime to try to relax and get some sleep because we had a long drive ahead of us. It was not entirely unlike the speech a flight attendant gives before the plane takes off, and I almost expected her to explain how to fit the metal buckle of my seat belt into the latch, and what to do if we experienced an unintended loss of cabin pressure.

I tried not to compare her to my mom any more, but it was difficult. My mother's instructions upon leaving for any sort of journey forth into the world typically consisted of the words "Hurry up, we're late," but Susan impresses me as someone who has never been late, or hurried, or wrinkled, or flustered, or held her breath to zip her jeans, or arrived with a shiny forehead ever in her life.

It's no wonder James kisses her like he does.

The sun has turned the sky above the highway the color of a forest fire. Soon it will peek over the horizon. I'm finally feeling sleepy and the thrum of the tires against the pavement and the perfectly cooled air spilling out of the vents is soothing somehow, and I think I might be able to sleep for a little while. I feel my whole body beginning to relax. I guess I didn't realize how tense I've been at home. There's a warm ease about sinking into this leather seat. Somehow I know I can close my eyes here and be safe even though we're speeding down the road at eighty miles per hour. As long as I'm here with James at the wheel and Susan riding shotgun, I don't have to worry. Everything is very clearly under control.

Later . . .

We're here! Finally. Lake Powell is the most amazing thing I have ever seen. I'll write more about that later. Anyway, we rolled in around 4:30 p.m. and went to the place where our houseboat rental was waiting. James signed some paperwork, and then we all loaded our stuff on board. Jill's parents have the master stateroom on the lower level. Jill and I put our bags in one stateroom on the main deck, and Jack and Rob took the other, but Jill says the guys usually sleep on these big cushions on the upper deck under the stars. I just wanted to write that we got here. I'm not sure why, but I feel this anticipation in my chest, an energy I'm not sure what to do with. I'm trying to figure out if I'm scared or excited. Maybe both?

The motor just roared to life, and the boys started whooping. Jack poked his head in the door. He has changed into a striped tank top and board shorts, and says I should put down my pen right this second and come to the upper deck or I'd miss my first sunset on the lake.

Later . . .

Jack was right about not missing the sunset. I followed him up the stairs to the top deck. We stood at the rail next to Jill and Rob. The engine was loud and the vibrations made my feet hum as the wind whipped through my hair. Jill smiled at me and I pushed my sunglasses up on my nose.

Slowly, Jill's dad maneuvered the boat out of the cove and

around the side of a sheer rock cliff that glowed the molten color of hot lava. As we made the turn, I saw the sun, blazing low on the water's razor edge. Fiery beams shot toward us across the flat surface of the lake, smearing orange and red across a bright blue summer sky crowned with clouds the color of royalty.

It took my breath away. I felt the radiant heat flash across my face and bore into my skin. My eyes watered at the brightness and the beauty and Jill must've heard me gasp, because I felt her hand over mine on the rail. Rob stood on the other side of Jill, and I felt him brush my shoulder as he placed his arm around Jill's shoulders. We watched in silence, the wind on our faces as the sun began to sink below the cliff line, almost as if someone had flipped a switch. As the four of us stood there transfixed I felt Jack's bare arm brush lightly against mine. I caught my breath again but didn't dare look at him. I felt my arm tense as he leaned against the rail, but he didn't move away, and I relaxed into him ever so slightly.

As the sun dropped out of sight completely, we made our way into the middle of the lake and heard people on two other boats in opposite directions far across the water clapping and cheering nature's fireworks. Rob and Jill joined in and we heard James whistling at the wheel one level below. Jack didn't move his hands from the rail to clap, and I didn't either. My heart was beating fast as I stared out across the purple sky, bruised from the blistering glory of the sunset. The buzz of the engine that I'd felt in my feet spread across my entire body, emanating now, it seemed, from the muscles of Jack's arm, taut and warm against my own.

No one was looking when he leaned closer and whispered two words into my ear: "So beautiful."

I nodded, and started to tell him it was the prettiest sunset I'd ever seen, but when I turned to face him, he wasn't looking at the sky.

I felt my cheeks flush, and I was suddenly glad I'd put on my sunglasses. Jack's eyes were kind and full. I tried to will my tongue to work, but I couldn't move or speak, until finally, Susan peeked her head over the top step of the upper deck and called to all of us, "Who's hungry?"

Sunday, June 17

Last night at dinner, we all helped Susan unload the coolers and boxes of food we picked up at the grocery store near the marina. She'd brought a few things from home and has the stocking and distribution of the boat's tiny kitchen down to a science. She unloaded and directed and pointed and explained like a well-oiled machine until the food was put away and the coolers whisked out of sight. Rob and Jack were shown where their stash of junk food was stored, along with a strict warning about breaking into supplies for family meals.

To that end, a menu has been posted on the refrigerator. It's laminated. (Just saying. Susan is like one of those women who has her own cooking show.) It maps out food for the week and I saw we'd be docking at a couple of restaurants along the way for dinner. The menu also stipulates which meals Jill's parents will be cooking and which ones will be "do it yourself" affairs. This mainly happens at lunch. Jill explained that those are times when we'll all just make sandwiches out of deli turkey or salads from the fresh organic romaine Susan brought in a cooler from home. Jill also noted that Jack typically consumes his own body weight in Twizzlers and Lucky Charms.

(How do guys eat *so much* and not gain a *single pound?*)

Anyway, after we got the kitchen unpacked, James fired up the grill and Rob and Jack were put in charge of flipping burgers and turning hot dogs. It was your basic cookout except Susan and James had flutes of champagne while grilling and white wine with dinner. There were bottles of Pellegrino and Mexican Coke ("no corn syrup," Susan said with a sniff) for everyone, and disposable silverware that was actually silver. Even the plates and napkins were thicker and more absorbent than the crinkly paper and Styrofoam my mom usually buys. We ate sitting on the top deck. There's a table that folds up next to the bench seats around the railing. I'm sitting on one of them now writing this, while Jill tans on one of the big cushions that stow away in cabinets but are big enough to sleep on. Jack and Rob slept up here last night. Jill was secretly thrilled when Rob tried to get her to sneak up after her parents went to bed:

Rob: C'mon. It'll be so romantic under the stars.

Jill: Until my mother catches me and tosses you overboard.

Rob: I'm a good swimmer. I'll risk it.

Jill had laughed and went back to . . . well, sipping Pellegrino. I swear that's all she consumed last night. It might be all she had yesterday, period. I realized she took a hot dog with no bun and cut it up into tiny pieces, and pushed it around in big pools of ketchup and mustard. She fed a couple pieces to Rob, who remarked that her plate looked like a battle reenactment, but I'm pretty sure she didn't actually have anything to eat. At all.

And come to think of it, when we stopped for coffee and lunch and snacks for the guys on the way out here, Jill always ordered a drink, but I can't remember her actually eating anything. At Starbucks she got a Venti iced coffee with two Splendas and poured a dollop of nonfat milk into it.

The thing is, she's still on her phone checking CalorTrack at least once an hour, and I'm curious. What is she keeping track of? I know she's really working hard in ballet and last night her mom mentioned seeing Misty Jenkins and her boyfriend Todd when she was coming out of the grocery store back home. Jill rolled her eyes and moaned.

Jack: What?

Jill: I will not dance behind her in *The Nutcracker* one more time.

Rob: My sister says she has a mustache. Last week Misty came into the salon where I worked and had her lip and cheeks and arms waxed.

Me: Her arms?

Jack: That's one hirsute ballerina.

Jill: Hirsute?

Rob (laughing): You think *your* vocab quizzes were hard this year? Just wait until Frau Schroeder gets ahold of you this fall.

Jack: You'll beat Misty out for Clara this fall, Sis. I know it.

Jill: If I don't, I'm not dancing.

Susan: Well, you've never been in better shape, honey.

Me: No kidding. You haven't eaten a carb since Christmas.

Susan: You know, they say that carbs are killing us.

Rob (stuffing an entire brownie into his mouth): Bring it on.

James: You deserve to be Clara because you're a fantastic dancer. Just because that girl is a stick figure doesn't mean she can sell it.

Jill: Thanks, Daddy.

Susan (raising her chardonnay): To Jill in the role of Clara.

Rob: And to mustachioed Misty. She'll make a great Sugar Plum *Hairy*.

Everybody laughed, and drank, and then Jill excused herself, headed in the direction of the bathroom down the stairs from the top deck. As she went, I saw the glow of her phone on her face.

Jack just climbed up the ladder on the side of the boat and told me I should jump in. Maybe he's right. I've been sitting here writing while he and Rob jump off the top of the boat into the water, then climb back up. Jill is lying here with her darkest sunglasses on pretending not to pay any attention to Rob, but I know she's watching him. He and Jack are both already completely tan from the pool and as they climb up the ladder their board shorts cling to their legs, pulling the waistbands lower and lower and . . .

Well . . .

Frankly . . .

It's distracting.

Later . . .

Jill brought a *scale* onto the *boat*.

I repeat: a *scale* on *vacation*.

We just went downstairs to get more sunscreen and water. I went into the bathroom and when I came out, Jill was standing on the scale in our room.

Me: What are you doing.

Jill (looks down at scale, back at me, blinks): Is this a trick question?

Me: You brought a scale with you on vacation?

Jill: My body doesn't know it's on vacation. It doesn't magically stop turning calories into pounds because we're on a boat for a week.

Susan poked her head in the door at this precise moment. She went up to the roof deck holding a bottle of water and a paperback book with a very shiny cover, all legs and sunscreen and visor and sunglasses. She smiled at us, then asked Jill how things were coming along.

Jill: Doing well. Holding steady.

Susan: I'm very proud of you, Jilly Bean.

Jill: Every time you call me that I die a little bit inside.

Susan (laughing): You'll always be my little bean, darling. I'm glad to see you fighting for what you want. That Misty doesn't stand a chance.

Susan turned to leave, then stopped and looked back at me: And *you* are a *good friend*. Jill tells me you've been keeping track of your calories, too. It's always easier when you've got support. It certainly has paid off. You've never looked better.

I opened my mouth to explain that I was keeping track of my calories in the opposite direction—making sure I got *more* calories, not fewer—but something about the look on Susan's face stopped me. The beaming smile, the admiration, it felt warm on my skin like the sun up on the top deck.

I smiled back at her and shrugged: What are friends for?

Susan winked at me and said she wasn't the only who had noticed.

Jill: *Mom!* Please!

Susan: What? Of *course* Jack would notice. I mean, look at the figure on this one. All this calorie counting and running is working out very well.

Susan put down her water bottle and book and draped an arm across my shoulders. She said she knew things must've been hard around home lately. I didn't really want to think about what was going on with my parents, much less talk about it, but Susan has this way of looking at you like you're the only person in the world who matters. Something about her smile makes you want to tell her everything. She should be a talk show host. Or a detective.

Me: I guess heartbreak is good for the abs.

Susan (laughing): That it is, sweetheart, that it *is*. But you hang in there, and keep doing what you're doing. All that baby fat has disappeared, and if you keep at it, you'll be turning every head in the hallway come fall. Jack will have his work cut out for him.

Jill must've seen me blush because she stepped off the scale, handed Susan her book and water bottle, and began pushing her out of our room.

Susan (laughing): Okay! Okay! I'm going.

Once she was gone, Jill turned to me and apologized.

Jill: Sorry about that.

Me: It's not a problem. She was just being sweet.

Jill: I haven't lost a single pound in the last two days.

Me: Is that a problem?

Jill: Yes. I've plateaued. You, on the other hand, look fantastic. When was the last time you weighed yourself?

Me: Not since our chocolate chip IHOP debacle.

Jill stepped off the scale and pointed to it. I sighed and stepped onto the square glass platform. The digital display flickered, then froze at 126.7. Jill screeched.

Jill: I can't believe it. You've been practically gorging yourself to keep running.

Me: Not so much lately. I haven't been hitting my calorie goals. I'm supposed to eat at least 2,500 to 2,800 calories on the days I run, and 2,000 to 2,500 on the days I don't.

Jill: Dear God. That's like an entire extra meal. Hope you're hungry.

Me: Well, I don't want to balloon out while I'm on the boat. I mean, I'm not running at all this week.

Jill said she was limiting her calories this week to 1,700 per day, and pointed out that it wasn't too far off from my 2,000-calorie "rest day" goal. She grinned and asked me if I thought I could do it with her.

I didn't know exactly what to say. Not being around my mom and dad and the unending sadness at our house for only two days had brought back my appetite. I hadn't been able to eat much for a week, and now that I could actually eat again, the idea of controlling it just because I could felt exhilarating. Besides, it was only three hundred calories less than I'd have been eating anyway, and I'd only be doing it to help Jill.

I nodded: Sure. Let's do it.

Jill: Excellent. You know, this is exactly what successful people do when they come up against hardships in their lives.

Me: Wait . . . what do they do?

Jill: They take *control*.

Me: Of three hundred calories?

Jill: It's a start.

Monday, June 18
Weight: 127

Jill is hard-core about the scale and the calorie tracking. I guess I knew she was doing it, but being on this boat with her and sharing a room is pretty intense. She insists we weigh ourselves before we go to bed, and again after we get up.

Sorry, scratch that. When we get up, *after* going to the bathroom. She made me redo it this morning because I hadn't pooped yet.

Jill: That's just extra weight that's going to come out of you anyway.

Me: I'd really like to not talk about my bathroom habits with you.

Jill: Go do your business and come back.

Me (fingers in my ears): LA-LA-LA-LA-LA.

In the end she was correct. I weighed less afterward.

You wouldn't think three hundred calories would make that much difference, but it *does*. It was the difference between eating dessert last night and just having some tea while Jill and I watched Jack and Rob scarf down s'mores they made over the grill.

Tonight we're docking and going ashore for dinner at this restaurant in the marina. I had two hard-boiled eggs and a cup of strawberry yogurt for breakfast this morning. According to CalorTrack that's 412 calories. For lunch the guys made deli sandwiches and Jill and I had turkey-and-cheese roll-ups. Each turkey slice had twenty-five calories and each cheese slice had eighty, so I used half a cheese slice with each piece of turkey and had six roll-ups for a total of 390 calories. That means if I stick to our plan of 1,700 calories per day, I've only got 898 calories left, which should be plenty for dinner tonight.

The problem is this: I'm hungry *now*, and it's only *two in the afternoon*. How am I going to hold out for another *five hours* until we get to the restaurant at seven tonight?

Jill and I are drinking so much water we've already run through a whole case of water bottles and we're going to stop to get more at the grocery store in the marina tonight. After lunch we were all floating on these big rafts tethered to the boat and Jill kept going inside to use the bathroom. Jack was making fun of her for not just peeing in the lake.

Jack: You have a bladder the size of a small walnut.

Jill: I will not pee in this lake.

Rob: Why not? The fish do.

Jack: So does Rob.

Rob (pushing Jack off the raft into the water): We won't tell anyone, I promise.

Jill: As a thinking vertebrate possessing the power of speech, limbs with which to climb a ladder, and a noted absence of gills, I will not be relieving myself in the water.

Jack climbed back onto the raft next to me as Rob followed Jill up the ladder to get a Coke and switch playlists on the iPhone playing through the speakers on the deck.

Jack: You having fun?

I smiled and nodded: It's beautiful here.

Jack: Did you know Lake Powell is man-made?

Me: No. Really?

Jack: Yep. Glen Canyon Dam was built across the Colorado River and flooded Glen Canyon.

As I stared up at the sheer cliffs, bright and orange, towering above us against a cloudless blue sky, I couldn't believe it. "Man," it seems to me, is so bad at coming up with truly beautiful things on a grand scale—especially in nature. My mom is forever talking about the Beautiful New Shopping Center, or the Beautiful New Hospital Wing, or that Beautiful New Condo Development, but none of those things seem very beautiful to me. I suppose they are nice in a certain way. I guess the new outdoor mall with the dancing fountains beats the old indoor mall from the eighties with the brown glazed brick and the orange-tile waterfall in the middle that smelled like chlorine and dirty feet.

Still, as I gazed around at the canyon walls I couldn't believe that someone had planned something so perfect and serene, so vibrant and brilliant, full of color and texture and endless sky. Something so . . .

Romantic, isn't it?

(That was Jack.)

I was blown away that he'd said that word just as I was thinking it. I blushed, but I don't think he could tell because my cheeks are a little pink anyway from the sun.

Me (softly): Yeah. It is.

Jack was lying on his back, one hand under his head. I'd been trying not to watch the drops of water that were slowly trickling off his chest and pooling in the little indentations between his abs.

I rolled over onto my back on the raft. The cool water against my legs and the sun warming the wet fabric of the new bikini top stretched across my chest gave me goose bumps. I felt Jack reach out with his free hand and grab my raft, pulling his over. I turned my head to glance at him through my sunglasses but he was staring up at the sky.

We lay there in silence letting the sight of the cliffs against the sky and the heat of the sun on our skin wash over us. There was something electric in the air that I'd never felt before—like someone or something had sucked all the air out of my lungs with a vacuum and I couldn't get a good deep breath.

I realized, floating there under the wide blue sky on rafts tied to the boat, that it was the feeling of anticipation. It felt like something was about to happen.

It felt like something *should* happen.

And then something did.

Jack: They named Lake Powell after John Wesley Powell.

Me: Who was he?

Jack: A one-armed Civil War vet. He explored the Colorado River and this canyon in a wooden boat.

Me: With one arm?

I felt Jack's hand against mine. His fingers were sure and steady as he threaded them through my own. This time when I turned my head, he was looking right at me, a sweet smile on his lips and a twinkle in his blue eyes, as clear and endless as the sky above us.

Jack: Better hold hands while we've still got 'em.

So we did. All afternoon. Even when Jill and Rob came back, Jack didn't let go. Finally, Susan called over the side of the boat from the upper deck and said it was time for us to get cleaned up so we could eat at the marina. We swam to the boat and as Rob and Jill climbed the ladder ahead of us Jack asked if I would be his date to dinner.

I told him yes.

Now I have no idea what to wear. Jill is in the shower and I've dumped both of our bags onto the big bed in our room and I'm trying to find the right top. Thank God Jill told me to bring a skirt. It's a white mini that's perfect for summer—not too short, but looks good with sandals. I got a new top that ties behind my neck. It's the color of a tomato. Jill swears it makes my blue eyes pop. As soon as she gets out of the bathroom I'll wash my hair and survey the sun damage. Hopefully my face isn't too red. I don't want to look like a lobster in this shirt.

I just realized I'm writing about what outfit I'm going to wear. I swear. One cute, sweet guy holds my hand and suddenly, I'm *that* girl. . . .

Whatever. I'm going to let myself be excited. Because I *am*.

I want to not worry about my parents' love life. I want to have one of my own.

Tuesday, June 19
Weight: 126.5

I woke up s-t-a-r-v-i-n-g this morning. No one else was awake yet because we were all up so late last night. (More on that in a moment. But first . . .) I went into the kitchen to get a cup of yogurt. I tried to take small bites and deep breaths in between.

Jill swears that this helps her to eat more slowly. She calls it being "mindful." Apparently the theory is that the food is more satisfying if you are truly aware and conscious of what you're eating instead of just scarfing it down. Which would seem like a good idea, and generally it is. I ate the yogurt slowly and "mindfully" and then drank a bottle of water very "mindfully" and had turned to put the bottle into the recycling bin when I saw the cabinet where Rob and Jack's junk food is stashed. The door was open, and I saw a pack of those little powdered doughnut gems. These doughnuts are my breakfast food kryptonite. I am powerless against their pull. I tore open the cellophane almost before I knew what I was doing and popped one of the tiny powdery doughnuts into my mouth in one bite. I was biting into the second one when I sort of came to. I stood there, frozen, like I had come out of a doughnut gem blackout wondering how I'd gotten here. The doughnut suddenly swelled in my mouth and I saw there was powdered sugar down the front of my sleep shirt. I felt my heart racing as I turned the package over to read the calorie information: 240 calories per serving. Serving size: four doughnuts. That meant every doughnut was sixty calories. Sixty calories in a tiny doughnut I could eat in one bite! The powdered sugar had melted in my mouth and the thick sludge of sweet cake felt like it might choke me if I tried to swallow. I rushed over to the trash can to spit out the doughnut in my mouth. At least I could save an extra sixty calories.

I opened my mouth over the garbage and pushed the mushy clump of calories out with my tongue. I watched the glob tumble from my mouth into the trash bag, and at that exact moment, to my sheer and utter horror, I realized I was not alone. Slowly, I looked up and my eyes met Susan's. I don't know how long Jill's mom had been standing at the counter, but judging from the look on her face, it had been long enough to see me cram a doughnut into my mouth, then check the label on the package and wheel around to spit it out.

There have been several embarrassing moments in my life, but none of them compares in even the smallest of ways with *this* moment. I am unsure how to even write how I felt except to say I wished a hole would open in the boat and I would be sucked to the bottom of the lake and drowned. I would rather have faced death than to have figured out what to say to Susan. Her eyes were sort of wide and I noticed that even this early on the fourth day of a vacation to the lake, her blond hair was thrown up in a twist that *looked* careless and jaunty but was actually planned and perfect. As her gaze drifted from the crumbs on my lips and the white powder dusting my T-shirt to the torn cellophane package in my hand, her perfectly lined lids slowly relaxed into a cool stare.

I straightened up, swiping at my mouth and shirt, trying to dust away the crumbs but only spreading the white confectioner's sugar in a small cloud. I tried to swallow but my mouth was a desert and the longer I stood there in silence the more panicked I became until finally, Susan said, "Well, good morning," and stepped to the counter to make coffee.

I was seized by the urge to make an excuse, to try to find some way to explain why I was covered in sugar and spitting doughnuts into the trash. I felt a fear in the pit of my stomach that didn't make sense. It wasn't a fear that Jill would find out or that Jack would care. It was a fear that I'd disappointed Susan. I folded the cellophane over on the doughnuts and slipped them back into the junk food cabinet and closed the door, then turned to Susan, stammering like a fool.

Me: I . . . I'm just . . . Wow. Those doughnuts are my Achilles' heel.

Susan: Well, we all have our secrets.

Me: Jill has been working so hard, and I want to be a good friend to her. Apparently powdered doughnuts make me a raving lunatic.

Susan: Yes, she would be disappointed, but I won't tell her. Besides. You don't have to worry about being in shape for ballet.

Something about her smile when she said this was like a knife slicing through my chest. It wasn't the extra sixty calories I'd just swallowed that made my stomach hurt, it was the crushing shame of having let Susan down. I was supposed to be a good friend to Jill. I wanted to be pretty enough for Jack. Susan's vision for her son's girlfriend was certainly lean and graceful like her, not wolfing down doughnuts over the trash can. Is this the person I've become? Sneaking bites like my mom? News flash: not a good way to keep a guy interested. If it didn't work for my dad it certainly won't work for a guy as handsome as Jack.

I didn't know what else to say to Susan so I slipped past her to go back to the room I share with Jill. As I did, she turned and stopped me with a hand on my arm.

Susan: You were so beautiful last night. Jack couldn't take his eyes off you. I just wouldn't want you to start forming bad habits that would get in the way of that.

My cheeks were burning, but I forced myself to meet her gaze. This was what tough love must feel like. Susan was telling me the *truth*. She was saying what I *needed* to hear instead of what I *wanted* to hear. Maybe if my mom had a friend like Susan she wouldn't have wound up sobbing into my shoulder while clutching a pint of ice cream. Maybe someone telling her the truth would have kept her from losing my dad.

I nodded at Susan, who smiled at me, then pulled me toward her and kissed my forehead, then poured herself a cup of coffee and asked where my new polka-dot bikini top was hiding.

Susan: Jill couldn't stop talking about what a knockout you

were when you tried it on in the store. I haven't seen it yet!

I smiled and she winked at me as I slipped out of the kitchen and back into my room, where Jill was still asleep. Quietly, I pulled off my sugarcoated T-shirt and fished the polka-dot swimsuit and a little pair of cutoffs from my bag. I also grabbed this journal so I could write about what just happened. I'm sitting in the bathroom on the edge of the tub writing.

It made me feel so good when Jill's mom said Jack couldn't take his eyes off me last night—mainly because I'd felt that too, but I wasn't sure if I was just dreaming. It's nice to have confirmation of good things. Sometimes I get excited about things, and then instantly I feel silly and afraid. This voice in my head tells me that this just *can't* be happening, and that I shouldn't be excited about it because somehow that will jinx it.

Last night Jill and I were getting ready while Rob and Jack helped her dad dock the boat at the marina. When we felt the boat stop and heard the dull roar of the engine go quiet, Jill was changing outfits.

Again.

For the seventh time.

You wouldn't think we'd have had that many outfit changes between us on a trip where we were limited to one bag each.

Let me assure you that this was not the case. We only had three skirts between us, not counting the white one I was wearing. Jill tried on almost every top with almost every skirt.

Me: He's already completely smitten with you. I'm not sure why you're in a panic about what you wear tonight.

Jill (wide-eyed pronouncement face): I am not reacting to panic. I am enacting perfection.

Me: We may miss the appetizers is all I'm saying.

Jill: You can't rush perfection.

Me: No, but you can't eat it either, and if I don't have some food soon, I may lack the strength to actually carry myself down the gangplank under my own power.

At that moment, we heard Susan call for us down the hallway from the stairs that lead out onto the main deck, and Jill took one last look in the mirror before turning and leading the way out of our room, onto the deck, and down the walkway to the dock, where Jack, his parents, and Rob stood waiting. Walking down the ramp, I felt like I was heading to dinner on the dock via a fashion show runway, and as I walked next to Jill, I could sense Jack's eyes on me immediately.

Naturally, Rob couldn't contain himself and let out a low whistle as Jill stepped onto the dock and took his arm. She smiled, then informed him that she was not a baseball game to be whistled at and shot him a look that silenced his joke about getting past third base before it had fully escaped his lips. In the awkward silence that followed, while James glared at Rob and Susan arched an eyebrow at Jill, I felt Jack's hand take mine for the second time that day. He leaned close and whispered into my ear.

Jack: You look great.

Me: I clean up okay.

Jack: Trust me, "okay" isn't the word I would use.

Me: And yet, I received no whistle.

Jack: Not my style.

Me: I like your style.

Jill had not been wrong about dinner: the restaurant was fantastic. The view across the lake was incredible. The sun set as the waiter offered us appetizers, and I caught myself having to ask Jack to repeat himself because I was trying to tally the rough number of calories contained in a small bowl of Southwest corn bisque as compared to the chopped salad. He asked me if I was nervous, and I smiled sheepishly and said maybe a little, even though I wasn't nervous about him, I was nervous about keeping my calories at 1,700 for the day. It dawned on me that I wasn't going to have very much fun if all I did was freak out about calories and lie about being nervous. I decided just to order what Jill was having and not worry about it. Luckily, the waiter went around the table starting with the ladies first in the order we were seated: Susan, Jill, me. Jill ordered the chopped salad to start and something called sixteen-spiced chicken with the mango butter sauce on the side. I followed suit.

Jack and Rob both got the barbecue ribs and Jack insisted I eat one of his, which I did. It was delicious, and I wished I'd gotten that instead of the chicken, but I knew pork ribs are not on a 1,700-calorie diet, so I savored the bite I had and left a little more of the sides on my plate. I kept checking to see if Jill was actually eating. I don't think she took more than a bite or two of her salad, and there was still so much chicken on her plate when the waiter came to offer dessert that her dad insisted he box it up so we could take it back to the boat.

Rob and James both ordered a Lake Powell Brownie Sundae, dripping in caramel and fudge, but Jack opted for the turtle cheesecake. Shockingly, Jill asked for a bite of her brother's dessert and I took one too. I held the rich, creamy bite in my mouth, savoring the combination of the slightly tart cheesecake with the buttery caramel sauce and crunchy graham cracker crust. I didn't realize I'd closed my eyes as I chewed until I opened them and saw Jack licking his fork with his eyebrow raised a little.

Jack: Good, huh?

Me: Transcendent.

Jack (offering another bite): Still hungry?

Me: No, thank you. Stuffed.

I wasn't stuffed, but I felt comfortable again. As I watched Jack place the last mouthful of cheesecake between his perfect lips, I realized I wasn't hungry for food. I was hungry for something else. I blushed when I had the thought, and glanced around quickly, as if I was afraid someone else at the table might've heard my thoughts or read my mind.

When we got back to the boat Jill's dad pulled out of the marina and charted a course for farther out in the lake, where we found a place in a secluded cove to drop anchor and spend the night. Susan seemed especially vigilant about sleeping arrangements after Rob's joke on the way to dinner, so she supervised the Saying of the Good Nights on the upper deck. While Jill made Rob work for a peck on the cheek, Jack smiled at me by the light of the almost-full moon and stuck out his hand toward me as if we were finishing a business meeting in a conference room. I laughed and took it, giving it my firmest pump up and down.

But he didn't let go.

Instead he pulled me in and held our handshake tightly between us while he wrapped his other arm around me in a hug and said, "John Wesley Powell couldn't do this either, poor bastard."

Me: But he did have a wooden boat.

Jack: He had three, actually.

Me: You should stop hugging me now. Your mom is watching.

Jack: She's watching Jill.

Me: She's a wise woman.

Jack: Would you kiss me if she weren't watching right now?

Me: On the first date?

Jack: Yeah.

Me: Not my style.

It took me a long time to fall asleep last night. First, I listened to Jill tell me all about how mortified she was that Rob made that joke, and how she's just not certain if he's mature enough for her. I kept drifting away from what she was saying and thinking about lying on the raft with Jack until finally she said:

Hello?

Me: Sorry. What?

Jill: Wow.

Me: What?

Jill: You've got it bad.

Me: What?

Jill: You've just said "what" three times in a row. You've responded thrice with the word "what."

Me: I was just thinking....

Jill: Yes, yes, about my brother, yes, I know. I am still somewhat dizzy from disbelief.

Me: I think that might be hunger. We didn't eat enough food today to sustain the life of a minnow.

Jill: Might I take this moment to say it is *so* much easier to do this diet *with* someone?

Me: Enjoy it now. I might not survive the boat trip.

Finally, we turned off the light and lay there next to each other in bed. Jill said she wished we could sleep on the upper deck with the guys under the stars. Then she asked me a question.

Jill: So. You and Jack?

Me: Maybe.

Jill: How did this happen?

Me: I don't know exactly. We were lying on the rafts when you and Rob climbed on board this afternoon, and all of a sudden we were holding hands.

Jill: There were no other warning signs? You've known each other for over a decade.

Me: True, but only as your big brother, and me only as your best friend. Generally, every time he saw me at your place I was a sweaty mess after cross-country practice.

Jill just woke up and kicked me out of the bathroom. I can't believe I was in there writing for this long. Sitting on the edge of the tub doesn't feel so good, but I do feel better about the Great Doughnut Gem Incident in the kitchen this morning. Just like folding up socks and T-shirts in my dresser, I know where it goes now. In light of everything else I've written down, it doesn't seem so bad. A few moments of embarrassment, neatly tucked away.

Besides, it was only sixty extra calories. I'll just go easy at lunch.

And no more sneaking food.

I will not turn into my mother.

Wednesday, June 20
Weight: 126

This morning when I woke up, I sneaked into the kitchen and got a cup of yogurt and a bottle of water, then climbed up onto the upper deck. Rob and Jack were already in the water, both of them wearing goggles, swimming laps—sort of. They'd swim out from the boat, then turn around and swim back. Neither of them noticed me until they climbed back up the ladder, laughing and panting. Rob shook his dark curls like a wet dog and I squealed and tried to roll out of the way.

Rob: I'm hitting the shower.

Me: Good luck. I think Jill is in there.

Rob: Maybe I'll join her.

Jack: Dude. I'm standing right here.

Rob: Maybe I'll rephrase.

Me: Maybe you'll bring me another water as penance?

Rob: Anything for you, hot stuff.

Jack: Dude . . .

Rob: I know, I know. You're standing right there.

Rob disappeared down the ladder with his patented hangdog smirk firmly in place, and I laughed while Jack rolled his eyes and ran a hand through his short blond hair. He threw both arms up in the air and turned around slowly, taking in the sights around us once more. The sun glinted off the water droplets that coursed over his shoulders and followed the beautiful curves and divots of the muscles in his back before trickling down the waistband of his board shorts.

That's one thing for sure about this trip: The view never gets old.

(And the lake isn't bad either.)

Later . . .

He kissed me.

It's funny how you think you *know* how certain things are going to happen. I have them all planned out in my head. It's like the movie scripts we worked on last year in English. Mr. DeWalt brought in sample scripts and put us in groups and we each had to adapt a different scene from *To Kill a Mockingbird*. Anyway, we learned about writing the locations and the camera shots and dialogue, and now sometimes I catch myself scripting the things I should say, or wish I'd have said, or hope to get to say.

I was hoping he'd kiss me. Only in the script I had in my head, it was late at night on the upper deck under the big yellow moon, which seems to be getting lower and lower in the sky every evening. It's a waxing gibbous—almost full. (See, Mrs. Brewer? I did learn something in earth science.)

EXT. NIGHT—HOUSEBOAT ON LAKE POWELL

A yellow summer MOON hangs low in the sky, lighting purple cliffs and the eyes of seventeen-year-old JACK, standing at the railing with ME at his elbow.

JACK: It's almost perfect out here.

ME: Almost?

JACK: Yep. It's just . . .

ME: Just what?

JACK: There's too much noise.

ME (*laughing*): Too much noise? It's just us talking.

JACK (*devilish grin*): I know. I have to make that stop.

JACK takes me in his ARMS.

EXT. NIGHT—CONTINUOUS

We push into a CLOSE-UP on JACK and ME kissing, first gently and then passionately, as we PULL OUT and swirl around them, circling them twice, then flying up and away over their heads and the boat zooming out across the water, up the side of the purple cliffs, and fading to white on the MOON.

But that's not how it happened.

We were lying on the rafts again, and Rob had just rolled off his into the water, splashing Jill into a narrow-eyed state of revenge that fueled her attempt to leap onto his head as he swam toward the boat, in an apparent attempt to drown him.

Of course, she weighs 108 pounds (as of this morning), and Rob just continued swimming toward the boat, dragging her along with him, until we were all laughing so hard that if they hadn't reached the ladder, they might actually have drowned in their own mirth. Rob asked Jack if he wanted something to eat and I realized I hadn't eaten since our turkey roll-ups at lunch, but today, I wasn't even hungry.

I realized my body has adjusted to Jill's 1,700 calories and I haven't even thought about it today. I've conquered 1,700 calories! It's almost dinnertime, and I haven't looked at the sun over the cliffs and tried to guess how close we are to being able to eat again, or asked Rob what time it is on his big waterproof watch. As I thought about this, I smiled to myself. Not a big, crazy smile, just a tiny "to myself" smile, and Jack looked at me as I did and he noticed my private smile and he got a tiny smile himself.

EXT. DAY—LAKE POWELL—CONTINUOUS

Camera floats above JACK and ME lying on separate rafts, facing each other.

JACK: What?

ME: Nothing.

JACK: It doesn't look like nothing.

ME: What does it look like?

JACK: I dunno. Like you're . . . happy.

ME: I guess I am.

JACK: When you smile like that it makes me want to kiss you.

ME: Oh, really?

JACK: Yeah, really.

JACK reaches out and pulls my raft closer, then puts one hand on my cheek and leans over and places his lips against mine. He is gentle and his lips taste like ChapStick, warm and smooth against mine. I feel the sun hot on my back, and the water is warm on my legs as I reach out toward his raft, trying to pull him closer to me. I feel his tongue brush against mine, and his breath on my cheek as he tries to adjust into a better angle on his raft, then—

CUT TO WIDE SHOT—EXT. LAKE POWELL—CONTINUOUS

JACK jerks away as his raft slips out from under him. He splashes and thrashes into the water, pulling ME along with him. We laugh and cough, then JACK drapes his arm around his raft and pulls ME close with the other. Suddenly, our legs are tangled up, and my arms are around his broad shoulders, holding on.

ME (*nervous laughing*): Don't want to pull you under.

JACK: You're weightless in the water.

ME (*rolling my eyes*): I am not.

JACK pulls ME even tighter.

JACK (*whispers*): I got you.

JACK kisses ME again. This time we melt into each other and we kiss for a long time, bodies wrapped around each other, his arm pulling me tightly against him.

CAMERA PULLS OUT—LAKE POWELL—CONTINUOUS

Camera pulls away from JACK and ME floating in the clear cool water, pans up the orange canyon walls standing guard around us, and fades into the bright rays of the desert sun.

I guess it wasn't particularly graceful. It wasn't the script I'd written, that's for sure, but when Jack kissed me it was perfect, just as it happened.

I'm ready for the sequel.

Thursday, June 21
Weight: 127

Today was our last full day on the water, and Jill was right
about one thing: her parents got tanked at dinner and were
downstairs in their stateroom by 11 p.m. After her parents
disappeared, Jill snuck downstairs with Rob and came back
with an open bottle of chardonnay they'd left on the counter
and cups for all of us. Dad let me have a sip of wine once
at his brother's wedding, but I'd never been handed a whole
glass.

Rob made a toast about "gorgeous scenery" and "lovely
ladies" and "a week to remember" and Jack laughed and rolled
his eyes, and then held his glass up and looked straight at me.

Jack: To more than friends.

If the moon hadn't been so bright, no one would've seen
me blush, but it was and they did. Rob made a horse sound. Jill
smacked his bare arm. Jack and I laughed, and then we pulled
out the big cushions the guys have been sleeping on all week
and lay down on them and stared up at the stars.

Lying next to Jack on the deck felt different from floating
next to him in the water. He had one hand under his head, and
I used his biceps and shoulder as a pillow. I fit perfectly against

him, my head tucked up under his chin. He felt so sturdy, every inch of him solid and strong. Jill was holding forth on the evils of light pollution and I knew without looking at her that she was wearing her wide-eyed pronouncement face. Then all of a sudden she stopped yammering on midsentence and I glanced over to see Rob kissing her. Jack knew what was happening without looking and groaned that they should get a room. Jill giggled and Rob said "gladly" and they went belowdecks, leaving Jack and me with the sound of the water against the boat.

The stars were so bright out here, and there were so many that the sky looked almost hazy with stripes of twinkling beams. Jack was quiet, and every time he took a breath, I felt his chest rise and fall against my body. It was a different kind of floating, a tide that made me feel like I was drifting closer to him—not physically, but on the inside. Jack must have felt it too, because right at that moment he turned and kissed my hair. He didn't say anything at all, just held his lips there, and he took a deep breath, like he was trying to breathe me in.

The wine was making my head warm, and I felt my heart speed up as I pressed my whole body closer to his. In one slow movement, he rolled toward me and slid his arm under the small of my back, pulling me tightly against him. His lips found mine and he kissed me long and deeply, like he was hungry and he couldn't get enough. I wrapped both arms around his broad shoulders and felt the strength pulsing through his whole body as he held me close. I felt so safe, tucked beneath him, his thick arm wrapped around me, holding on to me like he was drowning in the warmth of my breath and I was the only thing that would keep him afloat.

I slid my hands under the hem of his tank top and let my fingers wander up the knots of muscle in his back and shoulders. He rolled a little to the side, and I felt his hand on my cheek, then it slid down my neck and over my shirt. For a second I was worried. I wished my breasts were bigger and wondered how they felt under his fingers. His touch was firm like the rest of him, but gentle, and suddenly I had goose bumps on my arms. I wanted him to *like* touching me, to *like* the feel of my body as much as I liked the feel of his.

All at once I was so glad that I'd been watching my calories with Jill. I felt lean and pretty under the spell of Jack's hands. I reached up and touched his face, and he moaned softly as his hand found the soft bare skin of my stomach, and he moved his face there, planting tender kisses just above the waist of my shorts, my fingers tangled in his hair.

Right at that second, we heard Jill and Rob laughing on the

stairs. Jack moved back up for a quick kiss on the forehead and whispered one word in my ear:

Damn.

He looked at me with the sweetest smile, his eyes on fire, his cheeks flushed. I winked at him and whispered:

To be continued.

Rob had brought up another half-full bottle of white wine, and we all lay on the cushions laughing and talking and staring at the stars. We must've drifted off to sleep because at some point, Jill was shaking my shoulder and whispering that we had to get back downstairs before her mom got up. The light was gray and purple over the cliffs as I slipped out from underneath Jack's arm and tiptoed back belowdecks to the room I shared with Jill. She fell asleep as soon as we were between the sheets, but I couldn't think about anything but writing all of this down. I have to try to organize what is going on in my head, and inside my heart. I've never kissed a boy like that before. Mom is always saying I have to keep my head on my shoulders and keep boys' hands off to the side. I guess I've always been afraid of not knowing what would happen if a guy actually *did* touch me like that.

There's something about Jack—something I can see in his eyes, and hear in his voice, and feel in his touch—that I know will never hurt me. I wasn't afraid of having him touch me, only that I wouldn't be good enough somehow, and after what happened last night, I'm pretty sure that isn't an issue.

Jill is lying here snoring a little bit and drooling on her pillow a lot, and I'm scribbling in this food diary like a crazy person. I can't even think about closing my eyes. I have this floaty feeling just beneath my chin—almost like a bubble of pure happiness and excitement, mixed with that feeling when you go over the first drop of a roller coaster. I'm not sure I'd call it love. I don't think I've ever been in *love* before. That word seems so . . . serious. Maybe this is what Jill means when she says she's in *lust* with Rob, but I feel like this isn't *just* about Jack having a hot body, or being turned on by him. I think this feeling is probably a crush. It's been growing inside of me since that day at the pool when I first saw Jack as something different from my best friend's brother. It's a feeling that's grown a lot during this week on the boat. It's a feeling I think could grow into love.

I just heard Jill's mom start coffee in the kitchen. We're headed back to the marina this morning. The boat has to be returned by noon, and then we are driving back home this afternoon.

Ugh. Home.

I've barely thought about Mom and Dad and that whole situation since I got here. It makes my stomach hurt. I wonder if

Mom is still crying a lot. You know what? I'm not going to start thinking about it now. I've got one last whole day with Jack, and I'm not going to let myself waste it worrying about how my mom feels.

I'm also not going to let Rob sit next to Jack on the way home.

Sunday, June 24
Weight: 126

Two things were waiting for me when I arrived at home.

1. A shiny new hybrid SUV from my father with more luxury options than I have ever seen on one automobile in my entire life.
2. A shiny-headed, nearly comatose mother, asleep on the couch. I don't think she washed her hair the entire time I was away. She barely moved when I came in the door except when I asked her where the SUV came from.

Mom: Your father.
Me: Why?
Mom (pointing): Note on the counter.

I found a card on the counter, next to a key fob that looked like it might power a spaceship or hold the digital data of a blueprint for the colonization of Mars. In my father's square script were the words:

Want you to be safe on the roads. I know this won't fix things. Maybe it will help.
I love you,
Dad

I stood and stared at the key ring for a full five minutes. The TV was ablaze with a drag queen spatter-painting a bedroom wall, and Mom was staring at it glassy-eyed, not really seeing it. I crumpled the card up and tossed it into the recycling bin, then slipped the key into my pocket and dragged my bag upstairs.

Jack and I sat in the backseat together all the way home. He held my hand, and I fell asleep against his shoulder. I woke up as we drove into town, and the closer we got to my house, the worse my stomach felt. I realized I was dreading walking into the house, and when we'd pulled into the driveway, and I saw the only light coming from the windows was the TV, I knew I'd find Mom asleep in her scrubs on the couch.

It was totally depressing.

Susan gave me a hug in the driveway and told me how glad

she was I'd come with them, and that I was welcome anytime. She made a point of grabbing both of my shoulders and looking right into my eyes and repeating: *Anytime*.

Jack and Rob kept asking where the SUV in the driveway came from, and I kept telling them I didn't know, even though I deep down inside, I knew exactly where it came from. Dad was right. This SUV doesn't fix anything.

But it helps.

I unpacked and went to bed. Yesterday was Saturday, and when I woke up late and Mom was still on the couch, I put my foot down. I made her get up and take a shower. I called the salon we go to and made an appointment, and I dragged her down the stairs to the shiny new SUV, pushed her into the driver's seat, then took her to get a cut, her roots done, and her eyebrows waxed. While she was in the chair, I got a text from Jack.

Jack: Missed you at bfast.

Me: ditto

Jack: whose SUV?

Me: mine ;) peace offering from pop

Jack: NO WAY

Me: way

Jack: I want a ride.

Me: At salon on mayday mission with mom. Call you later.

It was good to get Mom out of the house. She looked

better on the outside after our salon trip and a salad at Lulu's Café across the street. She didn't feel any better on the inside, though. I tried to cheer her up by doing a school-report-worthy rundown of my vacation: My Week at Lake Powell. It was mildly edited. I showed her all the pictures and videos I took with my phone. Rob had brought along these thick plastic zipper bags that sealed tightly, and we took a lot of pictures out on the rafts. I flipped past a couple of Jack and me. I don't want to have to answer questions about him just yet. If I start telling everybody about him, I'm afraid I'll lose that floaty feeling under my chin. I want to keep it all to myself right now.

Mom smiled and halfheartedly munched on her salad, but back at home, she wound up on the couch again for another solid six hours. She was there again when I woke up this morning. All she can do is mope around and talk about how skinny and tan and beautiful I look. It makes me feel sort of frantic on the inside because I want to *do* something about this. It seemed she was doing okay with the whole divorce thing when I left. Now she appears to be falling apart.

I know this is a crappy thing to say about your own mom, but all I could think when I walked in the door on Friday night and saw her sleeping on the couch with greasy hair and dirty scrubs was that Susan would *never* let herself look like that. Ever. She'd go to the guillotine in tailored, matching separates, and her final request would be that someone blot the oil off her forehead so she wouldn't be shiny when she went to meet her maker.

I guess everybody is different.

I'm really glad I had that moment in the kitchen on the boat with the doughnut. It wasn't very fun at the time, but coming back and seeing Mom in this state makes me think it was a good wake-up call when Susan caught me sneaking food. That's how it starts, I think. First you sneak a doughnut, then it's a pint of ice cream, then you're fifteen pounds overweight and your husband is taking somebody else to Korean barbecue.

Monday, June 25
Weight: 126.5

When Vanessa and Geoff showed up to run this morning, they acted like they hadn't seen me since the Paleolithic period. Both of them talked at the same time while we did warm-up stretches. Finally, I just started running because I had to get them winded so only one of them could talk at a time. I thought my run would be horrible because I'd been on the boat for a week, but I think my body actually needed the rest because it felt great to stretch my legs. We decided to time ourselves on a five-mile run, and I couldn't believe it, but I beat Vanessa. I shaved almost a whole minute off my time. They started talking over each other again:

Vanessa: Did you eat anything on that boat?

Me: What? Yes.

Geoff: Your run was awesome, and you look great.

Vanessa: I can't believe it. How'd you manage to lose a couple pounds? You were floating around all day while I was running my butt off.

Geoff: Lighter equals faster!

Of course, that's when Vanessa reminded me we'd have to turn in our printouts from CalorTrack this week at practice. I just looked through my printouts and the numbers are really low. I was kind of surprised at how little Jill and I actually ate. The thing is, I still feel good. Plus, my run today was great. I'll just tell Coach that I cut back because I wasn't running. If she doesn't buy it, I guess I can tell her I'm still not feeling well after the split and everything. If I run as well on Thursday as I did today, she might not be worried about it at all.

Wednesday, June 27
Weight: 126

Mom was working tonight, and Jill called me to see if I wanted to go shopping with her. Jack came into her room while we were talking and this is what I heard:

Jill: What?

Jack: Lemme talk to her.

Jill: What? No. You also own a cell phone. Call her yourself.

Jack: I already did.

Jill: God! You're *hopeless*.

Jill: I've been telling my brother he can't call and text you every five minutes or he'll scare you off. I told him he needs to play it cool. I don't think he really understands the concept.

I was laughing, and I felt my cheeks get warm. Jack and I have been texting like crazy since we got back, and yesterday I drove by in my SUV and took him and Jill for a ride. Since my mom is working most nights, or comatose in front of the TV, I've been going to bed and talking to him before I go to sleep. I'd been sitting on my hands, trying not to call him—to let him make the first move—but it is hard! This feeling I have is more like a roller coaster and less like extreme happiness. Sometimes I think if I don't kiss him again soon, I might disappear in a little puff of white smoke. It made me relieved to know that he was having a hard time not calling and texting more too.

Jill: How did this happen?

Me: What?

Jill: You and Jack?

Me: I don't know. I just . . . saw him at the pool that day.

Jill: I *knew* it.

Me (laughing): What?

Jill: We were walking down that hill toward the car outside the swim club, and I turned around to find Rob. You had your eyes *glued* to Jack. You didn't even hear me when I asked if you wanted to ride with me or Geoff and Vanessa. You just followed us down the hill and climbed into the car with us.

It was true. She was right. That day had changed everything.

Me: Jack and Jill went down the hill . . .

Jill: And you came tumbling after.

Me: (laughing): Something like that.

Jill: You're the worst! You don't even deny it.

Me: Why should I?

Jill: My best friend has the hots for my brother. It goes against the natural order of things.

I could hear her smiling when she said it.

Me: Does that mean I have to choose between you?

Jill: Not if you'll come to the store with me.

She's on her way to pick me up now. I thought she wanted to go to the mall, but she wants to go to Whole Foods. She's got big plans for the next phase of our slim down, which apparently includes a lot of sugar-free gelatin desserts, organic brown rice cakes, dark, leafy greens, and hard-boiled egg whites. It sounds awful.

Jack just texted:

Come by before Jill drops u off. Wanna show you something.

I think I will. Maybe not having Dad at home at nights while Mom is working isn't such a bad idea.

Later . . .

Jill insisted on buying me the same groceries she got for herself. She said she's going to try to get down to 1,000 calories per day this week.

Me: I don't think I can do that.

Jill: Sure you can. You'll actually feel *more* full because these rice cakes totally swell up inside you and fill you up.

Me: Yeah, but I have to run a lot, and Coach is going to expect a lot more calories than I can get from rice cakes and leafy greens.

Jill: So? Just enter extra food. Just because you put it in the app doesn't mean you have to eat it.

This hadn't crossed my mind before. I really like Coach Perkins. She's been so understanding about the whole thing with my dad. I don't really want to lie to her, but my time did get a lot better after I lost a couple pounds. Plus, I know Jill likes having a friend to do this with.

Me: Maybe I can just stay at 1,200 calories.

Jill: Whatever you can do will help. I mean, you saw the

way Jack has gotten hooked on you over the last couple of weeks. What you're doing is working. I wouldn't stop now if I were you.

We pulled into her driveway, and Jack was waiting on the steps. He had this little smirk on his face. Jill took her bag of groceries in and said she was giving us ten minutes and then she was coming back out so we'd better not be steaming up the windows when she did.

Jack grabbed my hand and led me around the house, through the side gate, and into the backyard. My heart was racing the minute he touched my hand. Their backyard has always looked like one of those yards you see on TV shows. The grass around their pool is always perfect and green, and Jack led me down to the double porch swing that hangs at one end of a pergola near the fire pit. He held the swing still while I sat down on it, then he sat next to me and pushed us with his long legs.

I'd been a little nervous when he pulled me into the backyard. For some reason, my mind filled up with the idea that maybe he wanted to make out some more—go further this time. It's crazy what my brain can conjure up when left to its own devices. I had a horrible flash of his dad coming out onto the back steps and finding us practically naked, me scrambling for my bra.

I opened my mouth to say something, but he just said, "Sh!" and pointed up to a giant, round moon that was hanging low in the sky. I hadn't noticed it was full until that moment. He squeezed my hand, and the two of us just sat and stared up at the moon in silence.

As the swing slowed down, my heart sped up and I felt that thickness in the air again.

Me (whispering): Is this what you wanted to show me?

He nodded, then turned and looked at me. He slid one arm around my shoulders over the back of the swing, then reached up with his other hand and pulled my chin toward his. He kissed me once, lightly on the lips.

Jack: C'mon. Let's go say hi to my mom. She won't stop asking me about you.

Me: You showed her that picture on the raft, didn't you?

Jack: How'd you know?

Me: Because I knew my mom would never have let that one go.

He laughed, and my heart jumped at the light in his eyes and the cleft in his chin. Jack is the kind of guy I never had to worry about. This is the boy who wants me to come in and talk to his mom.

He's the boy who wants to show me the moon.

Thursday, June 28
Weight: 125.5

Vanessa is starting to get on my nerves. Ever since Jill and I got back from Lake Powell, she's been asking lots of questions—which is not abnormal or anything, just that they have *all* been on a single subject: eating.

Are you eating enough?

How many calories did you have?

Can I see your CalorTrack printouts?

Ever since we ran on Monday and I had a better five-mile time than she did, she's been all over it. At practice yesterday when we handed in our calorie printouts to Coach Perkins she wanted to compare totals. If Coach noticed I hadn't eaten very much on vacation, she didn't seem to care. She certainly *did* seem to notice when I clocked my best time ever on a five-mile run. We were doing cooldown stretches on the lawn in the big shadow cast by the gym when she walked over, put her hands on my shoulders, and announced my time to the whole team.

Coach: Ladies and gentlemen, *this* is what I'm talking about. Trimming almost a whole minute off a five-mile run isn't easy. It takes determination, and training as much during the summer as you do during the year.

Geoff made a couple of WOOT-WOOTs and then everybody started clapping. Vanessa just sort of looked at me. She was pretty quiet in the car on the way home, and then suggested we stop at Buster's Burgers for lunch.

Geoff: No can do, lovely lady. I'm on a strict budget that I plan to blow on dinner and a movie with you tonight.

Me: Yeah, we're all going out tonight. Let's just eat lunch at home.

Vanessa: I guess. Are Rob and Jill still coming?

Me: Last I heard. I'll text her to confirm.

We pulled into my driveway, and Geoff asked if I wanted a ride over to Jill and Jack's early so we could all leave from their place. I told him I'd just meet them there.

I had a rice cake and half a can of tuna for lunch, along with three full glasses of water, and I almost couldn't finish the last glass of water. I felt stuffed. As I was forcing down the last swallow my phone buzzed.

Jill: What r u doing

Me: Choking down 3rd glass of water

Jill: ATTAGIRL

Me: Rice cakes r tasteless but filling.

Jill: See you soon

I drove over to Jill's about an hour before I was supposed to be there because I was bored, and because I knew she wouldn't care, but mainly because I wanted to see Jack. He had just finished mowing the lawn. He was wearing only a pair of gym shorts, and he was covered in sweat. I parked at the curb and watched him push the lawn mower into the garage, then he turned around and walked down the driveway, his whole body glistening in the sun like somebody had oiled him up.

When I stepped out of the car, he had this mischievous grin on his face, and he came at me like he was going to hug me. I giggled like a total girl and squirmed away, squealing about how he was going to get me all gross.

Get me all gross? It's like I'm in sixth grade again. But you know what? I don't care. Jack makes me laugh.

We went inside, and I talked to Susan for a second. She said I looked fantastic, and I felt really great about my outfit. We were all going to dinner and a movie tonight, and I decided to just keep it casual, but I blew out my hair and put on some mascara and a little bit of eyeliner. I forgot that the whole week on the boat neither of us wore makeup or looked in the mirror much, so it was probably shocking for Susan to see me with eyelashes. Mine are so light that unless I put on mascara they disappear.

Jill called down to me from upstairs, and I followed Jack up to the hallway where her room is. At the top of the stairs, he pecked me on the lips before he went into his room.

Jack: Gonna hit the shower.

Me: Do more than hit it. Go ahead and get into it. Use a little soap.

Jack (smiling): Wanna come with?

Me: Don't make me regret organizing a triple date night.

Jack: This is a date, huh?

Me: That's it. I'm leaving.

He grabbed my hand, held it up to his mouth, and kissed it while he stared into my eyes. I almost fell down. His gaze makes my knees weak.

We both realized that Jill had come to the door of her room when she cleared her throat and we jumped and turned.

Jill: Thank you for that visual. It's as if there is a Disney movie happening in my hallway, only Jack is very sweaty and I think I can smell him from here.

Jack ran down the hall toward her with his arm raised, shouting at her to get a good whiff, while she ran shrieking into her bedroom and slammed the door. I was laughing when he passed me in the hall and paused.

Jack: You look beautiful tonight.

Me: You're not so bad-looking yourself.

Jack: And in a minute, I'll smell good enough to eat.

Me: Hurry up. I'm hungry.

He winked and headed into his bedroom. I watched him go,

then sighed and walked down the hall to Jill's room. I watched her try on fourteen different tops and T-shirts of a startling variety. She finally settled on the first one she had modeled for me some twenty minutes prior, then spent another five minutes picking out summer sweaters for both of us. We live in a place where summers are hot and dry, but even though it's still in the eighties after the sun goes down, Jill has an intense fear of being too cold in movie theaters. By the time she'd chosen outfit-appropriate sweaters for each of us, Geoff and Vanessa were in the driveway.

At dinner, Vanessa was on a mission about food:

Is that all you're ordering?

You ran like twenty miles this week.

Just a salad?

You didn't even finish it all.

Her obsession with what I was eating was so pointed even the guys started noticing her comments. Geoff looked really uncomfortable, and Rob smirked as he asked if she'd like to cook for us all next time, that way she could make sure we were all eating the right thing. Jill finally silenced her with an icy gaze and a firm tone while explaining that she and I were saving room for treats during the movie. This made Vanessa stop commenting, but also made her stop talking, and the rest of dinner was very strange. I saw Geoff slip his arm around her and squeeze her shoulder, and suddenly I felt really guilty. I could still sense Vanessa's eyes on me every time I took a bite, and again when I told the waiter he could take my plate.

Thankfully, Vanessa and Geoff had driven separately, and I'd been elected earlier by a show of hands to drive Rob, Jill, and Jack in my new car. The heady smell of new interior leather filled our nostrils, while Jack opened the sunroof and played DJ with my phone, which is synched via Bluetooth to the stereo system. By the time we arrived at the theater, the weirdness with Vanessa had been momentarily forgotten, and when we met her and Geoff at the ticket counter, she came with Jill and me to the bathroom, where we touched up lip gloss while Jack, Rob, and Geoff got tickets.

Jill and Vanessa and I stood in front of the mirror for a minute and laughed as Vanessa wondered aloud about the movie. How we'd gotten ourselves roped into seeing a blockbuster about killer alien robots disguising themselves as United States congressmen and the heroic Capitol Hill page who uncovers their plot to take over the planet I'll never be quite sure, but I have a feeling Rob's calves, Jack's eyes, and Geoff's grin had something to do with it. Somehow, the tension from dinner melted away in the bathroom and I thought maybe we'd get through the night without any more weirdness about calorie counting from Vanessa.

Then we met the guys in the line for concessions.

Rob and Jack ordered popcorn and large Cokes. The cups were so gigantic they appeared to be small barrels with straws. Rob wanted black licorice bites and Jill told him that he should under no circumstances expect her to kiss him if he ate black licorice bites all night, so he settled for Goobers. He also told Jill that *she* was a Goober, which she said was disgusting, and then he asked if she wanted anything. Jill and I had agreed to just get bottles of water because she had rice cakes in her purse for us to munch on. So we both got our water, and the guys balanced gigantic buckets of popcorn.

I should note that Jill carries an enormous designer purse she received from her mother for Christmas last year. In addition to being very stylish, it is large enough to hold a bicycle and still carry an immense amount of personal belongings. When we got to our seats, Jill opened her purse and pulled out a couple of rice cakes in a Baggie and our stylish summer sweaters, handing one of each to me.

Vanessa was sitting on the other side of Jack, next to Geoff, eating popcorn, and made a noise like a car backfiring.

Jill: What?

Vanessa: Those are your treats?

Jill: Indeed. These are the aforementioned treats. Do they not meet with the approval of the treat police?

Vanessa just looked at me and shook her head. Mercifully, at that moment the lights went down and the previews started. Jack leaned over and whispered in my ear.

Jack: What's up with her?

Me: She thinks we're not eating enough.

He held out the popcorn bucket.

Me (laughing): No. But I want a Junior Mint.

Jack grabbed the box before I could reach for it and placed it protectively on the other side of the popcorn.

Jack: No. We can't open the candy until the actual movie starts.

Me: Says who?

Jack: It's my movie candy rule. Otherwise, it's all gone before the movie starts.

Jill (not whispering): SHH.

About the time the incredibly buff, young Senate page discovered the body of his boss had been inhabited by an alien robot who was headed to the White House for a "meeting" with the president, I got really cold and pulled on the sweater Jill had loaned me. Jack folded up the armrest between us and I snuggled into him. He put his left arm around me and I could feel his heart beating in his chest against my shoulder.

As the Senate page led a Special Forces contingent to a final battle against the alien robots on the stairs of the Lincoln

Memorial, he was wearing only a white tank top that had been revealed when his suit and tie were blown off in an explosion. Instead of rolling my eyes, I smiled to myself. Sitting there with Jack, feeling the rise and fall of his chest, the warmth of his arm around me, I felt like I was starring in my own movie, and nothing could wipe the smile off my face.

Afterward, we all went back to Jack and Jill's, where Susan and James were polishing off a bottle of wine and insisted we all come in. Jill pulled a container of sugar-free gelatin out of the fridge while James scooped massive bowls of ice cream. The Jell-O was strawberry flavored and Jill had cut it into star shapes with a cookie cutter. It was cold and delicious and, best of all, calorie free.

We all went outside to the backyard, and while Rob and Jack ate ice cream and debated baseball standings with Geoff, I kicked off my sandals and sat down on the edge of the pool with my bowl of strawberry stars. The water felt cool, then warm, against my legs. Vanessa came over and joined me, rolling up her jeans, then sitting next to me with her bowl of chocolate ice cream. She told me she was sorry about earlier and that she was worried that I wasn't going to get enough calories for the week.

I told her not to worry, that I was keeping track of it. I said that I eat like a horse at home during the day and was just trying not to eat as much around Jill because she's working so hard on her ballet body. I told her everything she wanted to hear, and when Geoff looked at his watch and said he had to get home, Vanessa gave me a hug and all was forgiven.

I finished my Jell-O, but it didn't taste as good as it had before Vanessa sat down. Maybe it was because her chocolate ice cream looked so delicious. Or maybe it was because I'd just lied to my friend. I *am* keeping track of it. That part was true.

I took my bowl back into the kitchen and laid Jill's sweater on the counter, then told everybody I was tired. My stomach felt strange. Maybe it was the bizarre combination of food: half a salad, rice cakes, and Jell-O on top of the three Junior Mints I'd allowed myself during the movie. James and Susan both gave me a hug. Jill said she'd text me tomorrow. Jack walked me to my awesome/ridiculous new car and leaned against the driver's-side door.

Me: I need to get in there.

Jack: I'm going to need a kiss first.

Me: What if your mom is watching from the living room window?

Jack: Then she's going to see us kiss.

I just got home. Mom is working until 2 a.m., so it's quiet here, but my heart is still racing a little bit. When Jack kisses me it makes me breathless like I just ran for a mile. It's nice to feel like that, but sometimes, it's also a little tiring. After the past three weeks, between Dad leaving and vacation and Jack and this whole thing with Vanessa, I just feel really tired. ~~I'm going to take a long, hot bath and then~~

Jack just texted me. He left his wallet in my car. He's driving over to get it. My heart is racing. Seeing him again is better than a long, hot bath anyway.

Later . . .

Jack just left.

I met him in the driveway and unlocked my SUV. He climbed in and found his wallet wedged down by the seat belt in the passenger seat. When he got out, he looked up at my house.

Jack: So, this is where you sleep?

Me: Not so far tonight.

Jack: I wanna see.

Me: Me sleep?

Jack: That too.

I took his hand and led him up to the front porch. The sprinklers were *phrip-phrip-phripping* water all over the yard, and my bare feet got wet as we ran between them. When we walked through the front door, I told him I was breaking the rules.

Jack: What rules?

Me: No boys in the house when there isn't an adult present.

Jack: I turn eighteen in October. Does that count?

Me: No.

Jack: I guess I should go.

Me: No.

Jack: You'd break the rules for me?

Me: Just a little. Mom gets off in an hour.

I gave him the grand tour but didn't linger here in my bedroom, even when he sat down on the bed. Something about it felt like it was too much. We went back downstairs to the kitchen. I got him a Coke and a Diet Coke for myself, and we carried them into the living room and sat down on the sectional.

I leaned over his legs to grab the remote, and he wrapped his arms around me, then lay back on the couch, easily swinging me on top of him. Then we were kissing, and the remote and the Cokes were forgotten. It was like we were right back on the deck of the boat at Lake Powell, only this time my shirt came off too. When it did, he took a deep breath and lay back as his hands gently caressed my arms and chest. The only light was from the moon, leaking in through the window. It turned our skin a pale blue in the dark living room, and as he pulled my face gently back toward his lips, he breathed, "You are so beautiful."

Who knows what other articles of clothing might have come off if I hadn't had the sound turned up on my phone and heard the text message?

Mom: Headed home now. Need anything?

Me: No thanks. Sleepy. C u in a.m.

Jack rolled over on his stomach while I texted her back, and lay there for a second while I put my T-shirt back on.

Jack: I have to go home now, don't I?

Me: Well, you don't *have* to, but if you don't, my mother may kill me while you watch when she returns.

Jack: I'd never forgive myself.

Me: Then you might want to think about putting on your shirt.

He pulled his T-shirt on in a hurry and sort of tugged the hem down past the waist of his shorts.

Me (laughing): Little riled up, are we?

Jack: Hey, that's *your* fault.

Me: I will not stand for these wild allegations.

He put an arm around my shoulders as I walked him to the front door and we stepped out onto the porch.

Jack: Thanks for the tour.

Me: Thanks for coming by. Didn't know I'd see you again tonight.

Jack: I did.

Me (frowning): Really?

Jack: Whydaya think I left my wallet in your car?

Then a kiss, and a wink, and he was gone.

Saturday, June 30
Weight: Can't look yet.

The only thing missing from my birthday last night was Dad.

It's strange, but I can't remember a birthday without him. Because my birthday is never during school, he'd always take the day off from work at the dealership so we could have the whole day together. Every year for as long as I can remember, he always made chocolate chip pancakes for breakfast. He'd drop the chocolate chips in after he'd poured the batter to arrange them in the numbers of whatever birthday it was.

Yesterday was sixteen. But no chocolate chips—just a text from Dad:

HAPPY BDAY! Call me when you can. XO

I haven't talked to him yet. I feel guilty about it. I should at least call him and thank him for the car, but I haven't done it yet. Every time I think I'm ready to, Mom traipses into the kitchen looking like a zombie, and it makes me angry on the inside. Not burn-down-a-building angry. It makes me just angry enough to put down my phone.

Dad was always the one up and at 'em on weekend mornings. He liked to go to the gym before he went to the dealership. He was usually back making breakfast by the time I woke up on Saturdays and because Mom usually works Friday nights, it was just him and me eating omelets and talking on Saturday mornings.

When I got his text yesterday morning, I was lying in bed, listening to the silence of Mom sleeping late. My heart started pounding in this weird way, like I was going to be in trouble or something. I poised my thumbs over the screen to tap a message back to him, but I didn't know what to say, and I realized I was holding my breath.

I took in several long, deep breaths like I do when I find my rhythm running. It helped my heart to stop pounding so hard, and I sent him a little smiley face back:

=)

Maybe it's a start.

I didn't have high hopes for my birthday last night, but Mom managed to surprise me. Not only did she take Friday night off, she was dressed and looking nice when I got back from my afternoon run with Vanessa and Geoff. To top it all off she sprang a surprise on me. She'd called the whole gang and invited everyone over for taco night. She had a gigantic devil's food cake in the oven, and the whole house smelled so good my head got sort of light and loopy. I realized while I was standing in the kitchen with Vanessa and Geoff that I hadn't had a single bite of anything cakelike since that doughnut Jill's mom caught me eating on the boat. I made a decision right then and there that I was going to enjoy my birthday, and just not care about the calories for one day.

Vanessa and Geoff arrived at the same time that Jill and Rob showed up. Jack appeared on the front steps about five minutes later with a fistful of flowers. They were long-stemmed red roses, so bright and beautiful that they took my breath away. Let me stop here and say that I've only seen men arrive with flowers in movies. I've been trying to remember a time when my dad arrived at the door with flowers for my mom or me and I simply can't. Typically, when he showed up with a surprise, it was a car of some kind. As I stared at Jack's blue eyes, twinkling over the tops of the roses, I decided that flowers were better than an SUV any day.

Mom's tacos are delicious. They always are. There's something about the way she seasons the meat that knocks them out of the park. Everybody but Jill loaded up a big plateful. Jill took half a spoonful of ground beef and a sprinkling of shredded lettuce. Mom and the boys were back in the living room plugging the old video camera into the television so that my annual birthday humiliation of watching videos of myself as an infant could commence. I'd almost made it across the kitchen to where the great room becomes the living room on the other side of the island when I heard it:

Vanessa (to Jill): Is that really all you're going to eat?

Jill (quietly): That's your limit.

Vanessa: What?

Jill: You get one comment about what I'm eating tonight, Vanessa, and that was it.

Vanessa: I just want to make sure that—

Jill: Mind. Your. Own. Business.

I kept walking. Jill can hold her own.

I had a headache and a stomachache this morning when I woke up. I think it was all the sugar and calories. I had three tacos and two pieces of cake last night. It was so good, I felt like I was high. Or what I imagine it might feel like to be high. I've never smoked anything in my life.

Later . . .
Weight: 126.5

I just got on the scale in Mom's bathroom.

Mayday.

I was still at 125.5 on Thursday. Then I ran yesterday. I gained a full pound overnight, just from that crappy birthday cake and those damn tacos.

Mom was downstairs making coffee when I went into the kitchen earlier, and she was all chipper and smiling and asking if I wanted to try on the new outfit she bought me. She even wanted to make me breakfast. I poured a mug of coffee and told her I had to wake up before I could eat anything else. The cake was still sitting out, and she lifted up the tinfoil and swiped a little chunk of it off the side of the plate. Watching her lick the fudge frosting off her fingers almost made me throw up. I sort of wish I had. What was I thinking last night? I ate like I was going to the electric chair.

The worst part is that I know I let Jill down. She was *so disciplined* and didn't eat a single bite of cake, but still seemed to be having a great time with the rest of us. That's just it: I still think I *need* to eat food to be having fun with everyone else. The truth is, I don't want to be like everyone else. I want to be different. The reason Jack likes me is not because I look like every other girl; it's because I look *different* from any other girl.

Last night, everybody else left around midnight, and I walked him outside to his car. He leaned over and kissed me for a long time, then told me I was different from any girl he'd ever gone out with before.

I intend to stay that way.

As soon as Mom left, I took the cake and dumped it into the kitchen trash can, then hauled the trash bag outside and tossed it into the garbage can on the side of the garage. I don't need to have that in the house. And Mom *certainly* doesn't need to be sneaking bites from it all day and night. She'll end up eating the whole thing, and more devil's food on her thighs is *not* what she needs right now.

My head is pounding. I feel bloated. This is the price I pay for not sticking to my guns yesterday. I'm so stupid. I *know* better than this. I could see it in Jill's eyes when I got the second slice of cake and was licking the frosting off my fork. She gave me this little smile, this sad little smile as if she was saying, are you sure this is worth it?

The answer is *no*.

Nothing is worth feeling like this. There are far better feelings in the world: Jack's eyes on me as I cross the room. His hands on my body as I slide off his shirt. His lips on mine, breathing me in. Beating Vanessa by a full minute on a five-mile run.

Run.

That's what I need to do right this minute.

Run.

Sunday, July 1
Weight: 126

I feel so much better tonight. I ran seven miles yesterday, and Jill texted me while I was out. I called her after my run, and started crying on the phone about how I'd messed everything up, and lost control, and told her I was sorry for letting her down. I don't know how she does it, but Jill is one of the most completely calm people I know—especially when someone else is having a breakdown. She's in control *all the time*.

Jill: It's not a problem. You didn't let me down.

Me: I just don't want to end up fat and unhappy like my mom.

Jill: Not a chance.

Me: How do you know?

Jill: Because you called me crying about eating your own birthday cake.

Me: I threw the rest in the trash and ran seven miles just now.

Jill (laughing): See? Take a deep breath and meet me at the park.

So I did.

Jill showed me this aerobic workout she does that you can do anywhere. It's just isometric exercises mainly that give you some resistance training using your own body weight while also getting your heart rate up. It kicked my butt. She explained that if you do it correctly, it burns three hundred calories in twenty-five minutes. Anytime she feels like she's overdone it foodwise, she does this in her room, or jogs down to the park and does it outside, here in the grass.

Afterward, we went back to her place and lay by the pool for a while. Jack and his dad came home from a bike ride while we were out there. I heard a low whistle and when I turned around, Jack was standing there in these little spandex bike shorts and his cycling shoes. He kicked off the shoes and pulled off the helmet and his jersey, flinging sweat all over the place, then did a cannonball off the side of the pool and got us completely soaked. Jill calmly blinked the water out of her eyes and blotted her face with a heavy sigh while I shrieked.

Jill: Your boyfriend is so charming.

Me: And the only guy I've ever seen who looks sexy in bike shorts.

Jill: I'm going to pretend you didn't say that.

Tuesday, July 3
Weight: 125

If Vanessa asks me if I'm "okay" one more time, I'm going to implode. She just left, and all she could talk about was making sure that I'm getting enough calories so I don't lose any more weight, because if I do Coach is going to start to notice. The thing is, I've only lost eight pounds since we started keeping track. That's not too much. It's perfect. When I look in the mirror, I don't see baby fat covered in acne anymore. I see a face that looks more grown-up. (Pretty, even? I think Jack is convinced of that . . . I wonder if I'm really . . . pretty?)

I feel like I've finally mastered how to stay in shape and look the way I want to. After suffering through Mom convincing me to cut my hair off in seventh grade (huge. mistake.) and then zits on my forehead and nose like fireworks until she finally took me to the dermatologist in ninth grade, it's like I've come to a place where I'm not at war with my body anymore. It's like I've taken control of the way I look.

My phone just rang again.

It's Dad.

Again.

Every time I see his name flash up on the screen it makes my stomach hurt. He keeps leaving messages about coming to watch fireworks with him on July 4th. Mom has to work that night, so I guess I could, but I don't really want to see him yet. I don't know what to say. I know I have to talk to him at some point.

I can't just ignore him forever.

Friday, July 6
Weight: 124.5

I just got back from practice, and I want to strangle Vanessa. She's been great all week. She and Geoff and I have been running almost every day in the mornings. After we get back, Vanessa goes to babysit her nieces most days, and Geoff is working construction with his dad. So in the afternoons, Jill and I jog down to the park and do the workout she showed me, then we go back to her place and lay out by the pool.

Jill is still keeping her calories down to about 1,000 per day, and I'm doing around 1,200 or so. It's not that hard, and I feel full most of the time. I have two hard-boiled eggs for breakfast, a rice cake snack after we get back from running, and then a salad for lunch, and another salad for dinner, usually with a little chicken or tuna fish on it. Of course, I drink about twenty glasses of water every day, and I keep a couple bags of gummy fruit snacks in my bedside table. I let myself have one or two a day just to keep from going crazy. But it's not hard, and I can't believe how great I look in the mirror. I love my new body. I look like those girls in the workout ads for yoga clothes and running shoes. The other day when we were swimming, Jack said my six-pack was better than his. This is patently false; Jack has washboard abs like one of those European soccer stars in underwear commercials, but it made me smile and blush, so of course, I splashed him in the face so he wouldn't see how happy it made me, and he dove at me and knocked me off my raft.

Jill looks so thin her legs don't touch between her thighs anymore. I don't really understand the rules of how you have to look in ballet, but she tells me that it's all about being as light as possible so you can be lifted, and almost weightless in your jumps and spins. If "almost weightless" is the standard, Jill should have no trouble getting the roles she wants next week when her summer ballet intensives start. If she gets any more weightless, she'll float away.

All of this would be fine and good except that today at practice when we handed our CalorTrack printouts in to Coach Perkins, Vanessa lost her mind again. Coach glanced down at my sheets, then smiled and patted me on the back and told me I was doing a great job. I've been putting in a few extra things on the CalorTrack app that I don't actually eat, but nothing major. Just adding some toast to the eggs at breakfast and a turkey sandwich to the salad. Sometimes a brownie or some frozen yogurt for "dessert" after dinner. I don't do it for every day or anything—just enough to up the calories for the week by about 750 or so.

Vanessa heard Coach tell me I was doing a great job, and I heard her sigh really loudly like hearing this was *just so taxing* she simply *couldn't endure.* I shot her a dirty look, maybe a little dirtier than I should have, and she rolled her eyes. I'd ridden with her and Geoff, so after practice I was just completely silent in the car. Finally, she turned around and asked me what my problem was.

Me: No problem, Vanessa. None at all.

Vanessa: Right. Except for that look you shot me, and now you're not talking.

Me: You're the one sighing like there's a foreign missile crisis every time Coach tells me I'm doing a good job.

Vanessa: And you're the one *lying* about how much you're eating.

Me: Vanessa, do you see everything I put in my mouth each day?

Vanessa: All I know is that—

Me: Didn't ask what you *know*. Asked if you see everything I put in my mouth each day.

Geoff: Hey, you guys. Chill out. It's not that big a—

Vanessa and me: Shut up, Geoff.

Me: I'm eating plenty. I'm running better than I ever have. You're just jealous because you're not beating me in the five-mile anymore.

Vanessa: Oh. Yeah. That's it. You are such a liar.

Me: What?

Vanessa: You heard me.

I got out of the car and slammed the door. Geoff jumped like he'd been shot at. I was so mad I had to come straight upstairs and write about it. I'm sick of Vanessa's attitude. I look great, I feel great, I've got a great body and a great boyfriend, and she can't handle it because I'm beating her. Some friend. When she and Geoff started going out last year, I was so happy for her. I've been riding around as their third wheel for months now, and all of a sudden when things start to go well for me, she has to get all hot and bothered about it.

Screw her.

I don't need that noise.

Thank God for Jill. She's the only one who understands me. I'm going over there for dinner tonight. Rob is staying there this weekend while his parents are out of town for their anniversary. We're going to have a big cookout. Jill didn't tell Vanessa and Geoff. I'm glad. I don't think I could possibly deal with any more judgment from that direction this evening.

Monday, July 9
Weight: 124

Mom had the day off from work yesterday. When I woke up it was weird because I actually smelled coffee and bacon cooking. For a minute, I was confused because I imagined that Dad was downstairs making breakfast, and before I was really fully awake, I felt this funny excitement and actually smiled, and snuggled down into my pillows under my comforter, waiting for him to rap on the door and tell me the waffles or the omelets were ready.

Then it hit me: Dad doesn't live here.

My eyes flew open, and suddenly I was awake, and I had this strange sinking feeling. It was like I'd forgotten I was mad at Dad, and it made me feel stupid and sad at the same time;

stupid because I can't let him off the hook that easily, and sad because . . .

(Why is it so hard to even write this down?)

Sad because I miss him.

There. I said it. I miss him. I wish he'd been nicer to Mom. I wish they could have worked it out. When I was over at Jack and Jill's the other night having the cookout with Rob and these neighbors of theirs from next door, I couldn't help noticing how easy Susan and James were with each other. It's not that they don't ever have little "moments" where they disagree. It's just that they're nice to each other about it. It seems like they rarely have those "moments" at the same time. I saw Susan get briefly frustrated when James set down a knife he'd used to cut up some raw chicken on her clean cutting board, but instead of snapping at him about it, she glanced around the room and just asked him to rinse off that knife. It was a small thing, but it was such a big thing. My dad would've cursed under his breath and grabbed the knife and tossed it into the sink or something. Then Mom would've looked extra hurt and been crazily apologetic and scurried around trying to "fix" things and overcompensated, which would have annoyed Dad even more until he finally snapped at her to get out of his way. I saw that happen a lot between them, and it didn't matter who was around.

Anyway, I went downstairs and was thinking about all of

this and was surprised to see Mom sitting there with coffee and . . . bacon. No eggs. No waffles. Just a big plate of bacon.

Mom: Good morning, honey.

Me: That's a lot of bacon.

Mom: Want some?

Me: Not really the breakfast of champions.

Mom (moaning): I *know*. I just needed a little pick-me-up.

Me: Have you been exercising at all? You know working out fires up the feel-good in your brain.

Mom (sighing): I know. I just . . . I don't know how you do it. I'm so old, and I have no energy, and . . .

Her voice trailed off, and she popped another piece of bacon into her mouth. I ate a couple of hard-boiled eggs and drank a glass of water and a cup of coffee. When I was done, I rinsed out my mug and put it into the dishwasher. Then I picked up her plate of bacon and put it on the counter next to the sink.

Me: C'mon.

Mom: Hey! What?

Me: Put on your tennis shoes and some workout shorts.

Mom: What? Why?

Me: We're going to go for a jog.

Mom: Oh . . . no. Honey. I can't jog.

Me: How do you know?

Mom: I just haven't in like . . .

Me: Now. We're leaving in five minutes.

I couldn't actually believe it, but when I came back downstairs, she was lacing up her old running shoes.

The whole attempt was disastrous, naturally. We jogged down the block toward the park and had to walk the next block. Then I made her jog again. We did this all the way there, and the more she stopped and whined about how she was having a hard time breathing, or her ankles hurt, or her knee felt funny, the angrier I got. When we finally got to the park, I walked her over to the workout stations where Jill and I do sit-ups and push-ups, and dips and showed her how to start. I sat at her feet and she did four sit-ups before she lay back on the wooden bench huffing and puffing and said, I can't!

Me: Yes, you can.

Mom: Honey, you don't understand.

Me: Yes. I *do* understand. I understand perfectly. I understand that you don't care enough about yourself to take care of yourself. You don't care enough about me to take care of yourself. And you *certainly* didn't care enough about *Dad* to take care of yourself.

I didn't realize I was crying until I saw that she was crying too. I stood up and took off running across the park. I ran down the street, then turned away from our house and ran toward the mountain. I ran until the tears had stopped, which must've been at least four miles, then I turned around and ran toward home.

When I got here, Mom's car was gone. She'd left a note that she'd gone out with her girlfriend Pam. Pam is Mom's truly overweight friend from the hospital. They've worked nights together in the ER for years. Mom might have twenty pounds to lose. Pam is obese. She has big sacks of fat that wiggle on her arms, making her elbows just dimples from behind. She's always wearing sleeveless tops for some reason. Probably because sleeves on her arms look like sausage casings about to explode.

In the shower, I could just picture them sitting at Pam's favorite restaurant, this sports bar called Dick's Hot Wing Express. I could smell the buffalo sauce dripping off Pam's greasy fingers while she poured more light beer for my mom and listened as Mom cried and talked about how hard this has all been on her.

After my shower, I opened my drawer and realized I was almost out of clean clothes. I went down to the laundry room, and there was a load of whites just sitting in the washer, soaking wet. They'd been there overnight, so I set the machine to rinse again, and as I marched back upstairs, I saw the empty bacon plate sitting on the counter. Mom had eaten the rest of it when she got back, I guess. Something about that made me so angry, I wanted to throw it across the kitchen. Instead, I ran over to the couch and picked up a throw pillow off the floor and hit the couch with it over and over again. The living room was a wreck of Mom's dirty dishes and old newspapers, books, and ice cream bar wrappers. I thought about Jill's place. It was always gorgeous. It looked like a page out of a catalog for a furniture store—like Susan had styled the whole place.

Mom is still in bed this morning, but last night, I decided several things:

1. I'm getting a job. Now that Jill has ballet intensives for the next month, I can't stand being here with Mom all the time.

2. This wasn't all Dad's fault. I feel like since he's been gone, I'm seeing the things that must have driven him crazy about Mom. Maybe I'll call him this week.

Wednesday, July 18
Weight: 122

Turns out it's not as hard to get a job as I thought it would be.

On Saturday, Jill and I went to the Springs, which sounds like the name of a spa but is actually this big outdoor shopping mall near our neighborhood. They built the place around a big computerized fountain that squirts water in the air synchronized to music, then it splashes down and is pumped through the whole mall in little troughs along the walkways. It's sort of nice until you realize that there isn't a single blade of grass anywhere except for two strips in the medians near the parking deck. The entire shopping center is a giant slab of concrete.

Jill had to get new tights and toe blocks before she started ballet intensives on Monday, and while she was in the dance supply store, I noticed a Help Wanted sign in the window at this big chain Italian restaurant across the walkway called Parmesan's. I got an application and the hostess on duty explained that you start as a food runner, and then if it goes well, after a month or so they promote you to hostess. The pay isn't so great—minimum wage, but you do get "tipped out" by the waiters after every shift, and in my book, it seems that *not very good* still beats *nothing at all*. So I was happy when Melanie, the manager, called me in for an interview on Monday.

Melanie is tall and very excited about her role in management at Parmesan's, a member of the Brighton Restaurants LLC family, owned by Farnsworth Food Services Group. She asked me a number of the most high-energy, ridiculous questions I have ever heard regarding my strengths, my weaknesses, my overall level of commitment, and my goals in life. I am happy to report that I smiled and nodded and gave the Correct Answer each time. By the end of the interview you'd have thought I had only ever envisioned for myself a career in running bottomless bowls of salads and baskets of breadsticks to the lunch crowd here at the Springs location of Parmesan's. Satisfied with my enthusiasm, and after commenting on my clean fingernails and hair, Melanie offered me two starched white aprons, a photocopy of the Parmesan's uniform requirements and a firm handshake. I was hired on the spot.

My first shift was on Tuesday. Melanie explained that I'd work lunches until I proved I could handle a dinner rush, and filled me in on the Brighton Restaurant laws:

1. A smile on the face equals joy on the plate.
2. Full hands in, full hands out. (Of the kitchen.)
3. No questions asked.

When I first started, I was really nervous, but I just kept a big smile on my face and followed around this other runner named Angela. She showed me how to pop fresh breadsticks into the warmer and make sure they were smothered in butter and garlic salt before we loaded them into baskets. The salad bowls are premixed by the guys on the salad line, but then we have to pour the dressing on and toss it at the table. I'm also responsible for running around with water and iced tea pitchers, and Angela showed me how to approach the tables and serve plates over the person's left shoulder and clear from the right. In that sense the service flows like you'd read a book in English—from left to right. Serve to the left, clear from the right. I was worried I might drop something, or spill something, but I didn't. I did accidentally try to clear a salad bowl that had a single leaf of lettuce in it and looked empty to me. The woman at the table nearly fell out of her chair, covering the bowl with both hands:

Her: *No!* I'm not finished with that!

Me: Oh! I'm so sorry.

I blushed really hard, but I kept a big Parmesan's Team Smile on my face and picked up an armload of other dirty dishes from the table so that I could go back into the kitchen. That's what full hands in, full hands out means: on the way in I have to be carrying dirty dishes to the dish room, and on the way out I have to be carrying clean dishes full of food.

Andy was the waiter at that table, a smiley college guy who was studying premed. He spotted me refilling two more breadstick baskets for that table a few minutes later and told me not to worry about it.

Andy: I don't know where she put that extra bite of salad.

Me: Probably the same place she's going to put these two baskets of breadsticks.

Andy (laughing): I should check her purse.

Me: She'd try to stop you, but I think she's stuck in her chair.

As I carried the breadsticks and a fifth glass of Diet Coke to this table, I looked around and really noticed who was eating in this restaurant. Almost every single person was overweight except for the waiters. There were four women at Andy's table including the one whose salad I'd tried to clear, and each one of them seemed to spill over the arms of her chair. Suddenly, a wave of nausea swept over me. The smell of the butter and garlic on the breadsticks turned my stomach. I will *never* look like these people. I heard Susan's voice echo in my head. One night on the lake she'd watched with an approving grin as Jill refused a bite of Rob's dessert, and said something that now made total sense to me:

Nothing tastes as good as thin feels.

For the rest of the shift, those words rang in my ears. I picked up the pace while I walked around looking for dishes. I realized my new job is almost all exercise! I'm going to buy a pedometer to see how far I actually walk during a shift. I'm burning calories the whole time.

Later, Angela and I helped Andy carry out the entrées for his table. Each of these women had ordered a heaping plate of fettucini with creamy Alfredo sauce. As Angela and I slid the plates onto the table in front of each guest, Andy leaned over the shoulder of the woman who had panicked when I tried to take her salad with a grater and a block of cheese.

Andy: Fresh Parmesan?

Her: Oh my, yes! (conspiratorially to her friend) Hard cheese is on my diet.

When she said this, I almost laughed out loud. Instead, I bit my tongue until it almost bled and finished picking up the empty bread baskets that littered the table. One of the other women saw my big grin and commented that I had the prettiest smile she'd ever seen.

Andy followed me back into the kitchen and we stood at the dish stand and laughed.

Andy: Her *diet*?

Me: I *know*!

Andy (wiping his eyes): Whew! That was one for the books.

Me: I don't want to break it to her, but I'm afraid the hard cheese diet may not be working.

We carried clean dishes hot from the machine to the racks where the plates are kept, then I headed over to fill more baskets with breadsticks. After that, I wasn't nervous anymore. I fell into a good rhythm with Andy and Trish and the time flew by. A strange feeling came over me. I'd never had so much contact with so much food in my life: huge plates of carb-laden pasta covered in cream and butter; bread dripping with fat. Instead of looking good to me, it grossed me out. I kept having to turn my head or race off to find more dishes to carry every time I saw someone shovel a huge bite into their mouths or watched a customer dab a napkin at the butter dripping off his chin.

As I think about it now, there was something amazing and powerful about being around all that food and not being tempted to put a single thing in my mouth. Those people at Parmesan's couldn't control themselves. They were all stuffing their faces, their stomach rolls spilling over the arms of the chairs they'd wedged themselves into. Not me. I was in charge of my body. While everyone else was packing on the weight at the tables all around me, I was speed walking circles around them, getting even thinner than I already am.

As the lunch crowd waddled back to their offices nearby, things died down and the chef served a staff meal. I didn't have a bite. I sat next to Trish after we finished our side work. While she and the other employees ate spaghetti and meatballs I had two glasses of ice water and the two rice cakes I'd brought from home in my purse. As I was clocking out at the computer Melanie came by with my tip out from the waitstaff and told me Andy said I was the best food runner he'd ever worked with. She said it was *highly unusual* but she was going to schedule me for lunch the next day—today—not a training shift, but an actual shift on the floor.

I just got home, and I'm tired, but I feel energized. I did a great job again today, and it sure beats sitting here all day with Mom while Jill is in dance class. Jill texted me on the way home and said she was leaving ballet intensives and that she'd come by later. When I got home, Mom was on her way out the door to work.

Mom: Whew! Sweetheart, you smell good enough to eat.

Me: It's so gross, Mom. The garlic gets on everything.

Mom: There's leftover ham in the fridge and I made a bean casserole.

Me: They made us a staff meal at work.

Mom: Oh, good! I'm glad they feed you during your shift. You need to keep your energy up. I'm so proud of you for getting this job, honey!

She kissed me good-bye and wrapped her arms around me in a big hug. She took a deep breath and sighed.

Mom: Mmmmm. Breadsticks!

Me (laughing): Get out of here.

For a minute after she left, I felt sort of guilty about lying to her. Technically it was just a tiny white lie—not even a lie really. They *had* made us a meal at work. I just didn't eat it. I stood under a hot shower for a long time and washed my hair to get the smell of breadsticks out of it. Once I couldn't smell garlic anymore, I turned off the water and got dressed. I'm almost down to 120 pounds, and all of my shorts are loose. Jill is on her way over right now. She texted me and wants to go shop for jeans. We've both gone down a couple of sizes since we started tracking our calories, and there are back-to-school sales going on now, even though it's the middle of July. Can you believe it? Why is retail in such a hurry to get us back to school? It's like putting up Christmas decorations in October.

Thursday, July 19
Weight: 121

Vanessa and I went running this morning. Geoff has been working with his dad roofing a house early in the mornings before it gets too hot to be up there. I guess I was sort of quiet because Vanessa finally stopped in midsentence and asked if I'd even heard a word she'd said.

The truth is I really hadn't. I was too busy thinking about what happened last night after we got back to Jill's. Jill and I went shopping and both of us got new jeans and a couple of new tops. When we got back to Jill's bedroom, we took everything out and cut the tags off and tried them on in different combinations. Jill calls this Fashion Research. We always have to give outfits a test run together before we wear them out publicly to make sure they pass. Jill pulled on her second new pair of jeans, and the way the fabric hugged her legs was amazing.

Me: I've decided all clothes must be tried on by you first.

Jill (narrowing eyes, staring into mirror): That is ridiculous.

Me: No, what's ridiculous is how great you look in those jeans.

Jill (turning to check the back): They look okay.

Me: Okay?! They look incredible! You could stop traffic on the highway in those jeans.

Jill: They look pretty good, but *good* is often the enemy of the *best*.

Jill peeled off the indigo denim and tossed the pair onto her bed. She slipped the halter top she'd been wearing off over her head and walked over to her desk and pulled a red Magic Marker out of a pencil holder on her desk. It had the word "washable" printed across the side in big bubbly letters, and she handed it to me, then walked over to the tall mirror that leans against the wall next to her closet. It has a dark brown wood frame that goes with Susan's tasteful decorating scheme for the entire house. She stood in front of the mirror in her underwear. The indirect light from the pin spots in her ceiling and the halogen lamp on her desk softly bounced off her skin, accenting every muscle. Years of ballet have given Jill the core strength of a boa constrictor, and the graceful contours of her muscles taut beneath her skin gave her the look of a girl in an advertisement. I just stared at her for a second while she assessed her own body in the mirror. Finally she turned to face me.

Me (holding up marker): What's this?

Jill: There's always room for improvement.

Me: I'm sorry. Are you talking about improving your body?

Jill: Indeed.

Me: I think the only thing on your body that needs improvement is apparently your eyesight.

I moved to where she was standing and turned her shoulders back toward the mirror.

Me: My God, Jill. Your body is perfect.

Jill: No, it's not, but you're going to help me get closer.

Me: How?

Jill: Circle this.

Jill held up her right arm and pointed at the underside of her biceps.

Me: Why?

Jill: There's fat here under my arm.

Me: Where?

Jill: Can't you see that? It's right there. Circle it.

Something about her tone of voice stopped my questions. I took the cap off the marker and drew a red oval around the bottom of her arm as she indicated with her finger. Next, she pointed to the skin below her belly button, tracing with her index finger the path I should draw the circle. She didn't speak for the next few minutes, just pointed and turned, and pointed

142

and turned. It felt like a solemn ceremony of some kind, and as I drew one last circle around her upper thigh, just below the leg opening of her underwear, she began to nod, slowly, then stepped back from the mirror and held out her arms, turning around to survey my bizarre geometry.

Something about this motion—her head nodding, the slow turning, the determined glint in her eyes—was methodical and strange. It sent a chill down my spine, and I stared into the mirror with her, trying to see what Jill must be seeing.

But I couldn't.

It just looked like a bunch of red circles and ovals all over her arms and legs and sides and stomach. There was even one under her chin.

Jill: See? I still have a lot of work to do.

Me: I don't understand.

Wordlessly, Jill turned and smiled at me. It was almost a look of pity. She handed me her phone and told me to snap a picture of her so she could chart her progress. She held her head back so you could see the red circle under her chin but couldn't see her face or tell who she was. Then she took the phone and the red marker out of my hands and walked to her desk, where she opened her laptop and clicked to a website. After tapping and swiping at the screen on her phone several times, she clicked around on the laptop for a second, then

143

brought the computer to her bed and pulled me down next to her.

There was a message forum on the screen, and as Jill scrolled down the page, I saw images of models in ads I recognized from magazines. These pictures had been posted along with candid shots of dancers onstage and girls walking runways, and interspersed between all of these were inspirational quotations like "Craving is only a feeling" and "You've got to fight for every dream." Superimposed over pictures of Kate Moss with her rib cage clearly visible, these sentences seemed to take on a whole new meaning.

Jill clicked to make a new post. She uploaded the picture I'd just taken of her. Underneath the picture she wrote: "Everything that breaks you makes you stronger."

She clicked "submit," and after a few seconds, the picture appeared on the forum under her username: TinyDancer. A few minutes later, comments began to appear:

SkinnyNBones: Wow! Way to go TinyDancer! You have worked so hard.

ThinkThin: #youaremyhero

Thinspiring: Your dedication is uh-MA-zing.

I watched Jill type a response back and add one more picture that was saved on her desktop. It was a picture of a girl lying on her side. She was wearing only a pair of jeans, and you could see her ribs and every vertebra in her back very clearly through her thin skin. Just above her wrist on the inside of her arm there was a tattoo in dark, curly Latin script: "Quod me nutrit, me destruit." Jill typed the translation of the tattoo underneath the image and clicked to post it:

All that nourishes me destroys me.

Jill closed her laptop after that and picked up the red marker.

Jill: Now let's do you.

Me: Let's do *what* to me?

Jill: Circle your goal spots.

Me: No thank you.

Jill (smiling): Oh, c'mon! You helped me. Let me help you.

I shook my head and started gathering my stuff.

Jill: You're not *leaving*, are you?

Me: Yeah, I need to get home. I have to . . .

Jill: You have to what?

The way she leveled her eyes at me made me wince. She knew I was making an excuse. She knew my mom was at work all night. She knew there was nothing waiting for me at home but a big empty house and TV in the dark. Why did this feel so awkward?

Jill: Don't be scared. Be beautiful.

She held out the marker, and we both stood there staring

at it for a moment. Then I smiled at her and picked up the shopping bags with my new jeans inside.

Me: I don't think I'm ready to be quite that . . . beautiful.

Jill smiled as I turned toward her bedroom door, and as I stepped into the hall, I heard her say a single word:

Yet.

I ran into Jack in the kitchen. He and Rob were just coming in from soccer practice and groaning to Susan about having to start two-a-days in a couple weeks.

Jack: Hey, beautiful.

Rob groaned. Susan smiled. I blushed, caught off guard.

Me: Hey, sweaty.

Jack: I clean up real nice.

Me (laughing): So I've heard.

Rob groaned again.

Susan: You're staying for dinner?

Me: No—I have to get home.

She nodded and pecked me on the top of the head as she carried a colander of wet greens from the sink to the cutting board.

Susan: Join us tomorrow? Before you and Jack go . . .

She paused.

Jack: Mini-golf, baaa-by. Gonna tear up some putt-putt.

Rob groaned for a third time, this time loudly. I laughed and said that was my cue to leave, but Jack beat me to the door, spun me around, and kissed me lightly on the lips.

Jack: See you tomorrow.

Me: If you're lucky.

Jack: I always am.

Friday, July 20
Weight: 121

I couldn't get that picture of the girl with the tattoo and her bones poking through her skin out of my head last night. When I woke up this morning it was still there so I went for a run, but it didn't help. I just got out of the shower, and I can still see her.

I just pulled up that website on my tablet. I found Jill's picture with red circles. She's really thin. If she lost any more weight in all of those places she circled, she'd look like the girl with the tattoo. I have a weird feeling in my stomach about that. Somewhere there should be a balance, right? Not a scale, but a *balance* between not being overweight and not being underweight. I think that's what Coach Perkins was trying to do with these food diaries. I weighed myself when I got out of the shower, and I'm down to 121 pounds. I've lost twelve pounds in two months. I'm more in shape than I've ever been. I don't think I need to lose any more.

While I was running this morning, a plan started to form in my mind. I'm going to do a few things.

1. Stop limiting myself to 1,200 calories per day. Coach says I should be eating closer to 2,000, especially if I'm running every day.
2. After practice today, no more lying on my CalorTrack calories. I'm going to honestly type in what I have to eat.
3. I'm going to eat the staff meal at work today. At least I'm going to have a few bites.
4. I'm going to call Dad. I miss him.

Later . . .

Turns out, I didn't have to call Dad. He showed up at lunch today.

I wasn't really paying attention, and when Andy told me we'd just sat at table fourteen, I grabbed two glasses of ice water and a basket of breadsticks and was setting them down on the table before I realized who was sitting in the booth. I get into a zone at work, just running the food, looking for empty plates and half-full water glasses. I don't even look at the faces of the customers that much anymore. Usually they're chunky and chewing with their mouths open. It grosses me out. I might have dropped off the water and breadsticks and left without even noticing but Dad said my name.

Dad: What are you doing here?

Me: I work here. What are you doing here?

Dad: Having lunch. This is Annette.

Dad nodded across the table to a woman with the brightest red hair I'd ever seen and mesmerizing green eyes. She wore a silky white top that swooped low under her emerald blazer. She smiled and said hi. For the first time all day, my Parmesan's Team Smile faded. I couldn't smile, I couldn't say hello back, I couldn't look away. I just stood there holding a basket of breadsticks, staring at this woman.

Have you ever had a moment where you just *know* something out of the blue, no questions asked? I had one of those moments standing in the middle of Parmesan's, my nose full of garlic and ears full of forks scraping the final bits of bottomless salad drenched in Italian dressing from chilled ceramic bowls.

This woman was why Dad left Mom.

I'm sure I only stood there staring for a couple of seconds, but it felt like time stood still. Dad doesn't get flustered easily, but I could tell he was flustered when he spoke again.

Dad: When did you start working here?

Me: When did you stop having Korean barbecue for lunch?

I turned and headed toward the kitchen, blindly. As I walked around the food prep bar toward the dish room I heard Melanie chirp, "Full hands in!" at me, but I didn't stop. I walked past the dishwashers, through the door to dry storage in the corner, and leaned against a big metal rack stacked high with the boxed wine they use in the marinara sauce and to sauté mushrooms. I closed my eyes and took about ten long, deep breaths. All I could see was Annette's face, her bright red lipstick, her bright red hair, her bright green eyes. She was gorgeous.

And thin.

Mom never stood a chance.

I got a quick drink of water and found Melanie at the hot food counter. She took one look at me and knew something was up. I tried to plaster on my Parmesan's smile, but she doesn't miss much.

Melanie: Everything okay?

Me: Fine.

Melanie: Really?

Me: Yep. My dad's here.

Melanie (grinning): Oh, great! Which table?

Andy: Fourteen, and they need more water.

Me: Already?

Andy: Is that thirsty redhead your *mom*?

Me: Are you brain dead?

Melanie thought this was hilarious. I grabbed a pitcher of ice water and Andy followed me with their bowl of salad sputtering apologies. Melanie bought them dessert. Annette didn't eat a single bite. I stood there watching her refuse the bites of cheesecake Dad offered her while he tried to convince me to come to dinner with him the next night. I told him I'd think about it and that I had to go do my side work. He stood up and hugged me. When I tried to step back, he held on for a little bit longer, and something in his touch told me how much he missed me. His cologne smelled like pepper and peach blossoms and I heard myself whispering into his shoulder.

Me: Yes.

Dad: Yes what?

Me: I'll come to dinner.

Dad: Pick you up at seven o'clock.

Me: I'll meet you at Buster's. Some guy bought me this great SUV. I drive it everywhere.

I didn't tell Annette good-bye. I just walked to the back and joined Andy at the staff meal. I drank a glass of water and took a plate of chicken Parmesan. I picked off all the cheese and breading and just ate the chicken. Even without the fat and carbs it was delicious. I had a second piece and a small bowl of salad greens with no dressing. Andy asked me a bunch of

151

questions about Mom and Dad. I answered some of them, then told him I had to go.

Andy: Hot date tonight?

Me: Actually . . . yes.

My head was swimming. Maybe it was all the protein and roughage at once. Or maybe I was overwhelmed from seeing Dad with this Annette chick. Or maybe I just missed Jack.

When I got back home, Mom told me Dad had called her and said he'd seen me and that I'd agreed to go to dinner with him.

Mom: He was at Parmesan's?

Me: Yes. He came in for lunch.

Mom: By himself?

I opened my mouth to lie, but nothing came out. Mom saw in an instant, just like Melanie had earlier. A smile wasn't going to help any of this. And why should I be the one helping? This wasn't my fault.

As I trudged up the stairs to take a shower I heard the cabinets banging and the potato chip bags rustling and the spoon for some ice cream clank on the counter. I wanted to scream down the stairs. I wanted to yell at Mom: WHY DO YOU THINK HE LEFT? But what could I say? I was the one who had gobbled up a cubic ton of chicken during the staff meal. I had decided last night to eat lunch at work today. I told myself it was because I was freaked out by those pictures Jill showed me. Was it really? Maybe I was just eating my feelings too.

I stood in the shower and let the hot water pound onto my head. When I got out the house was still and I knew Mom had left for work. I let out a long, slow sigh and slipped into a clean T-shirt, then slid between the crisp, cool sheets on my bed.

I woke up a few minutes ago. My pillow is damp from falling asleep with wet hair. I'm going to blow it out as soon as I'm done writing. Jack is coming by to pick me up in an hour. I want to look perfect. I need to look perfect. I need to be close to him tonight. I need to feel his arms around me, and taste his lips on mine, and hear him tell me how beautiful I am.

Saturday, July 21
Weight: 120
Jack told me all of that and more.

Mini-golf devolved into Rob making chip shots at the windmill and purposely trying to hit the rotating blades. He finally succeeded, sending an orange golf ball ricocheting directly into Jill's leg. She was furious, and insisted we leave immediately so she could ice the purple welt halfway up her thigh. When we pulled into the driveway at their place, Jill stormed into the house, and Rob moaned and banged his head against the back of Jack's seat three times.

Rob: Why do I *do* this shit?

Jack (smirking): You're a glutton for punishment.

Rob: Or maybe I just like the makeup make-out session.

Jack (not smirking): Don't. Make. Me. Come. Back. There.

Rob got out of the car quickly. Jack rolled his eyes.

Jack: It's a good thing I like him. He's a scoundrel.

Me: I'm pretty sure Jill doesn't let him get away with a thing.

Jack: The question is, are *you* going to let me get away with anything?

Me (Southern accent): Why I de-*clare*, Mister Jack.

Jack laughed and reached over to take my hand. He brought it to his lips and kissed my fingers. He held on to it while he backed out of the driveway again, and as the moon rose over the mountain, we drove in silence. It was a comfortable silence, not a loaded one—no pregnant pause. It wasn't that either of us had something to say and was holding it back. Everything that needed to be expressed was happening in the way he laced his fingers through mine, and the way my thumb kept time with the music on the back of his hand.

I finally understood the phrase "Less is more."

Jack pulled into an industrial park behind the little airport in the center of town. He drove between the low adobe buildings filled with stores that sell construction contractors their windows, doors, and fixtures, scuba divers their gear, and mechanics their auto parts. Behind the last row of self-storage units was a twelve-foot-high chain-link fence that ran along the runway. Jack backed up against the fence, then pulled a stadium blanket out of his extended cab behind the seat. As the moon rose higher in the sky, we lay on our backs in the bed of his truck, holding hands, listening to the roar of the plane engines drown out the sound of the music filtering through the open window at the back of the cab.

Eventually, Jack rolled over on one elbow and stared at me. I felt his eyes on my face, then his hand sliding across my stomach, tucking beneath me, pulling me close to him. Both of his hands gripped my waist, and I realized that his fingers almost touched on either side. Something about this made me smile, and he smiled back.

Jack: You have such an amazing body. It's perfect.

I didn't speak, but I let my lips do the talking. I felt him pressing into me with that same reckless abandon he'd had on the deck of the boat last month, and I knew it was because he wanted me. I felt the thrill of his touch and the strength in his arms and legs. I recognized the fierce nature I'd stirred up inside him, and relished his passion. He wanted my body—this new, beautiful body of mine—and as his hands explored every inch of me, this time they slid under my clothes, taking my breath with their warmth and their tenderness. His hands were everywhere, his touch making me sure of his feelings for me even before he whispered, "I love you," into my ear. When he did, something rushed through me like the roar of the jets overhead, and using my perfect body, I assured him I felt the same without ever saying a word.

Saturday, July 21
Weight: 120.5

I can't believe he brought her.

When I walked into Buster's, Annette was sitting there next to him in the booth, smiling like it was Christmas morning and Santa had brought her a pony. When I saw her, I stopped short and just stared. When Dad spotted me and waved, he nudged her to slide over so he could get out of the booth, and she actually jumped up grinning, ran up to me, and gave me a hug.

A hug.

She pressed her enormous boobs, which were spilling out of her little strappy tank top, against me and said that it was great to see me again. Then Dad took a turn hugging me, and I whispered in his ear.

Me: Um . . . what is *she* doing here?

He tried to pull away, but I kept my arms around him, so his ear was close to my shoulder as he stuttered.

Dad: I . . . I . . . just . . . thought . . .

I plastered on my Parmesan's smile and peered over his shoulder at Annette.

Me: Would you excuse us just for a second? My mom gave me some stuff to give Dad, and I want to make sure I don't forget to get it out of the car later.

Annette nodded enthusiastically, and Dad sputtered protests as I dragged him by the hand into the parking lot, my smile now a grim line of determination drawn across my face, my cheeks hot with anger. In the parking lot, I let him have it.

Me: What the *hell* are you doing?

Dad: Now wait just a second—

Me: Nope. You don't get to talk right now. You get to listen. I did not sign up to have dinner with you and whoever that is, tonight. I agreed to have dinner with *you*.

His face clouded, and he crossed his arms like a toddler.

Dad: Her name is *Annette*. She's the office manager at the dealership. And she's my girlfriend.

Me: Really, Dad? *Really?* It's been what? Two months? Not even. It's been like *six weeks* since you walked out on me and Mom, and I'm just supposed to show up and have dinner with you and the chick with the tits in there?

Dad: You watch your mouth, young lady.

Me: I'll watch it all the way to my car.

I didn't look back as I walked to the enormous car he bought me. I didn't want him to see the tears sliding down my cheeks. He doesn't deserve to see me cry.

I get it that Mom is not a skinny, big-chested model. I understand that's what he wanted. I'd rather look like her than Mom, too. But he's my *dad*. Isn't he supposed to care about my feelings a little bit? Shouldn't he want to talk things over with me one-on-one at least *once* before I'm required to start having "family meals" with Boobalicious the office manager?

The worst part of it was that he didn't try to stop me. He didn't try to follow me. He just stood there in the parking lot and watched me go. This was supposed to be a special night. It was supposed to be this time when we regrouped, and talked, and cried—when he told me how sorry he was and when I told him that I understood more than he thought I did.

This was supposed to be the night when our relationship grew up. When he stopped being just my dad and started being my friend. I don't let my friends treat me this way. I'm not going to let him treat me this way either. I don't care if I never see him again.

It's just as well. There was nothing I could eat at Buster's anyway.

Sunday, July 22
Weight: 120

Couldn't sleep last night. Seeing Dad again ripped the scab off, and I couldn't stop thinking about him and Mom and everything that went wrong. Mom was up and in the kitchen in her sweatpants eating Lucky Charms and chirping to Pam on the phone. She was chewing with her mouth open and laughing really loudly, and I just couldn't deal with it. I drank three glasses of water, then brought a cup of coffee and a hard-boiled egg back up here to my room.

All I know for sure is that it grosses me out to watch Mom eat and act like that, and as much as Dad shouldn't have brought Annette to dinner last night, I can't blame him for wanting to be with her. In any sort of side-by-side comparison, Annette wins over Mom every time in the looks department.

As I finished my egg I glanced down at a picture of me and Mom and Dad on my desk. I was four years old, and we were at the water park here in town. I don't know who took this picture. Dad probably asked some stranger. Dad's tan and young and has a goatee. Mom isn't skinny, but she's curvy in all the right places. She's wearing a black one-piece suit that is cut just right for her figure and dark glasses. Her smile is beautiful and relaxed. She's laughing along with me as we try to pose in the shallow end of the wave pool.

We look happy.

I can't help but think we'd still be happy if Mom still looked like she does in this photo.

I was thinking about this and sipping my coffee as I opened my laptop. Maybe it was the caffeine, or maybe it was the web address I was typing into the browser, but my heart started to race as I scrolled the pictures on the site Jill showed me on Thursday. These girls are thin like Jill is. I remembered how Jack's hands had fit around my waist as he pulled me against him in the back of his truck. These girls in the pictures know what that feels like. They have control of their lives like Susan and Jill. They are the opposite of my mother.

I will be like them. I will have more willpower than my mother. I will not let Jack leave me the way Mom let Dad leave her.

Sunday, August 26
Weight: 119

School starts tomorrow. Jill just left. We planned our outfits and she posted the following on the website:

THE THIN COMMANDMENTS
1. Thin = Attractive. If you are not thin, you are not attractive.

2. Thou shalt do everything within your power to make yourself look thinner. This includes clothing, hairstyle, exercise, and taking laxatives when needed.

3. Thou shalt not eat without feeling guilty.

4. Thou shalt punish yourself for eating fattening foods.

5. Thou shalt always count and restrict your calories.

6. Thou shalt remember that what the scale says is the most important thing.

7. Being thin is more important than being healthy.

8. There is no such thing as "too thin."

9. Restricting calories and staying thin are the measure of true willpower and success.

I printed out a copy and taped it inside my notebook. I took a picture of it with my phone, so I can look at it if I'm feeling tempted.

Jill is down to only a hundred pounds. All of those areas she circled last month have somehow gotten smaller. I stopped writing for a while because all I could think about was Dad, and I didn't want to deal with it. I've been running every day whether Vanessa comes or not. I've kept my calories down to around 1,200 to 1,500 per day. Jill is restricting hers to 1,000 to 1,200 per day. She's never danced better. I've never had better times running.

I don't care if Vanessa is "concerned."

I'm fine.

I'm better than fine.

I'm better than ever.

(Just ask Jack.)

Sunday, September 2
Weight: 119

I came in second place at the invitational yesterday. Our team won the meet for the first time in four years. Coach Perkins hugged me and jumped up and down and cried when I crossed the finish line. Afterward, she gathered everybody and announced her decision to make me team captain. She told everyone that I was an example of what you could do if you put your mind to it and trained like a champion. Vanessa and Geoff could barely look at me, but I didn't care.

We won.

I won.

Dad showed up at the meet. No Annette. He gave me a hug

and told me he was proud of me. He should be. I kicked butt. He wanted to take me out to dinner, but I saw Mom standing at the edge of the parking lot talking to Jack and Rob, and I told Dad I had to go. Jack asked Mom if she wanted to come with us to get dinner after the race. She had to run home and then head to work, but it was just like Jack to offer.

We went to meet Rob and Jill at this restaurant where they bake your pizza in a wood-fire oven. Rob and Jack ate an entire pig's worth of pepperoni. I had a salad with Jill, dressing on the side, and I decided to allow myself a single glorious slice. I chewed the first bite slowly, and the gooey, salty, greasy deliciousness ran across my tongue and made my eyes roll back in my head. It was the best pizza I'd ever tasted. Then I took a second bite, and I realized something:

It never tastes any better than the first bite.

I put the slice back down on the plate while Rob and Jack ordered more Coke and talked to a guy from the soccer team they ran into, and Jill was checking a voice mail message on her phone. I thought about the salad I'd eaten most of, except for the croutons, and the bit of pizza I'd just swallowed, and I realized I was full. I didn't need the rest of that piece of pizza. I'd already enjoyed the first bite, and it was never going to taste any better than that.

The thought was like a cool breeze on a warm day, and I smiled really big at Jack as he and Rob finished talking to their friend and came back to the table. Just as they sat down, Jill's eyes went wide with the phone pressed to her ear and she started squealing and laughing and hopping up and down in the booth, and then tears started streaming down her cheeks.

Jill: I got it! I got it!

Rob: Holy cow. Watch it! You're gonna spill your water!

Me: Are you okay?

Jill: I'm better than okay. I'm *Clara* in the mother-effing *Nutcracker*!

Jack and I cheered like idiots, and we dragged her out of the booth and hugged her in the middle of the restaurant. I'm sure everybody thought we'd lost our minds. I didn't care. This is what discipline looks like. This is what willpower looks like.

Take *that*, Misty Jenkins.

Saturday, September 8
Weight: 119

Jack asked me to homecoming.

That sentence is amazing all by itself, but what's even more incredible is the *way* he asked me to homecoming. I went to Jill's last night after practice. Mom was already at work, so we hung out with James and Susan, who were watching some old romantic comedy about a hockey player and a figure skater who fall in love. Jill crushed up four rice cakes in a big bowl and made us "skinny-girl popcorn." If you pour enough salt on them, it almost works. I kept expecting Jack to come home, but James told me he and Rob were out shopping for supplies for some sort of science project they had to put together.

Rob and Jack arrived as the credits were rolling and both of them squeezed in next to us on the giant chesterfield sofa. Jack grinned and kissed me on the cheek. We talked with his parents for a while, then he asked if I wanted to go get yogurt at YouGoYum. I looked at Jill with raised eyebrows and she held up a hand like a stop sign.

Jill: No carbs for Clara.

Rob (yawning): Yeah, I gotta get home. My pops wants me to help him paint the garage door in the morning.

Me (to Jack): Shall I drive or do you want to?

Jack: I'll drive.

We held hands all the way there, and when Jack made a large swirl with caramel, hot fudge, bananas, and walnuts, I told him I'd just have a bite of his. The first bite was delicious. The second one he held out I politely declined. He shook his head.

Jack: I don't know how you do it.

Me: Do what?

Jack: Stay so disciplined—and gorgeous. You're like an Olympic athlete or something.

I decided to let him in on my newfound secret, and shrugged.

Me: It never tastes any better than the first bite.

He laughed and shook his head, then wolfed down the rest of his yogurt and dragged me back to the car. When we got to the intersection where he should have gone right to head to his house, he turned left and drove toward mine. Before I registered that my car was still at his place, we were turning into the driveway at mine, and as we did, a huge lit sign across the garage door blinked. There must've been *hundreds* of little white lights that spelled out my name and the words "Will You Go to Homecoming With Me? Love Jack." He had to have spent *hours* working on it—punching holes through giant sheets of foam board and arranging all the letters just right.

I sat there in shock as Jack reached behind the seat and pulled out a dozen roses.

Me: But—how did—

Jack: There's no science project. Well, there is, but Rob and I weren't shopping for that.

Me: How . . . ?

Jack: Did we turn them on? It's a timer. I nabbed a house key from your mom last week at your meet so we could set it up.

There were tears in my eyes. I'd always gone to the dances at school with either a random guy I didn't really like or as Geoff and Vanessa's third wheel. Now, for the first time, I was going to go with a boy that I really cared for—and not just any boy. I was going with Jack, the best-looking one of the popular senior guys.

Jack: Cat got your tongue?

Me: I . . . I can't—

Jack (whispering): Move over, cat. It's my turn.

He kissed me so gently and sweetly and fully on the mouth that the tears in my eyes spilled down my cheeks from the sheer joy of being me, in my skin, in my life at that moment. He kissed my neck and whispered in my ear.

Jack: Every taste of you is better than the last.

Jill was still up waiting for us when we got back to their house. Rob hadn't gone anywhere either. Everybody had been in on it, and we stayed up late in the hot tub, then I texted Mom at work that I was going to sleep over at Jill's, and this morning we went dress shopping for formals with Susan to celebrate.

Susan insisted on buying me a dress.

Susan: Please. Your poor mom is probably too exhausted from working her tail off to join us. I'll get the money from her later. *Besides*, this is a special occasion. We're celebrating what a great job you girls are already doing. Winning cross-country meets and ballet roles. I'm just so *proud* of you. Not to mention, you look *fabulous*.

Jill tried on seventeen dresses before choosing the first one she'd picked up (naturally), a short black sequined sheath with a black tulle pouf that wrapped on one shoulder. I tried on four but kept coming back to a dress I didn't have the nerve to pick up. Susan saw me eyeing it because when I opened the dressing room door, she was standing there holding it.

It was simple red organza silk, not shiny, but rich, textured and bright. It was fitted at the top with a plunging neckline and back line. No beads, no prints, no bangles, no tassels or trim. It just fell to a pool behind my feet with the tiniest train. When I opened the dressing room door so Susan could zip the back, Jill caught a glimpse of the front in the mirror and gasped.

Jill: That's it.

Me: I'm not sure if I can pull this off. It seems a little . . .

Jill: Dramatic. It's *amazing*.

Susan: I can almost get it closed. What size is this?

Me: It's a two. I'm really a four.

Susan: No, you're right in between. Let's get you this. You have six weeks and all you need to do is take off a couple more pounds and it'll be stunning.

Me: Are you sure?

Susan turned me back toward the mirror and told me to stand up straight. I did.

Susan: Now on your toes like you're wearing heels.

When I stood up on my toes, the hem at the front of

the dress cascaded down, just brushing the floor, and at that moment, Susan took my long blond hair from behind and wrapped it skillfully into a makeshift French twist, just like hers.

The effect was startling.

Jill: Wow.

Susan: This is the dress. You look like Grace Kelly.

Me: You really think I can do it?

Jill: As of right now, you don't have a choice.

This afternoon, Jill gave me something she calls "ballerina tea." It's made from the leaves of a plant that helps your body "cleanse." She told me to drink a mug every day, and then again at night before bed, but not to drink it before I was going to leave the house for anything important. I just had my first mug, and about an hour later I had my first "cleanse." She wasn't kidding. I'm going to have to stay close to home drinking this tea.

I'm sitting here staring at this dress hanging on my closet door. I'm feeling a little panicked about being able to fit into it, but I *have* to. I will *never forgive myself* if I don't. Mom came in a few minutes ago and asked me how it all went. I showed her the pictures I took of the sign on the garage door last night, and she hugged me. For just a minute, it was like I forgot all about the problems with her and Dad and how annoyed with her I've been lately. She was so happy for me.

Mom: Jack is a *good guy*.

Me (smiling): Yeah . . . he's pretty special.

Mom: Now! Let me see you in this dress!

It took me a minute to convince her that I needed to shower before I put it on, and that I really needed to find the right shoes first, and she wouldn't leave me alone about it until I promised her that we'd go shop for shoes together tomorrow. She wrote me a check to give to Susan for the dress and told me she was sorry she'd been so out of it and working so much. Now she's back downstairs, and I can hear the TV.

The work begins now. I know what I have to do. I have six weeks to fit in this dress, and I intend to if it's the last thing I do.

First I'm going to run.

Then I need to find a red marker.

Sunday, September 9
Weight: 118.5

I don't understand my mother. You'd think that after all she's been through, she'd see what I'm doing—what I'm trying to do, the sacrifices I'm making—and put it all together. You'd think she'd be able to see that I'm just trying my hardest not to end up unhappy and divorced. Instead, she's bound and determined to make me as miserable as she is.

It happened after my run yesterday morning. Usually, after I run, I feel *better* about things, but for some reason, when I walked into my bedroom and pulled off my sweaty clothes, I saw my homecoming dress hanging on the closet door and I just felt panicked. I caught a glimpse of my body in the mirror, and it looked way too big to *ever* fit into that beautiful red gown, and the idea of not being able to wear that dress in six weeks when Jack comes to pick me up in his tuxedo made me start to cry.

Usually I'm not so emotional, but I'd just run five and a half miles, and all I could see in the mirror yesterday were all the places on my body that stretched against that beautiful red size-two dress.

I dug through my desk until I found a red marker and stood in front of my mirror just like I'd seen Jill do. I circled every part of my stomach and hips and arms and chest that needed to go away, but it just seemed like the red circles on my skin made those places grow and swell until they were like gross, sagging bags of fat swinging from my body. I started to cry harder, and right at that very second, I realized I hadn't locked my door—just as Mom knocked softly and opened it to see if I was all right.

I saw from the look on her face that she knew *exactly* what I was doing. I screamed at her to get out of my room, and she didn't say anything or move at all. She just stood at the door, her mouth open, but no sound coming out.

I threw myself down on the bed and pulled my comforter over me and cried. I lay there for a long time, sobbing into my pillow, until I thought she was probably gone, but then I felt her hand on my back as she sat down next to me on the bed.

I thought she was going to lecture me.

I thought she was going to tell me all the things I already know about what she's afraid will happen to me.

Instead she just helped me up and into the shower, and when I got out there was a note on my pillow that said:

Come find me when you want to talk.

I love you.

Mom

I don't want to talk to her about this right now.

I don't think I can avoid her forever.

Monday, September 10
Weight: 118

Mom was waiting for me in the kitchen just now when I woke up. She was standing there with a big smile on her face and had a bowl of oatmeal with yogurt and strawberries on top. There was one for each of us. She asked me if I wanted coffee, and I told her I was going to make some tea. Thank God Jill gave me this stuff because Mom forced me to choke down the entire bowl of oatmeal. When I put it all into the CalorTrack app just now it was over four hundred calories with the berries and the yogurt.

I didn't try to argue with her. I knew that would just make things worse. Every bite felt like it lodged in my stomach, and I can feel it hanging there inside of me, making all the spots I circled last night stick out, making it impossible for me to fit into that dress.

The food wasn't the worst part of breakfast. No, it was Mom's new rules. She went on and on about the dangers of teenage girls and calorie restriction and the girls she's seen come into the ER who are so underweight that they can't hold a spoon and have permanent heart damage. I hadn't seen Mom this alive and fired up since Dad left. I have unwittingly given her a purpose in life now: keeping me as fat as she can.

So now, not only do I have to lose eight pounds in six weeks, I have to do it in spite of being forced to eat breakfast with Mom every morning before I go to school. This is her new requirement for letting me out the door.

Fine.

I'll just get up earlier and run before school. I'll put myself on two-a-day runs. I'll go in the morning before I have to eat breakfast and in the afternoon at practice. This is who I am now: the girl who doesn't back down. I will fit into that dress in six weeks. Nothing and no one will stop me. Not Mom. Not oatmeal. Not my own lack of discipline.

The tea just kicked in. Gotta run.

Wednesday, September 12
Weight: 118

Part of me is seething inside. Part of me wants to run down the hall right now after my mom and scratch her eyes out. I'm going to write until that part of me is silenced.

That's the part of me that is out of control, the part of me that must be contained. That's the part of me that will cause me to lose it and go berserk, to stuff my face with anything it sees to make these feelings go away.

I just got home from practice and passed Mom in the hall.

Mom: Did you talk to Coach Perkins?

Me: Yeah.

Mom: Everything okay, sweetie?

Me (Parmesan's smile): Yep! Everything's cool.

Mom: Good. I love you so much. I left you a barbecue chicken breast and some mashed potatoes on the counter.

Me: Thanks! I'm going to take a shower. Have a good night at work.

The fact that she called Coach Perkins makes me want to throw things. I closed the door and listened for the garage to open and close behind her. Then I hit my bed with a pillow about twenty times. When Coach asked me to stay behind after practice, I saw Vanessa's eyes shoot over at me, and I just *knew* she was hoping I was going to get into trouble. Coach was pretty calm about the whole thing, just said Mom was "concerned" and she wanted to make sure I was being truthful about my calories.

Coach: You're running better than you ever have. I just want to make sure you can keep it up.

Me: Everything is fine. Mom is just worried because I've lost a few pounds.

Coach: I know you've had a hard summer, but I want to make sure you keep winning. You have to eat right to make that happen.

Me: I'm eating a ton.

Coach: Winning is not more important than your health.

My face was so red it must've looked like it was going to catch fire. Vanessa tried to follow me to my car, but I walked right past her. She and Geoff still eat with us every day at lunch,

175

but I can barely talk to her. She just doesn't understand. She doesn't get it.

Jill just texted me back. I'm going to meet her at the park to do our workout.

Right after I bury those mashed potatoes in the outside trash can.

Thursday, September 13
Weight: 117

My mother is going to destroy me. She announced this morning over yet another bowl of carbohydrate-filled oatmeal sprinkled with fattening, sugary dried fruit pieces that she has decided to transfer to the day shift.

Why?

Well, me of course. She thinks I must be fed like a toddler. After talking with Coach Perkins on the phone about our little chat on Wednesday, she thinks it would be best if we "spent more time together. Especially *dinnertime*."

I could barely contain my rage.

But I did it.

My lip quivered, and my Parmesan's smile failed me, but I managed a nod and a quick "Great, Mom" and kept from shattering my bowl in the sink until she'd gone upstairs to get in the shower. By the time she was done, I had cleaned up the porcelain shards and was on my way out the door to school.

As I pulled into the parking lot, I took a deep breath, knowing that surely the very worst part of my day was over. I'd been up since 6 a.m., after all. I'd run a fast-paced five-miler, then showered, pooped, and weighed myself to find the scale said I was exactly where I'd been yesterday. Then I'd had to suffer through yet another breakfast while dealing with the worst news ever from Mom. This means she'll be hovering over me in the morning at breakfast, and again at night, when I usually don't have to eat anything after school. Now I'll have to contend with her at dinner at 8 p.m.

I cannot eat that late at night.

But no matter. I was finally at school. Jill brought me more tea bags. They kicked in during second period. We planned and strategized. We would meet and work out every night after my cross-country practice. I'd do double the running and double the workouts. From here, everything would look up. Nothing could make the day any more terrible.

Then Vanessa sat down at lunch. She reached across the table in front of Geoff, Rob, Jack, and Jill and grabbed my hand.

Vanessa (concerned): How did it go with Coach Perkins?

My blood froze.

Rob: How did *what* go with Coach Perkins?

Me: Nothing. It's fine.

Vanessa: Did she ask you about your food diary?

Me (firmly): Everything. Is. Fine.

I don't think I could have shot a more fierce look at her across the table, but it was like Vanessa was operating under a force field.

Vanessa: I just worry about you. You and Jill never eat very much.

Jill (icily): We eat plenty. And it's none of your business.

Vanessa (turning to me): It's just that you're so . . .

Jack: Beautiful?

It wasn't like him to jump in or even really pay attention to Vanessa, but all of a sudden his arm was around me, and I felt the warmth of his body on my shoulders. His gaze silenced Vanessa, and Geoff made some sort of stupid joke. Then Rob jumped in and started talking about the limo the guys want to rent for homecoming.

Jack kept his arm around my shoulders during lunch and walked me down the hall to my locker after we left the cafeteria.

Jack: She's just jealous.

Me: Really, I'm not worried about it.

Jack: She just wishes she was as fast as you, or as gorgeous.

He reached down and lifted my chin and kissed me lightly on the lips right there in the middle of the hall.

I went straight to the park after running and worked out with Jill. Mom still has a week and a half on the night shift, so when I came home, I did the whole workout again in my bedroom. Then I lay on the floor staring at the red dress in the clear plastic wrapper. All I could hear were Vanessa's words in my head. She acts so *concerned*, like it's her very own Lifetime movie and she's the best friend trying to keep everyone from going off the rails.

How dare she bring up my weight or my looks or my eating habits in front of Jack?

I looked around my room at all the little-girl crap that is still everywhere, and I couldn't stand the clutter anymore. I don't want stuffed animals in my bedroom. I don't want cute and cuddly. I don't want anything that reminds me of my dad, or my mom's knickknack crap all over everything. I want things to be clean and organized.

I raced down the stairs and grabbed garbage bags and started filling them up with all the lacy, frilly crap my mom puts everywhere. The flowers she dried for me from the Valentine's bouquet she gave me last year. The silly spoons and bells she used to bring back from all over the country when we went on vacation for "my collection."

This crap was never mine. It was hers.

I hauled most of it out to the trash. I kept a bag of stuffed animals and put them on the shelves in the garage next to a plastic bin of Christmas decorations. Then I vacuumed and dusted and straightened and organized until my room looked like a place where I wanted to be—a place of clean, sharp edges and symmetry, well arranged, with nothing but the absolute essentials, and the red dress, hanging on the closet door, reminding me that I can do anything, that I *must* do anything required to stay on track.

I can feel the places that I circled with that marker pulsing on my skin as I write this. I can feel that all my hard work today has paid off. I hope the scale won't tell a different story tmorrow.

Friday, September 14
Weight: 115.7

I am almost halfway to my goal. When I saw what the scale said this morning, I knew I was doing the right things. At school, Jill agreed, and hugged me when I told her how I was only five pounds away from 110. She texted me a link to a page of negative-calorie foods during second period. Negative calorie supposedly means that it actually burns more calories to digest the food than the food contains. The result is that your stomach is full, but your body burns up the calories from the food as you digest it.

Today at lunch, Vanessa and Geoff were right behind me in the lunch line at the salad bar in the cafeteria. My plate was piled high with the foods on the list Jill sent me: apple slices, celery sticks, and raw spinach.

Vanessa: Um . . . how are you going to make your calorie requirement for Coach if you're only eating apple slices and celery sticks? Don't you want some protein?

I pulled a bag of gummy fruit snacks out of my purse and tossed them onto the tray. I hadn't put one in my mouth for at least a couple of months, but she didn't need to know that. I like having them in my purse because it reminds me that I'm the one in control. At any moment, I could reach in and pour pure corn syrup down my throat.

But I don't.

Vanessa looked at the fruit snacks, then up at me. I could see the suspicion in her eyes.

Me: See? I eat. Lay off.

She opened her mouth again to speak. Geoff nudged her and shook his head.

Maybe Geoff is smarter than he lets on.

Tuesday, September 25
Weight: 114.5

I hate myself for begging. That was the worst part of it. I never want to be reduced to that again.

Vanessa was waiting for me at my locker today before we went to practice. I was grabbing the printout of my calories from the CalorTrack app when my ring slipped off my finger. It's from Tiffany. Mom gave it to me for my fifteenth birthday last year, and I tossed my books into my locker and hit my hands and knees. Everybody around me in the hall kept walking and tripping over me, and I saw the ring get kicked twice before I finally nabbed it.

I didn't understand why Vanessa wasn't helping me direct traffic or find the ring, until I stood up and saw her face. Apparently, all of my books had tumbled back out of the locker and she had scooped them up. When she did, she saw this notebook—the original food diary.

Her face was pale. She looked like she was going to cry. She held it out to me as I walked back toward her at the locker, a sinking feeling in my stomach that turned to panic.

Me: Wait. Vanessa. Wait.

Vanessa: What is *this*? What are you *doing*?

Me: Vanessa, it's not that big a deal. It's not—

Vanessa: It *is* a big deal. It is a *very* big deal. You are going to tell Coach right now, or I will.

That's when I started begging.

And bargaining.

And promising her anything.

She finally said she wouldn't tell Coach on one condition: That I start eating again. Every meal. Every bite. Enough calories. The recommended amount of 2,200 per day for my height and activity level.

She made me promise.

She made me swear.

I've still got four pounds to lose before two weeks from Saturday. I don't care what I said to Vanessa. I'm going to make it happen.

Wednesday, September 26
Weight: 114

Today is Mom's first day shift. She looked a little frazzled and I think it's going to take her some time to get on a normal sleep schedule. She just buzzed around the kitchen dropping things, and it took her three tries to get to the car after breakfast. She kept having to come in and get stuff: keys, sunglasses, wallet.

Something I realized as I sat there eating my required breakfast in front of her: she wasn't really watching me. I took a bite and then swallowed it, then took another bite and spit it out in my napkin when she wasn't looking. She didn't even notice. After that, I realized I could throw most of my oatmeal away in my paper napkin.

When the bowl was empty, I took it to the sink and rinsed it out. She kissed me on the cheek and scooted out to the garage for the third time. I made another mug of ballerina tea to keep the bites I did swallow moving on through me.

I have no idea what to expect tonight.

Later . . .

Dinner.

That's what I had to expect.

And of course, she made a big deal of it. She insisted we go out to get burgers at Buster's. I got a protein-style, and I didn't get any fries or onion rings.

Mom chirped on and on about how great it was going to be to finally work days like a normal person and not feel like a vampire. She's *very excited* about getting to spend more time with me, and talked about all the special dinners we could have together. She *totally understands* that I want to eat healthily so she talked and talked and talked about the food she was going to make me.

I'd never been so happy to see my phone light up when Dad called in the middle of her lemon-pepper chicken recipe. I pointed at my phone and said, "Dad," which stopped her midsentence, then I took a huge bite of hamburger and held it in my mouth as I slipped out of the booth and answered the phone with the wad of ground beef on one side of my mouth.

Dad: Hey, honey! Glad I got you on the phone.

Me: Hi.

Dad: Are you . . . eating? Did I call at a bad time?

Me: Hang on.

I pushed through the bathroom door and spit the huge bite of burger into the trash can. It was quieter in here.

Me: Hi. Sorry. Mom and I are at Buster's.

Dad: Oh! Great. Listen, I was wondering if you wanted to come over and stay the weekend at my place. Or maybe even Friday night? We could go to your meet together on Saturday? I finally got the guest room all set up and . . .

His voice trailed off. I just stood there waiting. It felt like I was supposed to say something now, and I didn't know what. I hated these silences between us now. Like it was somehow my job to be perky and cheerful and make everyone feel better about the crap they were putting me through.

Dad: You there?

Me: Yeah. Um . . . maybe . . . some other weekend, Dad. It's just . . . this weekend is really busy. I know you work late on Friday, and the meet is early on Saturday, and I have a date that night.

Dad: A date, huh?

Me: Yeah. Dad, I have to go.

Dad: Okay, sweetheart. Well, maybe the next weekend?

Me: Sure. Maybe, I'll look at my calendar.

He told me he loved me and then he hung up. All of a sudden, my stomach cramped up. I raced into a stall and threw up the bites of the burger I'd eaten.

Turns out there's a silver lining to phone calls from Dad after all.

Sunday, September 30
Weight: 113

I just got home from the hospital.

I sat and stared at that first sentence for a little while after I wrote it. I still can't believe I collapsed during the meet yesterday.

I didn't feel bad yesterday morning. The gun went off, and we started running. I pulled away from the pack with Vanessa right behind me, and two girls from the Riverside team in front of me. I don't like to try to run in the lead because it makes me nervous. I'm always looking over my shoulder for someone to be nipping at my heels. I like to hang back until I can tell the leaders are getting winded, then I try to make a move and come from behind in the last mile. The trick is not getting too far behind.

After two miles through the wash along the back edge of the school, we doubled back, following the markers along a golf course, and the mountains came into full view. They were majestic in shades of purple and blue, summits of torn construction paper stretched across the sky. Their fuzzy, jagged edges reached up toward the bright rays of the sun, which warmed my face. Everything else seemed to fall away. I stretched out my stride and made my move on the Riverside girls, sailing past them in a burst of speed. Now it was only me, out in front with a mile to go, then a half mile, then a quarter mile. I rounded the back of the fine arts building into the roped-off course that led toward the track. I heard the cheers of the small crowd of parents and friends watching from the bleachers near the finish line. I felt a rush through my head like a buzzing, and a smile formed on my lips. I sped up as I raced across the grass toward the edge of the track. I could hear my own heartbeat pounding in my ears as the white-hot light of the sun filled my eyes and then . . .

I heard a beep.

BEEP

BEEP

BEEP

BEEP

. . . and a voice:

Do you know where you are?

Can you tell me your name?

Do you know what day it is?

Slowly, the bright, white light of the sun narrowed into a single beam, which came from the end of a tiny penlight held by a woman with dark skin in a white jacket. She was asking me the questions.

Do you know where you are?

Do you know what happened?

Can you hear me?

I answered her questions:

No.

No.

Yes.

I looked around and slowly other faces came into focus: Mom, her mascara running down her cheeks; Dad, his eyes red and frightened; Coach Perkins, her lips set in a thin, straight line.

The woman in the white jacket was Dr. Nash, a friend of Mom's from the hospital, which is where I was.

Mom said I'd collapsed during the race.

Dr. Nash said I was dehydrated and beginning to show signs of malnourishment.

Coach Perkins said she'd gone over my CalorTrack printouts

and she had some questions about what I'd been eating.

Dad couldn't say anything. He just stared at me, lying there in the bed with a tube pumping fluids into my arm.

Mom said I had to start eating more.

Dr. Nash said I had to stay overnight for observation.

Coach said I was benched until I gained some weight.

Dad ran his hand over his face, kissed my forehead, and walked into the hallway, and I fell back asleep for what felt like a very long time.

When I opened my eyes this morning at 6:12 a.m., Mom was sleeping in the chair next to my bed. I guess she'd been there all night long. She had a blanket wrapped around her, and it was just the two of us, the beep of my heart monitor, and the gentle sound of her breathing, in and out, peaceful and slow.

My head felt clear, and I wasn't tired. There was a vase with bright yellow gerbera daisies and purple statice sitting on the little table next to the bed. I lay there trying to remember if they'd been there yesterday. I couldn't. I tried to remember anything at all between racing for the finish line and winding up in a hospital bed, but I couldn't. I watched Mom sleep in the chair, and I wondered where Dad had gone when he left.

Mom woke up when a couple of nurses who she works with in the ER came to check on us. When they went back downstairs, Mom told me Jack had come by yesterday evening, but I was sound asleep. He wouldn't let her wake me; he just left the flowers. When I checked my phone there was a single text from him:

Hope you're feeling better. I love you.

After I read that, I did feel better, even when Mom and Dr. Nash insisted I eat two bowls of Jell-O and a plate of scrambled eggs with cheese in front of them. As I ate, they asked me questions:

Had I been limiting my calories instead of keeping the goal set by Coach?

Why did I feel I needed to lose weight?

Did I know how dangerous it was for my heart and kidneys to be running long distances without proper nutrition?

Did I understand the long-term effects of not eating enough calories?

I answered all the questions correctly, but all I could hear in my head as I swallowed the cool, sweet gelatin squares was Susan's voice in my head:

Carbs are killing us.

Before she left the room, Dr. Nash looked right into my eyes and put a hand on my shoulder.

Dr. Nash: You are dangerously thin. You're a pretty girl, but you are more than ten pounds underweight. A young woman who is five seven should weigh well over 120 pounds; with your athletic frame, closer to 130. When was the last time you had your period?

I didn't say anything.

Mom: Sweetheart?

Dr. Nash: Did you have it this month?

I couldn't look at her. I shook my head.

Dr. Nash: Last month.

Me: No.

She turned to my mom.

Dr. Nash: We have worked together for how many years now?

Mom: Almost ten . . .

Dr. Nash: Would I lie to you?

Mom: No.

Dr. Nash: I need both of y'all to hear this. If you don't start eating more calories every day, you will be back. And if you come back, I'm going to send you to the thirteenth floor.

Mom has talked about the thirteenth floor for years. It's the psych ward, the floor in the hospital with a series of locked doors between the patients and the elevators.

Mom was quiet on the way home. When we walked into the kitchen, she gave me a hug and told me two things: I love you. Dinner is at seven.

I came upstairs and took a long shower, and when I came out of the bathroom just now, I saw the red dress hanging on the closet door. I sat and stared at it for the longest time. The hospital room seems very far away somehow—like a dream.

Was I really just there?

Did I really collapse?

Was it really because I've been dieting?

All I want is to fit in this dress. I started to get dressed, and then instead of pulling on my jeans, I walked over and took the dress off the hanger. I was able to zip it all the way up, and it's only a tiny bit snug. Three more pounds is all it would take.

I felt my heart begin to race, and for the first time in this whole ordeal, a tear slid down my cheek. I thought about Jack's face when I walked down the stairs in this dress. I'm three pounds away from that moment.

I don't want to end up back in the hospital. I don't want to be locked up on the psych floor. Why is it so wrong for me to want my body to be perfect?

I've come so far. I can't stop now, can I?

Mom just called up the stairs. Dinner is ready.

Monday, October 1
Weight: 114

I thought it would be all over school today, but if anyone had heard about me passing out during the race on Saturday, no one seemed that interested.

Except for Vanessa.

She met me in the parking lot this morning. As I pulled in, she walked toward my car, and I let out a long, slow sigh. I didn't think I could handle an "I told you so" this early in the day, but it looked like I wouldn't have a choice. I grabbed my bag, climbed out of the SUV, and braced myself for her scolding.

Instead, she gave me a hug.

Vanessa: I'm so glad you're okay. I was so scared.

It was Vanessa who got to me first. Vanessa who stopped running to roll me over and make sure I was still breathing. Now she was crying and hugging me, and instead of feeling her disapproval, all I felt was her love. We stood and cried in the parking lot.

Vanessa: I don't want to lose you.

Me: You won't.

Vanessa: I won't lie for you anymore. If your food diary isn't correct, I'm going to tell Coach. I'm going to speak up because I won't stand by while you starve yourself to death.

I followed her to the bathroom, where we fixed our makeup. I looked at her in the mirror and whispered, "Thank you."

Vanessa: For what?

Me: For being my friend.

She smiled, then we grabbed our stuff and hurried to first period. Jill was quiet all morning between classes, and went off campus with Rob for lunch. I texted her and she texted me back to say she'd call me tonight after her ballet class.

I wonder if she's worried. I can't help thinking that maybe she's afraid I'll tell people how much she's been restricting her calories. I would never do that to her. Her body is her business. Maybe she's not worried about me telling anyone else. Maybe she's worried I won't be as fun to hang out with? Or that I'll get preachy like Vanessa? I know I just need to talk to her so that she'll know I'm still the same old me, even if I have to eat more.

I checked in with Coach at practice and told her what I'd had for lunch: turkey wrap, apple, half a bag of fruit snacks. She hugged me too, and all of a sudden when she did, I just wanted to get out of there. I knew she wasn't going to let me run, but I resent having to tell her what I ate for lunch. The thought went through my head that I wished everyone would stop hugging me. Jill didn't hug me today. She kept her distance. She probably knew I needed some space.

Jill still gets me better than anybody else.

Except maybe Jack.

We talked on the phone last night after dinner, and I told him I wasn't allowed to practice until I'd fully recovered. I did not go into what "fully recovered" entailed. I didn't want him to think his girlfriend was going to become a blimp. He came by after his soccer practice just now. His hair was all sweaty and he was wearing soccer sandals and those big socks that normally go over your shin guards.

There is something undeniably sexy about a boy in soccer socks. We made out for a while on the couch, and then he just held me and we watched TV. Or I should say, the TV was on.

Jack: You okay?

Me: I will be.

Jack: Is there anything I can do?

Me: You're doing it.

I felt his big biceps tense around me as he squeezed me gently to his chest. I kicked him out at 7 p.m., when I knew Mom was clocking out at the hospital.

Jack: I liked it better when your mom worked nights.

Me: You and me both.

Wednesday, October 3
Weight: I DON'T KNOW

I don't *know* how much I weigh right now because Mom threw the scale away. She literally put it out with the trash yesterday morning. I weighed myself yesterday morning before school, then drove off to endure *another* day of Jill being standoffish, Vanessa being wildly huggy, and Coach making me recite what I had for lunch when I checked in at practice.

As I was driving home, it hit me: I'm cranky because I haven't been running. I have been missing my runner's high. My brain needs those chemicals to deal with stress. Of course, Mom and Coach would flip if they knew I'd started running again, but I'm so close to fitting in the dress, and I've been eating every single meal every single day since Sunday night.

I changed and did a quick four-mile loop around the neighborhood, then showered and stashed my shoes in my closet instead of leaving them by the back door like I usually do. I was working on chemistry when Mom got back from work.

She poked her head in my room and started asking me about my day, then started giving me the third degree about what I'd done after school.

Me: You're looking at it. Chemistry.

Mom: Have you talked to Jill?

Me: I saw her at school today. She's at ballet.

Mom: She called you Monday night, right?

Me: Yeah, on her way home from class.

Mom: And?

Me: And . . . what?

Mom: Honey, I'm just . . . worried.

Me: Worried about what?

Mom: I want you to be careful about hanging out with Jill.

I lost my mind. I yelled. Mom yelled back. I started crying. I told her Jill was my best friend and I didn't care. I was going to hang out with her. Mom brought up Susan, and how she was encouraging Jill to get too thin for ballet and how dangerous that was, and the longer I listened the more quiet I became. Sometimes when I get mad at Mom I just shut down.

This was one of those times.

She finally finished lecturing me and I took several deep breaths. When I heard her go back downstairs and start pulling food out of the fridge, I went to the bathroom to weigh myself. I don't know why, but it calms me down, knowing for sure what my weight is. Somehow the knowing makes it okay—makes it all measurable and manageable. It gives things an order, a number, a plan of action.

The scale was gone.

Sometimes Mom has borrowed it to weigh boxes when she sends something she's bought online back because it doesn't fit. I walked into her room and looked by her desk. It wasn't there either. I checked her bathroom. No luck. Finally I went downstairs and asked her where it was.

Mom: I threw it away, sweetheart.

Me: You *what*?

It came out louder and more shrill than I'd intended it to.

Mom: You are obsessed about how much you weigh and it's

not healthy. You were in the *hospital* on Saturday and Sunday
because you're not *eating enough*.

Suddenly we were shouting again. I kept screaming about
how I was supposed to make sure I was eating enough calories,
how I would know if it was working. She kept saying how
unhealthy it was until finally I'd had it.

Me: Unhealthy? I'm the unhealthy one? Have you looked at
yourself in the mirror lately?

Mom: That's *it*, young lady. You're *grounded*.

Me (laughing): Grounded? From what? The *scale*?

Mom: You are not to leave this house without my
permission. You are not to talk to or hang out with Jill unless
you tell me about it. And no dates with Jack for a week.

Me: Fine. I'll go stay at Dad's for a week.

Mom: Oh no, you won't.

Me: Watch me.

Thursday, October 4
Weight: 115.5

I've gained almost two pounds since Sunday, but at least I
know about it. This morning Mom left for work with strict
instructions that I go directly to school and then come directly
home. I smiled and nodded.

I drove directly to Jill's and texted her from the driveway.

She appeared at the front door and raised her hand to wave with a timid smile. I ran up the sidewalk.

Me: I need to use your scale.

Jill: I was afraid something like this might be happening at your house.

Me: You don't want to know.

Jill: I'll bet I can guess. Your scale disappeared, huh?

And just like that, we were back to normal. The swell of relief that started when I saw her smile at the front door flooded through me completely when I stepped onto the clear glass square in the corner of her bathroom and watched the cool blue glow of the digital numbers scramble up to . . . 115.5. I groaned.

Jill: Not so bad. At least you know. They pumped you full of all kinds of sugar water in the hospital.

Me: I only have two weeks before homecoming. I have to be at 110 for that dress to fit.

Jill: Five pounds is nothing. You're fine. You can't give up now.

Me: But I have to eat every single meal my mother puts on the table.

Jill: Do you?

I just blinked at her. She was right. I was standing in her house, hanging out with her even though Mom didn't want me to. I was using the scale even though Mom didn't want me to. I could eat or not eat whatever I wanted. What my mom wants or doesn't want really isn't my problem.

Jill saw the lightbulb go off in my head, and I smiled for what felt like the first time in days.

Jill: Welcome back.

I lay on her bed and we talked about how things were going in ballet for her. Classes had taken on a pretty competitive edge with Misty Jenkins always trying to outdo her now that casting for *The Nutcracker* had been handed down. When Jill was ready, we walked downstairs. Susan blew us kisses in the hallway as she sailed out the door in a trim navy business suit with an attaché case.

Jack was eating Lucky Charms at the island in the kitchen, and a big smile spread across his face when he saw me.

Jack: What are you doing here?

Me: Had to talk to your sister.

Jill: Confidential BFF assistance was required, *mon frère*.

He gulped down the pinkish milk at the bottom of his cereal bowl, then put his dishes in the sink and pulled me in for a kiss.

Jack: Wish I could wake up and have you here every morning.

It was the best start to a school day I'd had in a long time. I did well on my chemistry test in third period, and when I turned my phone on between classes, I had a voice mail from Dad:

Sure! I'd love for you to spend the weekend. Come over Friday night. I'll be home by eight, and we can go see a movie, or get food, or whatever you want.

Sunday, October 7
Weight: 114.5

Just got back from Dad's place. It was wildly depressing. He's living in this really nice condo not far from the dealership. It's full of new furniture that's comfortable, but it looks like he walked into a Crate and Barrel and just pointed at a sectional and chairs and beds and lamps and end tables. Also, there is n-o-t-h-i-n-g on the walls, which makes it feel sort of barren.

We went shopping to get bedding for the guest room where I slept. He had a bed already, but we had to go buy sheets and a comforter and pillows. He pulled out his Amex and kept asking me if I needed anything else, like if he just bought enough stuff for the guest room it would be more comfortable and might also ease the discomfort between us.

Dad: What else do you need?

Me: Well, there's no toothbrush holder in the bathroom.

We wheeled into the bathroom section and chose bath

accessories: soap dispenser and hand soap, a toothbrush holder, shower caddy, bath mat. I slipped a scale into the cart as well. He didn't blink.

Afterward, we went to dinner, just us this time. I ordered a soup and salad combo. Dad sent several text messages, and I assume they were to Annette. She probably thinks I hate her or something. I don't.

Last night, I asked Dad if Jack and Jill and Rob could meet us for a movie.

Dad: Your mom called me and said you're grounded. What'd you do?

Me: I told her I wasn't going to stop hanging out with Jill.

Dad: Why does she want you to do that?

Me: She thinks Jill is convincing me to starve myself.

Dad: Are you starving yourself?

Me: No! I just run a lot.

Dad: I know a lot of people who run a lot who don't wind up in the hospital.

Me: I'm fine. You saw me eat dinner.

In the end he relented. Jack met us at the theater with Jill and Rob. Annette met Dad. She smiled at me tentatively. I smiled back and gave her a polite hello. The movie was based on a book for teenagers about (surprise) teenagers. It was sort of a love story and sort of a story about a guy who is really depressed trying to figure out why. There are three main friends and they go riding around in a pickup truck listening to music. They take turns standing in the back of the truck as they drive through a tunnel in Pittsburgh, and at one point the main boy says, "We are infinite."

I don't know why, but that part made me cry. Big tears slid down my cheeks and I tried to be sneaky when I reached up to wipe them away, but Jack saw. You know what I like best about Jack? He didn't ask why I was crying, he just reached over and laid his hand on my leg, and I wove my fingers through his, and we sat like that until the movie was over.

This afternoon, I packed up all my stuff and came home while Mom was still at work. It gave me a chance to go for a run before she got home and also to stash the new scale Dad bought under my bed.

When Mom got home it was like nothing had happened last week—like we never fought. Maybe she got the message. Or maybe she's afraid of losing me. Whatever the reason, she brought home Thai food and called me downstairs. We sat on the couch and she ate curry while I pretended to, and we watched TV.

I'm heading to bed now so I can get up early in the morning and run before school. Mom will probably not be pleased, but I don't care. I've got almost two weeks before homecoming.

Thursday, October 11

Weight: 112.5

Only two more pounds to go. I've been eating nothing but lettuce at lunch, and Vanessa told me today she's going to turn me in to Coach Perkins tomorrow. I opened my mouth to answer but nothing came out. As I turned to walk away, she grabbed my arm.

Me: Let go of me.

Vanessa: *No!* I won't just let go of you. I don't want you to die.

Me: You are such a drama queen. I'm not dying.

Vanessa: I'm telling Coach.

Me: Okay.

Vanessa: Okay what?

Me: Okay fine. Tell Coach. I just don't care. I don't have the energy to fight with you about this.

Vanessa: She's going to kick you off the team.

Me: Yes, she probably will.

Vanessa: And you're just *okay* with that? We could win at *state* this year.

Me: Not without me you won't.

All of my clothes are really baggy on me now. My breasts have gotten smaller and a lot of my shirts don't fit the way they used to. I don't really fill them out anymore. Luckily, it's cooler now, and I've pulled out some of my cardigans and hoodies. When I wear long sleeves and baggier tops over leggings and jeans it's harder to tell that I'm a lot skinnier. Mom even saw me this morning in the kitchen and said I looked really nice before she ran out the door to work. She's going out with Pam tonight. Some sort of speed-dating thing Pam signed her up for. She's all excited about it.

At least she won't be here for dinner. I'm so tired of spitting food into napkins. Also, if I have to drink one more mug of that tea Jill gave me I might dissolve completely.

I just finished the workout Jill showed me, and I'm going to go on a quick run before Mom comes home from work. That should burn off about two-thirds of the 1,200 calories I've had so far today.

Friday, October 12
Weight: 112

Coach Perkins told me I was benched for the rest of the season unless I bring my weight up. There were tears in her eyes when she told me. She's going to call Mom to talk to her about "the situation." She announced to everybody that Vanessa would be the new team captain for the time being. I don't care. That's what Vanessa wanted anyway. I don't understand why everybody thinks sports are so important in high school. It's not like any of us are going to run cross-country professionally one day. And when the rest of them stop running, they'll get fat.

Not me.

Just because I'm benched for another two weeks doesn't mean I'm going to stop running.

Saturday, October 13
Weight: 111.5

Jill and I met Vanessa and Geoff to watch Jack and Rob's soccer game last night before Mom got home from work. Afterward, we went to this ancient diner Rob loves called Rick's. It's a greasy spoon attached to an old hotel. There's a ceiling fan over every table and you can tell from the color of the ceiling tiles that people used to sit in there and chain-smoke.

Our favorite waitress, Marlene, was wearing her signature metallic blue eye shadow. She sat us back in the corner booth, where Rob and Jack immediately ordered chicken-fried steak with gravy. Vanessa and Geoff got chocolate malts, and Jill and I both sipped hot water and lemon, and split a chef's salad—dressing on the side. The guys have been finalizing plans for homecoming next week, and they are so cute when they talk about it.

Jill told me she wants to see me in the dress and told me that she found the perfect shoes to go with it. I told her we'd have to figure out a time for her to come over while my mom was gone.

When I got home, Mom was really upset. She'd been crying and trying to call me. I had turned off my phone because I figured she'd hit the roof when she got the message from Coach.

She did.

Instead of getting angry with her, I just slowly and calmly walked upstairs to my room and started to get undressed. She followed me, warning and pleading, yelling and crying. As she did, I quietly pulled the dress out of its plastic bag and slipped it off the hanger. I slowly slipped one leg into it, and then the other. The light, slick fabric of the silk lining whispered over my thighs and hips. As I slid my arms into the sleeves, Mom began begging me to talk to her, begging me to be honest with her.

Mom: What is it that you want? What do you *need* from me?
Me: I need you to zip me up.

I turned my back to her, holding my hair up out of the way with one arm, while the other held the front of the dress across my chest. I watched in the mirror as she snapped out of her crying jag and really saw me for the first time since I'd gotten home. She realized that I was finally trying on the dress for her.

Slowly, she reached forward and slid the zipper up. I grabbed a hair clip and wound my hair up in a loose twist, then dropped my arms and pushed up on my tiptoes like I had done for Susan and Jill in the dressing room and took a step back from the mirror. The dress fit perfectly.

Mom gasped.

I glanced at her in the mirror, and her eyes were wide, like she was seeing a vision. She opened her mouth to say something, then closed it, then for the first time since I'd gotten home she spoke without sounding angry.

Mom: That dress . . . you look . . .

Me: Amazing. I look amazing.

We stood there staring at my reflection in the mirror for a moment.

Mom: You look like something out of a magazine.

After a minute or so, Mom sank down on the edge of my bed, and I slipped the dress off and back onto the hanger.

Me: This is all I wanted. I just wanted to look beautiful for Jack. Can you understand that?

Mom: Sweetheart, you were beautiful enough for Jack before you lost all this weight. It's getting dangerous now.

Me: Just let me have this one night. I just want a perfect homecoming dance, and then you can stuff me full of burgers and french fries. I promise.

I sat down on the bed next to her, and Mom put both arms around me.

Mom: I'm scared. I don't know how to help you.

Me: I don't need any help.

Mom: That's what scares me the most.

I've been thinking about why she said that. I've been wondering why she would be scared that I don't think I need any help. It makes me angry that she can't see what I've accomplished with my body. It makes me feel like throwing things at the wall that she could see me in that dress and tell me I look like something out of a magazine and not be *thrilled*. How could looking that beautiful ever be a problem?

Jill's coming over to pick me up and we're going to go buy the shoes.

Sunday, October 14
Weight: 111

Mom let Jill sleep over last night. I think she's decided that she can't keep me from hanging out with Jill, so she might as well keep both of us under her watchful eye. I don't know what it is she thinks she can stop by being in the same house with us, but I didn't try to figure this out. Sometimes my mother baffles me completely.

Jill was right about the shoes. They're silver heels with a slightly rounded toe and crystals embedded in a ring around a thick heel. They look like a souped-up version of something Marilyn Monroe would have worn. Something about them says old-school glamour just like the dress, and when I walk you can just barely see the silver toe flash through the drape of the skirt in the front. Jill was as loud as Mom was speechless when I slipped into the dress for the first time. She squealed and jumped up and down like she had when she got cast as Clara. She insisted on taking a picture to post on the website.

Jill: You have to provide some inspiration for all the other girls on the forum.

Me: I don't know. I'm not sure I want my face on the Internet.

Jill: I'll crop out your face. Oh! Or better yet, look over your shoulder and I'll take it from an angle where we can only see your hair.

Jill snapped the picture on her phone, then loaded it into an app and chose a filter that made the color wash out in the center just bit. She added a textured white frame that made the whole image appear to be a snapshot from the 1940s or '50s.

Jill: You look like a legend of the silver screen.

I blushed and giggled, then we logged on to the forum, and

Jill registered as a new user for me. After some debate we settled on a username: weigh2go. She posted the photo and underneath it wrote these words:

"Don't think about how hungry you are. Think about how skinny you're getting."

She tagged the picture "thinspiration."

Wednesday, October 17
Weight: 110

I hate myself right now.

Everything was going great today. Got up this morning and did a hard forty five-minute run. I weighed in a pound lighter than I was on Sunday, then ate an egg, a plum, and a spoonful of peanut butter for breakfast. At lunch I only had a salad, and then Mom grilled fish for dinner and I had a few pieces of broccoli. Then I was upstairs doing my homework and I smelled it: cookies.

I went downstairs to the kitchen, and Mom was taking out two giant silver baking sheets of homemade chocolate chip cookies—just like she used to make for me when I was a little girl on the last day of school.

Mom: Thought you might need a study break.

Me: Mom! You know I have homecoming in three days.

Mom: Oh, c'mon. One cookie is not going to kill you.

I couldn't *stop myself*. I *had* to eat one. The chocolate chips were all warm and gooey. The cookie melted on my tongue, and when I opened my eyes after the first bite, Mom was standing there holding a frosty glass of milk.

I ate *six*. I am such a fatty fatso. They were delicious, but I can't stop thinking about it now. I can almost feel my stomach growing as I write this. I hate myself for not being strong.

I just went onto the website a few minutes ago and posted about it. Jill must've seen it, because I got a text:

Jill: Cookies????

Me: I might throw up.

Jill: COOKIES???

Me: I know. I feel like total crap.

She called me after that and we talked. She suggested that I make a "Do This Instead" jar. This sounded like a great idea. I found an old shoe-box downstairs from my running shoes and I got some wrapping paper out of the hall closet and wrapped the box and the lid in bright solid red. Then I took a Sharpie and wrote "Do This Instead" in big, bold letters across the front.

I tore three sheets of paper out of my notebook and wrote out other things to do besides eating:

- Take a nap/go to bed early.
- Practice my Spanish.
- Text Jill for help.
- Look at "thinspiring" blogs online
- Really look at yourself in the mirror and remember *why* you're doing this.
- Read a book.
- Take a nice bubble bath.
- Read a book in a nice bubble bath.
- Weigh yourself and see how far you've come.
- Try on your tightest clothes.
- Go for a run.
- Research colleges.
- Do your cardio workout.
- Watch a movie.
- Write a note to slip in Jack's locker tomorrow.

I felt a little better when I was done, but I still made a mug of Jill's special ballerina tea. I posted a picture of my "Do This Instead" box on the forum. Jill saw it and posted right back:

Way to go, weigh2go!

It made me smile and hate myself a little less. We're going to have so much fun at homecoming.

Friday, October 19
Weight: 110

Tomorrow's the big day. Jill and Vanessa and I are meeting each other for mani/pedis tomorrow morning, and then we're going to Susan's stylist to get our hair and makeup done. Jill didn't want Vanessa to come.

Jill: After what she did to you with the whole cross-country thing, I don't know how you can stand her.

Me: It's not that big a deal. She didn't do this. I did this. I look better than I ever have.

Jill (sighing): I guess it won't hurt to have her in the pictures. It will give everyone else a point of reference for how thin and gorgeous we look.

Jill said Jack had already picked out my corsage. I actually bounced up and down on the bed.

Me: Please please please tell me he got roses and it's for my wrist.

Jill: Are you kidding? Like Mom would let him ruin the neckline of that dress. Yes. White roses, no baby's breath, wrist corsage.

Me: Is it pretty?

Jill: If it looks like the picture of the one he showed me on his phone, it's perfect.

Mom insisted that the limo come by our place so she can take pictures at our house instead of me going over to Jill's. I'm glad she did. It will be fun to walk down our big staircase in this dress and see the look on Jack's face.

Sunday, October 21
Weight: Don't know

The look on Jack's face when he picked me up for the dance was priceless. Dad had stopped by to take pictures, too. He and Mom have been talking again since they saw each other at the hospital after that race where I went down. Anyway, Jack was in midsentence joking around with Dad. When he saw me, his voice trailed off, and he just stared. I'd practiced walking down the stairs four or five times before he got there so I wouldn't trip on the dress or break my ankle in the heels. I felt like a model—a superstar. I took his breath away.

It wasn't the only time that it happened that night.

The limo was so long we could've fit twelve more people in it. Rob somehow managed to sneak a bottle of champagne under his jacket and Jack had another one stashed under the seat. Everyone but Vanessa had a glass on the way to the school, but thankfully, she didn't make a big deal out of it. She did roll her eyes when Geoff poured a second glass for himself, but who can blame him? He probably needed a third glass just to deal with her attitude. The driver dropped us off at the door, and Rob and Jack agreed on a time when he should come back to pick us up.

When we got out of the car, I wobbled just a little, then giggled. The bubbles and sugar had gone straight to my head. Jack offered me his arm and was the perfect gentleman for the entire dance. He never left my side for a second. We turned heads everywhere we walked, and girls who had never spoken to me in the halls for the past two years stopped me to tell me how beautiful my dress was. We danced for hours, and I was amazed that my feet didn't hurt in these heels. I guess you get what you pay for.

I got dizzy after a couple of hours, but I decided it must just be the champagne, and besides, I had the best-looking date at the dance (even if Rob was named homecoming king). After a while the band slowed things down, and I just leaned into Jack while we danced. I could feel him pressed up against me, and his breath on my ear sent goose bumps running down my arms.

Jack: Are you cold?

Me: No. You just do that to me.

Jack: Do you have any idea what you're doing to me tonight in that dress?

Me: I think I can feel what I'm doing to you.

Jack: Just a little?

Me: It's not so little.

He winked at me and smirked, but he was blushing. Hard.

Not long after that, Rob declared that it was time to hit the after-party. One of their friends on the soccer team had rented a room at an old hotel that used to be the estate of a movie star. Now it was a resort with three swimming pools and lush grounds where you could lie in a hammock or play a game of croquet, all with a view of the mountains.

Geoff and Rob broke open the second bottle of champagne and Jack and I shared another glass while Rob told the driver he needed a burger. We wound up taking the limo into the drive-through. My head was so buzzy from the champagne and I got really hungry all of a sudden. Not just hungry: ravenous. Jack asked me if I wanted anything, and I opened my mouth to tell him yes, but Jill caught my eye and gave me a look.

Me: I'll just have a couple of your fries.

Jack: You sure?

Me: Yeah, I'm good.

Jill looked at me across the limo and mouthed the words "stay strong." I smiled at her as Jack ordered, and mouthed back "thank you."

I should have eaten those fries. I wish I had ordered a whole value meal and a chocolate milk shake for myself. If I had, I wouldn't be writing this from a hospital bed on the thirteenth floor.

I still can't remember exactly what happened. I remember pulling up to the high front wall of the hotel. I remember the valets in salmon-colored pants opening the limo. I remember Jack stepping out of the car then turning back to offer me his hand. I remember stepping out of the car and the breeze on my cheek. I remember turning toward the tall, orange doors of the hotel lobby and walking through them on Jack's arm. The entire hotel has been designed in this retro 1960s glamour-puss style, and there are two suits of armor guarding the bathroom doors by the front desk. I remember thinking that Jack was my knight in shining armor, and I was about to tell him as we walked by the mod round fire pit by the back door, but the next thing I knew, I was lying on a couch by the door, and everyone was on their phones, except Jack.

Jack: Hey, babe. Are you with me? Can you hear me?

I tried to sit up and he gently took my hand and laid me back down.

Jack: I'm right here. I'm not going anywhere.

Me: I . . . I'm fine.

Jack: My dad is on his way.

When he said that, I got scared. If parents were involved, this was not going to be the night I had wanted. I'm not sure why I yelled at Jack. I think it was because I was scared.

Me: Why did you do that? God!

I pushed myself up on the couch. I tried to stand up but fell forward. I slipped through Jack's arm and hit my chin on the coffee table next to the couch. Blood was everywhere. Vanessa screamed; Jill ran between the two suits of armor and came back with paper towels. The hotel manager was there asking if I was drunk, and at that moment Jack's dad walked in. I don't remember what he said to Geoff or Rob, or Jill or Vanessa. I don't remember how he talked the hotel manager out of calling the police.

All I remember is Jack.

Holding me.

And crying.

Jack held me in the backseat of his dad's car all the way to the hospital. When we walked through the doors of the ER, every single head in the waiting room turned to stare, and I realized we were still wearing formal clothes. Jack slid off his tux jacket and draped it over my shoulders.

At that moment, Mom came through the doors from the parking lot into the waiting area. She stopped short at the sight of us standing there, me with blood pooling in a paper towel at my chin. She held up a finger to James, then disappeared through the double doors into the emergency room. James turned back to Jack and me. He had the kindest smile.

James: Everything's going to be okay.

Me: Everything's fine now. I don't think this cut is bad.

James nodded, and Jack held on to my shoulders as an orderly came back with my mom and a wheelchair, and Dr. Nash.

Me: I don't need that wheelchair.

Mom: Sweetheart, don't make this any worse than it is.

I turned to look at Jack. His eyes were red and glossy from tears, but he smiled and said one word.

Please.

Something about that word made me feel so tired, like I could fall asleep standing up. I nodded at him and let him help me into the wheelchair. He got down on his knees in front of me and said three more words:

I love you.

Then the orderly handed him his jacket and wheeled me away.

I passed out one more time after they got me onto a gurney in the back and started an IV. When I came to, Dr. Nash was talking to my mom:

Dehydrated

Overexercise

Her body is in a famine mode

Drastically restricted fats to the point that her liver is shutting down

Thirteenth floor

When I woke up this morning, Mom was sitting in my room. I tried to reach up and wipe the sleep out of my eye, but I felt something tighten around my wrist. I looked down and saw restraints. I looked at Mom, and she was crying.

Me: What the *hell*, Mom? Why am I *tied up* like a *crazy person*?

Mom: Oh, honey. You kept waking up and trying to pull the IV out of your arm.

Me: What is in this IV?

Mom: It's fluids and nutrients.

I knew what that meant. It meant they were pumping me full of sugar water. I couldn't help myself. I started shouting.

Me: You are pumping me full of calories! Of course I want to pull it out. You tell them to take it out of my arm this second. Don't you see what you're doing? I'm going to get so fat just lying here. Is that what you *want*? It *is* what you want, isn't it? You *want* me to be *fat and miserable* just like *YOU*.

I was out of breath, and Mom was sobbing, saying, "No," and "Oh, honey," over and over again. She stood up and I saw she had something in her hands. It was a mirror. She held it up to my face. I closed my eyes and turned my head away.

Me: *No!* I don't want to see how *fat* I'm getting. I don't want to see what the sugar you're pumping me full of has already done to my face.

She cried, but she wouldn't go away, and she wouldn't move the mirror. Finally, I turned to look into it.

Mom: Can't you see it? Your hair is getting thin and breaking off. Your cheeks are so hollow. Your eyes don't even shine anymore. Your skin is gray. Where is she? Look in this mirror and find my sweet girl! Where did she go? You're starving her to death.

As I looked in the mirror, I realized I didn't know when the last time was I'd actually looked myself in the eyes. I was always too busy looking at my body, checking for places that should be flatter or more toned. My eyes seemed dull and gray. Hadn't they been blue once? I stared until I didn't recognize myself anymore. The only way I knew it was me I was looking at was when I saw the tears start to fall, and I felt them, hot and wet, trickling down my cheeks.

Tuesday, October 23
Weight: 112

They released me this morning. Mom's insurance won't allow me to stay there for longer than seventy two hours without being sent to long-term treatment. Dr. Nash said if I don't start eating again, she'll make sure I get locked up for twenty eight days.

I hate her.

I want to text Jack and tell him I'm okay. I want to text Jill and ask her what I should do next. Mom won't let me have my phone back yet.

I hate her, too.

Wednesday, October 24
Weight: 113

This is a nightmare. Mom still wouldn't let me go to school today. She's taken some vacation days from work, too. Jack stopped by after soccer practice today. He brought me flowers. Gerbera daisies. Red this time. Mom invited him in and called me downstairs. Was it only five days ago I walked down the stairs to meet him and felt like a movie star? When I saw it was him, I wanted to run back up to my room. I stopped on the stairs for a second. Everybody just waited. I was staring at my feet, and then I started to cry. I didn't want him to see me like this. I guess I know in my head somewhere that I'm not really fat, but I *feel* so fat and ugly right now. I have stitches in my chin. I've been pumped full of crap at the hospital.

Jack set the flowers on the island and walked up the steps

toward me. Mom followed him and stood at the foot of the stairs in the living room. He wrapped his arm around me like I was fragile and might break in two if he squeezed too hard. Something about being close to him made me feel safe, and I leaned into the soft skin of his neck and just cried.

Jack: What is it, babe?

Me: I don't want you to see me like this.

Jack: You look amazing to me. I haven't seen you since Saturday night. That's way too long. I've been jonesing.

How does he know how to say the right thing every time? He turned to my mom.

Jack: Do you think it'd be okay if we took a walk down to the park?

Mom: It would be totally fine, but we have to leave in about twenty minutes to get to the doctor.

Me: What? What doctor?

Mom: I made an appointment for us.

Me: For *us*?

Jack: It's okay, babe. I'll come back tomorrow.

He kissed me on the forehead and left before I could stop him or figure out from Mom where this appointment was. Turns out Mom has booked us with a shrink. I'm so pissed off right now I can barely hold the pen. I shouldn't be going to see a therapist, I should be going to school. I should be walking down the street right now with my boyfriend, holding his hand, hearing about his day.

I told Mom she was ruining my life. She told me if I don't go with her, I wasn't going back to school.

I'll do anything to not have to sit at home with her all day.

Later . . .

The car ride to the therapist's office was complete silence. Mom tried to talk, but then gave up. Thank God.

Of course, once we were in Dr. Crane's office she let the floodgates open and it all gushed out. Dr. Crane is this little bald guy who is probably in his forties. He has a nice smile and bright eyes, and he was really friendly. I think he might be gay. He's in remarkably good shape and wears very cool glasses. The lenses are rectangular and sort of disappear because they're frameless. I kept staring at his glasses, sort of blurring my eyes a little, seeing if I could make out the lenses at all while Mom cried her eyes out about how scared she was. How upset she felt that she couldn't stop me. How angry she was that I didn't see what I was doing to myself and to her and to my dad.

Dr. Crane: How do you feel about that?

Me: How do I feel about what?

Dr. Crane: All of the things your mother just said.

Me: I feel like I don't want to be here right now. I feel like I don't want to talk about this. It's none of anyone else's business.

Dr. Crane gave me his little friendly, bright-eyed smile. He nodded. Then he asked my mom if she would mind stepping out so he could have some time alone with me. Mom looked sort of bewildered, but she dried her eyes and left the room. I settled back into the deep cushions of the couch, and Dr. Crane asked if I wanted any water or anything. I told him no.

Dr. Crane: Is there anything you want to tell me that you'd rather your mom not hear?

Me: No.

Dr. Crane: Do you trust me?

Me: I've actually watched television before in my life, so yes, I am familiar with the idea that psychologists are generally trustworthy.

It surprised me when he laughed.

Dr. Crane: You're funny.

Me: I bet you think I'm too skinny, too.

Dr. Crane: I don't really care what you weigh.

Me: You're the only one, then. The rest of us just can't get enough of it.

Dr. Crane: Who is this friend Jill your mom talked about?

Me: She talked about Jill?

Dr. Crane: Yeah. You were sort of staring at me during that part. I wasn't sure if you were actually listening or not.

Me: Yeah, I wasn't. I was checking out your glasses. They're really cool.

Dr. Crane: Thank you.

Me: Jill is my friend.

Dr. Crane: Your mom is pretty upset. She just told me that she wishes she'd never let you hang out with Jill.

Me: Jill isn't making me do this.

Dr. Crane: Do what?

Me: Count calories. Lose weight.

Dr. Crane: Does Jill do those things too?

Me: Yes.

Dr. Crane: But it's not your disease that makes her your friend.

Me: My . . . disease?

Dr. Crane looked at me with eyes full of concern. It made me angry.

Dr. Crane: Yes. The reason you're here is the disease of anorexia.

Me: I don't have a *disease*. I have *willpower*.

Dr. Crane flipped open a chart on the little glass table next to his chair.

Dr. Crane: What you have is a liver that is shutting down,

signs of scalp hair loss, elevated levels of serum sodium, potassium chloride, and carbon dioxide from continued dehydration, muscle wasting, and no regular period for months. Those are not signs of willpower. Those are symptoms of a disease called anorexia.

He said all this softly and gently, and then held my gaze as I sat there blinking at him.

Dr. Crane: Is anorexia what makes Jill your friend?

Me: No. Of course not. I'm not sure if she'll even want to be my friend anymore after this.

Dr. Crane: Why wouldn't she?

Me: She's got to do what's best for her. She's got to stay thin so she can be the best at ballet she can possibly be.

Dr. Crane: What other friends do you have? Your mother didn't mention anyone else by name.

I thought about telling him about Vanessa and Geoff and Rob and especially Jack. None of those names left my lips, though. When I opened my mouth, I didn't recognize my own voice.

Me: I feel like I am my best friend. When I'm able to get through a meal without eating too much, there's this thing I feel inside of me—this strength. It's like a place of power, and when I don't eat too much, or when I exercise enough, it makes me feel invincible. It keeps me company.

Dr. Crane: Your disease has become your best friend.

When he said those words, I couldn't speak anymore. I just looked at him, nodded, and cried.

Wednesday, November 7
Weight: 119

It's weird how two weeks can seem like two years. My life has been a completely different place since that night at homecoming. I've been seeing Dr. Crane three times each week. He runs an outpatient program for people with eating disorders at the hospital where Mom works. I go three days each week after school: Mondays, Tuesdays, and Thursdays.

On Tuesdays I see Dr. Crane one-on-one, and on Mondays and Thursdays, it's a "group therapy" session. Dr. Crane leads the conversation with seven or eight other girls. Most of us are in high school. Most of us are anorexic. A couple of the girls are bulimic and do a lot of bingeing and purging. A girl named Amy talked about eating a whole box of cupcakes, then making herself throw up. Just hearing her talk about it made me feel sick to my stomach.

This girl named Kim, who is a senior in Jack and Rob's class at school, is in the group. I was shocked to see somebody I knew there—especially her. She's a cheerleader and has big boobs and what Jill likes to call an "athletic spread," which means her butt and thighs are full and curvy. She doesn't look like she's missed a meal in quite a while. Today I found out that's because she hasn't. She's been what she calls "recovered" for three years.

Dr. Crane usually starts the group off with a topic. Today was about what we see when we look in the mirror. He calls it body image. When it was Kim's turn she said that she knows she needs to be careful when she gets too caught up in the mirror. She said that's when she knows her vision can start doing funky things.

Kim: Sometimes I catch myself staring at something in the mirror besides my eyes, and I know that's a trigger for me. I have to remind myself that I don't always see what's actually in the mirror.

Dr. Crane: Can you tell us a little bit more about that? What does it feel like?

Kim: Well, it used to be that I weighed about ninety-eight pounds, which meant for my height I was almost twenty-five pounds underweight, but I'd look in the mirror and see fat hanging over my waistband. I'd convince myself I had a muffin top, or that my thighs were too big under my cheerleading skirt.

Dr. Crane asked if anybody else had experienced this. Everybody in the circle raised a hand. Except me, at first.

When I saw everybody else's hand in the air, I sighed and put mine up too.

Dr. Crane smiled his little smile at me.

Afterward, Kim came up to say hi.

Kim: I'm glad you're here.

Me: I can't say that I am.

Kim: It gets better, I promise.

Me: I can't believe you aren't scared all the time.

Kim: Scared of what?

Me: Of becoming one of those girls that can't control how much she eats.

Kim smiled at me, a sad smile—almost like she could see something about me that I couldn't.

Kim: Just keep coming to group. It gets easier.

She gave me her cell phone number, and I typed it into my contacts, but I can't imagine actually talking to her about anything. When I think about Kim and her big boobs and the way her thighs touch when she walks, I get this sick feeling in the pit of my stomach. I have to take deep breaths so I don't gag. She just seems revolting to me.

I've gained three pounds each week since I got out of the hospital. Dr. Nash says I'm still fifteen pounds under my goal weight. I have a checkup with her once a week too. I told her I couldn't eat any more than I was.

Dr. Nash: You can, it'll just take time for your body to readjust. You'll know you're back on track when you get your period again. Should be in the next seven to ten pounds.

The idea of weighing ten more pounds totally freaks me out.

Dr. Crane: Why does it freak you out?

Me: I don't want to be ugly.

Dr. Crane: What if you were *more* beautiful because you were at a healthy weight? Not less.

Me: But I won't be. Jack is always saying how perfect I look.

Dr. Crane: Have you seen Jack lately? Since you put back on six pounds?

Me: Yeah.

Dr. Crane: When?

Me: He came over for dinner last night.

Dr. Crane: Did he act any differently around you?

I thought about this for a minute. Mom had made us spaghetti and meatballs. I only ate a little bit of pasta, but I had three meatballs and a slice of French bread with garlic butter on it. Jack had laughed and joked and slurped noodles in this way that made me giggle.

After dinner we hung out on the sectional in the living room reading our books for English class. He's halfway through *A Tale of Two Cities* and I'm finishing up *Little Women*. He didn't seem any different at all. In fact, he was actually smiling more than usual.

Dr. Crane smiled when I told him this.

Dr. Crane: Jack loves you. Your mom loves you. Let them love you while you learn how to love yourself.

Me: But what if Jack stops? What if he . . .

Dr. Crane: Leaves?

I nodded.

Dr. Crane: People break up sometimes. Even when they're married like your mom and dad. It happens all the time. You can't control that by controlling what you eat. I can't promise you Jack won't leave. I *can* promise you he won't leave because you weren't thin or beautiful enough.

Sunday, November 11
Weight: 121

Geoff and Vanessa came over tonight with Jack. I invited Jill, too, but she's been in rehearsals for *The Nutcracker* every waking moment she's not at school. I want to believe that's why I haven't been hearing from her as much, and why she's been so quiet at school, but I know it's because I've been eating more again.

I feel like I've lost two friends in a way—restricting my calories, and Jill. It used to be that we were friends for lots of reasons. Now it seems like we were only friends for one reason. Kim was talking about that at group on Thursday, and it made a lot of sense to me.

Geoff and Jack insisted on ordering a pizza with jalapeños on it, so Vanessa and I got one with just Canadian bacon and pineapple on it. Geoff and Jack got into a pepper-eating contest to see who could handle the most and both of them ended up red in the face with tears running down their cheeks.

I was laughing so hard with Vanessa that my stomach actually hurt, and all of a sudden, I realized what a good time I was having. I hadn't laughed like that in a really long time. It reminded me of how easy things used to be between Vanessa and Geoff and me. I want it to be like that again, but I get scared that it might not ever be. Even while I was eating delicious pizza there was this little voice in the back of my head saying: *You are disgusting. You are a fatty fatso. You should hate yourself.*

I was able to shut it out and not think about it when everybody was there. After they went home it was a different story. I was up in my room, and I saw my red "Do This Instead" box. Suddenly I didn't want to be alone in my room anymore. I grabbed that box and the scale from under the bed, and I went to find Mom. I gave her both things.

She hugged me really tight for a long time, and then asked if I wanted to join her. We're sitting on her bed right now. She's reading a book while I write. I feel really close to her right now—like being honest was a good thing. She told me that we'd keep the scale in the front bathroom, and as long as I was eating, we'd weigh in every day. It feels weird to bring someone else into the bathroom with me to weigh myself, but Dr. Crane has been talking about that in our sessions. He thinks it's one more way that I can ask for help, that I can admit I am not in control of my food. He's been helping me see how it's the other way around—that food has actually been in control of *me*.

Wednesday, November 14
Weight: 122

I felt really crappy this morning when I woke up. Mom and I did our little weigh-in in the bathroom, and then I took a shower and started to get dressed. The skinny jeans I bought with Jill before school started are a little snug now, and I had to take them off and wear a pair of my older jeans. Mom poked her head in the door and saw me just staring at the skinny jeans lying on the bed. She walked over and put an arm around me.

Mom: Let's go shopping after school today?

I nodded. My heart was racing like it might explode. I felt all panicky, and I think Mom felt me shaking because she pulled me in really close and held me tight.

Mom: Sssh. Sweetheart, it's okay. It just means you're *healthy* again. You're getting there. You look so much better than you did six weeks ago.

After she left, I kept looking in the mirror, trying to keep my eyes on my eyes like Dr. Crane talks about doing. Trying to take in the whole of myself, instead of just the physical part. I *know* on some level deep inside that I look *better*—that I don't look sick anymore. But I get so angry when I see magazines at the grocery store or Jill walking through the halls. How come those girls are able to be that skinny, and I can't be?

Dr. Crane calls it an "inside job." Meaning that my problems—the stuff that I have been trying to control by not eating—aren't actually anybody else's actions. It's my own thinking that has to change.

Kim stopped by the lunch table where I was to say hi today. Jill was sitting next to Rob and got this look on her face like she was really amused. I tried to ignore it, but after Kim left, I was cutting up the pieces of chicken in my salad and caught Jill staring at me. My face flushed, and I felt this hot flash of anger shoot through me.

Me: *What?*

Jill shrugged and started gathering her stuff to leave. Jack looked at Jill with a thunderstorm on his face, and the air around the table got really tense. He had a warning in his voice when he said Jill's name.

Jill: Oh, butt out, Mr. Perfect.

Rob: Whoa. What's going on?

I was trying not to cry, but it wasn't any use. I felt Vanessa reach under the table and squeeze my leg. That made me even more frustrated. I didn't want to have to choose between my friends.

Me: I have to *eat*, Jill. I don't have a choice.

Jill: You always have a choice.

Jack jumped out of his chair and almost out of his skin. He pointed toward the cafeteria doors and said a single word in a very low voice:

Go.

Jill shook her head at me and walked away.

I know I should talk about this at group tomorrow, but I don't know if I can. I feel like my heart is breaking on the inside. I don't want to hurt Jill, but I can't go on hurting myself anymore, either.

Thursday, November 22
Weight: 125

We're at Grandma and Grandpa's today for Thanksgiving. I was just watching the Rockettes perform in the Macy's Thanksgiving Day Parade. Those girls have legs for days. It made me miss Jill. It also made me worried.

I went into Grandma's bathroom and found her scale. It's really old and still has a dial on the front—no digital numbers. It creaked and wobbled a little when I stepped onto it, but when the dial finally came to a rest from spinning back and forth it said 125. That means I've gained a full fifteen pounds since homecoming. I felt an old familiar panic descend over me like a fog rolling in. I texted Kim. She called me back right away.

Me: Help. Freaking out.

Kim: Turkey panic?

Me: I don't know. I was just watching the parade and I had to come weigh myself.

Kim: Ah. The Rockettes?

Me: How'd . . . how'd you know?

Kim: Lots of dancers are anorexic. Did you know those girls have weigh-ins?

Me: Really?

Kim: Yep. If they can't fit in their costumes, their understudy goes on.

Me: How am I going to make it through this meal?

Kim: Breathe. Remember that you have a disease that wants to control you.

Me: I'm ballooning up. I've gained fifteen pounds in six weeks!

Kim: That's normal. You're still underweight. Your body is repairing itself.

Me: I feel so fat and bloated. My stomach pooches out in the mirror.

Kim: That's your disease distorting your vision. You're still ten pounds underweight for your height.

Me: How are you so calm about this?

Kim: Because I've been at it for longer. You're doing everything just fine. You called me, didn't you?

I took a deep breath. Maybe Kim was right.

Me: What do I do?

Kim: You keep a journal, don't you?

Me: Yeah.

Kim: Write all of this down.

Me: How will that help?

Kim: Write down what you're feeling. Write down this conversation. If it doesn't help, call me back.

Me: Okay.

Kim: Remember, your feelings are important, but they're not facts. They'll change. Just give them ten minutes.

Me: Thanks, Kim.

I started writing the second I hung up. I wrote down that whole conversation, but I feel hopeless somehow. I know in my head that Kim is right, but I have this fear in my stomach that I'm going to become a monster. My nose is full of turkey and pumpkin pie right now, and any second Mom is going to call me to dinner and try to stuff me full of Grandma's mashed potatoes.

Maybe Kim is right. Just breathe. This is my disease talking. I don't have to eat the entire table, just a normal plateful. Try a bit of everything. It's like being a little girl again. *I hate this.*

Just for today, I won't restrict my calories. Maybe I'll do it tomorrow. I could always start again tomorrow and go back down to 1,000 per day. That idea makes me feel a little bit better. I don't have to eat like a hog forever, I'm just not going to count my calories for this one meal.

Jack just texted me:

Hey gorgeous. Thankful 4U.

I have to make sure he stays thankful and doesn't get repulsed.

Friday, November 23
Weight: 125

I had a meltdown at the mall just now.

Mom and Grandma love shopping Black Friday sales. Grandma has been making a big deal about how pretty I look now that I've "filled out" again. Even writing those words "filled out" makes me want to throw myself into traffic. It's like I'm a form, covered in somebody else's ideas of what I should look like. To make matters worse, Jack called last night and invited me to come see Jill do *The Nutcracker* on Saturday night. He said the whole family is really excited about it, and he wanted me to be his date.

When Mom heard this, she was determined to buy me a new outfit for the ballet, and Grandma was determined to pay for it. I should have just told them that the idea of shopping right now *terrifies* me.

But I didn't.

Instead I let them shuttle me from Bloomingdale's to Nordstrom to Macy's and back again, until I thought they'd wear my skin off making me try on clothes. I told Mom I didn't want to look at the sizes, but of course, once I was alone in the dressing rooms, I checked every tag.

We were back at Bloomingdale's trying on the three dresses we'd put on hold there when Grandma said she thought one of them was a little too tight in the chest and I should get the next size up so I could really show off my "girls."

Mom froze when she said this, and I could see the daggers she was shooting at Grandma, but Grandma just acted like it was no big deal.

Grandma: Well, she's got to face facts at some point. She's

a four and that's all there is to it. No sense beating around the bush. She should be proud of the beauty God gave her. I know that Jack boy won't complain.

I smiled at Mom and nodded as if to say I was fine. She took the dress out and went to get the size four. I closed the dressing room door again and stood there staring at myself in my underwear.

I was disgusting.

I was so *fat*.

A month ago I zipped into a two no problem. Now I was squeezing into a four.

I started bawling. By the time Mom got back with the dress, I was lying on the floor in the dressing room, and she had to stand me up and help me get dressed.

Grandma bought me the dress anyway. In a four.

I guess my date with Jack tomorrow night will be my last. Susan will never let him date a heifer. Just thinking about it makes me want to throw up.

Saturday, November 24
Weight: 125

Jill was perfect.

She was the perfect Clara. She was tiny and athletic and

242

beautiful. The guys were all as muscular as Jack and they tossed Jill up over their heads in lifts and spins that made me gasp. Misty Jenkins was a beautiful Sugar Plum Fairy, but Jill stole the show.

I sat there next to Jack feeling like a sausage stuffed in a casing. When James pulled the SUV into the driveway to pick me up, Jack met me at the door in a suit and tie. I was wearing the new dress Grandma bought me and my dress coat. It was long and black and covered up everything except my favorite black heels. He just jumped up the stairs two at a time and kissed me square on the mouth. His cheeks were flushed.

Jack: Damn. You are a sight for sore eyes.

Me: Hi.

Jack: Did you survive Thanksgiving?

Me: Barely.

Jack: Let's go watch some dudes in tights kill mice.

I laughed in spite of myself, and I felt all my worries that he wouldn't like me disappear for an instant. Rob was in the SUV and when I climbed in he made room so I could sit by Jack, who put his arm around me and nuzzled my neck.

When we got to the lobby of the theater James suggested we go and check our coats, and my stomach dropped. I tried to think of what Kim would say. This is just my disease that's

worried. It's my disease trying to make me feel like I'm
worthless and fat. It's my disease that's telling me I'm ugly.

Jack helped me out of my coat, but instead of turning to
the girl at the coat check, he and Rob just stopped and stared.
The dress Grandma had bought me had a fitted, strapless black
velvet bodice with a short, flouncy skirt in red plaid taffeta.
I'd worn black stockings with a seam up the back, and as I
turned and caught them both staring, Rob whistled, and Jack
murmured:

Merry Christmas to me . . .

I laughed and could feel a blush burning its way across both
cheeks toward my ears. I felt Susan step up next to me and slide
an arm across my bare shoulders.

Susan: Well, well, young lady.

Jack: I'm sorry. I know it's not polite to stare.

Susan: No, no. You should stare.

She turned to me and gave me a little squeeze.

Susan: Plumping up has made you positively *radiant*.

Jack and Rob were checking coats and James was at the bar
fetching white wine. Nobody heard her say the words "plumping
up" but me. The blush on my cheeks turned from one of pleasure
to a sting of overwhelming shame. I don't remember exactly
what happened at the ballet after intermission.

I remember knowing that Jill was beautiful and that Jack

must be stroking my leg at the hem of my skirt so I didn't feel bad about being so plump.

It's been three hours since the applause in the hall died down, and two since Jack walked me to the door and told me something very sweet I'm sure was meant to spare my feelings. Susan's words, however, are the ones still ringing in my ears:

Plumping up.

The worst part is, she's right.

Thursday, November 29
Weight: 126

Just got off the phone with Jack. When he called he sounded so distant and far away that I thought he was calling to break up with me. I got really nauseous and lay across my bed, closed my eyes, and prepared for the worst.

He said there'd been an accident. Jill was performing in the matinee this afternoon and broke her foot. It's a stress fracture. Jack says she'll be out of the show for the rest of the run.

I was so relieved he wasn't calling to break up with me because I was too plump that I immediately jumped up and pulled on some shoes.

Me: I'm coming over right this second. What can I bring her?

He was silent. My heart dropped again. Something was *wrong*.

Me: Jack?

Jack: She's not here, babe.

Me: Is she still at the hospital?

Jack: Um . . . no. Not that hospital. She just left with my parents.

Me: Where did they go?

Jack: They're taking her to a place in Arizona. It's sort of a . . . hospital. It's like . . . a rehab.

Me: A rehab?

Jack: Yeah. It's a treatment center for anorexia.

I slowly slumped back down on the bed as the weight of this settled over me. Jack was quiet, but I could hear him breathing on the phone. Then I heard him sniff. It sounded like he was crying.

Me: Jack? Are you okay? Are you there by yourself?

Jack: Yeah. I'm fine. I just . . .

His voice trailed off, and I waited, holding my breath for what would come next.

Jack: I just . . . you looked *so beautiful* last night, and I am *so glad* that you're getting *better*.

Tears sprang up in my eyes and slowly rolled down my cheeks.

Me: Do you want to come over and hang out?

Jack: Is that okay? Will your mom mind?

Me: No. Come over.

I told Mom what was going on and she was glad I'd told Jack to come over. Rob came by too for a little while but left pretty quickly. I think he felt strange watching Jack and me together. It probably made him miss Jill. He's a big clown most days, but I can tell he really cares for her and that he was really scared.

After he left, Mom called Susan and left her a voice mail, just saying that she had heard what happened and that Jack was over at our place and to let her know if she could do something or if they needed anything. Mom went to bed and left me sitting on the couch with Jack, who laid his head down on my lap and fell asleep while we were watching TV.

I sat there running my fingers through his hair with a billion thoughts zinging through my brain at the same time. After a while, he woke up and smiled at me. He stretched and sat up and gave me a kiss, then looked at his watch and said he had to get home.

Me: I could sit here and watch you sleep all night.

Jack: If we spend the night together, I'm not gonna be sleeping.

He smirked, and I messed up his hair. We walked to the

front door with our arms around each other. He kissed me again and asked if he could come pick me up for school in the morning. I shrugged and said sure.

Jack: See you in the morning, beautiful.

I stood at the front door in the quiet house and watched until his taillights turned the corner, then I came upstairs and started writing.

When I was sitting there on the couch with Jack it crossed my mind how lucky I was that I hadn't gotten a stress fracture from running. Jill had gotten hurt so easily. I keep thinking about what Dr. Crane said about anorexia being a disease, and I wonder if I've done permanent damage. I still haven't had my period yet. What if my body is already giving out? What if I'm putting on weight too fast? Jack says he's happy that I'm getting healthy again, but what if they keep making me gain weight? Maybe fifteen pounds is plenty.

I just can't help thinking about those big girls who sit at the back of the cafeteria at school eating bags of cheese puffs and drinking soda with sugar in it. I swear, just walking by them you could get a corn syrup contact high. Is that where I'm headed? I don't want to end up thundering around in XXL sweatshirts covered in greasy fingerprints. I'm worried because I haven't been running at all since homecoming. Not even once. No wonder I've gained fifteen pounds so fast.

I need to go to sleep. My brain is in a spin. Reading all of that makes me feel silly for writing it, but that's what's going on in my head. Kim said something the other day in our group that caught my ear:

You're only as sick as your secrets.

Maybe writing all of these thoughts down isn't enough. Maybe I need to be talking about them more to Dr. Crane and to the other girls in group.

Jack is the sweetest, kindest guy I have ever met. I'm a lucky girl.

I hope Jill is okay. Wherever she is. Maybe we can learn to help each other stay healthy just like we helped each other not eat. That idea makes me smile.

Saturday, December 1
Weight: 128

All I could think about at the ice-skating rink was how fat my coat made me feel. I kept catching a glimpse of myself in the glass at the end of the rink by the snack bar. Maybe it was because it's curved, or maybe it's because I am a whale, but my jacket made me look like that cartoon man in the commercials who is made out of tires.

Jack seemed not to notice, or if he did, he didn't let it stop him from holding my hand the whole time. He and Rob are really good because they play in this hockey league during the winter. They can skate backward and do these "hockey stops" where they spray ice all over the place. It was all I could do to stand up at the beginning, but Jack was really patient, and by the end I was doing okay. Geoff and Vanessa came with us, and it was nice to be out with everybody, although it was weird not having Jill there. She's really good on the ice. She took lessons until we were in junior high, when she stopped to concentrate on ballet.

I've been talking a lot about my secrets at group this past week. I tell them almost everything I write down in here.

Almost.

If I just keep a few secrets that means I'm just a little bit sick, right?

I've been running again. I figure if I'm going to eat this many calories every day, I can at least run a couple of miles. I haven't told Mom I'm doing it yet. Or anybody, for that matter. I'm just running when I get home from school.

Also, I've decided I'm not drinking any calories. That seems like a fair rule. I'll eat whatever Mom gives me, but I'm just not going to drink anything with sugar in it. That's empty calories anyway.

It's funny how you can fool lots of people into thinking

you're completely better. Mom is thrilled with my progress. Dr. Nash told me my hair is coming back in really well where it had gotten thin at my temples, and she said once I was back up at 130 I'd be out of the woods.

I didn't fool Jack.

When the Zamboni came out to resurface the ice, Geoff and Vanessa went into the snack bar to get hot chocolate. Rob was talking to Jill outside. She gets to make two phone calls on Saturdays. I haven't gotten one of them yet. She calls her mom and Rob. When Jack ordered two hot chocolates, I put my hand on his arm.

Me: I want some Earl Grey tea.

He paused, and this funny look crossed his face. He turned back to the counter and changed the order. We walked over to a little table in the corner to wait for our drinks.

Jack: You're doing it again, aren't you?

I looked at him, my eyes wide and searching. Trying to appear innocent. Looking very caught.

Me: What? No. I'm . . . Jack. Look at me. I look like a blimp in this coat. I've gained so much weight since homecoming I'm practically—

Jack: I'm not a moron.

He wasn't angry, his tone was quiet, but his eyes were on fire.

Jack: I know there's a difference between the way you eat and the way you think.

I looked down at my skates. I just wanted him to hug me, to tell me how beautiful I was, that everything would be okay.

Our drinks were ready. He got up to get them, and when he came back, Geoff and Vanessa joined us. We all talked and laughed, and Rob came back in with a report on Jill. We finished skating, and Jack kept holding my hand. He didn't bring it up again, but when he dropped me off just now he kissed me and looked at me for a long time.

Jack: I just want you to be careful.

Me: I *am* being careful.

Jack: I don't want to lose you.

Me: You won't. *Look* at me. I'm *better*.

He nodded, but I could see the doubt behind his eyes.

Tuesday, December 11
Weight: 125

I stopped writing in this journal so I could stop sharing at group. Something about writing down what I'm doing makes it real. I've been restricting my calories again. I've been using the app to make sure I burn off most of what I'm eating. I've been running before Mom gets home from work and doing the cardio workout Jill showed me in my room early in the morning and again at night after Mom goes to bed.

The weight is coming off again. Just losing a few pounds last week made me feel like all my clothes fit better.

At group, Kim asked me if I was okay. We have to tell our weight every time we go, and she's been paying attention. So has Vanessa. At lunch today, she saw me throwing away most of my salad. I thought everyone had gotten over the idea that I wasn't eating enough. For a while there it was like I got a round of applause every time I swallowed a bite. Gradually, everybody stopped staring at me while I lifted a fork to my mouth. No such luck today.

Vanessa: Are you throwing all of that away?

Me: What? I'm full.

Vanessa: Of *what*? You barely touched that.

I couldn't handle it. I completely snapped.

Me: Damn it, Vanessa. Butt out! You're not my mom. You're not my doctor. This is none of your *business*.

I ran out of the cafeteria in tears.

Jack followed me. I was unlocking my car door in the parking lot when he caught up with me. As I tried to pull the door open he reached over my shoulder and pushed it closed.

I turned around and slumped against the car door and crossed my arms. It wasn't until I looked up at him that I realized there were tears running down his cheeks.

Jack: What do I have to do?

Me: This is not about you.

Jack: Yes. Yes, it *is* about me. You made it about me.

Me: How?

Jack: By being so beautiful. By being so smart and funny and such a good kisser. I fell in love with you. So this *is* about me now. I love you and I want you to know that, not up in your head, or in some greeting card sort of way. I want you to *know it* in your bones. This is my business, dammit. *You* are my business.

His cheeks were flushed, and his breath was coming out in sharp staccato bursts of white steam against the cold December air. I wanted to say I was sorry, but I couldn't.

Me: I'm not trying to hurt you.

Jack: But you *are*. When you hurt someone I love, you *hurt me*. Don't you get it? I *love you*.

I wanted to hug him. I wanted to tell him I would try harder, but I didn't. Everything he was saying was being drowned out by a voice that whispered into my ear: He doesn't really mean this. He's just being nice. He knows his mom is right. You're plump. If you really care for him, you'll walk away.

You'll spare him the humiliation of having a fat girlfriend.

He snapped me out of my thoughts when he reached up and gently touched my face.

Me: How could you love me like this?

When I said those words, I saw the same sad, faraway look that had sprung into his eyes at the ice rink when I changed my order from hot chocolate to tea.

Jack: I love you just the way you are. Doesn't that count for anything?

All I could do was shrug. He shook his head and took a step backward.

Jack: I don't understand how that doesn't make everything better. I keep thinking if I love you hard enough, or well enough, that you'll learn how to love yourself the way I do.

He turned to walk into the school building, then stopped and looked back.

Jack: I'm not giving up on you. Don't you give up on me.

Wednesday, December 19
Weight: 121

When Dad started crying, something in me snapped.

Jack called Mom. Dr. Crane called Mom. Dr. Nash called Mom. Mom called Dad.

Mom found me organizing all the clothing in my closet by color at 2 a.m. this morning. She woke up to go to the bathroom and saw the light on in my room. She took one look and knew the obsessive-compulsive part of this was back in full swing.

Today when I got home from school, she and Dad were sitting in the living room. Dad had a pamphlet and a website pulled up on his iPad. It's not the place Jill went to. That place is a gazillion dollars per day, but this place looks nice enough. It's here in town and Dr. Crane recommended it. Our insurance will cover it for twenty-two days.

At first I told them no way. I told them I was doing just fine. Then Dad asked if he could see my phone. He pulled out my laptop. He clicked to the website Jill had shown me. He'd found it in the history. I'd just posted a screen shot last night from CalorTrack. It showed that I'd done a cardio routine twice and run three miles after I got home from group. It also showed I'd only eaten 1,200 calories—most of which I'd burned off from overexercise.

I opened my mouth to defend myself. I was going to yell at him for snooping on my computer. When I looked up at him, there were tears running down his face.

I've never seen my dad cry before. Even when he was here and miserable and leaving Mom. Even when his dad died when

I was in sixth grade. Something inside me decided not to fight him.

I check into Hope House the day after Christmas next week.

Tuesday, December 25
Weight: 119

Dad came over this morning to open presents with me. He and Mom have figured out how to be nice to each other for my sake, I guess. Dad made pancakes for us and made sure I ate one. I mainly cut it up in little pieces and scooted it around in the syrup until it fell apart.

He's coming back tomorrow to help Mom take me to Hope House. Mom is visibly relieved that I'm going. She's probably glad not to have to feel like she's checking up on me every waking moment.

I woke up really early this morning and did my cardio routine twice. I know I shouldn't, but I can't help it. No matter how hard I tried, I knew I'd have to eat something really fattening today and if I didn't want to lose my mind, I had to get a jump on the calories.

I tried to get excited about Christmas presents this morning. I put on my biggest smile and squealed at the appropriate times when I opened my gifts. Dad went all out. I got a new iPad and a ton of gift certificates. Mom and Grandma went back to Bloomingdale's and got a bunch of the clothes I'd tried on there. By anyone's estimation, today was a success as far as loot goes, but the best thing I got was from Jack. He went with Susan and James to Arizona so they could spend Christmas with Jill, and then bring her back home in a couple of days. Mom usually crams my stocking full of lip balm and socks and candy. This morning, after I dumped out all of the usual stuff, I felt a heavy lump in the toe and pulled out a little blue box. It was a silver locket in the shape of a heart, and on the inside he'd engraved four words:

Just like you are.

I slipped it around my neck and for the first time I decided maybe I could face going to this treatment center. I logged on to the forum as weigh2go and there in the middle of all the posts about staying strong against Christmas candy and how not eating was the best gift you could give yourself, I wrote:

Going to get help tomorrow. I want to get better.

I clicked send, and as I did a new picture popped up at the top of the forum. It was posted under Jill's username, and it was a snapshot of the two of us at the pool back in seventh grade. We were tan and covered in freckles. My hair was frizzy, and hers was wet. We still had the round chubby cheeks of elementary school students, and we were laughing so hard our eyes were tiny slits. Neither one of us would have passed for "skinny" in this picture, but underneath it, Jill had typed a single word:

Beautiful.

Thursday, December 27
Weight: 122

Getting moved in was sad and exhausting. I'm sharing a room with a girl named Patricia who keeps to herself. We talked for a little while last night, and she said she's been here for a week. She's a bulimic and says she can't stop throwing up her meals. She's having major dental problems because the constant stomach acid in her mouth has eaten the enamel off her teeth. She's missing a tooth and the rest are a weird yellow color.

This morning we all had breakfast together. Everyone has to eat everything on their plate, no questions asked. My heart was racing as I shoveled in the eggs and oatmeal. I felt bloated by the time I stood up from the table. We all have chores assigned to us, and mine is to help wash dishes in the kitchen. I felt like a cow shuffling around the kitchen taking plates and glasses out of the dish dryer and putting them away.

After that I had my first appointment with my new therapist. It's a woman this time. She told me to call her Sharon. I like her, but I miss Dr. Crane. I talked about him and it turns out Sharon knows him. When I asked her how, she smiled.

Sharon: I'm here to help girls like you who are struggling with anorexia because I struggled with it too. Dr. Crane saved my life.

Me: You were an anorexic?

Sharon: Still am. But I've been recovered for over ten years now.

This startled me.

Me: So . . . you mean . . . I'll never get over this? I'll have to deal with it for the rest of my life?

Sharon: Anorexia is a disease. You can keep it in remission if you do the right things, but there is no cure. There's a line that you cross with any compulsive behavior. Once you cross that line, there's no going back. If you work hard, you can recover, but you'll always have to stay on your guard.

This scared me. I thought about the picture Jill had posted of us online a couple days ago. I wanted to go back. I wanted to have a rewind/erase button on the last year of my life. I wanted to never have crossed the line into this disease.

Me: How do I start?

Sharon: You start by using your *words* to tell me what's

wrong. Right now you're using your body. I'm going to ask you to use your *words* to tell me about what you're feeling instead.

This made sense to me—it was like a lightbulb clicked on in my head. Dr. Crane and I had talked a lot about what I was feeling, but he'd never put it like this. Or maybe he had, and I just hadn't heard him.

We talked for a long time during my session about what I was feeling about my dad, my mom, Jack, Jill, Vanessa. It wasn't so much about food or eating or how I looked on the outside. It was a conversation about how I felt on the inside.

When time was up, Sharon smiled and told me I was doing great.

Sharon: Remember, not eating, starving yourself, overexercise, those things aren't the problem. Those things are a *symptom* of the real problem. That's what you're here to figure out. What is the real problem? Once you know, we'll find other ways for you to deal with it that don't involve hurting yourself.

I had to come right back to my room to write that down. It sounded so exciting to hear her say it like that. When I was talking to Sharon I remembered back to a time when I wasn't all worried about the way I looked around Jack or other boys. Even just last summer at the pool I wasn't so focused on my weight. I think if I can find that place again, I'll be able to beat this. Hearing Sharon lay out a plan for finding the real problem made me feel so relieved. Like there's hope—a light at the end of the tunnel.

For the first time tonight, I feel like maybe I can win.

Tuesday, January 1
Weight: 124

I got called into Sharon's office this morning, and when I walked in, Mom was standing there. Turns out the insurance company reversed the preauthorization for my stay here at Hope House. Mom and Dad can't afford to keep me here, even though it's not as expensive as some of the other places.

Sharon and Mom and I had a session and talked about the issues I've been going over with Sharon every day in our individual sessions and sharing about on a group level. It was really hard to talk about how I blamed Mom for not staying slim enough and I blamed Dad for leaving. I could tell that it was killing Mom to take me out of this place, but on the way home, we talked about it, and I feel like I understand how my brain was tricking me into hurting myself.

Mom and I made a plan. I'm going back to the outpatient program with Dr. Crane and the group therapy meetings with Kim. I texted Kim as soon as I was in the car, and she called me and I told her what happened. Kim told me I could call her anytime and that she'd see me at group on Thursday.

When Mom and I got home, we headed straight to my room. We threw out all of my old fashion magazines. I used to keep every issue neatly stacked under my bed, and I'd look at the pictures and obsess about how I wasn't as skinny as the models. We hung sheets over the mirror in my room so I'm not tempted to obsess about how I look every time I walk past it.

Then Mom suggested we go get manicures, and on the way to our usual salon, she made a wrong turn.

Me: Where are we going?

Mom: Thought it would be fun for Jill to come with us.

I was nervous until I saw Jill. She was tan and smiling and had gained about twelve pounds while she was gone. She looked like a different person—one that I remembered from a long time ago.

She came running down the front walk, and I jumped out of the car and gave her a big hug. Jack wasn't far behind her. Soon I was squeezed in his big arms.

Me: Thank you for the locket.

Jack: Every time you think about not eating, I want you to read that.

I smiled. Jill was already in the backseat.

Jill: I'm sorry, but that's all the time we have for this episode of canoodling on the driveway. Tune in next time when we're back with beautiful nail enamel.

And just like that, everything seemed like it was going to be okay. Jack blew us a kiss as Mom pulled out of the driveway.

Tuesday, January 8
Weight: 126

I can't believe how much fun school was today. It was like the old gang was back together. Jill and I have been hanging out all the time again, and last weekend, Geoff and Vanessa joined us for a movie. This time when Rob and Jack ordered concessions Jill got popcorn and I got a hot dog. We even made Jack share his Junior Mints. It's sort of like I've been remembering myself—the old me who wasn't obsessed with food.

I've been sharing about all of this in group, and Dr. Crane even asked me to tell everybody in my own words about what I'd learned with Sharon at Hope House. Kim had a big smile on her face as I talked about how my anorexia was a symptom, not the problem, and by the time I was done sharing, there were tears in her eyes—and mine.

Sharon told me before I left Hope House that it was a good

thing to journal whenever I had feelings come up—especially hard ones—but that she wanted to make sure I wasn't tracking my weight or my food too obsessively, so I think this might be my last entry for a while. I'm still going to go to group, and I'm still going to be seeing Dr. Crane, but as I think about everything this food diary was supposed to be in the beginning and what it became later, it seems like a good idea to take a break. Writing in this journal has been all about calories and weight and food and restriction.

I feel like I'm walking into a new chapter of my life now—one that isn't restricted at all. It's a place where I feel free to love myself exactly the way I am.

Wednesday, January 16
Weight: 126

So much for not keeping track anymore.

Misty Jenkins stopped by our lunch table at school today. She took one look at Jill, sitting there all tan and happy, and couldn't stop herself.

Misty: Hey, Jill! Wow! You look so . . . tan.

It sounded nice, but it wasn't. The word "tan" was delivered instead of the word "heavy," which is what Misty was thinking.

Jack: Hey, twinkle toes. Get lost.

Rob: Yeah, don't you have some fairies to wrangle or sugarplums to eat or something?

Misty's smile was sickly sweet.

Misty: You guys are so funny. No fairies this spring. Just swans. Didn't Jill tell you we're doing *Swan Lake*?

Vanessa didn't get what was happening and took the bait.

Vanessa: No! Really? Oh, that's so exciting! I love that ballet.

Misty: Glad your ankle is better, Jill. Too bad about everything else. You're way too heavy to be a lead now.

Jack jumped up so fast his chair skidded into the wall of the cafeteria.

Jack: Get out of here. Now.

Misty smirked and glanced down at me.

Misty: Sure thing, Jack. If you ever get tired of being seen with that little scarecrow girl, give me a call.

I thought I would throw up. I left everything on the table, grabbed my purse, and ran into the bathroom. I locked a stall door and sat there crying.

When I got home tonight, I took the sheet off the mirror, got undressed, and really looked at myself in the mirror for the first time in several weeks. What I saw horrified me.

Misty is right: I *am* a scarecrow girl. My hair is like straw, and my body looks stuffed and ragged. I have lumpy curves in all the wrong places. Why has everyone been lying to me? Maybe Misty is mean, but at least she's telling the truth.

Wednesday, January 23
Weight: 122

It's been two weeks since I started using the CalorTrack app again. I've been keeping net calories at 1,200 per day so I don't get too skinny too fast. That also allows me to eat about 1,700 calories per day, most of which I pack into lunch so that Vanessa and Jack don't get on my case about not eating. I've started doing hard runs again in the afternoon instead of going to group. This helps me burn off as much as I can, and then I do my cardio routine at night after Mom's gone to bed.

I'm glad Misty was honest with me about how I looked. I will not lose Jack. As sweet as he is, he doesn't understand what he's asking. He doesn't want a girl who weighs 135 pounds. He won't know that until he sees me, so I'm not going to let myself take that risk.

It just feels good to be back in control. I'm sort of proud of myself for recognizing all this feel-good crap for what it is: people who don't have the willpower to stay thin and beautiful.

Wednesday, February 6
Weight: 118

Mom has flipped. Dr. Crane keeps calling to tell her when I
don't show up at my sessions. I told her I don't care. This is who
I am. I'm a thin, beautiful girl. Jack and Vanessa ganged up on
me. They pulled me aside after school the other day and told me
they can tell that I'm restricting again. I told Vanessa to get lost.
I held the locket around my neck up in Jack's face.

Me: So did you mean this or not?

Jack: What? Why are you being like this?

Me: Did you *mean* it? Did you actually mean that you love
me *just like I am*?

Jack: Of course.

Me: *This* is me, Jack. *This* is who I am.

We have a date next week for Valentine's Day. We're
supposed to double with Jill and Rob. I was just trying on
clothes and saw that I have these tiny dark hairs all over my
torso and arms. It's like the hair I shave off my legs, but softer.
I've seen girls post about this on the forum before. I called Jill.

Me: Mayday.

Jill: Yeah?

Me: I am getting hairy like an ape.

She chuckled.

Jill: You too, huh?

Me: You mean . . . ?

Jill: Of course. Come over. I've got some wax. We'll take care of it. Can't be hirsute for Valentine's Day.

Mom wasn't home from work yet, so I drove over to her place. We waxed. It was painful, but I'm smooth as a baby's bottom now. Jill has been restricting again, too. I sensed she was, but we'd both been careful not to talk about it.

It feels like we're sitting on a powder keg—that at any minute, everyone around us might blow up. Sometimes I think it's the level of discipline that makes people so angry and upset at us for not wanting to be fat slobs. Why shouldn't we look like models? Why do you think you buy the products these girls advertise? It's not because they're better than any other product. It's because you want to *look like the girl who is selling it.*

That's why I buy stuff.

Girls who look a certain way use a certain thing. If I use that thing, I'll be as pretty as the girl who is using it in the commercial or the magazine.

This isn't rocket science. If you want to look like a girl in a magazine, you eat and exercise like one.

Why is that such a problem for my mom? For Jill's dad? For Vanessa? For Kim? For Dr. Crane? For Sharon?

Because they know they could *never* do what we're doing.

They could *never* be this disciplined. Look at Sharon. She tried to once upon a time and failed.

Miserably.

Jill and I will not fail.

Thursday, February 14
Weight: 116

Trying to get back down to my homecoming weight, but dealing with it better this time. It feels right to be wearing my skinny jeans again. Mom has gone back to working the night shift because the pay is better and she needs to up our health insurance plan so she can send me to a better treatment center.

As if I'd go.

Dad stays away now for the most part. I think it's too hard for him to see me all grown up. I am my own woman now whether he likes it or not.

I made Jack bring me home tonight after our Valentine's double date. Jill and I looked amazing, but I could tell something was different with Jack. After dinner he and Rob took us for a carriage ride around the city. We were bundled under blankets in the back, and I felt his hand on my thigh. He flinched when he touched me. I can feel a difference in the way he puts his hands on me—almost as if he is afraid I will break.

But this is who I am.

This is the best version of me.

I can tell he doesn't love me.

After the carriage ride, we were supposed to go to the top of a big hotel downtown with a rotating restaurant for dessert. I laughed when I heard this.

Me: Dessert?

Jack: Yeah . . . do you . . . not want to go?

Me: I'm not going to have any.

Jack just stopped and stared. He reached out a hand and gently touched the silver heart hanging around my neck.

Jack: Okay. I guess I'll take you back.

He drove me home without a word. I sat there feeling stupid. He hates my body. He should hate my body. I hate it. I wanted it to be perfect. I should have done more. I shouldn't have let them shame me into eating so much. I should've measured the food I did eat perfectly. I should have tracked the calories perfectly.

If I could just get back down to where I was that night I walked down the stairs last fall in the red dress, everything would be better. It would fix his hesitance. If I still looked like that I'd feel his desire when he touched me instead of his repulsion.

He walked me to the front door and kissed me lightly on the lips.

Jack: I wish you could see how beautiful you are.

When I went inside the house, I came upstairs to my room and cried tears of anger for not being good enough for him. I wanted so badly to be the perfect valentine. Instead, he could barely touch me. He was repulsed.

I'll fix this. I'll make it all better. I'm going to be a hundred pounds by spring break. He'll see then. He won't be able to take his eyes off me. I'll be perfect.

Wednesday, February 20
Weight: 115

Mom found out today that the new insurance won't cover any treatment for my anorexia. It's a "preexisting" condition. She's still vowing to send me off to a treatment camp somewhere, but I won't go. I'm looking better than I have in a long time.

I don't need a "Do This Instead" box anymore. Now that Jill's working hard to get back in shape too, we stay in touch. Anytime I'm tempted, I just text her, and vice versa. We're limiting ourselves to 500 net calories per day. That means I can eat 1,200 and burn 700 or so. My thighs don't touch anymore. I'm getting down to homecoming weight! The lower I see the number drop on the scale, the better I feel about myself.

Jill and I are doing our workout routine twice each day until spring break. It's easier on our joints and bones than running. I don't want to get a stress fracture like she did. Casting for *Swan Lake* happens the first day of spring break next month.

I don't think I have time to keep this journal anymore. There's too much other stuff to do and all writing about this does is make me focus on the wrong thoughts and feelings. I don't want to think about how I feel. I just want to do the things I know will make me feel good about myself. I've got five pounds left, and four weeks to get there. I'm on track to look perfect in my swimsuit in Jack's hot tub the first day of spring break.

I'm not going to write again until I make my goal.

Friday, March 22
Weight: 110.5

Jack is coming over tonight. He said he's got a surprise for me, but I've got a surprise for him! I'm *finally* back down to the weight I was on homecoming night. When I got home from school today Mom was on her way out the door to work. She looked at me like she was seeing a ghost and just started crying.

Mom: What is it going to take?

Me: Mom. Please. Save it.

Mom: I am trying to *save you*. I don't know what to do anymore.

She went on and on about admitting me to the hospital and how Dr. Nash said my not eating enough could be doing real damage to my heart and organs.

Mom: I just want to get you some help for your disease.

Me: Mom! I am not diseased! Can't you see? I look better than all those other Fatty McFattersons. I am thin and gorgeous.

I swear it makes me so angry. If this is a disease, more people should catch it. All they can talk about on the news is how so many Americans are obese and overweight. You'd think my mom would be *happy* that I'm not some two-ton fatso thundering around the house. But no. She can't be *happy* for me. No, no. It must be a *disease*.

I stomped up to my room and started doing my exercise routine. I got really light-headed in the middle of it and couldn't stop coughing just now. I actually coughed up some blood. It was sort of amazing. I think I'm so thin my body is digesting itself.

I logged on to the forum and posted as weigh2go:

Finally back at my goal weight. Happier than I've been in MONTHS!

Jill called me right away.

Jill: Hey! Just saw your post.

Me: I *know*, right? It's amazing.

Jill: Congrats, lady. I think we should go for a jog to celebrate.

Me: Yes! I'm going to jog over to your place.

Jill: Excellent. See you in ten?

Me: Give me fifteen. I need to change clothes.

Hopefully, there won't be any more blood. I wonder if Jill has ever coughed up blood? I'll have to ask her about it.

Friday, March 22
EMERGENCY TRANSCRIPT

Dispatch: 911. What's your emergency?

Caller: My girlfriend collapsed. I need an ambulance.

Dispatch: Where are you?

Caller: I'm on Caballeros near the corner of Alejo.

Dispatch: Sending paramedics now. What is your name?

Caller: I'm Jack.

Dispatch: Jack, when did your girlfriend collapse?

Caller: I don't know. I didn't see it happen. She was jogging over to my house, and then she didn't show up and she didn't answer her phone, so we got in the car to go to her place to check on her.

Dispatch: Is someone there with you?

Caller: Yes. My sister.

Dispatch: Is your girlfriend breathing?

Caller: I can't tell.

Dispatch: Does it look like she's sustained other injuries?

Caller: She's got blood coming out of her mouth.

Dispatch: Is she lying on her back?

Caller: Yes.

Dispatch: Can you see if her chest is rising and falling?

Caller: Not really. I think it is. Just a little.

Dispatch: Are her eyes opened or closed?

Caller: Closed.

Dispatch: And she appears to be breathing.

Caller: Yeah, but it's sorta shallow. Oh, man! Please! Hurry up!

Dispatch: Jack? The ambulance is on its way. Stay on the phone with me. Jack? Are you there?

Caller: Yes! Yes, I'm here. My sister doesn't think she's breathing anymore.

Dispatch: Jack, do you know CPR?

Caller: Yes. My sister is starting compressions.

Dispatch: Make sure that you clean her mouth out with your finger to remove any blood or debris.

Caller: Okay. Okay. I did. I'm gonna set the phone down.

Dispatch: I'll hold the line.

Caller: Okay, I blew into her mouth and my sister is doing compressions. Oh—I hear the ambulance. Here they come. And a police car just pulled up.

Dispatch: I'll let you go. Thanks, Jack.

██████████████████ **MEDICAL CENTER—**
REPORT

Case #: 13-1612

Date: Friday, March 22, ██

Deceased: ████████████

Age: 16

Sex: Female

Race: Caucasian

Summary: ████████████ was pronounced dead on the 22nd day of March ████ at 5:29 p.m. by Regina Nash, MD, at ████████ Medical Center.

Hospital #: ED#098839520

Admitted: 22nd day of March ████ at 5:04 p.m. by ambulance from street corner of Caballeros and Alejo. Admitted by R. Nash, MD.

Symptoms: Cardiac arrest, bleeding from mouth

Remarks: History of anorexia nervosa/depression

Body identified by: ████████, decedent's mother, who was on staff in the ER at the time of arrival.

Immediate cause of death: Cardiac arrest

Due to: Anorexia nervosa

Other conditions contributing but not relating to the immediate cause of death: Natural cause

CASE REPORT

Informant: Pam Tomlin, RN

Incident:

The decedent is a 16-year-old female with a reported history of anorexia nervosa.

The decedent was last known to be alive this afternoon when her mother (an RN on duty in the emergency room when decedent arrived) left for work. Decedent spoke with a friend, Jill ██████████ then hung up the phone at 4:10 p.m., then left for a 15-minute jog to friend's house. After no word from decedent at 4:30 p.m., decedent's friend and brother (decedent's boyfriend) attempted to reach decedent via phone call and text message. After receiving no replies, decedent's friend and boyfriend drove toward decedent's house to look for her. Decedent was found unconscious on the southwest corner of Caballeros and Alejo.

Paramedics were summoned by decedent's boyfriend, Jack ████████, responded, and continued CPR initiated by friend and boyfriend while transporting the decedent to the hospital. The decedent was admitted to the emergency room of ██████████ Medical Center, where lifesaving efforts proved to be of no avail. Death was pronounced at 5:29 p.m., 3-22-██, by Dr. Nash.

This investigator viewed the decedent at ██████████ Medical Center. Close examination revealed no indications of trauma or foul play. Clothing (light blue jogging suit) and jewelry (silver heart-shaped locket) released to ███████████, decedent's mother. No additional information known by this investigator at this time.

Turn the page for a sneak peek at another anonymous diary.

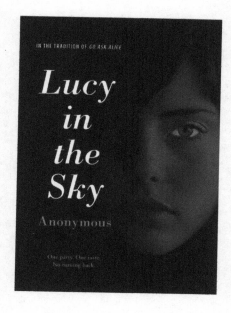

July 4

~~Dear Diary,~~

That's ridiculous. Who writes "Dear Diary" in a diary? I mean, who writes in a diary at all? Shouldn't I be blogging?

This is lame.

July 5

Okay, so this isn't going to be a diary. It's a journal. I guess that's the same thing, but "journal" sounds less like I'm riding a tricycle or something.

Yesterday was my birthday. I turned 16.

It's so weird sharing a birthday with your country. Always fireworks: never for you. Mom always plans an actual birthday dinner—usually the Saturday night after July 4th so that I can have a day where we celebrate just for me. It's fun, kinda like having two birthdays in the same week.

We're not big July 4th celebrators . . . celebrators? Celebrants? People. Whatever—we're not big on July 4th. Usually in the afternoon we have friends from school over and walk down to the beach to play volleyball. There are lots of nets at the beach just down the hill, then we haul ourselves back up the canyon to our house for a cookout in the evening. My brother, Cam, invites his friends from the varsity soccer team. Mom gets my favorite cake (the one with the berries in it).

After we gorge on grilled meat and birthday cake, we all crowd onto the balcony outside my parents' bedroom and watch the fireworks down the coast. You can see the display at the pier really well, and the ones in the cities just up the coast shoot off too. Last year Cam (nobody calls him Cameron except Mom) climbed onto the roof from the front porch so he could get a better view, but Mom freaked and said, CAMERON! Get. Down. This. Instant. Mom's big on safety.

I got a lot of cool presents yesterday. Mom got me the swimsuit I tried on at the mall last week. It's a really cute two-piece with boy shorts, and this fun, twisty top. Dad's present to me was that he's taking me to get my license this week. I've been practicing with him in the parking lot near his office at the college. He gave me a coupon for one "Full Day with Dad." On the back it says, "Good for one driving test at the DMV, followed by a celebratory meal at the restaurant of holder's choosing, and a $100 shopping spree/gift card to store of choice."

He made it himself out of red construction paper and drew this funny little stick figure on the front. It's supposed to be him. He draws curly hair on the sides of the round head so the little man is bald on top like he is. The coupon is sort of cheesy, but so is my dad. I think it's funny. And cute.

Cam got me this journal. We've been going to this yoga

class together, and the teacher is this woman named Marty with bright eyes who talks about her birds a lot. She told us to get a journal and spend a few minutes each day writing down our thoughts and feelings.

I just looked back at everything I've written, and it's mainly thoughts. Not very many feelings. I'm not sure how I feel right now. I mean, I guess I feel fine? Happy?

No, just fine. I feel fine.

I also feel like people who have birds are sort of weird.

July 6

It's funny that Cam bought me this journal. It's one of those things I would never have bought for myself but secretly wanted. I don't know how he knows that stuff. I guess that's what older brothers are supposed to do: read your mind. I mean, who actually goes out and tries the stuff that their yoga teacher says to do outside of class?

Cam got way into yoga last summer when he had a crush on this exchange student from England named Briony—like Brian with a y. (Really? Who names their kid that?) Anyway, she wouldn't give Cam the time of day, so when he found out that she went to this yoga class, he started going to the same one. He bought a mat and this little bag to carry it in and just happened to show up in her class like, Oh my God! Wow!

What a coincidence. Briony never went out with him. I didn't even know she'd gone back to London until I was teasing him about how he should be glad Briony didn't do something like synchronized swimming. He was like, Briony moved back to London right after school got out.

I asked him why he was still going to yoga, and he said he really liked it. And he said I should come.

I'm not sure why I did, really. I guess I was just bored last summer. But now we go to yoga together. It's this really great studio a block off the Promenade, and they run it on donations. You just pay what you can or what you think the class is worth. I didn't think I'd like it at first. It was hard, and I got sweaty and slipped on my mat and couldn't do any of the poses. But I sorta like spending time with Cam.

Who am I writing that to? It's not like anyone is reading this but me. This is exactly how it feels when Grams asks me to pray over dinner. I feel like I'm saying all this stuff that is bouncing back at me off the ceiling and landing in the spinach salad.

Cam probably didn't have to read my mind about wanting a journal at all. He's really smart. His early acceptance letter to this great college up north came last week. He's going to be a biochem major, which just makes me want to lie down on the floor and curl up in a ball. He's a brainiac. And on top of it he's

nice and enthusiastic—which has a tendency to be dangerous.

Last semester Mom was always telling me to ask Cam for help with my geometry homework. I did, but instead of telling me what to do, Cam always talks and talks and talks. It's like he knows so much about stuff and likes math so much that he has to say it all instead of just the answer.

I stopped asking questions. It sort of annoyed me. Just did it myself, and didn't really understand it. I got a C in geometry. You'd have thought I'd flown a plane into a building. (That's bad to say, I guess. I mean, I know people died and everything, but it was a really long time ago.)

Dad came unglued. He's the chairman of the music department at the college where he works. He made me sign up for tutoring this summer with a student that his friend in the math department recommended. Our session starts in a few minutes. I was relieved when Nathan showed up the first time. I was afraid I'd get stuck with some weird math girl.

Nathan is a freshman. He's from Nebraska and has brown hair that's cut short. He works out a lot, and he wears these polo shirts with sleeves that are tight right around his biceps. I just stare at his arms a lot instead of listening when he's trying to help me find the answer.

I wish somebody would just tell me the answer.

Nathan's here. Gotta go.

Later . . .

OMG.

I TOTALLY JUST INVITED NATHAN TO MY BIRTHDAY DINNER.

OMG OMG OMG OMG

And

He

Said

YES!

This is totally crazy. I can't believe I actually said the words out loud. I didn't mean to. We were just sitting at the dining room table and he was talking about the hypotenuse of a right angle, and while he was looking at the protractor he was using to draw lines, I was staring at the lines of his jaw and noticed that they were almost a right angle, and the hypotenuse of the right angle of his jaw was this line in his cheek with a dimple in the middle that he gets when he smiles, and then I heard myself saying, You should come to my birthday dinner on Saturday, and then I realized that Mom was looking RIGHT AT ME like my hair was on fire, and I realized that I'd just invited an 18-year-old over for dinner in FRONT OF MY MOTHER. OMG. I just wanted to CRAWL UNDER THE TABLE.

But he stopped with his pencil stuck into the protractor and looked up, and then glanced over at Mom like he was looking to see if she'd heard, and she smiled at him, sort of weakly. I guess he took that to mean that it was okay with her 'cause he looked me right in the eye and said, Sure. That'd be fun. Now look at this triangle.

I tried to look at the triangle for the rest of the half hour, but I have no idea what he was saying. When he left, I walked him to the door, and Mom said, Nathan, come by around 7:30. He said, Sure thing, and you can call me Nate. He waved at me before he got in his pickup truck and said, See you this weekend. Then, he drove away. Just like that.

I went running back up to my bedroom and buried my head in my pillow and did one of those silent screams where you just breathe out really hard, but with no sound; it's sort of a soft roar, but the excitement on the inside of me made it feel like my head would explode.

I could hear my heart pounding in my ears, and I took a couple of deep breaths and then I remembered what Marty said in yoga this morning about trying to meditate and how to focus on the breath, so I sat down on the floor and crossed my legs like Marty does in front of class, and I closed my eyes and took really deep breaths and tried not to think about Nate. I could do it for about 5 breaths at a time, but then I'd see that

line with the dimple in it behind my eyelids, and then the rest of his right-angle jaw would appear and I'd see a triangle fill in the space on his face.

I mean, it's really no big deal. My dad is two years older than my mom. Nate's only 18, and I'm 16, and it's not like he would be robbing the cradle or anything.

I think I really like him.

OMG I CAN'T BELIEVE THAT NATE IS COMING TO DINNER ON SATURDAY.

July 8

I was just standing in my mirror trying on a couple of different options for tonight. I passed my driver's test and got my license yesterday (YAY! OMG. Finally!), then Dad and I went shopping on the Promenade. I'm a really good bargain shopper. I worked at the Gap part-time last summer and I learned to never EVER pay full-price for anything 'cause they just mark it down every two weeks. Primary, secondary, clearance. Primary, secondary, clearance. Every week on Tuesday night the markdowns would come through from the home office, and we'd all run around with those price-tag guns the next morning, marking down tops that some poor dope had paid $20 more for 12 hours ago. So, anyway, I got a lot of great stuff. Even Dad was surprised with how many items I got for $100. Well, then

I splurged a little and added $40 from my savings to get these supercute sandals that I'd been wanting.

Anyway, I have all this stuff to try on, and I felt myself doing that thing I do where I put on, like, 12 different outfits and stand there and pick every single one of them apart, and I end up standing in front of the mirror in my underwear with this pile of really cute clothes with the tags still on them lying on the floor. I had just put on the second skirt I bought and could tell I was about to find something wrong with it, and then I just stopped, looked at myself, and thought: Don't be that girl.

I just don't want to be that chick who is always staring at herself in the mirror whining about how she looks and having a meltdown in the fitting room. I mean, I'm not a model or anything, but I think I look okay. I have already showered and straightened my hair. It's not frizzy or even curly really—just has some waves, and when you live this close to the waves it can get wavy. (God. Stupid joke.) Whatever, I stepped away from the mirror and saw my journal sitting on my desk, and I thought I'd write about it. I mean, this is a feeling. I'm not sure what kinds of feelings I'm supposed to be writing about in here, but maybe this is what crazy Marty the bird lady was talking about.

I'm SO EXCITED about Nate coming over and I want to

look really hot, but the excitement also feels like nervousness, like I'm going to barf or something. Mom is downstairs putting a marinade on some shrimp that she's going to have Dad grill, and the smell when I walked through the kitchen made me feel like I was going to hurl up my toenails—and I LOVE shrimp.

I know I look good in this skirt. Dad told me it looked "far out" when I came out of the dressing room to check it out in the mirror. He said this in his I'm-being-a-little-too-loud-so-the-other-people-present-will-hear-me-and-think-I'm-hilarious-when-really-I'm-just-torturing-my-daughter voice. I told him to please be quiet and offer his opinions only regarding possible escape routes in the case of a fire, or a random stampede of wild bison. In all other matters, I respectfully asked him to please refrain from speaking to me until we had reached the cash wrap.

I looked in the mirror again just now. This skirt totally works.

Weird how excited and scared feel like the same thing.

July 8—11:30 p.m.
I shoulda known.

I shoulda known when he walked up the front steps with flowers and handed them to Mom.

But he brought me a card with a joke about having pi on

my birthday instead of cake (guh-rooooan) and it had a $25 gift card for iTunes in it. Which was cool and so sweet of him, but he just signed his name. Shoulda known when he didn't write anything personal. Just "Happy B-Day! Nate."

But he was really funny and sweet at dinner. He sat across from me and told us all this hilarious story about when he was growing up in Nebraska and he and his brother raised sheep for the county fair. (Yes. Apparently people still raise animals and take them to fairs where they win ribbons and titles and scholarships. Thank you, CHARLOTTE'S WEB.)

One morning he and his brother went out to scoop food out of these big 25-pound sacks of feed for the sheep, and there was a mouse in one of the bags that ran up his little brother's jacket sleeve. He was telling us about how he thought his brother had been possessed by a demon because he kept screaming and shaking his arms and beating at his chest and running around in a circle while the mouse wriggled around inside his shirt. We were all crying, we were laughing so hard, and Cam almost inhaled a bite of shrimp, which sent him on a coughing fit that made the rest of us laugh even harder.

He jumped up and helped me clear the table when Mom asked who wanted dessert. When Mom told him he didn't need to do that, he smiled at me and said, Oh yes, ma'am, I do. My mama'd fly in from Grand Island and smack me if I didn't.

When we were in the kitchen, I started rinsing plates and he loaded them into the dishwasher like he lived here. We were laughing and joking around and no one mentioned geometry. He was so easy to talk to, easy to be near. I didn't feel nervous even once. I couldn't help but wonder what it would feel like if we were married and this was our house and we were loading the dishwasher together. That's probably stupid, but it made me feel hopeful inside, like maybe something like that was possible.

When Nate bent over to put the final plate in the dishwasher, a necklace fell out of his shirt. It had a tiny key on it, and I was about to ask him where he got it, but Mom came into the kitchen to get some coffee mugs and the French press. Nate tucked the necklace back into his polo before I could ask him about it, but I shoulda known.

There's a long porch on the back of our house that looks over the bottom of the canyon out to the water. We ate dessert out there. Dad lit the candles in the big lanterns on the table outside. Cam sat next to Nate and they talked soccer. The flicker made their skin glow like they were on the beach at sunset. Nate looked all sun-kissed and happy. I felt a foot nudge mine just for a second under the table and my heart started racing. I was glad that it was just the candles outside in the dark 'cause I started to blush like crazy. I thought maybe Nate had touched my foot, and I kept sliding mine a little bit closer toward him under the table, but his foot never touched mine again.

It was almost 10 when he pulled out his phone and checked it, then said, Whoa. I gotta go.

I felt really bummed all of a sudden, and then silly. What was I hoping? That he'd stay and walk me down to the beach? He stood up and shook my dad's hand, then gave Cam one of those weird hugs that guys give each other where they grab hands like they're gonna shake and then lean in and hug with their arms caught in between them. He kissed my mom on the cheek and told her what a good cook she was.

Then he looked right at me and said, Will you walk me to my truck?

I got so many butterflies in my stomach, I thought they might start flying out of my ears. I said SURE, and realized that nobody had really heard him ask that because Mom was pouring more wine and Dad was pouring more coffee and Cam was texting somebody. So I slipped into the house and out the front door.

He'd parked on the street, and when he got to the door of his pickup, he leaned against it and looked up at the sky and said, Huh.

I said, What?

He told me that in Nebraska at this time of night you

could see lots of stars. I followed his gaze up to the sky, but I knew there wouldn't be any stars. Out here, the sky just glows this weird purply color even on the darkest night here. It's the light pollution bouncing off of the marine layer, I said. It's what happens at night when 8 million people get jammed up against the ocean. I turned around and stood next to him with my back up against the truck.

He said it was funny how you always hear about all the stars in Los Angeles, but at night in Nebraska, it's like the sky is covered with diamonds. Then he looked over at me, and I don't know what happened, but I just knew that I had to feel his lips on mine. So I leaned in and kissed him.

Nate jumped like I'd shot him with a taser. He said, WHOA, what are you doing? OMG! I was SO EMBARRASSED I couldn't even LOOK at him. It was like we were having this PERFECT night, and then BLAM-O: I broke the spell. I was blushing and stammering and then I felt the tears come to my eyes, and I didn't wait. I just sprinted back across the street toward the house. I was not going to let him see me cry.

As my foot hit the curb on the other side of the street, he said WAIT!

There was something in the way he said it that made me turn around. And then he shook his head and smacked his forehead, and he walked over to me, and just looked at me.

He pushed my hair over my shoulder and said, No. I'm sorry.

He told me that I had come along two years too late. And that I was beautiful. And that he has a girlfriend.

I shoulda thought about that. I shoulda never invited him to dinner tonight.

I shoulda known.

Calling Maggie May

Calling Maggie May

Anonymous

Simon Pulse

New York London Toronto Sydney New Delhi

WW SIMON PULSE

An imprint of Simon & Schuster Children's Publishing Division

1230 Avenue of the Americas, New York, New York 10020

This Simon Pulse edition June 2015

Text copyright © 2015 by Simon & Schuster, Inc.

Cover photograph copyright © 2015 by Getty Images/Take A Pix Media

All rights reserved, including the right of reproduction in whole or in part in any form.

SIMON PULSE and colophon are registered trademarks of Simon & Schuster, Inc.

For information about special discounts for bulk purchases, please contact

Simon & Schuster Special Sales at 1-866-506-1949 or business@simonandschuster.com.

The Simon & Schuster Speakers Bureau can bring authors to your live event. For more information or to book an event contact the Simon & Schuster Speakers Bureau at

1-866-248-3049 or visit our website at www.simonspeakers.com.

Designed by Karina Granda

The text of this book was set in Adobe Caslon Pro.

Manufactured in the United States of America

10 9 8

Library of Congress Control Number 2015936199

ISBN 978-1-4814-3902-2 (hc)

ISBN 978-1-4814-3901-5 (pbk)

ISBN 978-1-4814-3903-9 (eBook)

Calling Maggie May

Wed, Sept 17

Swim meet: First place in the freestyle today! And second in backstroke.

Calculus test: 97%

Tues, Sept 23

Swim meet: First place in backstroke, third place overall.

American History: 80% on quiz

Wed, Oct 1

Chemistry: 92% on test, A on lab report

Math team: Fourth place in meet. (No prizes for fourth place, Mom notes.)

Fri, Oct 3

English: A- on essay

Swim meet: Third place in backstroke, second place in freestyle, didn't place overall.

American History: B on paper

I deserved an A, but Mr. Franklin hates me. Now I'm screwed.

Why do I even bother? I'm only keeping this journal because Mom is making me. Guess she's going for the Tiger Mom of the Year Award. "You're a junior now. You have to keep track of all your accomplishments so you'll have things to write on your college applications!" Right. Like colleges really want to read this litany of mediocrity. What's the point of noting all my near misses for the admissions committees? "It worked for Mark!" she singsongs in Chinese, smiling encouragingly.

I'm not Mark! Do you hear that, Mom? Mark had straight As all through high school. Mark lettered in three sports. Mark was editor of the newspaper. Mark won every debate, every Science Olympiad, every math team meet, every EVERYTHING. I get it, okay? Everyone gets it. Mark certainly does. . . . I can see the pity for me in his eyes every time he comes home from college. His poor, stupid sister, who can't do anything right.

The only person who doesn't get it is Mom, who still believes I have it in me to be a genius. Who still thinks I can get into Stanford, if only I really apply myself. Mom is living in an FOB fantasy.

Jenny Hsu taught me that the other day: FOB for Fresh off the Boat. Not that my parents are fresh anything. . . . They emigrated from Taiwan more than twenty years ago, before Mark and I were even born. But you'd never know it to talk to them. They still speak Chinese at home, and Mom switches into English only for words or phrases she has learned since coming here. A lot of these have to do with college applications.

Dad isn't as bad. He works as a hospital administrator, so he speaks English all day, but with an accent that makes me cringe. I think I'd actually rather listen to him speak Chinese, even though I understand only, like, 70 percent of what they say. Maybe it's better that way. It's all nagging anyway.

Sometimes I think Dad just wants me to be happy, but Mom would probably spit on that phrase. So American, she would say (in Chinese). Coddling kids, telling them anything they do is fine. How are they going to be happy if they are not successful?

She has a point, I guess. It's a tough world out there, and if you don't stay on top of it, you could be chewed up and spit out.

I know she just wants the best for me. She worries that I am too Americanized because my Chinese is crap (not like Mark's!) and I watch too much TV and my grades aren't perfect. But nothing is ever good enough for her. Well, that's not true. Mark is. But see above: I am not Mark.

She would be so pissed if she knew I was just spewing random crap about my life in my special college-prep journal. But it feels good to get it out. I'll just tear out this page later.

Mon, Oct 6

French: 96% on quiz

Swim meet: First place in backstroke, second place in

3

freestyle and butterfly, though that was a fluke. Second place overall.

Chemistry: 95% on test

Good day.

Thurs, Oct 9

Debate tournament: Fifth place

Newspaper: Got passed over for events editor even though I've been a reporter for four semesters and Chris has only done it for two. Totally unfair, but he's friends with the editor in chief. Of course.

Math team: Let's not even talk about it

How demoralizing. The thing is, I might do better at all this stuff if I actually cared about any of it. I'm only doing it for college. Well, I'm doing it for Mom, and she's the one who cares about college. Not that I don't care. It just all seems really . . . abstract to me. Does it really matter where I go to college? I'm not so sure it does. It just seems like a lot of money and a lot of debt, and I'm not sure what I'm supposed to get out of it.

But I keep showing up for all these stupid activities because Mom says it's important, and I'm a dutiful daughter. The only one I really like is swimming. I love swimming, which is probably why I'm better at it than any of the other stuff. Not that I'm that great. . . . I'm not even the best person on my team, let alone in the whole Seattle area. Definitely not good enough to attract serious interest from colleges.

But that's never bothered me.

I don't know, the other kids on my team all try so hard and work so hard. I work, but I don't seem to have that competitive drive. That Mark had. That I'm supposed to have. I don't care about winning or being the best or beating my best times. What I really like about swimming is the water.

That sounds dumb, doesn't it? But everything is better under there. I don't have to deal with other people—how they see me, what they want from me or whatever. When I'm underwater, I'm not a daughter or a student or a competitor. I'm just a body.

And when I lift my head to breathe, I hear the roar of the crowd and the echoing sounds of squealing kids, but it all feels far away, and a second later I'm down in that blue world again where everything is muted and wobbly. And I know it's only temporary, but sometimes it's the blue world that feels real and the dry world with all its noise and air and demands that feels like an uncomfortable dream.

Fri, Oct 10

American History: C+ on paper

Mom is going to kill me. Not even kidding. She'll . . . I don't even know. This is untested water. I've never gotten a C before. And obviously Mark never did. I bet Mom doesn't even know grades go this low.

I can't tell her. I'll just tell her it was an A. No, if I tell her it's an A, she'll be so proud she'll want to see it. God. Okay. I'll tell her it was a B+. She'll be mad, but she won't freak out. I'll just have to make sure I bring my grade up by the end of the semester. If I start getting As from now on, I can bring it up, and she never has to know.

I don't like hiding things, but what choice do I have? I guess I'll tear out this page later too, in case she goes snooping.

I don't know how to keep doing this. I've got so much bottled up inside, and one day it's going to blow up and destroy everything in my path like a tornado. I have to get it out, or I'll go crazy. And I have nowhere else to put my thoughts. Maybe if I had anyone to talk to . . .

I guess there are Jenny and Eiko and John and the others at the geek table, but I can't really talk to them. In the end, they're just like Mom. They might as well be spies for her. All they ever talk about is how they did on this or that test, or how nervous they are about the stupid Academic Decathlon. And if I told them I just got a C on something, they would judge me so hard. I can just imagine their faces. Jenny would be pitying: "Don't worry. You can totally bring it up if you work hard! Maybe you can ask for an extra-credit assignment!" All while calculating how much closer to valedictorian she is now. Eiko would furrow her brow, look concerned, and be like, "What's gotten into you? You used to be smart." And John would laugh at me and say I've let myself get distracted . . . and he wouldn't have to say anything more. Everyone at the table would crack up because they would all know what he meant. That I'm boy crazy. Just because Eiko told everyone that I have a crush on Tyler Adams.

I don't have a crush on Tyler Adams. . . .

I do have a small, and slightly unhealthy, obsession with Tyler Adams.

Who could blame me? Tyler's on the swim team, but he's not like me. He's amazing. I mean he actually wins things. That's not why I like him, though.

I know the reasons girls are supposed to like boys. I know that I'm supposed to love him from afar because he is intelligent, or kind, or generous, funny, and ambitious. But the truth is, I don't like him for those things. I don't even know if any of those things are true about him because I barely know him and have never spoken to him. What I do know is that he is intensely, painfully beautiful. That is something I know very, very well, because it is very difficult not to notice when you see him every day in a teeny-tiny racing suit.

So sue me. Tyler Adams is gorgeous, and there's nothing wrong with me for noticing—*not* that he would ever notice me. I am not gorgeous. I am a nerd. I am a geek. I am not cool or pretty or sexy or popular. I'm wallpaper. I'm worse than wallpaper, because people might notice an interesting wallpaper pattern. I'm beige, industrial-grade, institutional wall paint. The kind you never notice at all, unless it's to remark how totally boring it is.

Tyler would never talk to me. And besides, Mom would freak if she knew I was even looking at a white boy. John is right. I should stay focused on my schoolwork, since that's all I'm good for. Then maybe one day I'll be a huge success with my own biotech company, and then cute boys will date me. Will they? Does that work? Do cute boys want to date girls who can buy and sell them? Maybe not. Maybe I'll just buy and sell the cute boys, then.

Except I'm no good at schoolwork, either. So I really have nothing. Sixteen years old and already useless.

Wow. Colleges are going to be really impressed when I send them this. Better rip out more pages. Not yet, though . . . It makes me feel a little better to read over these rants, so I'll leave them a bit longer.

Mon, Oct 13

Calculus: 90% on test

French: 88% on test

Math team meet: Second place

And in far more interesting news, Tyler Adams almost kind of looked at me today! Wow, I am so pathetic. But it was the greatest thing that has happened to me since . . . since Dad took me and Mark to the amusement park for my fourteenth birthday? God, that was a long time ago. My life is sad.

But back to my miniscule triumph! It was on the bus home from swim practice today. I heard Tyler ask a friend of his when their next English paper was due. His friend had no idea, so Tyler stood up and called out to the whole bus, "Is anyone in my English class?" And, well . . . I am. I doubt he even knows that, since I'm sure he has never noticed me in class. But anyway, no one else said anything for a minute, and I saw my chance. I said, "Um . . . the paper is due next Thursday."

I was sitting three or four seats away from him, and there were people in between us, so he heard me but I don't think he knew exactly who had spoken. In any case, he sort of looked around in my general direction for a minute and said, "Thanks," and then went back to talking to his friend.

My brush with fame! Well, not fame but . . . attractive

boyness. Okay, writing that out, it seems so incredibly sad, it makes me ashamed of myself, but it was genuinely exciting at the time. I was proud of myself for having the guts to talk to him ... even if he couldn't tell it was me.

Tues, Oct 14

I saw Tyler talking to a girl today. I don't even know her name, but I hate her from the very depths of my being.

That's a little crazy, isn't it? I can't explain it, but when I saw them together, all this emotion swelled up inside of me. I've seen Tyler talk to girls before—he talks to and flirts with girls all the time. He's even dated girls on the swim team, but the thought of them doesn't twist my insides the way the girl today did.

Something about the way he looked at her ... It was different from the way he is with other girls. Somehow I knew right away: That's what I want. I don't care about college or the new debate topics or how I place in next week's swim meet. My only ambition is to be looked at like that.

What is it about this girl? I wish I knew. There's nothing special about her. As far as I could see, she's nothing but a pretty, dumb white girl, interchangeable with all the others at our school. So what was it that made him look at her like that? What does she have that the other girls don't? And how do I get it?

Thurs, Oct 16

Chemistry: 82% on test

Debate meet: Fourth place PF, no place LD.

English: 85% quiz

I was wrong about that girl. Ada Culver. The one Tyler was talking to.

I just assumed she was one of the popular girls, the ones who all blend together, with their honey-blond hair and their honey-tan skin and their skinny tan jeans. But she's not like that.

She's not exactly popular, for one thing. She eats lunch alone every day, and I never see her talk to anyone. That makes her sound like a loser, doesn't it? Like she's an even more hopeless case than I am. But that's not quite right either.

There's something sort of mysterious about her. I tried to cyberstalk her, but she's got almost nothing online. Usually the popular girls and the wannabes are all over the Internet, where they can control and curate their image from the safety of their bedroom. On the Internet, it's easy enough to make yourself look cool in front of the whole world, but her profile is totally locked down. Almost like she's hiding something.

I wonder if that's what Tyler likes: a little mystery. Or maybe it's just that she's beautiful . . . sheets of coppery blond hair and long legs like a model. I guess it's not so hard to understand the appeal there.

Thurs, Oct 23

I think I'm becoming a little fixated on Ada Culver.

Maybe it's not the sanest hobby, but it's something to do, something to think about other than the endless stream of tests and papers and competitions. I feel like if I just study her closely enough, learn everything I can about her, I could unlock her mystery.

There's something so different about her. Strange? Weird? A little off? But not in a bad way. I almost can't believe now that I ever mixed her up with the other girls at school. She doesn't dress like the popular girls. She doesn't dress like anyone else, really. It's like she doesn't even care about things like fashion and trends.

I guess people might say that about me, too (if they bothered to say anything at all about me). I don't seem to care about fashion because all I wear are baggy jeans and bulky sweaters and plain T-shirts. Definitely not the height of fashion.

But I don't think anyone could ever think Ada Culver and I have anything in common. If I avoid fashion, it's mostly because I don't have the time, don't have the energy, definitely don't have the money, and don't see the point in it. The result is that I look frumpy and invisible at all times. Whereas with Ada . . . it's not exactly that she's outside of popular style. It's more like she's above it.

Obviously money is not an issue for her, because even I can tell that her outfits don't come cheap. And it's not that she doesn't care or put in the effort, because she always looks amazing. Like, even the popular rich kids at school mostly just wear skinny jeans and tank tops or band T-shirts or whatever. They look cool, but they all look pretty much the same. But Ada . . . She dresses like a . . . like an adult, kind of? Or like a movie star. Maybe that's it.

Just an example: Almost everyone in school has these puffy ski jackets that are popular right now. And the people who can't afford those, or don't care enough to buy them, we have lumpy hand-me-downs or jackets from thrift shops that don't fit right. But Ada came to school yesterday in a perfectly fitted coat that swirls around whenever she turns, a deep blue scarf threaded with gold, and leather boots that *click-clack* on the pavement when she goes outside to smoke. No one else wears heels to school—not even the teachers.

The other weird thing is that even though she doesn't seem to have any friends at school, she's on her phone all the time. (A superfancy top-of-the-line phone, obviously, in a shiny pink case.) I always see her at lunch or between classes, looking like a model in a fashion magazine spread as she lounges against some wall and talks or texts on her phone. But who could she be talking to? And who picks her up after school? She's never on the bus. The other day I saw her get into the passenger side of a really nice car that I think was a Jaguar. I'm pretty sure no one at school drives a car like that. It must be her parents, and they must be loaded.

Okay, maybe I am being a little creepy. It's not like I spy on her. . . . I'm just curious, because she is so weird. I mean, interesting. And so different from me.

Fri, Oct 24

I did something crazy today. I wore a scarf. Blue paisley. Silk. My dad gave it to Mom for her birthday a few years back, but she's never worn it. When I was putting away laundry yesterday, I happened to see it, and before I even thought about what I was doing, I grabbed it. And I wore a dress today, too—my piano-recital dress. It's not particularly elegant or flattering. Actually, it kind of makes me look like a dumpling. But I had to do something.

This all probably doesn't sound that crazy, but for me, it is. The geek table noticed right away. They asked if I had a recital that afternoon and gave me a strange look when I said I didn't. But a strange look is better than no look at all, right? I'm not sure, but it seemed like it might be worth a try, anyway.

I don't know what I'm doing. I've been feeling a little nuts ever since I wrote that last entry. It's like expressing all those thoughts awoke something strange in me. And I know I should be worrying about my upcoming history test, and I am trying to study, but somehow all my mind wants to think about is what I can do to make myself less me and more . . . someone else. More Ada.

That's hopeless, I know, but school stuff feels hopeless too these days. If I'm not going to be the brilliant scientist Mom dreams of, maybe I can be cool and exciting at least. Enough so Tyler might know my name. I'd be happy with that.

I don't know why he doesn't just forget about her. She obviously has bigger things going on than him, though I can't figure out what. Who is she always talking to on her phone?

Wed, Oct 29

French: 84% on test

Math team: Meet, but I didn't place.

I haven't seen Ada and Tyler together in a while. Did they break up? Did he dump her? Did she dump him? A while ago I wouldn't have believed it was even possible to say no to someone as gorgeous as Tyler Adams, but I guess if anyone is in a position to turn him down, it's Ada Culver. She's probably dating someone even better now.

But who could be better than Tyler? It would have to be someone pretty amazing.

A celebrity. A prince. An alien. Or maybe no one at all. Maybe a girl like Ada Culver is so cool she doesn't even need boys.

Thurs, Oct 30

I spoke to Ada today. And to Tyler. It was so weird! I almost can't believe it really happened. Nothing this interesting has happened to me in . . . well, maybe my whole life. How can that be? How can a conversation with a couple of kids at school be the most exciting thing that ever happened to me? But Tyler is Tyler, and Ada's not just any girl, as I've already made pretty clear.

I want to get it all down now while it's still fresh in my head. I'm afraid if I go to sleep I'll wake up convinced it was all a dream. Even now I'm not so sure.

It was lunchtime. I was in line to collect my uninspiring rations of institutional-grade chicken fingers, stressing about this huge history test I bombed that morning, when I noticed Tyler moving across the lunchroom. I let my eyes follow him because even though it's painful to look at Tyler and see how

16

gorgeous he is and think about how hopeless it is to be in love with him, I prefer that kind of pain to thinking about what's going to happen when Mom sees my end-of-semester grades and realizes her dreams for me are dead.

So instead of dwelling on that, I watched Tyler. And as I watched, I noticed that he was heading toward the door out to the playing fields, and obviously if he went through that, I would lose sight of him. I don't know what came over me exactly, except that I really didn't want to go back to thinking about that history test or those chicken fingers. So I started moving. I stepped out of the line and I followed him.

It was drizzling a little outside, so there weren't many people around. I scanned the low wall and the steps where students usually gather at lunchtime, but I didn't see Tyler or anyone else. Then I turned and saw Tyler ducking down into a little passageway between the main school building and the auditorium.

I hurried toward where I'd seen him last, still with no fixed idea what I was doing or what I'd do if he spotted me. It's like I was on autopilot. That's when I heard the *click-clack* of heels on a small flight of concrete stairs, along with the soft thud of Tyler's sneakers. He'd been looking for Ada, of course. And now he'd found her.

From where I was, I could lean over a railing and see them both at the bottom of the stairs. Ada was wearing a short red trench coat that matched her nails. She slipped out of the rain under a little overhang and pulled out a cigarette and a book of matches.

"Dammit," she said in a low voice as one match after another went out. The wind had picked up. She was facing away from Tyler, and at first I thought she might not know that he was there, but then she said, "I don't suppose you have a lighter."

"I don't smoke," said Tyler.

"Of course you don't," said Ada, still not looking at him. Her straight blond hair fell like a curtain between them.

They stood together in silence a moment while Ada tried and failed to get another match to light. Tyler took a step forward. "I can help," he said. He leaned his body close to hers, rounding his shoulders to block the wind and blocking my view of her. After a moment, I heard her say thank you, and a plume of smoke rose to where I was standing. He didn't move.

"I said 'thank you,'" Ada repeated, more sharply this time.

"Don't be stuck-up," said Tyler. "I know what you are."

"Is that a fact?"

"I'll tell everyone."

"Be my guest," said Ada, not looking at him. Her phone trilled with a text message. "I've got to take this," she said.

"Okay."

"That was code for, 'Run along, now.'"

"Go ahead," he said. "I don't mind."

The phone trilled again. "Fine," said Ada, and she moved out from behind him, back into the rain. She started to walk up the stairs, but he reached behind him and grabbed her arm, tugging her back down to his level. "Ow," she said. "What's the . . . ?" But she didn't say anything else because he was kissing her.

"Hey," I cried out. Not stopping to think, I took the steps two at a time. "What are you doing? She said no."

Tyler stepped away from her, wiping his mouth with the back of his hand.

"No, she didn't," he said. "Who are you?"

At that point, my sudden attack of bravery wore off, and my throat closed over my voice. It's funny, because even then Tyler barely glanced at me. He kept staring at Ada until she said in a low, hard voice, "Get lost now. I mean it." At that he shrugged his shoulders, forced out a laugh, and wandered off toward the playing fields as if that had been his plan all along.

Ada's phone trilled again. "I've got to take this," she said, and she walked off in the other direction, leaving me alone in the rain.

I don't know exactly what to make of that whole scene. But I guess Ada doesn't really like Tyler.

Mon, Nov 3

I spoke to Ada again today. Or actually, she spoke to me.

I'd stayed away from her since our last interaction. I don't know why, but somehow I was embarrassed. I thought maybe she was mad that I interrupted what was going on between her and Tyler. And I definitely didn't want to see Tyler. So I did my best to stay out of sight, which is usually easy for me.

But Ada found me after school today. I was walking across the parking lot to the buses when she called my name. I was so surprised I didn't even answer. Ada Culver knows my name? It was hard to imagine, but she must have done some detective work after our last meeting.

I stopped and stared at her. She was standing by herself, away from the crowd, in a dun-colored coat with a cream fur collar that almost blended with her pale hair. She had her hands stuffed in her pockets, and she was shivering even though it wasn't that cold. I continued not to move, and eventually she approached and stood before me, maybe two feet away.

"Thank you," she said.

"For what?" I had thought of her before as beautiful and stunning, but now that she was close-up, I realized there was nothing unusual about her face or her body. She was skinnier and taller than me, but not statuesque. Her skin was pale, and a smattering of freckles on her slightly snub nose made her look almost wholesome. I had been fascinated before by her confidence, her coolness, but standing in front of me now, she seemed almost fragile. But that was fascinating too.

"The other day," she said. She pulled out a cigarette and lit it. She had a lighter this time. "Stuff like that . . ." She waved her cigarette vaguely. "We need to look out for each other."

We? I didn't know what she meant. Humankind? Women? Or me and her?

"It's fine," I said, and I turned to go.

"Why did you follow me outside?" she said abruptly.

I stopped again. "I wasn't following you."

She nodded as if she had half expected this answer. "You like Tyler," she said. It wasn't a question, so I didn't answer. She took a long drag. "A bit of advice," she said on her exhale. "Stay away from him."

I stared at her in surprise. Did she actually think I was a threat?

"You don't have to worry about me," I said.

"No?"

"Boys don't . . . do that to me."

"Lucky you."

I didn't say anything.

"You don't think you're so lucky," she said. "Is that it? You wanted it to be you he was mauling."

"No," I said quickly, but my hands were sweating. She was right. I hadn't even admitted it to myself, but there was a part of me that did wish it was me he had pushed up against that wall.

Ada shook her head, her hair catching what remained of the winter light. "You think that's what passion looks like, but it's not. Tyler's just a little boy, trying to be a big man." She dropped her cigarette on the pavement and crushed it under her heel. "Anyway, I should have said thank you the other day. So thank you."

"Sure," I said.

Ada turned away and walked toward a waiting car.

Wed, Nov 5

Screw this journal and screw Mom. I am so done with recording my pathetic attempts to distinguish myself for colleges, and I am really done with her nagging and demanding. I got second place overall at the swim meet today, but when I told Mom, she barely even looked up except to ask how the debate tournament went. Well, Mom, let me tell you: It was awful. I somehow got my notes out of order, and my opponent was really good, and the upshot was I didn't even place. Not that this is any surprise—I've never been good at debate. I hate public speaking. I never would have joined that stupid club except that Mark was awesome at it, of course, so

Mom naturally assumed that I should do the exact same thing.

How hard would it be for her to just say congratulations? Or nice job? Or maybe make a comment about how all my hard work in the pool paid off? But no. She has to fixate on the debate thing, which spiraled into a monster list of all my other shortcomings, until she cornered me into a two-hour lecture about what a worthless, terrible, disobedient child I am. Disobedient! That was the real slap in the face. All I ever do is obey. For as long as I can remember, I have done everything she asked, everything she told me to do, everything she wanted, up until and including this dumb journal. And what has it gotten me? Not a whole lot.

And the worst thing is, I don't even know why. Do I care about her approval? Do I even want it? Or is it just a failure of imagination? Maybe I let her direct every tiny aspect of my life because it's easier than thinking for myself, than actually deciding what it is I want and what's important to me.

Everything in my life has always been for her, from which classes I take to which activities I do to the food I eat and the clothes I wear. And I have never questioned any of it, but what's my reward? To be told that I've failed at being a dutiful daughter. The only thing I've ever really tried at.

Sometimes I wonder what she would do if she had a really bad daughter. It would blow her mind. I should do that, just to

23

make her appreciate how good I've been all this time. Just let everything go, let myself be bad.

Oh, who am I kidding? I'd never have the guts to do that.

Thurs, Nov 6

I did it! I can't believe it, but I actually did something, well, bad today. I guess I am officially a bad girl now. And weirdly, the world didn't end. In fact, I seem to have gotten away with it.

I feel like an idiot for spending so much of my life being well behaved and obedient, terrified that if I ever did anything wrong, anything for myself, anything fun, everything would come crashing down around me. I'm not even sure what I thought would happen, but I had to believe there was some terrible punishment awaiting me, or else why would I keep doing all that stuff I didn't want to do?

And now I feel like that was all a big lie. The world doesn't work like that at all, and I don't have to live in constant fear of messing up. I can live a little, breathe a little. Make my own decisions. And it will be okay.

Even if I do wind up getting found out and getting in trouble, I don't know that I care. I wouldn't change anything about today, because it was amazing. Even if I get grounded for a million billion years and never see sunlight again, I won't regret today.

It didn't start that great, honestly. In my fit of rebellion last night, I decided not to study for my chemistry test, and taking the test without any preparation felt pretty bad. I even felt a little sick to my stomach, just thinking about having to turn it in with basically nothing on it. I never do that. Usually I'm freaking out if I think I might get anything less than a ninety, so the very thought of what a zero might do to my average made me break out in a cold sweat.

I started panicking right there in the middle of the test, and I guess I must have looked pretty bad, because the teacher asked me if I was feeling all right. I took that as my cue. I just said "no" and got up and ran out of the classroom. Part of me was sure he would come after me, but the decision was made for me pretty quickly by my stomach. So I just ran for the nearest bathroom and barfed into one of the toilets.

I felt a lot better after that, but I didn't know what to do with myself next. I really didn't want to go back to class and finish the test. But I didn't want to go to the nurse either. So instead I just hid out in the bathroom until I could go to my next class.

That's when Ada walked in.

She was wearing a wrap dress that clung to every line and curve of her figure. She gave me a quick look and said, "Hey," before starting to reapply her lipstick in the mirror. "Shouldn't you be in class?" she asked.

"Shouldn't you?" I countered.

She shrugged and returned her attention to the mirror. "I won't tell if you don't."

That seemed like the end of the conversation, but I didn't want it to be. I cast around for something else to say to her, but before I could think of anything, she started up again. She capped the top of her lipstick with a delicate pop, then turned to me and said, "Why is it you never wear makeup at school?"

"Me?" I said, as if there were anyone else she could have been talking to.

"You," she said. "I always thought . . . you and your friends. None of them wear makeup. I always figured it was because you were above it. You seemed to have more important things to worry about than looking pretty for boys."

That in itself was a revelation. Ada Culver, of all the people on this earth, had not only looked at me and noticed me before we ever spoke, but it sounded like she might have been a little jealous of me. It's weird to even write those words down. I can't really believe that it's true, but I don't know. In the moment, I was so shocked I couldn't even say anything.

"But now," she continued, "now I know you're just as boy crazy as anyone in this place. You want boys like Tyler Adams to like you. So why don't you try?"

"What do you mean, try?"

"You're a smart girl. You can figure it out. Take some of that brainpower you put into your classes and apply it to your looks. You could have ten Tylers if you wanted."

I shook my head. "It would take more than a coat of lipstick to make a boy like that notice me."

Ada looked me up and down, appraising. "You'd be surprised what lipstick can do. Come here."

I opened my mouth to ask why, or maybe to put her off, but then I realized I didn't want to, and I didn't care why. I pushed myself away from the wall and stepped toward her. She smelled like jasmine and tobacco.

"Tilt your head up," she said, "and relax your mouth."

One of her hands came up and rested just below my ear, steadying my head. With the other, she carefully smudged the waxy pigment around my lips. "There," she said. "What do you think?"

She stepped away from me, and for a minute I just stood there rubbing my lips together, acclimating to the strange feel of it. Then I turned toward the mirror. If I had been expecting a miraculous, Hollywood-style transformation, I didn't get it. I guess I had been, because I couldn't quite stop a bubble of disappointment from welling up inside me. It was still my face, still my boring, blunt haircut, still my broad swimmer's shoulders and practical clothes. But now ornamented with a slash of bright red. It was definitely striking.

"Hmm," said Ada. "Not really your color. But I have more at home. You should come over. I haven't played makeover in years."

Ada Culver was inviting me to her house? I couldn't quite believe my ears.

"When?" I said.

She gave me a funny look. "What's wrong with now?"

"But it's the middle of the school day."

Ada started to laugh but swallowed it back down. "Yeah," she said. "That's right." Not like she had forgotten, but like she had forgotten that might mean something to other people. She dropped her lipstick tube into her purse and turned toward the door.

"Wait," I said, and she stopped. I thought about my fight with my mom, how just once I wanted to show her what real disobedience was. And how I'd never had the guts to really do it.

"I . . . ," I said, hesitating for a moment on the edge of this new me. "Okay. Let's go."

We took the bus. I kept expecting someone to stop us and ask us what we were doing out of school in the middle of the day, but no one did. Maybe it was the lipstick. I don't know if it made me look more grown-up, but it made me feel more in control. Like I was wearing a mask, almost.

Ada's house wasn't at all what I'd expected. Based on her clothes and her phone and how she carried herself, I just assumed her house would be some big mansion with a pool and a housekeeper and a badminton court in the yard. But we got off in front of a small, shabby ranch house covered in pale yellow aluminum siding, with a big hole sliced through the screen door. Ada unlocked the door and let me in. The rooms inside were cramped and dark, with junk mail and celebrity gossip magazines strewn over every surface. I've never thought of myself as one of the rich kids, but it made my house seem like a palace. I mean, at least we've got two floors and a piano and the beautiful garden Mom works so hard on. Ada's house looked like no one really cared about it at all.

Ada showed me down a hallway to her bedroom. Clothes were heaped on every surface, as well as scarves and shoes and a pile of coats in the corner.

"Sorry," she said. "I don't usually have people over."

I hovered between the desk and the bed, still not sure what I was doing there. Ada stayed on the other side of the room, leaning against the doorjamb with her hands behind her back. She looked nervous. "It's kind of a dump, I know."

"No," I said, thinking of my room back at home. It was clean and neat, with every little piece of my life squared away into its proper place, wallpaper and bedding chosen without consulting me. It felt like a prison. "I like it. Is it okay if I . . . ?" I indicated the bed.

"Go ahead." She nodded. "You can just dump all that stuff on the floor."

I couldn't bring myself to do that, so I just pushed some of the clothes toward the other side of the bed and perched myself on the edge. She tugged out her desk chair. On the seat was a rat's-nest tangle of jewelry.

"Right, the lipstick," said Ada mysteriously. "Let's see what we have."

She pulled a shoe box out from under the desk and opened it. It was cluttered with all kinds of makeup, from samples to cheap drug-store tubes to stuff that looked really fancy.

"Hmm, purple could be dramatic," she said, "but maybe too gothy. Coral . . . No, all wrong for your skin tone. Maybe something with some brown?"

"Brown?" I said dubiously.

"It sounds like it would be ugly, but it's very sophisticated. I promise. Here." She held up the tube she had been seeking, uncapped it, and twisted it to reveal a deep, earthy russet. "This will be great on you."

She grabbed a tissue from a box on the dresser and carefully wiped the other color away, then replaced it with the darker hue. She sat back to examine her handiwork. "Beautiful."

"That might be an exaggeration," I mumbled.

She leaned closer to me, and I could smell her perfume again.

"Oh, I don't know," she said, brushing the bangs off my face. "You don't know it, but you could break a lot a hearts with those cheekbones."

"Very funny."

She raised an eyebrow. "I don't get the joke."

"Sure you do," I said, feeling frustrated. "It's me. I'm the joke, and you're the one laughing. I can't have a guy like Tyler any more than I can have a diamond bracelet or a . . . a unicorn."

Ada laughed. It was the first time I'd heard her laugh, and it was a jagged sound, like a machine that hadn't been used in a while.

"I don't know about the unicorn, but you could have Tyler if you wanted him, and the diamond bracelet too. But you're too smart for that, right?" I didn't answer. "Right? You saw what he was like. And now that you've seen, you know better than to think that's a prize worth fighting for."

I think I managed to nod. In any case, she gave me a brief smile.

"Here," she said, pressing the tube of lipstick into my

palm. "You should take this. It looks awful on me. Now you just need some clothes to go with that pretty face."

Her long legs took her from the bed to the closet in two strides. She started going through the piles of clothes all over her room and tossing things at me. It seemed crazy at first. . . . She's tall and skinny and I'm short and dumpy, but she said not to worry.

"It'll look different on you, but good." And she was right. I put on a dress I've seen her wear—a clinging navy knit with small brass buttons—and a part of me had a fantasy that it would magically turn me into her. It didn't, but when I stood in front of the mirror, it didn't look bad. I looked curvy, not dumpy.

"There you are . . . all dolled up for a night out on the town."

I laughed. "Not like I have anywhere to go."

That's when it hit me. It was two thirty, almost the end of the school day, and Mom would be expecting me home soon. Plus, I needed to figure out an unfamiliar bus route. "I need to get going," I said, heading for the door to her room. Then I remembered I was still wearing her dress. I went to take it off, but she stopped me. "Keep it," she said. "It looks better on you."

That was definitely the lie of the century, but I appreciated it. Even if it didn't look better on me than on her, it definitely looked better than any of the clothes I currently owned. I stuffed my school clothes into my swim bag and hurried off.

On the bus home, I couldn't help smiling to myself. I felt like I had finally figured out what friends were. Technically, Jenny and Eiko and the other geeks were my friends, but I didn't much enjoy the time I spent with them, and if we got together, it was only to study or work on a project. With Ada, it wasn't like that at all.

All afternoon I had been on an adrenaline high from skipping school and hanging out with the bad girl, but on that bus, my normal self caught up with me and I started panicking about what would happen when I got home. Would my mom know? Well, obviously, if I walked in with makeup on and someone else's clothes, that wasn't going to help my case.

I dug a tissue out of my bag and carefully swiped off all traces of the lipstick. Then I got off the bus a few blocks from home and changed into my usual clothes in a restaurant bathroom. By the time I got to my house, I was back to my normal self, and only a few minutes later than usual. Still, as I opened the door, my heart was in my throat, not knowing what might await me. I heard Mom call me as the door swung shut behind me. I found her in the den, playing mah-jongg on the computer.

"Someone called this afternoon," she said in Chinese. The school. They called to let her know I ditched class. My heart pounded in my chest so hard I was sure she could hear it.

"Check the voice mail," she said without looking up from her game.

That's when it hit me. Mom never answered the phone unless it was a familiar number—someone from our family or the Chinese community. She didn't trust her English on the phone with strangers, so she let the voice mail get it and had me or my dad listen to it when we got home. This was perfect! I nodded meekly, obediently, and went off to listen to the message. It was the school, reporting me absent for my third-through sixth-period classes. I pressed delete.

Thurs, Nov 13

Oh God, I've never been so humiliated in all my life. I'm such an idiot! Why did I ever get it into my head that I could be like Ada? Ada . . . she's from a different planet from me. We're not the same species. As if a dress and some lipstick could change that!

All right, might as well record my foolishness, so I can read it over every day for the rest of my life as a reminder not to ever do anything risky again.

We had a swim meet. Remember when this journal was for tracking my success at things like swim meets? Yeah, well, forget it. I did terribly. I just couldn't focus at all. I don't know why; it just all seemed so unimportant.

Anyway, after my terrible swim, I was sitting there watching the boys get ready for the next event, dealing with pitying looks from the coach and a couple people on the team, and there was Tyler and . . . I know what Ada said. I know he's a creep, but he's just so incredibly perfect-looking. I haven't seen the whole world yet, but I swear there is no more beautiful physical specimen of masculinity to be found anywhere.

And that's when it came into my head . . . the most terrible idea in the universe. I remembered then and there that I still had Ada's dress and the lipstick she gave me in my gym bag, and I just thought, what if? What if I put it on? What if I got on the bus home tonight looking like . . . like . . . well, not like Ada, obviously, but like a person. Like a girl, instead of some invisible nothing, like I usually am. Ada said it. She said I could get Tyler if I wanted him. Well, goddammit, I want him, and if willpower and lipstick are all it takes, I have both of those.

So after the meet we were all getting changed, and I did it. I slipped on Ada's dress instead of my usual track pants and T-shirt. And I lined up with some of the other girls at the mirror to apply my lipstick. I made a mess of it, of course, because I'd never really done it before, and my hands were shaking with nerves. But eventually, by copying what I'd seen and felt Ada do, I managed a reasonable, not sloppy-looking mouth. Eiko, of course, gave me a hard time about it. She could not have acted more shocked and appalled to see me in a dress. I guess it was more than just a dress. I mean, it doesn't have a whole lot in common with my recital dress. She was all, "What are you doing?" I didn't know what to say, so I thought about what Ada would do in that situation, and I ignored her.

When we got on the bus, I was so scared my knees were shaking. But I took a deep breath and got a grip on myself, and I walked right by Eiko and the empty seat next to her and went to the back of the bus. Obviously, it would have been ideal if I could have approached him alone, but I couldn't think of any way to do that, so I just kept moving forward, deeper and deeper into this terrible plan, letting the momentum of it carry me through.

Tyler was sitting at the back of the bus, surrounded by all his friends. They were laughing and talking and not paying any attention to me at all. At first. One by one, they started to notice me . . . the friends, that is. Not Tyler. Some of them just looked at me in confusion or surprise, but at least a couple of them were looking at me in a particular way. A way I'd only ever seen boys look at other girls. Girls who aren't me. But I wasn't interested in them.

I thought about saying something to get Tyler's attention, but I knew I wouldn't be able to come up with anything that didn't make me sound like an idiot. And Ada didn't need to do a bunch of talking to get people to notice her. If there's one skill she has mastered, it's smoldering silently until every eye in the room is drawn to her. So that's what I did: I tried to smolder.

It probably looked pretty ridiculous.

Eventually, Tyler took note of his friends not paying attention to him anymore, and he looked in my direction. Plan on target! Unfortunately, I hadn't thought the plan through at all beyond this point.

"What?" he said at last. Which, all things considered, is not an unreasonable thing to say to someone who is staring at you. But it wasn't exactly the conversational opener I was hoping for.

So I just kept staring at him. Smoldering. In silence. Like a complete idiot.

He stared back. I kept staring. He raised his eyebrows. I stood like a statue. Finally, he said, "Could you, uh, leave? You're kind of creeping me out."

That broke the spell. I turned around and went back to my seat. Eiko, of course, asked me what the hell was going on, but I just stared ahead of me the whole ride back and tried not to cry. What the heck has gotten into me? I definitely won't be trying that again.

Fri, Nov 14

I saw Ada again today. Well, that makes it seem like I just ran into her, like I did the other times. This time was a little different. I went looking for her. I found her pretty easily, not surprising, given how well I'd committed her habits to memory back when I was basically stalking her. At lunch she was lurking in one of her usual corners with a cigarette and her phone, wearing a closely fitted dress with a subtle golden shimmer.

"Hey," she said as I approached, as if it were the most normal thing in the world. As if we were actually friends. It threw me off a bit. But then I remembered how angry I was.

"You lied to me," I said without preamble. I had to get it out before I lost my nerve.

Ada looked up from her phone, surprised. Then she narrowed her eyes. I got the impression that she was willing to accept she had probably lied to me at some point and was just trying to figure out what particular untruth I might be referring to.

"You said," I went on, building steam. "You said that if I really tried, if I wore your clothes and your lipstick and did everything just like you, I could have him. Did you really think it would work? Or did you know all along exactly how hopeless it was and set me up so you could have a good laugh?"

Ada gave me a puzzled look. "I'm pretty sure I never said any of that."

I opened my mouth to object, then closed it again. I guess it was true that she hadn't said precisely that.

"What I told you," she said pointedly, "is that boys like Tyler are interchangeable. You don't need Tyler—you need someone else to put him out of your head." Ada's eyes moved back down to her phone, and I seemed to have been dismissed from the conversation. But just as I was turning to leave, she looked up again and caught me in her gaze.

"Hey," she said without elaboration. She cocked her head and looked me carefully up and down, as if considering something. Whatever she saw must have made up her mind. "What would you say to a date tonight?"

"With you?"

Ada gave me a strange look—surprised or amused, maybe. "A date with a man, not a boy."

I shook my head. "I really don't . . ."

"You'd be doing me a favor. I double-booked by accident."

My mouth went dry, and I had a feeling in my stomach like I get before a test.

"I don't think anyone in the world would confuse me for you," I said.

"It won't make any difference. He's a nice guy, and he'll like you. I promise. I wouldn't set you up with a jerk."

A million objections ran through my head. The last real date I had been on was more than a year ago, with a boy from the swim team, and Mom drove us to the movie and home again. There was no way she was going to let me go out with a total stranger who was out of high school. It was a completely insane idea. But what came out of my mouth was, "I don't have anything to wear."

Ada smiled. "I'll take care of that."

Fri, Nov 14, later

Writing this while I wait. What am I even waiting for? I don't know exactly, but Ada says not to worry. I don't know why I trust her, but I do.

I am sitting in a hotel bar at the convention center downtown, with a Coke in front of me. They put a lemon in it, but I fished it out. Sorry. That was a stupid detail. I'm just nervous, I guess. But writing calms me down.

I told Mom I was going to sleep over at Jenny's so we could work on our Science Olympiad project, and I went home with Ada after school. She found an outfit for me—a minidress with a fun geometric print—then fixed my hair and did my makeup. Not much, though. Too much would make me look older, she said.

"Isn't that good?"

"Don't be in such a rush," she said.

She took me to the convention center and went in with me. She ordered this Coke for me, in fact, and said something to the bartender before she brought it over to the table. This is all so mysterious.

Then she said she had to go.

"You're not going to stay and introduce me?"

"I told you, I double-booked. I really have to run."

"How will he know who I am?"

She smiled. "He'll know."

Then she gave me her cell number and told me to call her if I needed anything, or if I wanted to get out of the date, and she'd take care of it. "We have to look out for each other," she said, just like the other day. She gave me a kiss on the cheek. "Don't worry. You'll be fine."

Oh, someone just walked in! Is it him?

Sat, Nov 15

Wow. I kinda can't believe where I am right now. Or what I've done. Or how much I can't wait to do it again.

Last night . . . I'm not sure I even have the words. It was the most incredible night I've ever had. I've never been on a date like that with a boy . . . with a man before. I didn't even know dates like that were real. It was like something out of a movie.

I was so nervous in the beginning, looking around at every person who walked in, trying to figure out if they were looking for me, because I totally didn't believe Ada that the guy would just know. I mean, how could he know? But then, just as I was craning over my shoulder to look at a dude in a baseball cap leaning against the bar, a man slid into the seat across from me. I jumped a little when I realized what had happened.

"Um," was my opening conversational gambit.

"Hi," he said. He put out his hand to shake mine and he introduced himself as Damon. By that time, I had caught my breath enough to take in what he looked like. And he looked good. Really good. He was older, definitely not in high school, or probably college even. Maybe twenty-five? And he had dark curly hair and friendly brown eyes, and his smile . . . When he smiled it made me feel like I was the most important thing in the whole world.

He asked if I wanted to get out of there and suggested we go for a walk in Myrtle Edwards Park. We walked and looked at the ocean. I told him about how I've lived in Seattle my whole life but I've hardly ever seen the ocean even though I know it's nearby. It always seems to be a touristy thing to do, to go down to the waterfront, and I just never bothered. He told me he was kind of a tourist, though he's been to Seattle before, and he loves coming here.

He asked me about myself, and I told him all about swimming and how I used to love it but how it had gotten complicated recently, tied up with competition, so it just wasn't fun anymore. I almost slipped up and told him about how I tried to make a pass at a boy on the swim team, but I stopped myself. It occurred to me that that maybe wasn't appropriate first-date conversation.

Anyway, we talked and talked, and he was just really nice. So much nicer than Tyler. Ada was right about that. And I couldn't believe it, but he seemed really interested in me. No one has ever been that interested in me other than my mom. Mom always has to know every single little detail of my day, and I think she would dig into my brain to know every thought I have too, if she could. But she has her own reasons for that. It's more about control than caring.

So we were walking and talking about being tourists in our hometown, and I happened to mention that I'd never even been to the Space Needle. There was a class trip there when I was in first grade, but Mom kept me home that day because she didn't see the point in me wasting time on something "nonacademic." I'd always regretted it. I mean, it seems like a silly thing, but every time I see it, it's just another reminder of how I'm never allowed to do anything for fun.

And then Damon was like, "Let's go." I was like, what, to the Space Needle? He said yeah; he was getting hungry, and they have a restaurant up there. So he took me to dinner in the Space Needle! How cool is that? Wait, no, it gets better. Did you know that the restaurant spins around? So you can see views of the whole city while you eat dinner. Basically, it was the most perfect, most romantic thing ever.

We walked around some more after dinner, and the moon was so pretty and the weather was just perfect, and we sat on a bench and just talked and talked. Or rather, I talked and talked. Damon was mostly listening. I started to feel really awkward about the fact that I was talking so much, so I shut up. I wanted to give him a chance to talk, but he didn't. So I looked at him and he was looking at me and . . . This is a terrible analogy, but it was like a car crash, or how people talk about them, anyway. How time slows down and you see your life flash before your eyes. Because I just had this moment of, *Oh my God, he's going to kiss me*, and then he did!

It was sweet. Honestly, the only time I've kissed anyone before was in seventh grade at a birthday party, and it was awful, really awful. Really wet, and the boy was basically choking me with his tongue. I remember thinking at the time, *I don't ever want to do that again*. But this wasn't like that at all. He was really gentle and slow, and he just held me there like that until all I could think was that I wanted more. So I put my arms around his neck and pulled him closer.

After a while I felt his hand on my knee. It shocked me. Literally. It felt like a shock of electricity, and I pulled away from him. He immediately pulled back.

"I'm sorry," he said, and he looked really guilty. "I shouldn't have done that. I can take you home now."

But I realized that wasn't what I wanted at all. I didn't want to leave and go back to my boring, awful, normal life. More than anything, I wanted to keep kissing Damon.

So I said, "Don't stop." And I moved closer to him again and pulled him in for another kiss. We kissed for what felt like ages, and it was fantastic, but after a while this feeling came over me and I wanted more again. So I reached out and took his hand, which was nice but not quite what I wanted. So I put it back on my knee. Except not really on my knee . . . farther up. And we kept kissing, and I noticed his hand creeping higher and higher until my breath caught in my throat. He pulled back then and looked me in the eyes and said, "Is this okay?" I nodded. And he said, "Are you sure?"

I meant to say yes, but instead what came out was, "Please don't stop." That was really embarrassing and I blushed hard, but he just smiled.

"We're starting to put on quite a show for all the people walking by," he said. I think I must have turned super red at that. I started to pull away, but he said, "How about coming back to my hotel room?"

I hesitated a second, and he started babbling, apologizing and saying he shouldn't have said it. But the truth was, it was exactly what I wanted. And I told him so.

So we went back to his room at the hotel, and I couldn't believe how nice it was. I've stayed in only a couple roadside motels in my whole life, and they were nothing like this. There was an iPod docking station, a huge flat-screen TV, and a bowl of pretty little candies. I grabbed the bowl of candies and took it with me as I checked everything out. The best part was the bathroom—there were heated towel racks, a huuuuge tub, and another flat-screen TV so you could watch from the tub! I turned it on, and they were having a *SpongeBob* marathon and I got so excited. I haven't seen that show in ages. Plus, can you imagine watching *SpongeBob* while taking a bath? The whole concept made me giggle.

I called out to Damon to come see, like a big dork—as if he doesn't know his own hotel room. And he found me lying fully clothed in the bathtub, watching *SpongeBob* with a bowl of candies balanced on my stomach. I must have looked like an idiot, but he just stood in the doorway, grinning at me. So I was like, "What?"

"I don't know," he said. "I had kind of thought you might like to see the view from the window. Maybe have a glass of champagne."

"Oh," I said. "I'm sorry." I was embarrassed that I'd been so rude when he was being so nice. "I'll come and see."

Damon shook his head. "I guess we got enough views from Space Needle."

"I don't really like champagne," I admitted. "Do you want

46

some candy?" I lifted the bowl toward him, and he crouched down to take some.

"You're cute," he said.

I laughed. "No, you're cute."

"Is that right?"

And I couldn't believe he didn't know how cute he was. I wanted to show him, wanted to prove it to him. So I grabbed on to his shirt and tugged him closer to me and kissed him. He tasted like candy—there were still little bits of it in both our mouths, like little pockets of hard sweetness mixed into the soft kiss. It was awkward and uncomfortable and delicious and amazing. Eventually, he pulled back and asked if I thought the tub was big enough for two. Which it definitely was. I mean, it was huge, so I tugged on him a bit harder until he got into the tub with me. It wasn't exactly comfortable, lying in a dry tub with all our clothes on, but kissing him felt so good it didn't matter. Except then I guess his elbow or something knocked into the tap and turned it on, and suddenly we were both getting drenched with freezing-cold water!

I screamed at first, and then when I realized what happened, I couldn't stop laughing.

"Maybe that was a sign," said Damon.

"Did you want to stop?"

"Do you?"

I told him no, and he grinned and said, "Me neither. But maybe we need a change of venue."

He got out of the tub and put out a hand to help me up.

"And clothes," I said. Ada's sopping-wet dress wasn't the most comfortable anymore. Damon reached behind me and tugged the zipper down, then slipped the dress off me until I was standing there in my underwear. He wrapped his arms around me.

"That better?"

And that's when it really hit me—we were going to have sex. I guess it seems pretty idiotic that I didn't realize that earlier. In some sense, I guess I knew when he invited me back to his hotel room. But I didn't really believe it. It just seemed so unlikely that this guy really wanted me. I kept waiting for him to realize what a boring loser I am and tell me to leave. But when he took my dress off, that's when I realized—he was not going to change his mind.

Suddenly I felt nervous and awkward. Kissing was great, but sex was scarier. I started worrying that it would hurt, that Damon would expect me to know what to do, or that he would notice all the blobby bits on my body and get grossed out. But Damon put me at ease. He was undoing the buttons on his shirt, and he leaned forward to whisper in my ear.

"Are you scared?"

I held my breath and nodded a little. I could feel his breath on my neck and his lips on my earlobe.

"Do you want to stop?"

And even though I was nervous, I didn't want him to stop. I was still just so shocked that it was happening at all. I mean, I had more or less given up on this whole idea, on anyone ever wanting me—especially someone I actually wanted back. At school no one ever looked at me that way, and I got used to the idea that I was invisible to the world except as a geek and a nerd. But here I was, in a situation I always thought was reserved for other girls—prettier girls, cooler and more confident girls. At best, maybe one day I'd talk another virginal geek into it, or someone gross and desperate, someone selfish. But Damon was none of those things.

Of course I knew it wasn't love—I'm not naive. I don't expect him to marry me or send me love letters or whatever. But what we were doing . . . It felt good. Just kissing him felt better than I had thought it possibly could, and I would have been happy to keep kissing him all night. But if he's so good at kissing, it made sense that he'd be good at other stuff too.

So I kissed him again by way of answer, and I let him pull me over to the bed. He was really slow and careful and it did hurt at first, but it also felt really good. Afterward I felt sore in places I hadn't even realized existed, but he held me and stroked my hair until I fell asleep.

I guess it sounds super slutty, since I'd only just met him. But it felt right, and you know what? I don't regret it at all.

Damon was gone when I woke up, which at first made me a little sad, but honestly, it was kind of a relief too. Last night was so amazing, and I needed some time to process it all this morning. I feel like if he were around, odds are I would do something stupid or embarrassing or awkward that would sour the whole experience. And I don't want that. I want to cherish this night forever, no matter what else happens.

He did leave a really sweet note saying that he was glad he got to meet me and apologizing that he had to catch a really early plane this morning. And he told me to go ahead and have breakfast sent up to the room, on his tab! The other hotels I've stayed in were definitely the "coffee and doughnuts in the lobby" kind of places, but the room-service menu here has all kinds of amazing things. Would it be bad to order one of everything?

Oh! I have to call Ada and tell her all about it. I can't forget I really owe all of this to her.

Sat, Nov 15, later

Ada's not very happy with me.

I don't totally understand it, and she says it's not my fault, but apparently it's a huge deal that I had sex with Damon. I was so excited to tell her all about it! And I was pretty sure she wouldn't judge me. But I guess I misread the situation.

I sent her a quick text about it, and she immediately texted back asking for the hotel room. And said she was on her way over. I thought she just wanted to hear all about it, but when she got here, she was in a terrible mood.

She kept saying it was supposed to be just a date, a regular, normal date. She told him no sex, which I thought was really confusing. I mean, how is it her job to decide if I have sex or not? I thought only my mom was that controlling. Then she asked me if I was a virgin. I mean, if I had been. I was like, well, obviously. At that she groaned and put her head in her hands.

"I am so fucked," she said. I had no idea what she was talking about. "I told him you were probably a virgin and he was *not* to have sex with you," she went on. "I'm such an idiot. I should never have told him that. It's like telling a kid that there's candy hidden in the closet that he's not allowed to eat. God, that bastard. He's going to get me into so much trouble."

"What are you talking about?" I said, still totally clueless. "What trouble?"

"Damon knows better than to scam a freebie off Irma's girls," she went on, but she didn't seem to be talking to me. "And now Irma is going to think I made off with the cash."

"Cash?" I said. "What cash?"

"That's just it. There wasn't any! It was supposed to be a favor. I asked if he'd take a friend on a date, show her a nice time. As a friend."

Suddenly some things clicked into place.

"Wait. You mean Damon only took me out because you made him? He didn't even want to?" My chest felt hollow, but Ada just laughed.

"Believe me," she said. "He got what he wanted. It wasn't just a favor to me. It was . . . mutual. Damon likes girls the wrong side of legal, but he doesn't like to feel like a sleaze. His thing is to be Prince Charming, do a whole fancy date. And his fantasy is to deflower a virgin. So I told him I had a virgin for him, just like he wanted—for free. The only catch was, he couldn't sleep with you. No money changing hands—just a fun evening for everyone involved. All I wanted was to give your self-confidence a little boost, show you that you can do better than assholes like Tyler Adams."

I was trying to follow her explanation, but one detail kept tripping me up.

"Why do you keep talking about money?" I asked. "And who is Irma?"

Ada looked up at me with a guilty expression. "Irma is my boss." She took a deep breath and seemed to brace herself. "I turn tricks for a living," she said. "Damon is one of my old clients."

For a long time, I couldn't speak.

"Turn tricks," I said at last. "You mean you're a . . . a prostitute?"

I had to sit down on the bed. On the one hand, I felt like I'd never been so shocked in my life. But on the other, I felt like an idiot that I hadn't figured it out earlier. So many things about Ada suddenly made sense now. How she always seemed to have so much money even though her family didn't. Why she was on her phone constantly, even though she didn't have any friends. Why she looked so sophisticated and adult even though she was still in high school. Why she left school so often during the day. And why she knew guys like Damon she could fix me up on dates with.

Damon! I had a sudden fear that last night meant something very different from what I had thought.

"Did I just have sex with Damon for money?"

"No," said Ada. "That's what I've been trying to explain. I've known Damon for a long time now. I'd even call him a friend. I just wanted him to make you feel better about yourself, and I can't believe he dicked me over like this."

"Oh," I said, and suddenly felt washed in a wave of guilt. "That wasn't totally his fault."

"What do you mean?"

"It was . . . It was my idea, kind of. I mean, I may have sort of . . . pressured him."

Again, I thought back to last night, and so many things

53

seemed clearer. Why Damon had been such an incredible listener. Why he showed me such a good time. And why he seemed so hesitant to take the next obvious step. "He kept trying to back off, but I . . . I was the one who wanted more."

Ada looked at me like she didn't know whether to laugh or cry.

"You poor thing," she said. "You really feel responsible. Look, honey, you're sixteen. He's twenty-seven. You're a virgin, and he is . . . Well, he's about as far from that as they come. Believe me, you didn't force him into anything." Suddenly a new look of horror came over her face. "Wait," she said. "You made him wear a condom, didn't you? Oh God. Please say you did. I will fucking murder him if he—"

I reassured her that he did wear one, though again I felt a little guilty that it hadn't been my idea. It hadn't even occurred to me until he brought it out. What had I thought would happen? I really felt like an idiot that I hadn't even given a thought to pregnancy or disease. I was just so caught up in the moment.

Anyway, that calmed Ada down a little. She took my hands and asked me really seriously if I was okay and how I was feeling. I said I was fine, just a little confused.

"Do you need anything?"

I shook my head.

"Did you . . . ? Well, did you have any fun, after all?"

I couldn't help smiling at that. "Ada, it was the best night of my life," I said honestly. That made Ada smile back.

"Good," she said. "Don't worry, then. It will be fine. We'll just have to hope Irma never finds out about this little mix-up."

Tues, Nov 18

I just read over that last entry, and it feels like a dream I had. It's hard to believe that's something that really happened to me. I mean, in some ways it's hard to believe it happens at all. High school girls working as prostitutes? But it is really hard to imagine that I came in any way in contact with that world.

Not that I'm a prostitute! I never asked for nor accepted any money. Or was even offered any, for that matter. So really I'm just a sixteen-year-old girl who had sex with an older man. Which isn't that unusual. That's probably pretty normal, actually. It definitely isn't illegal. Oh wait. Yes, it is. I guess technically that's rape. Wow. How ridiculous that anyone would think what happened between me and Damon could possibly be called rape. I knew what I was doing! I'm not that innocent. Although I guess he did know a lot more about the situation than I did.

But whatever. It was great! I had a lot of fun, and I didn't do anything illegal, in any case.

But all that's over now, and it's back to regular life for me. It was kind of weird and twisted that Ada set the whole thing up for me, but also kind of . . . sweet in a way. I guess she really did see something in me that I didn't, and so did Damon. And the weirdest thing is, it worked! I still see Tyler all the time at swim practice, but I'm not obsessed with him like I used to be. My world's a little bigger now, and I can see he isn't the only good-looking guy in it (though he is still really good-looking—nothing's going to change that). But compared to Damon? He is a twerp and a loser.

The other nice thing is that I expected to be horribly embarrassed around him all the time now, ever since I did my weird staring thing at him the other day. And it's true that he and his friends sometimes laugh at me or make comments when I walk by, and the old me would have been devastated by that. But now I just can't find it in myself to care. There are more interesting things in the world.

Too bad I still have to go through the motions of high school. It's harder than ever to convince myself that history term papers and debate tournaments and my mom's nagging are important. But that's life, I guess.

Wed, Nov 19

I had a chemistry test today that I totally didn't know about. Oops. It was probably announced during one of the periods I missed because I was hanging out with Ada. I guess I really have let things slide.

So, obviously, I failed it. I mean, I wasn't exactly doing great in chemistry even before, and that was when I was taking notes and paying attention and reading the chapters three times before each test. I've never really had a mind for it. And now I'm skipping classes and fudging my way through the homework and zoning out so bad that I don't even realize there's a test coming up. Honestly, I don't know how I'm going to come back from this. I used to calculate my average each time I got a B on a test and compute how well I needed to do on the remaining tests to bring it up to an A. But given my last couple of tests, that's just not possible anymore. Maybe if I got perfect scores on everything for the rest of the semester, I could still get a low B, but what's the point? Mom will still be furious. Stanford won't even look at me. It's hard to see how it's worth the constant struggle.

There's a part of me that has always wondered . . . what would happen? What if I just let go and stopped worrying over every little thing? But I guess that's pretty much what I'm doing now. It's weird—it's like, instead of being an active participant in my own life, I'm just watching it like a movie. Waiting to see what happens to me.

Fri, Nov 21

So it turns out that once you've decided to stop caring about your classes, school gets really boring really fast. I've spent so much of my life drowning in pressure and anxiety, and I guess I always assumed that people who didn't have that must be happy and relaxed all the time. I never imagined how depressing it would be to just . . . exist.

Even eating lunch with my old friends just feels impossible now. Today Jenny and Eiko were talking about our chances for Academic Decathlon this year, and they asked my opinion and I had nothing to say. I couldn't even really follow what they were talking about. The looks they gave me . . . It would have been embarrassing, if I cared at all.

Sun, Nov 23

I'm so bored.

Not just bored in this specific moment, from not having enough to do. God knows I have plenty to do. . . . In theory, I have tests to study for and papers to write and math team competitions to prepare for and helping Mom around the house, if I ever finish the rest of it. There is plenty of stuff to occupy my time. But I can't bring myself to do any of it, and none of it makes me less bored.

I can't stop thinking about that night with Damon. I can't stop wishing my life were more like that and less like this. It's like now that I've tasted that life, it is really hard to go back to my normal world of Mom picking on me and nagging me and never being satisfied with anything I do. And things between us are worse than ever now that I've pretty much stopped trying at all. My grades are plummeting. Half the time I don't even bother going to my activities. I haven't practiced the piano in ages, and as a result, every day when I come home from school, I get the same lecture about what a disappointment I am and how I am bringing shame on the family and will never amount to anything. I could bring real shame on this family if I wanted to! Maybe I should, just to show her. Mom is so sheltered. She has no idea what's out there.

I think a lot about Ada, too. Not that I don't see her. I mean, we're still friends, and sometimes I run into her in the halls and bathrooms at school. But I get flustered and don't know what to say. Her life is just so much more interesting than mine.

The other day she suggested we go shopping or something, and that sounded amazing. She always looks so glamorous and stylish. Maybe she could help me figure out how to do that too. But it's not like I have any money. It's kind of ironic, actually. Ada's family doesn't seem to have much money, but she personally has a lot of cash to spend, thanks to her work. Whereas my family is a lot more well-off, but that makes no difference in my life. I'm not like those rich kids with Daddy's credit card. I have to ask my parents to buy me things if I want them, and then they get to decide whether what I want is worth spending money on or not. Usually not. It's just another way they control me.

I can just imagine asking my parents for money to buy sexy boots or a gorgeous camel coat like Ada's. They'd think I was joking.

So in the meantime, Ada and I have less and less in common, and she has less and less reason to waste any time on a loser like me. And pretty soon the one bright spot in my life will disappear and it will all be nothing but drab and gray.

Maybe if I got a job? Then at least I'd have some cash I could call my own.

Sun, Nov 23, later

Well, forget the job idea. First of all, Mom totally did not go for it. I tried to use the angle that college applications ask about work experience, and it would show a sense of responsibility and hard work, but she wasn't having it. She said the last thing I needed was another thing taking my time and focus away from my schoolwork and my activities. She said maybe if I brought my grades up, she might think about it, but I don't see that happening anytime soon. Because the truth is, my grades lately are even worse than my mom realizes, and I'm just waiting for report-card day, when the whole truth comes out.

Not that I care that much. I mean, what can she really do? She can yell and complain and berate me all she wants. It can't be much worse than what I'm putting up with now.

And then the other thing is, even if I could talk my parents into it, I don't know if it would even be worth it. The only job I could possibly get would be part-time at minimum wage, and it would take me forever to save up any serious money. By the time I could afford a shopping trip with Ada, she would have forgotten all about me. Plus, they seem like kind of a drag. I mean, do I really want to spend hours every day mopping floors and scrubbing toilets? That sounds even worse than the stuff I currently have to do.

It all just feels so hopeless right now. Everything in my life is dull and pointless, and I can't even think of anything to look forward to. It's just a vast expanse of nothing, from here until forever.

Mon, Nov 24

It's the middle of the night, but I can't sleep. My brain won't shut down because there's this thought buzzing around in it—a totally crazy thought. But maybe if I write it out on paper I'll see just how ridiculous it is and my brain will finally leave it alone.

What if I did what Ada does? No, that's not good enough. I have to be able to say it. Okay. What if I became a prostitute? What if I were a whore?

Okay, see? Ridiculous! Crazy. I could never do that. That life isn't for girls like me.

Ada does it. But Ada's not like me. But could I ever be like Ada? I used to think no, definitely not. I remember when Ada seemed like she belonged to a different species. But it's not like that anymore, is it? We're friends. We share clothes. I look good in her clothes. And she herself said that I could be like her, if I wanted. I wonder if she was serious.

Back then I was a virgin and she was not. And that seemed like an unbridgeable gulf. But I'm not a virgin anymore—already I'm more like her. Damon wanted me, thought I was pretty. Thought I was sexy. A couple months ago, I couldn't even dream that. If Damon wanted me, other men probably would too. So I could do it. In principle.

But it's still nuts. I mean, what about my parents? Just imagining the look on Mom's face if she found out . . . She wouldn't believe it. She would never think me capable of such a thing. Because I'm not. Right? My mom should know.

But then, what does Mom know about me, really? I spend my whole life doing the things she expects of me, but is that who I am? I guess it is, in a way. I mean, you are what you do, right? But I'm not exactly happy with who I am right now. If I decided to do something different, something really crazy, would that make me a different person? Would I like that person better?

If she were more like Ada, then yes—I would like her better. Like me better.

And then there's the money. That would be nice, wouldn't it? I don't know. My family's not poor, like Ada's, so why should money be so important to me? It's not like there's a ton of fancy things I want to buy. But money isn't just about getting stuff. Having my own source of income would feel like . . . freedom. Independence. Right now I have to do whatever my parents want because I'd basically die without them. But if I had my own money, I could make my own choices.

Wow. Am I really considering this?

I'm sure in the morning I'll see what a terrible idea this is and drop it completely. But it's a nice fantasy for right now.

Tues, Nov 25

I'm excited. I shouldn't be, but I am. This is a bad idea, but honestly, who cares? I'm nervous and scared, but at least I'm feeling something. My whole body is buzzing, and it's partly fear and surprise at myself, but it feels better than all that dead nothingness before.

I didn't mean to say anything. I didn't think I was seriously considering it. But at lunch today I was sitting alone, eating a sandwich, thinking over the whole concept, not quite ready to let it go yet. But then Ada slid onto the bench across from me and asked me what I was thinking about. And I just blurted it out!

"I want to do it," I said, as if she'd been listening in on my thoughts for the past twenty-four hours.

"What?"

"I want to be a . . ." I hesitated over the rest of the sentence. Not because I wasn't sure, but because I didn't know the right word to use. I didn't want to accidentally give offense. "Do you think that I could do what you do?" I said.

Ada raised her eyebrows.

"Have sex," I clarified. "For money."

Ada blew out a long breath. "Shit," she said.

"You don't think I could do it? You think people wouldn't want—"

"It's not that." She pulled her coat tight around her, a dark expression on her face. "I shouldn't have told you. I was afraid at first that this might happen, but then I thought, no way, not her. She would never be interested in—"

"Why not? Why shouldn't I be? You think I want to be an invisible geek my whole life?"

Ada shook her head. "It's not what you think. Damon . . . they're not all like that. They're not at all like that. Damon was the worst possible introduction I could have given you to this business."

"I know that," I said, smiling a little. "I'm not an idiot, Ada. I have actually thought about this. I know it's not all dinners at the Space Needle."

She frowned. "You don't understand."

But I do! I mean, maybe not completely. Of course not completely—how can I understand something I've never experienced? But how can I learn without experiencing it?

"Do you want to quit?" I asked her.

"No," she said slowly.

"Is anyone forcing you to keep doing it?"

"No, but I—"

"If it were really that bad, you would quit, wouldn't you?"

Ada nodded, a little uncertainly. "But it's not that simple. You don't know—"

"How can I know if I don't try it? And if I don't like it, I can stop, right?"

Ada relaxed a little. "Yeah. You could always back out, if you wanted." She didn't look totally convinced, but she stopped fighting me. And when I pressed a little more, she agreed to introduce me to Irma. She said after that it would be between me and Irma and out of her hands.

I can't believe it. I can't believe I'm really doing this! I'm not sure I even recognize myself.

Wed, Nov 26

Ada just called. My big meeting with Irma is today! I'm so nervous and excited. I wanted to go home first to change. I'm worried that if I don't look really pretty, Irma won't want me. But Ada said not to worry about that. Irma is sending a car for me! I really can't decide if I am more nervous or excited.

Ada just reminded me *not* to mention anything that happened with Damon. I still don't quite understand why that's such a big deal, but I can do that. Okay, I have to run.

Wed, Nov 26, later

Well, I have a job! Kind of. I still have to wait until I get scheduled for my first date, and of course I can't get paid before then. But Miss Irma took me on! I feel . . . relieved, I guess.

One thing I definitely didn't expect: Miss Irma (that's what everyone calls her to her face) came here from Taiwan, just like my parents. She's probably about their age, too. Oh, wow. What if they've met? Given the size of the Chinese community here, it's not impossible. I definitely don't want to think too much about that, though. Let's keep those worlds separate.

It was surreal because Miss Irma speaks English with an accent that sounds a *lot* like my mom and all my aunts. I mean, obviously her English is much better. She's been doing business in English for decades now. So more like my dad, in that way. She speaks very carefully, slowly, and her sentences are always correct, but the accent is still there.

I can't even describe how weird it is, because Miss Irma is

like the complete opposite of my parents in every significant way. She is not obsessed with me going to college and doing all my homework and stuff like that. But it's not just that. Everything about her seems so much less rigid and controlling. It's kind of a revelation to meet someone Chinese who isn't a doctor or an engineer or a scientist or some other "acceptable" successful career, like my parents' friends are. Miss Irma has made her own success, in a completely original way.

It made me feel like maybe there are more options open to me than I thought. Not that I necessarily want to do what Miss Irma does when I grow up, but I'm starting to see that I don't have to limit my dreams to the ones my parents consider acceptable. I can follow a different, less-obvious path, if I want to.

Irma's office wasn't really what I expected either. It was in a big anonymous high-rise tower downtown, mixed in among dentists and lawyers and gynecologists. Her sign in the lobby was very discreet, and you would never have guessed anything at all about her line of work from it.

Even once you got upstairs into the reception area, it still felt a lot more like a doctor's office than like a . . . well, a whorehouse. It's all pastel wallpaper and tasteful paintings and fluorescent lighting. I figure this can't be where Miss Irma meets her clients. I can't see anyone being turned-on by that decor.

Anyway, there was a receptionist, a pretty woman named Anne who told me to wait a few minutes and then eventually let me in to Miss Irma's office. She was sitting behind a desk, and, again, I couldn't help a weird shiver of recognition because the layout of the room and the desk and everything were so much like my dad's office at the hospital.

Miss Irma was friendly and smiled a lot, but the whole thing felt much more formal and professional than I was expecting. She was wearing a well-tailored gray tweed suit and a fussy perfume that filled the whole room with notes of lotus and plum. The only hint that she wasn't an ordinary businesswoman or bureaucrat was a pair of pearl-gray stilettos so high they made my feet ache just to look at them.

She asked me a bunch of questions about myself and my family (but nothing too personal), and she asked me how I learned about her operation. I was careful not to say anything about Damon. I just said that Ada was my friend, and I learned about it from her. Miss Irma seemed to accept this, and she told Anne via her intercom to add my name to her appointment book.

Then she asked me what were the best times for me, and I sort of slipped and said, "I can't do nights anymore." I was thinking about my night with Damon, but obviously I can't tell my parents I have an overnight study session every time. I knew

I'd messed up the minute it came out of my mouth, but I was hoping Irma wouldn't notice. But she's sharp. She picked up on it right away.

"Anymore?"

"I can't do nights," I repeated, trying to sound confident. "My parents would cause problems. It's easier to get away from school."

Miss Irma nodded and I breathed an internal sigh of relief. "And your name?"

I repeated my name, even though I'd already introduced myself, and she gave me a sharp look over her reading glasses. "Not your real name. Never give a client your real name. You need a working name."

She tried to get me to come up with one on the spot, but I blanked completely, and after about half a minute, Miss Irma just sighed and said, "Sleep on it. You can let us know later." She made a few more notes in a big book on her desk, then looked up again. She told me I'd get a text in a few days, most likely, setting up my first appointment. Then she went over some ground rules:

> 1) Never accept money from the clients directly. Never discuss money with the client. All payment goes through Miss Irma.

2) Never discuss money with the other girls. Money talk is bad for morale, and Miss Irma doesn't like settling fights.

3) Never discuss clients with anyone. Spilling secrets is the fastest way to lose not just one client but all of them.

4) Never do anything you don't want to do. If a client asks for something that makes you uncomfortable, tell Miss Irma. Someone else will do it.

5) Safety first. If you feel unsafe, leave. Tell Miss Irma what happened as soon as possible.

6) If you are unhappy working for Miss Irma, you are free to quit at any time.

She asked me then if I understood everything. I said yes, and that was basically it! It was kind of anticlimactic, actually. I'm not sure what I was expecting, to be honest. Someplace with red shades on the lamps and mostly naked girls draped all over the furniture?

Toward the end she asked me if I had any questions, and for a moment I completely blanked and was about to shake my head no. But then I realized that actually yes, I had a ton of questions. The most obvious one being, what do we get paid?

Miss Irma smiled politely at this.

"Ada did not explain? It depends on the situation. Depends on the client, time of day, and nature of request. You leave that kind of thing to me."

"Oh," I said, feeling a little confused.

"Don't worry," she said, still smiling. "Everyone is paid fairly."

I was annoyed not to be able to get a more concrete answer out of her, but it's true that Ada had never complained about the money. It seems like a strange way to do business, but it can't be that bad or people wouldn't go along with it, right?

After that, all that was left was for me to check in with Anne. She had me pose against a bare wall for a quick photo, then handed me a pink phone just like Ada's.

"I already have a phone," I told her.

Anne explained that I needed a committed phone. One that Miss Irma controls. She doesn't like when the girls get their service cut off or their numbers changed. She needs to know that she and the clients can get in touch with us. Anne said it would take a day or two to charge and activate, but once it was all set, I should just wait for a text letting me know about my first appointment.

This is all so weird but exciting. It's like a strange dream, or something that's happening to someone else. Maybe once I do my first date, it will start to feel real.

Sat, Nov 29
Still no word from Irma. I'm starting to get nervous.

I'm not even sure what I'm nervous about. Part of me is afraid she's changed her mind and won't ever text me, and another part is terrified that she will. Sometimes I lie awake in bed thinking, *What am I getting myself into? Am I prepared for this at all?* I mean, I've had sex exactly once. Am I qualified to be a professional? Or is that a silly thing to ask?

What if it's weird and awful? What if I panic at the last minute and can't go through with it?

Yesterday I made Ada talk to me a bit about her experiences, to help calm my nerves. I made her describe an average date for me and what the guys are like and what they ask for. That helped a bit. Plus, she reminded me that I can always say no at any time. I can always turn around and leave if I'm not comfortable.

It helps to know that Ada has been through all this before. I want to be like her. I can be like her. I want to know something of the real world and not learn everything from books. I look at Ada, and I want all the experiences that made her what she is, even the bad ones. I can do it.

Mon, Dec 1

I got the text! I waited for ages. It felt like it was never going to happen. But I guess I have a client? This is all so weird. My handwriting is awful because I'm shaking a little, and I don't even know if it's fear or excitement. I mean I'm scared, but for the first time I feel like I'm living my own life and not just following someone else's path. Maybe this is a huge mistake, but it's *my* mistake and no one else's.

Miss Irma's car is coming for me at the same spot where I've seen Ada get picked up. That's basically all I know right now. I hope my dress is okay! (It's one of Ada's.)

Mon, Dec 1, later

I'm back from my date. I don't know what to say about it.

It was fine. It was . . . fine.

It wasn't fine.

I don't know. I feel like an idiot. Ada warned me. She told me most of my dates wouldn't be like Damon, and I heard her and I understood. I thought I understood. I knew they wouldn't all be as handsome as Damon or as kind. Or as young. But I thought . . .

I feel dumb even saying this, but I thought . . . at least they would appreciate me. Even if they were old and unattractive, they would at least make me feel sexy and wanted. But this guy . . . It's not that anything terrible happened. I didn't get hurt. He wasn't cruel. But I don't even know his name! I mean, I understand why people might not want to give their names, but not even a fake name. He was just so distant.

He had a drink in his hand when he came to the door, and I smiled and started to introduce myself when I realized I still hadn't thought of a fake name. So I was standing there with my mouth open like an idiot, trying to think of what to say, but I guess it didn't really matter, because he just grunted and turned his back on me. He didn't tell me his name or offer me a drink or tell me to take a seat or anything. So I just stood there. Eventually, he said, "What are you waiting for?" He was probably in his fifties, kind of fat, and wearing a nice collared shirt with gym shorts underneath, which was weird. He definitely did not turn me on.

At that moment, with everything so different from what I was expecting, I nearly turned around and walked out the door. But I knew if I did that, Irma would never book me for another date at all. I thought, this has to be a test. I don't even know if that's true, or if this guy was just the luck of the draw, but somehow it helped me to think of it that way. If there's one thing I know how to deal with, it's tests. Just focus and take deep breaths and do your best.

I did what he told me to, and I tried to do it well, though there was some stuff he wanted that was, well, more difficult than it looks in movies and stuff. But I think the worst thing is that through the whole thing, I had no idea if I was doing a good job or what I did well and what I did badly. The man was totally expressionless the whole time. It kind of hurt my feelings.

God, what a stupid thing to say. As if this is about my feelings! It doesn't matter what I want. It's about the client, not me.

Anyway, I guess it must not have been too terrible, because when I was done, he gave me a tip. Twenty bucks. I used it to get a cab home, because Irma's cars only take you to the appointment; they don't pick you up at the other end. We're on our own for that.

Now I'm pretty sore. But at least I'll get paid soon. It's funny. Now I can't remember why I was so eager for money.

Mon, Dec 1, later

I feel a lot better. Dumb, but so relieved. I just spoke to Ada. I hadn't planned to, but she called me, knowing that today was my first time. My first time for real. At first she just congratulated me, but I guess something in my voice must have given away how I was feeling, because she asked how I was and sounded really concerned.

I didn't mean to tell her. I didn't want her to feel responsible. But before I even knew what was happening, it was all spilling out of me, and I was sobbing into the phone. I told her I hated it. That I felt gross and used and like I wasn't even human. I asked her if that was normal and she laughed, though I don't think it was very funny. She said yes, that's normal. It's part of the gig.

I asked her how she put up with that, and she sighed and didn't say anything right away. Then, just as I was beginning to think we'd lost our connection, she said, "It isn't always like that."

"You mean like with Damon?" I said.

"Damon's great," she said. "But no, that's not what I mean. What I mean is, sometimes what gets you through is ... human connection. Even with someone who is gross-looking and kind of rude, sometimes you get just a moment, a brief glimpse of the person as a person. And you think, I have a chance to make this person feel good right now. And it might be the only good feeling he has in the next month."

"But how do you know ... ?"

"You don't. You never know. And maybe it's all a fantasy. Maybe the men are a fantasy to us as much as we are to them. Maybe there's no decent person under it all who needs you.

Maybe they are all dickbags. But you have to tell yourself something. I mean, there has to be something that gets you through it, week after week."

I thought about that for a while . . . tried to picture telling myself that story and believing it because I had to.

"Ada," I said after a while.

"Yeah?"

"I don't think I want to do it again."

I cringed as I said it, certain that she would be angry or disappointed or resentful. Angry, maybe, that I was passing judgment on the life she is living, or disappointed to lose a friend who understood her life, or resentful that I have the option of quitting and maybe she feels like she doesn't. But I didn't hear any of that in her answer.

"Good," was what she said, and she breathed out a heavy sigh that sounded like relief. "When you told me you were interested, I wanted to kick myself. I never meant to draw you into this."

"You're not upset?"

"Honey, no," she said sweetly. "It happens a lot. Loads of girls quit after their first date. It's fine."

I felt relieved too after that. I should have felt bad, giving up on this fantasy and going back to my normal life. Or embarrassed that I had given up so easily, after just one kind of crappy date that wasn't even that bad. But I think I'm doing the right thing. Even debate tournaments and chemistry tests don't sound so bad compared to the dead-eyed way that man looked at me.

Tues, Dec 2

Ada reminded me today that I still need to pick up my payment for my date. I asked if she would just do it for me so I wouldn't have to see Miss Irma again, but she said they don't like to do that because of that thing where no one's supposed to know what the others are earning, so I have to get it myself or just abandon it. I could do that, I guess. Wouldn't that make it better? If I don't take the money, I'm still not a whore.

But the man already paid the money, so maybe it doesn't matter. Besides, that feels almost worse in a way, if I did those things with that man for nothing. So I guess I'll go, even though it means cutting class again so I can go with Ada. I definitely don't want to go alone.

Cutting all this class is becoming a problem, though. At lunch Eiko asked me why I wasn't in French the other day. Awkward. I didn't know what to say, so I just mumbled something about not feeling well.

I really need to start putting more effort into school again. I've blown off so much lately, I think this semester may be a lost cause. But as long as I don't flunk anything, maybe I can have a fresh start next semester? Stanford is off the table (not that it was ever a likely outcome), but that doesn't mean all hope is lost. Right? I just need to buckle down.

Thurs, Dec 4

Went to pick up my fee today. It wasn't that bad. Well, the going wasn't that bad. I didn't even have to see Miss Irma, which was great. I don't know why I'm scared of her, since she's never been anything but kind to me. Maybe it's because of the way she reminds me of my mother. I just have this irrational fear that if I tell her I'm quitting, she'll look at me the way my mom did when I told her I wasn't going to play violin anymore: as if I had simultaneously slapped her across the face and broken a family heirloom.

But anyway, that part was fine because apparently Miss Irma does not hand out the money. I guess maybe I should have guessed that. We just went up to Anne's desk and gave our names and she handed us each an envelope.

But the not-so-good part was when I got outside and checked the envelope. First I thought there had to be some kind of mistake. I'm not exactly an expert in the going rates for call girls, but I wouldn't be doing much worse at those minimum-wage jobs I was looking at.

I freaked out a bit at Ada. Not that it was her fault, but it did feel like kind of a betrayal, that she and Irma had refused to give me any solid numbers but both let me believe the pay would make everything worth it. But Ada calmed me down. She said she forgot to warn me—the first envelope is always skimpy, because of all the setup costs. Like apparently I have to buy my own phone (even though I already had a perfectly good phone). And we all have to pay Anne's and the driver's salaries. And Ada says they take that in a monthly sum, instead of per date.

That still seems kind of unfair to me, but Ada says they only charge you if you're working. If you didn't take any dates the month before, you don't have to pay in. So at least I'm not going to wind up owing money now that I've decided to back off.

Still, it sucks that I'll never get to see any real money from this, even though I did the work. Now I just have this stupid phone.

Oh, that reminds me. I was going to turn in my phone when we went today, since I'm not going to work for them anymore, but I was so shocked by the envelope that I forgot all about it. So now I've got this phone. Do I go back tomorrow and deliver it then? I really don't want to go back. Is it wrong to keep it? I mean, I did pay for it.

I guess I'll just hang on to it for now.

Tues, Dec 9

Things are getting back to normal. That is to say, boring, but that's okay. I'm trying really hard to catch up as much as possible in all my classes, and that's draining all my energy for the moment. I've pretty much stopped all my activities for now, because I just can't with all the schoolwork. I expected Mom to give me a huge hassle about that, but she seemed to agree. School comes first, she said.

I've even quit swimming, which sucks, because I really do love that. But there isn't any point in showing up when I can't swim competitively right now. My head's just not in it. But I don't know, maybe I should start hanging out at the local YMCA or something, just to get in the water from time to time. Could be fun.

There is one other thing that is bothering me a bit. More than it should, maybe. It's this damn phone. I still have it, and I feel it weighing on me. The phone doesn't know that I've quit, and neither does Miss Irma. And neither does Anne, I guess. Which means my name is still in the appointment book, and I could get a call for a new date at any moment. Ada says all I have to do is say no. It's no big deal. People say no all the time, for all kinds of reasons—they're busy, or on their period, or have a cold or whatever.

And anyway, the phone hasn't rung. I haven't gotten a

peep out of it since my date. I wonder if that means the guy complained about me, so now Miss Irma doesn't even want me anymore.

I have no idea why that should bother me, of all things. I should be thrilled, if that's the case. But I guess even whores have pride.

I wish it didn't weigh on me, though. That one of these days the phone is going to buzz and it's going to be a text from Miss Irma setting me up on a date and it's going to make the whole rotten experience come flooding back. I kind of just want to pitch the phone into the ocean and never think about it again, but I have a feeling Irma wouldn't be too pleased about that. And I don't think I want to make an enemy of her.

Thurs, Dec 11

I got a text today—on the pink phone. But it wasn't Irma texting, and it wasn't Anne.

It was Ada.

That made the whole thing very different from what I was expecting. What I was worrying about. All it said was, *I need a favor. Call me.*

I called her right back, of course.

"I need your help," Ada said as soon as she picked up the phone. She sounded anxious.

"What is it?" I said. "What's the matter?"

Ada took a deep breath. "I know you're out of the business," she began, "and I really didn't want to have to do this. . . . Believe me, I'm the last person who wants to drag you back in. But I'm in a jam."

"I'll do it," I blurted out.

"What?" said Ada. "But I haven't even told you what it is yet."

"I know," I told her. "But if you're in trouble, I want to help. Whatever it is. Like you said, we need to look out for each other."

Ada didn't answer a moment as she weighed this over. "I did say that, didn't I?" she said at last. She took a breath. "Okay, then, if you're sure. Meet me at the pickup spot. I'll explain in the car."

Fri, Dec 12

Wow. I have so much to tell. I'm not sure how to put it all in words. And some stuff I'm not sure I want in words. . . .

But what does it matter? I had fun.

I can't believe I gave up so easily before. Maybe I just need to stick close to Ada. . . . She's my lucky four-leaf clover in all this. I wish she ran this business instead of Miss Irma. Then it would all seem like no big deal.

But I'm getting ahead of myself, and I do want to get all this down.

I met Irma's car outside the school and slid in next to Ada. She looked stunning as always in a charcoal dress with red detailing, which somehow made my patterned top and skinny jeans seem plain and boring. Ada explained then what the favor was about: A client wanted two girls at once.

I breathed a huge sigh of relief when she told me that, which I think surprised Ada. I guess she expected me to be shocked, and . . . Well, okay, it is a little weird. It's not exactly something I ever pictured myself doing. But when she told me she needed a favor, I figured it must have something to do with Miss Irma, and I assumed she double-booked again or something. So I thought I was going to have to do another date on my own, which made me really anxious. I mean, I'd do anything to help out Ada, but I really wasn't excited about that.

So when she told me what she needed and I realized that she'd be by my side and I didn't have to go into this alone . . . That was just so much better than what I'd been picturing. I was still nervous, but I felt like nothing that bad could happen as long as Ada was there.

Turns out Miss Irma had set up the date for Ada and another girl, Jen, who Ada's friends with, but Jen couldn't do it today. I wanted to know why, and at first Ada tried to be vague, but then she stopped herself.

"No, you know what?" she said, almost to herself. "You

should know what happened to Jen. I want you to know."
She turned and looked at me very seriously, her eyes dark and stormy. "Jen has a drug problem. She was doing smack last night even though she knew she was working today and knew I'd be furious with her. And I am. Not about the work, though." She sighed. "It's only because I worry." Ada paused a moment to collect herself, then went on.

"She was strung out this morning and could barely stay awake. Then her asshole roommate convinced her that the best way to deal with this problem was to snort a bunch of Ritalin. Jen should know better, given what happened to Ella last year. . . ."

Ada shook her head in sorrow and disbelief, but all these people were little more than names to me. Suddenly, she grabbed my hand, and the grip in those bony fingers was surprisingly tight and forceful.

"You have to promise me," she said. "I mean it. Never get mixed up in that stuff, okay? Don't kid yourself that you can handle it. It will destroy you. You have to keep your head about you in this business or it will eat you up."

None of this meant much to me. The closest I ever came to drugs was when my parents let me have a sip of champagne at a cousin's wedding, or the day they legalized marijuana here and I smelled something weird and pungent when I walked near the park on my way home from the bus stop. That world didn't seem to have much to do with me. But I tried to return her serious look while I nodded.

Ada explained then that since Jen was out of commission, Miss Irma was going to find someone else to go, but Ada didn't trust Miss Irma's choice of partners, so she asked if she could just do it with me, and Irma said fine.

I guess it's probably not a normal reaction, but I felt weirdly flattered at that. Still, I was kind of nervous. I've heard of this kind of thing before, mostly in locker-room jokes at swim meets, but I wasn't exactly sure what the client would be expecting.

"What will I need to do?" I asked her.

"It's nothing, really," Ada said. "He probably just wants to see us kiss and make out a bit, and then he'll want to get off. I'll take care of that part, and you'll still get half the money. And it will be at my rate, not yours, so a lot more than you got last time." She bit her lip as she looked at me. "I appreciate this so much. But you know you don't have to do it, right? If you're not comfortable."

I put a hand on hers and smiled. "It's okay. I don't mind."

And I didn't. I had been so filled with dread over even just the idea of a phone call, and I was so sure I never wanted to do anything for Miss Irma again, but this was different. Maybe I should have been more freaked out at the idea, but it didn't

86

seem gross or weird as long as it was with Ada. It seemed like fun, almost. Like we were playing a wicked little game. Which I guess we were.

I almost abandoned ship before we even began, though. Just as we got to the door, I felt a weird little rush as the memories of my last time came back to me. I had a vision of that same man coming to the door, or someone like him. I imagined how cold and impersonal it would all be, and my stomach turned and I had a sudden urge to run away, dash toward the fire exit, and run down sixteen flights of stairs just so I could breathe. But right then Ada touched my arm and smiled and I felt better.

She asked me what name I was using, and I realized I still hadn't come up with one. I got nervous that I would completely blank out, like the last two times it came up, so I just said the first name that popped into my head: Justine. It's my French teacher's name, and I don't even know why I said it, but Ada said she liked it, so I guess it's okay.

When the guy opened the door, Ada introduced me as Justine and herself as Brigid. The guy said his name was Marco, but who knows? That might be fake too. He was in his twenties, I'm pretty sure, and he said he worked for a record company. He asked if either of us knew how to sing, and I was worried for a second that he wanted us to sing for him, but he just laughed at the stricken look on my face and took a seat in a little sitting area near the window. Ada and I stayed standing. I wasn't sure what he was expecting. Should we sit on the bed? Take our clothes off? Start kissing? I figured I would follow whatever Ada's lead was, but she was as frozen as I was. She was smiling though. I tried to smile too, but it felt awkward and fake.

Marco grinned back and gestured at the love seat across from him as he pulled a little packet of papers and a bag of something out of his pocket and started rolling a joint. "You guys smoke?" he said.

"No," I answered automatically, but Ada shot a look at me.

"Are you sure?" said Marco. "It helps you relax."

"Go ahead," said Ada. "You should try it."

I looked back at her, trying to figure out what was going on in her head.

"But you said . . . ," I began, remembering our conversation in the car over.

Ada giggled. "That's different," she said. "I was talking about hard drugs. This is legal."

Marco had finished his joint and lit it, inhaling deeply, then taking a long time to exhale the thick smoke. He handed the joint to Ada, and she held it expertly in her fingers, taking a small, delicate drag. She handed it to me.

"Don't inhale too much, or you'll cough," she said. I started to bring it to my lips, but I hesitated at the last second.

"I don't know if—," I began, but Marco interrupted.

"Go on," he said. "Try it. You'll like it."

Ada gave me an encouraging nod, so I brought the joint to my lips once again and pulled. The heavy smoke filled my mouth and throat immediately. I struggled so hard not to cough that my eyes watered. I did let out a little cough/hiccup, but at least I didn't have a huge coughing fit. At first I was mostly aware of the smell and the taste of it, and the harsh burning feeling in my throat, but then I noticed that my head felt a little foggy. But I'm not even sure if that was the pot or just the weirdness of the situation. Honestly, I don't think I inhaled enough to really feel anything.

After a while Marco started fidgeting impatiently, and Ada took the cue to nudge me into a kiss. My mouth was so dry and hot, the wetness of her mouth felt like a relief, and I leaned into it. I had to admit, this was much nicer than anything that happened with that old man. Maybe even nicer than what I did with Damon. I realized right then that I still had never hooked up with anyone I actually knew for more than a few hours. So maybe it's not so surprising that it felt really comfortable and relaxed, like a natural extension of our friendship, instead of this awkward, artificial business arrangement. But that might also just have been the pot.

It wasn't quite how Ada had said it would be. Mostly Marco just watched, but sometimes he came over and put his hands on us, and sometimes he moved us this way or that to position us the way he wanted, as if he were a movie director. And he whispered directions and encouragement too, which was a little strange but not so bad. In a way, I started to see what Ada had been talking about the other day: that it could be fun to know you were giving pleasure to someone, fulfilling their fantasy. It made me feel sort of powerful.

Eventually he moved us to the bed and helped us take off each other's clothes, and then he mostly watched from then on. When he was ready to finish up, Ada took care of him while I just watched. A few times he reached for me, but I just giggled and kissed him a little, and each time Ada did something to distract him.

Ada's really talented. Watching her work was educational, in a way. It made me want to get better, so I could be skilled like her.

By the time they finished, my head was feeling a lot less fuzzy, but I was suddenly starving. Ada giggled when my stomach grumbled as we got dressed. We didn't really say anything until we got down to the lobby. Even though the whole experience had been sort of fun, it felt a little awkward afterward. But just as we were about to go through the big revolving doors, Ada stopped me with a hand on my elbow. I turned to look at her.

"Honey," she said, "are you . . . ? Are you all right? With everything, I mean . . ."

I nodded, and the smile that came to my face was completely unforced. "Yeah," I said. "It was okay. I mean . . . It was kind of fun, actually."

Ada smiled back. "Good," she said. "Hey, he slipped me a tip while you were getting dressed. You want to go get something to eat?"

We wound up at a diner Ada knew, and we both got burgers and fries and milk shakes, and it felt like an indulgence. Ada explained about how the guys tip sometimes, but I should never tell Miss Irma about it, or she'll insist on taking a cut. So that's good to know.

At one point I glanced at my watch and realized I was supposed to be in history class right then, and I couldn't help giggling. I also couldn't stop talking about how great the burgers were, and Ada laughed at me. I was like, "What?" And she said, "Nothing. It's just cute. You've never smoked pot before."

I looked down at my burger. "Oh my God," I said. "Is this what people mean by the munchies?" And we both lost it to giggles.

"But I don't understand," I said when we had recovered a little. "On our way over, you were telling me . . . I mean, didn't you say I should stay away from . . . ?"

"This is different," she said. "Jen was using heroin. This was just pot."

"So pot's okay, but nothing else?"

Ada pressed her lips together. "It's not that simple," she said. "Pot's not such a big deal, and it doesn't really count if it's with a client. Now, if the client offers you drugs and you don't want to do them, you can always say no. But it's more polite to accept. And everything goes a little more smoothly if you do it. But as long as you only do drugs when someone else offers them to you, you can't get into too much trouble."

I nodded slowly, trying to reconcile all this information with what she had told me before in the car. I'm still really new to all of this.

But today wasn't so bad. I'm still not quite sure what I want to do for the future. I need to think about it. Maybe it's one of those things that gets easier with practice, or as you get more used to the feelings and to the different types of clients.

The other thing is, it's nice to have something in common with Ada again. The truth is, when I'm not doing dates and stuff, but just living a normal life, I don't really have anything to say to her. I worry that she'll get bored with me. As long as I keep working like she does, we have this bond.

Sat, Dec 13

I've been thinking a lot about the date the other day with Ada. I had fun, but I also felt kind of like an imposter. I know I'm still

92

very new to all this stuff, but watching Ada work just made me aware of how much I don't know.

It's like when you go to a restaurant and the waitress says, "Hi! Just so you know, it's my first day," and you smile but inwardly you groan because you know she's going to mess up your order or forget about you completely or spill water on your shirt and generally be a big nuisance. That's how I felt. Like there was this whole encyclopedia of stuff I'm supposed to know, and I am pretty clueless about all of it.

I mean, not that I've never heard of a blow job, and on paper it doesn't sound like rocket science. But the mechanics of it are surprisingly . . . It's not easy to get the hang of. Also it's really gross, and I'm not sure how to get over that.

Miss Irma said it was okay to have things you won't do, but blow jobs probably shouldn't be on that list. I'll look like a real idiot if I won't do that, because it's not even that weird. Plus, I'd probably lose a lot of money to the other girls. So I just need to get better at it somehow.

And there are probably a lot of other things clients might ask for that I've never even heard of, so I don't know whether they should be on my list or not. I guess I need to do some research. Thank God for the Internet. . . . I don't even want to think about how girls like me had to figure this stuff out fifty years ago.

Wed, Dec 17

It's payday today! Ada and I are going to leave at lunch to go to Miss Irma's office together and pick up our envelopes. I'm not as scared this time, since I've seen how it goes. I only have to talk to Anne, not Irma. Plus, it will be sooo much better this time because my envelope will have actual money in it! No more start-up fees coming out of my pay. Maybe Ada and I can finally go shopping afterward.

Wed, Dec 17, later

Guess there's been a change of plans. I just got a call from Anne. She told me I'm not supposed to go to the office to pick up my envelope today. I'm supposed to go Saturday. And she gave me a totally different address to go to. I asked if Ada could wait until Saturday too, so we could still go together, but Anne told me that Miss Irma wants to see me alone.

Miss Irma wants to see me? I don't understand. I'm really confused. Why would Miss Irma waste her Saturday handing cash over to a newbie like me? And why at a different address? And why can't Ada be there?

I tried to ask Anne what was going on, but she told me not to worry. That Miss Irma just wants to have a private conversation with me. That doesn't make me worry any less, to be honest. I like Miss Irma so far, and Ada says she treats everyone well, but at the same time, the morning after my night with Damon, Ada seemed scared of Irma. At the very least, she is definitely intimidating. What does she want to talk to me about? Did she find out about Damon? Am I in trouble?

Should I even go? Maybe if I just don't show up and let her keep the money, she'll let it drop. Except I want the money. I mean, I earned it, didn't I? There wasn't much point in showing up to the date if I'm going to chicken out on picking up my payment.

Sat, Dec 20

That was . . . interesting. It wasn't what I was expecting at all, but I have a lot to think about now. I had to take three buses to get to Miss Irma's house, which was in an out-of-the-way suburb. I'd never been there before, but I've heard my parents mention it. A lot of people they knew from Taiwan live around there, though it's a mixed neighborhood.

From the outside the house looked nice but reassuringly normal. Not that different from my house. It has a pretty garden, and I wondered for a moment if Miss Irma works in the garden the same way my mom does. But Miss Irma has a career; she must be too busy for that. She must hire people.

Miss Irma welcomed me at the front door and invited me back to what she called her "office." She was wearing jeans and a pink shirt, which was a little strange, compared to how sharp and businessy she had looked when I met her the other time.

I guess it's not so strange for her to dress down on a Saturday, but it was weird to see her looking so . . . normal. But reassuring, too. I couldn't quite believe she would want to yell at me or fire me or whatever in her weekend clothes.

She told me to take a seat and offered me a glass of lemonade. Then she asked me how I was doing with the work. How I felt about how things were going. I was feeling awkward and not at all sure what she was looking for, so I just said everything was fine. Then she brought up my first client, and I got that feeling in my stomach like in class when the teacher starts handing back the graded exams. I wasn't exactly sure I had passed.

"The client contacted me," she said in that slow, precise way of hers. "He had a few . . ."

"Complaints?" I said, feeling queasy.

"Suggestions."

"I'm sorry," I said quickly, feeling like I was defending myself to my mom after getting yet another bad grade. "I . . . I'm still new to this. There's a lot of stuff I don't know, but I'm trying to learn. And I'm a . . ."

Irma held up her hand, and I closed my mouth, dropping my eyes in embarrassment.

"Don't apologize," she said. "And don't worry. In this business, skill and knowledge can be useful. But another kind of knowledge is even more useful."

96

I looked up.

"You might have guessed by now," she went on. "Men who are looking for skill don't hire sixteen-year-olds. Your innocence is a selling point. Keep it as long as you can."

"Oh," I said, surprised. "But Ada . . . She's so sophisticated. And talented. Don't men like that?"

"Some men, yes. But you have something Ada will never have. It can make you a lot of money, if you know how to use it."

I couldn't believe that. What could I possibly have that Ada didn't?

"Why do you think men choose you when I show them your picture next to Ada's?"

"I—I have no idea," I answered honestly. It seemed impossible that anyone would do that.

"You want to know what they say? They say, 'I want the Asian girl.'"

I looked up at her, startled.

"They pick me because I'm Asian? But . . . why?"

"Probably because they are racist pigs," Miss Irma replied with a delicate shrug. "But it's not important. What's important is if you keep them happy, they can make you rich. Those pigs have made me very rich."

I fidgeted in my seat, trying to take this information in.

"But if all they care about is my race," I said slowly, "why did that man complain about me?"

Miss Irma leaned forward and steepled her fingers on the desk.

"Try to understand, my dear," she said. "When clients ask for an Asian girl, they are not talking about skin color. Not really. What they want is the fantasy in their head. The fantasy they have been fed. You know this fantasy, because it has been fed to you too. They want a dragon lady. They want a kung-fu princess. They want a Japanese schoolgirl."

"But I'm not Japanese."

Miss Irma cocked an eyebrow at me. "For the right price, you can be Japanese enough." She stood up and stepped out from behind her desk.

"Come with me. I will show you something."

I got up and followed her into another part of the house. She opened a door and I noticed immediately that things were different here. The decor in most of the house was just normal, tasteful suburban, like the houses of most of my classmates. But in this part of the house, it was totally different, like something out of a Chinatown tourist shop or a Hollywood back lot.

Right away I was dazzled by all the red and gold in the room. Once my eyes adjusted to that, I was able to pick out other details: lacquer and jade and porcelain and bamboo. Dragons and peacocks and cranes and Buddhas. It was like a Pier 1 Imports had exploded all over her living room.

"Tell me," said Miss Irma. "What do you notice?"

"I . . . well . . . it's all Asian stuff," I said. "A lot of it reminds me of stuff my mom has lying around, or stuff I've seen when we visit family in Taiwan."

"And the rest?"

I felt a little embarrassed to say what I thought about the other stuff, but a look from Miss Irma reassured me that she wouldn't be offended.

"It looks more like stuff I've seen in some Asian restaurants, I guess," I said. "Kind of a mishmash of different countries and cultures and styles."

"Very good," said Miss Irma. "Perhaps you have guessed that I entertain clients in these rooms." So I had been right that she didn't have the clients visit her in that antiseptic office downtown. "Some of them have known me for a long time. They have certain expectations."

"But it's not real," I said. "It's all stereotypes."

Miss Irma shrugged. "What does it matter? We give them a fantasy, and they give us money. Everyone is happy that way."

She sat down on one of the low, cushioned benches and indicated that I should do the same.

"When I was young," she said, "almost as young as you, I worked in an Oriental massage parlor. It was run by a man, and he made it a very hard life. Not like you girls have now. Others who started with me couldn't take it. They let men abuse them until they were all used up. But I stayed focused. I saved my money. I

99

learned how to keep books, how to keep police away. I studied and used my head. One day all the other girls worked for me.

"You're like me, I think. A smart girl and hardworking. Keep your head, study what the clients want, and give them their fantasy." She leaned forward and patted my knee. "You will do better than the others."

I didn't know how to respond. I admit, I didn't feel totally comfortable with her suggestions. Miss Irma was so different from my mom, but in some ways they were remarkably similar. Always full of directions of how I should act and behave to be pleasing to anyone but myself.

Luckily, Irma didn't seem to expect me to say much of anything. When she had said her bit, she simply handed me a plain white envelope. I was surprised when I saw it and didn't reach for it immediately. Strangely enough, I had almost forgotten why I had come in the first place—not to receive lessons in making myself appealing to men, but to pick up my payment.

I was embarrassed to look through the envelope in front of Irma. It seemed rude, so I let her show me out her front door before I stopped and checked it. And as I flipped through the bills inside, I suddenly felt a lot better about our conversation and my new vocation. Living up to the images my mom and Miss Irma expected felt like being stuck in a cage, but having an envelope full of cash that I earned through my own work . . . that felt like freedom.

Sun, Dec 21

I got a text from Ada today just as I was helping clear the table from lunch. It couldn't have come at a better time. Mom was hassling me again about why she didn't see me working on my homework so much anymore, what's going on with my grades, and why am I so disobedient, blah, blah, blah. I couldn't wait to get out of there, so when Ada texted to see if I wanted to go shopping with her, I texted right back that I would meet her downtown.

Of course Mom the busybody wanted to know who I was talking to and why. Out of instinct, a lie rose to my lips about how it was someone from my English class, and we're working on a group project, and I have to go meet them at the Starbucks a few blocks away. But the words died in my throat. I just thought, *I can't do this anymore. I don't want to do it. I am sick of leading a double life.*

So I just told her. I mean, I didn't say, "It's my hooker friend and she's helping me pick out clothes I can wear while turning tricks." But I did say, "It's a friend. I'm meeting her to go shopping." Which, as far as Mom is concerned, might as well be the same thing. She nearly hit the roof when I said that. It stunned her silent for a second or two at first, and I could read on her face the internal battle she was waging between telling me off for disrespecting her and telling me off for doing something fun with my weekend when my grades were so disappointing. And maybe also joining the battle was the nosy part of her who couldn't bear to imagine I might have a friend she didn't know about.

But that was only a moment or two before she burst forth with her battle cry. The approach she went with was the grades— how I wasn't going anywhere until I had done all my homework and brought my grades up, etc., etc. Which almost made me laugh. As if there was ever really an "until." In my whole life, even when I was doing really well, my grades have never been good enough for me to deserve going off and doing something fun by myself. There would always be another task for me to complete, another thing I'm just not doing quite well enough at.

Well, I'm tired of living in her prison. If she wants me to stick around a minute longer, she's going to have to chain me to the radiator. And until she does that, I will go where I please. Her guilt trips can't affect me anymore.

Sun, Dec 21, later

Back from my shopping trip with Ada. After the scene earlier today, Mom is currently not speaking to me, which is a relief. I bet that won't last, though.

But the shopping trip! It was . . . well, it was definitely fun. But it was also, I don't know . . . I guess I couldn't help being a little disappointed. For so long, my fantasy was that I could become a little more like Ada. She is so beautiful and glamorous and sophisticated, and I've always been so bad at any of that stuff. Just dumpy and geeky and nothing anyone should have any reason to notice. A big part of why I got into this whole lifestyle in the first place was so I could be more like her: gorgeous and mysterious and set apart from all the other girls at school.

I wanted to make money so I could buy clothes and makeup like hers and not have to rely on her hand-me-downs. That was what the money was for. I didn't really have anything else I wanted or needed. But now . . .

After what Irma told me the other day, that's not really an option, is it? She was pretty clear about what the clients would expect from a girl like me. I'm supposed to look cute and young, like a schoolgirl, because that's their fantasy. Well, that's not my fantasy! But since when has anything I wanted ever mattered?

But I suppose if what I wanted was to be noticed, this new look will at least help me accomplish that.

I met up with Ada, and we stopped for coffee first while I told her about what had happened with Miss Irma and I explained to her all about the "look" I was supposed to have now.

Ada nodded and seemed to understand. She talked about it in another way, too. She said that when you think of it as playing a character, sometimes it was easier to get through a date. A bad client couldn't touch you or hurt you the same way if the person on the date wasn't really you. I guess that makes sense. I just wish I got to play a cooler character.

Ada did make me feel better about it. She thought the schoolgirl outfits were cute, and she wished she could get away with them. I don't really believe her, but it was nice of her to say. And she did take me to some stores where I could get stuff that looked better than I was expecting. I've seen the schoolgirls in Taiwan, and believe me, they don't look like anyone's fantasy. The school uniforms are almost as dowdy as my regular school clothes: plaid skirts down to the knee and shapeless white blouses that make everyone look puffy. And knee socks that are always slipping down. The stuff Ada picked out for me was like that, but the sexy version, I guess. The skirt was much shorter, the socks went up higher, and the shirt was a lot more formfitting. I came out of the dressing room feeling a bit shy, and Ada said I looked really cute.

I bought a few outfits along those lines, plus some decent makeup; then we went back to her place to play dress up. I stayed a couple of hours until it started to get dark, and then I got a little nervous about my parents waiting for me at home. I could call them, of course, but I wasn't quite ready to face that conversation yet. Instead, I asked Ada a question I'd wondered about before.

"Why aren't your parents ever home?" I asked her. "Do they work a lot?"

Ada barked out a laugh. "Work? I'm the only person in this household who works."

I didn't know how to respond to that. I just stared at her.

"So they just . . . ," I began.

"There's no 'they,'" she said. "I don't have a father."

"Oh," I said. "Did he die?"

"Beats me," she answered in a hard voice. "Maybe. I don't have the slightest idea who he is, and neither does anyone else, as far as I know."

"What about your mom?"

"She's here. Around. She always is."

"Why haven't I ever seen her?"

Ada shrugged. "She's in her room. Doesn't come out much."

"Oh," I said. "What does she do in there?"

"Mostly lies around in bed." Ada hesitated. It was clear she wasn't used to talking about this. "She's not . . . healthy," she said at last.

"What's wrong with her?"

Ada got up and moved around the room, picking things up at random and putting them back down. She seemed agitated, and I kind of hated myself for bringing up the conversation. It was none of my business. Why had I insisted on prying like my mom would? I was just about to tell Ada that she didn't have to say anything more when she spoke again.

"I don't know," she said. "She wasn't always like this, though she was never what most people would call a normal mom. She used to get . . . episodes, where she would take to her room and not talk and hardly move for days at a time. Then, after a couple of days, she'd snap out of it and put some clothes on and go to the store and get some groceries. Then, one time, she just . . . didn't come out of it."

"She's been like this ever since?"

"Not exactly. Sometimes she gets up and comes out and even tries to make some food. But it's not like before. The truth is, it's better for me when she keeps to herself," she said in a rush of breath. "She's easier to deal with that way."

I nodded as if I understood, though I didn't really. But at least I realized I didn't really want to know any more, and Ada didn't seem to want to give me more details than she already had.

It was getting late anyway, so I told her I had to catch the bus home and I got out of there.

Tues, Dec 23

Now that I have some new clothes, Miss Irma has suggested (via Anne) that I expand my page on the website to include more than just my old head shot from the day I started. It's funny. I didn't even realize Miss Irma had a website. I never thought before about what she did with that photo that Anne took. Now it seems obvious. Who doesn't have a website these days?

Immediately after I found out, I went to look for it online, but I couldn't get into the site. You need a password. The front page is surprisingly discreet, though. It's not like those porn sites that throw up a million pop-ups and start automatically playing a video of a girl and a horse (okay, maybe that was just one site I stumbled on to). You wouldn't have any idea what it was promoting if you didn't already know. There isn't even anyplace for entering your credit-card number. Just a form requesting your username and password but no way to sign up. I wonder how the whole thing works.

I'm honestly not sure about this, though. Do I really want seminaked pictures of myself on the Internet? That seems like the kind of thing people warn you about. Like, what if I want to become a Supreme Court justice or something at some point? Although maybe that ship has already sailed. Maybe once you start having sex for money, all regular ambitions are closed to you.

Still, it does seem like crossing a line of some sort to let someone take pictures. Right now I could stop tomorrow and no one would really know. Miss Irma has my real name, but she seems pretty good at keeping secrets, or else her whole business would fall apart. The clients know me only as Justine, except for Damon. And then there's Ada. As a group, that seems pretty safe. And even if Damon tried to tell someone at some point, he wouldn't have any proof. Just his story. Maybe it's better to keep it that way. . . .

I don't know. I'll ask Ada.

Wed, Dec 24

Last day of the semester today! Tomorrow we'll all go get dim sum in the city, and I'm looking forward to it. We don't really celebrate Christmas, but going into Chinatown is our tradition, since everyplace else is closed that day. We always have a huge meal and see loads of family and friends.

I'm so glad for a break from school! Except, spending 24-7 with my parents isn't much better. Especially since they saw my grades from this semester:

Chemistry: D

American History: C+

Calculus: D

French: B-

English: C

Art: B

Not good. Mom hasn't even really yelled at me—she just cries a lot and won't speak to me. Boy, you'd think I'd murdered someone! I think she's trying to make me feel guilty. Annoyingly, it's working.

I just have to keep reminding myself that I don't care. I don't care about school, and I don't care about my mom's stupid messed-up priorities. If she'd ever taken the time to really get to know me, she wouldn't be so surprised at how I've been acting lately.

At least Mark is home for school break. Now that I don't care about being the perfect daughter, it doesn't bother me so much that he is better than me at everything. It makes me feel a little better, actually. At least my parents have one kid they can't complain about. He's been really good at cheering Mom up, telling her all about his classes and how well he is doing and how all his professors love him.

I hope tomorrow everyone will be able to forget how awful I've been and just have a good time.

Mon, Jan 5

Back to school today. Mark went back to college right after
New Year's, which left me climbing the walls with Mom and
Dad all weekend. I'm almost glad to have a reason to get away
from them.

I wish I had a better reason than school, though. Ada says
it's normal that things get quiet with Irma's business over the
holidays and that it will pick up again soon. I hope she's right. I
need something to think about other than school.

I found out at lunch today that Jenny and Eiko and
everyone went to the movies together on New Year's Day and
didn't invite me. Not like I care. But still. In a way, we were
never very close, but for a long time, they were the only friends I
had. I guess they noticed that I've drifted away from them. And
maybe also that I'm not exactly keeping up my "nerd" image,
what with my last report card.

I wonder if Ada would go to a movie with me.

Wed, Jan 7

I still haven't been scheduled for any new dates. It's annoying,
because I spent all that money on the new clothes, thinking I would
make it back pretty quickly. But it's hard to make it back when the
phone doesn't ring. Maybe I should get those photos done.

I asked Ada about it and she said it's probably a good

idea. She told me more about how the website works, too. Apparently, it's all done by word of mouth. Everyone who signs up with Miss Irma has to come with a reference, and they never even hear of Miss Irma unless someone is willing to vouch for them. Ada says a lot of Miss Irma's clients are famous, and they could have their whole careers ruined if some nosy journalist found out what they were doing. So everything has to be really locked down.

Anyway, she said I would get a lot more dates if I put up a full photo shoot instead of just a head shot. So I said okay, but then Ada was like, just so you know, it will be expensive.

Of course. It hadn't even occurred to me that I would be expected to pay for all this, and of course Anne never mentioned it. But it shouldn't surprise me, after being charged for Irma's phone and the car service. I'm guessing the money for this will come out of my next date. I wonder when I'll ever actually start earning money from this work.

On the other hand, if I don't do it, it looks like I'll never have another date again. And that's no way to make money.

Sat, Jan 10

I had my photo shoot today. It was . . . awkward. And expensive, just like Ada warned me. I really, really hope it was worth it and this brings some more business to me!

I was really nervous about the whole thing, so Ada agreed to come with me for moral support. She helped me pick out some outfits to bring, since I wasn't sure what to expect or what the photographer would have in mind. Plus, I know the site is totally private and Miss Irma is superconcerned with confidentiality, but I still wasn't sure it was entirely a good idea to put seminaked pictures of myself on the Internet. So I went in there looking cute but basically fully dressed, and as I posed for the guy, he kept encouraging me to take this or that off, or hike up a hem or whatever. And every time he did, I would hesitate and resist a bit, then give in.

The guy was good. He made me feel really comfortable and relaxed, so I didn't mind doing it so much, but I was still kind of hesitant. Then Ada came over during a break and was like, "You should really try to speed this up."

"Why?" I said. "Jeb says I don't have to do anything I'm not comfortable with. I'd rather ease into it."

Ada smiled sympathetically and rubbed my arm. "I know," she said. "Jeb is a sweetheart, and he will let you take as long as you need, until you feel completely relaxed. The only thing is, Jeb gets paid by the hour. And he's getting paid by you."

That did put things in a different light. I thought about how I'd act with my clients . . . maybe dragging things out a bit on purpose if I thought I could get another hour's pay out of them. So after that I just bit the bullet and took off almost all my clothes and let Jeb pose me however he wanted. I tried to forget about the camera and my image being plastered all over the Internet.

Now that I look back on it, I'm kind of horrified at some of the pictures I let him take. If my mom ever saw those! I don't even want to think about it. As long as it works, I guess it doesn't really matter.

Thurs, Jan 15

Finally had another date today. I guess those pictures I took are at least doing their job. When I got to the client's room, I did my best to play up the whole Japanese schoolgirl angle, though it was hard to tell if the guy cared at all. He seemed pretty indifferent to everything I did or said. I think he mostly just wanted to pose me like a doll.

It was fine, nothing that crazy or weird, but let's just say that by the end, I was really looking forward to washing my hair. I almost asked if I could use the shower in the hotel room, but I wasn't sure if Miss Irma has a rule about that.

In any case, the guy seemed like he wasn't particularly eager for me to stick around longer than absolutely necessary, so I got out of there.

Made for a gross ride home on the bus though. Luckily, public transit passengers in Seattle are good at minding their own business.

Mon, Jan 19

This date was much better than the last one. The guy was older and kind of smelled weird, but I ended up enjoying my time with him. I think he was mostly lonely and wanted someone to talk to. He told me about his dead wife and about how he has to travel so much for work that hotels feel like home to him. Since he wanted to talk, I asked him to tell me stuff about all the places he'd traveled, and he seemed to enjoy that. I did, too. He had some really funny stories.

The only weird part was afterward, when he got very sentimental and wanted to kiss and cuddle for a while, and then he told me I reminded him of his daughter. Awkward. I'm just glad he didn't mention that at the beginning of the date.

Anyway, I can't really complain because he was a very nice man, and he also gave me a *huge* tip. I'll be honest—that goes a long way to putting me in a good mood. The money itself is nice, and it's also just nice to feel appreciated.

Wed, Jan 21

Another day, another date. This guy was a real creeper, but at least I felt like I was giving him his money's worth with the whole

Asian fantasy. As soon as I introduced myself, he said, "Do you know why I picked you?" I said no and started to undress, while he told me about how he'd been in the military for years, stationed in Okinawa and the Philippines, and how much he missed the whores there. I don't know why, but for some reason that grossed me out. It's weird that people consider me interchangeable with these random people on the other side of the world. But it's not like he knows any of us, so what does it matter?

Still, I hoped that he would shut up once we got down to business, but this one was another talker. He told me all about how he had traveled the world in search of whores who could re-create those experiences, and then he described in great detail what all his previous whores had looked like, including graphic descriptions of certain parts of their anatomy (for which he had a truly amazing memory) and how they compared to my own.

Then, at the end, when I was getting dressed, he said it was a shame he hadn't met me earlier, because he really "prefers them younger," and he grinned and asked me if I had a little sister. Yuck.

Also, no tip.

Mon, Jan 26

I got called into the office today because of all the school I've been missing when I'm off with clients. The assistant principal kept me there for almost an hour, making threats and trying to extort promises to reform. I just kept saying it wouldn't happen again. Easier than trying to fight back. They said they would get in touch with my parents, but what good will that do? It's not like my parents can control what I do or where I go in school.

Funny thing was, the whole time she was browbeating me about missing class, she never once asked me what I was doing in that time.

Fri, Feb 6

Originally I planned to write about every date I go on, but I've skipped a couple because, honestly, there's not that much to say. I guess it's like any job. . . . After a while, you're just going through the motions, and they all seem to blend together.

But the guy yesterday was kind of exciting. My first celebrity! Ada told me we get them from time to time, because everyone knows they can trust Irma to keep their names out of the papers.

I know this is my private journal, but before I went on this date, I got a special phone call from Miss Irma herself reminding me of the importance of confidentiality and how I really couldn't tell anyone. And it's not like writing it in here would be telling anyone, but who knows who might find this journal one day? So I'll just say it was a musician. A pop star, actually. From a boy band! I'll just leave it at that, because if I said anything more, it would become pretty obvious. Luckily, it's not a band I'm actually a fan of, so I didn't have to worry about being too starstruck.

The weird thing is that with a guy like this, you'd think he'd have no trouble getting a date. I mean, anytime it's announced that he's going to be somewhere, girls my age line up for hours and hours just for the possibility of seeing him. Surely a pretty high percentage of those girls would go to bed with him. But I guess I should know by now that it's a myth that guys go to whores only because they can't get it for free. Maybe for some guys, but there are a lot of reasons why people go to prostitutes—confidentiality probably being a big one, in this case.

The plus side of a date like this was that the guy was young (not much older than me, in fact) and really cute. Like, I'd always sort of figured with movie stars and pop stars that they look great in the magazines, thanks to all the airbrushing and stuff, but that in real life they probably look pretty ordinary and you wouldn't even notice them walking down the street. But that was definitely not the case here! I think part of it was him having a very expensive haircut and very carefully chosen clothes and stuff. But there's no question—he was really good-looking. And he had a certain aura about him. Or maybe "magnetism" is a better word. I kind of just couldn't stop looking at him. But I'm not sure if he's famous because he has this quality, or if he has it because I know he's famous.

The minus side was that he was kind of a spoiled little jerk. Like, he could be charming and powerfully compelling when he wanted to be, but the minute he got sick of that act, it was like flipping a switch. Then it was more like babysitting a two-year-old who hasn't had his nap. Draining!

Still, it was kind of exciting, and I didn't mind putting up with it for a few hours. I did feel kind of bad for his regular handlers, who have to deal with him all day, every day. Glad that's not my job.

Sun, Feb 8

I really don't know what I am going to do about my parents. How much longer can we keep up like this?

It's been some time now that I've been basically ignoring them: coming and going as I please and just slamming my bedroom door on all their lectures. I eat most of my meals out, or grab something and bring it back to my room, so it's not too hard to just avoid them.

And for a while it was really liberating. Just not caring what they thought. Doing whatever. I used to cower in fear of them, and now I don't even know what I was afraid of. Did I really think they were going to kick me out of the house or something just for getting a B on a test?

I don't know. Not really. Mom never did anything but yell a little and tell me how to do things better and tell me how disappointed she was. And what a no-good, worthless child I was. That used to hurt me so much! I think I was living my whole life to avoid that feeling of being told I wasn't good enough. But it didn't matter how hard I tried to avoid it, because nothing I did was ever good enough, so I heard it all the time anyway.

But I'm free from all that now. I don't care what they think of me, or how disappointed they are, or what a terrible child I am. And that means they can't hurt me anymore. I go where I want. I come home when I want. I blow off school whenever, and I don't even worry about the school's office calling anymore. What are they going to do to me? I've taken away their power.

Unfortunately, it doesn't work the other way. Just because I've stopped caring doesn't mean my parents have. And I guess it is a little hard to completely turn off my feelings. Mom doesn't yell at me like she used to, but she doesn't ignore me, either. She waits up every night I am late getting home, and anytime she sees me leaving the house in my new clothes, she wrings her hands and her eyes tear up, but she no longer bothers to say anything.

Most days I can shrug this off, but some days it's hard. Some days I just want to bow my head and put on my old clothes and get my books and sit at the kitchen table to study, just so I can see her approving smile again. But, obviously, I can't go back.

Tues, Feb 10

Mom came in my room today as I was taking off my makeup after a date. Out of instinct, my shoulders tensed up, but she didn't yell. She just looked at me silently for a moment and then sat down on the bed. She spoke to me softly in Chinese, asking what happened to me. What have I been doing? I turned to her to say something, but she held up her hand. "No. Don't tell me," she said. "I don't want to know. I think it would break my heart."

She stood up to leave, and just before she closed the door behind her, she turned and said, "What has happened to my little girl?"

I may have cried a little once the door shut. So much for not caring.

It's not fair for her to be nice all of a sudden. What am I supposed to do with this? It's too late. I can't go back to being her good little obedient daughter. Not after the things I've seen and done.

But I can't keep living here like this. School, too. Lately I just can't stand it. Other than Ada, it's so lonely, and since I've pretty much given up caring about my classes, it feels boring and pointless too. Why am I wasting six hours a day there, doing nothing? Wouldn't it make more sense for me to direct my own life?

I wonder what it would take. What if I quit school and moved out? Could I do it? Could I live on my own like a grown-up? Could I make enough money to support myself so I wouldn't have to answer to anyone but myself? Wouldn't have to face anyone's judgmental eyes? That sounds amazing. Now, that would be real freedom. But I would get lonely. . . .

What if Ada were with me? Her life at home with her mom is so different from mine, but it doesn't seem like such a great situation either. Maybe this is what we both need. To get away and be independent. Or be dependent only on each other, without all these expectations and pressures and people needing things from us.

I wonder how much money I would have to save up. How long it would take. Of course, it would mean fewer shopping sprees, but would I rather have a sparkly new belt or a life with Ada on our own, where we could be totally independent?

I think I will do some research on what rent on a decent apartment would be and how much we would need for food and stuff.

Thurs, Feb 12

I'm invited to a party! I don't know if I should really be that excited about it. I mean, it's a work party, which I guess are supposed to be lame, but it's not like work in a typical office.

I'm not sure the last time I went to a real party, but it was probably a kid's birthday party with pizza and cake and pin the tail on the donkey. Sometimes I hear about parties at school . . . real parties with making out and beer, but I only ever hear about those after they take place, on Monday mornings when everyone is dissecting the drama.

I am pretty sure this party won't be anything like those, but I don't know much else. Ada says Miss Irma does this every year around Valentine's Day. She presents it as a fun time for everyone. A way for her to show her love and appreciation for the "talent." But Ada says if it were really a gift, Miss Irma wouldn't invite the clients. Which she does. And the clients bring friends who are interested in becoming new clients, or they show up because they want to pick out their next date in the flesh instead of just using the website.

That makes it sound less like a party and more like dim sum . . . where we're the dumplings being brought around on trays and everyone gets to just grab what they like. Though Ada says that most years it doesn't turn into an all-out orgy. Most years. That's comforting.

Still, I can't help being a little excited about it. Most of all because it's a chance to meet the other girls. Ada mentions them from time to time, but I still haven't met anyone except her, and I want to put faces to names, or maybe even make a new friend or two.

Plus, all things considered, it probably wouldn't kill me to flirt with some of the potential clients. It would be nice to have as many regulars as Ada does and get a bit more cash coming in. Then I could tell Ada about my plan for us to get an apartment together.

Oh, the other thing is that the invitation made it very clear that you wouldn't be served alcohol unless you were over twenty-one. How's that for irony! We're there working as prostitutes, but we're not allowed to drink? Miss Irma says drunk teenagers attract cops like nobody's business, and she can't afford the risk.

But Ada said some of the talent bring flasks of liquor and share it around secretly, so everyone winds up getting kind of drunk anyway.

That does sound kind of fun. I think I like the idea of being included in the secret more than anything else. I never pictured myself as the kind of person who would get passed a flask.

Sat, Feb 14

I'm at Ada's house, prepping for the party! She looks so gorgeous, like a Hollywood screen siren from the 1940s. Her hair is ironed into perfect waves, and she's wearing a black bias-cut dress covered in shimmery beads. I wish I could look like her, or at least dress like her. I thought this party might be a place where I could break out of my persona and look sleek and sophisticated like she always does, but Ada said it would probably be better to stick to a version of my usual style. Some of the clients there will have already seen the pictures on the website, and they'll have an easier time recognizing me if I have the same "look." So I have to somehow pull off "cute," "sweet," and "sexy" all at once, which is actually kind of complicated. I've decided to go with a lot of white and pink and a flower motif, but still showing a lot of skin.

Ada said I looked amazing and kissed me on the cheek, so I guess that will have to do. I wish we got to trade characters for the night, but I guess no one wants that.

I am excited for the party but also a little nervous. I really have no idea what to expect. But Ada says not to worry and that Miss Irma keeps the clients on a pretty tight leash. Officially, there is no touching. That rule isn't enforced strictly, but if someone really starts mauling the girls, Irma is prepared to throw them out, and they know it.

I'm not sure I understand why Irma wouldn't just want to keep the clients happy by whatever means possible. That seems like her usual routine. Ada said Irma has learned from her mistakes. Once upon a time she treated it like a buffet. She had everyone pay a flat fee at the door, and then they could take what they wanted. But she didn't like the results.

"Have you ever seen people at a buffet?" said Ada. "They go crazy. Trying to get every last nickel's worth out of the talent. Plus, it took her ages to get the stains out of the upholstery."

(later)

omg the party was so much fun! except I drank too much and probably [illegible] don't care because I had sooooo much fun. and I met a boy! I mean a boy boy, not a client or whatever. [illegible] he was cute. ugh the room is spinning I better gotto got to go to bed.

Sun, Feb 15

Ugh. Now I know why people don't do this all the time. I feel like my brain went through the dryer or something. Maybe it's even still in there. . . . I'm not at all sure it's in my head. And my stomach might be in there with it, because it is definitely going around in circles.

And even worse than the physical stuff is thinking about how I behaved last night. What got into me? I mean, besides a few shots of whiskey. I want to vomit again just thinking about that.

I bet Miss Irma is so mad at me right now. I bet I was such a horrible embarrassment to her. To everyone. To myself.

Oh my God. I didn't even think about my parents. What must they think of me right now? What do they know? I honestly don't remember coming home last night, and I have no idea if I saw them or not. I am so embarrassed and ashamed even thinking about them seeing me in that state. Presumably they would have murdered me on the spot if they had, and I seem to still be here in my bedroom, so . . . maybe somehow I snuck past them.

I can't worry about that now. I need to start by piecing together what actually happened last night. My first clue is the previous entry, which I don't remember writing and I can barely read. That's kind of funny, actually, though also a little disturbing. Wait. Did I smoke pot again last night too? I seem to vaguely remember that. That probably didn't help matters.

All right. Let's start at the beginning.

The party was at Miss Irma's house, in those back rooms where Miss Irma had taken me the last time. She had added some holiday decorations here and there, but not that much, since the rooms were so ornate already.

At first I was really nervous and uncomfortable and kind of clung to Ada. Then I realized I was probably annoying her, so I tried to hide out behind one of the big screens. Ada found me after a bit and laughed. She said as the night wore on, it would be a bad idea to sneak behind the screens, since other people would have that idea too. And from the way she said it, I got the sense that she didn't mean they were shy like me.

Anne came over after a minute and took our coats and pointed out the bar and stuff, with a reminder that we wouldn't be served anything but soft drinks, so not to bother asking. Then she told us to make ourselves comfortable, because the clients would be arriving soon. I was confused by that, because there already were a few guys milling around the room, though they were younger and more attractive than the clients usually were. I thought maybe Irma was hiding a bunch of cute clients like Damon and fixing them up only with the more experienced girls.

Ada offered to show me around and introduce me to everyone, but it was too overwhelming. I felt really bad for holding her back and tried to put on a brave face, but she seemed to get it intuitively. Instead of bringing me over to the big gossiping groups exchanging greetings, she found a spot on a bench in a dark corner and tugged me down next to her.

"How about I give you all the dirt on everyone first?" she said in a whisper. "That way you'll already know who everyone is when you actually meet them."

I almost sighed with relief, and Ada started to point people out and tell me their names and their life stories. I have to admit that some combination of awe and anxiety prevented me from absorbing everyone's names, but almost everyone there had some pretty rough story in their past—violence or molestation or drugs or homelessness. They all seemed happy and okay now, but none of them were like me, with two parents who had plenty of money and didn't hurt them or abuse them. It made me feel sort of bad, like I had wandered into the wrong party. Is there something wrong with me that I took to this life without any trauma pushing me into it?

I did notice when Ada pointed out Jen, since she had mentioned her before. The one with the drug problem. Ada said that both her parents had died when she was little, and she wound up living with a distant relative who beat her, so she ran away and lived on the streets for a while, eating out of garbage cans. It was hard to believe that the person laughing and chatting right in front of me, wearing a designer dress and scarfing miniature quiches, could once have been so desperate. It gave me a newfound respect for Miss Irma, that she offered people like Jen and so many of the others a second chance at life.

Jen's roommate, Beth, was there too. Ada doesn't like her much. I guess there's some history there, but I didn't get the whole story. At some point I asked Ada about the guys who were at the party and who were they if not clients. She laughed.

"They're talent. I can introduce you to them, if you like."

"Wait," I said, resisting her attempt to tug me up by the hand. "What do you mean, talent? What kind of . . . ?"

Ada gave me a funny look. "They work for Miss Irma," she explained. "Just like us." I must have still look confused, because she laughed again, then leaned a little closer to me. "They have sex with men for money," she said slowly and clearly, like she was explaining it to a little kid.

"Oh," I said, trying not to look shocked. I don't know why I was so shocked, though. Why should it be so surprising that boys make money from this just like girls do? Now that I think about it, it seems like the most obvious thing in the world.

I couldn't help staring at this one boy who was standing in a group of girls and talking very animatedly. He was one of the most gorgeous guys I had ever seen, with dark skin and almond eyes and a delicate, heart-shaped face. He was wearing eyeliner and maybe even mascara, but I could tell that even without that he would be almost as pretty as any girl I had ever seen. I asked Ada about him, and she said his name was Shawn. She didn't tell me much about him, but I got the sense she didn't like him very much.

At that point there was a noise and the din in the room died down. Miss Irma was standing near the bar, tapping a glass for everyone's attention. I almost didn't recognize her in a flowing peacock-blue kimono. She had a drink in one hand and her phone in the other.

"Thank you for your attention," she said in her carefully clipped tone. "The clients will arrive in a minute or two. Some advice, if I may. Do not crowd them like a batch of hyenas. There will be plenty to go around. But do not spend the evening talking to one another as if this were a high school dance, either. Enjoy yourselves, but remember: The clients are our guests tonight. And last, alcohol is strictly forbidden to you, even if offered by a client. Is that understood?"

While she was talking, I leaned over and asked Ada about some men I hadn't noticed before in the room. Not ones like Shawn, but others that didn't seem like clients either.

"That's Miss Irma's security," said Ada. "'Goons' is a better word. She'll act like they're here to protect us in case any of the clients try to take something they haven't paid for, but don't kid yourself. They work for her, not for us. And if she has a problem with any of us, they won't hesitate to toss us out, or worse."

"Worse?"

Ada gave me a significant look but didn't elaborate.

A few minutes later, the clients started showing up. Just as Miss Irma had suggested, it was a little hard to resist the urge to surge toward them, especially when I saw other people doing just that. It was hard not to feel like the first people out of the gate were "winners" in some sense, but I held back. It made sense to wait until there were more in the room so you could actually take your time and pick one who seemed appealing. But then, even when there were more, it kept happening that every time I spotted someone who looked like a good bet, I'd try to catch his eye from across the room only to notice some other girl sidling up to him and running a finger down his arm. Obviously, I needed to be a bit more aggressive.

I did manage to give my cell phone number to a couple of guys, but they didn't seem all that interested. I wondered if my cutesy Asian girl getup had been a bad idea. Maybe it was too niche, and I would have been better off dressing more normal sexy like the other girls.

One guy did grab me as I walked toward the bar and pulled me down onto his lap, but he was pretty gross. He smelled awful and had a lot of hair on his knuckles. I was as pleasant with him as I could manage, and I did give him my number when he asked, but I was already thinking that if he contacted me, I would definitely pretend to be busy that day.

Eventually he let me up and I headed toward the bar, just hoping for a few moments of calm. I got a ginger ale and sipped it slowly, only gradually becoming aware that there was a man leaning against a bookshelf near me, sipping his drink and eyeing the room but not yet talking to anyone. He wasn't exactly good-looking—with a weak chin and a lazy eye—but he seemed pleasant enough and a much better option than most of the other men in the room. I took a deep breath and sidled up to him, running a hand down his arm as I introduced myself, just as I'd seen the other kids do. It didn't seem to work so well, though. He sort of twitched and shifted back a little.

"Nervous?" I said in what I hoped was a flirtatious tone.

He gave me an apologetic smile. "Maybe," he said. "I've never been to a party like this before."

I tried to think of something flirty and suggestive to say, but I drew a blank, so I wound up saying, "Neither have I." Surprisingly, this wasn't such a bad move, since it did give us something to talk about. Though that was awkward too. He kept starting in with questions like, "How did you get into this business?" but then cutting himself off as if maybe he didn't want to know. Still, it wasn't a bad conversation and I was proud of myself for holding up my end and not letting it descend into horrifying awkwardness.

The only problem was, I didn't seem to be making much progress with him. He still startled at all my little touches and still backed farther away every time I moved closer to him, until it looked as though he was trying to squeeze himself into the bookshelf.

I was starting to feel a little bad about it when I noticed someone standing at my elbow.

"Introduce me," said a voice near my ear. I turned and saw Shawn, the pretty boy I'd noticed earlier.

"What?" I said, caught off guard.

Shawn smiled at the client, then leaned in to me. "Introduce me," he said again.

"Oh," I said, and I made the introductions, feeling slightly annoyed that Shawn was distracting me from my awkward attempts to get this guy interested. That's when I noticed the guy's face. He was looking at Shawn with an intensity that I hadn't seen during our whole conversation. And when Shawn laid a hand on the man's forearm, he gave a slight shiver and leaned into it.

Ada's patient explanations popped back into my head. *Oh,* I thought. *Ohhhh.* Shawn gave me a quick grin, which I returned before coming up with some excuse to leave the two of them alone together.

I wasn't sure what to do with myself after that. I glanced around the room, but everyone appeared to be engrossed in conversations. I couldn't see any clients standing alone. Before long, though, I felt a hand at my waist. At first I thought it must be a client, but the cloud of expensive perfume gave Miss Irma away.

She whispered in my ear.

"Come," she said. "No prizes for standing about. You have to talk to people." I started to protest that there was no one to talk to, but she ignored me as her hand guided me toward an adjacent room I hadn't been in yet. A man standing alone was calmly surveying the snack table with his back to the room.

"Damon," said Miss Irma, "where have you been hiding? I want to introduce someone to you."

I don't know why it didn't occur to me that he would be there, but I couldn't have been more surprised. My brain froze in that moment, torn between trying to figure out an appropriate reaction to being suddenly confronted with the man I lost my virginity to and haven't seen since and the flaring memory of Ada reminding me that Miss Irma must never learn what happened between us. I stared up at him and said nothing.

He looked down at me, surprised but not half as dumbstruck as I was. "Oh," he said. "Yeah, we've met."

I felt more than saw Miss Irma's eyes narrow next to me as she processed this information. "You've met? But I don't remember . . ."

"It wasn't through . . . ," I said quickly.

"No," he agreed. "It was . . ."

But neither of us had a very good end to our sentences.

"I see," said Miss Irma, though she still sounded confused and, to my horror, more than a little suspicious. Luckily, I was saved from trying to dig myself out of this hole by Ada, who shrieked from across the room and then barreled toward our little group at full speed.

"Damon!" she cried, launching herself into his arms.

"Ada," he said with a laugh as she burrowed into his chest and squeezed him in a mighty hug. He kissed her forehead and mussed her hair a little. "Long time no see. What've you been up to, kiddo?"

A glance over at Irma revealed a bemused and not entirely pleased expression, but I didn't stick around to see how it played out. I took the opportunity of her distraction to get myself out of there.

That left me wandering the room with nothing to do again, and I was feeling awkward and sort of watching Ada out of the corner of my eye with a weird feeling as she talked with Damon. I don't know why. It's true that I had slept with Damon, but Ada had known him much longer and more intimately than I had, and I had hardly thought of him since that night. I'm not sure why seeing them together bothered me so much. In any case, I didn't have much time to consider the question because I was startled by a touch on my elbow. I tensed up, thinking it was probably Miss Irma about to lecture me again for not flirting with enough guys, but it was Shawn.

"Hey," he said gently. "I'm sorry about earlier. I hope you didn't mind that I jumped in on your conversation."

"Don't be silly," I said. "Obviously I was wasting my time with him." I looked down at my shoes, suddenly abashed. "Mostly I'm just a little embarrassed that I couldn't tell after talking to him for fifteen minutes, while you spotted it from across the room."

Shawn shrugged lightly. "It's kind of a sixth sense. You pick it up with experience. Hey," he said. "Keep an eye out for Miss Irma for a second, will you?"

I was confused, but I checked around for her. She seemed to be in the other room, so Shawn brought a silver flask up to his lips and took a swig, then pressed the flask toward me wordlessly, raising his eyebrows as if in offer. I was nervous, but I couldn't help a little thrilled shiver from going up my spine. Here I was, at a party, and someone was offering me a sip from their flask! As if he really believed I was one of the cool kids.

I giggled a little and took it from him.

"I'll keep an eye out for the Dragon Lady," said Shawn, "but try to keep your head down just in case. Don't draw attention to it."

I nodded and unscrewed the cap, but it's harder than you might think to keep your head down while at the same time tipping it back so liquid can slide down into your mouth. Plus, since the bottle was opaque, I couldn't really judge how much was in it, so it was really hard to figure out the best angle. I did my best, but wound up misjudging and sent a big mouthful of the stuff right down my throat. I was prepared for it not to taste too good, but the burning sensation it left in my throat took me by surprise. I tried to choke it back, but it was too late. . . . I choked and coughed and the stuff came right back up and all over Shawn's shirt.

I don't know if I've ever been more embarrassed in my entire life. This is why I can't have nice things! Because I spit up on them. So basically I wanted to die and was so close to just bolting for the nearest exit or screen or potted plant, but Shawn was really nice about it. He just laughed and said, "Guess you're not too experienced with whiskey, either." I blushed really hard at that, because I get tired of always being the innocent one, but he just rubbed my lower back gently, which made me feel a lot better, and said that it reminded him of his first time drinking whiskey.

He told me he was small as a kid, bullied by older boys, and didn't get any respect. He noticed that the older kids drank alcohol, and he thought if he did too, it would make him seem tough and cool and he wouldn't get picked on anymore. Well, there was this guy, a neighbor and an old friend of the family, who used to have him over all the time when his mom wasn't home, like, to babysit him. They played video games together, talked about school and stuff.

Then one day, the guy offered him some whiskey, so he took a small sip and it almost made him gag. The guy offered him more, and Shawn didn't want to seem like a wimp, so he kept accepting it. At first he tried to take really small sips, but even that made his eyes water. So finally he just took a swig and held it in his mouth, looking for an opportunity to spit it out. The guy kept offering him more, so he took a couple more swigs. Then the guy snuggled up and tried to kiss him, and Shawn spat whiskey all over him.

Shawn laughed at this point. "The dude was so pissed," he said. "I felt like an idiot."

I couldn't help laughing too, even though, now that I think about it, that's a pretty horrible story. But I guess, based on what Ada was telling me earlier in the night, pretty much everyone has a story like that. Maybe it's not such a big deal. I don't know. I always feel so sheltered around these people! Like I don't know a thing about the world. But then I think about all my old friends sitting around the geek table, and most of what they know of the world was compiled from newspaper articles in preparation for debate-team meets. I guess maybe it's not so bad to occupy the middle ground.

Shawn offered me another swig of whiskey, but I really

didn't even want to try it again. I could still feel that awful burning in my throat. Shawn noticed my cup of ginger ale on the table behind me and he said, "Here, try it this way. You'll like it better." And he poured some in. I was nervous to try it again, but it did taste better with the pop. I could still feel the burning in my throat a little, but it didn't instantly make me want to gag. And the flavor on my tongue wasn't bad at all. The whiskey cut the sweetness of the pop in a good way.

"Better?" he said.

I giggled and smiled. "Much better."

"I'm glad we met," he said. I realized that his hand was still on the small of my back. "You're a cool kid—you know that?"

I couldn't help grinning. No, I hadn't known that. Cool kid was about the last way I ever would have described myself. But there I was, sipping whiskey at a fancy party and talking to the prettiest boy there, and I thought, *Maybe he's right. Maybe I am a cool kid.*

I took another sip of the whiskey.

"Did you swallow it?" said Shawn. "Or are you just storing it up in your mouth?"

I let out a giggle.

"No," I said. "I swallowed it."

"Good," he said. He cast a quick glance around the room, clearly scouting for Miss Irma or her goons, but when he didn't spot them, he leaned in closer and he kissed me!

Honestly, I was so surprised I didn't know what to do. I just froze up completely, which is pretty embarrassing given that kissing people is one of the things I do for a living. I can only imagine that he was wondering how I make any money at all at this gig, given how I reacted. But it was different! Different because he is cute. Different because I like him. Different because I wasn't expecting it. But maybe most of all different because . . . Well, let's just say that I was confused.

As my senses started to come back to me, I pulled back. Shawn let me go, and he looked pretty embarrassed.

"I'm sorry," he said. "I didn't mean to—"

"No!" I interrupted. "It's not that. You didn't . . . ." We were both babbling pretty stupidly at this point. I stopped and took a deep breath. "It's just that I, well, I thought you were . . . I mean, aren't you . . . ?"

"Gay?" he supplied.

"Well, yeah. I mean, back there, with that guy . . . And Ada said . . ."

Shawn grinned. "Haven't you ever heard of 'gay for pay'?"

"What?" I said. I hadn't. "What do you mean?"

"I mean, it's a job. It's not who I am. Do you fall in love with all the men you date for this job?"

I made a face. "Definitely not."

"Are you attracted to all of them?"

"Hardly any."

Shawn shrugged. "Same for me. And these clothes you're wearing . . . Is this how you dress in your normal life?"

I laughed. "No. I only dress this way because Miss Irma told me to."

"Because the Japanese schoolgirl thing is what the clients want, right?"

I nodded.

"I bet you're not even Japanese."

"Nope."

"So you understand, then. This stuff isn't who I am." Shawn grinned. "When I'm with a guy, I just close my eyes and think about how much money I'm making."

"So you never enjoy any of it at all, then?" I asked. "You've never gotten any pleasure whatsoever from a date?"

Shawn sipped his whiskey. This line of questioning seemed to make him uneasy.

"I enjoy it exactly as much as I need to," he said at last. "For the client."

I was about to apologize for asking a kind of rude and nosy question when Shawn noticed something behind my left shoulder.

"Shit," he said. "The Dragon Lady is on the prowl. She'll

be pissed if she sees us flirting with each other instead of the clients." He gave me a mischievous smile and tugged at my elbow. "Come with me."

He pulled me toward the edge of the room, then slid open a glass door that opened onto a pretty garden and patio. A small group of kids were already clustered around on the patio furniture, talking quietly and trying to muffle their giggles. Shawn slid the door shut behind us. It was chilly outside in the night air but not too bad. Especially since once I shivered, Shawn wrapped his arms around me and squeezed. Then I felt a lot warmer.

"Come on," he said, nudging me toward where the other kids were assembled. I wished I'd remembered Ada's introductions better, but I couldn't remember who was who, and it was hard to even make out people's faces in the darkness. The only people I was sure of were Jen and her roommate, Beth.

Shawn nodded to the crowd like he knew them all, then found a seat on a bench near them and pulled me down onto his lap. I noticed they were passing a couple more flasks around, and some of them were smoking pot out of a little pipe, too. Everyone was quiet except for one girl, who seemed to be wrapping up a story she was telling. I couldn't figure out what had happened, exactly, but it was clear she was describing a very bad date. When she was done, a boy immediately jumped in and started telling a story he described as "his worst date ever." It was really bad! He got into a car with a guy and the guy took him out of the city so he had no idea where he was; then the guy wasn't happy with the sex, I guess, so he . . . well, raped him with a beer bottle. Then he left him in the middle of the woods somewhere. And he didn't even pay him! The kid had to walk all the way into the city while in a lot of pain before he could get a cell signal.

Then another boy jumped in with his worst-date story, about how he showed up at what seemed like a perfectly normal date with a client he knew well, but this time the client had invited a whole bunch of other men without asking, and they were all drunk and rowdy and got violent, and there was nothing he could do.

Then a couple of girls told their worst-date stories. Eventually they started to run together in my mind, maybe because of the effects of the whiskey. Not getting paid or paid enough was a common complaint, and being forced to do things that they explicitly said were off the table. Plus, clients getting violent or unpredictable, or treating them like disposable objects. It should have all been really scary and depressing, but it was hard to get too upset with the whiskey warming my belly and Shawn's arms around my waist. And everyone was sort of laughing and telling these stories like they were funny anecdotes rather than horrifying personal experiences. A big part of me felt terrible for them, and grateful that nothing that bad had ever happened to me. But another, smaller part felt a little . . . maybe jealous isn't the right word. But in some small way, I wished I had a story of my own to contribute, if only so I could feel more like part of the gang. There was something really comforting about that sense of shared camaraderie. I almost felt like people were sharing their worst stories to make each other feel better about what had happened to them. Like if they all went through it together, or if there was always someone who had it worse and survived, then it must not be all that bad.

Eventually, someone told a story that was particularly horrifying because it was her worst time, and it was also her first time. Not losing her virginity, but her first time having sex for money. I couldn't believe she'd actually continued with this profession after what had happened to her (let's just say it involved box cutters; I don't really want to think about it beyond that), but I guess, from the way she told it, she didn't have a lot of options.

But that was good in a way, because people shifted from telling worst-time stories to first-time stories. Maybe everyone in the group realized that after that one, we needed a change of mood. Something a little less grim. Not that the first-time stories were all rainbows and sunshine. There was still a lot of stuff that made me cringe. But it was more in the spirit of laughing together than staring in silent horror.

I was starting to feel pretty drunk at that point, but I happened to notice Ada and Damon slipping outside together. I hoped they would come over and join us, but instead they made their way to a bench at the other end of the garden and sat there talking quietly together. Occasionally, one of Ada's delicate bell-like giggles drifted through the chill night air over to me. I felt bad for my earlier flare of jealousy. Ada's life is hard. She doesn't get a lot of chances to just be happy and content. I was glad that she was enjoying the evening, even if Irma was undoubtedly pissed.

I had lost track of the conversation while watching them, but at some point Shawn squeezed me gently and said, "What about you? I bet you have a good first-time story."

"Oh," I said, blushing. "Well, yes. It was good, but not very interesting, I guess. He took me to the restaurant on top of the Space Needle. It was incredibly romantic, and I had a really wonderful time." I looked down, feeling almost guilty for having had such a good experience, compared to everyone else.

One of the girls laughed. "Was he at least gross-looking? Tell me he was really ugly."

I giggled. "You can judge for yourself," I said. "He's right over there."

Everyone turned to follow my gaze.

"Damon?" said Jen's roommate, Beth. "Your first time was with Damon?" She sounded incredulous.

That's when I remembered I wasn't supposed to tell anyone what happened with Damon. I clapped my hands over my mouth. "Oh my God," I said. "I wasn't supposed to tell anyone that. It was a secret."

"A secret?" repeated Beth. "Why would it be a secret?"

"I don't really know," I explained. "Ada just said I shouldn't tell anyone. Although I guess she didn't mean you guys. It's really just Miss Irma who isn't supposed to know."

"Miss Irma? Why not?"

I was really feeling the whiskey in my veins now. I was having trouble focusing on the conversation and my memories of Damon and what Ada had said about not telling anyone and the feeling of Shawn beneath me and around me. I felt confused. I shook my head, trying to clear my thoughts.

"I'm not sure. Ada just said she'd get in trouble if Miss Irma knew. I shouldn't have said anything. But you guys won't tell, will you?"

Everyone laughed a bit at that, which I didn't understand. One of the boys said, "Believe me. I don't think any of us is so loyal to Miss Irma that we're going to rat each other out to her. There's no good that can come of that. We're much better off standing together."

I nodded, feeling incredibly grateful.

"That's right," I said, remembering Ada's words. "We need to look out for each other."

Just then I caught the distinctive smell of expensive perfume carried toward me on the cold night air.

"What are you doing out here?" came a familiar voice. A voice with a very distinctive Chinese accent.

Everyone got really quiet, and I could almost feel my neighbors sitting up straighter. I kept replaying the conversation in my head, trying to figure out what Irma could have heard.

"Do you think I throw a party every year so you have a chance to talk together?" she went on. "If you want that kind of party, you can throw it yourselves. Right now this is not fun times. You are on the clock, and your job here is to make as many men want you as possible." She paused, but no one moved. "I'm not saying this just for me," she said. "The harder you work, the more we all benefit. Go on, now." She motioned toward the sliding door. "Get back inside and get to work."

A chorus of quiet, shame-faced "Yes, Miss Irma's" came from the group as people got to their feet and headed back toward the door. I stood up, feeling a little unsteady, and as Shawn stood up behind me, I stumbled forward and my feet went out from under me. I tumbled in a heap on the hard concrete of the patio, but it didn't hurt all that much. I said,

"Ow," anyway. Then, as I realized how ridiculous I must look, I started laughing.

Miss Irma froze and stared down at me. "What's going on here?" she said softly, her voice laced with danger. No one said anything, though I noticed a few people making their way quietly toward the door.

"Stand up," said Miss Irma severely. I managed to get to my feet, but the ground seemed to be swaying. I steadied myself on the patio table next to me. Miss Irma leaned in very close to me, looking up into my face. Then she sniffed. "Just as I suspected," she said. "You reek of liquor." She turned to face the others who remained. "And what about the rest of you? What have you been up to out here?"

No one answered.

"Idiots," muttered Miss Irma. "I give you so much, and this is how you repay me. You want us all to be out of a job, I suppose? You would prefer to go back to living on the streets, sleeping in Dumpsters, giving blow jobs for food? Is that what you want?"

Still no one answered, but they shuffled guiltily.

Miss Irma grabbed me by the arm and shook me. "Can you walk? Do you need a hospital?"

My head was still swimming a bit, but I didn't feel that bad. I was just upset that she was yelling at me. "I'm okay," I said quietly.

"I bet," she said. "Fine. Where's your little friend? Ada." She looked around behind her. "Ada!" she called out sharply.

"I'm right here," said Ada, and I had never been so glad to hear her soft, low voice.

"Can you get her home?"

Ada nodded.

"And have you been drinking?"

"No, Miss Irma."

"You are sure?"

"I haven't had anything to drink."

Miss Irma gave her a long sniff. "Fine," she said. "She's your responsibility. Take her home, and if there is any further trouble, you will all answer to me."

After that point, I can put together only bits and pieces. Flashes of me and Ada in a taxi, and trying to find my keys, and then next thing I knew I was waking up in bed and feeling like something you scrape off the bottom of your shoe.

Sun, Feb 15, later

Today has been so awful. Physically I feel a bit better than I did this morning (though still not 100 percent), but emotionally, mentally, I feel completely drained.

When I woke up this morning, based on what I remembered of the night before, I had some little hope that maybe I'd managed to sneak in and get to bed without my parents ever noticing. That was a nice fantasy while it lasted. I guess I temporarily forgot who my parents are. I learned exactly how wrong I was when I got dressed and went downstairs to dig up some breakfast. Mom and Dad were waiting for me, and the minute I saw their faces, I almost turned around and went right back up to my room. The way I was feeling, all I wanted was to drink a huge glass of water and maybe make myself some hot food. The last thing I wanted to deal with was getting yelled at in Chinese.

The weird thing is, they didn't really yell. I guess we're past that now. They didn't even act all that disappointed, like Mom did during our last big conversation. Mostly they just seemed worried. Concerned. Which was even worse. I used to feel guilty every time I did the slightest thing wrong, and I hated that feeling, but it's nothing compared to the guilty feelings I had today.

I sat across from them, starving and parched and feeling trembly and weak, and let the Chinese wash over me, exerting just enough energy to understand what exactly they were worried about. Of course their first question was the obvious: Where were you last night?

So I told them, accurately, if not completely, that I was at a party.

Then they wanted to know if there was alcohol at the party. I guess my drunken state when I got home was less obvious to them than it was to Miss Irma. But then, they have less experience with that type of thing.

Lying seemed pointless, so I told them yes.

They were quiet for a little while. Then my dad said, "Since when do you go to those kinds of parties where there are kegs and no parents?"

I knew it was rhetorical, and my role at this point was just to sit there and look sorry for the shame I had brought on our household, but I couldn't help almost laughing a little, if only internally. It just occurred to me at that moment that my parents were picturing me at a normal high school party. The kind of party that normal high school kids get into normal amounts of trouble for. How would they know any different?

I didn't say anything, but I couldn't help thinking, *If only you knew. It's so much worse than you are even thinking, and you are already so upset.*

Once they had said their piece, I finally got some food and started to feel a little better, so I was going to go back up to my room on the pretense of "doing homework" and take a nice long nap, but Mom and Dad had other ideas. I guess they had been talking while I ate, because afterward they cornered me and had a whole new plan in mind. I don't recall all the details, but I know it involved me never leaving the house again for pretty much anything but school. No extracurriculars, no meetings, and definitely no going out with friends.

And since they can't trust me anymore to tell them the truth about my life, Dad says he's going to meet with all my teachers on Monday to find out what my assignments are, and we'll go over my progress on them all every night. Oh, and I almost forgot the best part—if I don't obey these new restrictions, they're going to send me to Taiwan to live with my grandmother and my aunts!

No way. There's just . . . no way. I can't let that happen. I don't know anyone in Taiwan except a couple of family members, and I barely know the language. It would be just like prison.

And what about Ada? I can't just abandon her. I finally made a real friend. Someone who cares about me, and I care about her. Not just someone who tolerates me sitting with them at lunch or is willing to do group work with me in class. I know Ada acts tough, and she's pretty street-smart, but she is so alone in the world. She needs someone looking out for her.

I have to get away from here. Now.

Sun, Feb 15, later

I've calmed down a bit now. After my last entry I started throwing clothes into a suitcase so I could run away, but as I went through my stuff, I started to think over all the things they had said. I get so frustrated with how they try to control me, and I wish they would just relax and let me make my own decisions about my life, but I guess I have to ask myself if I'm making good decisions.

It's easy to be brave in theory, but some of the stories people told at the party should probably worry me more than they did. What will I do if some client wants to hurt me? If someone wants me to do drugs that leave me confused and not sure how to react? The drinking last night made me realize how out of control you can be when altered by chemicals. In a situation like that, I might not make the same decisions I would make when sober.

Do I have a plan for those circumstances? When I started, Irma said that safety always comes first, and if a situation seemed dangerous, I should leave. But what if I couldn't leave? If I called Anne or Irma or Ada, would they come rescue me? Would they come in time? What if I called the police? Irma wouldn't want that, but should I care? These are difficult questions, and I'm only just realizing I haven't thought them through completely.

I don't know. Maybe I really should just quit. Going back to my old life sounds pretty unappealing, but it's not forever. Once I graduate from high school, I can be on my own if I want. And even if I don't wind up going to college, a high school degree will at least give me a shot at a regular job that wouldn't be so dangerous.

But what about Ada? I can't just walk away from her. And as long as I follow my parents' rules, there will be no room for her in my life.

I guess there's really only one thing that makes sense: I have to keep working for Miss Irma. At least until I can save up enough money for me and Ada to rent an apartment together, like Beth and Jen have. I did some research on it, and I'm pretty close already. It won't take me long to earn that much, plus a bit extra for some security. Then, once we get on our feet, Ada and I can start looking for other kinds of work. I mean, yeah, we'd have to work long hours to make enough money, but normal people do it, so it must be possible. Somehow we'll make it work.

I love my parents, and I don't want to hurt them. But for now Ada needs me more. I just have to make sure I toe their line closely enough so they don't ship me off to Taiwan before I can put this plan into action.

Wed, Feb 18

My date yesterday got a little out of control. According to Anne, it was just supposed to be a normal, straightforward date. Easy peasy, no special requests. But when I got there, the client had lines of what I think was cocaine laid out, and he wanted me to do it with him.

I froze, just running through everything Ada had told me and trying to figure out what I should do. *Stay away from drugs so you don't wind up like Jen,* except I just saw Jen at that party and she seemed okay. *Some drugs are really bad, but others are basically okay, like pot and alcohol.* Which kind was cocaine? I was pretty sure it was a bad one, but then Ada had mentioned doing it a few times, so how bad could it be? Ada said it was always okay to say no, if you didn't want to do it, and I remembered how awful I felt after just a bit of whiskey and pot at the Valentine's party and how out of control they had made me feel. I really didn't want to put myself in that position with a client. But then, Miss Irma would say it's important to keep the client happy. And Ada had said they consider it rude if you say no.

The client was giving me a weird look at this point, and I realized I'd been standing there for way too long. He offered his straw to me again, and finally I decided I'd split the difference and just do a little bit, for politeness' sake.

It was a really weird feeling. The whole concept of sniffing something other than air into my nose was hard to get over, and it took me a couple of tries to even figure out the mechanics of it. Then, once I got it to work, I suddenly felt like I had a cold. My nose got all weird and congested, and there was this really wretched taste in my throat, hard and bitter like a chewed-up aspirin. Why do drugs taste so bad? But I guess that's not why people do them.

To tell the truth, I didn't really feel that much. Like, I didn't feel different the way I did with pot and alcohol. I did notice that I was talking a lot, when normally I talk the very bare minimum in these situations.

But that wasn't really a big deal. The problem was that the guy was taking forever. Technically, it's supposed to be an hour, and in the past I've had some clients go over a bit and I never said anything because I didn't care enough to make a stink about it. But these days I really need to make sure I'm home by the end of the school day, because I know that if I mess up even a little bit, my parents are prepared to ship me off to Taiwan. And I can't let that happen.

So I kept trying to hurry things along, but this guy just kept going. I wasn't sure exactly how much time had passed because I couldn't reach my phone, and from my angle I couldn't see the room's alarm clock. It started to feel like it had been a really long time, though, and I just wanted him to finish. But you can't exactly tell people to hurry up in this line of work—that would ruin the fantasy.

So I tried to suggest a different position, trying to make it sound like a sexy idea rather than a desperate attempt to speed things up, and he was just like, "No, this is the only position that works," and I could tell he was getting frustrated too. So I was trying to be encouraging, and then he says, "It's this fucking condom. I'll never be able to come with a rubber. I need to take it off." And I'm like . . . what? I didn't even know what to say. Condoms are required, obviously, Miss Irma tells all the clients that. Did he think I was insane?

Finally he got off me and I got off the bed and started to get dressed. I'd had enough of him. I just wanted to leave, but that pissed him off. First he couldn't believe it, and he tried to convince me to come back to bed. When that didn't work, he started yelling. "Fuck you, you fucking whore," and all that. And it's not like I've never been called a whore before, and it's not like it's inaccurate, but something about the way he said it upset me, and it scared me too. He just seemed out of control, unpredictable, and I was scared to be alone with him much longer.

So I kept getting dressed and getting my stuff together, and then he started really screaming at me. He hadn't touched me, and he wasn't being violent, but he was in my face screaming about how I can't leave him there with a fucking hard-on and he didn't pay three hundred dollars to have to finish off by hand. And how I was a shitty whore and he wasn't going to pay one cent and that I was lucky he wasn't charging me for all the coke

I did (even though I only did one line!). Then he called me a cokehead whore and said what could you expect from fucking crackhead whores (I was trying to figure out how I suddenly changed from being a cokehead to a crackhead), and how Miss Irma promised her whores were clean but clearly I was just a fucking addict and he was going to tell her to fire me. He was blocking my way to the door through most of this rant, and at some point I started crying a little.

This is the most ridiculous thing, but what started me crying is when he said I was a shitty whore who was no good at my job. Because I am good! I really do work hard at this. I've heard the jokes about how easy it is to make money on your back, but let me tell you, it is not easy. In addition to be dangerous and scary, it's actually a lot of work. And only a pretty small percentage of it is on my back. I always work hard and bring 100 percent to everything I do, and I just wish people appreciated the effort I put in.

He kept me there for quite some time, yelling at me for being a whore, for being a bad whore, for crying, for being a drug addict . . . anything he could think of. Called me fat and ugly too. And I just kept asking over and over, "Please let me through. Can I get through?" At one point I even started to take my clothes off again, in hopes that if I could just finish the date he would let me go, but that set him off again and he kept saying he didn't even want me and that I was no good and that he'd have more fun with a blow-up doll.

Anyway, finally he seemed to run out of steam and he wandered off to get a cigarette, so I made my escape. By then I was more than an hour late to get home, so I took a cab instead of wasting time on the bus. When I got home my mom asked where I'd been, and I didn't even bother to lie because I knew she would check any story I gave her about the bus breaking down or whatever. So I just didn't say anything and went up to my room and cried.

Today was awful, and now I'm terrified that Mom will use my outburst as an excuse to send me away. I better go downstairs with some story and make it up to her. But hey, at least I have a worst-date story now.

Thurs, Feb 19

Just when I thought things couldn't get any worse.

I went by Miss Irma's office today to pick up my fee, and Anne said she didn't have anything for me. I pointed out to her that I had an appointment clearly marked on the schedule and I needed to be paid for it, but she just said that if I thought there was some kind of mistake, I was free to take it up with Miss Irma. And she pointed me to Irma's door.

I didn't like the sound of that, but what choice did I have?

I went in to see her. Miss Irma started in right away about how furious the client was and how he had complained about me, so I tried to defend myself. I explained about how he had made me do drugs. Miss Irma asked if he had held me down and forced me, and I had to admit that he hadn't, but I did tell her about how he wouldn't let me go and how he was being abusive. Then she asked if he hit me, and I had to say no. She asked if he injured me in any way, but he hadn't.

So then she lectured me for a while about how important it is to keep the client happy at all times. And at the end she added, "Unless you are in danger," like it was an afterthought.

"I was!" I said. "He was threatening me and he wouldn't let me leave. And I was . . . I was scared."

Miss Irma was silent for a few moments, just looking at me over the top of her glasses.

"Of course," she said at last, "if you were in danger, you did the right thing. You must always leave if you don't feel safe."

I sighed with relief. "So you'll pay me?" I said.

Miss Irma smiled coldly. "How can I pay you if I did not get paid? Be reasonable."

"But you said—"

"The most important thing is to be safe. Surely your safety is more important to you than money."

"Yes," I said, "but—"

"You did the right thing. We all have to look after ourselves in this business."

"I thought . . . I thought we look out for each other."

Miss Irma laughed. "Who gave you that idea?" she said.

So on top of that being the worst date ever, I'm not even getting paid for it. And in fact, I'm in the hole since I blew money on the taxi home.

Fri, Feb 20

Chinese New Year. Normally this is my favorite time of the year, with so much good food, and firecrackers, and decorating the house. . . . But it's hard to celebrate family and community when I've spent the last few months making my parents hate me.

I'm really trying these days to stay in line and not give them a reason to make good on their threat, but it's hard. They just don't trust me anymore. Not that I can really blame them.

I know my parents would say that none of this would have happened if I could only have been the good, obedient girl they wanted, but sometimes I wonder if the problem is really that I've always been too obedient. Trying to live up to their expectations of the dutiful daughter nearly drove me crazy. I was living so much for other people, it hardly felt like living at all. Then I traded all that in for the "bad girl" life of a call girl, but even there, I spend all my time trying to be good, trying to be what people want, to fulfill their fantasies, to live up to Miss Irma's expectations, not to disappoint anyone. Where am I in all of this? What about me?

And what happens when all the people I am trying to obey disagree with each other? Or when obeying one person leads me in a bad direction? At a certain point, I have to start trusting myself and doing what I think is right, because the people around me don't always have my best interests at heart, or know what's best for me.

But then, how can I follow my own mind when I don't even know it? And how can I make the best decisions for myself when there's so much about the world I don't know?

I don't know, but after that last date, I am thinking again about quitting. Not for my parents, not for Ada, but because it might be the right thing for me. Maybe it's time to stop living in this crazy fantasy. Because it is starting to seem not so fantastic.

Wed, Feb 25

I haven't gotten called for another date since last payday. I'm guessing Miss Irma is mad at me for talking back and not just accepting whatever she says as law. But you know what? I'm just as glad. I'm still having nightmares about that last client, and when I even think about going out on another date, I just start to feel sick and panicky and my skin goes clammy. So I don't regret being left out of the loop for now.

The more I think about it, the more I realize I don't want to go back to that ever again. I had already been planning to quit at some point. I was just trying to save up enough money to have a nice amount for me and Ada. Since I didn't get paid for that last date, I have a little bit less than I'd been hoping for, but maybe it's enough. Maybe it has to be.

I'm going to call Ada and tell her about my plan. If she wants to talk me out of it, she can try, but I hope that she wants what I want. I just want to walk away from this mess and start over.

Wed, Feb 25, later

Just got off the phone with Ada. I'm still kind of . . . confused though.

I wanted to tell her my plan and hear her say, "Yes, we can do it. Let's make a new life for ourselves." Better yet, I wanted to hear that she had a better plan than mine, one that would solve all our problems. Or if she couldn't offer me any of that yet, I expected her to at least talk me out of quitting, so we could keep saving up. But nothing went quite how I expected.

"I'm glad you called," she said immediately upon answering the phone. "I need to talk to you."

"I need to talk to you too," I said, and before she could get in another word, I started in about my little dream of us living together in an apartment, getting real, legal jobs to support ourselves, and not getting pushed around by parents or Miss Irma or the clients anymore.

I kept talking for a while before I realized Ada hadn't said anything.

"Ada?" I said. "Are you there?" Still silence, but I could hear her breathing on the other end of the line. "Tell me what I should do, Ada. Should we quit? Or should we keep on with Miss Irma? I know we can trust her. I know she would never put us in any real harm, but—"

Ada barked out a humorless laugh.

"What?" I said. "What's going on?"

"Quit," she replied.

"What?"

"You should quit. You have to." Her voice sounded odd, broken. "I'm asking . . . I'm begging you."

"What's going on, Ada?"

"Nothing," she said with a sort of grim finality. "Nothing you need to worry about. I'm taking care of it, okay? It wasn't your fault, and it's not your problem. So don't worry about it."

"Okay, but Ada, did something happen? You sound upset." Actually, she sounded more than upset. She sounded scared.

164

"I'll be fine," she said. "I know what I'm doing. Just stay the hell away from Irma. Don't take any more dates. Don't respond if she contacts you. Ignore her, and she can't hurt you. In fact, take that stupid phone and throw it in the bay, like you wanted to that other time. I should have let you then. I should have made you do it then. Promise me you'll do it now."

"Okay. I promise. What's gotten into you? Why are you talking like this? Are you okay? Can I help?"

"I can't talk about it," she said, and hung up.

What was all that about? I'm worried about her.

Fri, Feb 27

I wish I knew what was going on with Ada. I've called and texted her a few times since the other day, but she's not answering. Not that that's all that unusual with her. Sometimes if she has a crisis with her mom or something, I won't hear from her for a couple of days. When I'm not working, we don't necessarily interact that much. And she's tough and smart. If anyone can take care of herself, it's Ada.

Still, something about my last conversation with her . . . I wish I knew what was going on. She sounded nervous and upset. A little desperate, even. But I trust her. And she did give me the answer I was looking for. I wanted her to tell me if I should quit the business or keep going a little longer, and she told me what I think I needed to hear. It's always tempting to work a little longer, turn just one more trick, in hopes of easy money, but the money's not so easy, and as I learned from my last date, sometimes there's no money at all.

I'm glad she said what she did. Quitting's hard, but I think it was the right decision. That lifestyle is not healthy. It grinds you down. I didn't even do it very long, and it has already taken its toll on me. And if I'm not doing it, at least it's easier for me to be obedient to my parents, so I don't have to worry about them sending me to Taiwan.

I just wish I knew what Ada thought about the other part of the plan . . . about us moving in together. All the time I was dreaming it, I don't think I ever allowed myself to wonder what I would do if Ada said no. If she wasn't interested. But what if she's sick of me? What if she'd rather live with someone like Jen? Someone cooler and more sophisticated? What if she just wants me to quit because she has figured out I'm not cut out for that kind of life, and she wants to just hang out with people more like her?

I don't know. Maybe she's right. Maybe to Ada it's really obvious how stupid my plan is and how I'm just too sheltered and ignorant to survive on my own. Maybe she knows I could never make it work and was trying to let me down easy.

Mon, March 2

I am trying very hard to be good, but it really sucks being on lockdown. My parents are sticking to their plan of not letting me go anywhere or do anything except for schoolwork. I'm so far behind in everything. I've missed so much. As overwhelmed as I used to feel by school, it's ten times worse now.

And it's not just the work. Back at the beginning of the year, I thought I knew what it meant to be invisible. I felt like a loser, an outcast, like no one really noticed me. I didn't know how good I had it back then. I had my regular table at lunch and I was in all those activities—no matter how I felt, I was part of the fabric of the school.

That's all gone now. I'm embarrassed to talk to my old friends, and they don't really seem to miss me. And Ada hasn't been coming to school, so other than answering the occasional question in class, I basically don't talk to or interact with anyone all day long. I'm like a ghost, haunting the halls of the high school.

There is something comforting in the ritual of it, though. I mean, as bad as it is, at least I don't have to worry about people assaulting me or making me do drugs I don't want. It's boring and frustrating, but it's not so scary. Scary was exciting at first, but I think I had enough. I'm still having nightmares about that last client.

I'm starting to get worried about Ada, too. I haven't heard from her in almost a week. I know she told me to throw Miss Irma's phone in the ocean, and I was going to sneak out of school and do it the other day, but I decided not to. What if Ada tries to contact me on it? She has my other number, but if she's in trouble, she might not have a chance to try both numbers, and if there is any chance she might try to reach me through Irma's phone, well, I'd never forgive myself if I wasn't there for her when she needed me.

It does make me nervous when I see it in my purse, but so far Irma hasn't contacted me on it since our last meeting, and that suits me just fine.

Mon, March 2, later

I convinced my parents to let me start swimming again! Not with the team. I don't know if I even want that anymore, but I really miss having something to do that was just for me. One thing in my life where I don't have to do what people tell me or care what they want. When I'm swimming, it's just me and the water.

I told them that my body was going to atrophy if they kept me locked up all the time, so they finally decided that I could go to the YMCA pool in the evenings. Only an hour, though, so it won't interfere with my homework. And they'll drop me off and pick me up. That's what they say, anyway. I know they're really afraid of me sneaking off.

I'm so excited to get back in the water again!

Fri, March 6

I feel gross.

I don't know what to do. I need to talk to someone, but who? I wish I could talk to Ada, but I still can't get in touch with her.

I thought things were supposed to be okay now. I thought if I just stuck to my parents' plan and behaved myself and did everything they told me to, I'd be safe and I'd never have to deal with the scary situations that hooking put me in. But it's like I can't go back to who I was. I should explain what happened. Maybe that will help me calm down.

I've been going to the pool every day all week now. It was nice. It didn't make everything better, but for an hour a day, at least I knew no one would be telling me what to do or hassling me or expecting stuff from me. That's what I thought, anyway.

So today I was doing some laps, not even trying for speed or perfect form or anything, just enjoying the feel of the water on my skin. And it was just a bit before closing, so I had the whole pool to myself. I was vaguely aware that there was someone standing nearby, but I didn't really pay attention, because I was off in my own little blue world. Soon I noticed the person had gotten in the water and was swimming next to me. He was really good, matching me easily, stroke for stroke, which is unusual given that most people at this pool are old folks or little kids.

So I stopped when I finished my lap and I looked up, and guess who it was.

Tyler Adams.

I wasn't expecting that at all. I felt like someone had just knocked the wind out of me. And even weirder than running into him at the pool was that he was actually looking at me and smiling, as if he knew who I was. Which was weird but sort of . . . nice, after everything that happened. These past couple of weeks I've been so isolated and alone, not speaking to anyone except my parents and everyone at school looking through me like I'm invisible. It felt nice to have someone treat me like I'm human.

And I couldn't help remembering how I used to feel about him. It's not like I could just instantly go back to that little-girl crush, not after everything I've been through, but there's no denying how good Tyler looks. A lot better-looking than the men I'm used to being with these days.

So we got to talking. I worried it would be superawkward and I would act like an idiot, just like I used to, but I guess at least one positive side effect of my recent career is I am less tongue-tied around boys. We talked about the swim team a bit and how they were doing, and I gave him a lame excuse for why I wasn't swimming with them anymore. Eventually I was like, "I better hit the shower. My ride will be here soon." And he put a hand on my arm and said, "Don't. Not yet." And he gave me this smile. I've seen him give that smile to other girls, but I never dreamed he would use it on me.

I admit, I melted a little. I stayed in the pool, and when he ducked into my lane and pressed up close to me, I didn't stop him. It was late, but the water was warm and the lights were glowing and it was almost romantic. And then he pulled in closer and started kissing me.

I was surprised, but too turned-on to really think too much about it. All that was going through my head was, *I wonder if it can really be this easy.* Tyler wasn't a client, and he wasn't twice my age or more, and he wasn't paunchy or bald. He's just a cute boy my age who likes me and wants to kiss me. And maybe I deserve that, after all I've been through. Maybe that would be the perfect antidote to all the gross stuff I've had to do for the past few months. Maybe I can just be with Tyler and be normal and happy, and it can all be uncomplicated.

That was what I was thinking until he stopped kissing me and started whispering in my ear. At first it was nice things, or nice enough. He was telling me how sexy I was and how much he wanted to touch me. He was moving pretty fast, I know, but the truth is, I wanted to touch him too.

But then he started saying other things like, "I bet you know all kinds of tricks. I bet you could make it good." I didn't know what he was talking about, but I started to feel uncomfortable. He was pressed all up against me now, and he said, "Why don't you show me what you know?"

So I was like, "What do you mean?"

"Don't play coy," he said. "I know what you are. I saw you hanging around with Ada Culver. You're like her, aren't you? You used to be a little nerd, but she made you a whore just like her."

I didn't like that. I didn't like him talking about Ada that way, so I stopped kissing and touching him and tried to wriggle away, but he had me pressed pretty firmly against the wall of the pool with his arms around me like a cage.

"Come on," he said in a whisper. "Don't try to act like you're some virgin." His lips were moving against my ear, and I could feel him pressed up between my legs. And he started whispering to me about Ada, how he had found out about her. He told me his uncle was one of her clients, and he had told Tyler all about her one day when he was drunk.

"My uncle's a real sleazebag," he said. "He told me all the things he did with Ada, all the things he made her do to him.

172

Why don't you show me what she taught you? I can pay, if you want. Then you'll be my little whore to do whatever I want with."

For a while I was just frozen, listening to him whisper those horrible words in my ear. I didn't know what to think. I felt like such an idiot, like I had been so naive. For so long I'd let myself believe I was living in two different worlds . . . that I had these two identities, but they were totally separate. On one hand, I was a highly paid call girl. On the other, I was an ordinary high school student, unpopular but high achieving. But that was a mistake, or a lie, because it was only one life all along. The same stinking life.

If Tyler knows about me, how many other people know? How many has he told? How many will he tell? What happens when Jenny and Eiko and John find out? What about the teachers? And my parents?

Finally I came back to myself and shoved Tyler away from me. He let me go without a fight, but his smug laughter echoed through the empty hall as I dragged myself out of the water.

Since then I have showered and toweled off and returned home and crawled into bed, but somehow I still can't stop shivering. What do I do now? Throughout this whole thing, I've always believed that there was a safety net. If I wanted to, I could pretend this was all a bad dream and just go back to the ordinary life I had before. But that's not possible anymore. Tyler had called me a dirty little whore. What's the point in getting offended? It was true. These aren't just words. This is who I am.

Sat, March 7

My phone is ringing. The pink phone.

It's like everything I have tried to do to walk away from that existence is falling apart around me. First that horrible experience with Tyler, so I don't even feel safe in the water anymore. I told my parents I don't want to go back to the pool again, and of course they are confused since I bargained so hard for this. Why don't I want it all of a sudden? And what can I say to them? But what does it matter even? They are going to find out all about me soon anyway. Now that Tyler knows, it's only a matter of time.

And now Irma's phone is ringing. And it's not Ada.

I don't understand it because usually when they want to set up a date, I get a text from Anne, or sometimes from Irma. And only if I ignore that, then they'll call. But there was no text this time, just a ringing phone. Even though I haven't heard from Ada in more than a week, I remember her last words to me. I remember how she told me not to talk to Irma ever again, to quit, to ignore all her attempts to contact me, to throw the phone into the bay.

So I won't answer. They called back three times in twenty minutes, but now it's been two hours with no calls, so maybe I am off the hook.

Sat, March 7, later

Phone is ringing again. I'm just staring at it, not answering. I mean, for all they know, I could have thrown it into the bay. I don't have to answer it.

It's weird, though. . . . Somehow, every time it rings, I feel like Miss Irma can see me.

Mon, March 9

They found me. I guess it didn't matter that I didn't answer the phone, because they just found another way to get to me. Now I'm in a mess, but maybe I can help Ada at least.

The phone kept ringing yesterday, and this morning while I was in school. It was getting more and more frequent, but I kept ignoring it.

Then, after school today, I was walking toward the buses and I happened to glance over to where Miss Irma's cars used to pick up me and Ada to take us to our dates. And there it was: Irma's car. At the sight of it, I sort of froze and stared. I certainly didn't have a date scheduled, and Ada hadn't been on the school grounds in almost two weeks, so who was it there for? I wondered if someone else at the school had started hooking. Maybe one of the younger kids. But some part of me knew that was not what was going on. I just had this dark sense, like something bad was about to happen, and all I could think to do was get away. I put my head down and forced myself to keep walking toward the buses, but I didn't make it more than a few steps before I heard someone call my name. More on instinct than by choice, I stopped and turned.

It was a big, solidly built man. Definitely not someone usually on the school grounds, but he looked strangely familiar. He said my name again, and that's when it clicked into place—I'd seen him at the Valentine's party. He was one of Miss Irma's security force. The people Ada had referred to as "goons." The people Ada had warned me about.

"You better come with me," said the man.

My feet felt frozen to the pavement. Everything in my body was screaming at me to get away from this situation. As long as I was here at the school, this crowd of students swarming around me, there wasn't much this man could do to me. Following him into that car, I'd be putting myself at risk. Of what, I wasn't sure. I couldn't think of anything Miss Irma would want to do to me, or why, but I couldn't ignore Ada's warning. Something had scared her, and that was enough to scare me.

Again he asked me to come with him. Calmly, quietly, but with just a hint of a threat.

I wanted to tell him no, but I couldn't find the words, so I just shook my head and turned away, back toward the buses. Then I heard his voice again.

"It's about Ada."

I turned around. "Is she all right?"

"I think you'd better come with me."

So I went. What choice did I have? Yes, it was risky and scary and I had no clue what I was getting myself into, but if there was any chance of finding out what happened to Ada, of helping her if she was in trouble, there was no way I was going to refuse that.

Once at the downtown office, Anne met me and showed me in to Miss Irma.

"I'm so glad you came," she said. "I got worried when you ignored my messages."

"I'm sorry about that," I said. "I can return the phone. I've . . . I've decided to get out of the business."

Irma looked slightly surprised. "Of course," she said. "You are free to leave anytime you want, as I said. But maybe you should keep the phone for now." That sounded a bit ominous. "It is inconvenient when people lose track of their phones," Irma went on. "You know I worry about my employees. I like to check on them, make sure they are okay. I'm very worried about Ada, because she doesn't answer her phone this past week. But perhaps you can tell me where she is."

My heart sank. I had hoped Irma would tell me where Ada was.

"I don't know anything about Ada," I said. "I haven't heard from her in a while."

"I see," said Irma. "Are you sure, though? Think hard."

What could I say or do to convince Miss Irma I had even less information than she did? When I didn't answer right away, Miss Irma changed her tack.

"Don't play dumb. You're in this together."

That had me confused.

"In what?" I said.

"I am not unreasonable," Irma went on. "I'm not some violent gangster. I'm a businesswoman. I respect free enterprise. I admire Ada's ambition to go into business for herself. We all have to start somewhere. But one thing I do not accept is poaching clients. Damon is my client, not yours. You girls think you are the attraction, but you are easily replaced. I earned my cut of your little scheme, and I want it."

So that's what this was about: Damon. I should have guessed. But how did she find out? Of course, my big mouth at the Valentine's party. She could have heard me, or anyone there could have blabbed to her. So this really was all my fault, then.

"We didn't earn anything," I rushed to explain to Irma. "It wasn't like that. I swear. It was a freebie. Ada was just setting a couple of friends up on a date. We didn't charge him."

I only realized once the words left my mouth how unlikely my story sounded, even though it was true. The look on Miss Irma's face showed that she was thinking the same thing.

"Really?" she said with more than a hint of sarcasm. "A whore and her virgin friend seduce a rich young client and no money changed hands?" Miss Irma shook her head. "Maybe an innocent idiot like you could wander into this situation by accident, but Ada is not so stupid. She knows very well the price of a virgin. She's far too clever to let that slide, even for a friend."

"I promise you it's true," I said a little desperately. "There was no money."

"Save your pleas," she said with an airy wave of the hand. "It doesn't matter one way or the other. It's not my fault if you were too stupid to charge him. I'm still owed the money I should have gotten. Ada owes me a debt and she ran out on it, so now you owe me a debt. Either pay me, or find Ada for me so she can pay me. Your choice."

So that was it. That was why Ada wasn't returning my calls. But that meant that if I could solve this problem, if I could settle her debt, she could come back.

I asked Miss Irma how much it was. When I heard the amount, I had a moment of relief combined with hopelessness. I have it . . . or almost. It's just a little bit more than I have saved for the apartment I was going to get with Ada. But handing it over to Miss Irma means the death of that fantasy, once and for all.

Well, since Ada's not speaking to me, I guess it was pretty much dead anyway.

I told Miss Irma I could get her the money. She looked surprised, and more than a little suspicious.

"You can? When?"

"I can pay you now," I said. "Or tomorrow," I corrected myself. "I just need to run home and get it."

Irma looked at me closely.

"You've been saving your pennies," she observed. I didn't say anything. "I underestimated you," she went on. "You're not as stupid as I thought, though you should pick your friends more carefully in the future. You can save all the money in the world, but it won't be any good if your friends skip town and leave you with their debts."

My face burned at the insult, but I tried to stay focused. "Ada skipped town?" This was the information I had come for

Miss Irma shrugged delicately. "As far as I know. My people have searched the whole city for her. If you think you know where she might be, by all means, hunt her down. As long as I get my money, it's all the same to me."

I have an appointment to drop off the necessary cash at Miss Irma's office in just under twenty-four hours. I've pulled my little savings from under my bed and counted it all out on the covers. I'm almost there but not quite. I hate to do this, but I think I'm going to have to sneak some bills out of my mom's mah-jongg jar. I know it's wrong, but I don't even know what Miss Irma's goons might do to me or Ada if I don't pay up. And I don't really want to find out.

Can I really do this? I have the money, but it's every last bit I saved. All my dreams for the future and all my hopes of escaping this awful life. What do I do after this? Go back to Miss Irma and start taking dates again, try to build it back up? But what's the point, with Ada gone? Without the money and without her, I don't even know what my dream is anymore.

Can it really be that what Miss Irma said is true? That Ada abandoned me to deal with this debt on my own, so she wouldn't have to? Of course, she did warn me not to talk to Miss Irma ever again. I guess she was hoping I could just avoid the problem and slip quietly back into my old life. But she must have known Miss Irma's goons would come after me. Why didn't she just come to me? If she had told me the situation, we could have fixed it together.

I called and texted her to let her know that I am paying her debt and that she's in the clear, but I just keep getting voice mail. I don't understand why she doesn't respond.

This is driving me crazy. I have to know what happened to her. I'm sure Miss Irma's goons have already checked Ada's house, but maybe her mom will be able to tell me something. It can't hurt to ask.

Mon, March 9, later

I'm at Ada's house. It was stupid to come here. I don't know what I expected to learn. Obviously Ada wasn't going to just be sitting here, watching TV. And if I was hoping her mom would be able to give me some clues, it doesn't look like that's going to happen.

When I got here, it was almost eerie how normal the place looked. Just sitting there in the gathering shadows of dusk, like all the other houses on the streets. The lights were on, giving it a cozy glow, and the twilight hid the shabbiness and disrepair of the place. I knocked on the door and waited a bit but didn't hear anything. I started to wonder if Ada's mom could have gone out and left all the lights on. I was about to give up and walk away when I heard a sound from inside the house. I held my breath and listened. Someone was definitely inside. Heart hammering, I raised my hand to knock once more, but just then I heard another sound, this time much closer. A door latch.

The door opened, but only a crack. The chain was still done up, preventing the door from opening more than a couple of inches. Behind it stood a haggard, anxious-eyed woman who I assumed to be Ada's mother.

"Hi!" I said brightly, trying to seem as nonthreatening as possible. "I'm a friend of Ada's. I used to come by and visit sometimes, but I don't think we ever met."

Ada's mom didn't say anything, but her eyes slid up and down my body, drawing in every detail. I couldn't tell if I was winning her over.

"I was just wondering if . . ." I hesitated. How much did Ada's mom know? How much should I give away, and how much should I hold back? I decided to keep it simple for now. "Do you know where she is?"

"Do you know where she is?" she said in a cracked, wavering voice.

I shifted uncomfortably. I honestly couldn't tell if she was asking me about Ada's whereabouts or just repeating what I said, as if she barely spoke the language but was trying out the sounds.

"No," I answered at last, trying to keep my voice calm and neutral. "I don't know, but I am looking for her. Do you remember when you last saw her? Do you know how to get in touch with her?"

"You're not one of them, are you?" she said. "You don't seem like one of them. Unless you're trying to trick me."

"One of who?" I wondered if she'd had some run-in with Miss Irma's goons. That might explain some of her behavior. "Have people been here, looking for Ada? Other people?"

"I think they got her," she said, leaning forward to whisper conspiratorially. "They were looking for her and then they must have come and taken her away."

"Taken her away?" I said. "Who took her away? When? What did they look like?"

I didn't want to stress her out or put too much pressure on her clearly fragile psyche, but I had to know what she had seen. I was feeling frantic. Was she talking about Miss Irma's goons? But if they had come and taken Ada away, why would they ask me where she is? Who else would be looking for Ada? Who would take her away? The police? Or was it possible that she was mixed up in something else?

"Please," I said. "Try to remember. Who took her away? If you remember anything at all . . ."

The woman shook her head. "You should stay away, if you know what's good for you. It's dangerous here."

"Dangerous?"

"We're being watched," she whispered hoarsely. "You have to act normal because they are always watching."

"Who is watching? The people who took Ada?" Instinctively, I jerked my head around to look up and down the street, but everything looked normal.

"She might be working for them. I didn't want to believe it either, not at first, but I don't think I can trust her."

She had figured out Ada was working for Miss Irma, then. That made some sense, even if she was confused about the details.

"Did she tell you where she was going?"

"She went with them, or they took her, or she is spying on me for them. I don't think I can trust her. She was always watching me, but I don't think it's her fault. They got to her."

"Who got to her?" I asked, growing desperate for any real information.

"Tom," said the woman in an anxious whisper.

"Tom?" I repeated. "Tom who?"

"He got to her, just like he got to Katie. Tom and Angelina and Miley. They're planning something. It's got something to do with me, but I don't know what yet. I tried to get Ada to help, but she was working for them already, watching me and reporting to them. I used to follow their messages to each other on the Internet, but then I realized they could see me too, so I had to stop. I turned it off, but that made them angry. That's when they got to Ada."

With a sick feeling in my stomach, I suddenly remembered all the celebrity gossip magazines I had noticed when I had visited Ada in the past. It was impossible to tell how much of my conversation with Ada's mom had been based in fact and how much based in her paranoid delusions. Ada had told me that her mom had "episodes," and she had hinted that they were getting worse. It seemed as though she was in the middle of a bad one.

I wondered if that was part of why Ada had left. Maybe even more than her debt to Miss Irma. If her mom had turned on her, had decided that Ada was part of some master conspiracy against her, that could be pretty hard to live with.

In any case, it was becoming pretty clear that I wasn't going to get any solid information out of Ada's mom, and the longer I talked to her, the more I risked her slotting me in with whoever else might be out to "get" her. I thanked her for her time and let her close the door. Now I'm sitting on the garden wall under a streetlamp, trying to decide what to do next. I guess this is a dead end, like I thought it would be. I'll try texting Ada one more time, letting her know I'm here. If she ever does check her messages, she'll at least know I cared enough to look.

That's weird. Something just caught my eye. Now I'm not even sure if I really saw anything, or if Ada's mom's delusions have gone to my head, but I could have sworn I saw a flash of light from that window. The window to Ada's bedroom. It's the only room in the house with no light on, but it looks like something flickered in there. Would it be crazy if I crept over there and peeked in the window?

Mon, March 9, later

Wow. That was the craziest thing I've ever done. Well, other than getting paid to have sex with strangers. Maybe my life is so weird now, I've lost all sense of proportion.

I went over to Ada's window after I saw that flash and I peered in, but it was all dark in there and I could barely make anything out. I don't even know exactly what I was expecting to see, but it definitely didn't look like Ada was in there. I was about to give up and go back home, but I couldn't stop turning the question over in my mind. What had I seen flash in there? Was it just my imagination? What would give off that kind of blue light?

Then I noticed the light again, but this time it wasn't coming from Ada's room. It was coming from my purse. It was my phone lighting up as a text came through. My parents, wanting to know where the hell I was. My first thought was panic that they had noticed I was gone too long, but before I could think too much about that, I realized something else. The flash of light I had seen had to be Ada's phone!

I tried Ada's phone again, calling this time. Sure enough,

a blueish light came on, illuminating Ada's room dimly as I listened to the ringtone. So Ada had abandoned her phone at home, which meant all my messages had gone unread. I felt my heart sink a little at this realization, but then another thought occurred to me. If I had Ada's phone, it might give me another clue as to where she was hiding.

Not really dreaming it would work, I gave the window a little shove and it moved. Ada must have left it unlocked. I checked around, looking up and down the street, my heart beating wildly at what I was about to do. But everything seemed quiet. As silently as possible, I slid the window up and hoisted myself up and inside. I gave a quick look around for any other possible clues, but I didn't want to stick around too long and risk getting caught by Ada's mom, so I just grabbed the phone and got out of there.

Now I'm on a bus headed back home and not totally sure what to do with my trophy. I thought it might be useful to see who Ada had spoken to last, but the last calls in her logs were me and Miss Irma. No new information there. Should I just start calling random people from her address book? I don't know if that might make things better or worse.

Jen's number is in here. At least I kind of know her. I'm not sure what she could possibly know that would be a help at this point, but it's worth a shot.

Mon, March 9, later

I texted Jen twice and called once, but she's not responding. Why doesn't anyone pick up their phones? What do I do? Do I give up?

I'm almost home now, but the minute I walk in the door, my parents are going to start talking about sending me away. How can I let them do that when Ada is so clearly in trouble? I've got to do something.

Should I try another number? Or Jen's address is in here. I suppose I could go over there. Maybe she'll be more willing to talk to me face-to-face.

Mon, March 9, later

That didn't go exactly as planned, but at least I have a new direction now.

I made my way over to South Downtown and found my way to Jen's place through a maze of old abandoned warehouses. When I found the building, it had a roll-up door, and I wondered if the owners even knew it was being used as living space. I banged on the door for a while until finally Jen's roommate, Beth, came down. I asked if Jen was there, but Beth just said, "Nope."

"Do you know when she'll be back?"

"Nope."

I was getting frustrated.

"Can I come in and wait for her, then? I really need to talk to her."

"You could be waiting a while," said Beth, lounging calmly in the doorway. "Jen's in jail. She got picked up last night."

I have to admit, that was the last thing I was expecting.

"For what?" I asked.

Beth laughed. "What do you think? Or were you unaware that your chosen profession is illegal? This could happen to any of us."

"Sure," I said, "but we're not streetwalkers. And Irma . . ."

"Irma only protects people as long as they're useful to her," Beth said, her voice hard. "Irma kicked Jen off the payroll two weeks ago because of her drug problem, so she started posting ads for her services online. One of the clients she got was a setup. They had sex, she asks for her money, and the guy whips out a badge instead."

"A cop would really do that?"

"You watch too much TV," she said. "Not all cops are heroes."

"Will she go to prison?"

"At sixteen?" said Beth. "Not likely. Probably she'll have to go to juvie, or she'll get stuck in the social services system or something. Either way, it will be a pain in the ass. What really sucks is how am I going to make rent without a roommate?"

At this point, I was almost on the point of crying from

frustration and worry. I leaned against the doorframe with all the fight gone out of me.

Beth narrowed her eyes. "What do you want with Jen, anyway? You guys aren't friends."

"I don't want Jen. I want Ada. I mean, I'm looking for her. She disappeared."

"She's not answering her phone?"

"No." I held up Ada's phone. "Look, do you know anything? I know you're not her biggest fan, but this is important."

Beth huffed a breath. "I bet it is. Everyone's always worried about Ada. I wouldn't be that worried about her. She knows how to take care of herself."

"What do you mean? If you know something, you have to tell me."

"You shouldn't trust her, you know. She'll take advantage of you just like she does everyone else."

I shook my head. "She wouldn't do that."

"Wouldn't she? You'll realize someday that I did you a favor. Ada was manipulating you and trying to put one over on Irma. She's done it before."

"A favor?" I repeated. "What kind of . . . ?" Suddenly I understood. "It was you," I said slowly. "You heard me talking at the Valentine's party about what happened between me and Damon. You went to Miss Irma."

"I wasn't trying to cause trouble for you," said Beth, looking sullen. "I was trying to protect you. Ada's a bad egg. You're better off without her."

"You're wrong. Ada would never do anything . . ."

"She got you into this life, didn't she? You're not like us. Me and Jen and Ada and the others . . . We didn't have much of a choice. Miss Irma looks like a walk in the park compared to the other options life gave us. But you could have been something. You had a good life and opportunities. Money, a future, a family that loves you. Ada couldn't stand it. She wanted to bring you down to our level."

Almost against my will, I thought about her words. Was it true what she was saying? Was it Ada's fault I got into this life? But I'd wanted to. I'd practically begged her, and she had always tried to stop me.

"Listen," I said, "I don't care what she did. If you know anything at all, you have to help me. Ada could be in serious trouble, and we need to look out for each other. Did she come by here? Did Jen mention that she'd spoken to her recently?"

Beth shook her head.

"Great," I said. "Dead end. Thanks anyway."

I turned my coat collar up and stepped back into the driving rain, tears of frustration prickling behind my eyes.

"Wait," said Beth. I turned around. "Before you give up, you might as well try Westlake Park."

"What have you heard?" I said sharply.

"I swear, I don't know anything. She could be a million miles away now, or around the corner, or dead, but Westlake Park is where a lot of Irma's old whores wash up when Irma's through with them. You could call it the Miss Irma Retirement Community."

I don't know what that means, but I'm off to find out.

Mon, March 9, later

Westlake Park is right in the middle of downtown Seattle, blocks away from the art museum and the convention center. Minutes from the business hotels where I used to meet most of my clients and only a few steps away from where I walked with Damon on our date. I've passed this park dozens of time and never noticed anything strange about it. I was always here in daylight, and it seemed perfectly nice.

But it's different after dark, and it didn't take me long to figure out why Beth thought Ada might be here. The women standing around the park are obviously streetwalkers. That's what she meant by Miss Irma's Retirement Community. When girls like me and Ada and Beth get too old or too difficult for Miss Irma's service, this is the only option left.

Still, even if I understood what Beth had meant, it's hard to picture Ada in this environment. These girls don't dress like Ada. They're streetwalkers, and they are dressed to make sure everyone knows it. They lean into car windows, negotiating deals.

I walked around the park a few times, my eyes instinctively seeking out Ada's tall, graceful form, her long swirling coat, her shimmery blond hair. But is that what she would look like now? Or would she be dressed in hot pants and fishnets and a lace bra? Would she wear a wig, as many of the girls seem to? I watched everyone carefully, trying to see past their performance to the person underneath.

Unfortunately, it wasn't long before people started to notice me. A couple of the girls started staring back. One wanted to know what I was looking at and what my problem was. I wanted to run away, but I knew that wouldn't get me any closer to Ada. So I screwed up my courage and approached her.

"I'm looking for someone named Ada," I said. "Maybe you can help?" I pulled up a photo of her on my phone, but the woman wouldn't even look at it.

"I mind my own business around here, and so should you," she said.

I swallowed my disappointment and slinked away, wondering if anyone else would be more helpful. That's when someone grabbed me roughly by the arm and spun me around.

"What's a pretty girl like you doing in the park tonight?" This time it was a guy in his twenties with a hood up, shading his eyes. "Are you working tonight?"

I tried to tell him no, that I was just there looking for a friend, but he sneered.

"I've heard that before. Who are you working for?"

"No one," I stuttered. "I mean, I used to work for Miss Irma, but I'm just . . ."

"This park isn't up for grabs, you know. No free agents. Now, if you're unattached, I'd be happy to . . ."

"Thank you," I said, hurrying away from him. "I was just leaving."

I wandered into a darker, more deserted area, far from the corners where the cars pulled up, and now I'm just sitting here, trying to stay out of everyone's way and figure out my next move. If I keep hanging around and asking questions, obviously I'm going to get myself into trouble, but I can't give up on Ada yet! Is there anywhere else I could look for her? Anyone else who might be willing to help?

Crap. There's a guy who has been lurking in the shadows near me for the last few minutes, and he is making me seriously nervous. Maybe I should find a different place to sit.

Tues, March 10? I think?

I am so confused. I wish I could remember exactly what happened last night and how I ended up here, but I'm only getting weird flashes, and I'm not sure what's real and what's a dream.

I'm in a bed right now, and from the light outside the window, I think it's very early morning. But it's not my bed, and it's not a hospital bed. Where am I?

I'd better try to reconstruct what happened after my last entry.

The guy lurking in my previous entry . . . I remember him. Just as I was thinking of moving, he walked up and asked if I had any money. I said, "Sorry, no," and he said, "Are you sure?"

I ignored him and started to walk away, but then he said, "How about you let me check?" I should have kept moving, but I chanced a glance at him and that's when I saw he had a knife. I kind of froze at that point. All I could think about was the envelope full of cash in my purse. The money I had saved up for ages. The money that was supposed to be the nest egg for my life with Ada. The money I had promised to deliver to Miss Irma tomorrow, to make sure Ada would be safe.

I started to walk away again, out of the shadows and toward a better-lit area, but the man grabbed my clothes and tugged me back toward him until I could feel the end of his blade against my back. I tried to struggle and cry out, but . . .

I don't know what happened then. Everything gets hazy at that point.

The next thing I remember is a familiar voice talking, saying my name, and hands shaking me awake. I opened my eyes to see who it was. It wasn't Ada. It was Shawn. The beautiful boy from Miss Irma's Valentine's party.

But that can't be right, can it? I must have been dreaming. But whose bed am I in right now?

Tues, March 10? later

I just investigated a bit, trying to figure out what the hell is going on. I'm still wearing all my clothes from last night, but my purse is gone. Which means all the money is gone. Not just that, but my cell phone, and Ada's too. At least I still have this journal—I was writing in my journal when I saw the guy, so I still had it in my hands when I went down.

I don't know what to do. I still don't know where I am. The room I'm in is a strange combination of shabby and swank. There are water stains and cracks in the plaster and the blinds are broken and hanging off the window, but there is also a huge flat-screen TV at the foot of the bed and these sheets are nicer than the ones on my bed at home.

The view out the window is totally unfamiliar. It doesn't look anything like the area around Westlake Park. Should I try to sneak out of this place and find my way back home? But what then? Irma's goons will be looking for me by nightfall, and now I have nothing to offer them. Leading them to my house will only put my parents in danger. They don't deserve that.

And even if I get out of that mess, it's guaranteed now that my parents will send me to Taiwan the first chance they get.

I wish I could go back to the days when everything felt like a choice. When I got to decide every day whether I was going to pick the dangerous path or the safe one. That safe path doesn't seem to exist anymore, and the dangerous one is more dangerous than ever.

I hear noises outside the door. Whoever's apartment this is seems to have gotten up. I wish I knew whether I'm his prisoner or not.

Tues, March 10, later

So this really is Shawn's apartment, and that really was Shawn from the Valentine's party moving around in the front room. He just came in and brought me a breakfast sandwich. I ate a few bites but had to stop when I suddenly felt really queasy. Shawn said it was probably from bumping my head pretty hard last night. That explains the painful lump and the memory loss, at least.

He asked me a lot of questions about how I was feeling and if I remembered my name and stuff. I kept trying to interrupt him to ask him what the hell he was doing in that park and what exactly happened, but he shushed me and told me not to worry about it for now. He said I needed rest and he didn't want to wear me out, but that we would talk more later.

I really feel like I would rest better if I weren't so confused. But I am awfully sleepy.

Tues, March 10, later

Shawn just came in and brought me half a burrito. I assured him I was feeling much better, so he finally agreed to tell me a bit about last night.

He said he was just hanging out in the park when he heard shouting and saw someone get knocked down. He ran over and found me there. He says he couldn't have been more shocked when he saw it was me. Small world, I guess. I would never have expected to run into him in a place like that either, but I guess that's what Beth was trying to tell me. Everyone who works with Irma winds up there sooner or later.

I asked him if he knew who beat me up, but he said the guy was making a run for it by the time he got there, and he thought it was more important to help me than follow him.

"Do you think anyone else who was there might know who he was?" I asked. "Or where I could find him?"

Shawn frowned. "I doubt it. I don't know if you noticed, but people who hang out at that park tend to keep their eyes to themselves. You know what I mean?"

Of course I did. I remember how people acted last night when I asked about Ada. I started to nod in answer, but instead I burst into tears. Shawn sat down on the bed with me.

"What's the matter?" he said. "You're safe now."

So I explained to him about the money and the phones.

"You had an envelope full of cash? In Westlake Park after dark? I'm sorry, kid," he said, "but that wasn't a very intelligent plan. What were you even doing there?"

"Miss Irma says we owe her money," I explained. "A lot of money. Ada disappeared, I'm not sure why, but maybe because she couldn't pay what Irma was asking. But I have the money. I was trying to find her to tell her I have it and we can go pay Irma and it will all be okay. Except I was saving that money for an apartment, and now I'm back to zero, and now someone stole the money so actually I'm still in debt and Miss Irma's goons are going to start looking for me and I still don't know where Ada is or if she's okay and everything is wrong and I wish I were dead."

"Hey," said Shawn soothingly, "don't worry, all right? Just rest for now. You lost some money. You owe some money. It happens. It's not the end of the world. I promise. You're okay now, so just relax."

"But what about Ada?"

"Let me worry about Ada. I have better resources than you do to figure out what happened to her. I'll put the word out, and it will only be a matter of time before we hear something. Trust me. I know how to get information."

Which made something occur to me. "What were you doing in the park last night?"

Shawn smiled. "I'm there pretty much every night. Keeping an eye on some friends, you could say. You're not the only girl who likes to get into trouble around here, you know."

"So, what . . . ? You're some kind of guardian angel or something?"

Shawn laughed. "Never been called that before. But that's one way to look at it."

Fri, March 13

I'm still at Shawn's. He just came in with half of a submarine sandwich he saved for me. He's sweet, but I get the feeling that all he eats is fast food.

I told him I'm feeling a lot better now. I have to start thinking about what comes next. What am I going to do about Miss Irma? And how am I going to find Ada?

"Relax," said Shawn. "I told you to let me take care of it, and I did."

"What do you mean?"

"You don't have to worry about Miss Irma anymore. I got her off your back. Her goons won't be sniffing around anymore."

"What? But why not? What did you do?"

"I paid her," he said simply.

"You paid her?" I said, incredulous. "You paid her what we owed? But it was a lot of money!"

"That's all relative. A lot of money to you is just a sound investment to me."

I took a second to process that. At first I felt like a huge weight had just been lifted from me. I hadn't even realized how worried I was about Miss Irma and the debt. But after a moment that good feeling got swept away by a low, sinking one.

"That's really kind of you," I said. "Too kind. How will I ever pay you back?"

"Don't worry about it," said Shawn. "Think of it like karma. Or like you said back at Miss Irma's party."

"What did I say?"

"We need to look out for each other."

I managed a smile at this, but the phrase only reminded me of my other problem.

"What about Ada, then?" I said. "Any news?"

Shawn shifted and dropped his eyes. "Not yet," he said.

I didn't like the look on his face when he said that. I had a feeling he knew more than he was letting on, and I was desperate to hear whatever it was. But when I pressed him for more information, he just told me to get some more rest and left me alone in his bedroom.

Sat, March 14

I got it out of him. Now I know what it was Shawn was trying to hide from me.

Ada . . . I can't say it. I can't write it. It's stupid, but it feels like that would make it real. Maybe if I just go to sleep, I'll wake up and realize this was all a terrible dream.

Tues, March 17

I can't hide from it anymore. Wishing and waiting isn't going to change things, so I might as well face it.

Shawn says Ada is dead.

He told me he asked around, put the word out to everyone he knows that we were looking for her. Three separate people came and told him the same thing. Hard to argue with that. I asked him how it happened, but he just shrugged.

"These things happen," he said. "It could have been any of us. It was almost you, the night I found you."

"You think she was murdered?"

"Maybe. Maybe killed for some cash, maybe an OD, maybe went to sleep in a Dumpster one cold night and didn't wake up. It happens all the time."

"But the police—"

"What do the police care about one more dead hooker? Unless she has family that are looking for her . . ."

I shook my head sadly, remembering my encounter with Ada's mom. Not likely that she was aware enough to even wonder what had happened to Ada.

I don't know what to do with myself. In a weird way, I don't even know who I am anymore. Ada's been the only person who really mattered to me for so long. My best friend. My only real friend. My only true family. The only person who really cared for me. How do I go on without her?

Mon, March 23

I haven't updated here in a little while. I didn't know how to talk about what's been going on, or maybe I just didn't want to. But I might as well say it.

I've been sleeping with Shawn. At first I didn't know what to make of it. All I knew was that it was something I needed right then, but I wasn't sure where it was going or what it all meant. And when it started, my head and my heart were still so full of Ada, none of it even felt real. But now it's the only thing that does feel real. The only thing I can hang on to in this life that isn't pure misery.

You might think that after all the experiences I've had, sex would be the last place I'd look for comfort. But this is different somehow. It doesn't feel at all like the sex I've had with clients. It doesn't even feel like that first time with Damon. Not just bodies and parts and fluids. For the first time, I don't feel like an object for someone else to enjoy.

The first night I found out about Ada, I just needed someone. I needed to not feel so alone. And Shawn stayed with me, held me while I cried, listened to all my ravings. He made me feel safe.

But at the same time, I didn't understand it, so finally I asked him. I asked him why he was being so nice to me. Why did he take me home that first night? Why did he pay off my debt? Why did he take up my search for Ada, and why was he putting up with me right now? He's been sleeping on the couch for two weeks now just so I can have the bedroom to myself.

Shawn smiled shyly.

"I guess some of us have to balance out all the assholes of the world," he said. I didn't know what to say to that, so I just looked at him with tears in my eyes until he got shifty and awkward.

"Also . . . ," he said, hesitating, "there's kind of something else, too."

I nodded for him to go on. He took a breath.

"I like you," he said. "I like you a lot, and I have ever since the night I met you. And I guess I was just hoping that if I was nice to you, maybe . . . maybe you would start to like me too."

I had nothing to say to that, so I kissed him. And I told him he didn't need to sleep on the couch anymore.

Sat, March 28

How do you know when you're in love with someone? This seems like such a silly question to be asking right now, with all that's been going on in my life, and as usual I feel like a naive idiot not to know the answer. But I don't think I've ever felt it before. Back in my old life, I wanted Tyler so much, and it was a really huge crush, but I don't think I ever would have said that I loved him. I mean, I didn't even know him, really, and what I did know suggested that he was kind of a jerk. (Which turned out to be incredibly true.)

Sometimes I have warm feelings toward some of my clients, and I did like Damon a lot, but I don't know them, and I know they don't really care about me.

With Shawn it's so different from how it always has been. I know he cares about me. He shows me every day how much. I know we haven't been together long, but the past couple of weeks have been so intense. I can't say exactly that I'm happy. How could I be happy after what happened to Ada? But I feel loved and cared for, and I think I feel it back. I want to take care of Shawn the way he has taken care of me.

At least he's not sleeping on the couch anymore. But the truth is, I have taken too much from him. I could never repay him for all he's done for me, but I have to at least start contributing. Plus, I need to get out and do something. For a while, being tucked away in his bedroom was just what I needed. An escape from all the crap I'd been dealing with out there. A chance to catch my breath and sort out my thoughts. But now I've done that, and I'm starting to feel cooped up. I need to make myself useful.

Sun, March 29

Shawn's going to let me help out! It's actually funny how it worked out. He came in today with lunch, and I could tell he wasn't himself. He seemed upset and preoccupied, though he was clearly trying to hide it from me. But I made him tell me what was up. I'm not some fragile flower. He doesn't have to keep protecting me.

He didn't want to say anything at first, but eventually he admitted that he'd been distracted from real life by taking care of me for a while, and now he wasn't totally sure how he was going to make rent. But he told me not to worry about it, that he was resourceful and always figured out something.

So I explained to him that this worked out perfectly, because I'd just been thinking how I wanted to start pulling my weight around here. He doesn't need to keep me under glass. I can work. I can contribute.

He kind of laughed and asked what I could do to raise rent money. It's true that I really know only one way to make money, but what's wrong with that? I don't mind, if it will help.

Of course he was really against the idea at first. He said he didn't want me doing that kind of thing anymore. But I was like, "Come on! Who are you kidding?" I've done it before, and so has he. It should be no big deal to us.

Then I asked him if the idea made him jealous, and he admitted that it did. So I told him he was being silly. There's such a huge difference between what we do out there for money and what we do together for love. Out there is just a show, and this is for real. I told him I could never mix the two up. . . . Could he? And he said he couldn't either. So it's settled.

Tues, March 31

Last night was my first night back at work. It's different from working for Miss Irma, but not so much worse, I think.

How we worked it out is, I go out and stand in the park, visible but not too visible. When a car drives by going kind of slow, I step out and try to get his attention. If he stops, at that point Shawn comes over to check him out and make sure he knows I have someone looking out for me. And he handles the money, too, so I don't have to worry about that. If Shawn thinks the guy's okay, I either get in the car with him for a blow job, or we drive to a hotel. That costs more.

Last night there weren't any hotel dates, just blow jobs in cars. It really wasn't so bad. It's all over pretty quickly, and it's easy to stay detached. And I feel safer knowing Shawn is right there than I did going alone to those hotel rooms. The money isn't as good, but you can do so many more people in one night, so it almost evens out.

One thing we need to worry about is cops. That used to be less of an issue with Miss Irma. It could be a real nuisance if I get arrested, especially if they send me back to my parents.

I was wondering whether my parents would come look for me at any point, but Shawn told me not to worry too much about that. Odds are they went to the cops when I didn't come home, but given my recent history of erratic behavior, the cops will assume I'm a runaway, and they don't usually bother looking too hard for runaways, especially if they don't have any idea where you might be. But if the cops pick me up and they recognize me, they'll send me home immediately.

Shawn also has his own problems to deal with in the park, it turns out. I came back from a trick at some point to see some girl yelling at him and getting in his face. He managed to calm her down, though. I asked him about it and he told me not to worry about it, just an old girlfriend.

Oh, there's another kind of weird thing I learned tonight. Shawn talks differently when he's in the park compared to when he's home with me. The first time I heard him talking to the other guys who hang around the fountain, I almost laughed! He talks like a gangster or something, which is *so* different from how he sounds with me. And really different from how he sounded at Irma's party.

I asked him about it and he looked a little embarrassed, but he explained about playing roles again, and how we all need to be different characters in different situations. He had to play one character when he was appealing to male clients, but in order to get respect on the street, he has to act different. I asked him what role he's playing when he's with me, but he just smiled and said that with me he gets to be real, and that's why he loves me.

Thurs, April 2

Some girl came by the apartment just now looking for Shawn. He told me not to open the door for people who come by (his neighborhood is not the greatest), but this girl kept knocking and calling his name through the door. I thought it was probably the same girl he was arguing with the other night, but when I opened the door, it was someone different.

I told her Shawn wasn't there, and she was like, "I see that. Who the hell are you?"

So I told her I'm his girlfriend, and she started laughing. She said, "Yeah, I've heard that before. Has he got you working the streets yet?"

She left after that, but I can't stop thinking about what she said. She made it sound like Shawn is my pimp or something. But it's not like that. It's not like he has a whole stable of girls. Obviously I am the only one living here. And I'm not working for him. We're both working to pay the rent and support ourselves. Right? I don't know. I'll feel better after I talk to Shawn about it.

Thurs, April 2, later

Shawn and I just had our first fight. I asked him about the girl at the door when he came home. He told me it was another ex-girlfriend. I didn't say anything right away, but he could tell I wasn't totally happy, so he asked me what was up. I wasn't sure what to say, exactly, so I tried to keep quiet, but he kept pushing and saying I should tell him what's wrong, so finally I asked him: "Is she an ex-girlfriend or an employee?"

He didn't answer right away, so I pressed harder.

"And what am I?" I said. "Am I your girlfriend or your employee? Am I the talent?"

"Don't do this to me," he said. "Don't act like that. You know I love you. And working the park was your idea, remember? I didn't force you into anything. You volunteered."

"You're right, I did," I said. "But what about your other girls? Did they volunteer?"

Shawn looked hurt at this. "I don't force anyone to do anything," he said. "I'm not like that. It's not my style."

After that I shut myself in the bedroom with my journal to think for a while. I don't like how this looks or how it sounds. I don't want to believe it, but at the same time, I wonder how I could have been so stupid and naive. Of course Shawn is a pimp. Look at all the signs: his willingness to let me work the street, his insistence that he handle all the money, all the other girls he's always talking to at the park, plus his lowlife pimp friends. . . .

And he's right. I agreed to it. I walked away from Miss Irma and fell right into his business.

So what now? The thing is, I'm upset . . . but am I upset at Shawn? Or at myself for thinking our arrangement was something other than it was? I could leave him now, but where would I go? And why would I be leaving? Pride?

He never outright lied to me. He never said I was the only girl he was managing. I just assumed it. I knew I was hooking to earn money for him and that he was my protection when I worked. It just never occurred to me that that's basically what a pimp is.

But now that I've woken up, what does that change? Should I leave? I don't know what other options I have, except to go back to Miss Irma. Between Irma and Shawn, at least I trust Shawn more. At least now I know what my cut is, instead of it always being a mystery with Irma.

This isn't ideal, and it's not what I dreamed, but maybe it's what makes the most sense for me right now.

Fri, April 3

I sat down with Shawn and had a long talk about our situation.

I was angry at first, but more than that, I was concerned. All I could think about was what Miss Irma had said about competition. She made it pretty clear that she didn't look kindly on her employees turning around and setting up their own businesses.

But Shawn had that all figured out. He's being smart about it. He's not going after Irma's customers, and he's not using her talent. Except for me, but that's why he paid off my debt to Miss Irma. He says he went to her office and paid up the debt, and now they have an agreement, fair and square.

I wasn't sure how I felt about that. It sickened me a little to think Shawn bought me like a piece of meat. But he said it was a little late to get picky about that sort of thing. Fair point, I guess. He says he did what it took to get Miss Irma off my back, and that's what I wanted, wasn't it? It's no different from what I was trying to do for Ada.

I asked him why he was doing all this. Setting up his own business, I mean. Why not just stay with Miss Irma? But he turned eighteen this year, and just like Beth said, he noticed his client list drying up as Miss Irma stopped referring people to him. You don't get fired, he explained. You just get called less. And it gets harder and harder to support yourself, until you are driven to supplement your income by other means.

"Miss Irma likes to keep tight control over everyone in her stable," he said, "and once they become adults, she worries they'll start asking too many questions, become difficult to manipulate. So we're basically disposable to her."

Shawn was afraid of what would happen to him once he lost her backing, so he started watching her closely and taking notes.

"I want something bigger for myself," he said. "I don't want to be just another two-dollar rent boy. I want what Irma has, and I think I can make it happen, if I work hard." He took my hands in his. "If you help me," he said, "we can have it together. And when we run the show, we can treat people right and make it a decent business."

I do like that idea. And when he puts it that way, it makes sense. I always knew I didn't want to be selling my body for the rest of my life. That wasn't realistic. But without a high school degree, or college, or any real work experience, I didn't know how I was going to support myself. What Shawn's talking about, this is the first plan I've heard that makes long-term sense. Who knows how to run a business like this better than we do? Irma worked her way up from the bottom. We can do it too.

But right now we've got some cash-flow problems, which is why I have to hit the park again tonight.

Sun, April 5

I had a bad night tonight. When I finally got home and crawled into bed, Shawn started to paw at me and I just couldn't stand it. We had a bit of a fight, and I wound up asking him why he doesn't work the park. He just laughed at that, but I was serious.

"We could take turns," I pointed out. "Or we could make more money if we both did it."

He shook his head. "I have a different job now. There's better money in managing than working the streets."

"Long-term, sure," I said. "And that's what we'll both be doing soon. But just for now, wouldn't it be good to bring in some extra cash?"

Shawn got out of bed. "Trust me, it's not a good idea."

"I don't see why not."

"Because," he said, growing exasperated. "You can't do both. I can't let the people in this neighborhood know I ever turned tricks, all right? They won't respect me anymore. And in this game, respect is everything."

"But people respect Miss Irma," I said. "And everyone knows how she started out. And you're expecting me to—"

"It's not the same, okay? Can't you see how it's not the same?"

I didn't say anything.

"It's different for guys," he said quietly. "The people in the park, the people in this neighborhood, can't ever find out what I did for Miss Irma. Do you understand? People might call a girl bad names if she turns tricks, they might laugh at her, but if people knew that about me, if they thought I wasn't the person I seemed to be, it would be worse. Guys like me get hurt. Guys like me get killed."

I didn't know what to say to that.

"Do you understand?" he said. "It's important. In here we're the same. We've been through the same shit. But out there you can never talk about what I did. Do you get that?"

I nodded.

"It's like I said before. It's all about playing the role. And to make people believe it, you can't ever break character."

Mon, April 6

Another long night last night. Then, even when I fall asleep, it's like all I can dream about is climbing into and out of cars in the dark. I wake up more exhausted than when I went to bed.

It's a little too crazy to think that this is my life now. It's hard to believe that less than a month ago I was living at home and going to school like a normal teenager. I wonder what my old friends are doing now. Jenny and Eiko and John. Visiting college campuses, studying for the SAT? I wonder what they would think of who I am now, if they could even believe it. Would they recognize me like this? Would they ever talk to me again, if I went back?

Wed, April 8

I just realized I don't even know how many girls Shawn has working for him. Whenever we're both working the park, I try to circle around in his direction to check up on him from time to time, and he always seems to be talking to a different girl. I can't help wondering, did he recruit them all the same way he got me? Well, obviously not exactly the same way, but who knows? That guardian-angel bit does work pretty well. Maybe he saw them getting beat up by a pimp or a john and swooped in to save the day. Then they start dating, and before long, they're working. And it's on to save the next victim. Is Shawn more victimizer than savior?

No, it's not like that. Maybe it's not ideal, maybe it's not a perfect fairy tale, but at least Shawn treats his workers like human beings, unlike a lot of the pimps around here. He splits the take fairly, he keeps them safe, and he never gets violent or cruel.

And he loves me, right? I'm not like the other girls. He tells me that every day. But then . . . maybe that's what he told the girl who came before me. What if that were me? What if some new damsel in distress came along and I got downgraded from girlfriend to employee? What if that became my life, and I was just another girl working the park and handing my money over to Shawn, while he took a new girl home to his bed? Would I keep working for him?

I want to say that I would not. But where else would I go at this point?

Sat, April 11 (after midnight)

God, I've really done it now. Why couldn't I leave well enough alone? Sure, things weren't perfect, and maybe Shawn wasn't the hero I wanted him to be, but I was getting by. We were building a life. Then I had to go and ruin everything.

I'm crying so hard, it's hard to see what I'm writing, and the page keeps getting wet and smearing my ink. But I'm scared and

I have to quit my sniveling and stay quiet or else who knows what might happen. So I'm trying to write to calm myself down.

It started at the park, of course. I was supposed to be working, but as usual, I kept circling back to see what Shawn was up to. Lately I just can't stop thinking about the day some other girl wanders into the park with a problem and Shawn turns into Captain Save a Ho again. I tell myself if I can just keep an eye on him, I can stop that from happening, but I don't know how I think that will work. And in the meantime, every time he catches me, he gets pissed that I'm wasting time when I should be earning money.

Anyway, I saw him talking to this or that girl during the night, but it all seemed pretty normal until one time I noticed him with one of the usual girls, but they were arguing. And I knew I should just stay out of it and get back to work, but I couldn't help being curious, so I kept drifting closer, trying to hear what they were saying. It seemed like something to do with money, or respect, or both. He was being really verbally aggressive toward her, yelling and telling her not to test him. She kept sort of backing off, but then she would come back after a minute with a new comment, and he was calling her names, calling her a smart-ass, and the other guys joined in, encouraging Shawn and egging him on.

I knew I should stay away, but it really bothered me, the way

219

he was treating her. I was anxious about him replacing me, but through it all, I had at least clung to the idea that Shawn wasn't so bad, as pimps went. He was a decent guy who didn't fit any of the usual stereotypes. But here he was, enacting them all.

All of a sudden, I was furious—at Shawn, and maybe even more at myself, for falling for his act. Shawn always said that what he did out here was an act and what he did back home was real, but the world doesn't work that way. He might think he was playing a role out here in the park, but none of this was make-believe. And I might have wanted to believe that what we had at home was real, but I was living a fantasy with Shawn just as much as with any other client I've been with.

I couldn't take it anymore. I knew I should wait until we were home alone to talk about it with him, but I wasn't thinking straight. I went right up and told him to leave that girl alone. The other guys in the park hooted and jeered at me, but I ignored them.

Shawn gave me a hard look. "Don't," he said simply, but I wanted an explanation.

"You told me you weren't like the others," I said, getting in his face. "You said you don't treat people that way."

"Don't do this right now," he said in a low voice. "We can talk about it later."

And the other guys started laughing again, but this time at

Shawn. Laughing about how he was letting a woman tell him what to do, I guess, but I wasn't paying much attention to them. I just wanted an answer out of him, and I wouldn't back down.

Then, the next thing I knew, there was a loud noise and I was reeling backward. It took a second or two before I even recognized the pain. Before I realized that he had smacked me. I stumbled back in a daze and somehow managed not to sink to the ground. After a few moments, I found my balance and stood up straight. Then, without a word, I turned and walked away from him, out of the park.

"Where do you think you're going?" he called after me.

"I don't know," I said, not turning around. "Away from you."

He jogged up and fell into stride beside me. "You can't take off by yourself. It's not safe," he said.

"Yeah? And I'm so safe here with you?"

"Fine," he said tightly. "Walk it off, if you have to. We can talk about this later."

After that he stopped following me and I just kept walking.

I went to the light-rail stop first, but at that hour it would be ages before one came by, and there were too many people around. Too many people who had watched what had happened and were eager to comment on it, offering advice or pity or criticism, or just wanting to stoke the drama for their own amusement. After a minute or two, I couldn't take it anymore and started to just walk toward our apartment. I figured I could follow the rail line, and it would take me back to our neighborhood eventually.

But after a few blocks, I realized . . . Our neighborhood? Our apartment? That place wasn't mine. It was all his. The apartment was filled with his stuff, and the neighborhood was filled with his family and friends. Without Shawn I was totally isolated.

I was really starting to feel sorry for myself, all alone and friendless on the empty streets of Seattle in the middle of the night, and I was about to just find a doorstep to sit in so I could have a good wallow and cry while I tried to sort out the mess of my life. But then I became aware of a sound. Footsteps. And they were getting closer.

I tried to calm myself down and reassure myself that they had nothing to do with me. It was just another person out late at night, dealing with their own problems, minding their own business. But as I forced myself to focus, I realized I'd been hearing these footsteps for some time. *Click-clack, click-clack.* The sound had echoed through my thoughts for the past fifteen minutes without me even realizing it. I was definitely being followed.

I thought about turning around and confronting whoever it was, but I had nothing on me that could possibly be used as a weapon. I thought about breaking into a run and trying to make it home, but it seemed like a bad idea to let the stalker know where I lived. And I still haven't replaced my phone since that night I got jumped in the park, since every penny I've earned went to Shawn. So I couldn't even call the police.

Not knowing what else to do, I just kept walking, and the footsteps kept following, sometimes a little closer, sometimes a little farther away. At last I saw the opportunity I'd been hoping for: The footsteps had grown more distant, and up ahead of me was a narrow alleyway lined with garbage bins. I slipped in and sank down to sit on my heels behind one of the bins, desperately hoping to lose my stalker. I could make out the footsteps for a little while, but they stopped before they got too close. I heaved a sigh of relief, but I was still too scared to come out.

So that's where I am now. Scribbling in this journal to pass the time and make absolutely sure there is no one out there.

Shit. I just heard it again. *Click-clack, click-clack.* It's getting closer.

Sat, April 11, later

I hardly know what to say. Never in a million years did I think . . . I can't even figure out what to write! My thoughts are scattered all over the place. I need to focus. I need to write out what happened or else I will never believe it.

I remember that sound drawing closer, and I remember

closing my eyes and holding my breath. After that I'm not sure what happened. It was like a gray mist was swirling around me, and I think I must have passed out for a minute from fear. In any case, the next thing I remember is the feeling of an arm wrapped around me while something slid down my throat like liquid fire.

I sat up, sputtering, and scrambled around to see who was there. I nearly fainted again when I saw.

She was filthy, her long coat torn, her hair matted around her face and tucked into an inelegant bun, and there was a battered flask in her hand. But there was no doubt in my mind: It was Ada.

"I didn't mean to scare you," she said as I fought for breath. "But Shawn was right. It's a dangerous neighborhood. I couldn't let you walk it alone."

For a while I couldn't speak. My heart was still racing and my breath was short, but even more, I didn't know what to say. I had so many questions, I didn't know where to begin. I didn't know whether to be happy she was back, or furious that she had let me believe otherwise.

"You were dead," I finally gasped out after a couple more sips of the awful whiskey. "Shawn told me you were . . ."

Ada raised an eyebrow. "And what was it about Shawn that made you think you could trust what he said? I told you back at the party that he was trouble."

"But then why . . . ?"

"I had to disappear for a while," she explained. "You must have seen that. I tried to keep you out of the whole thing, when Miss Irma came sniffing around about the Damon business. I told her to leave you alone, but I knew she wouldn't listen, so I told you to stay away from her. You should have done what I said."

My eyes filled with tears. It was too much to process: the euphoria of having her back, along with the pain of having disappointed her.

"I was worried about you!" I said, choking back my emotion. "You didn't tell me where you'd gone. You just disappeared. Miss Irma was the only person who had any chance of telling me what happened to you."

"I couldn't tell you," said Ada. Her voice was calm and steady, but there was guilt in her expression. "It was too risky. If Irma got to you . . ." Ada put a hand to my cheek and looked into my eyes. "You don't know what she's capable of."

"I wouldn't have told her," I insisted. "I'd never have betrayed you."

"I know," said Ada. "But this was safer for us both." She grimaced a little. "Or it would have been, if you'd only stuck to the plan."

"The plan you never told me about!"

Ada dropped her gaze. "I'm sorry," she said. "I didn't know. . . . It never occurred to me. . . ."

"What?"

"I never imagined you'd come after me. That you would care enough to—"

"Of course I would. I always would."

She smiled weakly. "We shouldn't stick around here," she said. "Anything could happen. Can you take me back to Shawn's place? I could use a shower."

"What if he comes back?"

"I saw him go off drinking with his little pimp friends," she said. There was something slightly vicious in her tone. "He won't be back before morning."

As we walked the rest of the way home, Ada told me her story. Beth must have tipped off Miss Irma right after the Valentine's party, because that's when Irma went after Ada. Of course, Miss Irma always knew that Ada didn't have the cash, but she was willing to strike a deal. She told Ada they could settle up quicker if Ada took on dates with some of the more . . . demanding clients. The ones who like to make special requests.

Ada balked, but Miss Irma told her to grow up. She told her she wouldn't be sixteen forever, and at some point she was going to need something other than her youth to build her career on. Taking on kinkier clients would be a good career move. And if she did it, Irma promised not to try to get the money out of me.

It seemed reasonable enough, so she went along with it. But after a couple of dates, she couldn't do it anymore. I asked her what happened, but she wouldn't tell me. She just got a hard look in her eyes.

On top of that, Irma's goons keeping an eye on her made her mother's delusions get worse, until one day she wouldn't let Ada in the house. Ada decided her mother would be better off if she just skipped out, so she called an aunt to come by and look in on her, and Ada disappeared.

"Disappeared," I repeated. "What does that even mean? Did you go to another country or something?"

"I might as well have. I was in the Jungle."

"The Jungle? Like . . . South America?"

"Close enough. It's right here in the city. A patch of land between the freeways, too narrow and steep to develop. It's turned into a kind of no man's land, reclaimed by nature but not like a park, with paths and flower beds. It's wild, and so are the people who live there. You go there when you have nothing left to lose and nothing to live for. It's all junkies and crazies, and the people who are neither are even worse. They call it the Jungle, but they should just call it Hell."

"Jesus, Ada. How could you—"

"I didn't mean for you to think I was dead, but I needed to stay gone long enough for Miss Irma to stop looking for me, and I didn't know how long that would be. As it happens, I got lucky. Some poor slut died in a Dumpster, and a handful of people decided it was me. That was enough to convince Miss Irma, and Shawn too, as it turned out. And you."

"But that was a while ago! Why didn't you come back before?"

"News doesn't travel quickly to the Jungle. I didn't hear about my own death until a couple of days ago. At that point, I went to Jen, but Jen's gone. Beth was there, though, and she told me you'd been around looking for me."

"And before that, you never even tried to get in touch with me?" Even in my relief at having her back, I couldn't hide how hurt I was that she had forgotten me.

Ada stopped me and looked me in the eyes. "I thought you were at home with your parents. I wanted to tell you, but I thought you were safe, and I knew I would only mess that up. All I could think of was how much better off you'd be if you'd never met me. I wanted to give you a second chance at your real life."

I grabbed her by the arm. "Ada," I said, "you are my real life."

I think she finally believes me.

Sat, April 11, early morning

Ada's out of the shower now. She was starting to put back on her grubby clothes that she's been living in God knows how long, but I stopped her and gave her something of mine to wear. It's funny. It's almost like we're back to where we started, only this time she's wearing my clothes instead of me wearing hers. I still think she looks better in them, though, no matter whose they were to begin with. Even as skinny as she is right now.

"So what are we going to do?" I asked her as she studied her new look in the mirror.

She caught my eye in the reflection. "What are you ready to do?" she asked.

"Ready?"

Ada turned around to face me. "You and Shawn," she said. "Is that over now?" She dropped her eyes when I didn't answer right away. "I know how it is," she said. "I've seen it a million times. A girl gets smacked around a little; she gets angry, says she's going to leave. In the morning, she's making him breakfast and saying how sorry she is that she upset him."

"Ada, no," I said in horror. I reached out to take her hand. "No," I said firmly. "It's not like that. Even before tonight, I think a part of me already knew he was no good and was looking for a way out. I was just scared of being on my own."

Ada smiled. "But now you're not."

"Now I'm not. But maybe we should leave soon. It's getting light out, so he could be home any minute. And I'd rather not see him again."

Ada squeezed my hand tighter. "One more time," she said. "Can you deal with him one more time? If you disappear, he'll look for you. We need to see him once more, to make sure he'll leave you alone." I nodded and she dropped my hand. "Good," she said. "Besides, me and him have a little business to transact."

Sat, April 11, late morning

We're at Beth's now. She and Ada never liked each other, and she definitely wasn't my friend either, but when we had no place else to go, she was the one who took us in.

It probably helped that we gave her money.

That's part of what Ada wanted to stick around Shawn's place for, it turned out. While we waited, she started ransacking the apartment, going through all the drawers and closets. I asked her what she was looking for.

"His gun," she said.

"He doesn't have one," I told her.

"Are you sure?" she said. She turned and stepped into my space, looking deep into my eyes as if she could read the truth of my statement there. "Are you absolutely sure? Because this information could be very important in the conversation we're about to have. Life and death."

I nodded, to show I understood.

"But he doesn't have one," I said. "It was one of the things he was saving up for, before I came around. There was one he wanted to buy. He was planning on it, but we didn't have the cash yet."

Ada nodded and relaxed a little. "Good," she said. "That will make this a little easier."

It wasn't much later that we heard his footsteps on the stairs. Ada motioned to me to be quiet, then silently moved behind the door just as we heard Shawn's key in the lock. He opened the door to see me sitting in his armchair and let out a sigh of relief.

"I'm glad you're here," he said. His words slurred a little, and I remembered Ada had said he was out drinking. But he was clearly trying to make up with me. "I'm sorry about last night," he went on. "You know I would never have done that, except—"

Ada slammed the door shut behind him.

Shawn jumped so high at the sound that I almost laughed. But that was nothing to how spooked he was when he turned around and saw Ada standing in front of him.

"Ada?" he said. "How in the hell? You—you're dead!"

"Not exactly," said Ada. "But you've done yourself a favor. You convinced me you really did think I was dead and you weren't lying before. That will make this go easier for you."

"What are you going to do?" he said. "Beat me up? I must have fifty pounds on you. And if you had a gun, you'd be pointing it right now."

"I don't have a gun," said Ada, "and neither do you. But you do have something that doesn't belong to you."

Shawn looked down at me, then back to Ada. "Take her," he said. "She's yours."

Ada made a disgusted face. "Really, Shawn? That's not what I meant. She's a person, not a thing, and you can't trade her back and forth. No. I want the money she earned that you never paid her."

Shawn hesitated, and even though I knew by now that he was a creep, it still hurt a little that he was more reluctant to give up the cash than me.

"How much did he pay you for all the streetwalking you've been doing?" Ada asked me.

"We were going to split it fifty-fifty."

"But how much did you actually see?"

"None yet. He was holding it for me."

"Not anymore," she said.

"You don't have a weapon," said Shawn. "Why should I do what you say?"

"I don't have a gun," agreed Ada, "but I do have a weapon. My weapon is your past. Give her what she's owed, or we'll go

232

door-to-door in this neighborhood like a couple of Jehovah's Witnesses, telling everyone you know what you were doing when you were employed by Miss Irma. What do you think they'll say, Shawn, when I tell everyone what a good little cocksucker you used to be?"

Shawn didn't answer right away, but I could see panic in his eyes. It was gnawing at him, preventing him from thinking of any way out of the situation. After a minute, he walked over to a small safe under his desk and opened it. We watched him count out half the money, and Ada made him hand it to me.

"Thank you," I said.

"Don't thank him," said Ada. "All that is yours."

After that we went back to Beth's and more or less threw ourselves on her mercy. Thanks to Jen still being mixed up in the correctional system, Beth is behind on the rent and on the point of being evicted, so I think she was actually pretty happy to see us and our wad of cash. Too bad that took a big chunk out of it, but there will be time to worry about that tomorrow.

For now we're both exhausted from running around all night. There's only Jen's narrow bed to sleep in, so we'll have to share, but I don't mind. To be honest, now that I have her back, I just want to keep Ada as close as possible, so she doesn't slip away again.

Sun, April 12

I'm worried about Ada. We fell asleep yesterday morning curled up together in Jen's bed, and I felt the safest and happiest that I have felt in ages. Ada was alive! And for the first time, my dream of us living together and leaving a life of prostitution felt like it might be within my grasp.

We slept like that through the day, but come night I woke up to find myself struggling to kick the blankets off me. I was boiling hot even though the apartment was chilly. That's when I realized it was Ada. She was burning up and making us both sweaty and miserable. I got up and got a cool, wet washcloth for her face, then managed to fall back to sleep. But this morning she still feels hot, and she hasn't woken up yet, even though she's been asleep for almost twenty-four hours.

If she's sick, I guess the rest is good for her, so I'm not going to wake her up.

Mon, April 13

I went out and got some orange juice, chicken soup, and vitamins for Ada, using a bit of Shawn's money. My money, I should say. I earned it, and it's mine. I guess I still have a ways to go, breaking out of the mental habits I learned with him.

When I got back, Ada was awake! So that's good news. I

made her soup and she took a shower, and after a little while she even started to get a bit of her color back. She says it's just a cold she picked up while living on the streets. It's been pestering her off and on for a while, but now that she has a roof over her head and a warm bed to sleep in, she'll shake it off soon. She's so skinny, though! That can't be good for her health. I have to make sure she eats well while she's getting better, even though it means dipping into our little pot of money.

Speaking of which, I guess we need to start thinking about what comes next. This place is dingy and kind of a dump, but it's good enough for now, and I think Beth will let us keep staying here as long as we can help out with the rent. But the money I earned with Shawn isn't going to last long, with Seattle rents being what they are. I really, really don't want either of us to have to go back to hooking, so we're going to have to think of another solution.

Wed, April 15

Ada's feeling a bit better, so we had a talk about the future. She wants to stay here with me, which is a huge relief. To her too, I think. She still finds it really hard to believe I don't want to just go home to my parents, and I know she worries that as soon as things get difficult, I'll change my mind and go back, but I'm doing my best to reassure her that's not true. That I would never abandon her.

But that still doesn't solve the money problem. She mentioned that as soon as she was feeling a little better, she'd get in touch with Miss Irma. Now that her debt's been paid, she doesn't have to hide out from her anymore.

Ada shook her head and laughed in amazement when I told her I wanted us to support ourselves with legal jobs and quit hooking for good. But she said that she believed in me, and if anyone could figure how to make that work, it was me.

I just hope I'm worthy of the faith she's putting in me. God knows I don't really have any experience in this area. But I have to try. That life was no good for either of us. There has to be something better.

I guess tomorrow I'll start looking for HELP WANTED signs and pick up a few applications. And online postings too. Maybe there will be some stuff there—Beth said she'd let me borrow her laptop, and I picked up a cheap prepaid cell phone so people can contact me. I know the money won't be what we're used to, but normal people support themselves with normal jobs in this city, right? I can make this work.

Thurs, April 16

I picked up some applications today. I'm going to work on filling them out tomorrow. And while I was out, Ada found some stuff online that has a lot of potential. The details are vague, but it looks like you can make a lot of money, which would be good right now.

Ada says she's feeling better, but she still seems pretty listless to me, and she's running a fever again. I'm going to try to make her eat some more soup, then get to work on these applications.

Fri, April 17

I'm stressed out about these job applications. Beth explained to me that I'll be better off if I lie and say I'm over eighteen, because sixteen-year-olds are only allowed to work twenty hours a week in this state. The idea is that you're not supposed to work too much while you're in school, but I haven't seen the inside of a school in ages. So how does this law help me?

It's so frustrating. I'm just trying to make an honest living. To support myself legally, without any help from my parents. The whole idea of this was to work at something legitimate, so I wouldn't have to be looking over my shoulder all the time, worrying about cops. But how legitimate is my new life going to be if I have to lie to maintain it? I'm still going to be worried all the time about being found out.

But there's no way Ada and I will be able to survive on part-time pay.

Maybe I'll work on my applications for those online postings. Those don't seem to ask so many questions.

Mon, April 20

I feel really productive today! I turned in a whole bunch of applications, both in person and online. Something has to come through.

Wow. I had no idea how exhausting this whole process was. I feel like I should write more about what's going on, but right now all I want to do is curl up in bed with Ada and watch bad TV. She's been sleeping all day, so hopefully that means her fever is down. All this will be easier when she's feeling better and we both have jobs. Then everything won't feel so desperate. We just have to hold on until then.

Fri, April 24

Ada's worrying me again. I ask her every day how she's feeling, and every time she smiles brightly and says, "Better!" But not fine, or good, or all better. Honestly, I'm not sure I believe her. I don't know if it's wishful thinking on her part, or if she's lying to protect me. All I know is that two weeks is a long time for anyone to be sick with a cold or the flu without any real improvement.

I haven't heard back about any of my applications yet, so I sent out a few more.

Fri, April 24, later

I got responses from one of the online applications! It says I can start right away. It sounds perfect. The money's pretty good, the work looks easy, and I can do it from home, so I can keep an eye on Ada.

The only problem is there are start-up costs. Basically, you have to wire them some money to pay for the materials you need before you can get started. Kind of like how I had to pay for my phone and stuff when I started with Miss Irma. It sucks because it's basically going to eat up the last of what we had saved, but you know what they say: You have to spend money to make money.

Wed, April 29

I haven't heard back from that online place since I wired them the cash. I've sent them a bunch of messages. Rent is due at the end of the week, and I don't have it. I know what we're going to do if they don't come through soon. I might have to turn some tricks to make ends meet, even though I really didn't want to fall back on that.

Ada offered to, but with how she looks right now, I'm honestly not sure anyone would take her up on it. At least she still has contact info for some of her old clients. Miss Irma wouldn't like us setting up dates behind her back, but it's a possibility.

Fri, May 1

Today was not good. Ada fainted in the shower, and I finally convinced her to let me take her to the hospital. I've been trying all week, but she always said it was just a cold, she just needed some rest, and I wanted to believe she was right. But a part of me has known for a while now that she's really not well, and we need to do something about it. I'm just so scared. I lost her once already.

No point in thinking about that. They admitted her to the hospital and said it looks like pneumonia. They said it had gotten pretty bad, but they also said that it would probably get better now that she's being treated.

I stayed there with her for a couple of hours, but eventually the nurses sent me home and told me to let her rest. Then Beth started nagging me about rent, so I did what I had to do. Called up a couple of the numbers Ada had written out, made some appointments. I had one this evening. I'll do another tomorrow, and that should see us through for a little while.

Mon, May 4

I got a job! A real, legal job.

I got a call this morning from one of the fast-food places where I applied. I went in for an interview, and they hired me on the spot! I'm so excited. I feel like things are finally coming together. Maybe I can even help Ada get a job there too, in a little while.

The job is basically working the cash register all day, plus mopping the floors and cleaning the bathrooms during the off-peak hours. Doesn't sound great, but it's better than nothing. I start tomorrow!

Tues, May 5

First day of work was okay. Too exhausted to write much more. Didn't even get a chance to visit Ada today, but I will make it to the hospital tomorrow. Hopefully, they will release her soon and I won't have to trek over there anymore.

Wed, May 6

I went to the hospital right after work today, hoping that this would be the day they released Ada and let her come home. When they let me in to see her, she really did look a lot better. Not so thin and gaunt anymore and with a lot more energy. But her expression was sad and serious, even when I tried to cheer her up with funny stories from work and stuff.

After a while she stopped me and said she had to tell me something. Then she told me not to freak out, which is never a good start to a conversation. I told her to just come out with it.

Ada has AIDS. Or HIV. I don't know. It's not totally clear right now. Ada was calm enough, but she didn't seem to have absorbed all the details. I guess I can't really blame her. It's hard enough just to wrap your head around something like that.

I had promised her I wouldn't freak out, but I couldn't help it. I started crying. Ada held my hand for a little while, but when I didn't stop, she scooted over a bit and let me climb into the hospital bed with her. She held me and stroked my hair as if I were the one dying, not her.

But I'm not supposed to say stuff like that. Once I had calmed down a bit, Ada whispered reassuring things to me about how it's not a death sentence anymore, and now that they know why she was so sick, they can treat it and she'll be healthy enough to come home soon. She'll have to take a lot of pills and be extra careful about certain things, but it's not like she's going to die tomorrow.

I know that, but still, it's not like it's going to be easy. This changes things. Realistically, we need to think about what this means for us, and our life.

I can't think about that stuff now, though. I just need to let it sink in. And I need to get to sleep. I have to be at work early tomorrow morning.

Fri, May 8

I asked Ada today how it happened. How she got sick. When I first found out, I was too shocked to even think about how she got infected, and after that I wondered, but I felt awkward about asking. But finally my need to know won out over my awkwardness.

Ada just sort of shrugged it off, though. She called it a "little souvenir" of her time in the Jungle. I don't understand, because she knows better. She always made me swear to use condoms with clients every time, no matter how much they tried to pressure me, but she just said that once you're living on the street, priorities change.

That's when I got angry with her, which I know isn't fair, but I couldn't help it. How could she let this happen to herself? How could she do it to me? That's selfish of me, I know, but it hurts.

After that she didn't want to talk about it anymore, and I felt like a jerk. I get the feeling that stuff happened when she was living out there. Stuff she can't talk about, even to me. Part of me wants to know everything, but another part of me thinks she's right. I don't know if I could handle hearing about it.

Some friend I am.

Fri, May 15

I haven't written in a while. To be honest, there hasn't been a whole lot to say. My days are split between work and visiting Ada in the hospital, and when I come home at night, I'm so exhausted that I can barely manage to microwave a frozen burrito before falling into bed. At least Ada is looking better these days.

But work is . . . I don't know. I keep telling myself that this is better than hooking, that this is a better life. And it is. It's safer. I'm not going to get beat up or infected with a disease or forced to take a dangerous drug. That's important. But in other ways . . . It sounds crazy to say, but sometimes this life doesn't feel so different.

I thought it would be less dehumanizing at least, but in a way it's even worse. All day long, for hours and hours, I'm doing the same actions, going through the same motions, until I feel like a machine. People say prostitution is "selling your body," but what am I selling at this job? Definitely not my mind. They just need someone to stand there, to work the cash register, to push the mop around. Any warm body could do it. But instead of doing an hour of work a day, I'm stuck there for eight or more. And I get paid half as much.

At least hooking was good training for this position. All that time I spent figuring out what clients wanted, smiling when I was miserable or in pain, making people believe I was enjoying myself, those are all pretty useful skills in the new job too. That whole idea of giving people their fantasy—I'm still doing it. Only instead of pretending to be a Japanese schoolgirl, I'm pretending to be a normal teenager who loves her job and is happy to serve them. Which is almost as much of a lie.

Oh, and I got my first paycheck and got to see how much was taken out for taxes and stuff. Not sure how this is different from when Irma and Shawn took their cuts from everything I earned.

Tues, May 26

I got fired today. They moved my shift around so I had to visit Ada in the morning before work, and then I wound up coming in late too many times. I know it's my fault. I'm such an idiot. But the time I spend with her is the only time I'm happy all day. It's so hard to make myself leave to go to that dark hole-in-the-wall that reeks of rancid meat. Well, I guess now I don't have to anymore.

I don't know what we're going to do for money, though. Even when I was working, it really wasn't enough to live on, so it's not like I had anything saved up. And it's going to take me a while to find something else.

I might try panhandling for a while. I hear sometimes people make okay money doing that.

Thurs, May 28

Beth is kicking me out. I can't say I blame her. I'm pretty useless as roommates go. Not only am I broke, but I'm also miserable all the time, so I'm not exactly good company.

She found someone else who wants to move in right away.

A new girl who just started working for Miss Irma. I met her tonight, which was awkward, but she seems nice enough. She's a little like me, actually. She grew up in a nice suburb, unlike most of the people who work for Miss Irma. But she says her father started raping her when she turned thirteen, and that's why she ran away. Jeez. Maybe she deserves this apartment more than I do.

Beth was surprisingly not a complete jerk about it when she told me. She just sat me down and said I had better find another situation, because this girl would be moving in tomorrow. And when I started to cry, she said maybe I should go back to my parents . . . which only made me cry more.

I don't know. Maybe she's right. It's true I'm not like the rest of them. My parents are tough, but they aren't abusive, and I know they love me and would take me back. But I also know that's not all they would do. After this, after all I've put them through—running away, stealing money, being completely out of contact for so long, to say nothing of how I treated them before I left—there's no question that the minute I came back they would book me on the next flight to Taiwan. And I understand it's not punishment. I know that when they made that threat, it was out of concern, not cruelty. They think they need to get me away all from all the bad influences that got me to this place. And how can I blame them? I see how it must look from their perspective.

But that's not the whole story. They would never understand about me and Ada. They can't possibly understand that none of this was her fault and she always did everything she could to protect me.

And they'll never understand that I promised I would stick with her and that I wouldn't give up and go home, no matter how bad things got. And with the way she is now, there's just no way I can abandon her, completely on her own, without a friend in the world. I know very well that going home means getting sent away, and that means leaving Ada. I can't do it.

So I'll figure something out. I have to. Even if it means living on the streets for a while. If Ada did it, I can too. And if it means turning tricks again, at least until I can get back on my feet, I can handle that. I did it before, and it didn't kill me. I'll do whatever I have to.

Wed, June 3

Why is it always raining in this damn city? I really don't want to sleep in a stinky old Dumpster, but I am so sick of being soaked all the time. At this point I'd be willing to blow someone just for a sandwich and a couple of hours in a bed. I bet Miss Irma would laugh at that, after the money I used to make with her, but it's hard to attract much attention from johns when you look like a drowned rat. And I don't even want to think about what I smell like.

In a few hours I can go visit Ada in the hospital. At least it's dry there, and I might be able to snag some food off her tray. Stealing food from AIDS patients! That's definitely a new low in my life.

Tues, June 9

I got caught sleeping in Ada's bed with her. It's not the first time I've been caught, but the nurses and orderlies always looked the other way before. They even let me stay past visiting hours a couple times. I think they probably had figured out that I didn't have anyplace else to go. Sometimes an hour or so snuggled up with Ada is the only real sleep I get all day.

But this time a nurse woke me up and made me leave the room. He stood out in the hall with me and explained about how sick Ada is. Yes, she is looking much better now, but she still has a severely compromised immune system, and any random bug I have could easily get passed to her. He was being really nice and gentle about it, but I got the message. All you have to do is look at me these days to see that I am probably crudded up with all kinds of diseases. Starving and sleeping in the rain and fucking random people for pocket change (even if I do always use a condom) is not exactly a healthy lifestyle.

I tried to just nod and show I understood, and I know he wasn't trying to be hurtful, but I couldn't help tearing up. I just felt so awful and guilty, thinking I could be the reason Ada gets sick again. I'm supposed to be visiting to make her feel better, but I've been so selfish lately, using my time in the hospital with her as a little vacation from my own wretched life.

So after that conversation, I basically just wanted to find a Dumpster to crawl into and die and not be a bother to anyone anymore, but the nurse wouldn't let me go. Instead, he took me to an office and had me sit down, and he brought me some food. After a while a woman came to talk to me. She said she was a social worker, and immediately I panicked that she was going to turn me over to my parents or the cops or get me put into foster care or something. I've heard enough stories not to want that.

But she calmed me down and said she wasn't going to make me do anything. She just wanted to talk and maybe see if she could help me. And she said I could leave if I wanted to, but she hoped I would stay and talk awhile. I almost walked out right then, because I didn't think anything good could come of this, but I could see out the window that it was still raining, and I just couldn't face going back out into that yet. Another hour in a warm, dry place didn't sound so bad.

So she asked me about my parents, and I told her I couldn't go back there. And I could see that she was thinking they beat

me or raped me or whatever, like so many of the other kids I've
run into, and I felt bad letting her think that, so I wound up
explaining the whole situation. About how they would send
me away and then I would never see Ada again, and there
isn't anyone else to take care of her (even if I'm not doing a
very good job of taking care of her right now). She listened
to my whole story and she didn't say I was wrong or stupid or
anything.

After I was done, she sat and thought for a while, and
then she asked me if she could call my parents. And I said
absolutely not. The less they know about where I am or how
I'm doing, the better. Then she said, "What if I can get them
to agree not to send you away? What if I explain to them that
you'll go back home with them, but only on the condition that
you get to stay in Seattle and you can visit Ada here in the
hospital every day?"

I didn't say yes right away. I was still really sure that
my parents would freak out and take me away from her, no
matter what this lady thought. But I stuck around and we
talked about it for a while. It was almost like a negotiation,
where she was trying to get me to agree to certain conditions
in exchange for certain promises. I wound up agreeing that
if my parents would let me see Ada every day, I would go
home and start going back to school and do whatever I had

to do to catch up in my classes. And I would promise never to run away again and not do any drugs or alcohol (which had never been a temptation for me anyway, but she wanted me to promise), and not contact anyone else who had anything to do with my life as a prostitute—Miss Irma or Shawn or any of the other talent or clients.

Honestly, that all sounded fine to me. I don't want anything to do with that world anymore. I won't mind going back to regular life and living with my parents and everything, as long as I can stay in touch with Ada and be there for her through her recovery. In all of this, Ada was all I really cared about.

So I wound up agreeing to everything the social worker was saying. And then she asked if she could call my parents right then and put me on the phone with them, but I wasn't ready to do that yet. I was scared that if I spoke to them, they would start telling me what to do and how it was going to be and I wouldn't know how to say no or stand up for myself. Or they would make promises but they might not keep them.

She said she understood, so we agreed that she's going to call them tomorrow and try to talk to them, but she won't give them any information about where I am or how to find me. She'll just tell them that I'm okay. I guess I would at least like them to know that.

And then, if they want me to come home, she'll explain about our agreement and we'll take it from there.

Wed, June 10

I spoke to the social worker (Jane) again today after visiting with Ada. She said she left a message with my parents, and they called back! And they were really, really happy to hear I was okay. That's nice to know, I guess. I think I was a bit worried that they would just be angry and disappointed and maybe not even want me back. But Jane said they had been really worried and they just want to talk to me.

She said she told them a bit about our agreement, and they're going to come meet with her later today to talk about it in person. She asked me if I wanted to be there, but I think it's better if I'm not. I just think that we would all get really emotional, and I'm not sure I'd make the best decisions with them right there in the room with me. I'd rather they agree to the terms we set out before I see them.

Thurs, June 11

Jane met with my parents yesterday and she says they agreed to our terms! She didn't want to go forward with anything without talking to me first, but she says if I'm okay with it, she'll arrange a meeting and I can go home with them. I think I'm going to do it!

I talked to Ada about it today too. I hadn't told her anything about Jane or my parents before, because I didn't want her to worry that I was thinking about leaving her. And I know how she is. She would always try to talk me into whatever she thought was best for me and not give a thought to herself. So I wanted to make this decision on my own, without letting her or anyone else influence me too much.

But I told her today that I was thinking about it, and she said she was really happy for me and that I should do it. And I explained about how I would still come see her every day, so she wouldn't even notice a difference really. And then she made a joke about how she hoped I would at least smell better. But her eyes were wet when she said it, and I started bawling, of course, and then the nurse made me leave again because he said I was getting Ada overexcited. But he let me back in after a few minutes.

I'm going now to tell Jane that I want to do it. I have to admit, I'll be glad to see my mom again. And to sleep in my own bed!

Wed, June 24

I haven't written in a while. At first I was just going through too much stuff to even think about this journal, and then, well, to be honest, things were going so well, I was afraid that putting it into words might jinx it all. Silly, I know.

But things are going well. Better than I had any right to expect, really. Ada's still in the hospital, but she is *so* much better, and starting to really get her strength back. The doctors say they'll probably release her at the end of the week. After that, it looks like she's going to move back in with her mom. I was nervous about this, but her mom's finally gotten on medication, so that should change things. She's even been to visit Ada a few times, and Ada says she is so much better. Plus, Ada's aunt helped her mom get signed up for Social Security disability insurance, which should help them out a lot. With that money coming in, they won't be dependent on Ada to support them.

As for me, I've been adjusting. My parents have been pretty great, all things considered. They were really happy to have me back, and they've been okay with me going to visit Ada regularly, even though I know they don't approve of her. My brother, Mark, came back from college for a while too, and that helped smooth things over. He told my parents that he is dropping his engineering major and switching to theater arts! That was a huge surprise to all of us and not a particularly happy one for my parents.

Mark took me out for milk shakes the other day and we talked about it. It seemed really out of the blue, but he said he'd actually switched over to mostly theater courses some time ago; he just hadn't felt brave enough to let our parents know. But when he found out everything that was going on with me, he decided to come home for a little while and tell them. He didn't say it in so many words, but I think he was trying to distract them. Maybe take a little of the heat off me. That was pretty cool of him.

I'm not sure if it worked, but we have all been getting along better lately, and I think Mom is coming around to the idea that she has to let us choose our own paths. In any case, there haven't been any more threats about getting sent to Taiwan, so at least they are holding up that end of the bargain.

I haven't gone back to school yet. The school year is practically over, and if I went back now I'd only flunk all my finals. Believe it or not, my parents actually suggested I take the rest of the semester off to just recover and get readjusted to living at home. Over the summer they're going to get me a tutor to help me catch up with everything I missed this spring.

It's weird. I always used to think of studying as a chore, but the truth is I'm kind of looking forward to learning stuff again. In any case, I don't find myself fantasizing about moving out on my own like I used to. I think living on the streets for a while cured me of my yearning for independence, at least for now.

I am nervous about going back to school in the fall, though. I have no idea what people have heard about why I disappeared for a while, or if anyone even noticed. I don't know what Tyler told people about me.

I wish Ada could come back to school with me, but everyone agreed that with her current health situation, she needs to be extra careful: Any random cold virus sweeping through the school could set her back. Once she's doing better, Jane found her a special program at one of the city schools, where they have more resources to deal with cases like hers. Which is great! But it leaves me on my own.

It's okay, though. It'll be weird for a few days, but I just need to be brave and work through it. I'm sure everything will get back to normal after that.

Editor's Note

This journal was found in the author's room shortly after her disappearance.

According to her parents, the author returned to classes in the fall. A few weeks into the semester, she went to school in the morning and never came home. A thorough investigation did not turn up any evidence at first. Police located her body two weeks later under a bush in the Beacon Hill area of Seattle between Interstate 5 and Interstate 90, referred to in this journal as the Jungle. Her body was mostly nude, covered in bruises, and forensic reports indicate the cause of death to be asphyxiation due to strangulation.

Witnesses recalled seeing her the previous week with a variety of different men, none of whom could be positively identified.

She was a good girl,

living a good life. One night, one party,
changed everything.

IN THE TRADITION OF *GO ASK ALICE*

Lucy in the Sky

Anonymous

One party. One taste.
No turning back.

**Read her story in her own words,
in the diary she left behind.**

She was an athlete

with a bright future. She only wanted
to lose a few pounds.

IN THE TRADITION OF *GO ASK ALICE*

Letting
Ana
Go

Anonymous

Once she started,
she couldn't stop.

Read her devastating journey in her own words,
in the diary she left behind.

simonTeen

Simon & Schuster's **Simon Teen**
e-newsletter delivers current updates on
the hottest titles, exciting sweepstakes, and
exclusive content from your favorite authors.

Visit **TEEN.SimonandSchuster.com** to
sign up, post your thoughts, and find out what
every avid reader is talking about!